John Forster

The Life of Jonathan Swift

Volume the First, 1667-1711

John Forster

The Life of Jonathan Swift
Volume the First, 1667-1711

ISBN/EAN: 9783337055189

Printed in Europe, USA, Canada, Australia, Japan

Cover: Foto ©Raphael Reischuk / pixelio.de

More available books at **www.hansebooks.com**

THE LIFE

OF

JONATHAN SWIFT

By JOHN FORSTER

VOLUME THE FIRST

1667—1711

NEW YORK

HARPER & BROTHERS, PUBLISHERS

FRANKLIN SQUARE

1876

PREFACE.

The subject of this book has been in my thoughts for many years, and to the collection of materials for illustration of it I have given much labor and time.

The rule of measuring what is knowable of a famous man by the inverse ratio of what has been said about him, is applicable to Swift in a marked degree. Few men who have been talked about so much are known so little. His writings and his life are connected so closely, that to judge of either fairly with an imperfect knowledge of the other is not possible; and only thus can be excused what Jeffrey hardily said, and many have too readily believed—that he was an apostate in politics, infidel or indifferent in religion, a defamer of humanity, the slanderer of statesmen who had served him, and destroyer of the women who loved him. Belief in this, or any part of it, may be pardonable where the life is known insufficiently, and the writings not at all; but to a competent acquaintance with either or both it is monstrous as well as incredible.

Swift's later time, when he was governing Ireland as well as his deanery, and the world was filled with the fame of *Gulliver*, is broadly and intelligibly written. But as to all the rest, his life is a work unfinished; to which no one has brought the minute examination indispensably required, where the whole of a career has to be considered to get at the proper comprehension of single parts of it. The writers accepted as authorities for the obscurer portion are found to be practically worthless, and the defect is not supplied by the later and greater biographers. Johnson did him no kind of justice because of too little liking for him; and Scott, with much hearty liking as well as a generous admiration, had too much other work to do. Thus, notwithstanding noble passages in both memoirs, and Scott's pervading tone of healthy, manly wisdom, it is left to an inferior hand to attempt to complete the tribute begun by those distinguished men.

Some such preface seemed necessary to so full an account of Swift's least important years as the present volume contains; and its minuteness of detail, in the fifth and sixth books more especially, must be left to the explanation its successors will supply. Here is laid the ground-work for the graver time which is to occupy exclusively the rest of the biography; and, excepting for illustration of the individual career, there will be no introduction of history.

Though the original materials thus far employed in the story will speak for themselves, it may be expected that the principal of them, as well as of other new matter to be used in the two remaining volumes that will complete the work, should have mention in this place. When the task was undertaken, Mr. Murray confided to the writer nearly fifty unpublished letters addressed by Swift to Archdeacon Walls after he was Dean of St. Patrick's; and this incentive to farther research led to many richer acquisitions. More than a hundred and fifty new letters have been placed at my disposal.

The value of the results yielded by collation of the later portions of the "Journal to Stella" with the original manuscript, can be judged only partially by the use of them in this volume. To later passages of the life their contribution will be extremely important. Some special blanks in the printed journal, on which Scott remarks, are filled up by them.

By the courtesy of a descendant of Archbishop Cobbe, some additions are made to the fragment of autobiography first printed by Mr. Deane Swift; and questions raised by that fragment in connection with Swift's university career, are settled by one of the rolls of Trinity College which fell accidentally into my hands. Two original letters written from Moor Park clear up that story of the Kilroot living which has been the theme of extravagant misstatement. Unpublished letters in the palace at Armagh, obtained through my friend, the late Sir James Emerson Tennent, show clearly Swift's course as to questions which led to his separation from the whigs. Others of the same date place it beyond doubt that Lord Somers, as early as the close of 1707, had urged his appointment to the see of Waterford.

At the dispersion of the library of Mr. Monck Mason, of Dublin, I became the purchaser of Swift's note-books and books of account; of his letters of ordination; of a large number of unpublished pieces in prose and verse interchanged between himself and Sheridan; of several important unprinted letters; and of a series of contemporary printed tracts for illustration of the life in Ireland, which I was afterward able to complete by the whole of the now extremely rare Wood Broadsides. At Mr. Mitford's sale there came into my possession the Life by Hawkesworth which Malone had given to Lord Sunderlin, enriched with those MS. notes by Dr. Lyon, who had charge of Swift's person in his last illness, on which Nichols and Malone, who partially used them, had placed the highest value. By subsequent arrangement, much favored by the courtesy of Mr. Edmund Lenthal Swifte, transfer was made to me of the papers given by Mrs. Whiteway to Mr. Deane Swift, altogether more than thirty pieces of considerable interest; comprising several of Swift's important writings in his own manuscript, and, among transcripts of other pieces with corrections by himself, a copy of the Directions to Servants, with humorous addition.

To Mr. Andrew Fountaine, of Narford, descendant of Swift's friend, my warmest thanks are due. Mr. Fountaine opened to me the manuscript collections at his family seat, where, amidst much other matter of a very attractive kind, I found unpublished poems and letters of much importance. Afterward I became the possessor of letters relating to *Gulliver;* of some to Stopford, and some to Arbuthnot of peculiar value; and of an unpublished journal, also in Swift's handwriting, singular in its character and of extraordinary interest, written on his way back to Dublin amidst grave anxiety for Esther Johnson, then dangerously ill. My friend, the Rev. Dr. Todd, late the senior fellow of Dublin University, procured for me this remarkable piece; and to the late Duke of Bedford I was indebted for the loan of a volume from the library at Woburn containing poems by Swift copied in the handwriting of Stella, which was given to the fourth duke by Sir Archibald Acheson, to whose father it had been given by Swift. For the use of a very striking unprinted letter to Delany, written from London during Walpole's ministry, I have to thank Lord Houghton.

The most rare of all my acquisitions, obtained from the late Mr. Booth, the book-seller, by whom it had been purchased at Malone's sale, remains to be mentioned. It is the large-paper copy of the first edition of *Gulliver* which belonged to the friend (Charles Ford) who carried Swift's manuscript with so much mystery to Benjamin Motte, the publisher, interleaved for alterations and additions by the author, and containing, besides all the changes, erasures, and substitutions adopted in the latter editions, several interesting passages, mostly in the Voyage to Laputa, which have never yet been given to the world.

Leaving to be named as they occur in the biography other illustrative pieces (among them some valuable unprinted marginalia of Swift's readings in Baronius, and other books in the Marsh and Christchurch libraries, for which I had the ready service of my friend Mr. Percy Fitzgerald), I prefix to my last acknowledgment some sentences from an unpublished letter of Sir Walter Scott to Lady Charlotte Rawdon, written from his "wilderness" of Ashestiel by Selkirk in the autumn of 1808, when he had just undertaken his edition of Swift. She had recommended him, hearing of the design, to apply for assistance to a distinguished Irish clergyman, himself a man of letters, the Rev. Edward Berwick; and thus (after promising, if she will visit him at Ashestiel, to "make up for narrow lodgings and sorry cheer by old ballads, family legends of feud and battle, and tales of ghosts and fairies without measure or limit") he thanks her for her suggestion. "Mr. Berwick has behaved toward me in the kindest way possible, and, what was still more flattering, has taught me to ascribe a great part of his civility to the interest your ladyship bestows on my undertaking. Every person to whom I have applied joins in representing him as most deeply skill-

ed in all that relates to the interesting object of my present researches. In short, *Go to Berwick* has not been more frequently
called for in a ball-room than it was returned in answer to all my
inquiries about Swift. So I went to Berwick accordingly, and have
every hope of profiting by my journey. I am only afraid of weary-
ing his kindness by the multiplicity of my demands."

With not inconsiderable success I may also claim to have gone to
Berwick. The son of Scott's friend, the president of Galway College, is an old friend of my own; and through him, among services
to this work which will have other mention, I succeeded in getting
access to the correspondence of Swift with his friend, Knightley
Chetwode, of Woodbrooke, during the seventeen years (1714–'31)
which followed his appointment to the deanery of St. Patrick's.
Of these letters, the richest addition to the correspondence of this
most masterly of English letter-writers since it was first collected,
more does not need to be said here; but of the late representative
of the Chetwode family I crave permission to add a word. His rare
talents and taste suffered from his delicate health and fastidious
temperament, but in my life I have seen few things more delightful
than his pride in the connection of his race and name with the companionship of Swift. Such was the jealous care with which he preserved the letters, treasuring them as an heir-loom of honor, that he
would never allow them to be moved from his family seat; and
when with his own hand he had made careful transcript of them for
me, I had to visit him at Woodbrooke to collate his copy with the
originals. There I walked with him through avenues of trees which
Swift was said to have planted, and was witness to his romantic interest in every minutest memory of the immortal Dean. A part of
this interest he was so friendly as to transfer to the work in which I
had engaged; and it is no common grief to me to include, in the list
of those now dead who encouraged the enterprise, Mr. Edward Wil-
mot Chetwode.

J. F.

PALACE GATE HOUSE,
KENSINGTON, *June*, 1875.

TABLE OF CONTENTS.

BOOK THIRD.

VICAR OF LARACOR.

1699–1705. ÆT. 32–38.

Pages 121-180.

I. CHAPLAIN AT DUBLIN CASTLE, 121–138.

II. LONDON LIFE, 138–154.

BOOK FIFTH.

WHIGS AND TORIES.

1709–1710. ÆT. 42–43.

Pages 271-373.

I. POWER CHANGING HANDS, 271–287.

BOOK SIXTH.

(APPENDIX.)

BIOGRAPHICAL NOTES FROM SWIFT'S
LETTERS TO ESTHER JOHNSON; AND
PASSAGES IN THE LETTERS CORRECT-
ED AND RESTORED FROM THE ORIGI-
NAL MANUSCRIPT.

Pages 377-473.

I. BIOGRAPHICAL NOTES, 377-420.

FAC-SIMILES.

BOOK FIRST.

ANECDOTES AND EARLIEST YEARS.

1667–1688. Æt. 1–21.

THE
LIFE OF JONATHAN SWIFT.

30TH NOVEMBER, 1667—19TH OCTOBER, 1745.

I.

ANECDOTES OF HIS FAMILY AND HIMSELF.

> " He'll treat me as he does my betters,
> Publish my Will, my Life, my Letters."

In the same year when Swift, playful in his bitter and kindly moods alike, so described a punishment then just invented, and inflicted ever since on famous men, he was doing his best to abate in some degree his own share of its penalties and pains. The anecdotes of his family and himself were begun at the time, as portion of an autobiography. They were laid aside and never finished; but such of them as he did complete are the highest authority for the matters to which they relate, and find their fitting place upon the opening page of the Life of Jonathan Swift.

Bathurst the book-seller published in 1755 Mr. Deane Swift's Essay upon the Life, Writings, and Character of Dr. Jonathan Swift, containing, as the title-page expressed, " That Sketch of Dr. Swift's Life, written by the Doctor himself, which was lately " (23d of July, 1753) " presented by the Author of this Essay to the University of Dublin." The Sketch had been given to him by " his old, faithful friend, and cousin-german, Mrs. Whiteway," Swift's nurse and last companion, whose daughter by her first husband Mr. Deane Swift had married; and from whom he derived the farther information that it was written " about six or eight and twenty years ago, as an introduction to his Life, which

Mr. Deane Swift's Essay.

VOL. I.—2

he had reason to apprehend would some time or other become a topic of general conversation." To this very valuable relic I am so fortunate as to be able to contribute several corrections, and **Additions to the Anecdotes.** a few not unimportant additions, undoubtedly authentic. Some years after the original was written, Swift permitted the then bishop of Kildare and dean of Christchurch (it was not until later years that the dean of St. Patrick's was also dean of the sister cathedral), Dr. Charles Cobbe, afterward archbishop of Dublin, to transcribe it; and this copy, already differing in some points from its predecessor, doubtless by suggestions made at the time when the copy was taken, appears to have been used by Dr. John Lyon, in or about the year 1738, for the insertion of corrections and additions manifestly derived from, and occasionally entered in the hand-writing of, Swift himself, at whose request Dr. Lyon was then engaged (*Scott*, i., 504) in biographical researches connected with his family. So it has remained, unused by any of Swift's biographers, in the possession of the bishop's descendants; and by their representative, Thomas Cobbe, Esq., of Newbridge, Donabate, Malahide, it was obligingly lent to me a few years ago, for the purposes of this work. The points in which it differs from Mr. **Collation of the MS.** Deane Swift's publication (which I have myself carefully collated in Trinity College with the manuscript in Swift's hand), as well as the variations from the original text of the copy as printed by Mr. Deane Swift, are noted at the bottom of the page; and the additions, all of which are indicated by inverted commas, will be remarked upon in their proper place in the biography.

FRAGMENT OF AUTOBIOGRAPHY: 1667-1699. The family of the Swifts are(¹) ancient in Yorkshire. From them descended(²) a noted person, who passed under the name of Cavaliero Swift, a man of wit and humor. He was created(³) an Irish Peer by King Charles the First, 20th March 1627,(⁴) with the title of Viscount(⁵) of Carlingford, but never was in that kingdom. Many traditional pleasant stories are related of him, which the family planted in Ireland hath(⁶) received from their parents. This lord died without issue male; and his(⁷) heiress, whether of the first or second descent,(⁸) was married to Robert Fielding, Esq., commonly called handsome Fielding.(⁹) She brought him a considerable estate in Yorkshire, which he squandered away, but had no children.

(¹) "Was": D. S.

(²) D. S. inserts in a note "Barnam Swift, Esq."

(³) "Made": D. S.

(⁴) D. S. inserts "or King James."

(⁵) "Baron": D. S.

(⁶) Incorrectly printed "had" in modern copies.

(⁷) "Daughter, Lady Margaret, an" inserted and erased.

(⁸) "Whether of the first or second descent" erased and restored.

(⁹) Dr. Lyon substitutes, "member of parliament for Gowran Co., Kilkenny, afterward pardoned, and died 12th May, 1712."

The Earl of Eglinton married another co-heiress of the FRAGMENT OF AUTOBIOGRAPHY: 1667-1699. same family.([1])
Another of the same family was Sir Edward Swift, well known in the times of the great Rebellion and Usurpation, but I am ignorant whether he left heirs or no.
Of the other branch, whereof the greatest part settled in Ireland, the founder was William Swift, prebendary of Canterbury,([2]) toward the last years of Queen Elizabeth, and during the reign of King James the First. He was a divine of some distinction. There is a sermon of his extant, and the title is to be seen in the catalogue of the Bodleian Library, but I never could get a copy, and I suppose it would now be of little value.([3])   Swift's ancestors.
This William married the heiress of Philpot, I suppose a Yorkshire([4]) gentleman, by whom he got a very considerable estate, which, however, she kept in her own power, I know not by what artifice.([5]) She was a capricious, ill-natured, and passionate woman, of which there([6]) have been told several instances. And it hath been a continual tradition in the family, that she absolutely disinherited her only son, Thomas, for no greater crime than that of robbing an orchard when he was a boy. And thus much is certain, that Thomas never enjoyed more than one hundred pounds a year, which was all at Goodrich, in Hertfordshire, whereof not above one-half is now in the possession of a great-great-grandson, except a([7]) church or chapter lease which was not renewed.

([1]) "As he hath often told me" written in and erased by Swift after the word "family."
([2]) In a note to this passage Mr. Deane Swift corrects his illustrious kinsman. "Had Doctor Swift," he says, "read the dedication of William Swift's sermon, it would have set him right. In that dedication we find that Thomas Swift, the father of William, was presented in the year 1569 to the parish of St. Andrew in the city of Canterbury: and, moreover, that upon the decease of Thomas, William Swift, in the year 1591, succeeded his father." The same error lends to the description, in the next following sentence, of "Philpot" as a Yorkshire gentleman. It was not William Swift, but his father, who first moved from Yorkshire to Canterbury. "I do not,"

adds Mr. Deane Swift, "find the name of William Swift in the list of the prebendaries of Canterbury; I suppose the Doctor took it for granted that the parish of St. Andrew's was one of the prebends belonging to that cathedral."
([3]) It is described as "On the 8th Rom. verse 18: printed London, 1622."
([4]) D. S. corrects to "Kent."
([5]) "I know not by what artifice" omitted by D. S.
([6]) "I": D. S.
([7]) This sentence is differently arranged, but substantially the same. Scott incorrectly prints "great-great-grandson" as "great-grandson;" confounding Mr. Deane Swift, who is so referred to, with his grandfather, Mr. Godwin Swift, named in the next sentence.

FRAGMENT OF AUTOBI- OGRAPHY: 1667–1699.

Family arms.

His original picture was([1]) in the hands of Godwin Swift, of Dublin, Esq., his great-grandson; as well as that of his wife, who seems to have a good deal of the shrew in her countenance; whose arms as([2]) an heiress are joined with his own; and by the last he seems to have been a person somewhat fantastic; for he altered the family coat of arms, and gives as his own device([3]) a Dolphin (in those days called a Swift) twisted about an anchor, with this motto, *Festina lente.*

There is likewise a seal with the same coat of arms (his, not joined with the([4]) wife's), which the said William commonly made use of; and this was([5]) also in the possession of Godwin Swift above mentioned.

His eldest son, Thomas, seems to have been a clergyman before his father's death.([6]) He was vicar of Goodrich, in Herefordshire, within a mile or two of Ross: he had likewise another church living, with about one hundred pounds a year in land (part whereof was by church leases),([7]) as I have already mentioned. He built a house on his own land in the village of Goodrich,([8]) which by the architect-

([1]) "Is now" erased by Swift, and "was" substituted. In first publishing the original Mr. Deane Swift described these portraits as "in the hands of Mrs. Elizabeth Swift, relict of Godwin Swift, late of Swiftsheath, in the county of Kilkenny, Esq. His picture was drawn in the year 1623, ætatis suæ 57: his wife's picture was drawn in the same year, ætatis suæ 54."

([2]) "Of" erased and "as" substituted by Swift.

([3]) "For these he gives as his device": D. S.

([4]) Incorrectly "his" in D. S. and modern copies.

([5]) "Is also now" erased, and "was also" substituted, by Swift.

([6]) Mr. Deane Swift explains this fact as made obvious by "the drapery in his picture, which was drawn at the same time with his father's, in the year 1623, ætatis suæ 28." Upon the statement in the next sentence "within a mile or two of Ross" his remark that it should have been "within four" would not be worth subjoining but that Scott, in copying it, has unconsciously left us an amusing illustration of his too hasty editorship. He probably made the memorandum "it should be four" when his eye first rested on Deane Swift's note, and he seems to have forgotten, when he came to use it, what it referred to. But finding allusion in a following paragraph to "certain pieces of iron with three spikes" he gravely appended thereto (and so it still stands in both his editions) the ridiculous correction "it should be four."

([7]) The words inclosed are interlined in Swift's hand in the original in Trinity College. They are not in the copy as printed by Mr. Deane Swift.

([8]) Deane Swift describes it as not in the village, but in the parish of Goodrich, and as a house of the oddest kind that certainly ever was built. "It has three floors, containing about twelve or fourteen rooms, besides vaults and garrets. The whole seems

ure denotes the builder to have been somewhat whimsical and singular, and very much toward a projector. The house is above an hundred years old and still in good repair, inhabited by a tenant of the female line; but the landlord, a young gentleman,(¹) lives upon his own estate in Ireland.

FRAGMENT OF AUTOBIOGRAPHY: 1667-1699.

This Thomas was much(²) distinguished by his courage, as well as his loyalty to King Charles the First, and the sufferings he underwent for that prince, more than any person of his condition in England. Some historians(³) of those times relate several particulars of what he acted, and what hardships he underwent for the person and cause of that(⁴) martyr'd prince. He was plundered by the Roundheads six and thirty, some say above fifty, times.(⁵)

An "eminent sufferer."

"The author of Mercurius Rusticus dates the beginning of his sufferings so early as October, 1642. The Earl of Stamford, who had the command of the Parliament army in those parts, loaded him at first with very heavy exactions; and afterward at different times robbed him of all his books and household furniture, and took away from the family even their wearing apparel; with some other

to be three single houses all joining in one central point. Undoubtedly there never was, nor ever will be, such another building to the end of the world. However, it is a very good house, and perhaps calculated to stand as long as any house in England. It was built, according to the date of one of the pillars, in the year 1736." He adds, with reference to the subsequent mention of the "tenant of the female line," that "she hath been dead these many years." Of course the "young gentleman" in the text was Mr. Deane Swift himself, from the information of whose son, Theophilus Swift, Scott tells us he derived the note he has substituted for the above: which note, however, here subjoined, is only a paraphrase of what Mr. Deane Swift had said in his Essay (*Appendix*, 21). "This house, now the property of Mr. Theophilus Swift, is still standing. A vault is shewn beneath the kitchen, accessible only by raising one of the flagstones. Here were concealed the provisions of bread and milk, which supported the lives of the family after they had been plundered by the Parliamentary soldiers. The vicar was in those days considered as a conjurer, especially when, his neighbors being discharged from assisting him, and all his provisions destroyed, he still continued to subsist his family. This vault is probably one of the peculiarities of architecture noticed by the Dean."

(¹) "Who" erased.

(²) D. S. omits "much."

(³) To the original MS. Swift himself subjoined, but Mr. Deane Swift did not print, the following note: "See a book called *Mercurius Rusticus*, and another in folio called The Lives of those who suffered Persecution for K. Cha. I."

(⁴) "Blessed": D. S. The word is erased by Swift from before "martyr'd."

(⁵) What follows this sentence is in Swift's hand in margin.

Fragment of Autobiography: 1667-1699. circumstances of cruelty too tedious to relate at large in this place. The Earl being asked why he committed these barbarities, my author says 'he gave two reasons for it: first, because he (Mr. Swift) had bought arms and conveyed them into Monmouthshire, which, under his lordship's good favor, was not so; and, secondly, because, not long before, he preached a sermon in Ross upon the text Give unto Cæsar the things that are Cæsar's, in which his lordship said he had spoken treason in endeavoring to give Cæsar more than his due. These two crimes cost Mr. Swift no less than £300.' "(¹)

About that time(²) he engaged his small estate, and, having quilted all the money he could get in his waistcoat,(³) got off to a town held for the king / where, being asked by the Governor, who knew him well, what he could do for his Majesty, Mr. Swift said he would give the King his **Swift's favorite ancestor.** coat, and stripping it off, presented it to the Governor; who observing it to be worth little, Mr. Swift said, Then take my waistcoat, and(⁴) bid the Governor weigh it in his hand; who, ordering it to be unripped,(⁵) found it lined with three hundred broad pieces of gold, which as it proved a seasonable relief, must be allowed an extraordinary supply from a private clergyman(⁶) of a small estate, so often plundered, and soon after turned out of his livings in the church.

At another time being informed that three hundred horse of the Rebel party intended in a week to pass over a certain river, upon an attempt against the cavaliers, Mr. Swift having a head mechanically turned, he contrived certain pieces of iron with three spikes, whereof one must always be with the point upward; he placed them over night in the ford, where he received notice that the Rebels would pass early the next morning, which they accordingly did, and lost two hundred of their men, who were drowned or trod to death by the falling of their horses, or torn by the spikes.

His sons,(⁷) whereof four(⁸) were settled in Ireland

<hr>

(¹) The passage within inverted commas inserted by Swift.

(²) So the original.

(³) As printed by Mr. Deane Swift, the passage runs "and gathered all the money he could get, quilted it in his waistcoat, got off," etc., etc.

(⁴) "He": D. S.

(⁵) "Ripped": D. S.

(⁶) "With ten children" written and erased by Swift.

(⁷) To this passage, in the MS. I am using, the following note is subjoined: "Tho. Swift married Elizabeth, daughter of Jonathan Dryden of Northamptonshire, gent, by whom he had six sons, viz. Godwin, Dryden, Thomas, William, Jonathan, and Adam. As also four daughters; Emily, Elizabeth, Sarah, and Katherine.—*Heralds' Office, Dublin.*"

(⁸) Mr. Deane Swift remarks (App.

(driven thither by their sufferings, and by the death of
their father), related many other passages, which they
learned either from their father himself, or from what had
been told them by the most credible persons of Herefordshire, and some neighboring counties: and which some of
those sons often told to their children; many of which are
still remembered, but many more forgot.

"In 1646"(¹) he was deprived of both his church livings sooner than most other loyal clergymen, upon account
of his superior zeal for the King's cause, and his estate
sequestered. His preferments, at least that of Goodrich,
were given "at first to one Giles Rawlins, and after to
William Tringham"(²) a fanatical saint, who scrupled not
however to conform upon the Restoration, and lived many
years,(³) I think till after the Revolution.(⁴)

"The Committees of Hereford had kept Thomas Swift
a close prisoner for a long time in Ragland Castle before
they ordered his ejectment for scandal and delinquency
(as they termed it), and for being in actual service against
the Parliament.   On the 5th July, 1646, they ordered the
profits of Gotheridge (Goodrich) into the hands of Jonath:
Dryden, minister, until about Christmas following; and
on 24th March they inducted Giles Rawlins into this parish: who in 1654 was succeeded by Tringham.   His other
living of Bridstow underwent the same fate.   For he was
ejected from this on 25th Sept., 1646, and it was given to
the curate, one Jonath: Smith, whom they liked better,
and ordered to be inducted into his Rector's cure.   What
became of him afterward I know not, but in 1654 one
John Somers got this living."(⁵)

The Lord-Treasurer Oxford told the Dean "of St. Patrick's, the grandson of this eminent sufferer,"(⁶) that he
had among his father's (Sir Edward Harley's) papers, several letters from Mr. Thomas Swift writ in those times,

to Essay 25) that he should have said
five.   "I suppose he forgot Dryden
Swift, who died very young and a
bachelor, soon after he had come over
to Ireland with his brothers.   He
recollects his name, however, in one
of the subsequent paragraphs."

(¹) "In 1646" omitted by D. S.

(²) Words within inverted commas
interlined by Swift.

(³) The two names put in a note by
D. S.

(⁴) "I have seen many persons at

Goodrich, who knew and told me his
name, which I can not now remember," erased by Swift, evidently upon
his obtaining the two names, and
ascertaining what he proceeds to
state.

(⁵) All within inverted commas inserted by Swift, the last line and a
half in his own hand.   Dr. Lyon had
supplied the other facts.   See Scott,
i. 504, 507.

(⁶) Words within inverted commas
inserted by Swift.

FRAGMENT
OF AUTOBI-
OGRAPHY:
1667-1699.

which he promised to give to the Dean ;([1]) but never going
to his house in Herefordshire while he was Treasurer, and
Queen Anne's([2]) death happening in three days after his
removal, the Dean went to Ireland, and the Earl being
tried for his life, and dying while the Dean was in Ireland, he could never get them.([3])

Mr. Thomas Swift died " May 2d,"([4]) 1658, and in the
" 63d "([5]) year of his age. His body lies under the altar
at Goodrich, with a short inscription. He died([6]) before
the return of King Charles the Second, who by the recom-
mendations([7]) of some prelates had promised, if ever God
should restore him, that he would promote Mr. Swift in
the church, and other ways reward his family for his extraordinary services,([8]) zeal, and persecutions in the royal
cause. But Mr. Swift's merit died with himself.

Uncle God-
win.

He left ten sons and three or four daughters, most of
which lived to be men and women. His eldest son Godwin Swift, of " Goodridge Co. Hereford, Esq., one of the
Society of Gray's Inn "([9]) (so stiled by Guillym in his Heraldry)([10]) was([11]) called to the bar before the Restoration.
He married a relation of the old Marchioness of Ormond,
and upon that account, as well as his father's loyalty, the
old Duke of Ormond made him his Attorney General in
the palatinate of Tipperary. He had four wives, one of
which, to the great offense of his family, was co-heiress([12])
to Admiral Deane, who was one of the Regicides. " She
was Godwin's third wife. Her name was Hannah, daughter of Major Richard Deane, by whom he had issue Deane
Swift, and several other children."([13])

This([14]) Godwin left several children, who have all es-

([1]) " Dean "substituted for "grandson, whose life I am now writing."

([2]) "The queen's ": D. S.

([3]) Strictly speaking, this paragraph
ought not to have been imported by
Mr. Deane Swift into the text of the
Anecdotes. It stands, in the Trinity
College MS., as in that which I am
quoting, as a marginal note in Swift's
hand.

([4]) " May 2d " substituted by Swift
for " in the year."

([5]) A blank in the Trinity College
MS., a year having been inserted and
struck out.

([6]) " About two years " erased by
Swift.

([7]) Plural in both MSS. Printed
in the singular by Mr. Deane Swift.

([8]) " And " erased by Swift.

([9]) Words within inverted commas
substituted for "the Inner Temple,
Esq."

([10]) " In his Heraldry " substituted
for " the Herald, in whose book the
family is described at large."

([11]) " I think " erased by Swift.

([12]) Mr. Deane Swift more correctly suggests " sole heiress."

([13]) Words in inverted commas inserted by Swift.

([14]) " This " inserted by Swift, and
new paragraph begun.

tates.   He was an ill pleader, but perhaps a little too dex- FRAGMENT OF AUTOBI- OGRAPHY: 1667–1699.
terous in the subtle parts of the law.(')
    The second son of Mr. Thomas Swift was called by the
same name, was bred at Oxford, and took orders.   He
married the(') daughter of Sir William D'Avenant, but
died young, and left only one son, who was also called
Thomas, and is now rector of Putenham in Surrey.   His Uncle Thomas.
widow lived long, was extremely poor, and in part supported by the famous Dr. South, who had been her husband's
intimate friend.
    The rest of his sons, as far as I can call to mind, were
Mr. Dryden Swift (called so after the name of his mother,
who was a near relation(³) to Mr. Dryden the poet), Wil- Other uncles.
liam, Jonathan, and Adam, who all lived and died in Ireland.   But none of them left male issue, except Jonathan,
who besides a daughter left one son, born seven months
after his father's death; of whose life I intend to write a
few memorials.
    Jonathan Swift, Doctor of Divinity, and Dean of(') St. Father.
Patrick's, was the only son of Jonathan Swift, who was
the seventh or eighth son of Mr. Thomas Swift above
mentioned, so eminent for his loyalty and his sufferings.
    His father died young, about two years after his mar-
riage: he had some employments and agencies; his death
was much lamented on account of his reputation for integrity, with a tolerable good understanding.(')   He married Mrs. Abigail Erick, of Leicestershire, descended from
the most ancient family of the Ericks,(') who derive their
lineage from Erick the forester, a great commander, who
raised an army to oppose the invasion of William the Con-
queror, by whom he was vanquished, but afterward employed to command that prince's forces; and in his old
age retired to his house in Leicestershire, where his family

(') The second sentence of this paragraph, after having been inserted
from the original into the MS. from
which I quote, is struck through with
a pen.   Mr. Deane Swift remarks
that the words "perhaps a little too"
appear, from the different shade of the
ink, to have been interlined in the
Trinity College MS. some time after
it was first written.
    (') "Eldest" erased by Swift.
    (') Mr. Deane Swift incorrectly ex-
plains, "aunt." See *post*, 35.
    (') In the Trinity College MS. the

initials only are given—"J. S. D. D.
and D. of St. P——."
    (') In the Trinity College MS. a
fresh paragraph is here begun.
    (°) "The family of Erick, which
has produced many eminent men, is
still represented by two respectable
branches, the Heyricks of Leicester
town, and the Herricks of Beaumanor.
Of both these branches, distinct pedi-
grees and many curious historical anecdotes are given in the History of
Leicestershire, ii., 215; iii., 148."—
Scott, i., 509.

Fragment of Autobiography: 1667–1699. hath continued ever since, but declining every age, and are now in the condition of very private gentlemen. This marriage was on both sides very indiscreet; for his wife brought her husband little or no fortune, and his death happening so suddenly([1]) before he could make a sufficient establishment for his family,([2]) his son (not then born) hath often been heard to say, that he felt the consequences of that marriage not only through the whole course of his education, but during the greatest part of his life.

30th November, 1667. He was born in Dublin, on St. Andrew's day, "in the year 1667;"([3]) and when he was a year old, an event happened to him that seems very unusual; for his nurse, who was a woman of Whitehaven, being under an absolute necessity of seeing one of her relations, who was([4]) then extremely sick, and from whom she expected a legacy, and being " at the same time "([5]) extremely fond of the infant, she stole him on shipboard unknown to his mother and uncle, and carried him with her to Whitehaven, where he continued for almost three years. For, when the matter was discovered, his mother sent orders by all means not to hazard a second voyage, till he could be better able to bear it. The nurse was so careful of him, that before he returned he had learned to spell; and by the time that he was Æt. 3. three([6]) years old he could read any chapter in the Bible.

After his return to Ireland, he was sent at six years old to the school of Kilkenny, from whence at fourteen he was admitted into the university at Dublin, " a pensioner, on the 24th April, 1682 ;"([7]) where, by the ill treatment of his nearest relations, he was so([8]) discouraged and sunk in his spirits that he too much neglected his academic studies; for " some parts of "([9]) which he had no great relish by nature, and turned himself to reading history and poetry: so that when the time came for taking his degree of bachelor of arts([10]), although he had lived with great regularity and due observance of the statutes, he was stopped of his degree for dulness and insufficiency; and at last hardly

---

([1]) Mr. Deane Swift tells us he was about twenty-five years old.

([2]) "That " erased.

([3]) Words within inverted commas inserted.

([4]) Substituted for " being."

([5]) "At the same time " is in both MSS., but was omitted from Mr. Deane Swift's copy.

([6]) "Three " is in both MSS., and so printed by Mr. Deane Swift; but Hawkesworth changed it to five, and Scott copied him. Swift first had written "two" years, for which he substituted " almost three," afterward erasing " almost."

([7]) Words within inverted commas inserted.

([8]) " Much " erased.

([9]) Words in inverted commas inserted by D. S. in previous line.

([10]) " Degrees of bachelor:" D. S.

admitted in a manner, little to his credit, which is called FRAGMENT OF AUTOBIOGRAPHY: 1667–1699. in that college "(¹) *speciali gratiâ* "on the 15th February, 1685, with four more on the same footing :"(²) and this discreditable mark, "as I am told,"(³) stands upon record in their college registry.

The troubles then breaking out, he went to his mother, who lived in Leicester; and after continuing there some months, he was received by Sir William Temple, whose Sir William Temple. father had been a great friend to the family, and who was now retired to his house called Moor Park, near Farnham in Surrey; where he continued for about two years. For he happened before twenty years old, by a surfeit of fruit to contract a giddiness and coldness of stomach, that almost brought him to his grave; and this disorder pursued him with intermissions of two or three years to the end of his life. Upon this occasion he returned to Ireland, "in 1690,"(⁴) by advice of physicians, who weakly imagined that his native air might be of some use to recover his health : but growing worse, he soon went back to Sir William Temple; with whom growing into some confidence, he was often trusted with matters of great importance.

King William had a high esteem for Sir William Temple, by a long acquaintance, while that gentleman was ambassador and mediator of a general peace at Nimeguen. (⁵)The King, soon after his expedition to England, visited King William. his old friend often at Sheen, and took his advice in affairs of greatest consequence. But Sir William Temple, weary of living so near London, and resolving to retire to a more private scene, bought an estate near Farnham in Surrey, of about £100 a year, where Mr. Swift accompanied him.(⁶)

About that time a bill was brought into the House of Commons for triennial parliaments; against which the King, who was a stranger to our constitution, was very averse, by the advice of some weak people, who persuaded the Earl of Portland that King Charles the First lost his crown and life by consenting to pass such a bill. The Earl, who was a weak man, came down to Moor Park by his majesty's orders to have Sir William Temple's advice, who said much to show him the mistake. But he continued

---

(¹) "In that college" erased by D. S.

(²) Words within inverted commas inserted.

(³) "As I am told" interlined.

(⁴) "In 1690" inserted by Swift.

(⁵) A new paragraph begins here, in the MS. I am using.

(⁶) The words "lived with him some time" had been substituted for "accompanied him" in the second MS., but were afterward erased by Swift, and the reading of the Trinity College MS. restored.

FRAGMENT OF AUTOBIOGRAPHY: 1667–1699.

still to advise the King against passing the bill. Whereupon Mr. Swift was sent to Kensington with the whole account of the(¹) matter in writing to convince the King and the Earl how ill they were informed. He told the Earl, to whom/he was referred by his majesty (and gave it in writing), that the ruin of King Charles the First was not owing to his passing the triennial bill, which did not hinder him from dissolving any parliament, but to the passing of(²) another bill, which put it out of his power to dissolve the parliament then in being, without the consent of the

Swift with the King.

house. Mr. Swift, who was well versed/in English history, although he was(³) under twenty-one years old, gave the King a short account of the matter, but a more large one to the Earl of Portland; but all in vain. For·the King by ill advisers was prevailed upon to refuse passing the bill. This was the first time that Mr. Swift had ever(⁴) any converse with courts, and he told his friends it was/ the first incident that helped to cure him of vanity.

(⁵)The consequence of this wrong step in his majesty was very unhappy; for it put that prince under a necessity of introducing those people called Whigs into power and employments, in order to pacify them. For, although it be held a part of the King's prerogative to refuse passing a bill, yet the learned in the law think otherwise, from that expression used at the coronation, wherein the prince obligeth himself to consent to all laws, *quas vulgus elegerit.*

Mr. Swift having(⁶) lived with(⁷) Sir William Temple some time, and(⁸) resolving to settle himself in some way of living, was inclined to take orders. "But first commenced M.A. in Oxford as a student of Hart Hall on 5th July, 1692."(⁹) However, although/his fortune was very small, he had a scruple of entering into the church merely for support, and Sir William,(¹⁰) then being Master of the Rolls in Ireland, offered him an employ of about £120 a year in that office; whereupon Mr. Swift told him, that since he had now an opportunity of living without being driven into the church for a maintenance, "he was re-

---

(¹) "That": D. S.

(²) "Of" omitted: D. S.

(³) "Then" omitted by Swift. A mark is also here attached in the MS. I am using, as if a correction were meant to be made: and in the Trinity College MS. the passage appears to have been written originally by Swift, and afterward erased, "under three and twenty years old." This would be the more correct date.

(⁴) "Ever" erased: D. S.

(⁵) A new paragraph begins here, in the MS. I am using.

(⁶) "Having" omitted: D. S.

(⁷) "Him": D. S. (⁸) "But": D. S.

(⁹) Words within inverted commas inserted.

(¹⁰) "Temple" inserted: D. S.

solved to go to Ireland, and take holy orders.(¹) In the
year 1694 he was admitted into deacon's and priest's orders
by Dr. William Moreton,(²) bishop of Kildare, who ordained him priest at Christ Church the 13th January that
year."(³) He was recommended to the Lord Capel, then
Lord Deputy, who gave him a prebend in the north worth
about £100 a year, "called the Prebend of Kilroot in the
Cathedral of Connor,"(⁴) of which growing weary in a few
months he returned to England, resigned his living in
favor of a friend "who was reckoned a man of sense and
piety, and was besides encumbered with a large family.
After which he "(⁵) continued in Sir William Temple's
house till the death of that great man, who beside a leg-
acy(⁶) left him the care, and trust, and advantage of publishing his posthumous writings.

Upon this event Mr. Swift removed to London, and applied by petition to King William upon the claim of a
promise his majesty had made to Sir William Temple, that
he would give Mr. Swift a prebend of Canterbury or Westminster. "Col. Henry Sidney, lately created "(⁷) Earl of
Romney, who professed much friendship for him, "and
was now in some credit at court, on account of his early
services to the King in Holland before the Revolution,
for which he was made Master-General of the Ordnance,
Constable of Dover Castle, Lord Warden of the Cinque
Ports, and one of the Lords of the Council,"(⁸) promised
to second Mr. Swift's(⁹) petition; but(¹⁰) said not a word
to the King. And Mr. Swift, "having totally relied on
this lord's honor, and having neglected to use any other

FRAGMENT
OF AUTOBI-
OGRAPHY:
1667-1699.
Swift's ordi-
nation.

(¹) Up to the word "orders" Deane
Swift prints the passage correctly.
Scott makes nonsense of it by omit-
ting every thing from the word "main-
tenance" to "he was recommended."
—*Works*, i., 50.

(²) Swift knew of this insertion, but
his orders both of dean and priest
were undoubtedly conferred by King,
then Bishop of Derry. The original
parchments came into the hands of
Mr. Monck Mason, at whose sale I
bought them many years ago, and
they are still in my possession.

(³) Words within inverted commas
inserted by Dr. Lyon.

(⁴) Words within inverted commas
inserted by Swift.

(⁵) Words within inverted commas
inserted by Swift. "And continued:"
D. S.

(⁶) After "legacy" in the Trinity
College MS. Swift inserts "of a 100
lb." subsequently crossed through
with a pen.

(⁷) "The ".erased: words within
inverted commas inserted.

(⁸) Words within inverted commas
inserted.

(⁹) "His" erased: "Mr. Swift's"
inserted by Swift.

(¹⁰) "As he was an old, vicious,
illiterate rake, without any sense of
truth or honor," inserted by Swift,
and erased. They are retained by
D. S.

FRAGMENT
OF AUTOBI-
OGRAPHY:
1667-1699.
instrument of reminding his majesty of the promise made
to Sir William Temple,"(¹) after long attendance in vain,
thought it better to comply with an invitation, given him
by the Earl of Berkeley, to attend him to Ireland, as his
chaplain and private secretary; his lordship having been
appointed one of the Lords Justices of that kingdom,
"with the Duke of Bolton and the Earl of Galway on the
29th June, 1699."(²) He attended his lordship, who landed
near Waterford; and Mr. Swift acted as secretary(³) the
whole journey to Dublin. But another person had so far
insinuated himself into the earl's favor, by telling him

Promises
broken.
that the post of secretary was not proper for a clergyman,
nor would be of any advantage to one who aimed only at
church preferments, that his lordship after a poor apology
gave that office to the other.

In some months the Deanery of Derry fell vacant; and
it was the Earl of Berkeley's turn to dispose of it. Yet
things were so ordered that the Secretary having received
a bribe, the Deanery was disposed of to another, and Mr.
Swift was put off with some other church livings not
worth above a third part of that rich Deanery; and at
this present time,(⁴) not a sixth: "namely, the Rectory of
Agher, and the Vicarage of Laracor and Rathbeggan in
the Diocess of Meath; for which his letters patent bear
date the 24th February following."(⁵) The excuse pretended was his being too young, although he were then
thirty years old.

ADDITIONS
TO FRAG-
MENT:
1700-1714.
(⁶)"The next year, in 1700, his grace Narcissus Lord
Archbishop of Dublin was pleased to confer upon Mr.
Swift the Prebend of Dunlaven in the Cathedral of St.
Patrick's, by an instrument of institution and collation
dated the 28th of September. And on the 22d of Octo-
ber after, he took his seat in the Chapter.

"From this time he continued in Ireland; and on the
16th of February, 1701, he took his degree of Doctor of
Divinity in the University of Dublin. After which he
went to England about the beginning of April, and spent
near a year there.

(¹) Words within inverted commas
inserted by Swift.

(²) Words within inverted commas
inserted.

(³) Mr. Deane Swift here prints
"during," but the word is not in either MS.

(⁴) "Time" inserted.

(⁵) Words within inverted commas
inserted.

(⁶) All that follows, to the end, inserted. As with all the other additions or insertions, indicated in these
notes, it is placed within inverted commas.

"He appeared at the Dean's visitation on the 11th of January, 1702; at a chapter held the 15th of April; and at the visitation on the 10th of January, 1703. He attended a chapter on the 9th of August, and the visitation of 8th of January, 1704. He was at two chapters held the 2d of February and the 2d of March following, and at the visitation the 7th of January, 1705. Also in April, August, and January, 1706; and in April, June, July, and August, 1707. Set sail for England 28th of November, 1707; landed at Darpool; next day rode to Parkgate; and so went to Leicester first.

"He was excused at the visitation in 1707 and 1708; and on the 9th of January, 1709, expected at the visitation, but did not come. He spent 1708 in England, and set sail from Darpool for Ireland 29th of June, 1709, and landed at Ringsend next day, and went straight to Laracor.   Was often giddy and had fits this year.

"He attended a chapter held the 15th February, 1709; also at a chapter 29th July and 11th August, 1710. Excused at the visitation 8th of January, 1710. He was not in Ireland after this till his instalment as Dean on the 13th of June, 1713. On the 27th of August he nominated Dr. Edward Synge to act in his absence as subdean; and came no more to Ireland until after the Queen's death. He set out to Ireland from Letcomb in Berkshire August the 16th, 1714; landed in Dublin the 24th of the same month; and held a chapter on the 15th of September, 1714."

To these Anecdotes reference will have to be made as occasion requires.   Imperfect as they are, they are found to illustrate Swift's career.   They show not alone the sense of worldly disadvantage that even during childhood and at school marred his enjoyment and chilled exertion, but the temperament which at later times fitted him as little to receive obligation as to endure dependence.   They exhibit disappointments such as fall to few men so endowed, and an eagerness to resent disappointments such as few men on earth are spared.   There is in them also, especially, a kind of family pride which he never more than half confessed, but which always strongly overruled him.   Comparing his claims on the side of both his parents with the imprudence of the marriage that had brought them together, he believed misfortune to have anticipated life, and that the world had been made bitter for him even before he opened his eyes in it.

II.

CHILDHOOD, SCHOOL, AND COLLEGE.

1667-1688.   Æt. 1-21.

On the 25th of January, 1665-'6, the Benchers of the King's Inns, Dublin, were met to consider a petition presented to them on the 14th of the previous November by a young Englishman who had been admitted an attorney and member of the society in Hilary term of the year preceding.   It humbly set forth that the stewardship of the King's Inns was become void by the death **Swift's father.** of Thomas Wale; that the petitioner, Jonathan Swift, his father, and their whole family, had always been very loyal and faithful to his majesty King Charles the Second and his royal father, and had been very great sufferers on that account; that for six or seven years last past the said petitioner had been much conversant about the inns, and was well acquainted with the steward's duty and employment, having assisted Wale in entering of their honors' orders; and that he therefore humbly prayed their honors **Steward of King's Inns.** to be pleased to make him steward.   The decision of the Benchers was favorable; and their direction, bearing date that day, admitted Jonathan Swift to be steward of the King's Inns.

Before this time he appears to have had no settled means of support.   With what his son calls a reputation for integrity and a tolerable good understanding, he had come over to Ireland, drawn by the success of his elder brother, on the final break-up of his father's house two years before the restoration; but though he obtained some employments and agencies connected with forfeited lands, he had no certain income, and, returning to England from time to time, was still wavering between such chances of a livelihood as either country presented, when a marriage contracted with Abigail Erick* (or Herrick), a Leicester-shire girl of old family but no fortune, determined him to settle finally to what had mostly occupied him since his father's death, and, having qualified himself in Hilary term 1664–'5 by membership of the inns, he had served as as-sistant in the steward's and under-treasurer's office until the date of his own appointment.

1667-1688.
Æt. 1-21.
Married to Abigail Erick.

Very brief was his enjoyment of this humble piece of fortune. He had held it little more than a year when there came under consideration of the Benchers another petition. On the 15th of April, 1667, the humble prayer of Abigail Swift, widow, was presented to them: setting forth that it had pleased God to take away unexpectedly her husband, the late steward of their honorable society; that, being left a disconsolate widow, she could not with-out their honors' assistance get in a debt of about six-score pounds sterling due to her husband's estate for commons and cost commons from members of the inns, several of whom, on being applied to by her brother-in-law, Mr. Wil-liam Swift, had denied him on pretense of his having no authority to receive the money; and she therefore petition-ed for an order to give him such authority. On the same day her petition was complied with, but her desire was as far as ever from fulfillment. As the days passed into months, her troubles and fears increased. She had been left with an infant daughter, but she carried another child unborn; and she had scarcely, in the seventh month of her widowhood, laid down that burden, when from her sick-room again the wail of poverty and anguish went up to the masters of the bench. Their new steward had been pressing her, even then, for payment of twelve pounds eighteen shillings and elevenpence, alleged to be owing from her dead husband. There was also another debt claimed by the doctors for his last illness, and his funeral

Dies before son's birth.

Widow's troubles.

* He settled upon her, at the mar-riage, an annuity of £20, purchased in England, and this was all she is   known to have possessed afterward in her own right.

1667–1688.
Æt. 1–21.
Petitions for help. expenses remained unpaid. But how, she implored their honors, were these debts to be discharged, while a hundred pounds of arrears due to his estate were still withheld from her? The reply was characteristic rather than munificent. As to the twelve pounds and shillings, their honors were content to balance it against an equal sum from their late steward's arrears; and as to the hundred of arrears, of which three-fourths were for commons actually served at their own bench table, they made order that "William Swift should exert his diligence" to recover it. Whether the diligence so re-exerted had that result, there is no evidence to inform us.*

The infant whose misfortunes thus began, upon 'the principle of Mr. Shandy's reckoning, eight months before he saw the light, and who at last had opened his eyes upon a world in which want and dependence were grimly awaiting him, lived beyond man's allotted term, and while conscious of any thing is alleged never to have omit-Jonathan's birthday.ted, as surely as his birthday came round, to repeat the words of Job in which he wished the day to have perished wherein he was born, and the night in which it was said there was a man-child conceived. Allowance is in this to be made for exaggeration, as in many other like things said of him. A man does not socially celebrate what he is always savagely denouncing; and Swift not only kept his birthday with unusual regularity, but rejoiced when those who loved him remembered it in his absence. "O, then, you kept Pdfr's little birthday: would to God I had been with you!" He had indeed a habit of reading on the day the third chapter of Job; and "What's here, now?" he writes of a letter from Esther Johnson reproaching him for not recollecting the proper date. "Yes, faith, I lamented my birthday two days later, that's all!" The habit grew upon him as years and disappointments grew, until at last the day became indeed an anniversary of unmitigable sadness. "It is a day you seem to regard,

---

* The facts stated in the text are | printed in Duhigg's *History of the* derived from the original documents | *King's Inns, Dublin* (1806, p. 216).

though I detest it," he wrote to Mrs. Whiteway three years 1667-1688.
ÆT. 1-21.
Readings of
Job.
before darkness closed upon his mind, "and I read the
third chapter of Job this morning." It was his way of
expressing, what more or less he doubtless felt all his life,
that with his birth had come inheritance of evil incurable
by philosopher or physician; but, beyond, there was also
much he was well content should be otherwise expressed,
and to show how far this counterbalanced the bitter disadvantage must be the task of his biographer. Before the
story is begun, some further notice of the Swift family,
with brief recapitulation of the principal points of his
own sketch, will explain both the kind of help the widow
and her children were to receive, and what it was that indisposed them to receive it gratefully.

The first notorious person of the name had been also Yorkshire
Swifts.
the first to connect the name with Ireland. Barnam Swift,
representative of the elder branch of an old English family which had long been settled in Yorkshire, and who for
his gallantry and jovial humor passed among his friends
as the Cavaliero, became one of Charles the First's Irish
peers under the title of Viscount Carlingford; but, dying
without male issue, this branch became extinct, and the
whole of the Yorkshire estates passed through the female
line by the marriage of his daughters, co-heiresses, one to
that Robert Fielding known as the Beau or Handsome
Fielding, who had for his second wife the famous or in-
famous Duchess of Cleveland, and the other to the Earl
of Eglinton. It was, however, from a younger branch of
the same family, through a representative equally but less
fortunately devoted to the Stuarts, in whose service he received nothing and sacrificed every thing, that the greatest of the name was directly descended. The Reverend
Thomas Swift, whose father, also a divine of good repute Hereford-
shire branch.
in the church, had wedded an heiress of whose lands in
Herefordshire only a very small portion descended to her
son, possessed in the same county, besides that temporal
estate increased by an inheritance from his father, the vicarage of Goodrich and cure of Bridstow, and lost them all

1667–1688.
Æt. 1–21. for his loyalty. In 1646 both lands and livings were sequestered; and at the close of that year, when Hereford
had been taken by the forces of the parliament, he was a
prisoner in Ragland Castle. It has been seen how exult-
ingly his famous grandson dwells upon these losses and
sufferings in the cause of the king.

Intermar-
riage with
the Drydens. Thomas Swift had in early life married Elizabeth Dryden, daughter of Sir Erasmus Dryden's brother,* who bore
him ten sons and four daughters; and it is a family tradition that, shortly after his sixth son, Jonathan, was born,
the soldiers of the parliament made forcible entrance into
his vicarage and stripped it, not merely of the last loaf
left in the kitchen, but of the very clothes of the infant
Godwin,
Thomas, and
Jonathan. lying in the cradle. Up to manhood, poor Jonathan the
elder seems to have had the same ill fortune; for when
his father died in 1658, he was one of the sons already
grown to man's estate who were left without a profession,
or any apparent dependence except on the elder brothers.
Of the latter, Godwin and Thomas had certainly received
advantages, while yet their father lived, not extended to
the rest. Thomas, who was bred for the church, obtained
an English living; and bettered his prospects, after the
Restoration, by marriage with the eldest daughter of Davenant, the poet. In earlier years his brother Godwin, the
eldest of the family, called to the bar at Gray's Inn while
yet the civil war was raging, had become favorably known
in the courts during the Protectorate, and had improved
his fortunes also by marriage, after the example generally
Uncle God-
win's four
wives. of his race. The first of his four wives was a cousin of
the old Marchioness of Ormond; through the third he became possessed of a portion of the family estate which
had been forfeited by her father, Admiral Deane, the regicide; the last was sister to Sir John Meade; and though
he had wedded his second and only undowered wife, Mrs.

---

* Sir Erasmus was the poet's grandfather, and the name of Jonathan was
taken by the Swifts from the Dryden
family, Jonathan Dryden, Mr. Thomas
Swift's brother-in-law, having received
the profits of the Goodrich living upon
its forfeiture by Thomas Swift in
1646.—*See Malone's Dryden,* i., 17.

Catherine Webster, before the restoration, his favor with _1667-1688._ _Æt._ 1-21. the Ormonds so far survived that new alliance as to secure for him, after the event, upon the first duke assuming his brief tenure of the government of Ireland, the office of Attorney-general for the palatinate of Tipperary. There _Connection with the Temples._ is evidence also that he was on friendly and confidential footing with the Master of the Rolls, Sir John Temple, father of the more famous Sir William.

By all his marriages Godwin Swift had issue; fifteen sons and three daughters survived him; his brothers had also representatives; and to his nephew Jonathan may be forgiven an alleged reproach, that when reputation and power were his he would not recognize, in all this crowd of cousinhood,* other title to notice than that of bearing a name made famous only by himself. But with the family increase Godwin's worldly successes kept pace, and at the date of his brother Jonathan's death he was undoubtedly a prosperous gentleman. It was the sunshine of his fortune at this time which had brought within its reach not alone that brother, but three others, Dryden, William, and Adam, who believed they might profit by its warmth in making Ireland their home. To him, then, as to the _The widow's dependence._ acknowledged head of the family, Jonathan's widow had turned naturally in her trouble. With exception of the small annuity of twenty pounds which her husband had been enabled to purchase at their marriage, she was wholly dependent on this supposed wealthy relative; and observing the circumstances in which her second child was born, and the privations of which she not unreasonably

---

* "I dined to-day with Patty Rolt at my coz Leach's, with a pox, in the city: he is a printer, and prints the _Postman_, oh! oh! and is my cousin, God knows how, and he married Mrs. Baby Aires of Leicester, and my coz Tompson was with us."—_Journal,_ 26th Oct., 1710.   "Did you ever hear of Dryden Leach?—he acted Oroonoko—he is in love with Miss Cross." (17th Jan., 1710-'11.)   Again, on a later day: "I went to-day into the city to see Pat Rolt, who lodges with a city cousin, a daughter of coz Cleve (you are much the wiser). I had never been at her house before. My he-coz Tompson the butcher is dead or dying." (2d March, 1712-'13.) Patty Rolt afterward married one Lancelot, whom Swift did his best to serve, being, he says, fond of Patty, as we shall see. _A crowd of cousins._

1667-1688.
Æt. 1-21.

complained, one sees what must have been the impression ineffaceably stamped upon Swift in his childhood, and imbittering every later experience of his uncle Godwin's bounty. The case is not altered by saying that the expectations disappointed were not such as it was entirely fair to entertain.

Swift's
birthplace.

In a small court in Dublin adjoining the Castle inclosure, on St. Andrew's Day (30th of November), 1667, Jonathan Swift was born.* Portions of this "Hoey's Court" are still standing; but the only house possessing interest in it, formerly numbered 7, and occupied within living memory by small dealers in rags, earthenware, and suchlike merchandise, was fallen into so ruinous a state a few years ago that it had to be pulled down, and the site was then taken into the Castle grounds. The principal houses now in the court are on the side opposite to that where Swift's mother lived; and, judging from the look of those still left on the side where number 7 stood, were probably of later date and of greater pretensions. How long she continued here after her son's birth, is not exactly known. She seems at all times to have made regular visits to her friends in Leicestershire, and Swift declared that at the time of his birth she was about to return there;† but it is

---

* Mr. Deane Swift says in his *Essay* (22), and in a letter to Mr. Nichols, which I will here quote, that the birth took place in Godwin's house. Writing nearly a hundred years after the event, he speaks of it with a minute particularity which will be always found to characterize his alleged facts in the exact ratio of their unlikelihood, or (if likely) of the impossibility of their being known to him. "Her husband having died a very young man about the time of the Spring Assizes in the year 1667, she was invited to my grandfather Counselor Swift's house in Dublin.' And as I have been told, and believe it to be true, she was then so young with child, that properly speaking she was not aware of it; and the

Doctor was born at my grandfather's house the 30th of November following." It would not be worth adverting to this if it had not imposed on Nichols and others, and if it were not an illustration of the entire untrustworthiness of all Mr. Deane Swift's family flourishes. It found a place in Joseph Spence's biographical sketch (printed in *Notes and Queries* of January, 1861), but no careful inquirer has adopted it. Spence's sketch is worthless.

† "As to my native country," he wrote to Mr. Francis Grant (23d March, 1733-'4), "I happened indeed by a perfect accident to be born here, my mother being left here from returning to her house at Leicester, and I

at least certain that there is no trace of her in Dublin aft- 1667–1688.
Æт. 1–21.
er Jonathan's school-days began.

Before the beginning of even these, however, or of the
second year of the little fellow's existence, an incident had
occurred claiming mention in his history. To the English Child carried
off by nurse.
nurse who had charge of him he had so endeared himself,
that, upon the occasion of a relative's death calling her suddenly to her native place of Whitehaven, she carried off
with her the child whom she could not bear to part from;
"stole him on shipboard, unknown to his mother and
uncle," says Swift himself; and did not take him back to
Ireland for more than two years. Her care of him had
not slept in the interval. Before his return he had learned
to spell; and "by the time that he was three years old,"* Æт. 3.
his fragment of autobiography has told us, "he could read
any chapter in the Bible." He had no pride of birth in
the country to which he was thus taken back, and with
which his name is eternally associated. He never called
himself, nor permitted others to call him, an Irishman.
He was an Englishman settled in Ireland. He was in the
habit of saying frequently to others what he wrote to the
second Lord Oxford in 1737. He happened to be dropped No pride in
Ireland.
there; was one year old when he left it first; and to his
sorrow did not die before he went to it again.

He had a sickly childhood; and it was his mother's fear
that a second sea voyage might be dangerous to him which
led her to consent that he should stay so long with the
woman who had shown him so strong an attachment.
Abigail Swift depended mainly at this time on her hus-

---

was a year old before I was sent to
England; and thus I am a Teague, or
an Irishman, or what people please,
although the best part of my life was
in England. What I did for this country was from perfect hatred of tyranny and oppression...... I believe the
people of Lapland or the Hottentots
are not so miserable a people as we."
Grant was a London merchant, who
wished to interest him in a fishery
scheme.

* "Almost three" is the first expression of Swift, altered by him to
"three;" and this followed the erasure of "two years," which at first he
had written. Mr. Deane Swift printed "three" correctly; but Hawkesworth altered the word to "five," and
was copied by Scott.

1667-1688.
Æt. 1-21.

band's eldest brother for help in her widowhood; and it was because he stinted, not what he gave, but the kindness with which he might have given it, that the bread of dependence was made very bitter to her. Godwin had the reputation of being wealthier than the sequel showed him to be; and, though a cold, unsympathizing man, there is no ground for thinking him an unjust one. "He gave me the education of a dog," said Swift; who thought, perhaps justly, that, but for his uncle's connection by marriage with the Ormond family, he would not have been taken from his mother's side at the early age of six years, and

At Kilkenny school.

placed, under the care of a Mr. Ryder, in the foundation-school of the Ormonds at Kilkenny. Whether at the same age the assistance was withdrawn which until now enabled the child's mother to continue her residence in Ireland, there are no means of ascertaining; but shortly after her boy had thus been taken from her care, she is found to be

School-fellows.

living among her own relatives in Leicester. Kilkenny school, however, had some repute in those days; and here, where a youth named Stratford well known to him in his famous time was in the same class with him, he was joined, after a couple of years, by his cousin Thomas, son of his Oxford uncle of that name; and he had for a later school-

William Congreve.

fellow a lad named William Congreve, two years his junior, son of a younger brother of a good English family, whose father was then managing Lord Burlington's Irish estate, who entered Trinity College under the same tutor as Swift two years later, and was to achieve a reputation only less famous than his own.

Swift remained till he was fourteen; but, except his name cut by himself on the sideboard of the seat of his class, no trace of him survived in the school. He told Doctor Lyon that the first Latin words which struck his childish fancy soon after entering it, "Mi dux et amasti lux," had touched him more durably than the graver teaching; for with them began his whimsical taste for the rhymed Latin-English indulged largely in his later years. There is also a hint in one of his letters to Pope and Bolingbroke

that other pursuits than of Latin or English may have oc- 1667-1688.
Æt. 1-21.
cupied him at Kilkenny, and we know with certainty that
what he mentions here was among his subsequent amusements at Laracor. "I remember, when I was a little boy,
I felt a great fish at the end of my line, which I drew up
almost on the ground; but it dropped in, and the disap-
pointment vexes me to this very day, and I believe it was A type of the
future.
the type of all my future disappointments."

Another school recollection, of less certain authenticity,
appears in some personal experiences with which he is alleged to have enforced an argument on the improvidence
of marriage where means were scant and health indifferent,
addressed to one of the many young clergymen helped by
him when Dean of St. Patrick's. "When I was a school- Story of
school-days.
boy at Kilkenny, and in the lower form, I longed very
much to have a horse of my own to ride on. One day I
saw a poor man leading a very mangy, lean horse out of
the town to kill him for the skin. I asked the man if he
would sell him, which he readily consented to upon my
offering him somewhat more than the price of the hide,
which was all the money I had in the world. I immediately got on him, to the great envy of some of my school-fellows and to the ridicule of others, and rode him about the
town. The horse soon tired, and lay down. As I had no
stable to put him into, nor any money to pay for his sus-
tenance, I began to find out what a foolish bargain I had
made, and cried heartily for the loss of my cash; but the
horse dying soon after on the spot gave me some relief."

An extract from the senior lecturer's book in Dublin
University exhibits the next step in Swift's career. It in-
forms us that on the 24th of April, 1682, from the school
of Mr. Ryder at Kilkenny, there were admitted into the
college as pensioners,* under the tuition of St. George Ashe
(who became afterward bishop of Clogher), "Thomas Swift,
son of Thomas, aged fifteen years, born in Oxfordshire;" Enters col-
lege.
and "Jonathan Swift, son of Jonathan, aged fourteen years,

* Stratford had been admitted under another tutor some months earlier.

1667-1688. born in the county of Dublin." For nearly seven years
Æt. 1-21. Jonathan remained here, taking his bachelor's degree in
February, 1685–'6, and passing the three following years
also in the college, which he did not quit until the "break-
Duration of ing-out of the troubles" at the opening of 1689. That is
residence. his own expression; and of all that has been written on
his university career, including a volume by a learned vice-
provost of the college,* there is hardly any thing really
authentic excepting what was written by himself. Famous
men may suffer quite as much by excess as by want of
curiosity about them, and more would certainly now have
been known of Swift if less had been written respecting
him in the half-century following his death.

His own anecdotes, in a passage it will be well here to
reproduce, inform us that by the ill-treatment of his nearest relations, in other words the insufficiency of the help
afforded him by his uncle Godwin, " he was so discouraged
and sunk in his spirits, that he too much neglected his academic studies, for some parts of which he had no great
relish by nature, and turned himself to reading history and
poetry; so that when the time came for taking his degree
of bachelor of arts, although he had lived with great regularity and due observance of the statutes, he was stopped
His degree of his degree for dullness and insufficiency, and at last hard-
by special ly admitted in a manner, little to his credit, which is called
grace. in that college *speciali gratiâ.* And this discreditable mark,
as I am told, stands upon record in their college registry." Here the truth substantially is related, no doubt;
but with coloring from the ironical tone which he so often
gave to his mention of the Irish college in the days when
it was written. Famous as he was then, any discredit from
the special grace would go to the giver; and while its im-
port may have been harmless enough, as will shortly be
seen, Swift preferred to tell the world that Trinity College
had thought him too dull for a degree. But this is not the

---

* *An Essay on the Earlier Part* | John Barrett, D.D., Vice-Provost of
of the Life of Swift. By the Rev. | Trinity College, Dublin. 1808.

view that has found favor with commentators and critics. They have made a very serious business of it indeed; though the matter would hardly have been worth even brief illustration, but for the light it throws on the claim to authenticity of the four earliest writers who have been accepted as original authorities for the Life of Swift.

First came, seven years after the death, the *Remarks* of Lord Orrery, who knew Swift only during his last six or seven years of consciousness, who had been shown by Mrs. Whiteway the anecdotes given by her afterward to her son-in-law, Mr. Deane Swift, and to whom the latter had told sundry stories of his kinsman's last illness. In the *Remarks* it is declared that Swift's sole occupation at the university had been to turn all its studies into ridicule except history and poetry; that on his appearing for a degree he was set aside for insufficiency, obtaining it only in a manner that was dishonorable; and that when, on presenting himself at Oxford for an *ad eundem*, he handed in his Irish degree *speciali gratiâ*, the English Dons took the words to signify a reward, not a reproach, and Swift never tried to undeceive them. Of the source as well as truth of this anecdote the reader will shortly be able to judge.

Two years after the *Remarks*, Doctor Delany published his *Observations*, in which he confirmed Lord Orrery's account of the degree, " which Swift hath been often heard to say was owing to his being a dunce;" and added that the disgrace of it had nevertheless a happy effect, for it made him immediately turn his thoughts to useful learning. His mistake at his outset in Trinity College, Doctor Delany stated, he had himself frequently explained to be " that he looked upon the study of Greek and Latin to be downright pedantry and beneath a gentleman; for that poetry, and plays, and novels were the only polite accomplishments." We shall soon see how near this is like to have been to the truth; and of the four authorities under illustration, Delany is undoubtedly the most to be esteemed.

A year after came Mr. Deane Swift, grandson of God-

1667–1688.
Æt. 1–21.

Earliest
writers on
Swift.

Lord Orrery.

Doctor Delany.

1667–1688.
Æt. 1–21.
Mr. Deane
Swift.
win by his marriage into the family of Deane the regicide, who published his *Essay* ten years after the death of his great kinsman; whom he personally knew only on the eve of that event, in his last year or two of consciousness; but of whom he speaks like one familiar with his prime, and says he took an opportunity of telling him that he certainly must have been idle in his college days. "But he assured me to the contrary; declared that he could never understand logic, physics, metaphysics, natural philosophy, mathematics, or any thing of that sort; but I will tell you, said he, the best part of it all was, when I produced my testimonials at Oxford in order to be admitted *ad eundem*, they mistook *speciali gratiâ* for some particular strain of compliment which I had received from the University of Dublin on account of my superior merit, and I leave you to guess whether it was my business to undeceive them." The reader who thus sees the origin of Lord Orrery's story, may appreciate also the value of such statements by consulting Mr. Deane Swift's own volume for the very copy of the Trinity College degree on which the Oxford *ad eundem* was granted.* The special grace does not appear in it. The proceeding *speciali gratiâ* was, in short, any thing but uncommon, and the degree thus granted, being as good as any other, was of course entered like any other.

Hawkes-
worth.
Hawkesworth's memoir appeared in 1755, but he had merely copied his predecessors; though ten years later he did excellent service, with Mr. Bowyer, Mr. Nichols, Mr. Wilkes, Mr. Deane Swift and Doctor Birch, in helping Collection of
the works. toward the gradual collection of the works, and addition thereto of the bulk of the correspondence, including the

---

* "Nos præpositus sociique seniores Collegii Sacrosanctæ et Individuæ Trinitatis juxta Dublin testamur Jonathan Swift die decimo quinto Februarii 1685 gradum baccalaureatûs in artibus suscipisse, præstito prius fidelitater erga regiam magistatem juramento: quod de prædicto testimonium subscriptis singulorum no- minibus et collegii sigillo quo in hisce utimur confirmandum curavimus. Datum die tertio Maii 1692. Rob. Huntington, Præpos. L.S. St. George Ashe, Rich. Reader, Geo. Brown, Ben. Scroggs." For Mr. Deane Swift's attempt to explain the contradiction, see *Essay*, 44–46.

several parts of what is called the "Journal to Stella."[*] 1667-1688.
Æt. 1-21. Hawkesworth was followed in 1780 by Johnson, who contributed some solid reflection, but neither novelty in the Samuel Johnson. way of facts, nor, happily, any pretense to it. Then, in 1784, came the edition with a Life by Sheridan, to which the habit of confounding the writer with his father, and its adoption by Nichols, who prefixed it to his valuable editions of 1801 and 1808, has given a factitious importance. A life by Swift's old friend would have been priceless; but this was a life, written fifty years after the death of Swift's friend, by Sheridan's son, the actor and author Sheridan. of the dictionary, himself not born until 1721, who was not nineteen in the year when Swift's mind was gone, who was little over sixteen when all personal knowledge or access had been closed by his father's death,[†] who had been three years on the stage when Swift died, but who nevertheless, like all the rest, speaks of him as a familiar and equal, and whose minutely elaborate statements, supported by no better authority than flighty histrionic inferences from detached fragments of letters and poems, are still accepted to explain the most disputed passages in Swift's life. "He told me that he had made many efforts, upon his entering the college, to read some of the old treatises on logic writ by Smeglesius, Keckermannus, Burgersdicius, etc., and that Fancy picture by Sheridan. he never had patience to go through three pages of any of them, he was so disgusted at the stupidity of the work. When he was urged by his tutor to make himself master of this branch, then in high estimation, and held essentially necessary to the taking of a degree, Swift asked him what it was he was to learn from those books? His tutor told him, the art of reasoning. Swift said that he found no want of any such art; that he could reason very well with-

---

* For the times and manner of publication of this, the most important of all the illustrations of Swift's life, *see* *post*, 420–'24.

† Of whom we can not but recall, too, Johnson's description, which, whatever in other respects its humorous exaggeration may be, describes only too faithfully the book about Swift. "Why, sir, Sherry is dull, naturally dull; but it must have taken him a great deal of pains to become what we now see him. Such an excess of stupidity, sir, is not in nature."

out it;" and so forth. "In going through the usual forms of disputation for his degree, he told me he was utterly unacquainted even with the logical terms, and answered the arguments of his opponents in his own manner, which the proctor put into proper form. There was one circumstance Swift before in the account which he gave of this, that surprised me his examin- ers. with regard to his memory; for he told me the several questions on, which he disputed, and repeated all the arguments used by his opponents in syllogistic form, together with his answers." Surprising indeed to a raw lad of sixteen! and still more surprising that a youth thus privileged to hear how Swift, when quite as young himself, had unsparingly handled the trained scholars of the college, should yet sum up and dispose of his Dublin-University career in these half-dozen words: "By scholars he was esteemed a blockhead."

Such was the amount of information possessed by the public concerning Swift at college when Nichols had completed in 1801 his collected edition; and he was on the eve of publishing the second impression of that important book in 1808, when Edmond Malone, who helped him with it, having heard, through an intimate acquaintance high Dr. Barrett's in the college who became afterward an Irish bishop, of essay. researches for trace of Swift's student days on which the vice-provost of the college, Doctor Barrett, had been some time engaged, obtained the use of them for his friend. The vice-provost had been moved to his inquiries by a published Samuel letter of Samuel Richardson, written to Lady Bradshaugh Richard- son's libel. on the appearance of Orrery's *Remarks*, in which, with other palpable misstatements, to be noticed in their place hereafter, he says:·"I am told my lord is mistaken in some of his facts: for instance, in that wherein he asserts that Swift's learning was a late acquirement. I am very well warranted by the son of an eminent divine, a prelate, who "—that is, the prelate—"was for three years what is called his chum, in the following account of that fact. Dr. Swift made as great a progress in his learning at the University of Dublin in his youth as any of his contemporaries; but was so very ill-natured and troublesome, that he was made Terræ Filius, on purpose to have a pretext to expel him. He raked up all the scandal against the heads of that university that a severe inquirer, and a still severer temper, could get together into his harangue. He was expelled in consequence of his abuse; and having his discessit, afterward got admitted at Oxford to his degree." Seizing on this clue, Doctor Barrett set to work with such eager desire to identify Swift as the expelled Terræ Filius, that, though he could not discover that he ever played that part of scholastic lord of misrule, or was ever at any time expelled, he gave him all the benefit of a discovery that both these things (substituting six days' degradation for expulsion) had occurred to a fellow-student named Jones, in whose offending "harangue," consisting of nonsense and filth in about equal portions, he so elaborately stated his belief that Swift must have taken part, because of preposterous alleged resemblances to ·the *Tale of a Tub* and *Gulliver*, that Nichols, and Scott after him (though not without misgiving in Scott's case), were induced to admit it into their editions. I have vainly attempted, in two careful readings, to discover in it any thing that should recall Swift, however distantly. It is simply an outrage on his memory to call it his.

Nor is the small residue of Doctor Barrett's research entitled to graver attention. The most important fact established by his " rakings " in the college books and registries, namely, that Swift's cousin and senior remained in the college during all the time that Swift remained, involves in quite hopeless confusion his attempts to identify either student satisfactorily with the rewards or the punishments he exhibits. He says that Swift senior (Thomas) obtained a scholarship, but supports it by no better reasoning than is used for establishing that Swift junior (Jonathan) had no scholarship: the presumption being that without a scholarship Jonathan could hardly, in his circumstances, have remained after his degree. He confirms Swift's own statement that up to the time of the degree (13th of Feb-

ruary, 1685–'6), he had lived with great regularity and due
observance of the statutes, for he declares that the attempt to find any earlier censures on him in the registries
had entirely failed. But he makes up for this by pro-
ducing a most astonishing number of unfavorable entries
from the buttery books, besides two public censures from
the college registry, subsequent to that date; with all of
which he discredits Swift junior, it must be said on the
most indifferent grounds. There is such a medley of senior and junior books; such a want of either, or both, at
critical points in the evidence; and a confusion between
Thomas or the two Sir Swifts (Christian names being never employ-
Jonathan? ed) so hopeless of settlement except when both are together
on the scene; that the only safe conclusion is, whatever
the increase at the latter time of Swift's discontents may
have been, to believe in no such violent change of his habits before and after his degree as Doctor Barrett attempts
to present to us. The just course might probably be to
divide between the two cousins the not very large amount
College fines of moral blame involved in the numerous fines and pun-
and cen-
sures. ishments; and in this view it is noticeable that both cousins appear in the first of the two public censures, of which
the date is a year after the degree: "Mr. Warren, Sir
Swift senior, Sir Swift junior, Web, Bredy, Serles, and
Johnson the pensioner, for notorious neglect of duties,
and frequenting the town, were admonished." On the
other hand, nothing is established by the second and
graver censure, which bears date on the day, two years
later, when Jonathan Swift completed his twenty-first
year, except that it applied to one of the two Swifts. The
offense was contumacious and contemptuous conduct to
the junior dean, whereby dissension was created in the college; and for this "Sir Web, Sir Sergeant, Sir Swift,
Maynard, Spencer, and Fisher," were to be suspended;
the principal offenders, "Sir Swift and Sir Sergeant," being directed publicly on their knees to beg pardon of the
dean. The suspension lasted for a month. There is no
means of knowing if the public pardon was asked; and

whether Thomas or Jonathan was the offender, the evi- dence does not in any way settle. Jones had been Terræ Filius five months before; and the attempt to fix upon Jonathan the later degrading punishment by connecting it with an alleged earlier offense of having had part in Jones's filthy and slanderous harangue, fails quite absurd- ly. The buttery-book entries remain, and Jonathan may accept his full share of them. It is more than likely he was a frequent offender in neglecting to attend the college chapel, in missing night-rolls or halls, and in haunting the town streets.*

The strange thing is, that all Doctor Barrett's most mi- nute searches, with every university record accessible to him, should have "raked up" nothing better than punish- ments or fines, and that from them no scrap of paper or other document should be forthcoming to indicate Swift's place in the college examinations relatively to his cousin and other students of his time. No such thing appears, and no surprise or regret is expressed at its absence. But it seems to have become matter of talk in the college ; and the well-informed historian of St. Patrick's Cathedral, Mr. Monck Mason, makes the following statement in his elab- orate chapter on Swift: "The learned Dr. Barrett, vice- provost of Trinity College, Dublin, informed me that he was present at a meeting of the board when the late Bish- op of Ossory, at that time a senior fellow" (Doctor Kear- ney, subsequently provost), "discovered among some loose papers a record of the judgments given at a quarterly ex- amination of this period. The name of Jonathan Swift

Marginal notes: 1667-1683. Æt. 1-21. Not proven.

Irregularities not un- likely.

Right clue found and lost.

---

* "Most of his punishments," says Dr. Barrett, "are for non-attendance in chapel. The amount is £1 19s. 4d. confirmed, and 19s. and 10d. taken off. For surplice (that is, for non- attendance in chapel at those times when surplices are required to be worn), 11s. 4d. confirmed, and 6s. 6d. taken off. Of his other punish- ments, those for lectures appear all confirmed ; and are, for catechism, 3s. ; Greek lecture, 9d. ; Hebrew lec- ture, 8d. ; mathematic lecture, 1s. 10d. ; and those for missing night- rolls, or town haunting (that is, for halls)" in other words, not being in the college-hall every night at nine when the students' names were called over, "amount to 3s. 4d., but are all taken off, the admonition being sub- stituted in their place."—*Essay*, 11, 12.

1667–1688. was discovered among the students; and upon his per-
Æt. 1–21. formance in some branches (but which, the learned doctor
could not recollect) the very opprobrious censures of ' pessime' and 'tacet' were pronounced—judgments which are
now rarely if ever given: that of 'vix mediocriter' calling
forth what is emphatically styled 'a caution' from the rul-
ers of that seminary of learning. I have endeavored to ·
obtain a sight of this valuable literary relic, but the representatives of the learned bishop have not been, hitherto,
successful in their search for it." It has been reserved to
the present writer, after this long interval of years, to ex-
Adventures plain why. The relic had been sent by the bishop to his
of a literary friend in England, Edmond Malone; and was found by
relic. me, only a very few years ago, in a copy of Doctor Barrett's book which belonged to Malone; in which were many
notes in his handwriting, with a packet of letters addressed
to him by the author; and which was said to have lain
undisturbed, since Malone's death, on the shelves of the
London book-seller from whom it was purchased by myself. The value of this remarkable discovery is as great
as its interest. It gives Swift an ascertained place among
the students at college with him, and it shows on what insufficient grounds later inmates of the college connected
" pessime " and " tacet " with his name.

Neither word is attached to it in the college-roll. This
contains 175 names, and those of the cousins Swift stand
together, twelfth and thirteenth. Christian names are not
in theirs or in any case given; but the order as well of admission into the college as of seniority in age, which I
have quoted from the senior lecturer's book, fixes it beyond the possibility of dispute that Thomas stands before
Jonathan. The internal evidence presented by this most
interesting roll is not less decisive. Its judgments, the result of one of the last important quarterly examinations in
College ex- Easter Term, 1685, which preceded the bachelor's degree
amination of in February, 1685–'6, not alone confirm Swift's own ac-
1685. count of his studies, but apply otherwise with a perfect
exactness to what is known of the characters of himself

and his cousin. In the fac-simile here made of the first twenty-one names, the reader will of course understand that Pⁿ., G L., and Tⁿ. signify respectively Philosophy, Greek and Latin, and Theology. The first is, in all the old university schemes, the general appellation for logic, metaphysics, and morality. It means mental philosophy, or the science of reasoning; it appears also in the roll as Loc., or logic, other entries presenting the contrast of Phys., or natural philosophy; and in it are comprised those subjects of college study which Swift says he had too much neglected, having no great relish for them by nature. How far he had neglected others; whether, as Lord Orrery tells us, he turned into ridicule every thing but history and poetry, or, as Doctor Delany says, he looked upon the study of Greek and Latin to be downright pedantry, or, as Sheridan avers, he was by scholars esteemed a blockhead; here are the means of determining. He was ill in philosophy; good in Greek and Latin; and negligent in theology. His cousin Thomas was mediocre in all. The pictures are life-like. What Jonathan was to be, and Thomas was to remain, are to be read off in them quite easily.

But can it be said, of the twenty-one names, that any one of them stands really higher in the examination than that of Jonathan Swift? Wade and Blany have the slight advantage of doing indifferently what he did badly, but in every thing else he compares favorably with the best; and "male" or "negligenter" is not the worst censure, though "bene" is the highest praise. There is "pessime," under which, in a later part of the roll not here presented, Sergeant, Cardiffe, and Sheridan fall, in the same branch of study where Swift was deficient; and in theology, where "negligenter" follows his name, "male negligenter" follows Vandeleur, Willson, and several others. With the exceptions stated, he is highest in the portion of the roll before the reader, where the first dozen names are of higher standing than his own; he beats his school and class fellow, Stratford; and some notes from its later portions, taken with the same impartiality, will show his position

1667–1688.
Æt. 1–21.

First twenty-one names on the roll.

Test of Swift's study.

The cousins.

Swift's position on the roll.

1667–1688.
Æt. 1–21.

Fac-simile
of portion of
Dublin Col-
lege Roll:
Easter, 1685.

relatively to the rest of the students who took part in this examination. Of the 175 upon the list, 56 were not examined at all; and out of 68 of the later students on whom judgment is passed in the same three subjects as the earlier, there are only 7 who have "bene" put twice to their names.* All the rest are under one or other of these several heads: "Bene, med^r, med^r;—med^r, vix med^r, med^r;—med^r, med^r, male negligr;—male, med^r, male negligr;—med^r, med^r, male;—med^r, male, vix bene;—med^r, med^r, bene;—med^r, bene, med^r;" nor is any thing more observable than the infrequency of any laudatory judgment, as in the two specially cited, for Latin and Greek. With those exceptions, there are only six† besides Swift that get a "bene" for those studies; and in the two other subjects "mediocriter" is the judgment on the whole six. Where the classification divides Latin and Greek, there is no instance of "bene" put to both. Mongumry and Phipps have "bene" for Latin and "mediocriter" for Greek, while for Travers and Mullan the epithets are transposed. Where the classification takes in four subjects (Log., Phy., G L., and Th.), the name of Tovey, already cited, is the only exception from the "male," "mediocriter," "vix mediocriter," and "male," applied exclusively to those examined in them. Finally, there is an ominous and comprehensive "mediocriter in omnibus" which swallows up 53; and leaves two for the yet lower deep of "vix mediocriter in omnibus." The names need not be mentioned; but there is one claiming remembrance for its contrast to the undistinguished crowd, the morsel of solid bread to those dozens of thin sack, standing solitary and apart from all the rest. Thewles alone, of the hundred and nineteen examined, receives a "bene in omnibus." He was a junior fellow before Swift left the college, and has not been heard of since.

Malone too evidently had not scrutinized this valuable

1667–1688.
Æt. 1–21.

Compared with other students.

Deeps and lower deeps.

Hero of the roll.

* Donavan, Alcock, Briom, Quin, Tovey, Touse, and Luther.   † Goodlett, Beecher, Pim, Garner, Williams, and Downing.

roll.   Eager after the false run started by Doctor Barrett, he missed the scent to which he was so close; thought only of the Terræ Filius; and employed for the mere authentication of Richardson's worthless letter, what was worthy of so much higher use.   Across the pages of Barrett's *Essay* (82 and 83) between which I found the roll, and in which remark is made by Barrett that notwithstanding the ambiguity of Richardson's phrase it may be safely supposed that what was meant to be asserted was, that his information was "originally" derived from a prelate who had been chum or chamber-fellow with Swift, there is this

Comment by Malone.

note in the handwriting of Malone: " This certainly was the meaning; and the prelate from whom the information originally came was the Rev. Doctor Edward Chandler (as Dr. Barrett afterward discovered), who was Bishop of Durham from 1730 to 1750, when he died.   He was bred in the college of Dublin, was in the same class with Swift, and stands next to him on a college-roll of Easter Term, 1685, containing a list of the students then examined, with their several judgments.   It is now before me.   Richardson's informer was this prelate's second son, who was a member of parliament.   He died about the year 1760.   The Bishop of Durham was in the same chamber with Swift under St. George Ashe.   He was in the college of Dublin from 1682 to May, 1688." It would have better justified Malone's sagacity, as well as his taste and love for

The point missed.

letters, if he had pointed out the extreme improbability of any part of a story being true, of which the two leading assertions, the appointment as Terræ Filius and the subsequent expulsion, had been clearly disproved; and if he had shown, by the remarkable evidence before him of the "several judgments" of 1685, that, in the university examination then held, Swift had taken higher place than the prelate so eager after more than sixty years to say an ill word of his old companion.*

---

* The reader is now in a position to estimate the historical and critical value of the opening of that portion | of M. Taine's *History of English Literature* which relates to Swift.   "In 1685, in the great hall of Dublin Uni-

Swift's bitter time in the college came doubtless after
his degree; but there is no ground for connecting it with
the manner in which the degree was granted, or with any
thing but considerations altogether personal. Two days
after Thomas Swift proceeded bachelor in the ordinary
manner, on the 13th of February, 1685–'6, Jonathan received his degree by "special grace" with Nathaniel Jones,
John Jones, Michael Vandeleur, and William Brereton:
but in the several cases the amount of reproach incurred
would be likely to differ widely with the differing circumstances. The specialis gratia took its origin from the necessity of providing, that what was substantially merited
should not be refused because of a failure in some require-
ment of the statutes; upon that, abuses crept in; but enough
has been said to show that Swift's case could not have been
one of those in which it was used to give semblance of
worth to the unworthy. What followed it, appears to be
hardly more clearly understood. Lord Orrery remarks
that so full of indignation was Swift at his treatment in
Dublin, that he at once transferred his studies to Oxford.
Very nearly to the same effect, Delany says that such preparation as he made for a mastership of arts was with a view

Margin notes: 1667–1688. Æт. 1–21. Specialis gratia. What followed the bachelor's degree.

versity, the professors engaged in ex-
amining for the bachelor's degree enjoyed a singular spectacle: A poor
scholar, odd, awkward, with hard blue
eyes, an orphan, friendless, poorly supported by the charity of an uncle, having failed once before to take his degree on account of his ignorance of
logic, had come up again without having condescended to read logic. To
no purpose his tutor set before him
the most respectable folios—Smeglesius, Keckermannus, Burgersdicius.
He turned over a few pages, and shut
them directly. When the argumen-
tation came on, the proctor was obliged
to 'reduce his replies into syllogisms.'
He was asked how he could reason
well without rules; he replied that he
did reason pretty well without them.

This folly shocked them; yet he was
received, though barely, *speciali gratiâ*, says the register, and the professors went away, doubtless with pity-
ing smiles, lamenting the feeble brain
of Jonathan Swift. This was his first
humiliation and his first rebellion.
His whole life was like this moment,
overwhelmed and made wretched by
sorrows and hatred." I quote the
careful translation of Mr. Van Laun
(ii., 116–'7), one of the masters of the
Edinburgh Academy, and will again
indulge the hope which I have had
occasion to express in a former work,
that the students of English literature
in that academy have safer guidance
than the brilliant but too often base-
less fancies of M. Taine.

Margin notes: Dangerous guide.

to Oxford exclusively; Hawkesworth, copying Delany, relates that such was his dread of the repetition of his disgrace, that from the date of his Dublin degree he studied eight hours a day for seven years; and finally Dr. Barrett, taking an opposite view, taxes all his energies to establish that after his bachelorship Swift became reckless of hall or lecture-room, violent and quarrelsome, a stranger to the chapel, a lounger in the town, and forever falling under fine or censure. Walter Scott not inaptly remembered, when he came to this picture by Barrett, how Johnson de-

scribed his Oxford life to Boswell. "Ah, sir, I was mad and violent. It was bitterness that they mistook for frolic. I was miserably poor, and thought to fight my way by my literature and my wit; so I disregarded all power and all authority." But there was a written sentence of Johnson's more nobly applicable both to Swift and to himself, when, in the life of the Dean, he said that the years of labor by which studies had been retrieved which were alleged to have been recklessly or negligently lost, "afforded useful admonition and powerful encouragement to men whose abilities have been made for a time useless by their passions or pleasures, and who, having lost one part of life in idleness, are tempted to throw away the remainder in despair."

Amidst all these varying accounts of opportunities lost and retrieved, one thing can yet be said with certainty, that before he left the college Swift had qualified himself for a master's degree, and that he did not leave it without
a more than competent acquirement in learning. He was never a profound scholar, nor perhaps entitled to the praise of a very exact one; but as early as in his first two years after quitting Dublin, he showed easy and varied knowledge of the principal classical writers, could use fluently the Latin language, was accomplished in French, and had a mass of general reading, in nearly every department of philosophy and letters, seldom equaled in its range and extent, perhaps never in the penetrating insight with which its leading subjects were mastered. He wrote *The Battle*

of the Books in 1696, and in that year had already designed 1667–1688. Æt. 1–21. the great satire which was to expose the corruptions of religion and learning. A foregone conclusion rises out of this, but we have otherwise no clue to the time or mode of the acquirement of what was then turned to such extraordinary use. It was as little Swift's habit in any part of his life to talk of his readings as of his writings, and it was Readings in youth. only for the power or pleasure derived from them to himself that he ever valued either. But, in even such scant allusion as he made in his later to the reading of his younger days, one may observe a taste and turn of thought very far from common. When the Dean of St. Patrick's was resisting the misgovernment of Ireland by England, he declared that he did not frequently quote poets; but he remembered there was in some of Mr. Cowley's love-verses Cowley's love-verses. a strain which he thought extraordinary when a lad of fifteen, but had since come to think might express very well the relation that England desired Ireland to hold to her. "Forbid it, Heaven, my life should be Weigh'd with her least conveniency!" He was not much older when another kind of strain attracted him, and he did not hesitate afterward to say, in his Advice to a clergyman entering into Holy Orders, that he had been better entertained, and more informed, by a few pages in the *Pilgrim's Progress*, Pilgrim's Progress. than by long discourses upon the will and the intellect, and simple or complex ideas.

Let it be finally assumed, then, that the truth of this portion of Swift's college life will be found between the two extremes of the accounts respecting it. He was a little over eighteen when he commenced bachelor, and his purpose in remaining afterward in the college was to qualify for a mastership in the same university. A passage in a letter of Sir William Temple, first published twenty years ago,* places it beyond doubt that Swift meant to A difficult time. have taken his master's degree at Dublin when the rebell-

---

* To be shortly quoted. The statement is confirmed by the master's degree at Oxford immediately following the *ad eundem.*

ion nearly emptied the college. But though he pursued his studies, he was "miserably poor;" and for so high a spirit this was a greater trial in the graduate than in the under-graduate days. What in the one had but barely supported him, had almost wholly ceased to be available in the other: though the lethargy which fell on Godwin Swift did not close in death until a few months before his nephew quitted the college, his estate had been so crippled some time before as to leave at that event a provision altogether inadequate for the sons and daughters who survived him; and but for William Swift, the only one of his uncles beside Godwin who had a settled residence in Dublin, Jonathan must have been nearly destitute. He long remembered as well the help thus received as the kindness that accompanied it, and he calls this kinsman "the best"[*] of his uncles. The house was open to him as long as his uncle lived or his aunt survived him; and on the walls hung the portrait of his favorite ancestor.[†]

"Best" of his uncles.

Uncle Adam. There was another uncle, Adam, who seems to have thriven in the world, for he and Lowndes, a man high in the

---

[*] Letter of November 29th, 1692: written to his uncle from Moor Park (first printed in Deane Swift's *Essay*, 56): in which he says: "My sister told me you were pleased, when she was here, to wonder I did so seldom write to you. I hope you have been so kind to impute it neither to ill-manners nor want of respect...... I always......thought that sufficient from one who has always been but too troublesome to you...... I am sorry my fortune should fling me so far from the best of my relations, but hope that I shall have the happiness to see you some time or other. Pray, my humble service to my good aunt."

[†] "O pray, now I think of it, be so kind as to step to my aunt, and take notice of my great-grandfather's picture; you know he has a ring on his finger, with a seal of an anchor and dolphin about it; but I think there is besides, at the bottom of the picture, the same coat of arms quartered with another, which I suppose was my great-grandmother's. If this be so, it is a stronger argument than the seal. And pray see whether you think that coat of arms was drawn at the same time with the picture, or whether it be of a later hand; and ask my aunt what she knows about it. But perhaps there is no such coat of arms on the picture, and I only dreamed it. My reason is, because I would ask some herald here whether I should choose that coat, or one in Guillim's large folio of heraldry, where my uncle Godwin is named with another coat of arms of three stags. This is sad stuff to write."—*Swift to Esther Johnson, Feb. 29th, 1711-'12.*

Treasury during Anne's last ministry, and to whom Gay 1667–1688.
Æt. 1–21. addressed some humorous verses "on the ingenious and worthy author of that celebrated treatise in folio called the Land-tax Bill," had married two sisters;* but almost all that is known of him in connection with his great kinsman is an allusion from the latter† which might lead us to suppose they had had personal intercourse in the North of Ireland, where presumably this uncle then lived. Of another relative something is more certainly known. While at Moor Park, Swift gave praise so unusual with him to a cousin Willoughby, Godwin's eldest surviving son by his Cousin Willoughby. first marriage, settled prosperously as a merchant in Lisbon, that it lends some color of probability to a story told by Mr. Deane Swift on the relation of Willoughby's eldest daughter,‡ and accepted by all his biographers. "It happened when he was at the University of Dublin that one day, as he was looking out of his window pensive and melancholy, his pockets being then at the lowest ebb, having spied a master of a ship gazing about in the college courts—*Lord! thought he, if that person should now be* Waiting on providence. *inquiring and staring about for my chamber, in order to bring me some present from cousin Willoughby Swift, what a happy creature I should be!* He had scarce amused himself with this pleasing imagination, when, behold, the master of the ship, having come into his chamber, asked him if his name was Jonathan Swift. He told him it was. Why, then, said the master, I have something for you that

---

* "Going to town this morning, I met in the Pall Mall a clergyman of Ireland, whom I love very well...... and with him a little jackanapes of Ireland too, who married Nanny Swift, Uncle Adam's daughter, one Perry...... His wife has sent him here to get a place from Lowndes; because my uncle and Lowndes married two sisters, and Lowndes is a great man here in the treasury."—*Journal, May 21st,* 1711. Another daughter of Uncle Adam was Mrs. Whiteway.

† "My uncle Adam asked me one day in private, as by direction, what my designs were in relation to you, because it might be a hindrance to you if I did not proceed."—*Swift to Miss Waring, the 4th of May,* 1700.

‡ Mrs. Swanton. "She had heard it many years ago from the Doctor himself;" but to Mr. Deane himself, I should say, its particularity has a suspicious likeness.

1667–1688.
Æt. 1–21.
A sailor "ex machinâ."

was sent to you by Mr. Willoughby Swift. Whereupon he drew out of his pocket a large greasy leather bag, and poured him out all the money that it contained on the table. As the sum which he had now received was much greater than ever in his life he had been master of before at any one time, he pushed over without reckoning them a good number of the silver cobs (for it was all in that specie) to the honest sailor, and desired he would accept of them for his trouble. But the sailor would not touch a farthing. No, no, master, said he, Ize take nothing for my trouble. I would do more than that comes to for Mr. Willoughby Swift. Whereupon Jonathan gathered up the money as fast as he could, and thrust it into his pocket. *For by the Lord Harry*, said he, *I was afraid if the money had lain much longer on the table he might have repented his generosity and taken a good part of it.* But from that time for-

Essay, 54–5.

ward he declared that he became a better economist, and never was without some little money in his pocket." That Swift did receive help from this cousin at Lisbon, and that the fact impressed gratefully both himself and his mother,* there is no doubt; but whether it came at this time, and in this way, can only now be determined by the degree of credibility in the story itself, which for that reason is here given with its particular "thought he's" and "said he's" exactly as first related. It is likely enough that such an

Habits of economy.

incident should have impressed the importance of economy and the uses of a little money in the pocket; and it is in any case certain that Swift acquired the habit, at an unusually early time, of keeping very minute record of the pence he expended and the shillings or pounds that were due to him. Many of his account-books are in my possession, and will be used to illustrate his life.

---

* "I wish and shall pray he may be as happy as he deserves, and he can not be more. My mother desires her best love to him and to you."— *3d June*, 1694. Swift to Deane Swift the elder, who passed some time in Willoughby's counting-house, and whose son and namesake is better known to us. Willoughby was the second son of Godwin's first marriage, but became the eldest by a brother's death "some years before 1688."—*Essay*, 50. See also *post*, 87.

Another of Mr. Deane Swift's stories it is impossible to 1667-1688.
Æт. 1-21. accept even conditionally. "Mr. Warren,* the chamber-fellow of Swift in the University of Dublin, and a gentle- Not credible. man of undoubted veracity, whose sister had made some very considerable impressions upon the Doctor's heart in the days of his youth, assured a relation of mine, whom he courted for a wife about eight or nine and forty years ago, that he saw the *Tale of a Tub* in the handwriting of Dr. Swift, when the Doctor was but nineteen years old; but what corrections or improvements it might have received before the publication in the year 1697 he could by no means declare."† The *Tale* did not appear until 1704, but Swift has himself informed us that the most part of it was written in 1696 during his second residence with Temple,‡ and there is certainly no evidence that any portion was in existence before that date. But he was familiar with Waring's family for more than three years beyond it; and Fellow-student Waring. it is not at all improbable that the story is true in every thing but place and (a more important drawback) date, and that the manuscript was seen by Waring before its publication.

For a third incident of the later college-time he is himself the authority. In the anecdotes, as we have seen, he relates that he happened, before twenty years old, to contract a giddiness and coldness of stomach that almost brought him to his grave, and this disorder pursued him with intermissions of two or three years (hazarding a sorrowful prediction) "to the end of his life." Sometimes Two life-long enemies. he a little altered the date of what he believed to have been the origin of these miseries, and, as in a letter to Mrs. Howard (Lady Suffolk) in August, 1727, fixed his giddiness at the first residence with Temple, and his deaf-

---

* The proper name is Waring. He stands 129th on the college-roll (*ante* 52), and was one of the batch of "mediocriter in omnibus" at the examination in 1685.

† *Essay*, 31.

‡ "The greatest part of that book was finished about thirteen years since, 1696, which is eight years before it was published."—*Swift's Apology* prefixed to the edition issued by Benjamin Tooke in 1709-'10.

ness at the second.* "About two hours before you were born, I got my giddiness, by eating a hundred golden pippins at a time, at Richmond; and when you were four years and a quarter old, bating two days, having made a fine seat" (having selected, he means, some favorite spot in the grounds at Moor Park) "about twenty miles further in Surrey, where I used to read, etc., there I got my deaf-

ness; and these two friends have visited me, one or other, every year since, and being old acquaintance, have now thought fit to come together." That the disorders did so pursue him, and may have had part, as he sadly foretold, in what at last overwhelmed him, there will be evidence enough. From those early days up to 1708, when he told Archbishop King that he had been persecuted with a cruel distemper of giddiness in his head for more than seven weeks which would not suffer him to write or think of any thing; through all the years that followed to 1727, when he told Knightley Chetwode that he had been nine weeks very ill in England both of giddiness and deafness, saying in the same year to Sheridan that he believed his giddiness to be the disorder that would at last get the better of him; from thence onward to 1733, when he wrote to the second Lord Oxford that he was just recovering after seven months' cruel indispositions of giddiness and deafness, the former of which he doubted would never quite leave him till he left it; and again to 1737, when he told Mr. Richardson that he had been troubled with a giddy head and deafness for nearly seven weeks that unfitted him for human conversation; the continual recurrence, for less lengthened periods, of these terrible and frequent visitors has large and reiterated mention in his letters.

His own belief as to the origin of the giddiness he never changed, and it is curious to observe how much it cost

---

* That the illness began in England he repeated ten years later; and if his memory is not at fault in the date given here, it must have happened during one of his boy-visits to his mother. "In England, before I was twenty, I got a cold which gave me a deafness that I could never clear myself of...... My left ear has never been well since."—*April 30th*, 1737.

him all his life to abstain from fruit, which he as passion- 1667-1688. *Æt.* 1-21.
ately liked as he steadily forced himself to resist; but
there is a remark upon it by Johnson which has his characteristic common sense: "The original of diseases is
commonly obscure; and almost every boy eats as much
fruit as he can get, without any inconvenience."

Swift was little more than two months past his twenty-
first birthday, when Tyrconnel let loose the Celtic popu-
lation on the English settlers in Dublin, and, quitting the Swift driven from college.
college with a crowd of other fugitives, he found his way
to his mother's house in England..

BOOK SECOND.

UNDER SIR WILLIAM TEMPLE'S ROOF.

1689-1699. Æt. 22-32.

I. First Residence at Moor Park.

II. In Orders, and at Kilroot.

III. Second Residence with Temple.

I.

FIRST RESIDENCE AT MOOR PARK.

1689-1694. ÆT. 22-27.

THE little that is known of Abigail Swift accounts for the admiration as well as the strong affection uniformly shown her by her famous son. Character, humor,* uprightness, and independence, are in all the traditions concerning her. She lived twenty-two years beyond the present date ; and, excepting two visits made to Jonathan in Ireland, never quitted the home in Leicester to which he is said to have traveled to see her rarely less than once a year : by coach when he could afford it, by the wagon or on foot in his poorer days. Though with a reservation of dislike for its fools and gossips, he always remembered Leicester kindly ; and when he was the familiar companion of dukes and first ministers, he took pains to choose a " Leicester† lad " for the making of his periwig. He was there in the winter of 1707, and saw a popular whig election, foreshadowing the general election so soon to follow, when, for the last time in the reign of Anne, whigs were to triumph at the polling-booths over tories and highfliers. But never did he see so much of the life that is

---

* This quality appears in a story told by Swift himself to Dr. Lyon, of the only visit she ever made to her son in Ireland, which was very shortly after he took possession of Larracor ; when she imposed on the credulity of the lodging-keeper to whose house she went, by pretending she had come to receive the addresses of a lover, and in that character received her son's first visit, before she confessed the truth. Mrs. Brent, Swift's housekeeper in later years, kept the lodging.

† "It has cost me three guineas to-day for a periwig. I am undone ! It was made by a Leicester lad, who married Mr. Worrell's daughter, where my mother lodged ; *so I thought it would be cheap.*"—*Swift to Esther Johnson, 15th Jan.,* 1710-'11. Nothing is found to be so characteristic of Swift as the invention of selfish reasons for doing unselfish things.

1689–1694.
Æt. 22–27.

Observation
of low life.

worth seeing, he used to tell the great men with whom he was already familiar, than when he saw it in his earlier travelings to and from that place. When life presented itself to him as he sat in a carrier's cart; when he would dine with peddlers and hostlers at obscure ale-houses; when, seeing written over a door, "lodgings for a penny," he would hire a bed, giving additional sixpence for clean sheets;* those were experiences that had been filled with all kinds of profit for him. Presumably they would belong to the days when Leicester knew him first; and what he thus learned of the ways and speech of the common people, enlarged and varied at every visit, is likely in sober fact to have been, thus far, not the least precious part of his education. The local historian naturally prefers to dwell on such traditions as that Sir George Beaumont received him at Stoughton Hall, and that the family connections of his mother, the Herricks of Beaumanor Park, and the Heyricks of Thurmaston, were not ashamed of him; but a greater probability seems to have been that his mother might for his sake be ashamed of them. Her worldly

Dignity in
poverty.

disadvantages never went before herself, in his own remark of her; and what is said in many varying tributes to her quiet independence† is in effect the same which afterward was said of one who also dignified poverty—that no circumstances external to herself ever prompted her to make the least apology for them, or to seem even sensible of their existence.

---

* "This practice Lord Orrery imputes to his innate love of grossness and vulgarity: some may ascribe it to his desire of surveying human life through all its varieties."—*Johnson.*

† "Her conversation," says Mr. Deane Swift, writing in 1754, "was so extremely polite, cheerful, and agreeable, even to the young and sprightly, that some of the family who paid her a visit near fifty years ago at Leicester speak of her to this day with the greatest affection......

She was a very early riser; was always dressed for the whole day at about six o'clock in the morning, in a mantua and petticoat, which, according to the fashion of those times, she constantly wore; and her chief amusements were needle-work and reading...... She declared in her latter days (for indeed she was a woman of an easy, contented spirit) that she was rich and happy, and abounded with every thing."

Her son had need of her counsel soon. "When I went 1689-1694.
a lad to my mother," he wrote to Mr. Worrall in January, Æt. 22-27.
1728-'9, "after the Revolution, she brought me to the
knowledge of a family where there was a daughter, with
whom I was acquainted. My prudent mother was afraid
I should be in love with her; but when I went to London
she married an innkeeper in Loughborough in that county, by whom she had several children." This was Betty Betty Jones.
Jones, who will re-apppear in his days of celebrity living
apart from her "rogue" of an innkeeper. She was an educated girl, notwithstanding the match she made, her mother and Swift's being cousins; and it was a legacy of five
hundred pounds from the mother on which she was living
at the time of his later knowledge of her. Hardly had
he escaped from this Betty Jones, however, when there
began to be talk of another; and long before the "some
months" passed which he describes as the duration of this
visit to Leicester, his mother must have been convinced of
the truth of what her son already had been told by a person "of great honor" in Ireland who was "pleased to stoop
so low as to look into my mind; and used to tell me that
it was like a conjured spirit, that would do mischief if I
would not give it employment."

How to give it employment was then anxiously consid- Application
ered, and it was his mother's suggestion that he should ap- to Temple.
ply to Sir William Temple. Besides the old connection
of Godwin Swift with Temple's father, Master of the Irish
Rolls, which sinecure office his more celebrated son inher-
ited from him, Temple's wife was a connection of her
own;* and Lady Temple still lived when Swift's application was made, and received with favor. He joined the
retired statesman at Moor Park, near Farnham, before the
close of 1689, and continued with him, not without intervals of absence, until just before Lady Temple's death in
1694. These five years are to be regarded as the first res-

---

* "Sir William Temple's lady," | 15). Orrery knew the Temples then
says Lord Orrery, "was related to | living, and his statement must be ac-
Doctor Swift's mother" (*Remarks*, | cepted implicitly.

1689–1694.
ÆT. 22–27.

First resi-
dence.

idence with Temple; but there was one interruption to it at the outset, which will be found, when closely looked at, to suggest a less confused and unintelligible story of it than has heretofore been given. It has been treated by all the biographers as a period of service, at the close of which Swift was on the same footing as at the beginning. Of the second residence this might be said; but not of the first.

He went from his mother's house to Sir William Temple's, in the summer of 1689, "a raw and inexperienced youth," as he described himself, but with mental equipment to set against this disadvantage; beginning thus early, there can be no doubt, to feel conscious of unusual powers, and with a ready observation for every thing around him. Temple then knew nothing of him but his family claim, and received him as on this ground entitled to protection; though very soon he had intimation of qualities of intellect noticeable for themselves, and not easily compressible within the limits of the kind of service that at first, perhaps, had alone been designed. The youth had not completed a year's* residence, when, as he says him-

Two periods
in the first
residence.

self, "he returned to Ireland by advice of physicians, who weakly imagined that his native air might be of some use to recover his health." Ill-health there was, but perhaps restlessness and impatience in greater measure; for the residence at Temple's, which was to prove in the end a priceless advantage to his young and teeming brain, could only have seemed at the beginning to make his future prospect more barren. Temple's behavior to him was nevertheless considerate. His friend Sir Robert Southwell went this very year to Ireland as Secretary of State, and to him he made intercession for Swift. The letter, writ-

Close of first
period: May,
1690.

ten from "Moor Park, near Farnham, May 29th, 1690," and discovered only very recently,† possesses remarkable inter-

---

* He calls it himself "two years" in the first draft of the anecdotes; but, as has been seen, this is corrected in my amended copy by the insertion, | in his own hand, of "1690" as the date of his first return to Ireland.

† It was first printed in Mr. Cunningham's edition (1854) of Johnson's

est. "This afternoon I hear, though by a common hand, 1689-1694.
Æt. 22-27.
Temple's let-
ter recom-
mending
Swift, May,
1690.
that you are going over into Ireland secretary of state for
that kingdom, upon which I venture to make you the offer of a servant, in case you may have occasion for such a
one as this bearer." (It may not be needless to remind
the reader that the word "servant" here used, according
to the custom of the time, carries no menial sense, but is
as the correlative of master, the person to receive employment or place from him who has it to give: "a gentleman to wait on you," as later words explain.) "He was
born and bred there (though of a good family in Herefordshire), was near seven years in the College of Dublin,
and ready to take his degree of Master of Arts, when he
was forced away by the desertion of that college upon the
calamities of the country. Since that time he has lived
in my house, read to me, writ for me, and kept all accounts
as far as my small occasions required. He has Latin and
Greek, some French, writes a very good and current hand,
is very honest and diligent, and has good friends, though
they have for the present lost their fortunes, in Ireland,
and his whole family having been long known to me
obliged me thus far to take care of him. If you please to
accept him into your service, either as a gentleman to wait
on you, or as clerk to write under you, and either to use
him so if you like his service, or upon any establishment
of the college to recommend him to a fellowship there, Suggesting a
college fel-
lowship.
which he has a just pretense to, I shall acknowledge it as
a great obligation to me as well as to him." The last lines
of the letter, like a lady's postscript, contain what was
probably Swift's object in getting it written. It can hardly be doubted that they expressed his own hope in regard
to the college, and his return to Ireland would be thus
better accounted for than by the reason put forward; but
though he must have placed the letter in the hands of
Southwell, among whose papers it was found, nothing
came of it except that he was shortly again at Temple's

Lives: being then in the autograph | heath. These have since been dis-
collections of Mr. Young, of Black- | persed, and it is now in my possession.

1689-1694.
Æt. 22–27.
Second peri-
od of first
residence:
Aug., 1690. on an improved footing. "Growing worse, he soon went back to Sir William Temple's, with whom growing into some confidence, he was often trusted with matters of great importance."

To service of that kind the account to Southwell would not apply, and far less the description by Richardson at the appearance of Mr. Deane Swift's book which has since found a place in all the biographies. It has been shown how little reliable is one half of that letter; and the other half compels the same distrust. "Mr. Temple (nephew to Sir William Temple), who lately died at Bath, declared to a friend of mine that Sir William hired Swift, at his first entrance into the world, to read to him, and sometimes to be his amanuensis, at the rate of £20 a year and his board, which was then high preferment to him; but that Sir William never favored him with his conversation because of his ill qualities, nor allowed him to sit down at table with him." There is no authority but this, for either the sum said to have been paid or the treatment alleged to have been received; and such authority should at once have condemned both averments. After Temple's death, Swift had disputes with the sister, Lady Giffard, and her nephews, arising out of Temple's bequest to him of the publication of his writings; and though these had been settled, and he was in not unfriendly correspondence six years later with the younger of the nephews, John Temple, they had been revived and imbittered by an advertisement from Lady Giffard on the appearance of the last volume, and at various times yet later there passed intemperate words. "I thought I saw Jack Temple and his wife pass by me to-day in their coach," he wrote on his arrival in London in 1710, "but I took no notice of them. I am glad I have wholly shaken off that family." In his next letter he says, "I will not see Lady Giffard until she begs my pardon;" and six weeks later he calls her an "old beast," repeating that in honor he can not see her.* For

<margin>More of the Richardson attack.</margin>
<margin>Worthless authority.</margin>
<margin>Temple quarrels.</margin>

---

* "The other day I saw Jack Temple in the Court of Requests; it | was the first time of seeing him; so we talked two or three careless words

all which she paid him back, perhaps more than suffi- 1689-1694.
Æt. 22-27.
ciently, when she permitted a friend of her family to transcribe a letter never yet seen in the original, which she had
indorsed as "Swift's penitential letter," and which Macau- Alleged lan-
guage of
penitence.
lay has characterized, with a degree of accuracy that will
appear when the story of it is told, as the "language of a
lackey, or rather of a beggar." In effect it takes blame
to himself for the troubles and infirmities that had closed
this first residence with Temple; and before the difference
which led to it is described it will be only fair to quote
what Swift wrote to the head of the Temple family some
years after the quarrel: "I own myself indebted to Sir Swift to Lord
Palmerston:
29th Jan.,
1726.
William for recommending me to the late King, although
without success, and to his choice of me to take care of his
posthumous writings. But I hope you will not charge my
living in his family as an obligation, for I was educated to
little purpose if I retired to his house on any other motive
than the benefit of his conversation and advice, and the
opportunity of pursuing my studies. For, being born to
no fortune, I was at his death as far to seek as ever, and
perhaps you will allow that I was of some use to him."
Thus to repel altogether the sense of obligation, was in
other words to say that he gave more than he received;
and taking as a whole his intercourse with Temple, from
the date of its resumption after the brief interval of absence at the close of 1690, there is every presumption that
he was entitled to say so.

A particular kindness now rendered is mentioned by Remarks, 17.
Lord Orrery, who says that Temple "most generously"
stepped in to Swift's assistance in the matter of his Oxford mastership of arts; and though he a little overpraises
it as "uncommonly magnificent," moving thereby much
wrath in Mr. Deane Swift, it was at least a timely service.
Writing a few weeks afterward to thank his uncle Wil-

---

and parted."—*5th December*, 1710.
Jack was the younger son of Temple's
brother, Sir John. His elder brother, William, was afterward created

Baron Temple Viscount Palmerston
in the Irish peerage on the 12th of
March, 1722, the year of his aunt
Giffard's death.

liam for his care in sending him the certificate of his Dublin degree required for his *ad eundem* at Hart Hall, as Hartford College was then called, Swift remarks that he never was more satisfied than in the behavior of the University of Oxford to him. He had, he says, all the civilities he could wish for, and so many favors that he was

ashamed to have been more obliged in a few weeks to strangers than ever he was in seven years to Dublin College. It is his first known success, and much that is not with exactness known may have dated from it. If he did not now first break into verse, it is certain that he wrote at this time his earliest piece that has survived; and some

of the lines of his eighteenth ode of the second book of Horace (of which a similar paraphrase is by far the most pleasing effort of Pope's boyhood) may possibly have been meant to involve an application to himself. He declares that he is content with what the gods have given him, and is unskilled to raise himself by unworthy arts. Thomas

Swift obtained his master's degree at Balliol concurrently with his cousin Jonathan at Hart Hall, and, a little later, was for a time Temple's chaplain. Jonathan told his uncle William that he was not himself to take orders till the King gave him a prebendary.

The remark is sufficiently decisive of the altered footing on which he now stood at Moor Park. Of that dwelling and its celebrated master not much needs here be said. Temple's part in public affairs was played out before Charles the Second's death; and through the tragedy of disaster which closed in the Revolution he. was only a looker-on. But it was natural that the Prince of Orange, on his landing in England, should have turned to the au-

thor of the Triple Alliance, of the treaty that ended the second Dutch war, and, above all, of the marriage that had placed himself on the steps of the English throne, as one of the first Englishmen from whom it behooved him to ask counsel. Temple had been on familiar terms with him at The Hague; and though he declined to be Secretary of State, he gave his advice freely. He then lived at Sheen,

near Richmond, where, says Swift, to whom that earlier 1689-1694.
residence was also personally known,* the King visited his Æt. 22-27.
old friend often, and took his advice "in affairs of greatest consequence." There was additional attraction for the
King when Temple finally changed Sheen for Moor Park, Temple at
Moor Park.
a place better suited to retirement, where, amidst the heath
and furze of one of the loneliest parts of Surrey, he had
created what might have been the retreat of a Dutch burg-
omaster, with terrace and canal, clipped trees and grounds
and flower-beds, laid out with quaint precision. If moral-
ists ever helped themselves, Swift might have profited betimes by the moral he was wise enough to draw thus early, in a very good couplet, from such a close to a life so
busy and aspiring.

> "You strove to cultivate a barren Court in vain,
> Your Garden's better worth your nobler pain."

Macaulay's essay on Sir William Temple mentions the
fact of his sister, Lady Giffard, living here with Temple
and his wife after their son's melancholy death, and adds
that there were others "to whom a far higher interest be-
longs. An eccentric, uncouth, disagreeable young Irish- Swift at
Moor Park
(Macaulay).
man, who had narrowly escaped plucking at Dublin, at-
tended Sir William as an amanuensis for board and twenty
pounds a year, dined at the second table, wrote bad verses
in praise of his employer, and made love to a very pretty,
dark-eyed young girl who waited on Lady Giffard. Little
did Temple imagine that the coarse exterior of his dependent concealed a genius equally suited to politics and to letters, a genius destined to shake great kingdoms, to stir the
laughter and the rage of millions, and to leave to posterity
memorials which can perish only with the English language.
Little did he think that the flirtation in his servants' hall,
which he perhaps scarcely deigned to make the subject
of a jest, was the beginning of a long, unprosperous love,
which was to be as widely famed as the passion of Petrarch

---

* See a note by Nichols in his second edition of the *Works*, i., 31.

1689-1694.
Æt. 22-27.

or of Abelard. Sir William's secretary was Jonathan Swift. Lady Giffard's waiting-maid was poor Stella." What John Temple said, at the close of his life, of the man with whom his family had bitterly quarreled, is the sole authority for the opening lines of this description,

Macaulay's insufficient authority.

though even that does not justify the "second," or servants', table; and a date will dispose of its closing state-ment, as far as relates to the first residence. When Swift went to Moor Park, Esther Johnson was little over seven years old. He spoke of her afterward as only six, which was the old impression about her always in his mind; but she was really in her eighth year. Her mother was some-thing more than waiting-woman, having rather the charac-ter of governess or companion ("friend and companion" Scott believed her to have been) to Lady Giffard, with whom she remained so connected until that lady's death, and long after Swift had reached his highest fame. Two

Inmates of Temple's house.

daughters, "Hetty" and a younger sister, Ann, whose at-tractive appearance and modest manners find mention in the Journal to Esther, lived with her in the house; and there is no evidence of either of them having "waited" on any body but herself. Proof is equally wanting that any thing "eccentric" had yet shown itself in Swift. At no time can it fairly have been said of him that he was "uncouth." And "disagreeable" as he doubtless had the power to be, his not less remarkable power of making him-self agreeable was more likely to have impressed itself on the persons named, at the time the description refers to. If he had little help from fortune, he had from nature a supreme gift, a charm in personal intercourse that none could resist, and which attracted to him in especial the favor and desire of women. But if he was really making

Occupations of Swift.

love at this time, it was not to "Stella;" and it was rather his misfortune than his fault to be writing bad verses.

Of Hetty Johnson he became first the playfellow and soon the volunteer teacher, and remembered long how he had guided the little hand in writing, and how his mind had given to hers its first impress. "I met Mr. Harley in

the Court of Requests," he wrote to her when great minis- 1689-1694.
Æt. 22-27.
ters were his obedient servants, "and he asked me how
long I had learned the trick of writing to myself. He had
seen your letter through the glass case at the coffee-house,
and would swear it was my hand; and Mr. Ford, who took
and sent it me, was of the same mind. I remember others have formerly said so too. I think I was little MD's
writing-master?" Not less was he trying to be agree- Hetty's writ-
ing-master.
able to his employer if he wrote verses to him, however
indifferent; and the poetical eulogy of Temple has at
least this much value for us, angry as poor Swift would
have been to think that any one should connect it with his
memory. No doubt it is bad, as are other things of the
kind then also written. An Ode to Sancroft, on the arch-
bishop becoming a non-juror; an Ode to the King, on Earliest
verse-mak-
ing.
his reduction of Ireland to obedience; and an Ode to the
Athenian Society, on Dunton, the book-seller, setting up in
a corner of his shop that now forgotten rival to the Royal
Society, are all of them productions which he seems to
have had no part in preserving or publishing. Poetry at
first is of necessity imitative; and it was Swift's misfortune
to have turned from the strong to the weak side of Cowley.

> "Forgot his Epic, his Pindaric art,
> But still we love his language of the heart."

It was his language of the heart Swift had been studying
at the age of fifteen, as we have noticed; but now a suggestion from those he desired most to please had directed
him to Cowley's odes, and under encouragement from Sir
William and Lady Temple he attempted his Pindaric Pindaric
flights.
flights.* He would hardly otherwise have permitted Dun-

* "The undertaking," says Scott, been written in his later time with "On the
speaking of the Pindaric odes, "is Temple, I can not bring myself im- Burning of
said to have been pressed upon him plicitly to believe in. Scott received Whitehall."
by Sir William and Lady Temple, it from an executor of Dr. Lyon, Mr.
who were admirers of Cowley." An- Thomas Steele (O'Connell's friend),
other poem, "On the Burning of with some undoubtedly genuine letters
Whitehall" (1697), alleged to have and pieces by Swift, and printed it as

1689-1694.
Æt. 22-27.
ton to advertise him among the wits as an inmate of Moor Park and a .friend of its master. That notorious person printed what was sent him with a letter signed Jonathan Swift, which described the writer's having heard of the society as he passed through Oxford, and his having " a while after come to this place upon a visit to Sir William Temple." Such a letter from a man living in the servants' hall on a wage of twenty pounds a year might indeed entitle him to be called " eccentric."

Three days before its date he had replied to some advice sent him by a clergyman of Leicester whom he calls his good cousin, in regard to some former love-making with one of his female acquaintance there; and the letter exhibits his character, and touches some points in his life. Mr. Kendall having heard of an improvement in his prospects, seems to have thought there was danger of his getting into a marriage entanglement in ignorance of rumors that were abroad about the lady. The people is a lying sort of beast, says Swift as to this, and particularly in Leicester; yet they seldom talk without some glimpse of reason. But as to marriage, he does not belong to the kind of persons, of whom he has known a great number, that ruin themselves by it. A thousand household thoughts always drive matrimony out of his mind whenever it chances to come there; and his own cold temper and unconfined humor are of themselves a greater hinderance than any fear of that which is the subject of his friend's letter. " I am naturally temperate ; and never engaged in the contrary, which usually produces those effects." At

A letter from Leicester, Jan., 1692.

Swift's reply.

Self-portraiture.

---

found "in his handwriting and with his corrections;" but he does not say that he saw the MS. himself, and its two allusions to Charles the First appear to me to be decisive against it. There is nothing in Swift's expressed opinions at any period of his life to render conceivably his a description of that king's death as "fifty tyrants executing one" amidst "eternal acclamations." I should otherwise have

rejoiced to give Swift the credit of such vigorous verse as this :

"Down come the lofty roofs, the cedar burns,
The blended metal to a torrent turns.
The carvings crackle and the' marbles rive,
The paintings shrink ; vainly the Henries strive,
Propt by great Holbein's pencil ; down they fall.   [all."
The fiery deluge sweeps and swallows

the same time he admits he has failings that might lead
people, in regard to such matters, to suppose him serious
while he had no design other than to entertain himself
when idle, or when something went amiss in his affairs: a
thing indeed so common with him that he could remember
twenty women in his life to whom he had behaved himself just the same way. "I shall speak plainly to you," he
added. And then came words that certainly foreshadow,
if they do not make intelligible, the fate that was to join
his name so strangely, through all future time, to that of
her who then lived under the same roof with him, a child
of ten years old. "The very ordinary observations I made   Views as to
with going half a mile beyond the university have taught   marriage.
me experience enough not to think of marriage, till I settle my fortune in the world, which I am sure will not be
in some years: and even then I am so hard to please myself that I suppose I shall put it off to the other world."
As to what Mr. Kendall said of his "great prospects of
making his fortune," it was a kindness that had "only
looked on the best side." He was busily engaged, but not
to much purpose. He found that he must be employed,   Necessity for
for when he was alone there was something that for want   self-employ-
of practice turned all into speculation and thought: "in-   ment.
somuch that, in these seven weeks I have been here, I
have writ, and burned and writ again, upon almost all
manner of subjects, more, perhaps, than any man in England." He closes, however, by telling his friend that
whenever the time came for taking sober resolutions, such ,
as that he now intended, of entering into the church, he
should not find it hard to "put off this kind of folly at
the porch."

That was at the beginning of 1692; and in the first
months of 1693 the time for soberness of resolution, and
for any kind of greatness of fortune, might seem to have
suddenly come. He was on his way to the palace at Ken-   On his way
sington, charged with a letter and message from Sir Wil-   to Kensing-
liam Temple, which he was himself to explain to the King,   ton Palace.
and to enforce by illustrations from the English history.

1689-1694.
Æt. 22-27.

Sent by
Temple to
the King.

History, vi.,
282-'3.

Swift known
to William.

Advice given
and not
taken.

The proposed Triennial Bill having alarmed William, he had sent the Earl of Portland for advice to Moor Park; and Temple, after doing his best with Portland to remove the King's fears, had a misgiving that his argument might not be safe in the Earl's hands, and, being unable himself to attend the King, resolved to send Swift to him. "The secretary," says William's noble historian, "was a poor scholar of four or five and twenty, under whose plain garb and ungainly deportment were concealed some of the choicest gifts that have ever been bestowed on any of the children of men,* rare powers of observation, brilliant wit, grotesque invention, humor of the most austere flavor, yet exquisitely delicious, eloquence singularly pure, manly, and perspicuous.... To William he was already slightly known. At Moor Park the King had sometimes, when his host was confined by gout to an easy-chair, been attended by the secretary about the grounds. His majesty had condescended to teach his companion the Dutch way of cutting and eating asparagus, and had graciously asked whether Mr. Swift would like to have a captain's commission in a cavalry regiment.† But now for the first time the young man was to stand in the royal presence as a counselor." The sequel may be told by Swift himself. What had weighed heavily with William was that Charles the First had passed such a bill. But Swift explained that Charles's ruin was not owing to his passing a bill which did not hinder him from dissolving any parliament, but to the passing another bill which put it out of his power to dissolve the parliament then in being without its own consent. "Mr. Swift, who was well versed in English history,... gave the King a short account of the matter, and

---

* A phrase taken by Macaulay from Swift himself, who characterizes Bolingbroke (in the *Enquiry*, 1715) as "adorned with the choicest gifts that God hath yet thought fit to bestow on the children of men."

† Mr. Deane Swift is the authority. "The King, as I have heard from the Doctor's own mouth, offered to make him a captain of horse, and gave him instructions, so great was the freedom of their conversation, how to cut asparagus (a vegetable his majesty was extremely fond of) in the Dutch manner."—*Essay*, 108.

a more large one to the Earl of Portland, but all in vain: 1689–1694.
for the King, by ill advisers, was prevailed upon to refuse Æt. 22–27.
passing the bill.   This was the first time that Mr. Swift First experi-
had ever any converse with courts, and he told his friends ence of courts.
it was the first incident that helped to cure him of vani-
ty." One may guess, from this, the confidence in himself
with which the young scholar had stepped into the closet
of the King.

But to the cure of his vanity the ill-success of his argument was not the only help administered.   Now was the
time when some disputes with Temple himself appear to
have begun, and when, from an unexpected quarter, the
literary aspiration most encouraged by Temple received a Other disap-
check.   Dryden, deposed from the laureateship, still ruled pointments.
at the Rose in Covent-garden ; and young Swift, already
well known to the chief of the rising men, Congreve, and
with the double claim on Dryden of brother-craftsman and
kinsman, had found his way to that resort of the wits.   "I
heard my father say," Joseph Warton tells us, in his *Essay* IL, 312.
on Pope, "that Mr. Elijah Fenton, who was his intimate
friend, and had been his master, informed him that Dryden, upon seeing some of Swift's earliest verses, said to
him, ' Young man, you will never be a poet !' " Johnson
also reports Dryden's sentence, "Cousin Swift, you will Dryden's
never be a poet !" and says that Swift never ceased to re- harsh sentence.
sent it.   The contempt would not be felt less bitterly because of praise from the same quarter lately lavished on
his school-fellow, Congreve ; but it is seldom that such per-
emptory sayings are in any case wise.   Equal disadvantages followed here from the hasty judgment and from
the anger it provoked.   A famous poet had to suffer, not
a little, for too sharply handling a young kinsman who
was able to strike back as heavy a blow ; and resentment Swift's retal-
at the greatest satirist in English verse proved to be no iation.
help to one having like ambition whom it indisposed to
profit by his highest example.   There can hardly be a
doubt that the war Swift afterward waged with the triplet
was no real distaste for it, but only part of his quarrel with

1689-1694.
Æt. 22-27.
its most consummate master; for in the poem shown to
Dryden, as well as in that which he addressed to Sancroft,
there were some that might have saved it from contempt.
The ode to the deprived archbishop has a note intimating
that it was written at the request of the Bishop of Ely.
Turner was deprived in 1690, the year following its alleged date; and if such a request was made, we must assume that Swift saw this bishop soon after he first went to
Moor Park.   But whether it was Turner or Temple who
put him first upon the writing of odes, there can be no
doubt who it was that brought to an end the too daring
enterprise.   After Dryden's verdict he wrote no more.
The close of the year when he went with Temple's message to the King is the time when he addressed to Congreve a poem in the heroic metre, which is one of the two
best of his uncollected pieces.   The tory Rose was now
become the whig Will's coffee-house; and in the chair so
lately filled by Dryden sat the young whig wit and dram-
atist, who by his comedies of *The Old Bachelor* and *The
Double Dealer*, produced a couple of years before, had
sprung into that highest seat.   None could have rejoiced
at this more than Swift, who told Pope truly, twenty-five
years later, that he had loved Congreve from his youth.
They had been familiar both in school and college, and
Swift never forgot his old companion when occasions came
that he could serve him.   But this is not yet; for, though
Congreve is two years the younger, he is far above Swift
in fame and influence.   Swift nevertheless addresses him
as " my Congreve," and has the boldness to tell him that
it will also be his mission some day to " make sin and folly bleed."   The lines, which forecast his later life and
have the ring of it in them, occur in his description of the
career of a dunce and fop of the lobbies, traced from its
beginning " just here at Farnham school;" of which the
case and mastery relish rather of days when he was dis-
secting knaves with Arbuthnot, or fools with Pope, than
of those he passed in difficult dependence and unsatisfied
desire.

Marginal notes:

No more
odes proper.

Congreve
and Swift.

Poem to
Congreve.

" He, in his idiom vile, with Gray's-inn grace,
Squander'd his noisy talents to my face;
Named every player on his fingers' ends,
Swore all the wits were his peculiar friends;
Talk'd with that saucy and familiar case
Of Wycherley, and you, and Mr. Bayes;
Said, how a late report your friends had vex'd,
Who heard you meant to write heroics next;
For tragedy, he knew, would lose you quite,
And told you so at Will's but t' other night."

1689–1694.
Æt. 22–27.

Not Irish
rhymes: see
Pope.

The Mourning Bride, Congreve's next production and his greatest success, was not played till more than two years later; but it is a fair inference from these lines that the writer already knew of such an effort impending.* To the same date belongs also the strongest expression ever given by Swift to discontents in connection with Moor Park. This is, in the other of the two poems named as of special worth, written on Temple's recovery from the illness that disabled him from waiting on the King; but the fault found in it is rather with himself than with others. He praises Temple. Lady Temple he thinks "the best companion for the best of men." Even Lady Giffard is "peaceful, wise, and great." Not so his own muse:

Poems on Temple's illness.

" Malignant goddess! bane to my repose,
Thou universal cause of all my woes!"

In other words, himself; and perhaps no clearer light could be thrown on his present disputes with Temple than is afforded by these lines. It would be less than just to him to call it restlessness, that he should wish to escape

Self-discontents.

---

* In a remarkable passage of one of his earlier prose pieces (on conversation) we have not only allusion to the coffee-houses thus frequented in his youth, but evidence of the clear insight brought even in those days to the detection of "false idols" of every kind, and the exposure of pretense or unreality. "The worst conversation I ever remember to have heard in my life was that at Will's coffee-house, where the wits (as they were called) used formerly to assemble......attended with an humble audience of young students from the inns of court, or the universities; who, at due distance, listened to these oracles, and returned home with great contempt for their law and philosophy, and their heads filled with trash, under the name of politeness, criticism, and belles-lettres."

1689-1694.
Æt. 22-27.

from dependence; but defects of temper and manner arc sufficiently indicated.

> "To thee I owe that fatal bent of mind,
> Still to unhappy restless thoughts inclined;
> To thee, what oft I vainly strive to hide,
> That scorn of fools, by fools mistook for pride;
> From thee whatever virtue takes its rise
> Grows a misfortune, or becomes a vice."

As he had risen by his services into favor with his patron, Temple's desire to retain them was on his part as natural as his own wish now to employ them for himself. He had reached his twenty-seventh year; and had passed so many of them in acquisition of a degree, as little qualifying him for medicine or law as for the King's first offer of

Resolution to enter the church.

a commission in a cavalry regiment, that the church was become really his only refuge. Nor did it then necessarily shut out from its ministers the chances of public employment. His later quarrel with the whigs, on the ground of their indifference to him, turned strongly on his own belief that it was easier to provide for ten men in the church than one in a civil employment.* The first chaplaincy he held, he only consented to take for the chance of a political secretaryship which he believed would accompany it; and he kept it afterward through two Irish viceroyalties, because political influences came to be blended with its personal considerations and duty. Important diplomatic serv-

Offices then open to a clergyman.

ice was still rendered by churchmen; secretary's places were often at their disposal; a bishop held a cabinet office in the succeeding reign; and when the rumor went abroad during Anne's last ministry that St. John was going to Holland, Swift was generally named to accompany him in that employment. These observations may help also to

---

* "The ministry know by this time whether I am worth keeping; and it is easier to provide for ten men in the church than one in a civil employment."—*Swift to Lord Peterborough, 4th May,* 1711. Compare this with what is said directly to the contrary effect, in Macaulay's paper on Addison, to explain the fact that while the whig statesmen loaded Addison with solid benefits, they only praised Swift, asked him to dinner, and did nothing more.

explain the direction taken by his high-church views. He 1689-1694.
would have increased her political power without enlarg- Æt. 22-27.
ing her domination over conscience. His churchmanship High-church views.
was neither intolerant nor tantivy; and he had as little
real sympathy with Atterbury as with Sacheverell, much
as he admired the one and despised the other. How far
he had thus early settled his own beliefs, no one can assume to say; and most certainly there is no later evidence
on which to found charges of disbelief. His respect for
the ordinances of the Reformed Church, his careful observance of her usages and ritual, and his sense of what the
world had gained by Christianity, there is no reason to Belief.
doubt or bring in question at any time of his life.* What
is said in his Anecdotes of the feeling with which his
thoughts first turned to the profession of a clergyman in
these early years, will be accepted also as evidence in favor of his sincerity in all that mainly concerns this weighty
matter. He had so decided a view, he says, of what the
sacred calling should be, small as its esteem was in those
days, as to shrink from resorting to it in mere despair of
other means of livelihood. But upon the King repeating
his offer of help in the acceptable form of a prebendary,
he became eager to enter into orders. Temple had been Misunder-
for delay, as we have seen, until what the King proffered standing with Tem-
was actually given; but, writes Swift to his uncle, "though ple.
he promises me the certainty of it, yet he is less forward
than I could wish, because I suppose he believes I shall
leave him, and upon some accounts he thinks me a little
necessary to him." This was written some months before
the verses to his patron, and it is easy to understand in
what way angry words arose afterward between them.

---

* Describing his impressive manner
in the pulpit, Hawkesworth adds that
"even in that transient act of adora-
tion which is called saying grace, and
which generally consists only in a
mutter and a bow in which the speaker appears to compliment the company and the company each other,
Swift always used the fewest words
that could be uttered on the occasion,
but pronounced them with an empha-
sis and fervor which every one around
him saw and felt, with his hands
clasped in each other and lifted to his
breast."—P. 15.

1689–1694.
Æt. 22–27.

What the one was become eager to apply for himself, the other wanted more and more for his own service; and every fresh display of his young kinsman's talents indisposed the old statesman to let him go. The position taken at last by Temple appears to have been, that whatever help toward the church he might hereafter be induced to give on continued good deserving, he would then pledge himself to nothing; but Swift might take, if he pleased, a clerkship of £120 a year in the Irish Rolls. The reply is in the Anecdotes: "Although his fortune was very small" (a remark that seems to show he had thus far been able to save something) "he had a scruple of entering into the church merely for support; and Sir William Temple, then being Master of the Rolls in Ireland, offered him an employ of about £120 a year in that office. Whereupon Mr. Swift told him, that since he had now an opportunity of living without being driven into the church for a maintenance, he was resolved to go to Ireland and take holy orders."* And so they parted.

Declines
clerkship in
Irish Rolls.

Leaves Moor
Park.

II.

IN ORDERS AND AT KILROOT.

1694–'96. Æt. 27–29.

1694–1696.
Æt. 27–29.

At Leicester
with his
mother.

On the verge of the step that was to determine finally his future life, Swift showed no misgiving. After leaving Moor Park he again went to Leicester; and Mr. Deane Swift found among the papers of his father, who was now at Lisbon employed in the mercantile house of his half-brother Willoughby,† a letter of Jonathan's written on

---

* Scott, in the reprint of the Anecdotes, in both his editions, omits the last eleven words, and goes on with the next member of the sentence, as if Temple had recommended him to Lord Capel; which, indeed, is implied in his text.—i., 38, 511.

† The same whose timely service to Swift in college has been told. In this letter warm thanks are repeated. "I had designed a letter to my cousin Willoughby, and the last favor he has done me requires a great deal of acknowledgment; but the thought of

the 3d of June, 1694, from his mother's house. "I forgot to tell you," he adds, "I left Sir William Temple a month ago, just as I foretold it to you; and every thing happened thereupon, exactly as I guessed. He was extremely angry when I left him, and yet would not oblige himself any further than upon my good behavior, nor would promise any thing firmly to me at all: so that every body judged I did best to leave him. I design to be ordained September next, and make what endeavors I can for something in the church. I wish it may ever lie in my cousin's way or yours to bring me in chaplain of the factory." Though he has now only his own endeavors to trust to, there is no hesitation, and he is even ready to go to Lisbon as chaplain to the English factory. The small immediate profit he would doubtless be glad of, but a greater ultimate gain by some experience of a foreign country was perhaps the stronger motive with him. His letter otherwise shows his interest in this direction. He says what a pleasure it is to himself to learn that his cousin sallies out of his road and takes notice of what is curious; and he points out to him what the advantages are to "so good an observer as you may easily be." His correspondent appears to have written with some horror of priestly displays in Lisbon streets, by way of holy intercession for rain or fine weather: to which Swift replies that he does not utterly dislike them, trifling as they are; since they yet may have some good effects, and at least the rabble get from them "a gaping devotion." But the priests had also been burning an old woman, and this, Jonathan adds, "unless she were a duenna, I shall never be reconciled to; though it is easily observed that

1694-1696.
Æt. 27-29.

Letter to Cousin Deane.

Interest in foreign countries.

my sending so many before, has made me believe it better to trust you with. delivering my best thanks to him, and that you will endeavor to persuade him how extremely sensible of his goodness and generosity I am. My mother desires her best love to him and to you, with both our services to my cousin his wife." There is also a letter of later date to the elder Deane Swift, in which Jonathan's mother writes: "Pray be pleased to present my best services to my good nephew Willoughby, and tell him I always bear in my heart a grateful remembrance of all the kindness he was pleased to show my son."

1694-1696.
Æt. 27-29.
Superstition
and trade.

nations which have most gallantry to the young are ever the severest upon the old." He is nevertheless sorry, and surprised too, at so much superstition in a country so given to trade, for he half used to think that commerce and superstition were incompatible.*

Results of
residence
with Temple.

Such remarks are valuable for the character that is in them, and for what they show of the result thus far that had attended Swift's life with Temple. He had become, when he left, too impatient of its disadvantages to remember perfectly his gains by it. Viewing the case impartially, the common conclusion respecting it can hardly be right. There may be a question for discussion hereafter upon the wisdom of making the church his profession; but the question whether, at his leaving the university, a college living or fellowship would have been as happily interposed as the intercourse with Temple and the leisure in Temple's library to qualify him for the work he was best fitted to do, can be answered only in one way. In all the compassion awakened by what has seemed to be the harder destiny, the circumstance is overlooked that what fate was to fashion out of this raw material was not a plump possessor of thriving benefice or bishopric, but a genius unrivaled for political controversy, and the greatest satirist and humorist that the world had known. Macaulay

Acquisition
of what was
most want-
ed.

thinks that but for Moor Park influences it would not be credible that Swift should have written political tracts, as he did within a year after Temple's death, not like a mere man of letters, but like a man who had passed his life in the midst of public business, and to whom the most important affairs of state were as familiar as his weekly bills. The remark applies equally to opportunities of study, as well in the literature of the ancients, and of the sciences and philosophy, as in that of humor and satire in his own and other languages, which may be traced in his notes of

* Swift kept up his correspondence with this cousin, though very little of it has survived. Writing to Esther Johnson on the 28th of March, 1712, he tells her he has been "writing to cousin Deane, in answer to one of his four months old, that I spied by chance routing among my papers."

books then read; and to his fragments of adventure in
the " kingdom of absurdity," which already he had written.
In that kingdom he had found bells of glass with iron
clappers, houses of gunpowder with fires in them, and
monstrous usages it would have been the easiest thing in
the world to destroy. "Ask the reason why they do not,
and they say it was their ancestors' custom of old."

1694-1696.
Æt. 27-29.
His "kingdom of absurdity."

The interval before the time of applying for ordination
was passed in Dublin, and upon its arrival a difficulty
arose. Having been so long absent from Ireland, the bishops required from him a certificate of behavior during his
absence. His application was in September, as he told his
cousin it would be; and the " two or three " bishops that
told him this were " acquaintance of our family." His
difference with Temple made him naturally reluctant to
ask a favor from him, and the intervening month before
his renewed application in October was passed in a fruit-
less effort to evade the necessity. But the Archbishop of
Dublin (Narcissus Marsh) having then declared that nothing would serve but a certificate from Temple, Swift wrote
to him on the following day. He had been all the while
trying to avoid, he said, what had proved necessary at last.
He begins, " May it please your honor;" admits that he
must have fallen low in his " honor's " thoughts; and repeats the phrase more than once. It is yet necessary to
remind those who call this the language of a lackey or
beggar, that it was not then unusual between persons of
the respective ranks of Swift and Temple; and that, to
go no farther for an instance, when Dr. Wotton, a few
years later, assailed the *Tale of a Tub* in a letter to his
wealthy acquaintance, Anthony Hammond, " honored sir "
and " your honor " are his modes of address. With other
kindly consideration, too, the letter should be read. A
man can have no harder task in the world than to ask a
superior with whom he has quarreled to do him a favor;
and Swift's reflection since he left Moor Park had perhaps whispered something to him of advantages underval-
ued, and anger unbecomingly indulged. " I shall stand in

Certificate required for ordination.

Applies for Temple's good word.

1694–1696.
Æt. 27–29.

Alleged
"peniten-
tial" letter.

Errors re-
specting it.

Living of
Kilroot.

The Waring
family at
Belfast.

need of all your goodness to excuse my many weaknesses and follies* and oversights, much more to say any thing to my advantage." He thinks he can not reproach himself with more than "infirmities;" but all is left to his honor's mercy. This, from which I have thus taken its most submissive phrases, is Lady Giffard's "penitential" letter; and Scott, following and followed by all commentators since, declares it to have been only written after five months' agonized delay. The simple truth respecting it has been stated here. Swift first knew what was required at the beginning of September; and finding, on the 5th of October, that there was but one way of compliance, he wrote on the 6th to Sir William Temple, requesting that the certificate might be in time for the ordination "appointed by the archbishop for the beginning of November." It reached him earlier. His deacon's orders bear date the 28th of October, 1694; his priest's orders are dated the 13th of January, 1694–'5; and into both he was ordained by King, Bishop of Derry, afterward Archbishop of Dublin. He had meanwhile been recommended by some family friends to Lord Capel, then Lord Deputy, who gave him the small prebendary of Kilroot, in the north of Ireland. His patent of presentation is enrolled under date of the 28th of January, 1694–'5.

Kilroot was a living somewhat over £100 a year, and the new incumbent became very weary there after not many months; the most memorable incident of his connection with it having had for its scene, not the small parsonage, which, with the poor little church, has long fallen to ruin, but the neighboring post-town of Belfast. Here lived his old college chum, Waring; and Swift, having no other sufficient occupation for his thoughts, did what he formerly described himself as then prone to do, and made love to his friend's sister. He changed her name of Waring to the more poetical Varina; two letters, with an interval of three years between them, tell the love-story;

---

* *And follies* is restored by me on collation with the transcript from | which the letter originally was printed. The original has never been accessible.

and the calm contents of the second will be found to con- 1694-1696.
trast not a little with the passionate phrases of the first. Æt. 27-29.
The lady had a small fortune (a hundred a year, it seems
to have been), but of that Swift desires nothing; he only
wants to marry her. She is less eager, and a reason for
her coldness appears to be suspected by him. After say- Letter to
ing that all the miseries of a man's life are beaten out on (Varina).
his own anvil, he gives her an apologue of a poor poet and
a rich beggar, which seems to imply some jealousy on his
part of a man who with himself has access to the Donegal
family and who writes execrable verses, but, being dunce
enough to be worth five thousand a year, has all the qualification to recommend himself to a woman. After which
he goes off into the wildest protestations, wishing to God
she had scorned him from the beginning; and declaring
that if he left the kingdom before she was his, he would
endure the utmost indignities of fortune rather than return, though the King should send him back as his deputy.
"And it is so, then? In one fortnight I must take eternal
farewell of Varina; and (I wonder) will she weep at parting, a little to justify her poor pretenses of some affection
to me? and will my friends still continue reproaching me
for the want of gallantry, and neglecting a close siege?"
Nay, he asks, would the friends of both, knowing well her
circumstances and his, be so anxious to get them married,
if it were likely to cross her happiness? On the other
hand, in a passionate burst of eloquent entreaty, he tells
her what she will forfeit by preferring the little disguises
and affected contradictions of her sex to the prospect of a
rapture so innocent and so exalted; and he warns her to
remember that if she still refuses to be his, she will quickly lose, forever lose, him that is resolved to die as he has
lived, all hers.*

---

* First printed in Monck Berkeley's   fixes this MS. note: "I have com-
Literary Relics (1789), of which I   pared this letter with the original,
possess the copy that belonged to Ed-   now in the hands of the Earl of
mond Malone, whose careful MS. col-   Macartney; and all the corrections
lation of the letter with the original   in the margin are taken from them.
gives it special value. Malone pre-   Some of them are of importance.—

1604–1696.
Æt. 27–29.

Invited back
to Moor
Park.

There is yet nothing to show that he had lived "all hers" for any thing like the full period of his twelve months' residence at Kilroot; a length of time, which, taken with the comment of this letter, would seem hardly to justify the alleged reproach of friends that he had not made close enough siege. He is to leave for England, moreover, in a fortnight; she is to make up her mind before he goes; and the sober facts that thus stand out from the exalted rhapsody are found to be all it contains that has any kind of importance for us. He had been absent from Moor Park little more than a year and a half; its master had written to have him back again; and he is resolved to go. "Sir William Temple," Swift's sister wrote afterward from Ireland, "was so fond of my brother that he made him give up his living in this country, and promised to get him one in England." This gives reality and meaning to the only passage in the letter to Miss Waring that appears to have either: "My Lady Donegal tells me that 'tis feared my lord deputy will not live many days; and if that be so, 'tis possible I may take shipping from hence, otherwise I shall set out on Monday fortnight for Dublin, and, after one visit of leave to his excellency, hasten to England; and how far you will stretch the point of your unreasonable scruples to keep me here will depend upon the strength of the love you pretend for me. In short, madam, I am once more offered the advantage to have the same acquaintance with greatness that I formerly enjoyed, and with better prospect of interest. I here solemnly offer to forego it all for your sake. I desire nothing of your fortune. You shall live where and with whom you please till my affairs are settled to your desire; and in

E. M., Feb. 17th, 1804." Dr. Lyon says, in his MS. corrections and additions to Hawkesworth's Life, that three other letters, now lost, were directed to Miss Waring at Belfast: 20th December, 1695, from Dublin; 29th June, 1696, and 28th August, 1697, from Moor Park: but for this no authority is mentioned. I shall have occasion to make important use of other notes in this curious volume, given by Mr. Nichols to Malone and by the latter to his brother, Lord Sunderlin, and which passed into my possession on the sale of Mr. Mitford's library.

the mean time I will push my advancement with all the 1694-1696.
Æt. 27-29.
eagerness and courage imaginable, and do not doubt to suc-
ceed." Whether he obtained the interview is not known;
but he certainly departed for England, and nothing more Departure
from Kil-
root.
is heard of Varina until after Temple's death, when the
second letter turns the tables on the first, and the lady is
supposed to be impatient for a marriage which the gentleman more prudently declines.

That it was a sudden departure, and upon request from Departure
accounted
for.
Moor Park, is manifest from his letter as well as from his
sister's; and much talk, among his own and Miss Waring's
friends, followed naturally enough. Two stories explaining it, and his later surrender of the prebend, opposed to
each other in every thing but extravagance, found their
way into the biographies. According to one, he was seized
by a sudden desire to befriend an aged curate with eight
children and forty pounds a year, borrowed his black mare
(the curate being richer than himself in that particular),
rode off to Dublin, resigned the prebend, and obtained the
old gentleman a grant of it then and there. The other, ·
traceable to a time when incredible scurrilities assailed
him, accounted for his resigning by his having been exam- Absurd in-
ventions.
ined before a magistrate named Dobbs for a criminal at-
tempt on a farmer's daughter: its one grain of reality being that a Mr. Dobbs lived near him, and they used to lend
one another books. The first romance Scott gravely admits into his text as "highly characteristic of Swift's exalted benevolence;" and in a note disposes of the second
as the invention of a mad parson who afterward held the
prebend. The circumstance as it actually occurred has
in it nothing sensational; but it is extremely interesting,
and Swift himself has related it, in letters addressed to the
clergyman in whose favor he resigned, and who was collated to the living in March, 1697-'8.

Mr. Winder, whose acquaintance he had made at Hart
Hall (the second letter reminds him of "our chapel at Ox- The truth
told by him-
self.
ford"), being in the North of Ireland when his application
for absence was made to Bishop Walkington, undertook

1694–1696.
ÆT. 27–29.
the duty of the prebend until the prebendary should return ; but that there was strong probability he might not return, and that in such case he would do his best to get the prebend for his friend, appears to have been not only said at their parting, but repeated in kind and friendly letters.   At a break in the correspondence, Winder, who had the anxieties and "fastenings to the world" of a wife and children, was afraid he should be blamed as its author ; to which Swift at once replied that, as he had "never in his life entertained one single ill thought" of him, he did not impute his silence to any bad cause, but to a custom that broke off commerce between abundance of people liking

Correspond-
ence with his
successor
(MS.).
each other very well.   "At first one omits writing for a little while, and then one stays a while longer to consider of excuses, and at last it grows desperate, and one does not write at all."   (Are there any who have not had the experience thus expressed with his exquisite common sense?)   A remark followed more flattering to Mr. Winder than complimentary to Miss Waring: "I believe, had I been assured of your neighborhood, I should not have been so unsatisfied with the region I was planted in."

The resolu-
tion to re-
sign.
These expressions lead us to the resolve taken a year and a half after the return to Moor Park.   Shortly before, Winder had sent him some intimation from the bishop about the prebend, but without any hint at a resignation, so that the reply inclosing one gave great surprise, and set all the gossips busily to work.   Swift had surrendered Kilroot, they said, because of the Miss Waring affair ; and Winder had artfully intrigued for it by passing himself off for what he was not.   The resignation meanwhile steadily went on ; was completed by obtaining the succession for Winder ; and then, from Moor Park on the 1st of

Letter to Mr.
Winder: 1st
April, 1698
(MS.).
April, 1698, Swift wrote him a letter delightful for its illustration of his own character, and for what otherwise it reveals at this early time:

"Since the resignation of my living and the noise it made among you, I have had, at least, three or four very wise letters, unsubscribed, from the Lord knows who, de-

claring much sorrow for my quitting Kilroot, blaming 1694-1696.
Æт. 27-29.
my prudence for doing it before I was possest of some-
thing else, and censuring my truth in relation to a certain
lady.... From what they say relating to myself, either as
to my prudence or conscience, I can answer sufficiently for
my own satisfaction, or for that of any body else who is
my friend enough to desire it. But I have no way of con-
vincing people in the clouds." Of imputations against his
friend he then speaks: "One or two of the anonymous
letters talkt of you as one who was less my friend than
you pretended; with more of the same sort, too tedious
to trouble you or myself with." Such things were not
believed by him, and therefore he needs not answer them.
"For I was ever assured of your good intentions and justice and friendship; and though I might suspect them,
yet I do not find any interest you can have either to wish
or to use me ill." Winder himself had been conscious of
what his enemies were saying, and had written in some
fear that it might be believed by Swift. "For what you
say of my having no reason to repent any of my endeavors to serve you, I am and have always been of the same
opinion; and therein yourself may bear me witness, when
you remember that my promises and designs relating to
your succeeding in the prebend were not of a sudden, or
by chance, but were the constant tenor of what I said
when we last parted, and of most of my letters since.
Neither did that inclosed letter of the bishop's hasten it
at all, for Sir W. T. desired to write for my further license, Part taken
by Temple.
and I would not consent to it. Besides, I had several ac-
counts from others that it was your opinion I should not
give it up so soon.... This I thought fit to say to set us
both right and clear in each other's thoughts." In the
same unaffected way he speaks of his own share in the
service done: "I am very glad you have finisht the affair
and are settled in possession. I think you may henceforth
reckon yourself easy, and have little to do besides serving
God, your friends, and yourself: and unless desire of place
or titles will interfere, I know nothing besides accidents

can hinder you from being happy, to which if I have contributed either by chance or good-will, I shall reckon it among the lucky adventures of my life."

Outstanding accounts.

What is added of the outstanding accounts of the prebend, and a claim for abatement made by a farmer of the glebe, is not less worthy of note. He wisely expresses himself as " ever very much for that custom of making accounts the clearest especially with nearest friends," and he asks that they should be arranged with his uncle Adam *Ante*, 58. when the latter should be " down in the North." On the other hand, he would do " nothing rigorous " in the matter of the abatement, not being on the spot to judge of the circumstances ; but as he had himself half promised a renewal of the farm this year, " if you have disposed it to another, in consideration of that disappointment let him take the whole abatement in God's name." The measure of this kindness is in what he adds : " I want money sufficiently ; and have nothing to trust to but the little in your hands."

Directions follow about books and papers left behind him, of which Winder is to send a list, not dispatching any to Dublin till he gets them all together, and those that were not in the parsonage were to be collected. " Jack Tisdall will do it. He has my trunk, and some books and papers which you are also to get. Pray use messengers and pay them at my charge. And for God's sake see about paying Taylor of Laughbritland (I have been an hour thinking of the town's name) for something about grazing a horse and the farrier's bill. You will buy a wooden box for my books, and get the new ones put up in brown paper. . . . I will not pardon you the loss of any.*

Brother to
William :
post, 148.

Directions
as to books.

---

* So particular were these instructions about the books, that poor Mr. Winder takes alarm, and, sending the list, mistakes Swift's reason for requesting it ; whereupon his friend tells him he only wanted to know what they were, because some might be worth his keeping and others not worth his sending back. Among the latter certainly was " the old musty Horace ;" and, on the other hand, Reynolds's Works (the Puritan divine), the quarto collection of sermons, and Stillingfleet's *Grounds*, might be useful to the new prebend, and he was to write in them, in large letters, " Ex

Take time rather than not finish as you and I shall like, 1694-1696.
tho' it be but about a trifle. And pray give my service Æt. 27-29.
to your wife and family." It is all full of character.

To expressions of interest in his own future which it Hopes as to future career.
was natural that the friend he was so serving should send
him, his reply is very striking: "For my own fortune, as
late in my life as it is, I must e'en let it drive on its old
course. I think I told you in my last, that, ten days before my resignation, my Lord Sunderland fell, and I with
him. Since that there have been other courses, which if
they succeed I shall be proud to own the methods, or if
otherwise very much ashamed." Sunderland, William's
friend, was also the friend of Temple; during the King's
last absence had taken part in the administration of the
kingdom; and had probably renewed to Swift William's
old promise of preferment, when, with his sudden fall,
hope again had fallen. Swift nevertheless, though Temple would himself have written for a further extension of

---

Dono Jon. Swift." *Sceptis Scientifi-
ca*, an abominable piece of fustian virtuoso rubbish, belonged to old Mr.
Dobbs, from whom he was to get back,
in returning it, Temple's *Miscellanea*,
a book worth his keeping and reading.
The folio paper book he might copy
sermons in, or give to his wife for
receipts, or family accounts: but the
sermons written by himself which
Winder had been transcribing, and
proposed to preach, were "the idlest
trifling stuff," a perfect lampoon upon
him, and what he had resolved to
burn. A rather interesting item follows next, which Winder is himself
to burn: a packet of "letters to Eliza
writ in his youth:" discovery of which
might imply that his love-letters either
did not go from him always, or sometimes came back. "There were par-
cels of other papers," he adds, "that I
would not have lost, and I hope you have
packt them up so that they may come
to me. Some of them were Abstracts

and Collections from Reading." His Papers left at Kilroot.
final sentence makes evident, and cer-
tainly not agitated, allusion to something Winder had written of Miss
Waring. "You mention a dangerous rival for an absent lover; but I
must take my fortune. If the report
proceeds, pray inform me." I have
to add that through my late friend, the
Rev. Doctor Todd, senior fellow of
Dublin University (who gave me valuable help for this work, which, alas!
he has not lived to see even on its way
to completion), I was enabled to procure, a few years ago, from "Mrs.
Winder," the original of the letter of
the 13th Jan., 1698, quoted in the
present note. It had been printed,
but with very grave omissions, as I
found on collating it, and have found,
almost invariably, in numberless similar cases. The earlier and more important letter in the text I obtained
recently, on dispersion of the auto-
graphs of Mr. Young, of Blackheath.

his license to be absent from Kilroot, persisted in resigning it.   What were the "other courses" of which the success or failure was to bring him pride or shame, can only
now be inferred from the tenor of the life that awaits us.

One word may be added.   If acceptance is to be given
to the statement of Waring, reported on authority more
than doubtful, that he had seen some portion of the *Tale
of a Tub* before its publication, this can only have happened during the residence at Kilroot; and it seems to
be more likely, indeed only too probable, that now first
were derived Swift's impressions of the fanaticism of the
Northern Presbyterians, against which so much wrath was
launched in that great satire, and which unhappily warped
his wonderful intellect on the single question of Irish government and policy in which time has proved him to have
taken the wrong side.

III.

SECOND RESIDENCE WITH TEMPLE.

1696-1699.   Æt. 29-32.

WHEN Swift returned to Moor Park, Hetty Johnson,
whom he had first known there as a child little over seven
years old, was become a girl of fifteen.   Her mother was
still in the same relation to Lady Giffard; in which, indeed, she continued until that lady's death, nearly thirty
years later.*   The two daughters both remained with her;
and with them lived another inmate of Temple's house
who was much their elder, a kinswoman of the family
named Rebecca Dingley, whose name was to be lastingly

---

* Lady Giffard was not placed under the monument for which her brother had written the inscription twenty-
four years before ("To Martha Giffard his best of sisters"), until 1722,
in her eighty-fourth year.   It was the
close of a story which had romantic
beginning, for Sir William Giffard had
been struck by mortal illness while he
was courting her, and only married
her when at the point of death, that
she might bear his name and inherit
his estate.

associated with Esther Johnson's as her life-long friend *1696–1699.* *Æt. 20–32.*
and companion. Of the terms on which these ladies were
at Moor Park, except that Mrs. Dingley was there as a relative and that Mrs. Johnson's husband had been closely in
the confidence of Temple, nothing is really known with
certainty. Temple left a small fortune to Esther, calling
her in his will "servant" to his sister Giffard; but it can
not have been a service implying any thing menial. The
language of Swift himself is our only secure guide: "Her *Swift's ac-*
father was a younger brother of a good family in Notting- *count of Es-* *ther John-*
hamshire, her mother of a lower degree; and indeed she *son.*
had little to boast in her birth. I knew her from six *Ante, 70.*
years old, and had some share in her education, by direct-
ing what books she should read, and perpetually instruct-
ing her in the principles of honor and virtue, from which
she never swerved in any one action or moment of her
life. She was sickly from her childhood until about the
age of fifteen; but then grew into perfect health, and was
looked upon as one of the most beautiful, graceful, and
agreeable young women in London, only a little too fat.
Her hair was blacker than a raven, and every feature of
her face in perfection. She lived generally in the country, with a family where she contracted an intimate friendship with another lady of more advanced years. Never
was any of her sex born with better gifts of the mind, or
who more improved them by reading and conversation."

Words of another famous English writer have been *Ante, 73.*
quoted, and others remain to be given, which sound
strangely beside these. Macaulay repeats in his *History*
what in substance he had said in his *Essays;* but the passage in the later work becomes necessary here as his deliberate and confirmed conclusion in regard to Swift's second residence. It repeats the old tale of the board and *Macaulay*
twenty pounds a year, and of the dining at the second ta- *as to second* *residence.*
ble. "Sometimes, indeed, when better company was not
to be had," Swift "was honored by being invited to play
at cards with his patron; and on such occasions Sir William was so generous as to give his antagonist a little sil-

1696–1699.
Æt. 29–32.

Statements
without evi-
dence.

ver to begin with. The humble student would not have dared to raise his eyes to a lady of family; but, when he had become a ·clergyman, he began, after the fashion of clergymen of that generation, to make love to a pretty waiting-maid who was the chief ornament of the servants' hall, and whose name is inseparably associated with his in a sad and mysterious history. . . . IIis spirit had been bowed down, and might seem to have been broken, by calamities and humiliations. The language which he was in the habit of holding to his patron, as far as we can judge from the specimens which still remain, was that of a lackey, or rather of a beggar. A sharp word or a cold look of the master sufficed to make the servant miserable dur-

History, vi.,
382-'3.

ing several days. But this tameness was merely the tameness with which a tiger, caught, caged, and starved, submits to the keeper who brings him food. The humble menial was at heart the haughtiest, the most aspiring, the most vindictive, the most despotic of men."

False under
color of true.

There is no safe test for language in which true and false are so strongly colored, yet subtly mixed, but that which has been applied to similar phrases in the same masterly writer's essay on Temple. It is, however, decisive. For the love-making there is not only entire absence of all ground whatever, but, as will hereafter be shown, the strongest presumptive evidence to the contrary. For the lackey-like speech, or any kind of speech held to his patron, the "specimens which still remain" are confined to one letter; and its self-depreciatory tone has been seen to involve neither dishonor nor shame to the writer. The card-playing is taken from these words to Esther John-

Card-play-
ing like and
unlike.

son in 1712: "I was playing at one-and-thirty with Lord Treasurer and his family the other night. IIe gave us all twelve-pence apiece to begin with: it put me in mind of Sir William Temple." There is nothing here to show the "better company" that "was not to be had," or that the retired statesman under such deprivation would have condescended to the worse company of his own servants' hall. As little likely is it that a "servant" should droop or re-

cover at a look or word from his "master;" since it is not
such intercourse that anger interrupts, or a fit of coldness turns into misery. The only ground for the statement supports this view of it; and there is perhaps no better clue to a correct appreciation of the terms on which Swift stood with Temple. It occurs in the same series of letters written during Harley's ministry.

It begins with an observation made at a dinner at St. John's, who was probably the last person on earth to whom Swift would have mooted any thing of his relations or his intercourse with Temple, if they could even be suspected to have stood on the footing of master and servant. Prior and Lewis, as well as himself, had observed a change in their host, "who seemed terribly down and melancholy;" and two days later he went to him, and, telling him he had seen the temper he was in, gave him this warning: "Never to appear cold to me, for I would not be treated like a school-boy; that I had felt too much of that in my life already (meaning Sir William Temple); that I expected ev- ery great minister who honored me with his acquaintance, if he heard or saw any thing to my disadvantage, would let me know in plain words, and not put me in pain to guess by the change or coldness of his countenance or be-havior; for it was what I would hardly bear from a crowned head, and I thought no subject's favor was worth it." To which he added, the next day: "I think what I said to Mr. Secretary was right. Don't you remember how I used to be in pain when Sir William Temple would look cold and out of humor for two or three days, and I used to suspect a hundred reasons? I have plucked up my spirit since then, faith! he spoiled a fine gentleman." From this may be gathered with perhaps some exactness the terms on which Swift stood generally with Temple. There was just so much equality of intercourse as made any in-terruption to it sensitively watched and felt. No political reputation stood higher than Temple's; he was the retired adviser of more than one sovereign; and it was the fame above all others so attractive to Swift that there was plenty of veneration at first, no doubt. But though Temple's nature was cold, those first relations could not but be changed by the help which Swift was found able to render, not alone in arranging his writings, but by coming to his relief in a controversy where the master of Moor Park very sorely needed protection. Between the undistinguished and the distinguished man, the measure of distance would lessen as the measure of service increased. Then would follow what can easily be imagined: occasional assumptions of overfamiliarity, rebuked by caprices of reserve. To make a man feel that he is treated like a school-boy is as mortifying a check as you can give him, and from such a temper as Temple's arose perhaps not unfrequently this kind of suffering; but that any secret savageness of pride was eating into Swift's heart at the time has as little foundation in fact as the rest of Macaulay's picture.

Sensitive not savage pride. Swift's pride was the reflection or consciousness of power. It did not come to him without a clear perception of strength; and by the feeling that it could so sustain itself, and make other odds ultimately even, every pang it inflicted at Moor Park must surely have been lightened and consoled. Universal as is now the practice of associating Temple's house with Swift's greatest misery, this is decidedly not the impression to be derived from himself. There is nothing that is not on the whole kindly and grateful in his memories of it. It is a fact not insignificant to me, though commentators and biographers have overlooked it, that he made the first garden of his own which he ever possessed, at his living of Laracor, a sort of small imitation *Temple disputes.* of the Moor Park garden. Even in the heat of his dispute with Lady Giffard, nothing mean or sordid in his relation to her brother was hinted at on either side. The extent of her reproach is measured in his reply, that he pretended not to have had the least share in Sir William's confidence "above his relatives or his commonest friends," having but too good reason to think otherwise. The reason to think otherwise expressed a complaint he was then entitled to make, that the Temple bequest had paid insufficiently the labor which it also bequeathed. But he visited the house 1696–1699.
Æt. 29–32. repeatedly after Temple's death; and in 1706, more than two years before the worst rupture with Lady Giffard, he wrote to the younger of her nephews, in a letter now first to be printed in his Life, " I am extremely obliged by your *Gratitude to Temple.* kind invitation to Moor Park, which no time will make me forget and love less." Nay, after thirty more years were passed, and while the elder of the nephews, Lord Palmerston, still remembered bitterly the old disputes, he wrote to the same John Temple of one of the Moor Park elms, on which he told him that he had carved a Latin *Affection for Moor Park trees.* verse commending its shade to Temple's descendants. His recollection of it is not, what he supposes the letters to have become, " widened and grown shapeless by time." He remembers exactly the spot on which the tree stood, in the hollow ground just before the house.

The only clear glimpse afforded of its interior while he lived there is given to us in a fragment of a letter written in the autumn after his return, and most probably ad- *The house in 1696.* dressed to Esther Johnson's mother.* Temple with his sister, and all their following, are away in London; but Swift has had a kind letter which " Robert " has delivered by word of mouth, and he calls it a vast condescension in them to have thought " of us " in their greatness: the " us " being himself, " Mr. Mose, of Farnham," Mrs. Bridget Johnson's second husband, who was now acting as agent or steward for Temple's estate, and some pet of Lady Giffard's whom he calls " Loory." As for what is going forward in London he expects to hear nothing from them for five months but " we courtiers," and he begs they will remember his and Mr. Mose's love to the King, and let them know how he looks. It was the time of Pe- *The Temples in London to see Czar Peter.* ter the Great's famous visit to England; and " Robert," having stated that the Czar was fallen in love with his correspondent, and designed to carry her to Muscovy, he

---

* It is in the correspondence as having been written to his sister, which Scott saw to be unlikely; but his belief that it was written to Esther Johnson is much less probable than the suggestion in my text.

1696-1699. advises her to provide herself with muffs and sable tippets.
Æt. 29-32. There are two good touches of character at the close of
Swift in state. the fragment. Swift describes himself desiring "their absence" heartily, for now, he says, he lives in great state,
and the cook comes in to know what he will please to
have for dinner, and he asks very gravely what is in the
house, and ends by giving orders for a dish of pigeons.
The rooks. His other allusion concerns the rooks. "Æolus has made
a strange revolution in the rooks' nests. But I say no
more, for it is dangerous to meddle with things above us."

He was nevertheless busily meddling with things above
him after not many weeks were over; if 1697, as he says
himself, was the time when he wrote the greater part of
the *Tale of a Tub*, as it certainly is the date of the *Battle
of the Books*. Into the dispute which Swift was thus led
to join, his patron had been drawn by a silly question
Ancients and Moderns controversy. raised in France on the respective merits of ancient and
modern writers, wherein somebody having declared Cor-
neille to be as much superior to Æschylus as Pascal was
to Plato, Temple took up the cudgels for the ancients, on
whose behalf he made assertions quite as preposterous, and
incidentally declared the Epistles of Phalaris to be one of
the triumphs of antiquity. Then came Wotton, a so-styled
youthful prodigy of learning in those days, defending the
moderns against Temple; then the new edition of Phalaris, produced on behalf of Temple by Charles Boyle, after-
Scholars who took part. ward Lord Orrery, his tutor Atterbury; and other Oxford
scholars; and then from the other university the scornful
challenge of Richard Bentley, first of scholars, who in a
second edition of Wotton's book declared the Phalaris
epistles to be the egregious forgery which they too truly
were. At this stage of the conflict, while Boyle, Atterbury, and Smallridge were preparing the reply that elic-
ited Bentley's crushing rejoinder, Swift came to the pro-
Battle of the Books. tection of Temple with the *Battle of the Books ;* and of
all that constituted once the so famous controversy, its
prodigious learning and its furious abuse, this triumphant
piece of humor alone survives. It was circulated widely

before Temple died, and not until four years later appeared 1696-1699.
Æt. 29-32. in print, as portion of a volume which weakened the side on which the writer had engaged as much as it strengthened that of the enemy. Swift could not help himself. The ancients could show no such humor and satire as the *Tale of a Tub* and the *Battle of the Books*.

Other allusion to them, for the present, is restricted to such personal illustration as they afford of opinions now held by Swift, or of the bent given to his genius in Moor Park days. When Wotton made feeble reply to the terrific onslaught in the *Battle*, he affected to have been "assured" that the satire was a mere copy from a foreign piece "entitled *Combat des Livres*, if I misremember not." Wotton's reply. "Which is to call me at a venture," retorted Swift, "a plagiary, than which I know nothing more contemptible." He meets it with the emphatic assertion that it is a falsehood; and that through the whole book he had not borrowed one single hint from any writer in the world. Johnson nevertheless rejected the denial and repeated the charge, though too evidently as little acquainted as Wotton with the alleged original; and Scott, taking his information from Nichols,* produced by way of countenance to Wotton's attack, Coutray's exact title, which at the same time he showed to be all he knew of Coutray's book, by describing as a poem what was merely a lengthy prose tract contributed to the Fontenelle and Perrault controversy, which it might as fairly be said to have originated as to have supplied a grain of material to Swift. If Wotton had charged him with plagiarizing Homer, Swift with a laugh might have owned it; for its broadest fun arises from the Homeric burlesque, which is also its most original feature. Only Wotton could have doubted this; but Charge of plagiarism. Disproved.

---

* Who first gave the title: *Histoire poétique de la Guerre nouvellement déclarée entre les Anciens et les Modernes*. A prolonged inquiry and great good fortune enabled me at last to obtain a copy of this very rare little work; of the contents of which, so variously criticised by writers who had never read or seen them, I write with the advantage of some personal acquaintance. Coutray's Combat des Livres.

1696-1699.
Æt. 29-32.
of course a writer under such an assault as Swift's had no alternative but to try, however feebly, a fall with his assailant.

Swift's ideal of criticism.
· Wotton figures in the *Battle of the Books* as the favorite and darling son, by an unknown father of mortal race, of a malignant deity called Criticism; dwelling in a den on the top of a snowy mountain in Nova Zembla, extended on the spoils of numberless volumes half devoured; at her right hand, her father Ignorance, blind with rage; at her left, her mother Pride, dressing her up in the paper scraps torn by herself; her sister Opinion beside her, light of foot, hoodwinked and headstrong, yet giddy and perpetually turning; and her children Noise and Impudence, Dullness and Vanity, Positiveness, Pedantry, and Ill Manners, playing about her. From this powerful mother Wotton gets a place in the army of the Moderns, under a leader "tall, but without shape or comeliness; large, but

Bentley.
without strength or proportion;" in other words, Bentley; in armor patched up of a thousand incoherent pieces, of which the sound as he marches is loud and dry, like the fall of a sheet of lead. Together they sally forth to attempt some neglected quarter of the Ancients; and coming to the spring of Helicon, one of the prizes of Parnas-

Temple.
sus for which the battle is raging, they fall in with Temple, "General of the Allies to the Ancients," who, having been educated and long conversed among them, "was of all the Moderns their greatest favorite," and was now refreshing himself at their fountain. An incident of this episode, which ends in the transfixing of both the Moderns with one lance and trussing them like a brace of woodcocks, is characteristic of Swift. Temple receives a "light graze" of which he is wholly unconscious; and though it has no effect whatever on the fortunes of the day, it serves to intimate that in the opinion Swift had formed of the

Flaw in Temple's armor.
Phalaris dispute he did not believe the armor of his friends, though "the gift of all the gods," to be entirely unassailable.

The battle meanwhile had been raging with no doubt-

ful issue, for the exploits of Homer alone went far to de- 1696–1699.
cide the day.*   "Mounted on a furious horse, with diffi- Æt. 29–32.
culty managed by the rider himself, but which no other Exploits of Homer:
mortal durst •approach, he bore down all before him."
Not here may be written the list of his victims, beyond
remarking as not without significance that such indisputa-
ble moderns as Chaucer, Spenser, Shakspeare, and Milton
are altogether absent; but his condign execution on the
beginners of the fray is part of my narrative. "He took
Perrault by mighty force out of his saddle, then hurled
him at Fontenelle, with the same blow dashing out both
their brains."   Only second to him in efficiency is Virgil, and of Virgil.
who, mounted on a dapple-gray steed of the highest met-
tle and vigor, busily seeks out objects worthy of his valor,
"when, behold, upon a sorrel gelding of a monstrous size,"
appears a foe making less speed than noise, "for his horse,
old and lean, spent the dregs of his strength in a high trot,
which, though it made slow advances, yet caused a loud
clashing of his armor terrible to hear."   But as the stranger comes nearer, lifting his visor for a parley, what is Virgil's disappointment to discover his own translator, "the
renowned Dryden," whose head appears situate far in the Dryden and Blackmore.
hinder part of a helmet nine times too large for it, "even
like the lady in a lobster, or like a mouse under a canopy
of state, or like a shriveled bean from within the penthouse
of a modern periwig."   Near Dryden is Blackmore, who
must have fallen under the lance of Lucan had not Escu-
lapius, unseen, turned off the point :† which may be taken,

---

* "Swift used often to declare that in his opinion Homer had more gen- ius than all the rest of the world put together."—*Swiftiana*, ii., 176. The special authority is not given, but there is certainly no writer for whom Swift expresses so frequently an ex- alted admiration; and the reader of the Voyage to Laputa will recollect what Gulliver says when, upon desir- ing to see in Glubbdubdrib the great- est of the writers of the antique world,

Aristotle and Homer are presented to him, and he observes the former stoop- ing much and making use of a staff, while Homer is taller and comelier, walking very erect for one of his age, and "his eyes the most quick and piercing I ever beheld."

† The return for this compliment made by Blackmore, who cared less for his physic than his poetry, was a fierce attack on Swift.

1696-1699.
Æt. 29-32.
Pindar and
Cowley.
perhaps, to signify that Swift was some time or other indebted to the Doctor's skill. Nor in less danger was Cowley from Pindar's lance, under which Mrs. Behn, "Afra the Amazon," and hosts of others had fallen, when Venus interposed to save him : by which, with the adverse comment suggested in a note that "Cowley's Pindarics are much preferred to his Mistress," we have both sides of a question that had interested Swift from his boyhood, and which doubtless had been frequently discussed at Moor Park.

Concentrated writing.
There is, in short, not a line in this extraordinary piece of concentrated humor, however seemingly filled with absurdity, that does not run over with sense and meaning. If a single word were to be employed in describing it, applicable alike to its wit and its extravagance, *intensity* should be chosen. Especially characteristic of these earliest satires is what generally will be found most aptly descriptive of all Swift's writing: namely, that whether the subject be great or small, every thing in it from the first word to the last is essentially part of it ; not an episode or allusion being introduced merely for itself, but every minutest point not only harmonizing or consisting with the whole, but expressly supporting and strengthening it.

Apologue of
Spider and
Bee.
The apologue of the Spider and the Bee is so marvelously good as almost to cheat one into the belief that there is a question to fight over ; the Spider boasting of his native stock and great genius, displaying his large skill in architecture and improvement in the mathematics, and attributing it all to the fact that he spins and spits wholly from himself, and scorns to own any obligation from without ; while, on the other hand, the Bee glories in pretending to nothing of his own but his wings and his voice, his flights and his music, which enable him, by infinite labor and search, to range through every corner of Nature, and to fill his hive, not, like his adversary, with dirt and poison, but with honey and wax, " thus furnishing mankind with Sweetness
and Light. the two noblest of things, which are Sweetness and Light."

The same argument is in the greater satire which Swift had in hand at the same time ; and proper significance has

never, by any of his biographers or critics, been given to 1696-1699.
Æт. 29-32.
the fact that the corruptions of religion and the abuses of A greater
entire in-
baud.
learning handled in the *Tale of a Tub* are but the contin-
ued pursuit, in another form, of the controversy between
the claims of ancients and moderns. Peter, Martin, and
Jack do nothing for the first seven years after their father's
death (by which are expressed the seven centuries of early
Christianity) but carefully observe their father's will; and,
while they travel together, and have a reasonable number
of hazardous but victorious adventures, they keep their
coats in very good order. It is not until they fall in love
with Covetousness, Ambition, and Pride, that, becoming
slaves to a then prevailing religion that the Universe
is only a large suit of clothes, and Man himself nothing
more (what the world calls suits of clothes being really the
most refined species of animals), they take to embroidery,
fringes, and gold lace, and fall into all their misfortunes.
And as with Religion, so with Learning. At the time Corrup-
tions of Re-
ligion and
Learning.
when this befalls the brothers, there has ceased to be any
such thing; and a method of becoming a scholar without
the fatigue of reading or of thinking has come into vogue.
A book being governed by its index as a fish by its tail,
thorough insight into an index is become all the labor necessary for mastery of a book; and it has been found also
that books may be served as some men do lords—first study
their titles exactly, and then brag of their acquaintance.
Nor is there any lack of books for the purpose. The modest computation of that "present month of August, 1697,"
was, that nine thousand seven hundred forty and three Wits of En-
gland in
1697.
persons (a stroke of wit lying underneath this number,
which was exactly that of the church livings then in England) were reckoned to be pretty near the current number of wits in the island, and corresponding numbers of
books were produced with every revolution of the sun;
though it was unhappily the case that books, which, like
men, had only one way of coming into the world, had ten
thousand ways of going out of it: the business of the last
volume being merely to displace the first, and mock the

1696-1699.
Æt. 29-32.

Books compared to clouds.
lookers-on with a fresh set of titles. "If I should venture in a windy day to affirm that there is a large cloud near the horizon in the form of a bear, another in the zenith with the head of an ass, a third to the westward with claws like a dragon; and you should in a few minutes think fit to examine the truth, it is certain they would all be changed in figure and position: new ones would arise, and all we could agree upon would be, that clouds there were, but that I was grossly mistaken in the "zoögraphy and topography of them." To this remarkable passage, whose writer must have known perfectly well the famous lines in *Antony and Cleopatra*,* may be added one other which probably took its rise, half jestingly, half sadly, in the comparison of books to dissolving and dispersing clouds. It is very affecting to me, because it is the only passage in Swift's writings where he seems openly to ask for some foretaste in life of what so often fails to come until life is passed away. "I have a strong inclination, before I leave the world, to taste a blessing which we mysterious writers can seldom reach till we have gotten into our graves:

Posthumous fame.
whether it be that Fame, being a fruit grafted on the body, can hardly grow, and much less ripen, till the stock is in the earth; or whether she be a bird of prey, and is lured among the rest, to pursue after the scent of a carcass; or whether she conceives her trumpet sounds best and farthest when she stands on a tomb, by the advantage of a rising ground, and the echo of a hollow vault."

The Tale not printed for seven years.
Yet the man by whom those words were written showed himself so far indifferent to any fame that might arise to him from enriching English literature with its greatest

---

* "Sometime we see a cloud that's dragonish;
A vapor, sometime, like a bear or lion,
A tower'd citadel, a pendent rock, [ry
A forked mountain, or blue promonto-
With trees upon't, that nod unto the world,
And mock our eyes with air: thou hast seen these signs:
They are black vesper's pageants....
That which is now a horse, even with a thought

The rack dislimns; and makes it indistinct,
As water is in water."—*Act* iv., sc. 12.

Swift was very often in his writings (especially these earlier pieces) figurative in a high degree, and fond of imagery, though Johnson absurdly says of him that "the sly dog never ventures at a metaphor."

prose satire, that the bulk of it remained in MS. for seven years, and was then alleged to have been printed from a copy in possession of a friend which had not had the advantage of his own final correction. There is some doubt about the story that will have again to be referred to, and Swift studiously refrains from clearing it up. "How the author," he says, "came to be without his papers is a story not proper to be told, and of very little use, being a private fact; of which the reader would believe as little, or as much, as he thought good." One thing is certain, that portions of both pieces got into the hands of Thomas Swift, never named by his great kinsman without contempt, but latterly become resident chaplain to Temple; and this position at Moor Park of the "little parson-cousin," as his great cousin always called him, during the composition of both works, which the bearing that both were meant to have on the Temple controversy would necessarily make him privy to, may hereafter somewhat explain the mystery. What further belongs to the present point of time is the personal description Swift gave, when he undertook the writing of his greater satire, of the qualifications he believed himself to possess for discharging such a task. By the assistance, he said, of some thinking and much conversation, he had endeavored to strip himself of as many real prejudices as he could; the study, the observation, and the invention of several years had yielded as their product what he then wrote. He often blotted out much more than he left; and if his papers had not been a long time out of his possession, they must have undergone corrections still more severe. "He resolved to proceed in a manner that should be *altogether new*, the world having been already too long nauseated with endless repetitions upon every subject."* He kept his word: having rare qualifications for keeping it. He was young, his invention at the height, and his reading fresh in his head.

Such was Swift during his second residence with Tem-

Swift's qualifications for satire.

Resolve in writing it.

---

* He has a pregnant remark on this: "It is reckoned that there is not at the present time a sufficient | quantity of new matter left in nature to furnish and adorn any one particular subject to the extent of a volume."

1696-1699.
ÆT. 29-32.

Other employments at Moor Park.

ple; and of the character of his employment over Temple's writings when he was not engaged in writing for himself, there is some account in a letter to Lady Giffard of some years' later date, replying to her attack upon him for publishing a third part of her brother's *Memoirs*, which she alleged to have been taken from an "unfaithful copy," containing laudatory notices of Godolphin and Sunderland it had been her brother's intention to omit, and omitting a remark on Sunderland which he meant to have retained. "By particular commands," wrote Swift,* "one thing is understood, and by general ones another. And I might insist upon it that I had particular commands for every thing I did, though more particular for some than others. Your ladyship says, if ever they were designed to be printed, it must have been from the original. The first *Memoirs* was from my copy; so were the second *Miscellanea;* so was the *Introduction to the English History;* so was

Revision of Temple's writings.

every volume of *Letters*. They were all copied from the originals by Sir William Temple's direction, and corrected all along by his orders; and it was the same with these last *Memoirs;* so that whatever he printed, since I had the honor to know him, was an 'unfaithful copy' of it, were it to be tried by the original." Then came what

Ante, 90.

has been quoted of his not pretending to share in Temple's confidence above his relatives or commonest friends.

"A thing in my way."

"But this was a thing in my way. It was no more than to prefer the advice of a lawyer, or even of a tradesman, before that of his friends, in things that related to their callings. Nobody else had conversed so much with his manuscripts as I; and since I was not wholly illiterate, I can not imagine whom else he could leave the care of his writings to. Your nephews say the printed copy differs from the original in forty places as to words and manner of expression. I believe it may in a hundred. And that passage about my Lord Sunderland was left out by his consent; though, to say the truth, at my entreaty; and

---

* This letter has not been included in any of the editions of Swift. It was partially printed by Mr. Courte- | nay in his *Life of Temple* (10th November, 1709).

I would fain have prevailed to have left out another.... He told me a dozen times, upon asking him, that it was his intention they should be printed after his death; but never fixed any thing about the time. The corrections were all his own; ordering me, as he always did, to correct in my copy as I read it." He closes by telling her that, knowing her opinion to be against the publication of this particular portion of the *Memoirs*, he had published it without her knowledge, on purpose to leave her wholly without blame.

All this is proof that Swift did not live idle days at Moor Park; and his own memorandum of one year of his reading, from 7th January, 1696–'7, to 7th January, 1697–'8, shows a strenuous employment of his leisure. He had read the *Iliad* and *Odyssey* of Homer, Virgil twice, and an elaborate edition of Horace, eminently a favorite with him. Thrice he had read Lucretius, and thrice Lucius Florus, Petronius Arbiter, the first volume of Ælian, Cicero's *Epistles*, and the *Characters* of Theophrastus. Of English books he had read the folio translation of Thucydides by Hobbes, making an abstract of it, which was an excellent habit he had; and three other folios—Lord Herbert's *Harry the Eighth*, Camden's *Elizabeth*, and Bishop Burnet's *Reformation*. He had made abstracts of Sleidan's *Commentary on the Reformation*, of Father Paul's *Decrees of the Council of Trent*, of Cyprian and Irenæus, and of Diodorus Siculus. And, in addition to several out-of-the-way voyages and travels, and curious French books,* the same year's reading comprised Temple's *Memoirs* and *Introduction to History*, Sir John Davies *On the Soul*, two volumes of French *Dialogues of the*

Marginal notes:
1696–1699.
Æt. 29–32.
Temple and his editor.

One year's readings at Moor Park.

---

* The memorandum specifies, besides those in the text, the following as having been also among his readings of that single year: *Voiture; Prince Arthur; Histoire de Chypre; Voyage de Syam; Mémoires de Mau-* rier; *Count Gabalis; Conformité de Religion; Histoire de M. Constance; Histoire d'Œthiopie; Voyage de Maroc; Bernier's Grand Mogol,* 2 vols. ; *Œuvres Mêlées,* 5 vols. ; *Vossius de Sibyllinis.*

VOL. I.—8

Dead, and two volumes of *Essays* by Jeremy Collier, with whose assault on the indecency of the stage, published in the following year, he expressed always the strongest agreement.

Occupied thus in his hours of business or leisure, there is other proof that his relaxations were hardly less active.

Strenuous exercise. A hill was long pointed out near the house as the scene of his daily exercise; and Mr. Deane Swift, professing to correct what Dr. Delany related from Swift himself—that for seven years from the time of taking his Oxford degree he 'studied at least on the average eight hours a day—declares it as a fact known to the family "that from the time Swift went to Sir W. Temple in 1688 until the death of Sir W. in 1699, he spent ten hours a day, one with another, in hard study, abating only the time which he consumed in bodily exercise, for every two hours (since we are fond of the most trifling anecdotes) he ran up a hill that was near Sir W. Temple's, and back again to the study: this exercise he performed in about six minutes, backward and forward: it was about half a mile." The anecdote may be believed; notwithstanding "the family," and the absurdly obstinate particularity, already named as Mr. Deane's never-failing characteristic. All his life long,

Passion for walking. sharp exercise was essential to Swift, who protested continually that without his walk or ride he could not exist at all. He walked to make himself lean, he said, in describing his long walks with Prior a dozen years later, and his fellow-poet walked to try and make himself fat. Irishwomen could not abide walking, he would add, and that was why he disliked them. He always cried shame at them, as if their legs were of no use but to be laid aside. It is his first and last advice to Esther Johnson never to lose the opportunity of using her legs, and he bought a little horse for her to ride which was called by her name. "At your time of life," he wrote in his declining years to Pope, "I could have leapt over the moon;" and his "walks like lightning" in the parks, between London and Chelsea, and in the Windsor avenues, have prominent mention in his journals. There also he mentions a design he had, on leaving for Ireland after he obtained the deanery, to 1696–1699. Æt. 29–32. "walk it" all the way to Chester, his man and himself, by ten miles a day. "It will do my health a great deal of good, and I shall do it in fourteen days." One special walk of his earlier years, also recorded there as if not in- 14th April, 1713. frequently taken, deserves a line to itself. It was from Farnham to London, a distance of thirty-eight miles.

The death of Sir William Temple in 1698–'9 closed Close of a profitable time. what without doubt may be called Swift's quietest and happiest time. In the three peaceful years of that second residence he had made full acquaintance with his own powers, unconscious yet of any thing but felicity and freshness in their exercise; and the kindliest side of his nature had found growth and encouragement. The soil had favored in an equal degree his intellect and his affections. More than one feeling of this description, we may be sure, contributed its earnestness to his pathetic mention of the day and hour of Temple's death. "He died at one Death of Temple. o'clock this morning, the 27th of January, 1698–'9, and with him all that was good and amiable among men." There was afterward some natural disappointment at the smallness of the legacy left for editing the writings; but though Swift in a not undignified way (as we have seen) referred to this when he repelled Lady Giffard's charges against his editorship, it never colored unfavorably any other of his allusions to Temple. The opinion now expressed he never changed. He continued, speaking rather with affection than judgment, to characterize him as a statesman who deserved more from his country by his eminent public services than any man before or since, and as the most accomplished writer of his time.

Temple's legacy of money to Swift was in express ac- Legacy of Temple's writings. knowledgment of the pains already taken with the writings. This is apparent from the date of the codicil, which was executed less than a year before the death, and four years later than the will. But it left also to Swift the emolument derivable from the works so edited, or, as Swift expresses it, "the care, and trust, and advantage, of publishing his posthumous writings;" and, as Temple was

never in the habit of undervaluing any part of himself,
he may have taken this to represent a larger return in
money than Swift would think likely. The amount received for the five volumes was about £40 apiece, which
by present money value would be upward of £600. Nor
was Temple otherwise without fair expectation for his
kinsman. Swift himself still believed in the royal pledge
for the first prebend that should become vacant at Westminster or Canterbury; and though he was in his thirty-
second year when, upon Temple's death, he removed to
London, it could not be said that the future, which then
at last seemed to be opening to him, was devoid of reasonable promise.

At this turning-point of his life his paper of resolutions
"When I Come to be Old" was probably written. It has
the date of 1699, and was found by Mrs. Whiteway at his
death. Too much importance may be given to such things,
which are just as likely as not to represent a whim or
mere passing fancy; but as the original is in my possession, a fac-simile of it will have interest. One can hardly
help connecting the first and fifth of the resolutions with
what must still be called the mystery of his life, whatever
the solution offered for it; and something of a strange and
even touching character is suggested by the erasure in the
fifth, under which the words originally written are traceable still. The erasure was not Swift's, but that of the
person who in printing it would have shielded his memory
from an apparent coldness of nature implied. But may it
not bear a meaning other than hard and unfeeling? "Not
to be fond of children, *or let them come near me hardly.*"
Such a fondness had begun at Moor Park in his youth, and
all that was to follow it he did not yet know; but if, in
the pain of quitting Moor Park, the thought had risen to
him not to renew the same kind of intercourse in his age,
who will say it was harshness that prompted the fancy?
We do not fortify ourselves with resolutions against what
we dislike, but against what in our weakness we have reason to believe we are only too much inclined to.

[facsimile of handwritten manuscript]

* WHEN I COME TO BE OLD. 1699.

Not to marry a young woman.

Not to keep young company, unless they reely desire it.

Not to be peevish, or morose, or suspicious.

Not to scorn present ways, or wits, or fashions, or men, or war, &c.

. Not to be fond of children, [*or let them come near me hardly.*][1]

Not to tell the same story over and over to the same people.

Not to be covetous.

Not to neglect decency or cleanliness, for fear of falling into nastiness.

Not to be over severe with young people, but give allowance for their youthful follies and weaknesses. .

Not to be influenced by, or give ear to knavish tattling servants, or others.

Not to be too free of advice, nor trouble any but those that desire it.

To conjure (altered to "desire") some good friends to inform me which of these resolutions I break or neglect, and wherein; and reform accordingly.

Not to talk much, nor of myself.

Not to boast of my former beauty, or strength, or favor with ladies, &c.

Not to hearken to flatteries, nor conceive I can be beloved by a young woman; *et eos qui hæreditatem captant, odisse ac vitare.*

Not to be positive or opiniative.

Not to set up for observing all these rules, for fear I should observe none.

Resolutions for old age.

[1] Words in brackets erased in printed copy.

BOOK THIRD.

VICAR OF LARACOR.

1699–1705. Æt. 32–38.

I.

CHAPLAIN AT DUBLIN CASTLE.

1699–1701. ÆT. 32–34.

The death of Temple did not alter the position of Lady Giffard, or the relation to her of Esther Johnson's mother, who continued to manage the house and act as her companion.* But Temple's legacy to Esther (" of a lease of some lands I have in Monistown in the county of Wicklow in Ireland ") gave her the means of living independently of his sister; and, soon after Swift's removal to London, she and her friend, Mrs. Dingley, who had at her disposal a small property of which Swift had undertaken the management for her, were living together in lodgings at Farnham. Mrs. Dingley was older than Swift by two or three years. Esther Johnson, born fourteen years later than Swift, was in her eighteenth year when the second residence closed.

He had known her from seven years old; and his ascertained position to her during the whole of the Moor Park life, confirming all that followed on the life breaking up, forbids the possibility of his having ever assumed to her, thus far, the pretensions of a lover. There is not the shadow of a ground for assuming it. It was the tenderest possible connection, but in no respect that of the mistress and admirer. They were playfellows, as father and child are; they were master and pupil, as the growth of her mind began to interest him; and in all the attempts to ex-

---

* At what time Mrs. Bridget Johnson became Mrs. Bridget Mose does not exactly appear. Swift calls her "Mrs. Johnson" as late as March, 1710–'11; but this may have been a slip, from old habit. Mose managed the Giffard property after Temple's death, and it seems unlikely that the marriage should have been delayed so long.

1699-1701.
Æt. 32-34.

plain the "mystery" of their later connection, sufficient weight has never been given to the character in which respectively they thus stood to each other, and to all that was implied in it, at the very outset of her life and the maturity of his. One thing between them, common alike to the later and to these earlier years, is itself a proof of the durability of such first impressions, and of the difficulty of changing the relations they involve. There can not be a doubt that what he afterward called "our own

The little language.

little language," hitherto all but suppressed by those who have supplied the materials for his biography existing in his Journals, began at Moor Park; and began in the man's imitation of a child's imperfect speech. The loving playfulness expressed by it had dated from Esther Johnson's childhood; it in some way satisfied wants of his own nature, or he would not have continued so lavishly to indulge it; and the passion for good-humored trifling, punning, and such innocent indulgences, which attended him all his life and often contrasts so strangely with his great robust intellect, is perhaps mainly due to its influence.

During Anne's last ministry he wrote to her of a dispute at Bolingbroke's about the house of a Colonel Graham

Moor Park memories.

at Bagshot-heath. "Psha! I remember it very well, when I used to go for a walk to London from Moor Park. What! I warrant oo don't remember the golden farmer neither, Figgarkick Soley." That is a bit of their peculiar language of which the mystery will never be solved; and abundant addition might be made, from the same source, to the proofs already given of the interest which Moor Park had for them both, and which he seizes every occasion to remind her of. Had she forgotten one Trimnel, whom they saw there on his travels with the lord's son, to whom he was tutor? That was the man who had since become Bishop of Norwich, and had just preached so whiggish a sermon before the commons that the question for thanking him and printing it was negatived. He brings to her recollection a high-church parson they used to laugh at together—one Savage, who preached at Farnham on Sir William

Temple's death—who had lately been seen in Italy in red and yellow, not content with the extravagance of kissing the pope's toe, but kneeling to him at the Palm-Sunday ceremonies. The neighborhood's commonest folks, in those grand days of his, were still vividly borne in memory. When the Farnham carrier, "Smithers," brings him a letter from her mother, he tells her he has been asking him all about the people at Farnham, and adds, by way of news that will specially interest her, that "Mrs. White" had left off dressing, being troubled with lameness and seldom stirring out; but that her old hang-dog husband was as hearty as ever.

1699-1701.
Æt. 32-34.

Farnham news.

What now befell Swift, and the next step to be taken in his life, is the final bit of autobiography told in his fragment; and there are some not unimportant new touches in the version I have been enabled to give, to which the reader is referred. In substance the relation is that Swift, after applying by petition to the King for the promised prebend, had relied, for the support necessary to back it efficiently, upon Lord Romney, who professed much friendship, but said not a word to the King. That having totally relied on this lord's honor, and having neglected to use any other instrument of reminding his majesty of the promise made, Mr. Swift, after long attendance in vain, thought it better to comply with an invitation from Lord Berkeley to attend him to Ireland as chaplain and private secretary on his appointment as one of the Lords Justices of that kingdom; and that he acted as secretary the whole journey to Dublin. On arrival, however, such arts and insinuations were practiced on Lord Berkeley by a person bent on obtaining the secretaryship for himself, who said it was not proper for a clergyman, and could be of no worth to one who was bent only on church preferments, that the earl, after a poor apology, gave it to the other man. Upon this Mr. Swift had held himself entitled, and his claim seems to have been admitted, to the next church preferment that should fall to the Lords Justices. But, upon a deanery falling vacant which it was Lord Berke-

Swift's account of present dis-appoint-ments.

1699-1701. ley's turn to dispose of, again the new secretary interfered,
Æt. 32-34. having received a bribe of a thousand pounds from a ri-
Loss of Der- val candidate; the deanery of Derry was given away from
ry deanery. Swift; and he was "put off" with church livings which
the new dean was required to resign for him, "not worth
above a third part of that rich deanery, and at this present
time not a sixth," the excuse pretended being that he was
too young, "although he was then (above) thirty years
old."* The result of it all was, that, in the summer of
1699, Swift was again resident in Dublin, quartered for a
time in the castle with Lord Berkeley's family; and that
in the February following he became Vicar of Laracor.
Other evidence amply confirms this account.

Chaplain at   The chaplainship had been accepted for the sake of the
the castle. secretaryship, and it was only in the hope of some immediate preferment that the one was retained without the
other. The same feeling existed now as at the later time,
when, upon a vague hint from Harley while his patent of
earldom was preparing, Swift promptly exclaimed, "I will
be no man's chaplain." Even with the promise now received, he would probably not have continued as the Lords
Justices' chaplain but for the connection with public affairs incident to a residence in the castle, and the liking
for him that had at once sprung up (where success never
seems to have failed him) among the women of the family. Then came the incident of the Derry deanery; his

---

* What Lord Orrery says of the interference of Bishop Wm. King, of Derry, to prevent Swift's acquisition of the deanery would not have been worth mention but for its adoption by the biographers. "I have no objection to Mr. Swift," he represents King saying. "I know him to be a sprightly, ingenious young man. But instead of residing, I dare say he will be eternally flying backward and forward to London; and therefore I entreat he may be provided for in some other place."—*Remarks*, p. 36. This is manifestly sheer invention, suggested by the mention of youth in the fragment; by the fact that King at a later time, when Archbishop of Dublin, objected to the habit Swift then had (which certainly he had not exhibited yet) of flying backward and forward to England; and by the opportunity it gives Lord Orrery to point a moral against the bishop, who, having denied a deanery to Swift on account of his youth, was himself afterward denied the primacy of Ireland because of his age.

exclamation thereon, by way of intended final salute to
the earl and his secretary, being recorded by Sheridan, "Confound you both for a couple of scoundrels;" and not till he had gibbeted both in some satirical verses did his anger begin to subside. Then the women again triumphed. He was brought back to the castle, which he had quitted in a rage; and after not many weeks he was Vicar of Laracor, the new Dean of Derry (Doctor Bolton) Vicar of Laracor. being required to resign to him this and the other livings he held. With the vicarage was united in one benefice the adjacent rectory of Agher; and to it was added the living of Rathbeggan, also in the diocese of Meath; Laracor, where the church was, giving its name to the whole. Swift remained chaplain at the castle; continuing his service, for political as well as personal reasons, to two later viceroys. But with none had he so much intimacy as with the Berkeley family; and he passed much time with With the Berkeleys. them.* Certainly not an unhappy time, unsatisfied wishes notwithstanding.

The countess he afterward described as a woman in whom the most easy conversation joined with the truest piety might be observed, united to as much advantage as ever they were seen apart in any other person. By this he meant to say that the sincerity and strength of her religion did not weaken her relish for a jest, which he tells The countess and daughters. us that she shared with her two lively daughters, Lady

---

* One of the few passages worth preserving from Mr. Deane Swift's dull and incoherent *Essay* may be this anecdote. From what source obtained he does not say, but its absurdly minute particularity is all his own.' "I can not tell whether it be worth recording among the anecdotes of his life; but in the year 1699, Swift had like to have burnt the castle of Dublin, and the Lord Berkeley in the midst of it. For the doctor, whose bed-chamber was the next room to his excellency's, having grown drowsy over his book while he was reading in bed, dropt asleep without extinguishing his candle, which, happening to fall upon his quilt, set it on fire, and burnt its passage quite through the bedclothes until it reached his thigh. Swift, roused by the pain, leaped out of bed and extinguished the fire, which by this time had burnt part of the curtains. He took care to have the damages repaired; and by throwing away some guineas in hush-money, the accident was never made known in the castle."

1699–1701.
Æt. 32–34.
Mary and Lady Betty, who, under their wedded names of Chambers and Germaine, re-appear in his later story. There was a third daughter, Penelope, who died soon after they reached Dublin; and it is pleasing evidence of Swift's liking for the members of this family, that, after two-and-thirty years were gone, we find him placing over the altar-piece of the church where she lay a marble tablet to

Lady Betty. her memory. Her sister Betty, then become old like Swift himself, writes to him concerning the date of her little sister's death, and at the close rebukes him for having written to her not in his old familiar strain, but in the style (not unusual then, be it said, even with closest friends) of formal "humble servant," with his whole name at the bottom as if she were asking him his catechism.

In youth Lady Betty, after her own fashion, had also been given to turn a verse; and a doggerel of hers, found tacked on to some unfinished verses by Swift descriptive of the card-playing and other employments at the castle, picked up by her in the chaplain's room,

Doggerel on
the chaplain.

"With these is Parson Swift:
    Not knowing how to spend his time,
Does make a wretched shift
    To.deafen them with puns and rhyme,"

may doubtless be taken to compensate by its accuracy for its failure in elegance. The parson punned and rhymed for want of better occupation; and thus opened another page of the wonderful book of that busy brain, which, after a couple of centuries, gives as vivid life to the homeliest forms of our every-day common speech as when it moved to anger or laughter the world of its contemporaries. This

Swift's earliest poems of
humor. is the date of his "Ivory Table-book;" of his "Cutpurse" and other ballads; of the lines to "Biddy Floyd," an inmate of the Berkeley house; and of "Mrs. Francis Harris's Petition on the Loss of her Purse of Money," with its rhythm, of which the author was also inventor, made of long irregular prose verses tagged at the end, and with truth at the heart of them as incomparable as the comedy. Scott thought that in the felicity and spirit of this kind

of writing Swift was unequaled, and he wonders that so
powerful an intellect should be able so to bind itself to the
sentiments and expressions of cooks and chamber-maids.
The secret is not far to seek.   He brought to this, as to
more serious things, the pre-eminent quality of which I
have spoken.   There is in all of it, as in what we have
thus far seen of the graver parts of his writing also, an intensity which is the singular mark of genius.   The lowest
subject is the same as the highest, in such treatment; each
part runs over with the meaning of the whole; and my
lady and my lady's maids, in their ways of thought or
speech, are deciphered with equal accuracy.   As when
first they lived in these playful poems, therefore, they
went on living, and they exist still.   To Lady Betty Germaine's memory, for example, at the time when she was
doubting the date of her little sister's death, Mrs. Francis
Harris sprung up quite untouched by age; and, in order
to solve her doubt, Lady Betty wished that she had but
her dame Wadgar's or Mr. Ferris's head for a memorandum, and might settle at once if it was at "the time of
gooseberries."

Petition of Mrs. Francis Harris.

"Lord! madam, says Mary, how d'ye do?   Indeed, says I, never worse;
But pray, Mary, can you tell what I have done with my purse?
Lord help me! says Mary, I never stirr'd out of this place!
Nay, said I, I had it in Lady Betty's chamber, that's a plain case.
So Mary got me to bed, and covered me up warm:
However, she stole away my garters, that I might do myself no harm.
So I tumbled and toss'd all night, as you may very well think,
But hardly ever set my eyes together, or slept a wink.
So I was a-dream'd, methought, that we went and search'd the folks round,
And in a corner of Mrs. Duke's box, tied in a rag, the money was found.
So next morning we told Whittle, and he fell a swearing:
Then my dame Wadgar, and she, you know, is thick of hearing.
Dame, said I, as loud as I could bawl, do you know what loss I have had?
Nay, said she, my Lord Colway's folks are all very sad;
For my Lord Dromedary comes a Tuesday without fail.
Pugh! said I, but that's not the business that I ail.   [spring,
Says Cary, says he, I have been a servant this five-and-twenty years come
And in all the places I lived I never heard of such a thing.
Yes, says the steward, I remember when I was at my Lady Shrewsbury's,
Such a thing as this happen'd just about the time of gooseberries."

1699-1701.
Æt. 32-34.

Mrs. Harris's
fellow-serv-
ants. They are all real people: even the old deaf housekeeper's Colway and Dromedary are the other Lords Justices
Galway and Drogheda; the steward is Ferris, who re-ap-
pears not pleasantly in the "Journal to Stella;" Cary is
clerk of the kitchen; Whittle is Lord Berkeley's valet;
Mary is wife to one of the footmen; and the way in which
they each and all regard, from their own point of view only,
and without any sort of sympathy for hers, the unfortu-
nate housemaid's loss, is the perfection of humorous character.   To Dame Wadgar's brain there is no possibility of
access for any thing not already there; Mary's great anxiety, with all her good-fellowship, is to show that she could
not have taken the money herself; Ferris remembers one
such similar case at my Lady Shrewsbury's; Cary remembers no such thing in all his five-and-twenty years of places
come spring; and Whittle can only fall a-swearing.   The
satire that in hour of need had come to Sir William Temple's aid was hardly richer than the humor thus placed at
the service of the Berkeleys; and it was a conversation
with the earl, in less than a year from this date, that led
Other scenes
opening. to the first employment of Swift's pen in its next field,
which was that of its greatest worldly triumphs.   But
some passages of his present Irish life claim attention before he is again in London, publishing the works of Temple and launched into political controversy.

Varina, the sister of his old college chamber-fellow, Waring, re-enters the scene; quitting it again suddenly, finally, and mysteriously as ever.   The complete story can but
be guessed at, and no interpretation of the portions of it
known to us can be other than unsatisfactory.   Though
Sequel to
Miss War-
ing's story,
Ante, 90-96. the second of the two letters by Swift, constituting the sole
surviving testimony on which judgment can be formed,
belongs more than the first to the region of fact, there are
expressions in it, if less high-flown, not less hard to understand.   Abundant reasons why their intercourse should
cease are followed by a list of conditions essential to the
pleasing of a man so deeply read in the world as himself,

by which alone it might be possible for her to continue the intercourse which he has just shown can be good for neither of them. ' The most plausible solution, or way of escaping the difficulty, may be that, while the lady herself had not become really less indifferent than when her ad. mirer three years before reproached her for that failing, his present acquisition of church preferment had set on third parties to intermeddle for her; whereat Swift, in whom a cool self-possession had soon replaced his first passionate heat, was not sorry to get altogether out of the affair. The only thing clear in his letter is the hopelessness of settling differences which exist on both sides. He had made strong resistance to the place she lives in and the people she lives with, and she had refused both changes asked for. She had made his want of income, and her own want of health, the obstacle to marriage; and he points out to her that it is out of his power to remove either objection. "My uncle Adam asked me one day in private, as by direction, what my designs were in relation to you, because it might be a hinderance to you if I did not proceed. The answer I gave him (which I suppose he has sent you) was to the effect that I hoped I was no hinderance to you; because the reason you urged against an union with me was drawn from your indisposition, which still continued; that you also thought my fortune not sufficient, which neither is at present in a condition to offer you; that if your health and my fortune were as they ought, I would prefer you above all your sex, but that, in the present condition of both, I thought it was against your opinion, and would certainly make you unhappy; that had you any other offer which your friends and yourself thought more to your advantage, I should think I were very unjust to be an obstacle in your way." This left no more to be said; and what else was attempted to be said could mean nothing. But, for what it reveals of his own position at the time, the substance of the rest of the letter may be given. The statement of his income is below

Margin notes:
1699–1701.
Æt. 32–34.

Third parties interfering.

Treatment of his objections.

Ante, 53, 96.

Message by his uncle Adam.

1699-1701. what had been asserted as the value of Laracor, but is
Æт. 32-34. found to be strictly true.

She had asked as to the altered style of his letters since
he last came over.   Abundance of times had he told her
the cause.   The company she was with, and the place she
was in, were disagreeable to him; yet she had answered
only by a great deal of arguing, often in most imperious
style.   She had expressed in her letters some suspicion of
Important   "thoughts of a new mistress," but at once he declares, upon
declaration. the word of a Christian and a gentleman, that it is not
so: neither had he ever thought of being married to any
other person but herself.*   True, she had often belied that
great sweetness of nature and humor which he believed
her to possess; but he knew this to be a thing only put
on as necessary before a lover, and he had striven hard
not to impute it to any want of common esteem for him.
She resented his having asked for an account of her fortune.   But it was not for the reason she suspected.   It
was simply to ascertain if it were sufficient, with the help
of his own poor income, to make one of her humor easy
in a married state.   She had £100 a year: enough, at any
rate, to save her from dwindling away her life and health
"in such a sink, and among such family conversation :"
yet she had entirely disregarded all his strong feelings as
Dismal but to that.   She had called his account of his livings a dismal
true picture. one.   It was a true one; and their joint incomes would be
perhaps less than £300 a year.†   Let her, then, draw her

---

* No one acquainted, however
slightly, with the character of Swift
ought to hesitate in accepting unre-
servedly this statement as decisive
against any love-passages, thus far,
between himself and Esther Johnson.
  † Scott calculates that the addition
of Dunlavin to Swift's other preferments raised his income to betwixt
£350 and £400; but this is an estimate formed on the flighty and never
trustworthy flourishes of Mr. Deane
Swift, who puts down Laracor at £200

a year, and the rest in like proportion.
The value of all the livings, including
Dunlavin, worth very little, was probably within £230 yearly. From his
note-books for 1702 it would seem
that Laracor and Agher were let in
that year by Parvisol for "£143 in
money, besides Stokestown and
Readstown drawn, and hay to value
of £17 10s., in all £160 10s." From
the same very interesting memorials,
now in my possession, I take the account of what he paid of "charges

conclusions. The former incumbent, Doctor Bolton, still kept with his deanery the place he lived on ; and the place of residence given to himself was within a mile of a town called Trim, twenty miles from Dublin : so that his only alternative was to hire a house at Trim or to build ; the first hardly to be done, and the other he was too poor to do. He could not go to Belfast at present : his attendance on the Lords Justices was so close, and so much was required of him : but the Government sat loose, and he was apt to believe the Berkeleys would be involved in the

1699–1701.
Æt. 32–34.
Real state of affairs.

---

belonging to Laracor and Agher" from July, 1702, to August, 1703, in which will be seen traces of "work done in the garden." To this I add from the same authority, in a parallel column, where every entry is also written by himself, his receipts from Laracor and Agher during 1703.

Paid.	£	s.	d.
July 31, 1702.—Paid Mr Smith the remaindr of a Quartr euding Jul. 12, 1702	9	5	2
Dec. 24.—Pd Mr Smith in part for a Quartr ending Octr 12, 1702	8	0	0
Feb. 2, 1702-3.—Pd Mr Smith in full	11	5	0
— For work done in the Garden below to Mar. 14, 170½, making Trenches and walks, and planting Sallyes	1	12	7
Apr. 6.—To Andr Maluly for all accts	1	10	0
May 10.—Proxyes, School, and Bps Clerk, 1s	2	7	9
— Schoolmaster of Trim for the year 1703	0	10	2
— Two dinners at Visitations	0	10	9
— For making the well-hide Ditch and other work, Salley, &c.	0	13	8
May 25.—To Glascock, Pd in Dublin, Parvisll has his Acqnittance, for 20 parts for 3 Parishes	0	14	2
May 28 to July 31.—Cleaning Sallyes 3 times and drawing Stone	0	4	6
July 31, 1730.—For Hay money pd May 28	0	4	0
— To Mr Smith for 2 sermons	1	3	0
Aug. 5.—Pd an old Arrear of Crown rent for the year 1688, due by Dean Bolton	7	11	8
— Pd for setting money of the Corn drawn	0	19	0

Received.	£	s.	d.
Decr 2.—From Mr Parvisol	1	9	0
Jan. 7, 170½.—Allowd on Acct then stated	15	2	0
— More received	5	0	0
— More allowed on Account	0	13	9
— 8.—Allowd to ballance the great Account	1	9	5
— Received	10	6	0
Feb.2.—Allowd to clear Mr Smith	14	5	0
— 9.—Recd	0	13	0
— 17.—Recd by the Conch	4	3	1
— 22.—In mild shillas, &c.	0	16	10
Mar. 11.—6 Pistolls	5	11	0
Mar. 14.—Recd	2	9	0½
Aprl 21.—Recd on Acct for Horse & Coach, Malaly, Skelton &c.	6	16	4
May 17.—Recd Cash	11	0	0
— 23.—Recd (and lent in part)	2	18	6
Jan. 23.—By Coach	2	18	10
Aug. 1.—Recd in money at Laracor	2	11	6
— 8.—In money at Laracor	5	10	0
— 5.—For the Queen's Crown rent, being the old arrear due by Dean Bolton	7	11	8
— 22.—In money	5	0	0
Sept. 12.—In money	4	11	10
— 20.—In money	2	10	4½
Oct. 23. — Overplus of Corn Money allowd	1	0	0½
— 24. — Allowed on Horse, Grazing, &c.	2	8	4½
— In money at Laracor	1	4	6
— 30.—In money sent me to Dublin	4	1	6
	£122	1	6

change now probable, in which case leisure would fall to himself. But he hopes other friends, more powerful than he, will before that time persuade her from the place she is in. He desires his service to her mother, in return for that lady's remembrance: "but for any other dealings that way," is his significant addition, "I entreat your par-

don; and I think I have more cause to resent your desires of me in that case than you have to be angry at my refusals. If you like such company and conduct, much good do you with them! My education has been otherwise." His concluding sentence was not less characteristic. Whenever she could heartily answer yes to all he had said, he should be blessed to have her in his arms, without regarding whether her person were beautiful or her fortune large. Cleanliness and competence were all he looked for. He had singled her out from the rest of women at first, and he expected not to be used like a common lover.

No more is heard of Miss Waring; and the most correct impression derivable from so strange a courtship would probably be, that Swift was fortunate in being rejected by his mistress at the first, and Miss Waring not less so in losing her lover at the last.

Another question of the prudence or imprudence of marrying arose in the Swift family at the time, and he has been as sharply, perhaps as little justly, criticised for
the part he took in it. His sister Jane married a currier in Bride Street named Fenton, and the match, though sanctioned by her mother and uncles, was so determinedly opposed by her brother, that when remonstrance failed he broke off intercourse for a time. Lord Orrery says it was nothing but rage at her marrying a tradesman, "which seemed to interrupt those ambitious views he had long since formed;" and Mr. Deane Swift parallels this nonsense by saying that the brother never saw the sister again, having offered her £500 if she would but show a "proper disdain" of Fenton, but that, on Fenton's dying bankrupt two or three years after the marriage, the widow received

from her brother a small annuity on condition of her never again showing her face in Ireland. The case was really a simple one, and Swift's conduct in it intelligible and manly. He could not have liked such a marriage, being undoubtedly always sensitive on the point of family connections; but there is no evidence that he opposed it on those grounds. He opposed it because he disliked the man, and believed his alleged fortune of five thousand pounds to be sheer imposture; nevertheless, upon Fenton's subsequent bankruptcy, he contributed more than he could well afford to his sister's support. There is no pretense for saying he refused to see her; and when she went to England, it was not because but in spite of his wish, for she went, greatly to his dislike, to pass some time at Moor Park with Lady Giffard. This was during Anne's last ministry; and even then Fenton was not dead, but living still with his wife, though his worthlessness had by that time made itself known, even to those who had approved the marriage. Swift told Esther Johnson, in January, 1710–'11, of a letter from his sister about money of hers "that is entrusted to me by my mother, not to come to her husband;" and eight months later he wrote that he pitied "poor Jenny" for her deafness, but that her husband was a dunce, and with respect to him she lost little by it. She was not the worse for not hearing any thing he said. Poor Jenny survived her dunce some years, and was wholly dependent at last on her brother. She lived upon an annuity from him until within seven years of his own death, and died in the same lodging with Esther Johnson's mother, Mrs. Bridget Mose, in the village of Farnham.

At Lord Berkeley's recall Swift accompanied him to England, but he had shortly before gone down to take possession of his livings at Laracor. Tradition followed him, and has been, as the great master of nature expresses it, believed into truth. It has given us many stories for which brief reference here may suffice. There is the walk all the way on foot, with a clean shirt and one pair of

1699–1701.
Æt. 32–34.
Misrepresentation.

Truth of the case.

Swift kind to the last.

Taking possession at Laracor.

1699-1701. stockings in his pocket, and sarcastic couplets dropped on
Æt. 32–34. places passed in his way.* There is the meek curate's
fright at the loud knock and yet louder voice that blunt-
ly self-announce "the master." There is his poor wife's
puzzled consternation at the shirt and stockings committed to her charge. There is, finally, the substantial kindness that afterward takes the place of these airs of domination, and changes terrible alarm into grateful respect.

Truth and   Scott found such stories fit in so well with his own bio-
tradition. graphical impressions that he was more than ready to believe them. It was so like Swift to evince satisfaction
under cover of complaining, to make threats the prelude
to benefits, to put irony into grave things and satire into
light ones, that Scott did not care to inquire if it was likely that stories of the kind referred to should have contributed to form a character, or if it were not likelier still that
they had grown and settled round a character already famous as well as formed. It is difficult to distinguish truth
from its resemblance, when a man with such marked peculiarities becomes so widely known as Swift.

There is another story of this time which we could ill
afford to lose, and of which Scott is, perhaps, entitled to
say that Swift was more likely to do such a thing than
Orrery to invent it. "When he went to reside at Lara-

Remarks, 32. cor," says Lord Orrery, "he gave public notice to his parishioners that he would read prayers every Wednesday
and Friday. Upon the subsequent Wednesday the bell
was rung, and the rector attended in his desk, when, after
having sat some time, and finding the congregation to consist only of himself and his clerk Roger, he began, with
great composure and gravity, but with a tone peculiar to

"Dearly be- himself, *Dearly beloved Roger, the Scripture moveth you
loved Rog-
er."   *and me in sundry places;* and then proceeded regularly
through the whole service."

---

* "High church and low steeple, | Navan for a market, Ardbracken for
    Dirty town and proud people." | a cow."
  Or again :   [a plough, | Etc., etc.   And so forth.
  "Dublin for a city, Dunshaughlan for |

The tradition of his surprise and indignation at his first sight of the church at Laracor may be accepted without question. A couple of miles from Trim, in a dull farming country at the northern extremity of East Meath, with a few huts around it, a parsonage-house too dilapidated for decent residence, and a glebe of one acre, rose the old, plain, barn-like structure with its low belfry, in manifest neglect and decay.* Swift's resolve was taken on the instant, that it should not remain so; though with his narrow means he could proceed but slowly in the self imposed duty of repair. The greater part of his first year's income was expended in making the vicarage tenantable; and gradually, through the next half-dozen years, extraordinary improvements were effected in the church and glebe. An extensive garden was laid out, having for its boundary a small stream, of which he so enlarged the current and smoothed the banks as to turn it into a canal, in the Dutch style that Moor Park had made pleasant to his memory; and along the pretty winding walk, formed by the side of it, he planted regular ranks of willows in double rows. Long before even Scott wrote, the willows had decayed or been cut down, the garden could not be traced, and where the canal had been there was a ditch; but, in the letters to Esther Johnson, they will continue to live as long as the name of Swift survives with the language he wrote in.

Other solider additions to the living I assume still to

Margin notes: 1699-1701. Æt. 32-34. First sight of his church. Restoration and improvements. The willows planted.

---

* Among my papers I find the subjoined extract from some official register in the diocese of Meath, dated after Swift's possession of his deanery, and mentioning some of the improvements in the original glebe. Unfortunately, I can not remember where I obtained it:
"No. 76. Larachor als Leicor. Jonathan Swift Vic. Stafford Lightburn, Curate. There were originally in this Parish a Rectory & a Vicaridge ye Rectory was appropriated to ye Monastery of St. Thomas Dublin but 12th of Charles ye 1st was grant-

ed to ye Vicar under a crown rent of 20 L. Irish.
"The Church-yard is inclosed partly with a stone wall and partly with a ditch. The original glebe belonging to this parish contains about an acre & is exceedingly well inclosed there is a good garden and a neat cabbin made by ye present Incumbent and valued at 60 L. tis situated near ye Church.
"The Incumbent is resident on his deanery of St Patrick Dublin & serves this parish by a curate who resides in Trim."

Margin note: Notices of Laracor in Swift's time.

1699–1701.
Æt. 32–34.
Additions to glebe.

remain as when he left them.* He increased the glebe from one acre to twenty, and endowed the vicarage with tithes which he had himself bought, and which by his will he settled on all future incumbents, subject to one condition. Language more eloquent than mine may be here

Condition of Laracor in 1875.

* The note subjoined is from Scott (1814): "'The house appears, from its present ruins, to have been a comfortable mansion. The present Bishop of Meath (whom the editor is proud to call his friend), with classic feeling, while pressing upon his clergy, at a late visitation, the duty of repairing the glebe-houses, addressed himself particularly to the vicar of Laracor, and recommended to him, in the necessary improvements of his mansion, to save, as far as possible, the walls of the house which had been inhabited by his great predecessor." Through the kindness of a friend I have been favored with a statement from the present vicar of Laracor, the Rev. Charles Elrington M'Kay, of the existing condition of a place never to be disconnected from Swift's name and memory. The date of this interesting communication is the 21st of January, 1875.

"(1.) The fragment of the wall of the old vicarage is still standing, and remains in the same condition in which it was on my succeeding to this incumbency in 1865. I have not observed any process of decay in it, nor (as far as I have noticed) does there appear any symptom of that gradual abstraction of stones which frequently takes place from celebrated memorials, by the hands of enthusiastic tourists. There it remains, gaunt and solitary, a most interesting relic of the abode of an extraordinary man. It is, as you say, all that is left of the 'old vicarage.'

"(2.) The church of the Dean is no longer standing: it was taken down in the year 1856, and a new one built

on the old site. As the old site is very inconveniently situated for the majority of the parishioners (being at the extreme verge of a large parish), it was proposed that the new church should be transferred to the centre of the parish. However, the then incumbent, thinking that the 'genius loci' was worth deferring to, had the old site maintained, and consequently the new church stands precisely where the Dean's was.

"(3.) There are, unfortunately, no written entries whatever regarding the Dean: the parish registries are comparatively modern. Nor are there any traditions worth relating. Of memorials there is what is known as 'the Dean's well;' which is situated somewhat near the old vicarage gable on the roadside, and which is greatly used by the neighbors. It was of this that tradition says the Dean used the phrase 'that he had a cellar which never went dry.' It is at one end of the small garden attached to the old glebe.

"(4.) The place consists now, as far as I can learn, of what it did in his time. There never was a village, or county town of Laracor. The church stands at the junction of four cross-roads, where there are four or five scattered cottages. This is the only sign of habitation about. The vicarage in which I reside is about six minutes' walk from the church. The present glebe consists of two distinct portions—one of 20 acres Irish, the other of about one acre. This one acre is detached from the 20, and comprises the old glebe of Dean Swift." As to the last remark, see above.

interposed. "When Swift was made Vicar of Laracor," 1699-1701.
said Mr. Gladstone to the House of Commons in March, Æt. 32–34.
1869, "he went into a glebe-house with one acre, and he Mr. Gladstone's reference to Swift in 1869.
left it with twenty acres improved and decorated in many
ways. He also endowed the vicarage with tithes purchased by him for the purpose of so bequeathing them;
and I am not aware if it be generally known that a curious
question arises on this bequest. This extraordinary man,
even at the time when he wrote that the Irish Catholics
were so downtrodden and insignificant that no possible
change could bring them into a position of importance,
appears to have foreseen the day when the ecclesiastical
arrangements of Ireland would be called to account; for
he proceeds to provide for a time when the Episcopal religion might be no longer the national religion of the
country. By some secret intimation he foresaw the short-
ness of its existence as an establishment, and left the
property subject to a condition that in such case it should
be administered for the benefit of the poor."* Not quite
so. The incumbents were to have the tithes for as long
as the existing church should be established; and Mr.
Gladstone having withdrawn that condition, the living
loses the tithes. But it is "whenever any other form of
Christian religion shall become the established faith in
this kingdom" that the condition arises handing them Stipulations of Swift's will.
over to the poor, securing that their profits shall be giv-
en in a weekly proportion "by such other officers as may
then have the power of distributing charities to the parish," and excluding from this benefit Jews, atheists, and
infidels.

It is a bequest which certainly raises a "curious question," whether we regard it with Scott as a mere stroke

* A similar provision appears in the clause of Esther Johnson's will (which Swift is alleged to have dictated), endowing a chaplaincy to Steven's Hospital. "And if it shall happen (which God forbid) that at any time hereafter the present Established Episcopal Church of this kingdom shall come to be abolished, and be no longer the national Established Church of the said kingdom, I do, in that case, declare wholly null and void the bequest above made of," etc., etc.

1699–1701.
Æt. 32–34. of Swift's peculiar humor, or with Mr. Gladstone as a quasi-forethought for the "downtrodden" Irish Catholics.

Shortly after his institution to Laracor, Swift received from the Archbishop of Dublin (then Marsh, the founder of the library) the prebend of Dunlavin in St. Patrick's Cathedral, entitling him to a seat in the chapter; and a few months later, on the 16th February, 1700–1701, he Degree of
D.D. took his doctor's degree in Dublin University.* At the beginning of April, he set sail with the Berkeleys for England; where for the present, notwithstanding his professional preferments, the most memorable portion of his life is to be passed. But let the reader disposed to be severe on such abandonment of clerical duties, remember always See letter to
Arbp. King,
6th Jan.,
1709. what the Irish Church then was, and that when the Vicar of Laracor turned his back on Ireland he left behind him "a parish with an audience of half a score."

II.

LONDON LIFE.

1701–1705. Æt. 34–38.

1701–1705.
Æt. 34–38.
Impeach-
ment of
whig lords. LORD BERKELEY had been recalled on the success of the tories in the general election at the close of 1700; and, upon the news then also reaching Ireland of the tory impeachment of the four whig lords, Swift had remarked to the earl that the same manner of proceeding, it appeared to him, had ruined the liberties of Athens and Rome, and that it might be easy to prove this from history. "Soon after," says Swift, "I went to London; and in a few weeks drew up a discourse under the title of *The Contests and*

---

* His account-books show that in "fees and treat" this degree in divin- | ity cost him forty-four pounds and up- | ward.

Dissentions of the Nobles and Commons in Athens and Rome, with the consequences they had upon those states. This discourse I sent very privately to the press, with the strictest injunctions to conceal the author; and returned immediately to my residence in Ireland." He had been in England from May to September, visiting Leicester before his return to Dublin. It was not a long visit; but it contributed to his future existence much that determined its color and character. His public career began with his plunge into politics; and a visit now made to Esther Johnson at Farnham gave lasting influence to what remained of his private life.

He found her and her friend, Mrs. Dingley, still in the trouble and discomfort that had followed the changes consequent on Temple's death. Her fortune at this time, which he reckons to have been in all not above fifteen hundred pounds, and which we should now call nearly treble, he characterizes as but a scanty maintenance in so dear a country for one of her spirit. This fact, and the circumstance that what Temple had bequeathed to her was a leasehold farm in County Wicklow, might of themselves have suggested a removal to Ireland; but Swift, with perfect frankness, says more than this. Moved to the advice he gave, not by those considerations only, but, "indeed very much for my own satisfaction, who had few friends or acquaintance in Ireland, I prevailed with her and her dear friend and companion, the other lady, to draw what money they had into Ireland, a great part of their fortunes being in annuities upon funds. Money was then ten per cent. in Ireland, besides the advantage of returning it, and all necessaries of life at half the price. They complied with my advice, and soon after came over; but I happening to continue some time longer in England, they were much discouraged to live in Dublin, where they were wholly strangers. But the adventure looked so like a frolic, the censure held for some time as if there were a secret history in such a removal: which, however, soon blew off by her excellent conduct. She came over with

1701–1705.
Æt. 34–38. her friend in the year 1700,* and they both lived together until this day."†

The "secret history" that "censure" so readily invented was not blown off so readily; but remark may confine itself for the present to "the frolic" which thus first set Dublin gossip. on foot the gossip of Dublin, that two unmarried ladies should come over from England for mere companionship and social intercourse with an unmarried clergyman in Ireland. There was no affectation of concealment. Out of what is said of the discouragement and strangeness of Swift and his Moor Park friends. Dublin by which the ladies were met at their arrival, the arrangement probably arose by which, at first, Swift's lodgings were opened to them as long as he should be absent; and among other considerations held to justify its continuance for the most part of the subsequent years, we may be sure that a regard to economy had prominent place. Manner of life. The mode of life so adopted was not afterward greatly changed, though it was by no means kept up unalterably. This, however, is certain, that when Swift was in England the ladies used his Dublin residence; and when he returned, they went into a lodging of their own. They were always near each other, if not together; and Swift could very rarely have seen the girl who thus fearlessly linked her name to his, except under the same roof with the woman chosen for her guardian and companion, who was some years older than himself. The like arrange-

---

* The circumstances prove it to have been, not 1700, but the first months (reckoning the beginning of the year from March 25th) of 1701.

† Written by Swift on the day of Esther Johnson's death, Sunday, the 28th of January, 1727-'8. The "censure" to which he refers, and the character of much of the gossip that doubtless long held its ground, may be inferred from a passage in a letter of the "little parson-cousin" as late as 1706. Thomas there asks "whether Jonathan be married? or whether he has been able to resist the charms of both those gentlewomen that marched quite from Moor Park to Dublin, as they would have marched to the North or anywhere else, with full resolution to engage him." Mr. Deane Swift, who first published this letter, has the boldness and bad taste to infer from it, in direct contradiction to the statement of his great kinsman, that it was Esther Johnson who proposed to go over to Ireland, and that her "prime intention was to captivate the affections of Dr. Swift." This is the way that lies come to pass themselves off for truth.

ments were made also at Laracor. They were there as often as they pleased, when Swift was away; and when he was in residence, they had lodgings in Trim, or were guests of the vicar, Doctor Raymond, or occupied a little farm-cottage near Knightsbrook-gate, half a mile from Laracor, of which the site is now marked with the name of "Stella" on the ordnance survey of Meath. All the reserves were, to outward appearance, scrupulously kept up to the last. "I wonder how you could expect to see Mrs. Johnson in a morning," wrote Swift to Tickell in July, 1726, "which I, her oldest acquaintance, have not done these dozen years, except once or twice in a journey."

1701–1705.
Æt. 34–38.

Swift had an interview with the King before he went back to Dublin, probably to lay before him another volume of Temple's remains. "I remember" he afterward said, "when I was last in England, I told the King that the highest tories we had with us in Ireland would make tolerable whigs in England."[*] The poor great-hearted King had found the problem of constitutional government a very thorny one. What with tory doubts of his title and whig doubts of his prerogative, he passed an unenviable time; and one can fancy him repeating to Swift what he had said to the elder Halifax, that between them he could really see no difference except that the tories would cut his throat in the morning and the whigs would let him live till the afternoon.

Again with
the King.

Close of a
great life.

In April of the following year Swift, after a visit to his mother in Leicester, was again in London, and found his position somewhat changed. He had received a foretaste of it before he quitted Dublin, when, being in company with Bishop Sheridan, of Kilmore, he heard much praise of a new pamphlet that the Bishop of Salisbury had written, replete with political knowledge. It was the *Dissentions in Athens and Rome* which had been making a great deal of noise. Was the bishop certain of Burnet's authorship? Swift asked: and was told he must be a "positive

Swift's tract
ascribed to
Burnet.

---

* Letter on the Sacramental Test.—*Scott*, viii., 364.

1701-1705. young man" to doubt it. Nevertheless the doubt was
Æt. 34-38. repeated; and upon being then more sharply rated as a
"very positive young man," Swift was fain to confess that
he was himself the writer.   The anecdote may be believed*
on the authority of Swift's own relation of what he heard
and experienced on his return to England.

In the tract itself there is nothing that calls for detailed
remark.   It is chiefly noticeable for its statesman-like use
of book-knowledge in the practical affairs of public policy;
but it is right to say that the charges against the author
which have been based upon it, of having afterward turned
against men whom it had compared and identified with
such faultless heroes as Aristides, Themistocles, Pericles,
Misde-   and Phocion, are simply not true.   It has no such strained
scribed.   comparisons, for its applications are in no respect personal.
With perfect truth Swift says in it: "I am not conscious
that I have forced an example, or put it in any other light
than it appeared to me long before I had thought of pro-
What it was. ducing it."   It is an extremely able argument, supported
by reasonings and illustrations both dispassionate and ap-
posite, to show that states can only be kept free by just
balances of power at home as well as abroad; that any
conflict between the great authorities in a commonwealth,
as in this case between commons and lords, has an ultimate
tendency, through whatever immediate consequence, to
anarchy or a single tyranny: and that ancient history was
filled with such examples.   His parallels are slight, and
only meant to give point to the historic application.   All
Moderns and that is said of Somers to liken him to Aristides is that he
ancients not
compared.   was a man of exact justice and knowledge in the law, as
well as thoroughly acquainted with the forms of government; of the victor of La Hogue, for likeness to Themistocles, that he was a fortunate admiral; of Halifax, for a
parallel to Pericles, that he was an able minister, orator,
and man of letters; and of Portland, for a representative
in Phocion, that he was renowned for success in treaties as

---

* Johnson tells the story with undoubting faith and evident enjoyment.

well as battles. The subject-matter of the impeachment
of the modern statesmen receives hardly an allusion ; but
there is a pregnant warning of danger in any permitted
preponderance of the power of France, and a wise protest
against blind and unreasoning subservience to party. Of
the effect produced by it, Swift will himself speak :

"The book was greedily bought and read ; and charged
some time upon my Lord Somers, and some time upon the
Bishop of Salisbury ; the latter of whom told me afterward
'that he was forced to disown it in a very public manner,
for fear of an impeachment, wherewith he was threatened.'
Returning next year for England, and hearing of the great
reputation this piece had received (which was the first I
ever printed), I must confess the vanity of a young man
prevailed with me to let myself be known for the author :
upon which my Lords Somers and Halifax" (Charles Montagu), "as well as the bishop above mentioned, desired my
acquaintance, with great marks of esteem and professions
of kindness—not to mention the Earl of Sunderland, who
had been my old acquaintance." (In the Moor Park time.)
"They lamented that they were not able to serve me since
the death of the King ; and were very liberal in promising me the greatest preferments I could hope for, if ever
it came in their power. I soon grew domestic with Lord
Halifax, and was as often with Lord Somers as the for-
mality of his nature (the only unconversable fault he had)
made it agreeable to me."* The last few lines anticipate
a little. But from the date of this second visit to England, after Temple's death, there was no more prominent
figure than Swift's among the wits and men of letters in
London.

How formidable a body they had become it hardly
needs that I should say. The press, set free by the Revolution,† had made itself the most powerful intermediary

---

* *Memoirs relating to that change which happened in Queen Anne's Ministry in the year* 1710.—Scott edition, iii., 186-'7.

† The censorship of the press expired in 1694, and no man of any party was found to suggest its renewal. It passed away forever.

between the commonalty and the lower house of legisla- ture, to which the Revolution had at the same time com- mitted the highest authority in the state. At the critical moment when the people were rising into the first impor- tance, men who could best use the pen found themselves best able to influence and persuade them. Speakers to either lords or commons had no such influence, for the reporting of debates was unknown, and their speaking Orators and remained within their four walls. What the orator now writers. is, the writer was then, with the world for his audience. Such power was to Swift an irresistible temptation; hence- forward, for some years, it was to divide the occupations of his life in nearly equal portions between England and Ireland; and with some confidence it may be said that its fascination to him was far less the help it might avail to give to any special public object, than the unspeakable en- joyment which its exercise gave himself. Though he led the greatest party fight ever fought in England, he was never, strictly speaking, a party man. In Addison's last letter he spoke of him as having so much compass in his character that there was room in it for all sides to admire; and this was in other words to describe his character as having too much room in it to satisfy one side only. It was at all periods of his life his favorite saying that no one who really valued the church would commit himself to the extremes of whig, and that all who cared for the Avoidance state would avoid the extremes of tory. What, indeed, of extremes. was wanting to him as a whig while he was a whig, and what was still more wanting to him as a tory when he went over to Harley, will soon be apparent enough; but he was otherwise as far as possible removed from the taint of Grub Street. He had nothing in him of the hired scribe, and was never at any time in any one's pay. The minister he supported had to hold him by other ties. He might fairly look to future preferment; but the immedi- Conditions ate condition of his party service was to " grow domestic " of party with those he served, exacting from them increased per- service. sonal consideration. His familiar footing with the leading men alike of whig and tory, and his exception to the *1701-1705. Æt. 84-38.* "unconversable" Somers, have in this their explanation; and what in later life he laughingly wrote to Pope was not without its gravity of meaning:. "I will tell you that all my endeavors, from a boy, to distinguish myself, were only for want of a great title and fortune, that I might be used like a lord by those who have an opinion of my parts; whether right or wrong is no great matter; and so the reputation of great learning does the office of a blue ribbon, or of a coach and six horses."

Swift's English visit in 1702 closed in October by his *Visits to England.* return to Ireland; and his visit the following year lasted from November, 1703, when he arrived at Leicester and traveled thence to London, until May, 1704. This he calls, in his note-books now in my possession, his tenth voyage between the two countries; and its first and its last day are thus recorded: "Novr 11th 1703. Thursd. I went to sea, landed in Eng^d on Saturd. 13th 1703. Tuesd. May 29th 1704. I went to sea, landed in Irel^d on Thursd. Jun. 1 1704." Again, in 1705, he was in England, and in the winter of 1707–'8; Esther Johnson, who is supposed nev- *Esther Johnson in London with Swift.* er to have recrossed the Channel but once after her settlement in Ireland, having also paid short visits (accompanied by Mrs. Dingley) in both those years. Swift's entry in his note-book of his English residence, which began in the winter of 1707–'8, and extended to June, 1709, will be found to have a special significance. "In suspense I was all this year in England."

Great were the changes in those years. For the first half of them, the tories retained the power thrown into their hands by the King's death, and confirmed to them, as they believed, by the bigotry of his successor, Queen Anne. *Character of Anne.* But though they had good reason for the belief that her weak religious fears would place her permanently in the power of the high-church party, they had not yet discovered how much the same obstinate feebleness of mind would bind her to a slavery more resistless and abject. Thus far the woman-favorite she had chosen was helping

them; the Marlboroughs being still tory, and Mrs. Freeman not untender to the conscience of her beloved Mrs.
Morley.* But the spirit of the great survives them; and,
as the foreign policy which William had bequeathed was
Effect of
Marlbor-
ough's vic-
tories.
carried to its height by Marlborough's transcendent military genius, not he and his wife only, but the chief of the
cabinet in which Rochester and Nottingham still sat, began to see the wisdom of making common cause rather
with those who exulted in such victories than with those
who viewed them with dismay. The battle of Blenheim,
fought in 1704, not only put the seal upon this change,
but brought to the front a man who had been silently
working, from even before the King's death, to keep in
check both the party extremes. It then seemed safe to
Marlborough and Godolphin to begin to alter their course
in a way as little startling as might be; and they consented to receive as colleagues two yet moderate tories,
Harley joins
Godolphin.
Robert Harley, the ex-Speaker, and his brilliant young
lieutenant, Henry St. John, not committed to any extreme
church policy, and not supposed to have any doubts of
that act of settlement and royal title which Blenheim had
finally secured against foreign arms. But the effect of
Marlborough's triumphs soon began to take wider range.
Whigs still
rising.
The general election of 1705 gave the whigs a sufficient
preponderance in the House of Commons to enable Marlborough and Godolphin, with less caution than had characterized their previous change, to get rid of what remained of their high-church colleagues. Cowper became
lord chancellor, Somers and Halifax were sworn of the
council, and Addison, appointed under-secretary of state,
had for his chief the son of Swift's old acquaintance, Sunderland, the most uncompromising of whigs. A year and
a half later, though the interval had been marked by many
Harley
turned out.
strange alliances, even Harley and his friends had to retire. He had made the important discovery, that Mrs.

---

* The names under which the queen and the duchess masqueraded in their
private apartments.

Morley (the queen) was growing tired of her dear Mrs. 1701-1705. Æt. 34-38. Freeman (the duchess), but he too prematurely made use of his valuable secret.* Though his Abigail was ready, the Marlboroughs were too powerful, and Harley had to bide his time. Then came the general election of 1708 with its decisive whig majority. Somers was at last made president of the council, Wharton went to Ireland, and all further compromise with the church party closed. Ministry all whig.

Whether, with his particular church views, Swift had not a more difficult part to play in the last four than in the first four of these years, when the whigs had obtained power rather than when they were struggling to obtain it, is a question open to considerable doubt. He has himself, however, by hints dropped in his letters, given us some means of forming an opinion upon it; and a part of his correspondence available for this purpose illustrates also, in a very striking form, his present personal relations with Esther Johnson.

A clergyman first known to him when he lived in the North, who had been a minister in Belfast, and was now incumbent of a small Dublin parish, the Rev. William Tisdall, had stepped into some favor at this time by civilities to Esther Johnson and her friend; and we find him in 1703 asking Swift to tell him of public affairs in London, reporting to him news of the ladies in Dublin, and confiding some little ambitions he had to try his own hand at writing for the press. Swift replies pleasantly; but with touches of irony in his good-humored regret, that he can not persuade his correspondent of his insignificance so far as to get himself treated with a proper distance and Correspondence with Tisdall.

---

* See Swift's letter to Archbishop King, Feb. 12, 1707-'8. "Mr. Harley had been for some time, with the greatest art imaginable, carrying on an intrigue to alter the ministry, and began with no less an enterprise than that of removing the Lord Treasurer, and had nearly effected it, by the help of Mrs. Masham, one of the queen's dressers, who was a great and growing favorite, of much industry and insinuation...... He had laid a scheme for an entire new ministry, and the men are named to whom the several employments were to be given. And though his project has miscarried, it is reckoned the greatest piece of court skill that has been acted these many years."

1701-1703.
Æt. 34-38.

A distinguished lodging.

respect by him; which he supposes must arise from the credit that is pretended with two ladies who came from England. " I allow indeed the chamber in William Street to be Little England by their influence; as an ambassador's house, wherever it is, hath all the privileges of his master's dominions; and therefore, if you wrote the letter in their room, or their company (for in this matter their room is as good as their company), I will indulge you a little." So great the indulgence, that his letters are to be answered, in future, " the first after the ladies; for I never write to any other friend or relation till long after;" Tisdall is, moreover, selected for the privilege of giving messages to her from himself about her investments; and he is told how, after the new court amusement which all the fashionable folk were mad for, he is to outwit the

A bite.

young lady by the way of a bite. " You must ask a bantering question, or tell some damned lie in a serious manner, and then she will answer or speak as if you were in earnest; and then cry you, *Madam, there's a bite.*"

But even his playful messages take the tone which gives its prevailing color and specialty of meaning to his interest for this young girl. He is mightily afraid that the ladies are very idle, and don't mind their book, wherefore he prays that Tisdall will put them upon reading, and " be

Teacher still.

always teaching something to Mrs. Johnson, because she is good at comprehending, remembering, and retaining." His correspondent's literary aspirations he decidedly discountenances; from all meddling with public affairs by the way of writing he strongly dissuades him; and what on this point he says to Tisdall himself in these friendly days, is exactly what he said later to others, when, after

Letter to Dr. Jenny, 1732.

thirty years, he described him as an honest fellow enough, who had been unhappily misled all his life by mistaking his talent, which he had been trying, against all nature, to apply to wit and literature. He tells him now it is a " terrible mistake" to imagine he can not be enough distinguished without writing for the public. He is to " preach, preach, preach, preach, preach, preach ;" that, certainly, was his talent; and if he was ever to be a writer, there would be time for it many years hence. Nothing so bad, in Swift's judgment, as to be "hasty to write for the world." Tisdall had pleaded his wish to be heard on a leading question then in agitation. "A pox," cried Swift, " on the dissenters and independents. I would as soon trouble my head to write against a louse or a flea. I tell you what: I wrote against the bill that was against occasional conformity; but it came too late by a day, so I would not print it."*

1701-1705.
Æt. 34–38.

Time enough to write.

The bill against occasional conformity, of which the drift was to disqualify dissenters for all civil employments, had been forced upon Godolphin by his high-church colleagues, twice passed by the commons, and twice sent back by the lords. The excitement for and against it was extraordinary. Party and faction, says Swift, had never run so high. "I observed the dogs in the streets much more contumelious and quarrelsome than usual; and the very night before the bill went up, a committee of whig and tory cats had a very warm and loud debate upon the roof of our house. But why should we wonder at that, when the very ladies are split asunder into high church and low, and, out of zeal for religion, have hardly time to say their prayers?" His own position in regard to it had troubled him at first. " The whole body of the clergy" being violent for it, and " some great people" urging him "mightily" to publish his opinion, he was at a loss for a time what to do. But observation of what was passing showed him that the bill was not a wise one, and that resistance to it was quite compatible with love for the church and a dislike of presbytery. "I put it close to my Lord Peterborough, just as the bill was going up, who assured me in the most solemn manner, that, if he had the least suspicion the rejecting this bill would hurt the church or

Occasional Conformity Bill

Dogs and cats in debate.

Swift's doubts.

---

* He thus closed his letter: "But you may answer it if you please; for you know you and I are whig and tory. And, to cool your insolence a little, know that the Queen and Court, and House of Lords, and half the Commons almost, are whigs, and the number daily increases."

do kindness to the dissenters, he would lose his right hand rather than speak against it. The like profession I had from the Bishop of Salisbury, my Lord Somers, and some others; so that I know not what to think, and therefore shall think no more." It ended in his writing against the bill, and not publishing what he had written. His position was not unlike that of the queen's husband; taking one from the view of a churchman, and the other from

Non-con-
formist
prince.
that of a dissenter. Poor Prince George was himself an occasional conformist, but the tories laid violent hands on him. With a remark to Wharton which that eminent whig would be likely to think rather foreign than germane to the purpose, "My heart is *vid* you," he went with his vote into the other lobby.

But the Tisdall correspondence was to take another and startling turn. In the letters just quoted, of which the date is February, 1703-'4, Swift had told him that he seemed to be mighty proud (having, indeed, good reason, if it were true) of the part he had in the ladies' good

Tisdall's ad-
dresses to
Esther John-
son.
graces, "especially of her you call *the party;*" and had added, half jocosely, that he was very much concerned to know it. Upon this appears to have followed a letter from Tisdall, and a reply to it by Swift, of which all that is known to us is Tisdall's description of the reply given

Swift's reply.
in Swift's rejoinder of the date of April, 1704. "You have got three epithets for my former letter, which, I believe, are all unjust: you say it was *unfriendly, unkind,* and *unaccountable.* The two first, I suppose, may pass but for one; saving (as Captain Fluellin says the phrase is) *a little variations.* I shall, therefore, answer those two as I can; and for the last, I return it to you again by these presents, assuring you that there is more unaccountability in your letter's little finger than in mine's whole body." Then, with sarcastic allusion to "a mystical strain" in his correspondent, as if he had found out in some marvelous way what others were trying to conceal, the case between them is put with singular simplicity and unreserve. No one has written of this passage in Swift's life

without imputing to him a grave disingenuousness,* but 1701-1705.
Æt. 34-38. the sufficient answer is in these words: "I might, with good pretense enough, talk starchly and affect ignorance of what you would be at; but my conjecture is that you think I obstructed your inclinations to please my own, His own in-
clinations. and that my intentions were the same with yours; in answer to all which I will, upon my conscience and honor, tell you the naked truth. First, I think I have said to you before that, if my fortunes and humor served me to think of that state, I should certainly, among all persons on earth, make your choice; because I never saw that person whose conversation I entirely valued but hers: this was the utmost I ever gave way to. And, secondly, I must assure you sincerely that this regard of mine never once entered into my head to be an impediment to you, but I judged it would perhaps be a clog to your rising in the No bar to
Tisdall's. world, and I did not conceive you were then rich enough to make yourself and her happy and easy; but that objection is now quite removed by what you have at present and by the assurances of Eaton's livings. I told you, indeed, that your authority was not sufficient to make overtures to the mother, without the daughter giving me leave A proper
condition. under her own or her friend's hand; which I think was a right and prudent step. However, I told the mother immediately, and spoke with all the advantages you deserve; but the objection of your fortune being removed, I declare I have no other; nor shall any consideration of my own misfortune of losing so good a friend and companion as her prevail on me against her interest and settlement in the world, since it is held so necessary and convenient a thing for ladies to marry, and that time takes off from the lustre of virgins in all other eyes but mine. I appeal to "In all other
eyes but
mine." my letters to herself whether I was not your friend in the whole concern; though the part I designed to act in it was

---

* "From the time of her arrival in Ireland he seems resolved to keep her in his power; and therefore hindered a match sufficiently advanta- geous, by accumulating unreasonable demands and prescribing conditions that could not be performed."—*John-son.*

1701-1705.
Æt. 34-38.
purely passive, which is the utmost I will ever do in things of this nature, to avoid all reproach of any ill consequences that may ensue in the variety of worldly accidents : nay, I went so far to her mother, herself, and, I think, to you, as to think it could not be decently broken ; since I supposed the town had got it in their tongues, and therefore I thought it could not miscarry without some disadvantage to the

Esther John-
son de-
scribed by
Swift.
lady's credit. I have always described her to you in a manner different from those who would be discouraging ; and must add that, though it has come in my way to converse with persons of the first rank, and of that sex, more than is usual to men of my level and of our function, yet I have nowhere met with a humor, a wit, or conversation so agree-. able, a better portion of good sense, or a truer judgment of men and things—I mean here in England, for as to the ladies in Ireland I am a perfect stranger. As to her fortune, I think you know it already ; and if you resume your designs, or would have further intelligence, I shall send you a particular account." Are these expressions capable of other construction than they suggest to an ordinary understanding?

Tisdall desired to marry Esther Johnson ; and submitted the proposal to Swift as the friend in whom she most trusted, with some misgiving as to what his own views

Honest ad-
vice in a dif-
ficult case.
might be. Swift replied that if his fortunes or his humor led him to marriage, she was, of all persons on earth, the one he would choose ; but as this was not the case, her lover had nothing to apprehend on that score. His advice, nevertheless, was against the marriage, on the ground of prudence, and because he judged Tisdall to be not rich enough ; but, upon assurances that removed these objections, he had spoken to the young lady's mother ; whereupon came Tisdall's letter characterizing the advice as unkind and unaccountable. What had most jarred upon him appears to have been the intimation that Swift could not communicate with the mother unless the young lady under her own hand desired him to do so ; and whether such sanction ever was obtained seems open to much doubt.

There is, in fact, no proof whatever that Esther Johnson had herself approved of Tisdall's suit. But Swift did not really press the objection far. Though he made it the condition on which he would speak to the mother, this was when he imagined Tisdall's means to be inadequate; and he may have thought it no longer necessary after Tisdall's reply on that head. He then also went so far as to say, both to Esther Johnson and her mother, that perhaps the affair could not "decently" be broken; but this was said on the supposition, which we infer to have been a mistake, that there really was an engagement, and the town might have got it on their tongues. With the letter all, direct information ends; and Tisdall's name is hardly again found on Swift's lips uncoupled with some epithet of scorn. When he wanted a phrase of contempt for Steele, he called him a "Tisdall fellow."

But, for the memorable disclosure thus made, Tisdall will always have a niche in Swift's story. Written when Esther Johnson was in her twenty-second year and Swift in his thirty-sixth, the letter describes with exactness the relations that, in the opinion of the present writer, who can find no evidence of a marriage that is at all reasonably sufficient, subsisted between them at the day of her death; when she was entering her forty-sixth year and he had passed his sixtieth. Even assuming it to be less certain than I think it, that she had never given the least favorable ear to Tisdall's suit, there can be no doubt that the result of its abrupt termination was to connect her future inalienably with that of Swift. The limit as to their intercourse expressed by him, if not before known to her, she had now been made aware of; and it is not open to us to question that she accepted it with its plainly implied conditions, of Affection, not Desire. The words " in all other eyes but mine " have a touching significance. In all other eyes but his, time would take from her lustre; her charms would fade; but to him, through womanhood as in girlhood, she would continue the same. For what she was surrendering, then, she knew the equivalent; and this, al-

1701–1705.
Æt. 34–38. most wholly overlooked in other biographies, will be found
in the present to fill a large place. Her story has indeed
been always told with too much indignation and pity.
Not with what depresses or degrades, but rather with what
consoles and exalts, we may associate such a life. This
young friendless girl, of mean birth and small fortune,
chose to play no common part in the world; and it was
not a sorrowful destiny, either for her life or her memory,
to be the star to such a man as Swift, the Stella to even
such an Astrophel.

The words that closed the Tisdall letters had a touch
of sadness in them. Giving him joy of his good fortunes,
and envying very much his prudence and temper, his love
of peace and settlement, Swift adds that the reverse of all
Restless
thoughts. this had been the great uneasiness of his own life, and was
likely to continue so. And what was the result? What
was to grow in the fields he had sown? He found nothing
but the good words and wishes of a decayed ministry, whose
lives and his own would probably wear out before they
could serve either his little hopes or their own ambition.
Therefore he was resolved suddenly to retire, like a discontented courtier, and vent himself in study and speculation,
till his own humor, or the scene in London, should change.

As he said, he did; but not till he had given sanction
to an act which proved to be of the deepest moment to
him. He went suddenly to Ireland at the beginning of
From June,
1704, to
April, 1705. June; the battle of Blenheim was fought in August; before winter was over, the decayed ministry had been built
up and strengthened; and before the March winds ceased,
Swift had again crossed the Irish Channel, and was once
more in London, in April, 1705. The eve of that flight to
Ireland is the date of one of the most important passages
in his life. His title to take higher intellectual rank than
any man then living, and his perpetual exclusion from the
rank in the church which in those days rewarded the most
commonplace ability and questionable character, were settled by the same act. The *Tale of a Tub* had been published.

III.

TALE OF A TUB.

1704. ÆT. 37.

1704.
ÆT. 37.
Ante, 104–'6.

I have spoken of the probable origin of this famous
production, and of the tone given to it by the time at
which the bulk of it was written. Why it should have
remained incomplete and unprinted so many years, has not
been cleared up; but perhaps the "book-seller's" explanation, though itself partly intended to mystify, had in it
more of the truth than has been supposed. The papers See "Book-
seller to
Reader."
came to him in 1698, he says, the year after they were
written; and he had delayed to print them until express
authority to do so should be given. This he had not received, owing (he was credibly informed) to the author's
having supposed that the papers in his possession were lost
by "the person since dead" to whom they had been lent;
and he would not have ventured on the present publication, being indeed ignorant if his copy had received the
author's last touches, but for having been "lately alarmed
with intelligence of a surreptitious copy which a certain "Surreptitious copy."
great wit had new polished and refined." In the "Apology" prefixed to the edition of 1710, Swift substantially
admits this "book-seller's" explanation to have been his
own; but declares that the copy to be called "surreptitious"
was rather that which Mr. Tooke had printed, and that the
original remaining in his own hands was "a blotted copy "Blotted
copy."
which he intended to have writ over with many alterations." Putting aside from this a very evident device to
free himself from direct responsibility for phrases found
open to censure, what may fairly be inferred is, that with
the transcript of the *Battle of the Books* certainly made
for Temple (the "person since dead"), a fair copy had also
been made of portions of the greater satire, which after

1704.
Æt. 37.

See letter of
Doctor Dav-
euant: Nich-
ols's Select
Poems, iv.,
358.

Temple's death had fallen into Thomas Swift's hands; and that Jonathan took his sudden resolve to complete and print his own copy because of some foolish brag by his namesake. The "little parson-cousin" certainly induced his uncle Davenant to make interest to procure him a war-chaplaincy on the ground of his having had some hand in the *Tale*. The same pretense had undoubtedly imposed upon Wotton, who, in his assault upon the *Tale* in 1705, says that Thomas Swift was its author; and perhaps nothing in that effusion so much galled the real author, who afterward referred to it with emphatic contempt, when corresponding with Tooke about the printing of the Apology, which had been written in the summer of 1709. Remarking on Curll's scurrilous *Key* sent him by Tooke, describing the *Tale* as "performed by a couple of young clergymen who, having been domestic chaplains to Sir William Temple, thought themselves obliged to take up his quarrel," he expresses wonder that the law should allow any rascal to publish names so boldly; tells Tooke that he shall take a little "contemptible" notice of the thing; and suspects his "little parson-cousin" to be at the bottom of it. "If he should happen to be in town, and you light on him, I think you ought to tell him gravely that *if he be the author he should set his name to the &c.*, and rally him a little upon it; and tell him *if he can explain something, you will, if he pleases, set his name to the next edition.* I should be glad to hear how far the foolish impudence of a dunce could go." In the little "contemptible" notice, printed as a P.S. to the Apology, he wrote to the same effect: "If any person will prove his claim to three lines in the whole book, let him step forth, and tell his name and titles, upon which the book-seller shall have orders to prefix them to the next edition, and the claimant shall, from henceforward, be acknowledged the undisputed author."[*] Swift never put his own name

To his pub-
lisher: 29th
June, 1710.

"Contempti-
ble" for con-
temptuous.

---

[*] The authorship became a thing known to all his intimates, and we shall find him writing to Esther John-son of its having helped him to his great successes; but excepting to her, and to Ben. Tooke, no avowal of it

to the *Tale of a Tub*, but he took sufficient care that no
other name should be put to it; and a few words thrown
into *Gulliver's Travels* identified the handiwork of both
as one and the same.

The earliest of the two greatest prose satires in the English language, remaining with *Gulliver*, after the test of
nearly two centuries, among the unique books of the
world, might here have passed without other tribute to its
fame, but for its influence on the life of its writer requiring a particular description. The description will be brief,
for it can not deal with all the wonderful wealth of wit
and learning that sustains the allegory. Three brothers
born at a birth, none knowing which was the elder, Peter,
Martin, and Jack, have for some time enjoyed from their
father each a special legacy of a coat having two miracu-
lous virtues—that of lasting all the life with good wearing, and that of lengthening and widening of itself so as
always to fit the changes of the body. The will of the father bequeathing these coats had enjoined strict directions
for their wearing and management, and the brothers, faith-

1701.
Æt. 37.

Unique
books.

Three broth-
ers and their
coats.

exists under his hand; though he so
far forgot himself, in drawing up a
list of "subjects" for an intended
volume in 1708, as to include "Apology for the Tale, &c." It is yet quite
possible that he contemplated for it
then, not the form it assumed when
he wrote it a year later, but one that
would less openly have broken the reserve which he maintained steadily to
the close of his life. In the only edition of his writings overlooked before
publication by himself (Faulkner's
first four volumes had, as I believe,
this advantage) it did not appear until
after his death. When he was nearly seventy, on his cousin, Mrs. Whiteway, asking him to give her the book,
he excused himself at the moment;
but after a week or two she received
it from him with these words on the
fly-leaf: "To Mrs. Martha White-

way, a present on her birthday, 29th
May, 1735, from her affectionate
cousin, Jonath. Swift." "I wish,
sir, you had said *the gift of the author*," was the remark of Mrs. Whiteway. "No, I thank you," was his
answer, with a good-humored smile.
As I have mentioned Faulkner's edition, I will add a note of Mr. Deane
Swift's to his publication of a letter
of the second Lord Oxford mentioning that edition (Aug., 1734). "These
were the first four volumes in octavo,
which were actually revised and corrected by Swift himself, as indeed
were afterward the two subsequent
volumes printed by Faulkner in the
year 1738." The writer was then in
the habit of seeing Swift occasionally
and Mrs. Whiteway frequently, and
spoke for once with competent knowledge.

Faulkner's
edition.

1704.
Æt. 37.

ful to that condition, had lived together in friendship for the first seven years after their father's death (thus being expressed the first seven centuries of true because primitive Christianity). They carefully observe their father's will, and, while they travel together through several countries, encountering a reasonable quantity of giants and slaying certain dragons, they keep their coats in very de- cent order. Then unhappily worldly temptations come in their way. They arrive in town, and fall in love with the great ladies, Duchess d'Argent, Madame de Grands Titres, and the Countess d'Orgueil; in other words, Covetousness, Ambition, and Pride; and this leads them also to become acquainted with a strange sect who hold the universe to be only a large suit of clothes, and humanity to be noth- ing but its outside covering;* what the world calls im- properly suits of clothes being in reality the most refined species of animals. Hence that remarkable sect gave their worship to an idol that created men daily by a kind of manufactory operation; trimming up a gold chain, red gown, and white rod, into a lord mayor; placing together furs and ermine for a judge; and converting lawn and black satin into a bishop. Under this teaching the broth- ers, no longer satisfied with the simplicity of their vest- ments, resort to their father's will for authority to make changes; into which they plunge accordingly. By call- ing in much subtlety of distinction, they adorn themselves with shoulder-knots; by help of tradition, get themselves gold lace; they line themselves with flame-colored satin, by a supposed codicil; cover themselves with silver fringe, by critical erudition; and embroider their coats all over with Indian figures, by abandoning the commonplaces of a too literal interpretation. Once dressed up in their shoulder-knots, however, and walking about as fine as lords in their fringes and satins and "the largest gold lace in the parish," Peter somehow comes out first, showing a superior

Marginal notes: Exploits and temptations. Clothes-wor- ship. Not totidem verbis or tot- idem sylla- bis; but ter- tio modo, or totidem lit- eris.

---

* Of the depth and range given to this fancy by the most original think- er and greatest writer of our century, it is not necessary that I should speak.

turn for worldly advancement. He worms himself into the confidence of a great lord, installs himself in comfortable quarters by turning out his lordship's family, tells Martin and Jack he is their father's eldest and sole heir, orders them no longer to call him brother, and sets himself up as my Lord Peter. Then, for support to his grandeur, he launches into a variety of projects to bring in money; turns off his own wife, bundles out the wives of both Martin and Jack, and orders in three strollers from the streets; curses his brothers in the most dreadful manner if they make the least scruple of believing the huge palpable lies he tells them; sets a brown loaf before them which he declares to be true, good, natural mutton as any in Leadenhall Market, praying God to confound them, and the devil to broil them, both eternally, if they offer to believe otherwise; and in short goes so distracted with knavery and pride that his brothers resolve to leave him. They had before taken part in locking up their father's will; but now, having managed to get at a true copy exposing all Peter's lying pretenses, they have dismissed their concubines, have sent for their true wives, and are in the act of telling a Newgate attorney who has brought money for a pardon to a thief who was to be hanged next day, that not Peter, but only the Sovereign can grant such pardons, when Peter himself interrupts them with a file of dragoons, "kicks them both out-of-doors, and would never let them come under his roof from that day to this." Hereupon they take a lodging together, and a resolution to reform their coats into the primitive state enjoined by their father's will. It was high time; for what with lace, ribbons, fringe, embroidery, and silver-tagged points, hardly a thread of the original vestments remained to be seen. But in pulling off these trimmings, differences of temper showed themselves. Martin began rudely enough; but proceeded more moderately as he found that parts of the ornamental covering, especially the silver-tagged points, could not be got away without damage to the cloth; and in the end he was content to leave whatever was not removable without

Margin notes:

1704. *Æt.* 37.

Peter sets up as Lord Peter.

Peter's lies and misconduct.

His brothers turned out-of-doors.

Martin and Jack reform their coats.

injury to the substance of the stuff. Jack, on the other hand, would have no such compromises. In three minutes he made more dispatch than Martin in as many hours; and such indeed was his tearing zeal that he rent the main body of his coat from top to bottom, and had to darn it with pack-thread and a skewer. Clumsy by nature as well as impatient of temper, he left even part of Peter's livery upon his own rents and patches; so that, as it is in the nature of rags to have a mock resemblance to finery, there were some people that could not distinguish between Jack and Peter.* His rage against his brother Martin's patience vents itself in a million of scurrilities, and ends at last in a mortal breach. The rest of this portion of the *Tale* is taken up with the extravagances of Jack, and with those extremes of absurdity in which he and Peter are found to be continually meeting. The victory remains with Martin; if not of absolute compliance with his father's will, of the nearest practicable approach to it.

The satire had an effect apparently without example in matters of the kind. The hit was admitted by all who most strongly objected to the book. Congreve, to whom many strokes in it must have been distasteful, tells a friend

---

* "It was among the great misfortunes of Jack to bear a huge personal resemblance with his brother Peter ...... the similitude between them frequently deceived the very disciples and followers of both." Swift knew not only that there were extremes of belief in direct inspiration where Quakerism and some other forms of dissent ran into Roman Catholic neighborhood, but that excess of zeal for religious liberty by no means implied a corresponding regard for civil freedom; and he was old enough to have witnessed the support given by William Penn to James the Second's claim for a dispensing power. But let me add that among his papers at his death which had been treasured by him was found a letter, now in my possession, printed by Scott, with the date of "Chilad" instead of "Philad" (for Philadelphia), 29th March, 1729. "Friend Jonathan Swift, Having been often agreeably amused by thy *Tale*, and being now loading a small ship for Dublin, I have sent thee a gammon, the product of the wilds of America, which perhaps may not be unacceptable at thy table, since it is designed to let thee know that thy wit and parts are here in esteem, at this distance from the place of thy residence. Thou needest ask no questions who this comes from, since I am a perfect stranger to thee." We may be very sure that Swift never felt so kindly to the Quakers as when he received this delightful and substantial tribute.

that, though several passages had diverted him, he can not quite think of it as the million do, and he is in the minority of "very few" against a "multitude."* Doctor Charles Davenant writes to his son that it had made as much noise as any book these last hundred years. Atterbury, after saying that nothing could please more than the book did in London, tells Bishop Trelawny of some famous men at Oxford (among them "Rag" Smith and the author of *The Splendid Shilling*) charged with the authorship, but goes on to remark that if he has guessed the man rightly he has reason to continue to conceal himself, because its profane strokes would be more likely to do harm to his "reputation and interest in the world" than its wit could do him good. Smallridge, afterward Bishop of Bristol, replied to a compliment from Sacheverell on his supposed authorship of it, that not all which they both possessed in the world could have hired him to write it. Sir Richard Blackmore speaks with horror of such an audacious and impious buffoon being caressed and patronized by people of great figure and of all denominations. De Foe characterizes its author, with a happy touch of censure in the compliment, as a learned man, an orator in the Latin, a walking index of books, who had all the libraries in Europe in his head, from the Vatican at Rome to the learned collection of Doctor Salmon at Fleet Ditch. Doctor King, the civilian, prefaced an attack upon it by saying it had been bought up by all sorts of people, not only at court but in the city and suburbs. And Wotton justifies his onslaught by declaring that he thought it might be useful, to the many people who pretended to see no harm in what had been "so greedily bought up and read," to lay

Works, I., 318–325.

How it struck contemporaries.

Works, I., 216.

Wotton's attack:

---

* Congreve to Keally, Berkeley's *Literary Relics*, 340. Of Voltaire's admiration there will be occasion to speak hereafter, but he placed Swift even above his great countryman, the Curé of Meudon. "C'est Rabelais perfectionné," he said, in his *Siècle de Louis Quatorze*. For the monstrous absurdity that ascribed the book to Lords Shrewsbury and Somers, to Lord Shaftesbury and Sir Wm. Temple, see Maddock's *Life of Somers*, 34; and Cooksey's *Life*, 21. It pairs off with Harley's alleged authorship of *Robinson Crusoe!*

1704.
Æt. 37.

turned to
profit by
Swift.

Assailants of
good books.

The charge
of irreligion.

Offense in
rendering
service.

open the mischief of the ludicrous allegory. Open he laid it accordingly, by illustrating its several recondite allusions with elaborate explanation of the subtleties and mysteries referred to; and what thereupon was done by Swift completely turned the tables upon him. He printed these illustrations as notes contributed to the elucidation of its text by the worthy and ingenious Mr. Wotton, bachelor of divinity; and its most envenomed assailant has thus, in countless editions since, figured as its friendly illustrator. Poor Mr. Wotton has been the slave in the victor's chariot, swelling the triumph he had so desperately fought against. He might nevertheless, unpleasant as this was, think it better than to be wholly forgotten with the other assailants of the *Tale*. Already, said Swift finely, while extracting Wotton's venom, "such treatises as have been written against the ensuing discourse are sunk into waste paper and oblivion, after the usual fate of common answerers to books which are allowed to have any merit. They are like annuals that grow about a young tree, and seem to vie with it for a summer, but fall and die with the leaves in autumn, and are never heard of more."

Imputations, nevertheless, survived which Swift strongly felt. Charges of irreverence and irreligion came from quarters to which he fairly might have looked for protection. Scott says the *Tale* had been written with a view to the interests of the high-church party; but unreserved adoption of that epithet would be misleading. As a churchman, Swift was only high in the sense of a vigilant regard to church interests in state matters, and of a stout resistance to the extremes, on either hand, of popery and dissenting non-conformity. It is the English Reformed Church which the satire exalts at the expense of her rivals; and Scott truly says that it rendered her the most important service, "for what is so important to a party, whether in church or state, as to gain the laughers to their side?" But the satire went too deep. It reached the truth on too many sides, and what it was written to keep aloof it was thought likely to encourage. As it is the seamen's prac-

tice to fling overboard a tub to turn a whale from mis- **1701.**
chief,* Swift had thrown out the *Tale* to divert danger- **Æт. 37.**
ous assailants from objects that invited attack in church
and state. But the clergy understood their portion of the
danger in another sense, and preferred the mischief to his **High-church**
remedy. They would rather the whale should swallow **extremes.**
them than have such a diversion. A powerful section of
them were now making head in the Reformed Church who
were high in another sense than Swift's, to whom gold lace
and silver tagging were as dear as to Peter himself, and
from whose pulpits had been heard not only approval of
auricular confession, sacerdotal absolution, and prayers for
the dead, but express teaching of the real presence, and of
the claim of the church to stand above the state. The men
most clamorous against toleration, said De Foe, and most
eager for more power to ecclesiastics, are that part of the
clergy who have made most manifest advances to Rome.
These men understood the satire too well; a majority of
the rest of the clergy would not be likely in the least to
understand it, and all were ready to join against the *Tale
of a Tub*. It was a parallel case to De Foe's. The dissenters gave up their stoutest champion because his banter was unintelligible to them; and for a similar reason
Swift was thrown over by the party in the church whom
he had most materially served.† The one was pilloried **Mistakes of**
thrice, and the other punished for life. Yet he could **dullness.**
hardly have been quite unprepared for this defection of
his professional brethren. He quietly remarks in his

---

* Originating, doubtless, in this
practice, the title chosen by Swift had
passed into a common phrase, and
had already been used by two men
before him of whom Englishmen are
proud. "Why, this is a Tale of a
Tub!" exclaimed Sir Thomas More,
at an incoherent speech in his court
by an attorney named Tubbe; and
the title was given by Ben Jonson to
an early comedy, of which his hero
was one "Squire Tub," into which

he afterward introduced some satire
against Inigo Jones.

† When Gulliver in Lilliput extinguished the flames that would have
consumed the royal palace, his manner of doing it offended the queen
mortally. All evils have some com-
pensation, however; and but for her
majesty's persistent hostility on this
point, Captain Gulliver might never
have left Lilliput.
·

1704.
Æt. 37.

Ill-judgment
of clergy in
church af-
fairs.

Apology the very frequent observation he had made (which Lord Clarendon made before him), that that reverend body were not always very nice in distinguishing between their enemies and their friends; he declares his belief that if he had written a book to expose the abuses in law or physic, the learned professors in either faculty would have been so far from resenting it as to have given him thanks for his pains; of the book he had actually written he challenges its assailants to show that it had advanced any opinion which the discipline and doctrine of the Church of England rejected, or condemned any which they received; and he offers to forfeit his life if any one opinion could be fairly deduced from it contrary to religion or morality.

Blame well-
founded.

So much, which he said after he knew that the plea had availed to exclude him from the highest dignity of his calling, he was thoroughly entitled to say. But there was a grave objection on which the enemies of the *Tale*, with more show of justice, had also fastened, and which remained the unhappy peculiarity of Swift's writing in later days than these. If to owe nothing to other men is to be original, a more original man than Swift never lived; but, with the wonderful subtlety of thought so rarely joined to the same robustness of intellect which placed his wit and philosophy on the level of Rabelais, he had the same habit as the great Frenchman of turning things inside out, and putting away decencies as if they were shows or hypocri-

Coarseness
of language.

sies. In both it led to an insufferable coarseness. Replying himself to the charge, he said very earnestly that no lewd words would be found in the book, and that its severest strokes of satire were leveled against the prevailing fashion of employing wit to recommend profligacy. This was true, but it did not touch the imputation of indecency, for which he could only partially plead the example of contemporaries; and he might have been better guided by one of his own wittiest illustrations in the *Tale*. You do not treat nature wisely, he says, by always striving to get beneath the surface. What to show and to conceal, she

knows; it is one of her eternal laws to put her best fur- *1704.*
niture forward; and in making choice between the inside *Æt. 37.*
and the outside, though it be but skin-deep, better follow *With and*
without
her suggestion. " Last week I saw a woman flayed, and *one's skin.*
you will hardly believe how much it altered her person
for the worse." Under the process of flaying applied by
himself so indiscriminately, he altered much for the worse,
and did not get really nearer to the innermost depth of
things.

But this objection admitted (and, with full allowance
for the manners of the age, it is a very grave one), hardly
any praise can be deemed excessive for the *Tale of a Tub.*
To the corruptions of learning it applies the same handling
as to those of religion; and in it first appears that great
invention of a Grub-street *Dunciad* to which Pope later *Prose Dun-*
was to bring his poetry and personalities, but by which *ciad.*
Swift thus early cleared an important ground from what
might otherwise have left it the property of dunces to this
hour. Something to such effect has been shown; but in *Ante, 109.*
additions on the eve of publication the looser threads of
the satire were knitted up and the purpose more closely
interwoven in the texture of the whole. One or two illustrations may express this part of his design, though it
would be difficult to give with them the faintest notion of
the astonishing and never-ceasing play of wit and raillery.
The book-seller, observing *Detur dignissimo* written large *Dedication.*
on the covers of the papers, fancied the words might have
some meaning. " But it unluckily fell out that none of
the authors I employ understood Latin, though I have
them often in pay to translate out of that language." So
he has to get the meaning from the curate of his parish;
and, finding that the book is to be given to the worthiest,
he asks of a poet in an alley hard by (" he works for my
shop") who it can possibly be that is intended: on which
the poet tells him, after some consideration, that vanity is *A poet's*
a thing he abhors, but by the description he thinks he must *modesty.*
be the person aimed at, and kindly offers to write *gratis*
a dedication to himself. Trying a second guess, however,

1704.
Æt. 37.
at the book-seller's request, he names Lord Somers; and as the same thing occurred with several other wits of his acquaintance, it had finally dawned upon himself that the best title to the first place was likely to be his to whom every body allowed the second, and that the "dignissimus"
Choice of worthiest.
must be Lord Somers. To him therefore the book-seller dedicates the book.

The same turn is given to the author's Epistle Dedicatory, addressed to Prince Posterity, in which intercession is made with the prince against the malice of his governor, Time, in ruthlessly hurrying modern authors off the scene. Such had been his inveterate dislike to the writings of the age, that, out of several thousands produced yearly from that renowned city of London, not one was to be heard of by
Immortal productions swamped.
the next revolution of the sun. Many were destroyed even before they had "so much as learnt their mother-tongue to beg for pity.". If the prince doubts this, let him ask his governor *where they are.* The author was himself acquainted with the names of "a hundred and thirty-six poets of the first rate" not one of whose immortal productions was likely to reach the prince's eyes. Of course his governor (of whose designs the writer was well informed) would ask the prince what was become of them, and would even pretend that there never were any because none were then to be found. Not to be found, indeed! Who, then, had mislaid them? Were they suddenly sunk in the abyss of things? Certain it was that in their own nature they were light enough to swim upon the surface for all eternity.
Fate of one hundred and thirty-six first-rate poets.
No, no; there could be no doubt, with any one who noticed the large and terrible scythe the prince's governor affected to bear continually about him, who was really the author of this universal ruin. The writer of this book, however, was bent upon doing his best to baffle the destroyer by composing "a character of the present set of wits in our nation;" and meanwhile he offered to the prince "a faithful abstract drawn from the universal body of all Arts and Sciences."

In what are called the "Digressions" of the *Tale* that

deeper plunge is accordingly taken, the Arts and Sciences being called to render account. Frankly at the same time the author describes himself as a man who had written, under three reigns, four-score and eleven pamphlets for the service of six-and-thirty factions;* who had therefore passed a long life with a conscience void of offense; and who now, finding the state has no further occasion for his pen, had willingly turned it to speculations more becoming a philosopher. He then proceeds to show that the philosophers who meet at Gresham's (the recently founded Royal Society), and the wits to be met with nightly at Will's (Congreve, Vanbrugh, and the rest), are only two junior start-up societies that have branched of from Grub Street; and that the two prodigals, whenever they should think fit to return from their virtuoso experiments and comedies of high life, "their husks and their harlots," will be received back with open arms. The several platforms of modern intellectual display are next ranged under three "oratorical" machines—the Pulpit, the Ladder, and the Stage; illustrations pregnant with rarest humor and wit being applied to each kind respectively; from which he afterward breaks off, for a correct estimate of results, to a digression concerning critics. These are shown to have proved beyond contradiction, with unwearied pains, that the very finest things delivered of old had been long since invented by much later pens; and that the noblest discoveries those ancients ever made, of art or of nature, had all been produced, on the three several platforms, by the transcending genius of the existing age. A digression in the modern kind follows; whereby, among other things, the assertion that a certain author called Homer ("though otherwise a person not without some abilities, and, for an an-

Margin notes: 1704. ÆT. 37. — Conscientious writing. | Offshoots from Grub Street. | Oratorical machines. | Homer's deficiencies.

---

* That is the passage to which an exact parallel was discovered in Swift's later and greater satire. "On each side the gate," says Gulliver in Lilliput, "was a small window not above six inches from the ground; into that on the left side, the king's smiths conveyed four-score and eleven chains, like those that hang to a lady's watch in Europe, and about as large, which were locked to my left leg with six-and-thirty padlocks." This curious discovery was made by Professor Porson.—*Tracts by Kidd* (1815), p. 316.

cient, of a tolerable genius") had embraced *omnes res humanas* in his poem, is shown to be absurd by proof of his "gross ignorance in the common laws of this realm, and in the doctrine as well as discipline of the Church of England;" to which is added the hope that some famous modern may yet attempt a universal system in a small portable volume of all things that are to be known, or. believed, or imagined, or practiced, in life. That part of the book, in which we have the germ of the whole of Martinus

Scriblerus, exposes the falsity and pretenses of prevailing forms of learning. The next digression is in praise of digressions, which are justified on the ground that the society of writers would quickly be reduced to a very inconsiderable number if men were put upon making books with the fatal confinement of delivering nothing but what was to the purpose; and then, though not so entitled, there is a digression in regard to a sect who maintain the cause of all things to be wind, being, in fact, progenitors of the innumerable wind-bags to which attention has been since directed. These are the Æolists, whose primary rite, or mystery, is to stuff themselves to enormous sizes with the "spirit or breath or wind of the world," and who then, by disemboguing the same in varied and surprising ways, blow out their disciples to the same extent. Hence the expression that learning puffeth a man up, which they prove by a syllogism: "Words are but wind, and learning is nothing but words; *ergo*, learning is nothing but wind." From

this too he is led—Jack having now launched into extravagances as mad as Peter's in the other extreme—to enter upon a consideration whether great things have not been done by people with their brains shaken out of their natural position like Jack's; and whether madness so called, being but a redundancy rising up into the brain of the same vapor or spirit which the Latins called *ingenium par negotiis*, might not by re-adjustment be turned into the sort of frenzy never in its right element "till you take it up in the business of the state." He proposes a commission, therefore, to report upon the fitness for employment, in a way useful to the public, of the inmates of Bedlam: *1704. Æt. 37.* supporting it as well by illustrious examples of the mad-*Utilization of Bedlam.* men of history, as by homely resort to the requirements of the existing world. "Is any student tearing his straw in piecemeal, swearing and blaspheming, biting his grate, foaming at the mouth ... let the right worshipful the Commissioners of Inspection give him a regiment of dragoons and send him into Flanders among the rest. Is another eternally talking, sputtering, gaping, bawling, in a sound without period or article? What wonderful talents are here mislaid! Let him be furnished immediately with a *Fixed fare for lawyers: three-pence.* green bag and papers, and threepence in his pocket, and away with him to Westminster Hall." The war in Flanders fixes the date of this passage, and adds another to the many proofs, all mystifications notwithstanding, that the publication of the *Tale* was exclusively the act of Swift.

That Johnson should have doubted it, and even the au-*Johnson on the Tale.* thorship altogether, shows how strangely unreasoning a strong personal dislike may be. To think the thing not good enough to be Swift's, one might have understood; but to find it too good to be his, is a touch not intelligible from such a critic. In the life he speaks of it as a "wild" book, of which the authorship was never owned or proved by any evidence; though it was not denied when Archbishop Sharp first, and the Duchess of Somerset afterward, debarred Swift of a bishopric by showing it to the queen.*

---

* Doctor William King (principal of St. Mary's Hall, Oxon), says in his *Anecdotes* (p. 60) that Lord Bolingbroke told him "he had been assured by the queen herself that she never had received any unfavorable character of Doctor Swift, nor had the archbishop, or any other person, endeavoured to lessen him in her esteem. My Lord Bolingbroke added that this tale was invented by the Earl of Oxford to deceive Swift, and make him contented with his deanery in Ireland; which, although his native country, he always looked on as a place of banishment. If Lord Bolingbroke had hated the Earl of Oxford less, I should have been readily inclined to believe him." No belief can be given to such an alleged statement by Bolingbroke, who would have had ten thousand reasons for disclosing it to Swift himself; from whom, if it were true, he carefully withheld it. But even Doctor King, headlong Jacobite as he was, could not have put credence in his informant. And see what had gone before, *post*, 223.

1704.
Æt. 37.
Odd reason
for a doubt.

Wit's disad-
vantages.

Cobbett's
first knowl-
edge of
Swift.

In the life, also, Johnson remarks that it is not like Swift, because it has (what every one versed in him knows him pre-eminently to have had) vehemence and rapidity of mind, copiousness of images, and vivacity of diction. More than once the same was said to Boswell. It was said at one of their earliest meetings at the Mitre, when they were together in the Hebrides, and when they met at the club. Often as it was repeated, no question was made of its reasonableness or fairness. Swift was to lose a bishopric in one generation because a piece of writing was thought too witty to be fathered on any body else, and in the next he was to lose the credit of having written the piece because it was thought too witty to be fathered on him.* No-

---

* "The *Tale of a Tub* is one of the most masterly compositions in the language, whether for thought, wit, or style."—*Hazlitt.* "An effusion of genius sufficient to redeem our name in that century's annals of fiction. The *Tale of a Tub* is, in my apprehension, the masterpiece of Swift; certainly Rabelais has nothing superior even in invention, nor any thing so condensed, so pointed, so full of real meaning, of biting satire, of felicitous analogy."—*Hallam, Lit. of Eur.*, iv., 336. Another tribute should not be omitted. Cobbett had a passion for Swift, to whom he often refers as the first writer with whom he made acquaintance "after Moses:" the book that seized upon his fancy being the *Tale of a Tub.* He was, curiously enough, a native of Farnham, and at eleven years old employed there as a gardener's lad, though he did not then know Swift's connection with the place; when he heard of the beautiful gardens at Kew, and had the ambition to go and get work there. So he set off on a June morning, with no clothes except those on his back, and in his pocket thirteen half-pence; of which he spent twopence on bread-and-cheese, a penny on small-beer, and somehow lost a half-penny before he got to Richmond in the afternoon with threepence left. "With this for my whole fortune, I was trudging through Richmond in my blue smock-frock, and my red garters tied under my knees, when, staring about me, my eyes fell upon a little book in a book-seller's window, on the outside of which was written *The Tale of a Tub, price threepence.* The title was so odd that my curiosity was excited. I had the threepence; but, then, I could not have any supper. In I went and got the little book, which I was so impatient to read, that I got over into a field at the upper corner of Kew Gardens, where there stood a haystack. On the shady side of this I sat down to read. The book was so different from any thing that I had ever read before, it was something so new to my mind, that, though I could not understand some parts of it, it delighted me beyond description, and produced what I have always considered a sort of birth of intellect. I read on until it was dark without any thought of supper or bed." He slept by the stack till the birds woke him, went on to Kew next day, still reading his little book, and got work from the kind

where is there proof of the authorship so irresistible as in   1704.
the reasons against it thus expressed by Johnson : " There . Æт. 37.
is in it such a vigor of mind, such a swarm of thoughts, so
much of nature, and art, and life." These words exactly
describe it. Swift could have desired no better to vindi-
cate the claim. They might have risen to him on that   Touching in-
day of the dark close of his life, when he was seen by his cident.
kinswoman and nurse turning over the leaves of the copy
he had given her, and overheard to mutter to himself as
he shut them up, unconscious of any listener, *Good God,
what a genius I had when I wrote that book!*

IV.

BAUCIS AND PHILEMON.

1705. Æт. 38.

SHERIDAN would have his readers believe that Swift was   1705.
not familiarly known at clubs or coffee-houses until after __Æт. 38.__
suspicions connecting him with the *Tale* had stirred curiosity about him. But this is not better founded than the
statement on the same page of the memoir, that he now
first met Arbuthnot in the coffee-house where Addison
gave " his little senate laws."* The " senate " did not   Addison's
come into existence for six or seven years, nor was " But- senate.
ton's " before then in vogue ;† and Swift certainly did not

Scotch gardener, who, seeing him fond | to be found there. He published it
of books, lent him some on gardening. | in the *Evening Post*, when he was ap-
" But these I could not relish after | pealing to reformers to pay for return-
my *Tale of a Tub*, which I carried | ing him to Parliament.
about with me wherever I went, and | * Or than his other assertion that
when I—at about twenty years old— | the *Battle of the Books* was published
lost it in a box that fell overboard in | two years before the *Tale of a Tub.* | Loss of his
the Bay of Fundy, in North America, | They appeared together. threepenny
the loss gave me greater pain than I | † The date of Swift's last friendly Tale.
have since felt at losing thousands of | intercourse with Ambrose Philips is
pounds." One would naturally look | 1708 and 1709; and in July of the
for ·this interesting passage in the | former year he thus mentions to his
writer's *Autobiography*, but it is not | correspondent their place of resort :

1705.
Æt. 38.

know Arbuthnot, who was not of Addison's party at all, until after six years :* but Prior or Congreve was not better known at Will's than he was. At the St. James's, which for the present was the whig resort, he had turned the laugh against Vanbrugh a year and a half before by some verses on the house he had built in Whitehall; and his note-books fix the present year as the beginning not of his acquaintance, but of his more intimate intercourse, with Addison. A batch of entries, clustered on the same page, are dry enough; but vividly behind them rise the

Suppers of the gods.

noctes cœnœque deorum: "Tav^{rn} Addison 2*s*. 6*d*. Tav^{rn} Addison 1*s*. Tav^{n} Add^{sn} 1*s*. 6*d*. Tav^{rn} Addis^{n} 4*s*. 9*d*. Tav^{n} Addis^{n} 2*s*. 6*d*." "I have heard Swift say," says Delany of such memorable nights in London and Dublin, "that often, as they spent their evenings together, they neither of them ever wished for a third person to support or enliven their conversation." There is a well-known

Real conversation.

saying of Addison that the only real conversation is between two persons, and his own charm in this respect Swift has explained in what he says of Prior. He liked him, and thought him one of the best of the talkers of that day; but he would say that he was not a fair one, because he left no elbow-room for another, which Addison always did. There was, however, one point in which Swift had perhaps the superiority in friendly talk over all his

Swift's talk.

lettered friends. He was better able than either Prior or Addison, or even Steele, or any of the wits, to tolerate wit of a less grade than their own. This, in fact, arose from his regarding literature as less of a serious employment than they did, and it is a peculiarity to be always noted in him. "Col. Froud," he writes to Ambrose Philips, "is just as he was, very friendly and *grand rêveur et distrait.*

"St. James's coffee-house is grown a very dull place upon two accounts: first, by the loss of you, and secondly, of every body else. Mr. Addison's lameness goes off daily, and so does he, for I see him seldomer than formerly, and, therefore, can not revenge myself of you by getting ground in your absence."

* Their first meeting is mentioned in the Journal to Esther Johnson.

He has brought his Poems almost to perfection, and I have great credit with him, because I can listen when he reads, which neither you, nor Mr. Addison, nor Steele ever can." Froud or "Frowde" was a small poet who had written two tragedies,* and whose recommendation to Swift was his intercourse with Addison. That most pleasing of writers and zealous of whigs, who was next year to have his party reward by appointment as under-secretary of state, had this year (1705) published his *Travels in Italy;* and I possess a large-paper presentation-copy with an inscription in Addison's hand,† which is itself an emphatic memorial of one of the most famous of literary friendships.

1705.
Æt. 38.
A small poet.

Addison to
Swift.

That "the Authour" had then read the *Tale of a Tub,* and knew who had written it, we need not hesitate to believe.

Nor is it incumbent on us to reject all that even Sheridan tells us, upon the authority of Ambrose Philips, of Swift's so-called first appearance at the whig club. The

---

* *Philotas* and the *Fall of Jerusalem,* long forgotten. Not to be confounded, as he is by Scott and others, with "Old Froude," the squire of Farnham, who repeatedly appears in the Journal. And see *post,* 305.

† "To Dr. Jonathan Swift, The most Agreeable Companion, the Truest Friend, and the Greatest Genius of his Age, This Book is presented by his most Humble Servant the Author."

misdate and misplace throw discredit over it; but what the old whig poet, to whom in his youth Swift had shown many kindnesses for Addison's sake, related to the young Irish player must have had some substance of truth. He says that they had for several successive days observed a strange clergyman come into the coffee-house, who seemed utterly unacquainted with any of those who frequented it; and whose custom it was to lay his hat down on a table, and walk backward and forward at a good pace for half an hour or an hour, without speaking to any mortal, or seem-ing in the least to attend to any thing that was going for-

ward there. He then used to take up his hat, pay his money at the bar, and walk away without opening his lips. The name he went by among them, in consequence, was the mad parson. On one particular evening, as Mr. Addi-son and the rest were observing him, they saw him cast his eyes several times on a gentleman in boots, who seem-ed to be just come out of the country, and at last advance as intending to address him. Eager to hear what their dumb, mad parson had to say, they all quitted their seats to get near him. Swift went up to the country gentleman, and in a very abrupt manner, without any previous salute, asked him, "Pray, sir, do you remember any good weather in the world?" The country gentleman, after staring a little at the singularity of his manner and the oddity of the question, answered, "Yes, sir, I thank God I remem-ber a great deal of good weather in my time." "That is more," rejoined Swift, "than I can say. I never remem-ber any weather that was not too hot or too cold, too wet or too dry; but, however God Almighty contrives it, at

the end of the year 'tis all very well." With which re-mark he took up his hat, and, without uttering a syllable more, or taking the least notice of any one, walked out of the coffee-house. It has something of the same turn, and not without the same philosophy, as his own anecdote of

"Will Seymour the general" fretting under the excessive heat, at which a friend remarking that it was such weather as pleased the Almighty, "Perhaps it may," replied the general, "but I'm sure it pleases nobody else" (as there was not the least necessity that it should). There is, however, as small. probability that this was Addison's first knowledge of his great friend, or Swift's first introduction to Steele, as that the incident occurred in 1703. That year was the date of the earliest of the verses on Vanbrugh's house, "built from the ruins of Whitehall;" and their writer was already as well known on the neutral ground of Will's as at the whig St. James's. But what Philips tells has in it a smack of the same grim humor that turned the laugh of the poorer wits against the prosperous architect and playwright.

1705. Æt. 38. Satisfying nobody.

It had not been Swift's intention at first to give to the Vanbrugh poem the form which his printed works have made familiar. It was to laugh, but not without decorum, at a wit who, after building comedies, had taken to build a house.* There was plenty of banter : but the wits were not to be shown running up and down Whitehall, everywhere looking for, and always overlooking, what their brother Van had raised for himself to inhabit; asking every body for its whereabouts, appealing to the watermen, even invoking the Thames, till at length they

Poem on Vanbrugh's house.

> "in the rubbish spy
> A thing resembling a goose-pie"

(which it probably did resemble, if a brother architect was justified in comparing it to a flat Dutch oven). Those jibes were in the second version of the poem. It was not

---

* Vanbrugh had not quite got over the effect of the verses even after seven years were gone. Swift writes to Esther Johnson of a dinner with him and Congreve at Sir Richard Temple's on the 7th November, 1710. "Vanbrugh, I believe I told you, had a long quarrel with me about those verses on his house; but we were very civil and cold. Lady Marlborough used to tease him with them, which had made him angry, though he be a good-natured fellow." It is, however, to be added that what had given him most offense was not the first of the poems (printed with the date of 1706), but some supplementary verses (printed in 1708) on the selection of him by Marlborough to build Blenheim.

"For if his grace were no more skill'd in
The art of battering walls than building,
We might expect to see next year
A mouse-trap man chief engineer!"

1705.
Æt. 38.
Earlier un-
printed ver-
sion.

in his first plan to give so strong a personal coloring as they express, or as the witty parallel between play-building and house-building conveys. His design was rather to jeer at the successes of the stage of the day (against which he had always the grudge which its profligacy too well warranted), and to show how structures out of nothing rise to the sky, while the solider and heavier can not get above the ground. "After hard throes of many a day," verse-building Van is triumphantly "delivered of a play"

> "Which in due time brings forth a house,
> Just as the mountain did the mouse:
> One story high, one postern door,
> And one small chamber on a floor."

**Swift MSS.
at Narford.**

The MS. version of the poem from which these lines are taken exists still in Swift's handwriting at Sir Andrew Fountaine's house in Norfolk; and at Narford,* which remains the property of Sir Andrew's descendant and representative, Mr. Andrew Fountaine, the present writer discovered it. The lines just quoted, and the subjoined satirical parallel between a play-writer and a silk-worm, which in this earlier version occupies the place given in the later to a comparison of house-building to play-building, have never until now been printed.

**Unprinted
poem on
Vanbrugh.**

> "There is a worm by Phœbus bred,
> By leaves of mulberry is fed,

**Sir Andrew
Fountaine.**

* Fountaine's father built Narford in 1704, and, after his death there, in 1708, the house was let on lease for a time. His son, Swift's friend, educated at Christchurch, was selected by the dean, as one of the best Latinists of his year, to make the oration on King William's visit in 1699; and he then received knighthood. He was afterward much abroad. He had formed a friendship with Leibnitz while at the court of Hanover in 1701; and in Italy became acquainted with Lord Pembroke, having much the same taste as a collector in matters of art and vertu. He was very rich in medals and coins, of which the greater part went ultimately to Wilton; and of the wealth of his possessions in old pottery and ware, magnificent indication still exists at Narford. There is a bust of him by Roubiliac at Wilton as well as at Narford; and a painting in oils in the library at Holland House, which, till very recently, had peculiar honor as the portrait of Addison, was a few years ago discovered to be Fountaine. Addison had probably received it after his marriage with Lady Warwick, as a present from Sir Andrew, of whom there will be other frequent mention in these pages.

Which, unprovided where to dwell,
Consumes itself to weave a cell:
Then curious hands this texture take,
And for themselves fine garments make.
Meantime a pair of awkward things
Grow to his back instead of wings:
He flutters when he thinks he flies,
Then sheds about his spawn, and dies.
　　Just such an insect of the age
Is he that scribbles for the stage:
His birth he does from Phœbus raise,
And feeds upon imagin'd bays:
Turns all his wit and hours away
In twisting up an ill-spun Play:
This gives him lodging, and provides
A stock of tawdry shift besides,
With the unravel'd shreds of which
The under-wits adorn their speech:
And now he spreads his little fans
(For all the Muse's geese are swans),
And, borne on fancy's pinions, thinks
He soars sublimest when he sinks:
But, scatt'ring round his fly-blows, dies;
Whence broods of insect-poets rise."

1705.
Æt. 38.

Nor was this the only discovery made by me at Narford. Another and more important was that of the first
draught of a poem of 1706, a year after the present date,
to which peculiar interest belongs. Among the papers in
Swift's handwriting I found the original version of the
poetical piece which Swift is known to have altered at
Addison's request.* Nothing is better established in his
literary history than that he made, at Addison's suggestion, extensive changes in one of the happiest of his poems,
Goldsmith's favorite, the *Baucis and Philemon;* "on the
ever-lamented loss of the two yew-trees in the parish of
Chilthorne, Somerset. Imitated from the eighth book of
Ovid." Scott speaks more than once, with something of a
poet's wonder, of the "forty verses struck out, forty added,

Interesting
discovery.

Baucis and
Philemon as
first written.

---

* "He himself," says Doctor Delany, "was often wont to mention that
in a poem of not two hundred lines
(*Baucis and Philemon*), Mr. Addison

made him blot out fourscore, add fourscore, and alter fourscore."—*Observations,* p. 19.

1705.
Æt. 38.
and forty altered," in that brief poem; and much surmise has been hazarded whether changes so great in the first conceptions of such a master in his art could possibly all of them have been improvements. Swift's own account makes the number of changes twice as large: "Mr. Addison," he says, "made me blot out fourscore, add fourscore, and alter fourscore;" to which he adds, confounding naturally enough in his memory the original with the altered piece, "though the poem did not consist of more than one

The poem as printed.

hundred and seventy-seven verses." The poem, as printed, contains one hundred and seventy - eight lines; the poem, as I found it at Narford, has two hundred and thirty; and the changes in the latter, bringing it into the condition of the former, by which only it has been thus far known, comprise the omission of ninety-six lines, the addition of forty-four, and the alteration of twenty-two. The question can now be discussed whether or not the changes were improvements, and in my opinion the decision must be adverse to Addison.

The story of the little poem is of course familiar, in other shapes as well as Swift's; and though M. Taine is angry that so touching a legend should be degraded by what he calls travesty, turning the two gods into begging friars and the two lovers into elderly "Kentish" peasants, it must be said, with deference to our French critic, that the

Legend according to Swift.

travesty is in his own mind. The license of putting antique fables into homely modern dress is not disallowed to poetry; and, worthily executed, is no violation of the ancient beauty or nobleness, but a homage widening and diffusing it. "Two brother hermits, saints by trade" (on whose holiness, that is, attends the power of miracles), while exercising their trade in an English country village by putting to the test the hospitality and Christian kindliness of its inmates, are so unlucky as to find them by no means able to stand the test, and that, in fact, they possess nothing whatever of the desired qualities. The saints are scouted and flouted from every house, gentle and simple; until, having arrived at the farm of Baucis and Philemon, they are hospitably received and entertained with the best; upon which they reward the good old couple by transforming their cottage into a church, and Philemon, at his own request, into the parson of it, and by finally metamorphosing the worthy pair, after sundry more years of happy life, into a couple of yew-trees in the church-yard.

> "Old goodman Dobson of the green
> Remembers he the trees has seen;
> He'll talk of them from noon till night,
> And goes with folks to show the sight;
> On Sundays, after evening prayer,
> He gathers all the parish there;
> Points out the place of either yew,
> Here Baucis, there Philemon, grew!
> Till, once, a parson of our town
> To mend his barn cut Baucis down:
> At which, 'tis hard to be believed
> How much the other tree was grieved;
> Grew scrubby,* died atop, was stunted;
> So the next parson stubb'd and burnt it."

Asked to describe briefly the two versions, reply might be made that, in the poem printed as it was altered for Addison, the story is very succinctly told, with completeness as of an epigram; and that, in the Narford MS. as originally written, the narrative is not so terse or close, but has more detail and a greater wealth of humor. It is the old distinction (applicable to so much work that is yet entitled, either way, to more than common praise) between correctness and enjoyment, regularity and abundance. The reader shall have the means of pronouncing for himself, by restoration of the lines struck out by the side of those which were substituted for them; and whatever his judgment may be, Swift's will not be brought in question. That he not only made such changes, but spoke of them always with pride as his friend's suggestion, never hinting at the existence or desiring any revival of the original poem, is evidence simply of his manliness of character.

---

* An amendment on the "scrubbed" of the printed version.

1705.
Æt. 38.
A contrast.
Having sought his friend's advice, he acted upon it, and there was an end. In the advice Addison might be right or wrong; but Swift knew that he was honest, and what matter if he should be wrong? When Pope found he had enchanted the town by putting the sylphs into the *Rape of the Lock*, he quarreled with Addison for having advised him not to make the change; but this was not Swift's way of holding the balance between a poem and a friend. The poem would always kick the beam. Doctor Delany tells a story of his having in later life asked one of the clergymen of his chapter to look over a piece of writing for him, the result being a recommendation, at once acted upon, to alter a couple of passages, which on the thing's

No vanities
of author-
ship.
appearance the critic saw to be a mistake. "Sir," said Swift, after hearing his regret, and his surprise that such changes should have been acquiesced in so easily, "I considered that the passages were of no great consequence, and I made without hesitation the alterations you desired in them, lest, had I stood up in their defense, you might have imputed it to the vanity of an author unwilling to hear of his errors." If Addison, after seeing the printed *Baucis and Philemon*, ever hinted a misgiving of the judiciousness of his own advice, Swift doubtless would have told him it was either way a thing "of no great consequence."

Original and
alteration
compared.
It is nevertheless of some consequence now to recover lost fragments of such a writer; and, apart from the interest of the discovery, the lines are capital specimens of Swift. The earliest and most important are in the treatment of the disguised holy men by the villagers whose virtue they are trying; and as this is the ground-color as well as main inducement to what follows, the whole piece turning upon the contrasted rudeness and hospitality, there can be little doubt that Swift was right in his first notion of showing both in detail.

In the printed poem it stands thus:

Opening as
printed.
> "It happen'd on a winter night,
> As authors of the legend write,

Two brother hermits, saints by trade,
Taking their tour in masquerade,
Disguis'd in tatter'd habits, went
To a small village down in Kent,
Where, in the strollers' canting strain,
They begg'd from door to door in vain,
Tried every tone might pity win ;
But not a soul would let them in."

1705.
Æt. 38.

From Swift's manuscript at Narford here is the corresponding passage :

" It happen'd on a winter's night,
As authors of the legend write,
Two brother hermits, saints by trade,
Taking their tour in masquerade,
Came to a village hard by Rixham,*
Ragged, and not a groat betwixt 'em.
It rain'd as hard as it could pour,
Yet they were forc't to walk an hour
From house to house, wet to the skin
Before one soul would let 'em in.
They call'd at every door—' Good people!
My comrade's blind, and I'm a creeple!
Here we lie starving in the street,
"Twould grieve a body's heart to see't,
No Christian would turn out a beast
In such a dreadful night at least!
Give us but straw, and let us lie
In yonder barn, to keep us dry!'
Thus, in the strollers' usual cant,
They begg'd relief which none would grant ;
No creature valued what they said.
One family was gone to bed :
The master bawl'd out half asleep
' You fellows, what a noise you keep!
So many beggars pass this way
We can't be quiet, night nor day ;
We can not serve you every one ;
Pray take your answer, and be gone!'
One swore he'd send 'em to the stocks :
A third could not forbear his mocks ;
But bawl'd, as loud as he could roar,
' You're on the wrong side of the door;'

Opening as
first written
(MS.).

---

* The " village hard by Rixham " of
the original has as little connection
with " Chilthorne " as the " village
down in Kent " of the altered version,
and Swift had probably no better reason than his rhyme for either.

1705.
Æt. 38.

One surly clown look't out and said,
' I'll fling a brickbat on your head!
You sha'n't come here! nor get a sous!
You look like rogues would rob a house.
Can't you go work, or serve the King?
You blind and lame?   'Tis no such thing!
That's but a counterfeit sore leg!
For shame!   Two sturdy rascals beg!
If I come down, *I'll* spoil your trick,
And cure you both with a good stick!'"

Superiority
of the MS.
version.

To say nothing of the rich filling-in, and coloring of humorous character, so much description as this we must think almost essential to give the proper sharpness of contrast to what ensues, when the holy men at last, leaving this "pack of churlish boors" behind them, come to

"Where dwelt a good old honest ye'man,
Call'd thereabout good man Philemon,"* (Narford MS.)

by whom they are heartily invited to pass the night, which Goody Baucis and he busy themselves to render comfortable; she mending the fire, and he taking a flitch of bacon from off the hook in the chimney.   Here is the printed version:

The saints
entertained
(after Addi-
son).

"And freely from the fattest side
Cut out large slices to be fried;
Then stepp'd aside to fetch them drink,
Fill'd a large jug up to the brink,
And saw it fairly twice go round;
Yet (what is wonderful) they found
'Twas still replenished to the top,
As if they ne'er had touch'd a drop.
The good old couple were amazed,
And often on each other gazed;
For both were frighten'd to the heart,
And just began to cry, ' What ar't?'
Then softly turned aside, to view
Whether the lights were burning blue.
The gentle pilgrims, soon aware on't,
Told them their calling and their errand:

---

* More characteristic than the printed couplet,
       " Where dwelt a good old honest ye'man
          Call'd in the neighborhood Philemon."

'Good folks, you need not be afraid,   1705.
We are but saints,' the hermits said ;   Æт. 38.
'No hurt shall come to you or yours :
But for that pack of churlish boors,
Not fit to live on Christian ground,
They and their houses shall be drown'd ;
While you shall see your cottage rise,
And grow a church before your eyes.' "

Swift's first version does more justice to the old couple's
hospitality. Baucis is seen at her cookery, and Philemon
as he taps the kilderkin brewed for a riper time. Their
fright at the first miracle, too, and the doubt that besets
Philemon (marked in Swift's manuscript with a long dash)
before he pronounces them "saints," are strokes of humor
incomparably better than the lights "burning blue" of the
printed poem. What follows is from the Narford MS.:

"And freely from the fattest side   Hospitality
Cut out large slices to be fried ;   to the saints
Which, tost up in a pan with batter   (before Ad-
And serv'd up in an earthen platter—   dison).
Quoth Baucis, 'This is wholesome fare ;
Eat, honest friends, and never spare !
And if we find our victuals fail,
We can but make it out in ale.'

  "To a small kilderkin of beer,
Brew'd for the good time of the year,
Philemon, by his wife's consent,
Stept with a jug, and made a vent ;
And having fill'd it to the brink,
Invited both the saints to drink.
When they had took a second draught,
Behold, a miracle was wrought.
For Baucis with amazement found,   MS. version.
Although the jug had twice gone round,
It still was full up to the top,
As if they ne'er had drunk a drop.
You may be sure so strange a sight
Put the old people in a fright.
Philemon whisper'd to his wife,
'These men are——saints ! I'll lay my life !'
The strangers overheard, and said,
'You're in the right : but don't afraid :

1705.
Æt. 38.

No hurt shall come to you or yours:
But for that pack of churlish boors,
Not fit to live on Christian ground,
They and their village shall be drown'd;
Whilst you shall see your cottage rise,
And grow a church before your eyes.'"

No sooner said than done:

House turn-
ing to church
(Swift MS.).

"Scarce had they spoke, when fair and soft
The roof began to mount aloft;
Aloft rose every beam and rafter;
The heavy wall went clambering after."*

A wooden jack, fallen into disuse of roasting, is turned
to a clock, and its friend, the chimney, to a steeple. The
humor of the contrasts of jack and clock is dropped from
the printed lines.

Other
changes
(Swift MS.).

"It now, stopt by some hidden powers,
Moves round but twice in twice twelve hours.
While in the station of a jack
'Twas never known to show its back,
A friend in turns and windings tried
Nor ever left the chimney's side—†
The chimney to a steeple grown,
The jack would not be left alone;
But up against the steeple rear'd,
Became a clock, and still adher'd;
And still its love to household cares
By a shrill voice at noon declares,
Warning the cook maid not to burn
The roast meat which it can not turn."

Philemon's old creaking chair becomes a pulpit: the
printed poem thus describing the change:

The pulpit
(printed ver-
sion).

"The groaning chair began to crawl,
Like a huge snail, along the wall;
There stuck aloft in public view,
And with small change, a pulpit grew."

---

* According to the printed version:
"They scarce had spoke, when fair and
soft
The roof began to mount aloft;
Aloft rose every beam and rafter;
The heavy wall climb'd slowly after."

The last is a good line; but the
"clambering" it replaced has more
of a humorous picture in it.

† These turns and touches of enjoyment are not in the printed version:

"But, slackened by some secret power,
Now hardly moves an inch an hour.
The jack and chimney near allied
Had never left each other's side:
The chimney to a steeple grown," etc.

1703.
Æт. 38.

Swift's MS. includes a font as well as the pulpit, and is
so much better that one wonders what Addison's objection
could have been, if it were not one of those touches of ex-
tra-solemnity in convivial hours which led to Mandeville's
nickname of "a parson in a tye-wig."

> "The groaning chair began to crawl
> Like a huge insect, up the wall;
> There stuck, and to a pulpit grew.
> But kept its matter, and its hue,
> And, mindful of its ancient state,
> Still groans while tattling gossips prate.
>
> "The mortar, only chang'd its name,
> In its old shape a font became."

Pulpit and
font (Swift's
MS.).

The next transformation is of the pictured ballads pasted
on the cottage wall, into the rude painted inscriptions so
common in old days of country churches, and to be met
occasionally even yet, where Jacob's ensigns may be seen
standing for the tribes of Israel, and here and there an
aspiring church-warden will have found beside them a place
for his own family heraldry.

Other
changes.

> "The ballads, pasted on the wall,
> Of Chevy Chace, and English Moll,*
> Fair Rosamond, and Robin Hood,
> The little Children in the Wood,
> Enlarged in picture, size, and letter,
> And painted, lookt abundance better,
> And now the heraldry describe
> Of a church-warden, or a tribe.†

Swift MS.

Next come into sudden shape the pews, out of a bedstead "such as our grandfathers use" (Addison's odd

What the
bedstead be-
comes.

---

* In Percy's *Reliques* will be found
a popular ballad on Molly Ambree and
her exploits in Flanders.

† The printed version is certainly
not so good.

> "The ballads, pasted on the wall,
> Of Joan of France, and English Mall,
> Fair Rosamond, and Robin Hood,
> The little Children in the Wood,
> Now seem'd to look abundance better,
> Improv'd in picture, size, and letter:

> And, high in order placed, describe
> The heraldry of every tribe."

The "painting" is wanted here, as
well as the characteristic touch of
the "church-warden;" and though
"Joan" pairs with "Moll" (or
"Mall" as it is printed), the worthy
couple are more likely to have been
students of "Chevy Chace."

1705.
Æt. 38.

What is
made of
Philemon.

amendment is "ancestors"), and which retains in its new
character its "former virtue" (better than Addison's "ancient nature") of lodging folks disposed to sleep; after
which we have the grand metamorphosis of Philemon into
the parson.   Of this I have placed in a note the version
as printed,* and comparison of it with what follows here,
from Swift's manuscript, will show what excellent traits
of character were sacrificed at Addison's suggestion.   The
reason the good man gives for desiring to be made the
parson, the gait and the look which he takes thereon, his
changes of demeanor to his equals and to the squire, and
the decent uses of his gown on market-days, are Swift all
over: but no trace of them will be found in the altered
poem.

Parson
Philemon
(Swift's
MS.).

"The cottage, with such feats as these
Grown to a church by just degrees,
The holy men desired their host
To ask for what he fancied most.
Philemon, having paused a while,
Replied in complimental style:
'Your goodness, more than my desert,
Makes you take all things in good part:
You've raised a church here in a minute,
And I would fain continue in it:
I'm good for little at my days—
Make me the parson, if you please.'

"He spoke, and presently he feels
His grazier's coat reach down his heels:

---

* In print Philemon thus became
parson:

Parson Phi-
lemon (as
printed).

"The cottage, by such feats as these
Grown to a church by just degrees,
The hermits then desired their host
To ask for what he fancied most.
Philemon, having paused a while,
Return'd them thanks in homely style;
Then said, 'My house is grown so fine,
Methinks I still would call it mine.
I'm old, and fain would live at ease;
Make me the parson, if you please.'

"He spoke, and presently he feels
His grazier's coat fall down his heels:
He sees, yet hardly can believe,
About each arm a pudding sleeve;

His waistcoat to a cassock grew,
And both assumed a sable hue;
But, being old, continued just
As threadbare and as full of dust.
His talk was now of tithes and dues:
He smoked his pipe and read the news;
Knew how to preach old sermons next,
Vamp'd in the preface and the text;
At christenings well could act his part,
And had the service all by heart;
Wish'd women might have children fast,
And thought whose sow had farrow'd
last;
Against dissenters would repine,
And stood up firm for 'right divine;'
Found his head filled with many a sys-
tem;
But classic authors—he ne'er miss'd 'em."

The sleeves, new border'd with a list,
Widen'd and gather'd at his wrist:
His waistcoat to a cassock grew,
And both assum'd a sable hue;
But being old, continued just
As threadbare and as full of dust.
A shambling, awkward gait he took,
With a demure, dejected look,
Talkt of his Off'rings, Tythes, and Dues,
Could smoke, and drink, and read the news;
Or sell a goose at the next town
Decently hid beneath his gown.
Contriv'd to preach old sermons next
Chang'd in the preface and the text.
At christenings well could act his part,
And had the service all by heart;
Wish'd women might have children fast,
And thought whose sow had farrow'd last;
Against dissenters would repine,
And stood up firm for ' right divine;'
Carried it to his equals high'r,
But most obsequious to the squire.
Found his head fill'd with many a system;
But classic authors—he ne'er miss'd 'em."

Swift did not return to Ireland, until, in the autumn of 1705, the whig majority in the elections had restored Somers and Halifax to the council; and this, presumably, was the date of the remonstrance he describes himself to have made personally to both those statesmen upon the way in which the clergy were treated by both parties in the state. The tory lords, with plenty of profession of zeal for the church, treated "not only their own chaplains, but all other clergymen whatsoever," with haughtiness and insolence; the whig lords, with great courtesy to the persons of particular clergymen, showed "ill-will and contempt for the order in general;" and here, for one of the results, was poor old Parson Philemon. Swift was carrying back to Ireland that picture in his mind, but the artists responsible for it were the great men of the state. It was probably on the same occasion he told Somers that he was himself, from his reading having given him a love for liberty, and from thinking it impossible on any other principle to ac-

Remonstrance on treatment of clergy.

Both parties alike to blame.

1705.
Æt. 38.
cept the Revolution, much inclined to be a whig; and that he thought that party would strengthen themselves in Ireland if they could obtain for the poor Irish clergy the same remission of first-fruits and tenths which had been conceded to the English in the preceding year. Some sort of promise to this effect had already been given, at the Bishop of Cloyne's intercession, before the whig prospects brightened; and on the eve of Swift's leaving for London

Translated
from Derry
in 1705.
on his present visit, he had written to Archbishop King to beg of him also to press " that the crown-rent should be added, which is a great load upon many poor livings, and would be a considerable help to others. And I am confident, with some reason, that it would be easily granted;

Desire to
help the
clergy.
being, I hear, under one thousand pounds a year, and the queen's grant for England being so much more considerable than ours can be at best."

Return to
Ireland.
Easy as it might be, however, he went back without any step made toward it, or any better hopes for himself. Some pieces are in his works, and some letters, with the date of this visit; but, excepting a few witty trifles for entertainment of the Berkeleys, they are more than a couple of years antedated. The only piece which may have been written before he left, and that has any thing of a personal significance or bearing, is a little poem to Lord Peterborough, filled with movement and life; and as his will be one of the most familiar figures of Swift's later London days, a few of his vivid lines shall place it here on the page for us. One of the characters in the book called *Macky's Memoirs*, to which Swift gives rare approval as " for the most

Lord Peter-
borough.
part true," sketches Peterborough as mightily affecting popularity, given to preach in coffee-houses, inconstant and fiery of temper, giddy in running from party to party and from place to place, with a good estate and not seeming expensive, yet always in debt and very poor, " a well-shaped, thin man, with a very brisk look." All, doubtless, extremely true, and such as a drawing by Jervas or Hudson might express. But Reynolds and Hogarth have no finer lines, more firm and more vigorous, than these that follow:

"Mordanto fills the trump of fame,   1705.
The Christian worlds his deeds proclaim,   Æt. 38.
And prints are crowded with his name.

"In journeys he outrides the post,
Sits up till midnight with his host,
Talks politics, and gives the toast.

"Knows every prince in Europe's face,
Flies like a squib from place to place,
And travels not, but runs a race......

"A messenger comes all a-reek
Mordanto at Madrid to seek;
He left the town above a week.

"Next day the post-boy winds his horn,
And rides through Dover in the morn:
Mordanto's landed from Leghorn......

"So wonderful his expedition,
When you have not the least suspicion,
He's with you like an apparition.

"A skeleton in outward figure,
His meagre corpse, though full of vigor,
Would halt behind him were it bigger."

Swift was now to be resident in Ireland longer than
usual, and I propose to give some description of his ways
of life in Dublin and Laracor.

BOOK FOURTH.

IRELAND AND ENGLAND.

1706–1709. Æt. 39–42.

I. Life in Laracor and Dublin.

II. Waiting and Working in London.

I.

WITH the Ormond family at the castle, during 1703 and 1704, when the duke was in residence as lord lieutenant, Swift lived in the same friendly association as with the Berkeleys; a touch of even greater intimacy being, perhaps, derived from the old Ormond connection with his uncle Godwin. When the daughters, Ladies Betty and Mary, had grown to womanhood, and after brief interval of absence he met them in London in 1710, he describes the "insolent drabs"* coming up to his very mouth to salute him: the epithet, of course, meaning nothing, but that, being fond of them, he was free to call them what he pleased. Lady Mary was his greatest favorite; he found a likeness in her to Esther Johnson; and extremely pathetic was his remark upon her early death, not many months after a happy marriage to Lord Ashburnham: "I hate life when I think it exposed to such accidents; and to see so many thousand wretches burdening the earth while such as her die, makes me think God did never intend life for a blessing."

Swift's relation to these Irish viceroys, as already hinted, was something more than a mere chaplain's. It continued through the government of Lord Pembroke, after his appointment at the close of 1706; and when discovery was made, in 1708, that Lord Wharton was to bring over

Marginal notes: 1706–1708. ÆT. 39–41. Duke of Ormond's family. Lady Mary Butler.

---

* Grave mistakes have been made by giving importance to such chance words as these, which are frequent as they are meaningless in the speech of Swift. When he calls duchess's daughters "insolent drabs," the Irish bishops "insolent, ungrateful rascals," and Lord Somers himself a "rascal," the words ought not to be, as there will be other occasions more particularly to point out, credited with meanings such as would be given to them in present ordinary use.

1706-1708.
Æt. 39-41.
Swift's chaplaincy.

his own chaplain, the Archbishop of Dublin expressed great concern. "If you can attend the next lord lieutenant," he wrote to Swift, "you, in my opinion, ought not to decline it. I assure myself that you are too honest to come on ill terms; nor do I believe any will be explicitly proposed. I could give several reasons why you should embrace this." But already, to the Irish primate, Swift had transmitted from London sufficient reasons why he

Objected to by Wharton.

could not. Doctor Lambert's appointment in his place had been made at the express instance of the lord treasurer, Godolphin, and of influential English bishops,[*] by whom, Swift slyly added, "it was thought absolutely necessary, considering the dismal notion they have here of so many high-church archbishops among you; and your friend made no application, for reasons left you to guess."

Primate and archbishop.

Narcissus Marsh, the primate, and William King, the archbishop,[†] were pretty nearly the only two men of superior ability in the existing Irish episcopate, and with both Swift was on friendly terms; his communication with King being necessarily frequent. Their agreement in church policy was unfortunately but too close; though, in King's objection to the Northern Presbyterians, there was much less of Swift's general dislike of fanaticism and far more of

William King.

the mere churchman's prejudice. King was a whig in politics; and, though a good, well-disposed man, possessed of very considerable learning, and unselfishly anxious to promote what he believed to be for the benefit of Ireland, he never could understand Swift's contempt for the parliament, intolerance of the convocation, and belief in the general government corruption. Nevertheless, through many differences, they did not lose respect for each other; and when, at a later momentous time, Swift, on behalf of Ireland, declared war against the government of England, King, with great courage, took a place by his side.

---

* The low-church Archbishop Tenison took the lead in this: "The dullest good-for-nothing man I ever knew," says Swift. See post, 223.

† Whately edited (Oxf., 1821) a discourse by King *On the Right Method of Interpreting Scripture, preached at Christ Church, Dublin, in May,* 1709.

Thus far no such questions had been raised. Until his later life Swift can not be credited with so much interest in the country as to be thought likely to have even brought under consideration how best it might be governed; but no one so keenly saw the extent of the misgovernment, and no clearer light has been thrown on its causes than may be found in his casual utterances from time to time. He had for the present persuaded himself that his proper task in Ireland was to give more strength to the Established Church and a better provision to its clergy; though it would be extremely difficult to say of which class of Irish residents he was even now least tolerant, the colony from England or the native population. John Temple wrote to him from Moor Park in June, 1706, to ask his help in some necessary arrangements of valuing and leasing on his estates in Armagh. "'Tis an advantage to you," after replying on the points of the letter Swift goes on to say,* "that land in this kingdom was never lower than now—I mean where it is far from Dublin; and therefore, if you have a fair return, you can not well be a loser whenever we have Peace. Nothing can be righter than your opinion not to let your lands at a rack-rent. They that live at your distance from their estates would be undone if they did it, especially in such an uncertain country as this. Therefore I should advise you to let it so easily to your under-tenants, when you renew, that they may be able to repay you part of your fine, and then your rent is secure. If you have thoughts of selling it, your best way will be to offer it among the gentlemen of the neighborhood that will give most; but I hope you will consider it a little longer, or else you may be in danger of selling you know not what; which will be as bad as buying so. I forgot to tell you that no accounts from your tenants can be relied on. If they paid you but a pepper-corn a year, they would be readier to ask abatement than offer

1706–1708.
Æt. 39–41.

As to government of Ireland.

Letter to John Temple: 1706.

---

* This letter ("for John Temple, Esq. at his house at Moor Park near Farnham in Surrey, England," dated | "from Dublin, 15th June, 1706"), is now first printed.

1706–1708.
Ær. 39–41.
Tenants and
landlords.

Love of
Moor Park.

Changesince
early days.

Party in
Ireland.

An Importa-
tion from
England.

to advance. It is the universal maxim throughout the kingdom. I have known them fling up a lease, and the next day give a fine to have it again. It has not been known in the memory of man that an Irish tenant ever once spoke truth to his landlord."

The close of the letter, in which he speaks of an invitation from Temple, and of a common friend, a landed proprietor living near Laracor, whose opinions of Ireland were said to resemble his own, has much personal interest. " I am extremely obliged by your kind invitation to Moor Park, which no time will make me forget and love less. If I love Ireland better than I did, it is because we are nearer related, for I am deeply allied to its poverty. My little revenue is sunk two parts in three, and the third in arrear. Therefore if I come to Moor Park it must be on foot; but then comes another difficulty, that I carry double the flesh that you saw about me at London, to which I have no manner of title, having neither purchased it by luxury nor good humor. I did not think Mr. Perceval* and I had agreed so well in our opinion of Ireland. I believe it is the only public opinion we agree in; else I should have had more of his company here; for I always loved him very well as a man of very good understanding and humor. But whig and tory have spoiled all that was tolerable here, by mixing with private friendship and conversation, and mining both; though it seems to me full as pertinent to quarrel about Copernicus and Ptolomee as about. my lord treasurer and Lord Rochester; at least for any private man, and especially in our remote scene. I am sorry we begin to resemble England only in its defects. About seven years ago frogs were imported here, and thrive very well; and three years after, a certain great man brought over whig and tory, which suit the soil admirably. But my paper is at an end before I am aware."

---

* The chief of the family, also known to Swift, who mentions in his Journal occasional dinners at his house (23d March, 1710–'11, etc.), was Sir John Perceval, created Baron and Viscount Perceval by the whigs after the queen's death, and ultimately made Earl of Egmont.

He nevertheless found space for a postscript characteristic 1706–1708. of him as any thing in the letter. "I, was desired by a Æt. 39–41. person of quality to get him a few cuttings of the Arboyse and Burgundy vines mentioned by Sir W. T. in his *Essay on Gardening*, because they ripen the easiest of any. Pray be so kind to order your gardener to send some against the season, and I will direct they shall be sent to London, and from thence to Chester."

He was himself now engaged in planting at Laracor, not indeed Franche Comté or Burgundy vines, but cherry-trees in his river-walk, a grove of hollies, and quicksets on the flat in his garden. He was strengthening his river-bank Improving against possible floods, putting in fresh willows, and in- and plant- creasing the number of his apple-trees. From nature, as well as by early association with Temple, he had a liking for such occupation; and a little went a great way with him. "Pray keep the garden *for me*," he wrote to Dean Sterne, when changes were in hand at the deanery-house during his absence in London; and it is a real sadness to him when his poor "half-dozen of blossoms" at Laracor are killed by frost. "Spes anni collapsa ruit!" he exclaims, uncertain whether the words are his own or Virgil's. When away in London his thoughts travel continually to Love of his garden. "I should be plaguy busy if I were at Laracor gardening. now," he says at the opening of March, 1710–'11, "cutting down willows, planting others, scouring my canal, and ev- ery kind of thing." The useful activity, the movement and variety of scene, were the charm to him. When Ad- dison took him to see his sister's garden at Westminster, where her husband was a prebend, he found it to be a "delightful" retreat; "yet I thought it was a sort of mo- nastic life in those cloisters, and I liked Laracor better." Never a spring day breaks with sunshine on his London life that he does not think of his willows beginning to His quicks peep and his quicks to bud, and what work he should have and willows. upon his hands if he were but beside them. He is always urging Esther Johnson and her friend to betake them- selves to Trim and tell him of his river, his banks and

1706–1708.
Æt. 39–41.
Trouts and
pike. *Ante,*
41. groves of holly, his apples, and his cherry-trees. "And now they begin to catch the pikes, and will shortly the trouts (a pox on these ministers!), and I would fain know whether the floods were ever so high as to get over the holly bank of the river-walk? If so, then all my pikes are gone; but I hope not." Here was another of his summer amusements; and one may still bring vividly back the enjoyment he derived from it, in the years of which I am speaking, as one reads, in these London letters to his lady friends, what his injunctions were that they must do at his own return in the summer. They were to go and make the Raymonds a visit at Trim, and were to be joined by him there, and they were to have "another eel and trout fishing;" and then, too, Mrs. Johnson on her namesake would ride by Laracor, and would see and greet himself in his garden in his morning-gown, and they would go up 21st Feb.,
1710-'11. with "Joe" to the hill ·of Bree, and round by Scurlock's town. "O Lord! how I remember names! 'faith it gives me short sighs."

Not for itself, I should add, did he care for Trim, but only for its nearness to Laracor, and for the sake of one or two living in it. When the vicar asked him to help "Joe's" father to be elected portreeve, he said he would Trim people. do any thing for Joe that he could; but the Trim people had behaved ill in disregarding advice he had given them, and though he wished them their liberty to choose whom they liked, he would not trouble himself for them. Nor, 30th November, 1710. upon their failure to carry the election against the influence of a neighboring squire, Tom Ashe,* the Bishop of Clogher's brother, did he scruple to say that he was glad to see the town "reduced to slavery" again: for "the peo-

---

* Tom was the eldest of the three brothers Ashe, "descended from an ancient family of that name in Wiltshire," which had settled in Ireland. He had an estate of land of more than a thousand a year in county Meath. Nichols's description of him is derived from Mr. Deane Swift, but may be accepted: "He was a facetious, pleasant companion, but the most eternal unwearied punster that ever lived. He was thick and short in his person, being not above five feet high at the most, and had something very droll in his appearance." —*Nichols,* second edition, xix., 185.

ple were as great rascals as the gentlemen." Joe Beau- 1706-1708.
Æt. 39-41.
mont was one of the exceptions. Engaged in the linen
trade, he had put forth some inventions recommended by Joe Beaumont.
Swift, for one of which a government reward was given;
but the too common fate of inventors befell him. His
ingenuities withdrew him from the necessary attention to
his business, bankruptcy followed, and, a few years after
Swift was made Dean of St. Patrick's, on the eve of a supposed discovery in mathematics which had overtaxed his
brain, he died by his own hand. To the last he had Swift's
sympathy, and always some kindly allusion.* When Trim
is mentioned there is commonly a word for Joe. Pressing on Mrs. Johnson the necessity of country air and exercise, and that she should "take a good deal of it," he
asks, " where better than Trim ? Joe will be your humble
servant, Parvisol your slave, and Raymond at your command, for he piques himself on good manners."

Isaiah Parvisol, an Irishman of French extraction, was Parvisol, the
steward.
Swift's tithe-agent and steward at Laracor. Raymond, as
already stated, was Vicar of Trim. He was a commonplace, worthy man, not provident in money matters, and
only enabled to repay some advances from Beaumont
through a windfall that had come to his wife.† He visited Swift during his great time in London, and by him was
introduced to the solicitor-general, Sir Robert Raymond, Vicar Raymond, of
Trim.
who acknowledged the family connection claimed by the
vicar.‡ But, though he called on Swift many times oftener than he had the good fortune to be seen, he was grateful when admitted ("drank a pint of ale cost me fivepence,
and smoked his pipe"), overflowed with pleasure when put

---

* It is Joe to whom there is allusion in the delightful verses, "On the
little house by the church-yard of
Castleknock" (1709-'10):

"Whoever pleases to inquire
Why yonder steeple wants a spire,
The gray old fellow, poet Joe,
The philosophic cause will show."

† "I am heartily glad of Raymond's
good fortune, and I write this post

to congratulate him upon it. I hope
you will advise him to be a good
manager, without which the greatest
fortune must run out." — *Swift to
Walls, 9th November*, 1708. Unpublished letter *penes me.* "In money matters he is the last man I would
depend on."—*Journal, 7th June*, 1711.

‡ Journal, 11th December, 1710;
10th January, 1710-'11.

1706-1708.
Æt. 39-41.
Vicar's visit
to London.
Post, 381. among the beef-eaters to have a good look at the queen, and was altogether so easy and manageable, that, when he took his way back to Trim, Swift was "a little melancholy" to part with him, and remorseful for having seen him so seldom. He has kind words for his wife also, though a grudge at her excess of motherly qualities, and not the highest opinion of her conversational powers. " Will Mrs. Raymond never have done lying-in ?" is more than once his whimsical question ; and when he wants to describe the fall of a celebrated Toast from the brilliancy of London to the dullness of Lynn, only fancy, he says, " Poor creature ! It is just such a change as if Pdfr (himself) should be banished from Ppt (Esther Johnson), and con-

Vicar's wife. demned to converse with Mrs. Raymond." Even the vicar's grammar does not always escape ; for when he has written to Mrs. Johnson so that he can not read his own hand, he consoles himself with " I'll mend my hand if oo please ; but you are more used to it nor I, as Mr. Raymond says."*

Out of Trim, but in the Laracor neighborhood, Swift's principal friends were Mr. and Mrs. Perceval, John Temple's acquaintance ; Mr. and Mrs. Garret Wesley (the latter a daughter of Sir Dudley Colley), for both of whom he had such regard, that very often, when Mrs. Wesley was ill in London during Anne's last ministry, he would leave the great tables to go and read prayers to her ;† Sir Arthur Langford ; a friendly farmer named Johnny Clark ;

Friends near
Laracor. and his curate Mr. Warburton, who did not resign to marry a second wife, "Mrs. Melthrop of my parish," until four years after Swift was dean. Altogether, with Squire Jones " and other scoundrels," the congregation at its most populous time mustered under a score. " I am this minute very busy," he writes to Dean Sterne before setting out for London in 1710, " being to preach to-day before an audience of at least fifteen people, most of them gentle

---

* Journal, 7th January, 1712-'13.

† "She is much better than she was. I heartily pray for her health,

out of the entire love I bear to her worthy husband." — Journal, 4th of March, 1712-'13.

and all simple." It can hardly be said that he stinted his 1706-1708.
Æt. 39–41.
Dubliu club. preaching in giving alternate Sundays with his curate to this audience of fifteen. "Pray let the ladies continue to be part of the club," he had written from London to Archdeacon Walls two years earlier, "and remember my Saturday dinner against I return: it was a cunning choice that of Saturday, for Mrs. Walls remembered that two Saturdays in four I was at Laracor."* The club, of which the day was altered thereon to Friday, takes us back from Laracor to Dublin: its principal members, who dined or Its members. supped and played cards at each other's houses, during the autumn and winter evenings, being the Walls family; a worthy Dublin alderman, Stoyte, afterward lord mayor, his wife, and his daughter Catherine, great favorites with Swift; Mrs. Johnson and Mrs. Dingley; the Dublin post-master, Manley, and his wife; Dean Sterne; and himself. It largely contributed to Esther Johnson's enjoyment during his longest separation from her; it survived many vicissitudes; and it found mention, among graver things, in a letter from Swift to Walls in the autumn of 1713, when he had returned to London to complete that famous and eminently religious compromise by which one member of the club had been made a bishop that another might be made a dean. "Our club is sadly broke! The ladies tell Its break-up. me they are going to live at Trim. The bishop" whilome dean " at Dromore, I " now the dean " here; and none but you and Stoyte left. Our goody Walls, my gossip, will die of the spleen.... My service to the alderman, and Goody, and Catherine, and Mr. Manley and lady."† The club nevertheless did not finally break until Esther Johnson passed away.

Walls, a Dublin clergyman who held the rectory of Cas- Archdeacon Walls. tleknock, near Trim, created archdeacon in the summer

---

* Swift to "The Reverend Mr. Archdeacon Walls at his house in Cavan Street, Dublin, Ireland." Unpublished letter *penes me.*

† Swift to "The Rev. Mr. Arch-deacon Walls at his house over against the hospital in Queen Street, Dublin, 7th September, 1713." Unpublished letter *penes me.*

1706-1708.   of 1708, had been intimate with the Vicar of Laracor for
_Æt._ 39-41. some years, and long after the vicar became Dean of St.
Patrick's continued to be a great poster in his affairs. He
is the hero of a charming little poem which is like a page
out of a poetical *Gulliver*, where Swift describes his country
An Irish   rectory as composed only of bits of wall, roof, and weath-
rectory.   er-cock blown down from his church steeple by a western
breeze ; the walls in tumbling getting a knock, and the steeple a shock : " From whence the neighboring farmer calls
The steeple Knock ; the vicar Walls."*   But in Dublin he
had a more commodious dwelling, which was a second home
to Esther Johnson ; and though Swift's humorous objection
Archdea-   to Mrs. Raymond applied equally to Mrs. Walls, her kind-
con's wife. ness to his dearest friend insured her his regard.   Already
Post, 404.
he was sponsor to one of her children, when he was asked to
stand again ; but he protested he would not be " godfather
to Goody *that* bout," and he hoped she'd have no more.
Nevertheless " gossip Doll " succeeded in obtaining his
consent twice more ; and by his influence her " son Jacky "
was painted by his and Pope's friend, Jervas.   Her husband he called " a reasoning coxcomb," which only meant,
however, that the archdeacon, though not a man of note
in any respect, was apt to go his own way, relying much
upon himself ; and, excepting that stinginess is sometimes
hinted, and too much deference to his wife, we hear of no
other objection.   His five days' visit to London, while

* The drift of the poem is a delightful exaggeration of the minuteness of the house, into which nevertheless

"The vicar once a week creeps in,
Sits with his knees up to his chin ;
Here cons his notes and takes a whet,
Till the small ragged flock is met."

Nothing will persuade people that it *can be* a house. Horsemen ride over it : crows and blackbirds are taken in by it : Swift's curate likens it to "a pigeon-house or oven, To bake one loaf, or keep one dove in."

"Then Mrs. Johnson gave her verdict
And every one was pleased that heard it ;

All that you make this stir about
Is but a still which wants a spout."

But matters are brought to a crisis by one of the children of Doctor Raymond :

"The doctor's family came by,
And little Miss began to cry,
Give me that house in my own hand !
Then Madam bade the chariot stand,
Call'd to the clerk, in manner mild,
Pray reach that thing here, to the child :
That thing, I mean, among the kale,
And here's to buy a pot of ale.

"The clerk said to her in a heat,
What I sell my master's country-seat,
Where he comes every week from town :
Why, he wouldn't sell it for a crown."

Swift was all-powerful there, gives rather a favorable im- 1706–1708.
pression of him. He took no gown or professional equip- Æt. 39–41.
ment, rode from Chester to London on horseback, lodged Visit of arch-deacon to London.
with his horse in Aldersgate Street, and intruded only
once on his celebrated friend; who was thereby piqued
into saying that he had no more curiosity than a cow, that
his wife would not let him stay in London longer, and
that all he did there was to buy her a silk gown and himself a hat, and go with Dilly Ashe once to the play.

Dilly Ashe* was one of three brothers—the Bishop of Brothers Ashe.
Clogher, Tom Ashe, and himself—who, with Swift, Bishop
Lloyd of Killala, and Sir Andrew Fountaine, now passed
a great many pleasant nights with Sterne at the deanery
of St. Patrick's. Fountaine had come over to Dublin with Sir Andrew Fountaine. *Ante*, 176.
Lord Pembroke, as usher of the black rod in the new vice-
roy's court; and Swift, who at this time first knew him,
told Sterne the following year that he had left him in London, declaring he should never be satisfied till he was
happy again in the little room at Dublin at the expense
of the dean's wine and conversation. The dean's claim to
Swift's liking was the same as that of Walls, and at this
time only second to his, no other houses being opened so
familiarly to Esther Johnson; and her great friend would
often plague her to reveal her favorite, the tall brown archdeacon or the black little dean. In that competition it Dean Sterne.
was Sterne's disadvantage to be unmarried; considerable
eagerness in looking after his own interest is also often
objected to him. Nor is he to have credit for any special
ability; but it was something to have an agreeable house,
a well-furnished library, and a liberal table,† and, though
Swift quarreled with him later, they had now much inter-

---

* Tom Ashe has been referred to. Dilly (Dillon) was Vicar of Finglas. He had held the living since 1694, and Parnell (the poet) succeeded him in it in 1718. There will be other notices of him.

† "The Dean of St. Patrick's lives better than any man of quality I know," wrote Swift to Sterne in 1710. "The worst dinner I ever saw at the Dean's was better," he said of a din-ner with Sir Thomas Mansell, who was enormously rich with a stingy wife. Mansell was afterward one of the famous "twelve."

1706-1708. course.   The hospitable owner of good bits, good books,
Æt. 39-41. and good buildings, Swift calls him; adding, with allusion
to a much dearer friend, that those were "three b's" that
Bishop of the Bishop of Clogher would envy him for.   The bishop
Clogher.   was another of Mrs. Johnson's kindest allies, and for his
own sake had inspired the strongest regard in Swift.   It
began in the old college days in 1682, when St. George
Ashe was tutor to Jonathan, and it continued uninterrupt-
edly until the close of Ashe's life in 1717.   Swift told
Lord Halifax in 1709 that it was "only the bishop and
perhaps one or two more that rendered Ireland tolerable
to him;" and in the same year he heard from Addison
with what warmth of expression the bishop had spoken
of him, and reciprocated his esteem.   Four years later
they both stood with Addison behind the scenes at Drury
Lane to witness the rehearsal of the tragedy of *Cato*.
Likings born . They would not like each other less for a weakness
of a common shared in common.   The bishop and both his brothers
infirmity.   were notorious for punning.   As far back as the Tisdall
letters, Swift sent a message to Esther Johnson that she,
in this as in all else his pupil, was to forbear punning after
the Finglas rate when Dilly was at home;* and it may be
doubtful if the Ashe family took it first from him, or he
from them, as far back as even his college days.   But, at
the time under description, no one came near to Swift
either in making puns himself or infecting others with
a frenzy for it.   High or low, every one punned that came
within reach of him; and at the castle, under his influence, the disorder so raged for a while, that a language
A new Cas- constructed chiefly of puns was invented, and called the
tilian.   Castilian.
Earl of Pem- The new lord lieutenant, Lord Pembroke, occupied
broke.   worthily the viceregal seat.   He had served the highest

---

* "Squire Tom lived not far away from his brother at Finglas. "I won-der," Swift adds, "she could be so wicked as to let the first word she could speak, after choking, be a pun. I differ from you; and believe the pun was just coming up, but met with the crumbs, and, so struggling for the wall, could neither of them get by, and at last came both out together."—*To Tisdall, 3d February, 1703-'4.*

offices at home, was first plenipotentiary at the peace of Ryswick, and, concurrently with his present appointment, still held that of president of the council in England. But he was more than all this. He was a man of independent conduct and capable of a great generosity; had been displaced from the lieutenancy of Wiltshire for fidelity and spirit in the Monmouth rebellion; in the strife of parties since, had been so temperate as to win consideration from all; and, under any other than the prevailing system, might have left his mark on Ireland. He took with him George Dodington as secretary, whom Swift characterized as not disposed to give threepence to save from the gallows all the established clergy in both kingdoms; but in this there was strong coloring from his own church views. The utmost reproach against Pembroke himself was that his mind too readily took impress from stronger minds, and that there was a want of fixity in his opinions; but of the many who veered, as he did, between tory and whig, there were few so little overruled by factious or unworthy motive. Not born to the earldom, he had received the advantage of a younger brother's education, and was a man of books* and travel; had brought from Italy the noble antique sculptures that are still the pride of Wilton; and justly was it set down by Swift as "a very great mark of honor and distinction" conferred upon an Englishman, when, during Anne's last ministry, Pembroke was elected into the French Academy. A yet greater honor had nevertheless been his, when, soon after the Revolution, Locke inscribed to him his *Treatise on the Human Understanding*, in gratitude for kind offices in evil times. Swift and he had taken mightily to each other. Attending to pay his respects, Doctor Delany relates, the Vicar of Laracor found the viceroy listening to a lecture from a learned physician on the qualities of bees, which in every other sentence he called a commonwealth or a nation. "Yes,"

Margin notes: 1706-1708. Æt. 39-41.

Secretary Dodington.

An earl's highest distinction.

---

* When Swift first went to visit Pembroke in England, "it was to see some curious books."—*Journal, 5th March*, 1712-'3.

1706–1708.
Æt. 39–41.

Swift's first
pun to Lord
Pembroke.

interposed Swift, " no doubt, and very ancient.   Moses numbers the Hivites among the nations Joshua was appointed to conquer."   Pembroke was delighted, and punning became his great enjoyment after that day.

It was Swift's remark later that he first hit Lord Pembroke with a pun ; and the blow hit wider than the laugh it raised.   Nor was it, at the worst, a missile with any

Why puns
are despised:

harm in it.   The pun is not a high kind of humor, because it is a thing that can be made by almost any body ; and of course, on the viceroy's taste becoming known, every body about him took to the manufacture.   But the best things in even this kind of wit remain, notwithstanding, the property of only the best intellects ; and there is also a sort of them so execrably bad, so far above ordinary intellects in the extent and degree of atrocity, as to claim

and popular.

rank on that very ground.   These, and indeed the art or habit generally when taken up by superior men, are among those condescensions of the great which will always be attractive ; and low as the intellectual achievement is, a pun. is mostly tolerated, and very rarely fails to amuse.   Best and worst have contended for the palm of laughter, and Swift was unapproached in both.*   In the two extremes of witty meaning and extravagant absurdity the best that

Puns by
Swift.

have been preserved are his.   "A fellow hard by pretends to cure agues, and has set out a sign, and spells it egoes. How does that fellow pretend to cure agues? said a gentleman observing it with me.   I did not know, I said ; but I was sure it was not by a spell."   An admirable pun. " I will tell you," he says in another letter, " a good thing I said to my Lord Carteret.   So, says he, ' My Lord (blank) came up to me and asked me,' etc.   ' No,' said I, ' my Lord (blank) never did, nor ever can *come up* to you.'   We all

---

* So was Charles Lamb ; a man of most delicate genius, who had also Swift's habit of saying, without a thought of irreverence, the most startling things.   I once heard him express a wish that his last breath might be drawn through a pipe and exhaled in a pun.   He had then given up tobacco, but would go where smokers were, to enjoy

"Its by-places
And the suburbs of its graces,
And in its borders take delight,
An unconquer'd Cananaite."

pun here sometimes." Then follows an atrocity by Prior: 1706-1708. Æт. 39-41. "Lord Carteret set down Prior the other day in his char- 25th Dec., 1710; 4th January, 1710-'11. iot, and Prior thanked him for his charioty. That was fit for Dilly. I do not remember to have heard one good one from the ministry, which is really a shame." A su- per-eminently good one by himself belongs to the days when Carteret was viceroy. At one of the Castle enter- tainments, a lady, whisking about her mantle, swept down with a crash a Cremona fiddle; and Swift, who was by, re- Delany's Ob- servations, 213. peated Virgil's line—

> " Mantua, væ miseræ nimium vicina Cremonæ."*

Such specimens of the Castilian language as I now add to these will not be thought so good; but as they have not been printed, and are all that remains in this form of so peculiar a speech, they will be worth preserving. I found them in Swift's handwriting, entitled by him *Dia- logues in Castilian,* among the manuscripts at the seat of Sir Andrew Fountaine.† The reader is to imagine Lord Pembroke at the Castle, and around him the three mem- Dublin Cas- tle dialogue. bers of the Ashe family, the Bishop, Tom, and Dilly; two doctors, named Howard and Molyneux; Sir Andrew Fount- aine, and Swift. LORD LIEUT. "Doctor Swift, you know Gemelli says"—TOM ASHE (interrupting quick). "Jem- mie Lee,‡ my lord, Jemmy Lee, I know him very well, a

---

* The reader must be warned against the many alleged productions of Swift in this form of wit, with which he had nothing whatever to do, and of which not a few have found their way into his collected writings by the carelessness of his editors. Any thing in the shape of a pun or an indecency it was long the fashion to father on him, without the least regard to either truth or probability. Almost the only genuine piece con- nected with this subject is his *God's Revenge against Punning,* in which he shows the miserable fates of per- sons addicted to the crying sin. One may be quoted for sample of the rest: "George Simmons, shoe-maker, at Turnstile, in Holborn, was so given to this custom, and did it with so much success, that his neighbors gave out he was a wit. Which report com- ing among his creditors nobody would trust him, so that he is now a bank- rupt, and his family in a miserable condition."

† For other examples of Castilian, in letters, also found at Narford, see *post,* 248, 275.

‡ Jemmy Leigh and Tom Leigh were friends who played cards with Mrs. Johnson, and visited Swift in

very honest gentleman." Dr. HOWARD. "My lord, there is a great dispute in town, whether this parliament will be dissolved by your excellency, or only prorogued." LORD LIEUT. "Doctor Swift, I did not see you at the society last meeting." Dr. HOWARD. "My lord, your excellency, I hope, is pleased with their proceedings this session." LORD LIEUT. "Doctor Swift, won't you take another cup of coffee?" An amusing hint is thus given of the degree of attention his excellency was disposed to bestow upon that most surprising of all constituted things, an Irish par-
"Castilian" from Narford MSS.
liament of those days. The subject is resumed in Castilian. ·TOM ASHE. "Pray, Doctor Howard, which is the way to dissolve a parliament? Should it be done in vinegar or aquafortis?" But a more pertinent question is put by his brother: BISHOP OF CLOGHER. "My lord, has your excellency considered whence comes the common saying among us of tag, rag, and bobtail?" LORD LIEUT. "No; but now on the sudden I should think it were a description of the three ways that beggars order their dress. Tag —that is, when their rents are sewn, tackt, or pinn'd together. Rag—that is, when they hang down in tatters. Bobtail—that is, when the rags are torn off, and daggle in
Dublin Castle dialogue.
the dirt." SIR ANDREW FOUNTAINE. "Pozzitively 'tis so, my lord bishop." BISHOP OF CLOGHER. "Be assured it is, Sir Andrew. But pray, my lord, whence comes the way of calling a man fellow, when we have a mind to abuse him as base fellow, pitiful fellow. I believe it may be a corruption of the French word *filou*." LORD LIEUT. "It may be so, my lord, or it might be from the word *felo*, which signifies all sorts of rogues, and was formerly more used in common speech than now. However, your lordship's may be the truer one." BISHOP OF CLOGHER. "Oh, my lord, your excellency's is much more natural." Tag, rag,

London during his famous time there. "Tell Jemmy Leigh that his boy that robbed him now appears about the town." 5th March, 1711–'12. "I saw Tom Leigh in town once, 9th Oct., 1712." See also Journal, 23d Dec., 1712; 9th Jan., 1712–'13, etc., etc. And particularly 16th March, 1711–'12; 30th Dec., 1712; and 20th Jan., 1712–'13. Tom was not popular with Swift.

and bobtail, fellow and rogue, are the associations brought 1706-1708.
Æt. 39-41. up by mention of the Irish parliament.

Meanwhile Doctor Molyneux has launched into a learn- "Castilian" from Nar- ed argument against Doctor Swift's continued acceptance ford MSS. of the cups of coffee handed to him, for which he suggests a more wholesome preparation. DR. MOLYNEUX. "My lord, I do not think coffee so proper to help those who are troubled with a lacochymia, or dyspepsia, as the concha of testaceary fishes pulverized. I mean not only those to which nature has denied motion, but all that move in armatura articulata, and are crustaceous, as the Astacus major and minor. Which latter I take to be the crayfish, and both are indeed but a species of the Cancer marinus. In all which the chèlæ or acetabula, that is, the extremity of the forceps (improperly called crab's eyes), reduced to powder, Paracelsus recommends as a noble alkali." DR. HOW-ARD. "Chalk or powdered egg-shells are full as good." TOM ASHE. "Doctor, what do you think of powdered beef?" DR. HOWARD. "Mr. Ashe, if I had an engine to shut your mouth, I should value it more than that we make use of to stretch open the mouths of our patients." Sir ANDREW FOUNTAINE. "The doctor says that, I suppose, by way of os-tentation." DR. HOWARD. "Well but, os— a—why os, ay, oh, oysters! As for oysters, my lord, Pliny seems to prefer those of Brundusium; Martial thinks the best come from the Lacus Lucrinus; and the British oysters were much celebrated by others. I find, in short, my lord, that the ancients differ very much, and are divided in their opinions about oysters." LORD LIEUT. "Sir Andrew, do not some authors call that an ostra- Dublin Cas-tle dialogue. schism?" DR. HOWARD. "Oysters, why, a—yes, I think our best oysters come from Colchester; my Lord Rivers, as I take it, has for one of his titles Lord Colches-ter. He is not Earl of Rivers: he is only Earl Rivers. His name is Savage; the seat of the family is called Rock Savage in Cheshire, as Sir William Dugdale takes notice. 'Tis a noble family, my lord, a very noble family." DILLY ASHE. "Pray, my lord, what town in England is that

1706–1708.
Æt. 39–41.
Punning at
its lowest.
where the people may afford to keep the best fires, and the lord is best able to put them out." Sir Andrew Fount-aine. "'Tis Newcastle, I suppose; because there are the most coals; and the Duke of Newcastle is very rich, and rich folks can do any thing, and so they can put out fires." Dilly Ashe. "No, 'tis Cole-chester, and the lord is Lord Rivers." Dr. Molyneux. "Ay, but, Mr. Ashe, there are no coals at Colchester, you should have named a place famous for coals κατ' ἐξοχὴν." Tom Ashe. "Pray, doctor, when *a cat takes a cane* what does she design to do with it?" Dilly Ashe. "Well—a— But if puss were tied to a post, how would she be useful in a library?" Dr. Molyneux. "Why, to scratch those that came to steal the books." Dilly Ashe. "What, and' be tied to a post; no, no, she would be useful as a cat-a-log." Bishop of Clogher (whispering Doctor Swift). "There's another Catherine, to make up my set. Mrs. Catherine Logg, Kattylog."

The ladies'
club.
But more than enough of what we may hardly call exquisite fooling.* The bishop's whisper to Swift takes us back to the club of Walls and Stoyte, of which Mrs. Catherine was a member; and an unpublished letter of Swift's to Walls, a few months later, not only brings back the bishop's pun, but will fitly finish the sketch of the punning circle, by again showing Swift at his best and worst in Swift to
Walls (MS.)
22d Jan.,
1707-'08. that form of facetiousness. "I have received your three letters, though I have not had the manners to answer any of them sooner. By manners we here mean leisure, but you Irish folks must have things explained to you.... I am glad the punning trade goes on. Sir Andrew Fountaine has been at his country-house this fortnight.... Pray, is your Dorothy, as you call her, any kin to Doctor Thindoll† (you know h is no letter).... She should have

---

* One or two specimens of Castilian will be found also in the printed works among letters addressed to Lord Pembroke. One of them contains "The Dying Speech of Tom Ashe," which Mr. Deane Swift, who first published

it, says was given by Sir Andrew Fountaine to Doctor Monsey, from whom he received it. — *Miscell.* (1765), ii., 380.

† Swift was at this time writing his *Notes on Tindal.*

call'd it Mrs. Catherine Logg, not Katty Log: that leaves 1706-1708.
Æt. 39-41. nothing to guess.... Tell her a pun of mine. I saw a fellow about a week ago hawking in the Court of Requests Puns for the
club. with a parrot upon his fist to sell. Yesterday I met him again, and said to him, ' How now, friend, I see that parrot sticks upon your hand still ?'*—When you had done with the Dean's books, I believe you were very glad of your liber-ty. Your cat-alogue puts me in mind of another pun I made t'other day. A gentleman was mightily afraid of a cat: I told him it was a sign he was pus-illanimous. And, Lady Berkeley talking to her cat, my lord said she Punning at
Lord Berke-
ley's. was very impertinent; but I defended her, and said I thought her ladyship spoke very much to the poor-pus.— Do you call Dorothy's puns a spurious race because they turn your stomach ? If you do not like them, let the race be to the Swift, and I am content to father them all, as you direct me.—Tell her I thought she had been a New-man,† but I find she is the old woman still.... I give no service to her because I write this to you both."‡ Another unpublished letter of some months' later date winds up with humble service to his "punning spouse. The Dean Swift to
Walls,
1707-'8. of St. Patrick's repeats strange ones after her and the other ladies. *They* wash their hands of it, but how clean I can not tell. Let them look to that."

Some view of Esther Johnson among these friends will Esther
Johnson. complete, for the present, the Irish scenes. How she fared among them in Swift's absence, and what her general ways of life and recreation were, will tell us also, with more or less vividness, his ordinary relations to her, and what remains to be said of his manner of existence in Ireland during the years I am describing, when troubles spared

---

* The probable doubt and puzzlement of the parrot-seller may hereafter pair off with the effect of Swift's famous question when he met a countryman carrying a hare, and struck him dumb with inability to reply by asking him, " Is that your own hare or a wig ?"

† Mrs. Walls's maiden name was Newman.

‡ From the original *penes me.* "London, 22d of January, 1707-'8. For the Reverend Mr. Walls at his house in Cavan Street, Dublin, Ireland."

him, and his grave employments left him leisure. The authority will be his own. It will be that wonderful Journal already often quoted, that unrivaled picture of the time, in which he set down day by day the incidents of three momentous years; which received every hope, fear, or fancy in its undress as it rose to him; which was

Journal written for her. written for one person's private pleasure, and has had indestructible attractiveness for every one since; which has no parallel in literature for the historic importance of the men and the events that move along its pages, or the homely vividness of the language that describes them; and of which the loves and hates, the joys and griefs, the expectations and disappointments, the great and little in closest neighborhood, the alternating tenderness and bitterness, and, above all, the sense and nonsense in marvelous mixture and profusion, remain a perfect microcosm of human life. Charles Fox had a theory that Swift must have been a good-natured man, for an ill-natured one never could have written so much designed absurdity as he did; but no one would have made this a question who was well acquainted with his private life. What is over and over

Swift by nature cheerful. again remarked by himself was undoubtedly true, that he had a spirit naturally cheerful, and that spleen was a disease he was not born to.

30th June, 1711. What shall be our first picture? "Go to bed and sleep, sirrahs, that you may rise to-morrow, and walk to Donnybrook, and lose your money with Stoyte and the Dean; do so, dear little rogues, and drink Pdfr's health. O, pray, do not you drink Pdfr's health sometimes with your Deans, and your Stoytes, and your Walls, and your Manleys, and your everybodies, pray now? I drink MD's to myself a hundred thousand times." A little later in the same let-

Esther's habits and ways. ter come additional touches. "So, go to your Dean's, and roast his oranges, and lose your money; do so, you saucy slut. Ppt, you lost three shillings and fourpence the other night at Stoyte's, yes, you did, and Pdfr stood in a corner, and saw you all the while, and then stole away." When he is not watching from a corner, he may himself be tak-

ing part in the game. "An insipid sort of day; I hope 1706–1708. Æt. 39–41.
MD had a better with the Dean, the Bishop, or Mrs. Walls.
Why, the reason you lost four and eightpence last night Card-playing.
but one at Manley's was because you played bad games.
I took notice of six that you had ten to one against you.
Would any but a mad lady go out twice upon manilio,
basto, and two small diamonds? Then, in that game of
spades, you blundered when you had ten ace. I never Bad play: 5th October, 1710.
saw the like of you. And now you are in a huff because
I tell you this. Well, here is two and eightpence half-
penny toward your loss." Or follow, on another occasion,
when they have gone with Walls to the Dean's, and he
has warned her not to play small games when she is losing. "You will be ruined by manilio, basto, the queen,
and two small trumps in red. I confess it is a good hand Mistakes at ombre.
against the player; but then there are spadilio, punto, the
king, strong trumps against you, which, with one trump
more, are three tricks ten ace. For, suppose you play
your manilio—"

And what does her friend and duenna do all the time?
"Poor Dingley fretted to see Ppt lose that four and
elevenpence t'other night." Dingley is always at hand
for a background to set off the picture. "How does Ppt
look, Madam Dingley? Pretty well? a handsome young Duenna Dingley.
woman still? Will she pass in a crowd? Will she make
a figure in a country church?" Answering, sympathiz-
ing, helping, Dingley is the resource in difficulties. "Can
Dingley play at ombre yet? Enough to hode the cards "Hode" for "hold."
while Ppt steps into next room?" If Ppt can not write,
she dictates to Dingley; if too ill to read, Dingley reads
to her; for "she is a naughty healthy girl, and may drudge
for both." They are gone to Wexford together to drink
the waters, and poor Ppt is fretting at the place, the company, the diversions, the victuals, the wants, the vexations;
but the active Dingley is sending all over the town for a House cares.
little parsley to a boiled chicken, "and it is not to be had,
the butter is stark naught, except an old Englishwoman's,
and it is such a favor to get a pound from her now and

1706–1708.
Æt. 39–41.

then." Or suppose them at dinner at home, with their loin of mutton and half a pint of wine, and the mutton underdone, and "poor Ppt can not eat, poor dear rogue;" well, then, "Dingley is so vexed: but we'll dine at Stoyte's to-morrow."

Winter morning.

Or take Mrs. Johnson earlier than at dinner or cards. On a winter morning with a visitor, for example. "Starving, starving, uth, uth, uth, uth, uth. Don't you remember I used to come into your chamber and turn Ppt out of her chair, and rake up the fire on a cold morning, and cry uth, uth, uth." Or suppose it to be a Sunday morning.

Sunday morning.

"Ppt will be peeping out of her room at Mrs. de Caudre's" (her lodgings) "down upon the folks as they come from church. And there comes Mrs. Proby, and that's my lady Southwell, and there's my lady Betty Rochfort."* Or yet

Every-day pictures.

earlier on a week day. "Ppt is just now showing a white leg, and putting it into the slipper. 'Present my service to her, and tell her I am engaged to the Dean, and desire she will come too; or, Dingley, can't you write a note?' That is Ppt's morning dialogue, no, morning speech I mean. Morrow, sirrahs, and let me rise as well as you; but I promise you Walls can't dine with the Dean to-day, for she is to be at Mrs. Proby's just after dinner, and to go with Gracy Spencer to the shops to buy a yard of muslin, and a silver lace for an under-petticoat." A couple of days before this we are shown her walking in Dublin streets; it having come into his head to remind her, in the same letter, that from the very time she first went to Ireland he had been always plying her to *walk and read*.

A November walk.

"I wish Ppt walked half as much as Pdfr. If I was with you, I'd make you walk; I would walk behind or before you, and you should have masks on, and be tucked up like any thing. And Ppt is naturally a stout walker, and carries herself firm; methinks I see her strut, and step clever

---

* Journal of the 22d January and 25th March, 1711. Explanation will hereafter be given of the Ppts, MD's, and Pdfrs, which appear in Swift's note-books as early as 1702, and were afterward used in his journals. See *post*, book vi. (Appendix), § ii.

over a kennel. And Dingley would do well enough if her 1706-1708.
Æt. 39-41.
petticoats were pinned up; but she is so embroiled and so
fearful; and Ppt scolds, and Dingley stumbles, and is so
daggled. Have you got the whalebone petticoats among *The hoop.*
you yet? I hate them. A woman here may hide a moderate gallant under them. Pshaw! what's all this I'm saying? Methinks I am talking to Ppt face to face."* Is
he not audibly talking still, and do not we see again, vividly as himself, what had passed before his eyes so often?

There is a ride in June, too, as fresh as the November *A ride in*
walk, and claiming a place beside it. She had told him at *June.*
the time that she was riding every day, and it interrupted
her writing somewhat; on which his comment is that if
she "rid" every day for a twelvemonth she would be still
better and better. "O Lord, how hasty we are! Ppt can't
stay writing and writing; she must write and go a cock-
horse, pray, now. Well, but the horses are not come to *Going out.*
the door; the fellow can't find the bridle; your stirrup is
broken; where did you put the whips, Dingley? Marg'et,†
where have you laid Mrs. Johnson's riband to tie about
her? 'Reach me my mask.' 'Sup up this before you
go.' So, so, a gallop, a gallop. 'Sit fast, sirrah, and don't
ride hard upon the stones.' Well, now Ppt is gone, tell
me, Dingley, is she a good girl? and what news is that you
are to tell me?" She gives him all the news, and in due
time Esther returns. "O, Madam Ppt, welcome home! *Coming*
Was it pleasant riding? did your horse stumble? how often *home.*
did the man light to settle your stirrup? ride nine miles!
'faith you have galloped indeed!"... "Ah, that riding to
Laracor gives me short sighs as well as you. All the days
I have passed here have been dirt to those."‡ More than
once had he told her that his journeys to Laracor did him
more good than all the ministries for twenty years. Not
that he was unhappy among his great friends, but that

---

* Journal of 12th, 4th, and 10th of November, 1711.

† Mrs. Marg'et (Margaret) was Mrs. Johnson's maid.

‡ Journal, 30th of June, 1711; and same of the 15th of November, 1711.

1706–1708.
Æt. 39–41.

Common
interests
and ways.

China and
books.

Keeping
Lent.

Punning.

things were tasteless to him for not being where he would be. No such cooler of making court as the want of health; and in England he had not the opportunities he had in Ireland of preserving his health by riding, which now she so wisely did. Thus are his own ways shown by hers, and illustrations borrowed from his journal serve for both.

When he lays injunction on her that she is to get somebody to come and play shuttlecock if she can not walk or ride, he tells her he hopes soon himself to join her in the game. He rebukes her for being too fond of china; but admits that he once took a fancy of resolving to go mad for it himself, and confesses to an itching of his fingers at a book-stall just as hers do in a china-shop. When he wishes her a happy new year on the 25th of March, the then statutory beginning of the year, he tells her that now she must leave off cards and put out her fire, it being his intention, on the 1st of April, cold or not cold, to put out his. The same letter that he hopes will find her peaceably in Pdfr's lodging, or riding little Johnson at Trim, intimates his own resolve to turn her out at Christmas, when he shall either have done his business, or found it not to be done. Having occasion to remind her that he had passed his last Michaelmas at Laracor, with this is coupled an express intention to eat his next Michaelmas goose in his goose's lodgings. When he wishes her to have a merry Lent, she may infer that he does not mean himself to pass a gloomy one; for he adds that he hates different diets, and furmity and butter, and herb porridge, and sour, devout faces of people who only put on religion for seven weeks. When he tells her that he had made a "good" pun to the lord keeper* which Prior swore was the worst he had ever heard, he adds the characteristic admission that he said he thought so too, but at the same time thought it was most like one of Ppt's that ever *he* heard. He relates to her his practice, at the most luxurious tables, of

---

* This was his remark on seeing spread between Lord Harcourt and Prior a doily napkin fringed at each end, that he was glad to see there was such a *fringeship* between them.— *Journal*, 21st *April*, 1711.

hardly ever eating above one thing, and the plainest ordinary meat, because he loves it best and believes it whole-
somest; but it is to contrast such simplicity with her love
for rarities. "Yes, you do love them; and I wish you
had all that I ever see where I go."*   To his information
that the caps Dingley made for him are wearing out and
he does not know how to get others, is appended a confession of how strangely he wants what he calls a necessary
woman, and how he finds himself "as helpless as an ele-
phant." Upon her announcement to him that she and
Dingley are going to Wexford, he jokes Dingley about
the carking, caring, and scolding with which she'll set
about the preparation for it; laughs at Ppt for the "millions of businesses" she will have to do before she goes;
and, with his own character running over at every word,
makes whimsical pretense of his entire ignorance as to
all such places in Ireland, which they are to enlighten by
writing a book of their travels. "Pray walk while you
are there. I have a notion there is never a good walk in
Ireland. Do you find all places without trees? Pray
observe the inhabitants about Wexford: they are old
English: see what they have particular in their manner,
names, and language. Magpies have been always there,
and nowhere else in Ireland, till of late years. They say
the cocks and dogs go to sleep at noon, and so do the people. *Write your travels.*" .... "Don't fall and hurt yourselves, nor overturn the coach. Love one another and be
good girls; and drink Pdfr's health in water, Madam Ppt,
and in good ale, Madam Dingley."†
    The usual touching tenderness winds up that letter,‡

---

* Later he reminds her how, during former days in Ireland, "Ppt used to maunder" when he came from a great dinner, and Dingley had provided for her that day "but a bit of mutton. I can not," he adds, "endure above one dish, nor ever could since I was a boy and loved stuffing."—*Journal, 12th March,* 1712–'13.

† *Journal,* 9th July, 1711; and the same of 26th June, 1711.

‡ "Farewell, my dearest lives and delights, I love you better than ever, if possible, as hope saved. I do, and ever will. God Almighty bless you ever, and make us happy together; I pray for this every day; and I hope God will hear my poor hearty prayers."

1706–1708.
Æt. 39–41.
Three
wishes.

and there is one expression at the very end which should perhaps be singled out. He declares that he is, as long as Ppt and DD are, WELL; and he sums up all they want in three short rhymes—little wealth, much health, *and a life by stealth.* They were to live in their own way, and the world was not to share their confidences.

II.

WAITING AND WORKING IN LONDON.

1707–1709. Æt. 40–42.

1707–1709.
Æt. 40–42.
Pembroke's
recall.

LORD PEMBROKE was recalled to England (leaving the primate and chancellor* as lords justices until he should return) in November, 1707. He had been lord admiral in the last years of William's reign, and the queen thought he might protect her husband, his successor in that office, and now sinking under a mortal disease, from the onslaught against the naval administration in which Somers and Wharton had lately joined with a section of the tories, and which led to the complete ascendency of the whigs at the close of the following year. Swift and Sir Andrew Fountaine left Dublin with the lord lieutenant, but they separated on landing; Pembroke and Fountaine going to Wilton, and Swift to Leicester, on a visit to his mother.

Swift at
Leicester.

From Leicester, on the 6th of December, he wrote to the Archbishop of Dublin; and the letter, in many ways characteristic and here first printed,† shows strongly with what political leanings he was about to take his departure for London.

---

* Freeman was now lord chancellor.

† This and other very interesting letters from Swift to the archbishop, now first made public, were discovered by the Rev. Mr. Reeves (Vicar of Lusk, County Dublin), in the record-room of the see of Armagh; and, by permission of the primate (obtained for me by my dear old friend, Sir James Emerson Tennent, through the then member for Belfast, Mr. Dunbar), careful copies were most kindly taken for me by Mr. Reeves—now, alas! fifteen years ago.

After stating his intention to join Lord Pembroke and 1707–1709.
Æt. 40–42. Sir Andrew in London as soon as the latter should give him notice of their arrival, he speaks of Leicester: "I came round by Derby to this town (where I am now upon a short visit to my mother), and I confess to your grace that, after an absence of less than four years, all things appear new to me. The buildings, the improvements, the dress and countenance of the people, put a new spirit into one, et tacitò circum præcordia ludit. This long war has here occasioned no fall of lands, nor much poverty among any sort of people; only some complain of a little slowness in tenants to pay their rents, more than formerly. There is a universal love of the present government, and few animosities except upon elections, of which I just arrived to see one in this town upon a vacancy by the death of a knight of the shire. They have been polling these three days, and the number of thousands pretty equal on both sides; the parties, as usual, High and Low; and there is not a chamber-maid, prentice, or school-boy in this whole town but what is warmly engaged on one side or t'other. I write this to amuse your grace, and relieve a dull letter of business."

Letter to Arbp. King (MS.).

An election for the county.

The "business" is what had lately passed between him *Business of first-fruits.* and his correspondent in regard to the chances of obtaining for the Irish clergy the same remission of first-fruits and tenths that had been conceded to the English. "I confess I was always of opinion that it required a solicitor of my level, after your grace had done your part in it; and if my endeavors to do service will be thought worth employing, I dare answer for every thing but my own ability. When your grace thinks fit to send me the papers, I would humbly desire your opinion, whether, if occasion should require, I may not with my lord lieutenant's approbation engage the good offices of any great person I may have credit with, and particularly my Lord Somers, and the Earl of Sunderland,* because the former by his great

---

* Sunderland, the Duke of Marlborough's son-in-law, was now secretary of state.

influence, and the other by his employment and alliance, may be very instrumental.   I would not have mentioned this at such a distance if I had not forgot it when your grace discoursed this matter with me last." In a post-script he says he shall be at Sir Andrew Fountaine's house in Leicester Fields before the archbishop's reply, there directed, could reach him.*

Believing both the war and the whigs to be popular, having still reason to think he had influence with the most powerful of that party in and out of office, Sunderland and Somers, and unchanged in his opinions against further meddling with the church, Swift found himself in London in the middle of December, and acknowledged on the 1st of January the archbishop's reply.   The Houses were then up for the recess, but he had ascertained the probability of some attempt at compromise in regard to the naval miscarriages; the Duke of Marlborough, whose brother, Admiral Churchill, was of course deeply involved, having "made lately a speech with warmth unusual to him, and with very great effect.   The admiralty is certainly to continue in the same hand, nor do I yet hear of any change in the privy council."   But what he adds is in decisive sympathy with the line taken by Somers in opposition, whose ground of most effective attack upon the inefficiency of the sea-service had been even less the dishonor

---

* These sentences may also be worth giving: "Others would make excuses for taking up so much of your grace's time to read their impertinence.   But I shall offer none, I, who know that no man's time is worse taken up than your grace's: which I am sorry to say of so great a person, and for whom upon all other accounts I have so high a veneration.   The world may contradict me if they please. But when I see your palace crowded all day to the very gates with suitors, solicitors, petitioners, who come for protection, advice, and charity, and when your time of sleep is misspent in perpetual projects for the good of the church and kingdom, how successful soever they have been, I can not forbear crying out with Horace, 'Perditur hæc inter misero lux.' No doubt, the public would give me little thanks for telling your grace of your faults, by which it receives so much benefit.   But it need not fear: for I know you are incorrigible, and therefore I intend it purely as a reproach, and your grace has no remedy but to take it as it is meant.   And so, in perfect pity to that very little remnant of time which is left in your own disposal, I humbly kiss your grace's hands."

to English arms than the injury and loss to English com- 1707–1709. Æt. 40–42.
merce. "The sea commanders seem mightily pleased as at Whig and tory attacks on the admiralty.
a great point gained, and speak hardly of the merchants,
who are yet louder against them; and those gentlemen
who go into the city return with melancholy accounts
from thence. I shall enter into the merits of either cause
no further than by telling your grace a story which perhaps you may have already heard. After the Scots had
sent their colony to Darien, it was proposed here what
methods should be taken to discourage that project without coming to any avowed or open opposition. The opinion of several merchants was required to that purpose.
Among the rest, Haistwell advised to send over to them Unpopulari-ty of "my lords."
the lords of the admiralty; and if that would not ruin
them, nothing could! Such a liberty of speech people are
apt to take when they are angry." Other indications appear also in the letter of its having probably been written
after personal communication with Somers, but there is no
avoidance of other matters in which their opinions widely
diverged.

Swift had led the opposition in the Dublin convocation Irish discon-tent with Test Act.
to a revival, in the last sittings of the Irish parliament, of
agitation for repeal of the Test Act; and though Lord
Pembroke's government, acting on direction from Lord
Sunderland, had thrown out a hint of some such measure,
a majority of four to one in the debate that ensued discouraged the introduction of any bill. But Swift has now
to tell the archbishop, in connection with the business of
the first-fruits (as to which he still waited to receive promised formal instructions, and appears already to have felt
the intermediate order referring him at all stages to Lord
Pembroke as a bar to his chances of success), that he had
heard it whispered by some who were "fonder of political
refinements" than himself, that "a new difficulty may
arise in this matter; that it must perhaps be purchased by
a compliance with what was undertaken and endeavored
in Ireland last sessions; which I confess I can not bring
myself yet to believe, nor do I care to think or reason

1707-1709.
ÆT. 40-42.

Profiting by
an experi-
ence.

upon it." This was undoubtedly the ground subsequently taken both by Godolphin and Somers, to the former of
whom was attributed, with what truth will shortly appear,
the saying that as nothing had been gained from the English clergy "after" the concession, it might be well to get
something from the Irish clergy "before" any like concession to them; but Swift, though with a powerful motive
at the moment for not placing himself in a direct antago-
nism to Somers, declined to entertain it. He follows up
some remark of the archbishop's on the difficulty that attended every effort to help the clergy with a somewhat

Swift on the
Irish clergy.

notable comment of his own: "I should be surprised at
what your grace tells me of the clergy if I were not sensible how extremely difficult it is to deal with any body of
men who seldom understand their true interest, or are able
to distinguish their enemies from their friends. Your
grace's observation is so great a truth, that there is hardly
a clergyman in Ireland whose revenue is not reckoned in
the world at least double what he finds it, besides the accidents to which the remainder is subject. For my own
part, I hope to live to see your grace very ill used; that
is, in other words, I wish this affair may succeed, and then
you will be sure to be rewarded with a good conscience
and detraction."*

Other personal allusions were in the same vein of cor-
diality. The archbishop had taxed his correspondent with
injustice in denying him all talent for trifling. "I observe your grace's artifice," says Swift, with pleasant confession of his own weakness that way, "to bespeak my

"Merit of
trifling."

good opinion by pretending to the merit of Trifling; but
I, who am a strict examiner and a very good judge, shall
not be so ready to allow your pretensions: without some
better title than I ever yet knew or heard you were able
to set up. And, if this trifling you boast of were strictly
inquired into, it would amount to little more than talking

---

* A personal allusion not now ex-
plainable lurks under what follows:
"And then likewise those Woodcocks
may have a better reason for hiding
their heads. They may hide them
for shame."

with a friend an hour in a week, or riding to Clontarf on
a fair day. Would Socrates allow this, who at fourscore
was caught whistling and dancing by himself; or Augus-
tus, who used to play at hucklebone with a parcel of boys?
Your grace must give me better proof before I shall admit your plea." Hardly less interesting in a personal
sense are the opening and closing words of the letter. In
the former Swift relates the incident of treasonable correspondence discovered in Harley's office, which, though
Harley was cleared of complicity, loosened the last hold
for their places that he and St. John possessed; and in
the other he mentions the great storm of 1703. "The
storm your grace mentions did not reach England; and I
remember about the same time four years ago I came just
to have my share of a much greater in this town, when
Ireland received no damage. I am glad your grace says
nothing of any people killed or hurt." By the storm that
Swift shared, whole fleets were cast away and cities deso-
lated; high and low were swept down alike; and a bishop
and his wife were buried under the ruins of their episcopal palace. But we are not all "alone" either unhappy
or happy. The success of a simile suggested by that awful tempest was Addison's first step upward in his life
of fortune.

While yet writing his letter to the archbishop, Swift
might have thought that at last his own foot was on the
ladder. A vacancy had fallen in the see of Waterford;
Lord Somers, though not now a minister, but indeed rather strongly opposing the court, had promised to do what
he could to recommend his claim for it; and, probably
through Lord Sunderland or other influence from the
Somers party in the government (though Swift had as yet
seen only the ex-minister), his pretensions had been placed
strongly before the queen and Archbishop Tenison. But
the cup, to appearance so near his lip, was promptly dashed
away, and in the middle of January he knew that Doctor
Thomas Milles, a person very distasteful to him, was the
new bishop. Walls had written to him from Dublin at

1707–1709.
Æt. 40–42.

Famous
triflers.

The great
storm of
1703.

Swift named
for a bishop-
ric: Jan.,
1707–'8.

His account
to Walls
(MS.).

the occurrence of the vacancy, and on the 22d Swift replied: "I thank you heartily for the care, and kindness,
and good intentions of your intelligence, and I once had a
glimpse that things would have gone otherwise. But now
I must retire to my morals, and pretend to be wholly without ambition, and to resign with patience. You know by
this time who is the happy man; a very worthy person,
and I doubt not but the whole kingdom will be pleased
with the choice. He will prove an ornament to the order, and a public blessing to the church and nation.
And after this if you will not allow me to be a good
courtier, I will pretend to it no more. But let us talk
no further on this subject. I am stomach-sick of it already."* He goes back to it, nevertheless, with an allusion pointing at Lord Pembroke's great present influence
with the queen, and that this, if set in motion through
their common friend, might have given the affair another
turn: "Sir Andrew Fountaine has been at his country
house this fortnight. And he has neither influence nor
effluence from thence to London, else perhaps things would
not have gone as they did." The quiet bitterness that
closes the letter may be forgiven him: "Pray send me an
account of some smaller vacancy than a bishoprick in the
government's gift." To Archbishop King, a fortnight
later, he wrote with a dignified reserve: "Your grace
knows long before this that Dr. Milles is Bishop of Waterford. The court and Archbishop of Canterbury were
strongly engaged† for another person not much suspected
in Ireland; any more than the choice already made was, as
I believe, either here or there." Hitherto, it has been matter of guess-work only that such a disappointment had so
early befallen Swift, and that, five years before the hopes
which the tories had raised so much higher were also dashed
to the ground, he had been so near promotion by the whigs;
but here the fact is established in place of mere surmise,

The man
who got it.

Swift to the
archbishop.

Proof of
what was
only sur-
mised.

---

* A portion of this letter, descriptive of the punning at Lord Berkeley's,
has been printed *ante*, 210.

† In other words, interceded with,
or pressed.

and a passage in a letter of a year's later date fixes the 1707-1709. part taken by Lord Somers, to whose friend and then fel- Æt. 40-42. low-minister, Lord Halifax, it is recalled by Swift.* The minister had written to him shortly before to assure him of continued efforts in his behalf,† and Swift replied by asking him to use his credit, that, "as my Lord Somers thought of me last year for the bishopric of Waterford, so my lord president may now think of me for that of Cork, if the incumbent dies of the fever he is now under." The strength of Swift's case was to himself the misery of it also. The leader of the whigs who thought of him for a bishopric was at the time out of office, and especially hateful to the queen ; but when she had been so far won back to him as to admit that he at least had never deceived her, Dartmouth's and the same leader, with all the extreme whig party, had note on Burnet. obtained for a time uncontrolled power, there is no evidence of a renewal to Swift of any thing but promises. Through every disappointment he was still to have courage, till, as Halifax told him, his "worth would be placed in that light where it ought to shine." He was not to be raised too high by encouragement, or sunk too low by denial. He was to be left as he was found, "a man of hopes, a man of levees ;"‡ the doubt was to remain whether the

---

* This is one of two interesting letters, dated respectively the 13th of June and 13th of November, 1709, from Swift to Lord Halifax, existing among the MSS. of the British Museum ; of which careful copies were taken for me several years ago by my friend Mr. John Kemble, then engaged on his volume of Hanover state-papers ; and which subsequently were printed (not very correctly, and the first with the erroneous date of the 13th of January) in Mr. Cunningham's edition of Johnson's *Lives of the Poets.*

† Lord Halifax to Swift, London, 6th October, 1709 ; also among the MSS. of the British Museum.

‡ This expression is from one of his letters to Ambrose Philips not in Letters to the printed correspondence (some of Philips. the later, *penes me,* will now first be printed), which seem to me the perfection, the *decus et deliciæ,* of easy, natural, unstudied letter-writing ; where every sentence, simple as it appears, has some point of humor, or one of those unexpected turns of good-natured raillery that are the delight of witty conversation. Ambrose had been extremely impatient at not getting some piece of preferment, and, says Swift to him, "Your saying that you know nothing of your affair more than when you left us puts me in mind of a passage in *Don Quixote,*

1707-1709.
Æt. 40-42. lord president would renew what Lord Somers had set on foot; and his own description was to lose nothing of its applicability. "*In suspense* I was all this year in England."

22d Jan.,
1707-'8.
"At Cran-
ford from
22d to 27th." It is nevertheless the date of not a few of the best of his minor writings, some account of which may delay for a while what remains of this part of his story. On the day he wrote to Walls of his punning with the Berkeleys, his note-books mention his having gone with that family to Cranford for five days;* and there will be nothing strained in supposing such kind of talk to have ensued with these old friends, upon the recent disappointment, and some suspected charge of irreverence or infidelity in connection with it, as determined him to write his *Argu-*
Probable
origin of two
famous
tracts. *ment to prove the Inconvenience of Abolishing Christian-ity*, and his *Project for the Advancement of Religion and the Reformation of Manners.* They were published anonymously, but the authorship was not concealed from any to whom it concerned the writer to be known; and in his published correspondence there is a brief note of Lord Berkeley's, hitherto misdated,* in which, pressing Swift to come as much as possible to Cranford, he earnestly entreats him, if he has not done it already, not to fail of having his book-seller "enable the Archbishop of York to

---

where Sancho, upon his master's first adventure, comes and asks him for the island he had promised, and which he must certainly have won in that terrible combat. To which the knight replied in these memorable words: 'Look ye, Sancho, all adventures are not adventures of islands, but many of them of dry blows, and hunger, and hard lodging; however, take courage, for one day or other, all of a sudden, before you know where you are, an island will fall into my hands as fit for you as a ring for the finger.' In the mean time your adventures are likely to pass with less

danger and with less hunger, so that you need less patience to stay till midwife Time will please to deliver this commission from the womb of Fate." Swift had great experience in applying to himself those lessons of patience which he here recommends to Ambrose.

* The date put to it is "Cranford, Friday night, 1705," an error for 1708. I found the original among the British Museum MSS. addressed "For Dr. Swift at his lodgings in the Haymarket," and indorsed by himself "Old E. of Berkeley about 1706-'7."

give a book to the queen,"* being entirely of opinion that
her reading of the *Project* for the increase of morality and
piety might be of very great use to that end. Assuming
it to be possible that the end might thereby be secured,
morality and piety increased, religion advanced, and manners reformed, the author, to whom indirectly such effects
were attributable, could hardly continue to be kept out in
the cold even by queens and archbishops.

1707-1709.
Æt. 40-42.

Hope to influence the queen.

Both tracts are indeed admirable; and, unwise or vis-
ionary now as are many suggestions in the second, both
inspire unhesitating confidence in the absolute sincerity,
of the writer. Irony does not always so recommend itself; but its effect in the *Argument* is quite as impressive
as the plain speaking in the *Project*, both having also that
indefinable subtlety of style which conveys, not the writer's knowledge of the subject only, but his power and superiority over it. The *Argument* begins by admitting
that the general humor and disposition of the world appear to be for abolishing Christianity, and by nevertheless
declaring that even if the attorney-general were to come
down upon him with an *ex officio*, he must still confess
that he does not yet see the absolute necessity of extirpa-
ting the Christian religion. But in the second paragraph
a possible misapprehension is cleared away. He is not
going to be so weak as to stand up in the defense of real
Christianity, such as used, in primitive times, to have positive influence on men's actions as well as their beliefs.
That, indeed, would be a wild project; and he begged every candid reader to understand his argument, therefore,
as no more than a defense of nominal Christianity; the
other having been, by general consent, for some time wholly laid aside, as quite inconsistent with existing schemes of
wealth and power. The ground thus cleared, he sets forth

Swift on the inconvenience of abolishing Christianity.

Real v. nominal religion.

---

* Scott puts a quite wrong color
on this by remarking of the tract that
"it was very favorably received by
the public, and appears to have been
laid before Queen Anne by the Arch-

bishop of York, the very prelate who
had denounced to her private ear the
author of the *Tale of a Tub* as a
divine unworthy of church preferment."

1707–1709.
Æt. 40–42.
Swift on
the incon-
venience of
abolishing
Christianity.
the many inconveniences that would attend the abolition, and one or two of these may be given as examples of the rest. He allows, for instance, that it does seem a most ridiculous custom for a set of men to be suffered, much less hired, to bawl one day in seven against the lawfulness of such modes of pursuing greatness, riches, and pleasure, as are the constant practice of all men alive on the other six; but he points out that more than half the pleasure of enjoyment to most people consists in the thing enjoyed being a thing forbidden. He is not blind to the advantage of turning out of their pulpits as many as ten thousand parsons, and making them useful in the fleet and armies, because he sees that so great a number of able (bodied) divines would be a recruit worth having; but might there not be some disadvantage in thus leaving tracts of country "like what we call parishes" without a solitary soul in them able to read and write? With some reason it had been urged that the revenues of those ten thousand parsons would suffice to maintain, as ornaments to the court and town, at least a couple of hundred young gentlemen of wit, pleasure, and freethinking, enemies to priestcraft, narrow principles, pedantry, and prejudices; but, after the present refined way of living, was it not to be feared that, upon even all the incomes of the clergy, not half the number of young gentlemen could be accommodated? A good

deal was expected from making the churches themselves of more use by turning them into theatres and the like, but he would fain know how it could be pretended that they were already misapplied? Where were more appointments of gallantry? Where more care to appear with greater advantage of dress? Where more meetings for business? Where more bargains driven of all sorts? And where so many conveniences or incitements to sleep? But supposing the churches to go, and the parsons, and that Christianity itself were got out entirely of the way, had it been considered what would become of the freethinkers, the strong reasoners, the men of profound learning? How would they ever be able to shine or distin-

guish themselves on any other subject? Who would ever 1707-1709.
Æt. 40-42. have suspected A for a wit, or B for a philosopher, or C Argument against abolishing Christianity. for a sage, but for their invectives and raillery against religion? For who on earth could have any doubt that a hundred such pens employed in her service would immediately have sunk into silence and oblivion? Nor is the exposition of unavoidable inconvenience more clear than the warning against expected good effects; one quite certain conviction at which he arrives being, that to abolish Christianity will be the very readiest way to bring in Popery. Reserving to the last the greatly prized and hoped-for advantages to trade, he offers ground, on the other hand, for "very much" apprehending that, in six months after the passing of the act for the extirpation of the Gospel, Bank and East India stock, instead of rising, might fall at least one per cent.; "and since that is fifty times more than ever the wisdom of our age thought fit to venture for the preservation of Christianity, there is no reason we should be at so great a loss merely for the sake of destroying it." The reader would be a very superficial person whom this light banter did not move to some consideration of the grave purpose underneath it, weighting the writer's wit with a message of the last importance, that it would, on the whole, be best for you, not only to retain, but to try and improve, your Christianity.

Not inferior in design or spirit is the *Project for the* Project for advancing religion and reforming manners. *Advancement of Religion and the Reformation of Manners*, which, though it proposed some remedies not very practicable, for those evils of the time of which it gives a striking picture, suggests others that have not long been effected, and some that still remain to be done. This was the treatise which Steele said every man in the town had Steele's opinion of it. read and none had disapproved; and the whole air of which, as to its language, sentiments, and reasonings, gave the impression of being written by one who had seen the world enough to undervalue it with good-breeding, whose virtue sat easy about him, and to whom vice was thoroughly contemptible. Some one had remarked of it in his company (Addison, there is little doubt) that the author wrote much like a gentleman, and went to heaven with a very good mien.

Its principal suggestion, that religion and morality should be made a necessary condition to all appointments, and that the continued practice of both should be insured by reports of inspectors making annual circuits of the kingdom, may be dismissed with Swift's own remark upon it that "this might increase hypocrisy among us, and I readily believe it would;" to which his only opposing set-off that "it is often with religion as it is with love, which by much dissembling at last grows real," must be rejected as inadequate. But his accompanying observation is still full of wise meaning, that characters of marked and notorious impiety in high life ought not to receive the countenance ordinarily extended to them; that care should be taken as far as possible to exclude such from the magistracy; and that some check should be found for the indifference with which, in the common callings of life, the practice of fraud was too much regarded. "The vintner
who, by mixing poison with his wines, destroys more lives than any one disease in the bill of mortality; the lawyer, who persuades you to a purchase which he knows is mortgaged for more than the worth; the banker who takes your fortune to dispose of when he has resolved to break the following day; do surely deserve the gallows much better than the wretch who is carried thither for stealing a horse." In like manner he singles out the "fraud and cozenage of trading men and shop-keepers;" adverts again and again to that insatiable gulf of injustice and oppression, the law;" condemns the "corrupt management of men in office," and the "detestable abuses" of parliamentary elections; denounces the open traffic for civil and military employments "without the least regard to merit or qualification;" and, in defense of the general suggestions and reasoning of his project, offers the pregnant remark that of nine offices in ten that are ill executed, the defect is not in capacity or understanding, but in common hon-

esty. As a correction to the immoralities of the stage, he
proposes a censorship to be exercised by "men of wit,
learning, and virtue;" whereby the theatre might become
"a very innocent and useful diversion, instead of being a
scandal and reproach." He ventures to say, even, that
among other public regulations "it would be very convenient to prevent the excess of drinking;" and he called attention to a scurvy custom, the parent of the former vice,
which had grown up among "the lads" at the universities, of taking tobacco in excess. In addition to his pub-
lic-house bill, Swift has even his permissive bill, for, besides that, "all taverns and ale-houses should be obliged to
dismiss their company by twelve at night," and that wom-
en should be altogether excluded from them, he would
have, upon the severest penalties, only a proportioned
quantity served to every company, so that the drunken or
disorderly should not have more drink : but it is needless
to add that he had small success with either suggestion.
What is said of his own calling is full of character; the
purport of it being that the clergy, instead of using all
honest arts to make themselves acceptable to the laity,
shut themselves up in special clubs and coffee-houses, con-
sorted only with their own class, accepted the level at
which they were put, nor ever cared to rise above it by
appearing in all companies as other gentlemen, and taking
that agreeable part in the conversation of the world for
which a learned education gave them great advantage, if
they would but improve and apply it. "No man values
the best medicine if administered by a physician whose
person he hates or despises." The same reasoning led
him to doubt if the gown and cassock should be held on
all occasions indispensable, and if the clergy should be
"the only set of men among us who constantly wear a
distinct habit from others. In my opinion," Swift continues, "it were infinitely better if all the clergy, except
the bishops, were permitted to appear like other men of
the graver sort, unless at those seasons when they are doing the business of their function." His final recommen-

1707–1709.
Æt. 40–42.

Public-
house and
stage im-
moralities.

Advice to
clergymen.

dation was, that church accommodation should be provided in a somewhat fairer proportion to the numbers of the people; regarding the want of it as a shame to the country and a scandal to Christianity. In many large towns of the kingdom, and particularly in London, so prodigious had been the increase of houses and inhabitants, and so little care taken for the building of churches, he pointed out that there were five parts in six of the people with no means of attending divine service; and there were cases of a single minister, with one or two sorry curates, having the care "sometimes of above twenty thousand souls." As he penned this passage, Swift must have had strange thoughts of his own Irish congregation of half a score; nor was the subject overlooked by him in his days of power. Fifty new churches were built in London during the last ministry of Anne.

The *Project* was inscribed to Lady Berkeley in what Scott justly calls an elegant yet manly and independent style of eulogy, which simply desires the good opinion of a person of her " piety, truth, good sense, and good nature, affability, and charity," and has nothing in it more high-flown than a mention of her "two incomparable daughters." She had no quality more agreeable to Swift than her liking for lively talk; while her very enjoyment of this, on the other hand, and of his occasional jesting even at her own expense, led her to airs of gravity about the books she might be reading, which made it easy to impose on her in that respect with any thing sufficiently solemn and decorous. He would sometimes read aloud to her; and she would ask him to select, not trivial things, but a thoroughly good book like the Honorable Mr. Boyle's *Meditations*, which accordingly he would do; until one day, quite tired of its commonplaces, he substituted for one of its pages a meditation of his own, taking a broomstick for his subject, and, reading it out to her with steady gravity, obtained for it her highest commendation. He traced the stick from its flourishing state in the forest, through a gradation of diversities of fortune so resem-

bling human accidents, that at last he exclaims, "Surely 1707-1709.
Man is a Broomstick!" He shows him strong and lusty, Æt. 40-42.
wearing on his head the branches proper to a reasoning
vegetable, until the axe of intemperance lops them off,
whereupon he flies to art, valuing himself on an unnatural
bundle of hairs covered with powder that never grew on
him, and drawing down on himself contempt and ridicule
for his vanity. "Partial judges that we are of our own
excellence and other men's defaults!" The Broomstick
had a great run among the wits, though Swift more than
once refused to assist in its circulation. "Though you
won't send me your Broomstick," wrote Anthony Henley, "I'll send you as good a reflection on death as even
Adrian's himself, though the fellow was but an old farmer
of mine that made it."*

He was a man of fortune, son of Sir Robert, at Henley of the Grange.
whose house of the Grange in Hampshire, famous also in
our own day for hospitable association with letters and
the wits, the wits in those old days used to meet. Indeed,
he had himself some rank with the fraternity. He wrote
humorous papers for Steele, stood by the whigs *in extremis*,
and received from Garth the dedication of the *Dispensary*.
"I han't the honor to know Colonel Hunter," he wrote to
Swift from the Grange in the autumn of this year, "but I
never saw his name in so good company as you have ·put
him in, Lord Halifax, Mr. Addison, Mr. Congreve, and the
Gazetteer." Hunter, for whom Swift had a special re- Colonel Hunter.
gard, deserved this company. He was among the most
scholarly and entertaining of his correspondents; some of
Swift's own best letters were written to this friend; and

---

* Swift afterward used it in his
*Thoughts on Various Subjects, Moral
and Diverting.* The old farmer, dying
of asthma, replied to the inquiries of
those about him, "Well, if I could but
get this same breath out of my body,
I'd take care, by ——, how I let it
come in again!" This, Henley adds,
"if it were put in fine Latin, I fancy
would make as good a sermo as any
I have met with." Steele put it into
the *Tatler*, but did not improve it by
making the poor man's disorder "a
colic." Nor has Scott, with the other
editors of Swift, improved Henley's
remark by printing "sound" instead
of "sermo." The old dy-
ing farmer.

the judgment he had formed of him may be taken from the fact that, when all the world were giving to himself the authorship of Shaftesbury's (anonymously printed) *Letter on Enthusiasm,** Swift believed Hunter to have written it. When Addison introduced them, Hunter was designed for, and had accepted, the governorship of Virginia under Lord Orkney; but ultimately that of New York and New Jersey was substituted for it, and he went out later to Jamaica as captain-general. "Sometimes,"

wrote Swift to him at the close of 1708, "Mr. Addison and I steal to a pint of bad wine, and wish for no third person but you; who, if you were with us, would never be satisfied without three more." Perhaps the so-desired three might be Halifax, Congreve, and Steele.

Certainly they were never oftener together than in the spring and summer of this year. Swift's note-book contains entries of dinners to or with them all, and of frequent coaches to the houses of Halifax in New Palace Yard or at Hampton Court. We trace them dining at the "George," with Addison for host, at the "Fountain" with Steele, and at the "St. James's,"· where Wortley Montagu entertains. Nor did they fail to see each other frequently even in such intervals of their not coming together as are mentioned by Swift to Ambrose Philips. "The triumvirate of Addison, Steele, and me, come together as seldom as the sun, moon, and earth; but I often

---

* See Correspondence, 12th January, 1708-'9. In a letter to Ambrose Philips, not in the Correspondence, but now before me in his MS., he says (14th September, 1708): "Here has been an *Essay of Enthusiasm* lately published, that has run mightily, and is very well writ. ' All my friends will have me to be the author, sed ego non credulus illis. By the free whiggish thinking I should rather take it to be yours; but mine it is not, for though I am every day writing my speculations in my chamber, they are quite of another sort." To give the *Essay* to Ambrose was only for a laugh at his ultra whiggery; and to this, noticing the fact of his being still left out in the cold, Swift has another allusion: "Lady Betty Germaine is upon all occasions stirring up Lord Dorset to show you some mark of his favor, which I hope may one day be of good effect, or he is good for nothing...... For my part, I think your best course is to try whether the Bishop of Durham will give you a niece and a golden prebend, unless you are so high a whig that your principles, like your mistress, are at Geneva."

see each of them, and each of them me and each other." 1707-1709.
Æt. 40-42.
Just before March,* Swift had launched his joke against
the astrological-almanac-makers; and all the town was
now laughing over the relation of the accomplishment of
the first of Mr. Bickerstaff's predictions. These almanac-
makers were then a wicked nuisance, as they have even
been in days of so-called greater intelligence, and the present chief offender was John Partridge, bred originally a
cobbler. Author of various astrological treatises, and editor of the yearly *Merlinus Liberatus*, he, with the rest of
the villainous tribe, had come to exercise despotic sway
over the vulgar in high as well as low life, not alone in
matters of weather or seasons of blood-letting and physick-
ing, but in all kinds of knavish devices to swindle money
out of the hopes or fears of besotted ignorance. Writing
in the character of a genuine astrologer as opposed to such
charlatans in the divine science, and giving himself a name
which his eye had caught over the sign of a lock-smith's
shop,† Mr. Isaac Bickerstaff professed it to be his aim to
rescue a noble art from the illiterate impostors who set up
to be artists, and who delivered from no greater a height
than their own brains what they pretended to have come
from the planets. [With exquisite gravity he contrasted
their ludicrous methods of observation and prediction, so
loose as equally to suit any age or country or individuals
in the world, with his own careful and precise procedure;
wherein the month and the day of the month were set
down, the individuals named, and the great actions or events
of the forthcoming months particularly related as they

Side notes: Mr. Bicker-staff's pre-dictions: 1708. — Astrologer Partridge. — Joke against him.

---

* "It was toward the conclusion of the year 1707, when an impudent pamphlet crept into the world entitled *Predictions, etc., by Isaac Bickerstaff*," says "John Partridge," in the pamphlet called *Squire Bicker-staff Detected;* but "John Partridge" here meant William Congreve and Thomas Yalden, who made that con-tribution to carry on Swift's jest, of which it was an essential part to pre-tend that the *Predictions* had come out nearly at the same time with the other almanacs for 1708.

† A real Irish name, as it after-ward turned out, and borne in Gold-smith's time by a facile playwright who had a very wretched end.—See my *Life of Goldsmith*, ii., 136.

1707-1709.
Æt. 40-42.

Seriousness
of Swift's
laugh.

were sure to come to pass. He went on to apologize for not being able to offer more than a specimen of what he intended for the future, having employed most part of the previous two years in adjusting and correcting the calculations he had made for some years past; but, by way of challenging something of confidence for his results, he brought forward the testimony of private friends to establish* that in the preceding year he had predicted, in every article except one or two extremely minute, the miscarriage at Toulon and the loss of Admiral Shovel, and had foretold to the very day and hour, with the loss on both sides and the consequences thereof, the Battle of Almanza. His present predictions, which were only a sample, he had forborne to publish until he could make himself master of the several almanacs for 1708; and having found them to be in the usual strain, he entreated the candid reader only to make

Prophecies
of Isaac.

comparison of himself and them. His own prophecies he had begun after the 25th of March, when the sun was entering into Aries, taking that to be properly the beginning of the natural year; and for the present he had not gone farther in his calculations than that busy period when he was entering Libra, the 25th of September. He was rather ashamed of ushering in the more grave part of his undertaking with an announcement of singularly small moment; but, as it came earliest in date, he could not help it. "My first prediction is but a trifle, yet I will mention it, to show how ignorant those sottish pretenders to astrology are in their own concerns. It relates to Partridge, the almanac-maker. I have consulted the star of his nativity by

Death of
Partridge
predicted.

my own rules, and find he will infallibly die upon the 29th of March next, about eleven at night, of a raging fever. Therefore I advise him to consider of it, and settle his affairs in time." After which came, promptly on the dawn of the 30th, "a letter to a person of honor" from a writer who, having been employed in the revenue, had come to

---

* "That is, I gave them papers sealed up to open at such a time, after which they were at liberty to read them; and there they found my predictions."

know something of Partridge, and who related the accom- 1707–1709.
plishment, on the very night of the 29th, of the first of Mr. Æt. 40–42.
Bickerstaff's predictions; detailing all the circumstances Partridge dies accord-
with irresistibly truthful particularity, but showing that ingly:
Mr. Bickerstaff had been mistaken in his calculation *al-*
most four hours. " In the other circumstances he was
exact enough. But whether he has been the cause of
this poor man's death, as well as the predicter, may
be very reasonably disputed. However, it must be confessed the matter is odd enough, whether we should endeavor to account for it by chance or the effect of imagination."

What, of course, Swift calculated on was that Partridge
himself should take up the matter gravely, and he was
not disappointed. Putting forth an almanac for 1709,
the indignant philomath informed his loving countrymen
that Squire Bickerstaff was a sham name assumed by a but will not admit he is
lying, impudent fellow, and that, blessed be God, John dead.
Partridge was still living, and in health, and all were
knaves who reported otherwise. To this Mr. Bickerstaff
lost no time in retorting with a "Vindication" more diverting than either of its precursors, rebuking Mr. Partridge's scurrility as very indecent from one gentleman
to another for differing from him on a point merely spec-
ulative. This point was, as he went on to explain, whether or not Mr. Partridge was alive; and with all brevity,
perspicuity, and calmness, he proceeded to the discussion.
First he pointed out that about a thousand gentlemen,
having bought Mr. Partridge's almanac for the year mere- Swift retorts and proves it.
ly to find what he said against Mr. Bickerstaff, had been
seen and heard lifting up their eyes, and crying out, at
every line they read, " they were sure no man alive ever
writ such damned stuff as this!" But the proof that no
man alive wrote it appeared in his own very language of
denial, that " he is not only now alive, but was also alive
upon that very 29th of March which it was foretold he
should die on;" whereby his opinion was plainly announced that a man *may be* alive now who was not alive

1707–1709.
Æt. 40–42.

twelve months ago. And here lay, in truth, the whole
sophistry of his argument. "He dares not assert he was
alive ever since that 29th of March, but that 'he is now
alive, *and was so on that day.*' I grant the latter; for he
did not die till night, as appears by the printed account of
his death, in a letter to a lord; and whether he be since
Evidence of the fact. revived, I leave the world to judge." The close of the
"Vindication" is a remonstrance with the writer of a letter
to a lord for having taxed him with a mistake of nearly
four hours in his calculations, whereas he shows the mistake to have been under half an hour: and, for a final
word, he remarks it as no objection against Mr. Partridge's
death* that he should continue to write almanacs, this being a common thing, and no one feeling any surprise at
Gadby, Poor Robin, Wing, and Dove continuing their lucubrations yearly, although notoriously all of them were
dead even before the Revolution.

All the wits take part. The jest had by this time diffused itself into so wide a
popularity that all the wits became eager to take part in
it. Rowe, Steele, Addison, and Prior contributed to it in
divers amusing ways; and Congreve described, under Partridge's name, the distresses and reproaches Squire Bickerstaff had exposed him to, insomuch that he could not leave
his door without somebody twitting him for sneaking
about without paying his funeral expenses.† The poor
astrologer himself, meanwhile, was continually advertising
The astrolo-ger at bay. that he was *not* dead; and he actually wrote to the Irish
postmaster Manley, as unconscious still of his real torment-
or as that Manley was Swift's intimate friend, to prevent
the people of Ireland also from being imposed upon by a

---

* To an elegy Swift gave the dignity of verse, and showed, with as delightful humor, with how much light
derived from his original trade Partridge could illuminate his favorite science:

". . . that slow-pac'd sign Boötes,
As 'tis miscall'd, we know not who 'tis;
But Partridge ended all disputes;
He knew his trade, and call'd it *boots.*"

† Addison's friend, Yalden, was said
to have written this paper, but there
seems to be little doubt that Congreve
was joint author, and contributed the
best hits. Yalden succeeded Atterbury in 1713 as minister of Bridewell,
and was under arrest ten years later
on suspicion of being concerned in the
Atterbury plot.

pack of rogues headed by a fellow under a sham name, 1707-1709. Æt. 40-42. whose real name was Pettic, and who was always in a cellar, a garret, or a jail. There was at the same time such accompaniment of real gravity as heightened the comedy by its contrast. The company of stationers applied for an injunction against the continued publication of almanacs by Partridge, as if he were dead in earnest; and Sir Paul Methuen wrote to Swift that the Portuguese Inquisition had condemned to the flames Mr. Bickerstaff's predictions. Steele spoke afterward with no exaggeration when he gave Swift the merit of having rendered Mr. Bickerstaff's name famous through all parts of Europe, and of having raised it, by his inimitable spirit and humor, to as high a pitch of reputation as it could possibly arrive at. Yet Steele Good-natured Steele. had then done much to carry it even higher. He started the *Tatler** while the jest was going on: gave to its lucubrations the name which had become a synonym for mirthful gravity; and closed those charming papers, as he began them, by giving all the praise he could to Swift. He characterized him as a gentleman well known to possess a genius quite unapproachable in its power of surrounding with pleasing ideas occasions altogether barren to the common run of invention; and, with all the generosity of his frank and sweet nature, confessed his personal obligations. "I must acknowledge also that at my first entering upon this work, a certain uncommon way of thinking, and a turn in conversation peculiar to that agreeable gentleman, Swift's "turn" in conversation. rendered his company very advantageous to one whose imagination was to be continually employed upon obvious and common subjects, though at the same time obliged to treat of them in a new and unbeaten method." One

---

* On Tuesday, the 12th of April, Steele published, as the first of the lucubrations of Isaac Bickerstaff, Esquire, the first number of the *Tatler*, which he continued to issue, unintermittedly, every Tuesday, Thursday, and Saturday, until Tuesday, the 2d of January, 1710-'11, when he brought the *Tatler* to a close; and on Thursday, the 1st of March, 1710-'11, he published the first number of the *Spectator*, which, with regular help from Addison, was continued daily, without a single intermission through 555 numbers, up to the 6th of December, 1712.

1707-1709.
Æt. 40-42.

of the secrets of Swift's extraordinary social charm was thus very happily expressed.

He had another advantage of which a word may be said. The portrait of him now painted by Jervas confirms the

Personal appearance.

general statement at the time, that his personal appearance was very attractive. Features regular yet striking, forehead high and temples broad and massive, heavy-lidded blue eyes, to which his dark complexion and bushy black eyebrows gave unusual capacity for sternness as well as

Picture by Jervas.

brilliance, a nose slightly aquiline, mouth resolute with full-closed lips, a handsome dimpled double chin, and over all the face the kind of pride not grown of superciliousness or scorn, but of an easy, confident, calm superiority. Of the dullness which Pope saw sometimes* overshadow the countenance of his friend, of the insolence which Young declares was habitual to it, of the harsh, unrelenting severity which it assumes in Bindon's picture at the

Pope (Spence's Anecdotes).

deanery, there is no trace at present. By one who loved him he was said to have a look of uncommon archness in eyes quite azure as the heavens; and he was himself told

Hester Vanhomrigh (1714).

by one who did not love him less, that he had a look so awful it struck the gazer dumb; but only the first is in Jervas's picture, the years that are to bring the last being still to come. To the date when it was painted belongs also the amusing illustration which Young gave to Spence of his figure and person. Mentioning that Ambrose Philips was a neat dresser and very vain (Pope laughed at him for wearing red stockings), he says that in a company where Philips, Congreve, Swift, and others were, the talk

Gnesees at JuliusCæsar.

turned on Julius Cæsar, and "What sort of a person," said Ambrose, "did they suppose him to be?" To which some one replying that the coins gave the impression of a small, thin-faced man, "Yes," rejoined Philips, proceeding to give an exact likeness of himself, "for my part I should take him to have been of a lean make, pale complexion,

---

* This was his remark to Spence, at the same time when he said that Jervas's portrait was "very like."

extremely neat in his dress, and five feet seven inches 1707-1709.
high." Swift made no sign till "he had quite done," and Æt. 40-42.
then with the utmost gravity said, "And I, Mr. Philips,
should take him to have been a plump man, just five feet
eight inches and a half high,* not very neatly dressed, in
a black gown with pudding sleeves."

To that professional costume in social intercourse we Ante, 232.
have seen that he strongly objected, but it is not difficult
to imagine its giving even increased relish to the charm
of his talk. Wonderful in his influence over women, to
enumerate thus early his female friends would be to name
the principal whig and some tory toasts of the time. The
Berkeley and Ormond daughters were all their lives in Beauties
correspondence with him; and with Lady Betty Germaine's and toasts.
great friend, Mrs. Biddy Floyd, who could thaw a bitter
frost by looking out on it with both her eyes;† with Mrs.
Finch, who became afterward Lady Winchilsea; and with
Mrs. (soon to be Lady) Worsley, whose daughter was to
marry Lord Carteret, poems‡ written in the present year

---

* Spence reports "just five feet five inches," but, not to lose the whole point of the story, I venture to think his memory was at fault, and I have substituted Swift's real stature.

† "'Tis a loss you are not here to partake of three weeks' frost, and eat gingerbread in a booth by a fire upon the Thames. Mrs. Floyd looked out with both her eyes, and we had one day's thaw: but she drew in her head, and it now freezes as hard as ever."— *Swift to Hunter, 12th Jan., 1708-'9.*

‡ The poem to Mrs. Worsley I print for the first time, having found it among Sir Andrew Fountaine's MSS. in Swift's handwriting. Some ladies, among whom were Mrs. Worsley and Mrs. Finch (herself the writer of pieces that have had high praise, and to whom is addressed, under the name of Ardelia, his celebrated poem in which he calls himself, what he says she despises,

"A whig and one who wears a gown"),

appear to have written verses to him from May Fair, offering him such temptations as that fashionable locality supplied to detain him from the country and its pleasures; and thus he replies:

1.

"In pity to the emptying town   Original
    Some god May Fair invented,   poem by
When Nature would invite us down,   Swift (MS.).
    To be by Art prevented.

2.

"What a corrupted taste is ours
    When milkmaids in mock state,
Instead of garlands made of flow'rs,
    Adorn their pails with plate!

3.

"So are the joys which Nature yields
    Inverted in May Fair,
In painted cloth we look for fields,
    And step in booths for air.

4.

"Here a dog dancing on his hams,
    And puppets mov'd by wire,

1707–1709.
Ær. 40–42.

attest his friendly familiarity. Those decided whigs, Lady Stanley (wife of Sir John), Lady Lucy Stanhope, her daughter Moll, and her sister Armstrong, were his sworn admirers. "Mrs. Long and I are fallen out," he wrote during the year to Hunter: "I shall not trouble you with the cause, but don't you think her altogether in the wrong?

Best public intelligencers.

Mrs. Barton is still in my good graces.... The best intelligence I get of public affairs is from ladies, for the ministers never tell me any thing; and Mr. Addison is nine times more secret to me than he is to any body else, because I have the happiness to be thought his friend. The company at St. James's coffee-house is as bad as ever, but it is not quite so good. The beauties you left are all gone off this frost, and we have got a new set for spring, of which Mrs. Chetwynd and Mrs. Worsley are the principal.... I am now with Mrs. Addison, with whom I have fifty times drunk your health since you left us." Mrs. (or

Mrs. Barton and Mrs. Long.

as we should say Miss) Barton, niece of Sir Isaac Newton, with whom she lived, and the admired of Lord Halifax, who left her a fortune at his death, was one of the famous whig beauties, and a special favorite. But, for Mrs. Long, sister of Sir James Long, of Draycott, and a well-known toast at the Kit-kat, he had even a more particular liking. "She was the most beautiful person of the age she lived in," he says in one of his note-books which I possess: "of great honor and virtue, infinite sweetness and generosity of temper, and true good sense." Her first advance to his friendship, and the despotic condescension with which all

Whimsical decree:

such advances were mirthfully received, appear in a whimsical decree drawn up in his handwriting under date of the present year, which for another reason also is rather memorable in his story.

"When I lived in England," he told Bishop Hoadly's daughter in later days, "once every year I issued out an

Do far exceed your frisking lambs
   Or song of feather'd quire.
5.
"Howe'er, such verse as yours, I grant,
   Would be but too inviting:
	Were fair Ardelia not my aunt,
	   Or were it Worsley's writing."
	Some playful allusion is in that last stanza, not now decipherable.

edict, commanding that all ladies of wit, sense, merit, and quality, who had an ambition to be acquainted with me should make the first advances at their peril." At pretty nearly the same date (1730) he told the Duchess of Queensberry and Lady Suffolk that it had been "a known and established rule above twenty years in England that the first advances have been constantly made me by all ladies who aspired to my acquaintance, and the greater the quality, the greater were their advances." From the decree in the case of Mrs. Long,* however, it would seem that while humbly acknowledging the general right of Doctor Swift to such advances, she yet claimed exception for herself as a lady of the Toast ; and hence had arisen, to the female friend and her family at whose house the meeting was proposed, the necessity of resolving this delicate question, which, being referred to the eldest son, after weighty consideration had gone against Mrs. Long, who within two hours, without essoin or demur, had to make the advances required. The decree has the signature of Ginckel Vanhomrigh, whose mother and eldest sister, " Mrs. Vanhomrigh and her fair daughter, Hessy," are by one of its clauses strictly forbidden " to aid, abet, comfort, or encourage her, the said Mrs. Long, in her disobedience for the future." Bartholomew Vanhomrigh, a Dublin merchant of Dutch extraction, to whom King William had given profitable employments in Ireland, had left his wife, at his death in 1703, the life-income of a fortune of nearly twenty thousand pounds, with which she and her two sons and two daughters came ultimately to England ; and she had been some time living in London in fashionable style, visited by the best company, when, early in the present year, Sir Andrew Fountaine introduced Swift.

At the time when Hester Vanhomrigh, a girl seventeen

Margin notes: 1707–1709. Æt. 40–42.
requiring ladies to make first advances:
resisted by Mrs. Long.
The Vanhomrighs.

---

* This decree was first published at pp. 147–150 of a little volume (1719–'20) containing the *Art of Punning* and *Letters found in the Cabinet of that celebrated Toast, Mrs. Anne Long, since her decease.* It has an admirable engraving by Vertue from Jervas's portrait of Swift, but not a line of his writing except the decree, though the "Punning" pages have been most improperly included in his collected works.

years of age, thus first saw Swift, Esther Johnson also was
in London, on the last visit she ever made there; but
Swift had not named to her these new acquaintances.
She was ignorant of them, and of their mode of life or
the company they kept, when Swift mentioned them to
her nearly three years later. She had come over with
Mrs. Dingley shortly after Swift left Dublin, and she
went back at the end of April; but in his present letters
there are only two allusions to her. She had brought her
little dog, whom he reports to Dean Sterne in April as very
well, and liking London wonderfully, "but Greenwich better, where we could hardly keep him from hunting down
the deer;" and a few weeks earlier he had told Walls that
"the ladies of St. Mary's are well, and talk of going to
Ireland in the spring. But Mrs. Johnson can not make a
pun, if she might have the weight of it in gold. They
desired me to give you their service when I writ."

The same letter shows that further observation had
brought him doubts of the popularity of the war. "As
for politics, I know little worth writing. The parliament
this year is prodigiously slow; and the preparations for
war much slower. So that we expect but a moderate
campaign, and people begin to be heartily weary of the
war." Three weeks after that was written, however, politics again became exciting enough; and it took only
about as many more months, and the victory of Oudenarde, to make the war as popular as ever. Swift's interest had been strongly re-awakened by the turn which the
close of the previous campaign had given to some political questions at home. The disaster of Almanza brought
into sudden and unexpected prominence the recall of Lord
Peterborough in the preceding year, and the whigs found
it hard to justify their treatment of that eccentric but triumphant general. "It's a perfect jest," Swift had written in one of his letters to Archbishop King soon after his
arrival, "to see my Lord Peterborough, reputed as great a
whig as any in England, abhorred by his own party and

caressed by the tories." Nor was the letter at any pains 1707-1709.
Æt. 40-42.
to conceal that opinions on all sides had been rather rough-
ly shaken. It was well, he said, that he did not himself Peterbor-
ough and
the torles.
feel disposed to make reflections on the facts he detailed;
for if he were, he could not tell what to make, so oddly
were people subdivided. Seven days later he wrote again
to tell of the dismissal of Harley, at the break-down of the 5th Feb.,
first Masham intrigue; and of his having just heard from 1707-'8, mis-
dated 1706
a friend of Mr. St. John that he also intended to "lay down by Scott.
in a few days." This last letter otherwise was curious for
its remark on Harley's scheme. The attempt to bring
together the moderate men of both parties, he calls the
"greatest piece of court-skill that has been acted these
many years;" and this immediately follows an observation that "you sometimes see the extremes of whig and
tory driving on the same thing."

Entering on a part of Swift's life which was the turning-point of his political career, which led to his approaching connection with Harley and St. John, and to which
there has not been even an attempt by his biographers to
do any kind of justice, I here interpose what his own opinions really were at this time. They are taken from a tract
now written by him, entitled *Sentiments of a Church-of-* Sentiments
England Man with Respect to Religion and Government, of a Church-
of-England
and they will best explain what remains to be given from Man.
the letter last quoted.

Johnson says of the tract that it is written with great
coolness, moderation, ease, and perspicuity; and the presence of such qualities when party heats were so intense
may well be noted as a marked singularity. He had indeed put forward this piece of writing to declare the danger of such heats to both sides.* He thought it just as
foolish in the whigs to charge the tories with hankerings

* Swift does not decry party, though
he deprecates its heats and passions.
It must always exist, as he well knew.
Reading a history, or sitting at a play,
we can not help taking sides; and no
wonder we should do so in public

affairs "where the most inconsiderable have some real share, and, by the
wonderful importance which every
man is of to himself, a very great
imaginary one."

after Rome and arbitrary power, as in the tories to charge
the whigs with designs to bring in presbytery and a commonwealth. Both might with profit have gathered from
this what it was meant to convey. To such party antago-
nism it was incident on either side that the greatest power
should expose its possessors to the greatest danger, because
of the temptation to use it; and if the whigs had taken
the advice now given, and let the church alone, they might
have escaped the disasters of the five following years.
Swift stated fairly his qualifications as a moderator: " I
believe I am no bigot in religion, and I am sure I am none
in government. I converse in full freedom with many
considerable men of both parties; and if not in equal
number, it is purely accidental and personal, as happening
to be near the court, and to have made acquaintance there
more under one ministry than another."

What he had to say, then, as the friend to both, was,
that the whigs should not think the Church of England so
narrow as not to be able to fall in with any regular kind of
government, and that the tories should not hamper themselves with the belief that any one kind of government
was more than another acceptable to God. He warned
the whigs of what was meant by an Establishment in religion: that, while sects should have full liberty of conscience, they should not have such political authority as
might be used to overthrow the church; and that the government which desired to retain their allegiance could not
give them too much ease, or trust them with too little power. On the other hand, he warned the tories of the in-
expressible folly of permitting any section of their party
to set up distinctions between kings *de facto* and *de jure*.
Every limited monarch, he told them, every sovereign sub-
mitting to conditions, was a king *de jure;* and he was the
only king who could claim to be so entitled, because he
governed by the only authority sufficient to abolish all precedent right, namely, the consent of the whole.* In this

---

* One of its many remarks of a
shrewd wisdom is this upon the Dutch:

" They are a commonwealth founded
on a sudden, by a desperate attempt

part of the tract, all the questions of right divine, non-resistance, and passive obedience, are handled with admirable
good-sense, and it is clearly shown that none more than the
tories themselves were interested in frankly accepting the
doctrine, that, where security of person and property for
all is insured by laws which none but the whole can repeal, the great ends of government are thereby obtained,
whether administration be in the hands of one or of many.
" It is a remark of Hobbes that the youth of England are
corrupted in their principles of government by reading the
authors of Greece and Rome, who writ under common-
wealths. But it might have been more fairly offered for
the honor of liberty, that, while the rest of the known
world was overrun with the arbitrary government of single persons, arts and sciences took their rise and flourished
only in those few small territories where the people were
free."

    If the truth of the case, then, and the wisdom of it, lay
as he thus stated, it was not matter of surprise to him that
the extremes of whig and tory should, as he had written to
the archbishop, drive on the same thing. " I have heard,"
he went on to say in that letter, " the chief whigs blamed
by their own party for want of moderation ; and I know a
whig lord in good employment who voted with the highest tories against the court and ministry with whom he is
nearly allied." In short, it is clear enough that Swift,
whose earlier misgivings in the same direction have before
been indicated, had a dread of the extreme whigs getting
too much of their own way ; though if, amidst unsettled
and disturbed opinions, he was secretly working in any
one's interest at the time, it was certainly in that of Somers,
who next to Sunderland had been Harley's most unsparing
enemy, and whom in this very letter he says he is " going

Margin notes:
1707-1709.
Æt. 40-42.
Sentiments of a Church-of-England Man.

Extremes meeting, 12th Feb., 1707-'8.

Ante, 144, 147.

---

in a desperate condition, not formed
or digested into a regular system by
mature thought and reason, but hud-
dled up under the pressure of sudden
exigencies ; calculated for no long
duration ; and hitherto subsisting by
accident, in the midst of contending
powers who can not yet agree about
sharing it among them."

1707–1709.
Æt. 40–42.
Swift with
Somers.

this morning to visit." But Somers had his difficulties still. Writing to the Archbishop of Dublin in the middle of April to assure him of Lord Pembroke's intended return to his post, "which we certainly conclude will be toward the end of summer, there being not the least talk

To King:
April, 1708
(MS.).

of his removal," Swift adds: "I was told in confidence three weeks ago that the chief whig lords resolved to apply in a body to the queen, for my Lord Somers to be made president: but t'other day, upon trial, the ministry would not join, and the queen was resolute, and so it has miscarried."*

Success, nevertheless, was at hand. At the end of October, when Marlborough had strengthened his colleagues

Whig triumph.

by another great victory, came the event some time expected; and to the appointments rendered necessary by Prince George's death the queen found herself powerless to offer further resistance. Somers was made president of the council; the viceroyalty of Ireland was given to Lord Wharton, Pembroke being restored to the admiralty;†

Unpublished
Swift letters.

* Swift to Arbp. King, 15th April, 1708. From the same letter (MS.) these allusions may be taken: "I most humbly thank your grace for your favorable thoughts in my own particular; and I can not but observe that you conclude them with a compliment in such a turn as betrays more skill in that part of eloquence than you will please to own, and such as we whose necessities put us upon practicing it all our lives can never arrive to...... Sir A. Fountaine presents his humble duties to your grace, and will get you the *Talmud* if you please. He is gone this morning to Oxford for three or four days. Your bill shall be made up when the *Talmud* is in it."

Pembroke's
first pun.

† I found in Swift's handwriting, among the MSS. at Sir Andrew Fountaine's seat in Norfolk, the draft of an address in which "The Doctor," as Pembroke always called

Swift, congratulates the earl in the Castilian, or punning, language, and in the names of himself, Sir Andrew Fountaine, the Bishop of Clogher and his brothers, Dean Sterne, Doctor Howard, and the rest of the punning circle, on his appointment to the admiralty. The "Arundel" allusions are explained by the ex-viceroy having just taken the Lady Arundel for his second wife. It is so characteristic of Swift to show him thus amidst the graver matters pressing upon him at the time, that I shall perhaps be pardoned for giving the dignity of print to these rather laborious and not very successful jokes. "*The Address of the Doctor and the Gentlemen of Ireland, Humbly Sheweth*, That since your lordship is new *Deckt* for the sea, your petitioners have been excluded as ig-*navi* or *cast-aways*; whereof they can not *fathom* the cause. For your lordship is the Doc-

and Addison was made Irish secretary in place of Doding- 1707–1709.
ton. "A new world!" Swift called it, writing immediate- Æt. 40–42.
ly after to the archbishop. "On my return from Kent, A new world.
the night of the prince's death, I staid a few days in town
before I went to Epsom: I then visited a certain great
man, and we entered very freely into discourse upon the
present juncture. He assured me there was no doubt now
of the scheme holding about the admiralty, the govern-

tor's peculiar governor, since he that pleased with your new office, consid- Letter in
is admiral of the *fleet* must be so of ering the mischiefs likely to happen Castilian on
the *Swift*. You were not used to look under your administration. First, Pembroke's
Stern upon your visitants, nor to keep the seamen, in complaisance to my admiralty
abaft while we were *afore*. Pray, lady, will take a young *Arundel* into (MS.).
my lord, have a *car'-in-a* new office every ship, whom they begin to call
not to disoblige your old friends. by a diminutive name, *A-rundelet*.
Remember, be-*fore-castle* puns, you Then, upon your lordship's account,
never heard any in your life. We the merchant will turn gamester, and
are content to be used as the *second* be ready to venture all upon any
rate, as becomes men of our *pitch*. *Main*, without fearing a *Cinque*.
If Tom Ashe were here, he would Again, while your lordship is admiral,
never keep at land, but *pump* hard I doubt we shall lose all our *sea-fear-*
for a new sea - pun. I designed to *ing* Men, for, as you are likely to man-
have Mr. *Keel-hawld* to your lord- age it, every seaman that has any mer-
ship yesterday, but you saw no com- it will soon be *landed*. What a con-
pany. Thus we are kept under fusion must this cause! and more
hatches, and can not *compass* our still, when our boats must be all
point. I have a *Deal* of stories to troubled with a *Wherry-go-nimble*,
tell your lordship, and tho' you may and our ships new-trimmed must all
have heard them before, I should be dance *Rigg - i' Downs*. We agree
glad to *Chat'em* over again; but I your lordship will certainly beat the
am now sick, tho' I hope not near French; but what honor is that?
Grave's-end. But your lordship must Alas, they are all *Galli - Slaves* al-
give me leave to say that if we lose ready. My lord: your petitioners
the sight of you in England as well beg one hour a week to attend, for
as in Ireland, Fortune who is a Gray which they shall ever pray; That aft-
and not a *Green-Witch*, is much in er your lordship has subdued the
our *Dept-for't*. But how can your French and Spaniard, and given us
friends of Ireland approach, while the an honorable Peace, you may retire
seamen *punch* us away, to get at you? many years hence from the wet to the
But, while you *canvas* their affairs, dry Downs; from the boats-*swains*
can they not drink their *can* vas, to looking to their *ship* to the *swains*
your health at home? and swallow looking to their *sheep*, and, that my
Ph'lip at a sup? and when they see meaning may not be mistaken, from
your lordship's *Flag-on*, toss up an- those Downs where *Sails* are hoist
other of their own? But your peti- and mis'd to those of *Sailsbury*"
tioners with humble submission can (Wilton by Salisbury).
not see why you should be much

1707-1709.
Æt. 40-42.

Wish to be
out of it.

Would like
to go as sec-
retary to
Vienna.

Swift's party
position.

ment of Ireland, and presidency of the council, the disposition whereof your grace knows as well as I; and although I care not to mingle public affairs with the interest of so private a person as myself, yet, upon such a revolution, not knowing how far my friends may endeavor
to engage me in the service of a new government, I would
beg your grace to have favorable thoughts of me on such
an occasion; and to assure you that no prospect of making
my fortune shall ever prevail on me to go against what
becomes a man of conscience and truth, and an entire
friend to the Established Church. This I say, in case such
a thing should happen; for my thoughts are turned another way, if the Earl of Berkeley's journey to Vienna
holds, and the ministry will keep their promise of making
me the queen's secretary, by which I shall be out of the
way of parties, until it shall please God I have some place
to retire to, a little above contempt: or, if all fail, until
your grace and the Dean of St. Patrick's shall think fit to
dispose of that poor town-living in my favor."* He closed
by referring to the possibility of a peace: and this might
certainly have been effected with many advantages that
winter, if the opportunity had not been strangely missed.

Swift's position at this critical time is thus clearly explained. He did not think his own prospect improved by
the fact of power without control having fallen to the
whigs. He at once finds his ground to be unsafe. Al-

---

* In the letter to Walls (MS.) on the
disappointment of the bishopric (ante,
224) he had put this postscript: "I
wish you would desire Dr. Smith to
speak to Dean Syng as from himself,
to inquire whether Dr. Sterne designs
really to give me the Parish that has
the church, for I believe I told you
that at parting he left me in doubt,
by saying he would give me one of
them. If he means that which has
the church to build, I would not accept it, nor come to Ireland to be deceived." So quietly was Swift then
prepared to accommodate himself to
his fortunes. A letter to the same
friend (MS.), of the same date as that
in the text to the archbishop, says:
"If Mr. King dies, I have desired
people to tell the archbishop that I
will have the living; for I like it, and
he told me I should have the first
good one that fell; *and, you know,
Great Men's promises never fail.*"
Sterne's conduct in regard to the living
here named was one of several grave
charges afterward preferred by Swift
against him. See letter of July, 1733.

ready since the disappointment of the bishopric he had-
turned his thoughts in another direction, as to which,
though he has "promises," as usual, he has yet nothing
more certain; and now, though the party to whom he had
rendered special service is become stronger than ever, the
very circumstance has brought with it a doubt if he can
continue to be politically "engaged" for these whig friends
without a sacrifice of opinions of vital moment to him.
After a few days he wrote in the same vein to Dean
Sterne, telling him that Lord Pembroke took all things
mighty well, and they punned together as usual : but adding that the ex-viceroy either made the best use or the
best appearance with his philosophy of any man he ever
knew; for it was "not believed he is pleased at heart on
many accounts." His own position is taken up, with, if
possible, greater explicitness, in a letter to Walls of the   Letter to
same date, hitherto unprinted, and he is more than ever   Walls (MS.).
anxious that the promise of a secretaryship should be re-
deemed. "My journey to Germany depends on accidents
as well as upon the favor of the court. If they will make
me queen's secretary when I am there, as they promise, I   ·
will go; unless this new change we expect on the prince's
death should alter my measures, for it is thought that
most of those I have credit with will come into play.
But yet, if they carry things too far, I shall go to Vienna,
or even to Laracor, rather than fall in with them." A
couple of months swept away this hope also, and his lan-   Failure of
guage then to the archbishop is in many respects remark-   the Vienna
able : "My Lord Berkeley begins to drop his thoughts of   project.
going to Vienna; and indeed I freely gave my opinion
against such a journey for one of his age and infirmities.
And I shall hardly think of going secretary without him,
although the emperor's ministers here think I will, and
have writ to Vienna. I agree with your grace that such a
design was a little too late at my years; but considering
myself wholly useless in Ireland, and in a parish with an   Why Swift
audience of half a score, and it being thought necessary   desired a sec-
that the queen should have a secretary at that court, my   retaryship.

1707-1709.. friends telling me it would not be difficult to compass it,
Æt. 40-42. I was a little tempted to pass some time abroad, until my
friends would make me a little easier in my fortunes at
home. Besides, I had hopes of being sent in time to some
other court."

One thing only in the new arrangements he dwelt upon
with unalloyed pleasure, though it involved a contrast that
might have given to it a not unpardonable touch of bitter-

Addison
made Irish
secretary.

ness. "Mr. Addison," he told the archbishop, "goes over
first secretary. He is a most excellent person; and being
my most intimate friend, I shall use all my credit to set
him right in his notions of persons and things. I spoke
to him with great plainness upon the subject of the Test;
and he says he is confident my Lord Wharton will not attempt it if he finds the bent of the nation against it. I
will say nothing further of his character to your grace at
present, because he has half persuaded me to have some
thoughts of returning to Ireland." "Vous savez," he
wrote to Hunter, "que Monsieur d'Addison, notre bon
ami, est fait sécrétaire d'état d'Irlande; and unless you
make haste over, and get me my Virginian bishopric,* he
will persuade me to go with him, for the Vienna project
is off; which is a great disappointment to the design I had
of displaying my politics at the emperor's court." The

Addison and
Swift of each
other.

friends, nevertheless, did not leave London together; but,
though widely different fortunes were for the most part
in future to divide them, a mutual admiration and affec-

Playful
allusions.

* In a letter to Hunter of a few
. weeks' later date (22d March, 1708-
'9), written while Addison was in the
room with him, he returns to the
project of a bishopric in Virginia,
which his editors take gravely, and
say that the design for it was drawn
out with power to ordain priests and
deacons for our colonies in America
(*Scott*, i., 97). I have, however, failed in finding any authority for it but
these letters to Hunter, who may
have started such a notion to him,
but who, as I have shown, gave up
Virginia, after all. "I shall go for
Ireland some time in the summer, being not able to make my friends in
the ministry consider my merits, or
their promises, enough to keep me
here; so that all my hopes now ter-
minate in my bishopric of Virginia."
At the end of the letter he says of
Addison: "I pray God too much
business may not spoil *le plus honnête
homme du monde;* for it is certain which
of a man's good talents he employs in
business must be detracted from his
conversation."

tion remained which was only closed by death. What
Addison said of Swift as the *greatest genius of his age*
we have seen, and what Swift exclaimed of Addison two
months before his Irish appointment is in a letter to Ambrose Philips lying before me, *That man has worth enough
to give reputation to an age.* The world has no other instance of two intimate friends speaking thus with perfect
truth of each other, and with something so like, yet so unlike, in what with strange caprice was dealt out to them
by destiny. Addison went to Ireland, where a deanery
was awaiting Swift, and Swift remained in England, where
a secretaryship of state awaited Addison; yet never was
shrewder remark than Sir James Mackintosh made, when
he said that Addison as the dean and Swift as the secretary of state would have been a stroke of fortune putting
each into the place most fit for him. Incalculable the gain
to themselves, though the world might have lost Captain
Gulliver!

The First-fruits and the Test still kept Swift in London, and two letters written before the prince's death, here
first printed, enable me to show his course on 'both subjects very clearly. The first was to the archbishop; and
the second had apparently been drawn up for Primate
Marsh's information, with a desire that it should be sent
on to King, in whose archives it was found. Writing to
the latter on the 15th of April, he says that upon consulting with Southwell and other friends familiar with Ireland, they were strongly agreed in recommending him to
solicit the affair himself with Lord Godolphin himself.
"I told Lord Somers the case, and that by your grace's
commands, and the desire of several bishops and some
of the principal clergy, I undertook the matter; that the
queen and lord treasurer had already fallen into it these
four years; that it wanted nothing but solicitation; that
I knew his lordship was a great friend of Lord Sunderland's, with whom I had been long acquainted, but, hearing he forbore common visits now he was in business, I
had not attended him. Then I desired his lordship to tell

Margin notes:

1707–1709.
Æt. 40–42.

14th Sept.,
1708 (MS.).

What was
and what
might have
been.

Business
that kept
Swift in
London.

1707-1709.
Æt. 40-42.
Lord Sunderland the whole matter, and prevail that I
might attend with him upon my lord treasurer. Yesterday my Lord Somers came to see me, and told me very
kindly he had performed my commission ; that Lord Sunderland was very glad we should renew our acquaintance ;
and that he would, whenever I pleased, go along with me
to lord treasurer. I should in a day or two have been
able to give your grace some further account, if it were
not for an accident in one of my legs* which has for some
time confined me to my chamber, and which I am forced
to manage for fear of ill consequences. I hope your grace
will approve of what I have hitherto done. I told Lord
Somers the nicety of proceeding in a matter where the
lord lieutenant was engaged, and design to tell it Lord
Sunderland and lord treasurer, and shall be sure to avoid
any false step in that point; and your grace shall soon
know the issue of this negotiation, or whether there be
any hope from it."

Conferences
with Lord
Somers.

Interview
with Lord
Treasurer.
The story was continued in a letter to the archbishop of
the 10th of June. He described the interview with Godolphin, who to all the pressure put upon him had but one
reply; that small good had been got by the remission to
the English clergy, and he should not consent to it in the
case of the Irish unless assured it " would be well received,
with due acknowledgments." What, asked Swift, was to
be understood by this? " Nothing under their hands,"
said Godolphin; " but I will so far explain myself to tell
you, I mean better acknowledgments than those of the
clergy of England." Again Swift pressed to be advised
Godolphin
and the
clergy.
what sort my lord would think fittest. " I can only say
again," replied the dry Godolphin, " such as they ought."
Little, therefore, had come of the personal soliciting with
the lord treasurer; and all that was left to Swift was to

---

* The accident is mentioned in a
letter to Dean Sterne of the same
date : " I wonder whether, in the
midst of your buildings, you ever
consider that I have broke my shins,
and have been a week confined this
charming weather to my chamber,
and can not go abroad to hear the
nightingales, or pun with my Lord
Pembroke."

pursue the cold scent of asking his. excellency the lord 1707–1709.
Æt. 40–42. lieutenant once a month how the affair went on.

Wearied of this kind of waiting, however, Primate Marsh appears to have written to Pembroke's secretary, Dodington, from whom in reply he had received such an account of no-progress made, as left hardly room for as-surance more encouraging than that any satisfactory issue could not now be expected "before a peace." This was communicated to Swift, and hence the second letter to which reference has been made as found in the archives of the Armagh diocese. "I hope you will excuse" (the First-fruits
negotia-
tions, Aug.,
1708 (MS.). date is 28th August, 1708) "my want of ceremony occa-sioned by my desire to give a full answer to yours of the 12th. What hindered my writing was the want of confi-dence to trouble you when I had nothing of importance to say; but if you give me leave to do it at other times, I shall obey you with great satisfaction, and I am heartily sorry for the occasion that hath prevented you, because it is a loss to the public as well as to me. The person who sent you the letter about progress made in that matter, is one* who would not give three-pence to save all the Estab-lished clergy in both kingdoms from the gallows. And to talk of not encouraging you to hope for it before a peace, is literally *dare verba*, and nothing else. But, in Maxim of
the great. the small conversation I have had among great men, there is one maxim I have found them constantly to observe, which is, that in any business before them, if you inquire how it proceeds, they only consider what is proper to an-swer, without one single thought whether it be agreeable to fact or no. For instance, here is lord treasurer assures me that what you ask is a trifle; that the queen would easily consent to it, and he would do so too; but then he adds some general conditions, as I told you before. Then comes lord lieutenant; assures me that the other has

---

* Mr. Dodington, he means. To the same effect, on the prince's death, he wrote to King: "I spoke formerly all I knew of the" (first-fruits and) "twentieth parts; and whatever Mr. D—— has said about staying until a peace, I do assure your grace, is noth-ing but words."

nothing at all to do with it, and that it is not to come before him, but that *he* has made some progress in it; and also hints to you, it seems, that it will be hardly done before a peace. The progress he means must be something entirely between the queen and himself, for the two chief ministers assure me they never heard of the matter from him; and, in God's name, what sort of progress *can* he mean? In the mean time, I have not stirred a step further; being unwilling to ruin myself in any man's favor, when I can do the public no good. And therefore I had too much art to desire lord treasurer not to say any thing to t'other of what I had spoke, unless I could get leave, which was refused me; and therefore I omitted speaking again to Lord Sunderland. Which, however, I am resolved to do when he comes to town, in order to explain something that I only conjectured. Upon the whole, I am of opinion that the 'progress' yet made is just the same with that of making me general of the horse; and the Duke of Ormond thinks so too; and gave me some reasons of his own. Therefore I think the reason why this thing is not done can be only perfect neglect, or want of sufficient inclination; or perhaps a better principle, I mean a dislike to the conditions, and unwillingness to act on them. I think Mr. Southwell and I agree in our interpretation of that oracular saying* which has perplexed you, and have fixed it upon *the Test.* Whether that be among the trifling or wicked meanings you thought of, I need not ask. Whatever methods you would please to have me take in this, or any other matter, for the service of the public or yourself, I shall readily obey. And if the matter does not stick at that mystical point before mentioned, I am sure, with common application, it might be done in a month."†

Progress
without pro-
gressing.

Secret of
failure.

Swift and the
gazetteer.

* The "as they ought" of Godolphin: *ut supra.*

† This letter (MS.) was written during the period of intense expectation that preceded the taking of Lisle, and its closing sentences show not only Swift's interest, but the influence he exercised over the then gazetteer, Richard Steele. "We are now every day expecting news from abroad of the greatest importance. Nothing less than a battle, a siege, or Lisle taken...... Wagers run two to one for the last. In the last *Gazette* it

The matter was thus brought back to the point from which Swift had started at the first,* that attempt would be made in that way of bargain between the First-fruits and the Test, the one to be a bribe for the repeal of the other, to which he had declared a persistent hostility. But, before adverting to the course which this determined him to adopt on the more important question, the sequel to the present attempt to obtain remission of the first-fruits may be briefly told. When the arrangements involving Lord Pembroke's resignation were made on the prince's death, Swift wrote to the primate, that, upon putting Pembroke in mind of the first-fruits before he went out of office, Pembroke told him that the thing was done; sent him word, as he afterward explained, " by Sir Andrew Fountaine, that the queen had granted the thing, and afterward took the compliment I made him upon it;" but a sudden attack of his· old disorder of giddiness disabled Swift, till toward the middle of January, from announcing this to King, whom he then told of it, with the addition that two great men in office, giving him joy of it, very frankly said that if he had not smoothed the way by giving them and the rest of the ministry a good opinion of the justice of the thing, it would have met with opposition.† Yet the thing had not been done, after all! Upon closer inquiry, Swift learned from the ex-lieutenant that it was a matter purely between the queen and himself, and there was no doubt that my lord had received from her, who during the past year would hardly have denied him any thing, a promise for the remission. But know-

Marginal notes:
1707-1709.
Æt. 40-42.
Attempted bargaining.

Supposed success at last.

Only a promise.

---

was certainly affirmed that there would be a battle; but the copy coming to the office to be corrected, I prevailed with them to let me soften ·the phrase a little, so as to leave some room for possibilities; and I do not find the soldiers here are so very positive. However, it is a period of the greatest expectation I ever remember, and God in his mercy send

a good issue. This is all I have to say at present. I will soon write again, if any other thing be worth sending. And then it shall be in more form."

　* See *ante*, 219.

　† " Upon which I only remarked what I have always observed in courts, that when a favor is done there is no want of persons to challenge obligations."

1707-1709.
Æt. 40-42.
Swift and
Lord Whar-
ton.
ing Godolphin's determination to exact conditions, and ascertaining through Addison that no grant had passed the
treasury, Swift went to Wharton himself, "which was the
first attendance I ever paid." He was in a great crowd
and much haste, and Swift had to be satisfied with the as-
surance that he was well disposed, but must have the usual
application made to all lord lieutenants before he could do
any thing. With which the matter ended, and is thus dismissed by Swift: "It is wonderful a great minister should
make no difference between a grant and the promise of a
grant.... Had I the least suspected it...I would have
applied to Lord Wharton about two months ago...which
might have prevented at least the present excuse....
Though others might, I suppose, have been found."

"Test".
trouble.
Godolphin's "conditions" remained, however; and, long
before the appointment to the lord lieutenancy of the
most eager advocate for a repeal of the Test, there had
come foreshadowings of trouble from that question which
some other occurrences gave prominence to. The Irish
Presbyterians, taking advantage of an alarm of invasion
in the spring of 1708,* obtained the lead in addresses of
loyalty to the queen while the church party still were silent; and it was supposed that this might recommend on
the English side their claim to be relieved from the Test.
At the same time there came over to England the speaker
of the Irish house, who held also the office of chief-justice,
with the declared object of agitating for the repeal by
the English parliament on the ground that the Irish would
Letter to
Arhp. King
(MS.).
not give way. "We have been already surprised enough,"
Swift wrote to the archbishop on the 15th of April, "with
two addresses from the dissenters of England; but this
from Dublin will, I fear, be very pernicious; and there is

---

* See the letter to Dean Sterne of
the 15th April about the good use
made in England, by the dissenters,
of the fright in Ireland upon the intended invasion. Observe, too, what
he writes to King, on the 10th of
June, of the endeavor he is always
making "to take off that scandal the
clergy of Ireland lie under of being
the reverse of what they really are,
with respect to the revolution, loyalty to the queen, and settlement of the
crown; which is here the construction of the word *tory*."

no other remedy but by another address from the uncor- *1707-1709.*
rupted part of the city, which has been usual in England *Æt. 40-42.*
from several counties, as in the case of the Tack; and I
should hope, from a person of your grace's vigilance, that
counter-addresses might be sent both from the clergy and
the conforming gentry of Ireland, to set the queen right
in this matter.   I assure your grace all persons I converse
with are entirely of this opinion, and I hope it will be
done.*   Some days ago my Lord Somers entered with me *Somers*
into discourse about the Test clause, and desired my opin- *and Swift.*
ion upon it, which I gave him truly, though with all the
gentleness I could; because as I am inclined and obliged
to value the friendship he professes for me, so he is a person whose favor I would engage in the affair of the first-
fruits. . . .   If it became me to give ill names to ill things *Brodrick,*
and persons, I should be at a loss to find bad enough for *afterward*
the villainy and baseness of a certain lawyer of Ireland, *dleton.* *Lord Mid-*
who is in a station the least of all others excusable for
such proceedings, and yet has been going about most in-
dustriously to all his acquaintance in both houses toward
the end of the session to show the necessity of taking off
the Test clause in Ireland by an act here, wherein you
may be sure he had his brother's assistance.   If such a
project should be resumed next session, and I in England,
unless your grace send me your absolute commands to the
contrary, which I should be sorry to receive, I could hardly forbear publishing some paper in opposition to it, or
leaving one behind me, if there should be occasion."

The occasion arose with greater urgency on the success
of the extreme whigs a few months later; and, under the
double apprehension of an attempt by the new viceroy in

---

* The subject, I ought to add, was
resumed at the close of August by another urgent recommendation that the
proposed addresses should be strengthened, by making the utmost possible
use of the fact that the university had
expelled one of its members (Forbes)
for disrespect to William the Third's
memory.   The desire to connect, in
every possible way, respect for the
doctrines of the revolution with eagerness to support the church, is Swift's
marked peculiarity.   He is, and in
principle was to the close of his life,
as his verse to Mrs. Finch declared,
"A whig, and one who wears a gown."

1707-1709.
Æt. 40-42.

Letter
against re-
peal of Test.

Of the na-
tive Irish.

Of the Scotch
settlers.

Ireland, and, supposing it defeated, of its almost certain
resumption with success in England, Swift wrote his
pamphlet. He called it *A Letter from a Member of the
House of Commons in Ireland to a Member of the House
of Commons in England concerning the Sacramental Test,*
and dated it as from Dublin in December, 1708. Three
things very noticeable pervade its reasonings. There is a
strong personal dislike of the Presbyterians, dating probably from early associations. There is an obvious dread of
the insecurity of the Establishment, as well from the smallness of numbers in her pale, as from the greater energy of
her assailants. There is, above all, a contempt for the
Roman Catholics as an inferior race, so fettered by penal
laws as to make their numbers a weakness to them. The
last was of course Swift's grand mistake, from the point
of view he had taken. His desire was to strengthen and
extend Protestantism, and the only policy that could have
united Protestants he rejected with scorn. Churchmen
and dissenters were the only two parties he saw, and the
church would have to fall to the strongest. He saw nothing outside. He believed the Catholic population, as a
power in the country, to have been shattered at their last
rally under James. They were become to him as "inconsiderable" as women and children. The lands were taken
from their gentry. The fact of the priests being register-
ed made it easy at any time, by refusing to renew the
licenses, to diminish if not abolish them. And as for the
common people, without leaders, without discipline or natural courage,* being little better than hewers of wood and
drawers of water, they were out of all capacity of doing
mischief, if they were ever so well inclined. Having
drawn this picture, Swift placed beside it that of the Scots
in the northern parts of Ireland, as a brave, industrious
people, extremely devoted to their religion, and full of an
undisturbed affection toward each other. He portrayed

---

* There are no better or braver soldiers than the Irish; but Swift would
call that trained courage.

numbers of that "noble" nation, invited by the fertility 1707–1709.
Æt. 40–42.
of the soil, as eager to exchange, by a voyage of three
hours, their barren hills of Lochaber for the fruitful vales
of Antrim and Down, "so productive of that grain which,
at little trouble and less expense, finds diet and lodging
for themselves and their cattle."* He depicted them Virtues of
Presbyte-
rians.
growing speedily into wealth from the smallest beginnings,
by extreme parsimony, wonderful dexterity in dealing,
and firm adherence to one another; showed them never
rooted up where once fixed, but rather increasing daily;
and pointed it out as their invariable habit, on finding
themselves the superior number in any tract of ground,
not to prove patient of mixture, but speedily to remove
such as they could not assimilate.† That there might be
something in such qualities to suggest a better feeling than
distrust never occurs to him. What he has to add imbit-
ters all the good. This brave, industrious, frugal, clannish A fault out-
weighing
all virtues.
race had unhappily brought from Scotland a most formi-
dable notion of episcopacy; and if they thought it, as most
surely they did, three degrees worse than popery, where

---

* Swift delights as much as Johnson did in every opportunity for a
laugh against the Scotch and their
country, and when Ambrose Philips
goes with Lord Mark Kerr to the
North of England, he warns them that
the ladies in even those regions will
think them too Southern by three degrees. "I am not so good an astron-
omer to know whether Venus ever
cuts the arctic circle, or comes within the vortex of Ursa Major; nor can
I conceive how love can ripen where
gooseberries will not." Philips had
been with Kerr to Copenhagen and
written verses in a sledge there.
"Your versifying in a sledge," wrote
Swift (MS.), "seems somewhat parallel to singing a psalm upon a ladder;
and when you tell me that it was upon
the ice, I suppose it might be a Pastoral, and that you had got a calenture,
which makes men think they behold

green fields and groves on the ocean. . . .
I suppose the subject was Love, and
then came in naturally your burning
in so much cold, and that the ice was
hot iron in comparison of her disdain. Then there are frozen hearts
and melting sighs, or kisses, I forget
which. . . . . But I believe your poetic
faith will never arrive at allowing
that Venus was born on the Belts, or
any part of the Northern Sea." Mr.
Shandy would probably have ascribed
Swift's inveteracy against the Scots
to the fact of his having perversely
come into the world on St. Andrew's
Day. To Ambrose
Philips
(MS.).

† "I have done all in my power on
some land of my own to preserve two
or three English fellows in their neighborhood, but found it impossible,
though one of them thought he had
sufficiently made his court by turning
Presbyterian."

1707-1709. was the common enemy for churchmen to join against?
Æt. 40–42. Naturalists might agree that a lion was a bigger, stronger,
more dangerous enemy than a cat; but bind the lion fast,
draw his teeth, and pare his claws to the quick, and determine whether you'd have him in that condition at your
throat, or "an angry cat in full liberty." It was a mistake
the shrewdest man might make, but not pardonable in a
wise one.

Upon other points in the tract which perhaps more than
its leading argument gave it a singular run and popularity
in Ireland, it would be beside the present purpose to dwell;
but powerful use was made of the fact that it was from
English, not from Irish, ministers the proposal for the repeal came, and that the country it was to benefit was not
Ireland, but England. On one side of the channel was
Irish lover Cowley's abject lover, and on the other his despot mis-
to English tress.* The life of the one was to be a ready sacrifice if
mistress. the little finger of the other did but ache; but should the
Irish give what was thus exacted and fain be content, it
was surely too much to expect them to be grateful. "If
there be a fire at some distance, and I immediately blow
up my house before there be occasion, because you are a
man of quality and apprehend some danger to a corner of
your stable, yet why should you require me to attend next
morning at your levee with my humble thanks for the favor you have done me?" Great was the relish and enjoyment of this in Ireland; and of the light thrown on Non-
conformity by contrasting its wail for conscience when it
was low, with its shout for persecution when it got upon
its feet; and then again by comparing its acquiescent hu-
milities, as Swift remembered them in his childhood, with
the noisiness of its demands since the revolution, not one
of which had been made but as a step to enforce another.
Here was Cowley's lover reversed. The Puritan swain

---

* On a former page (77) reference in the text was one of Swift's favorite
is made to Cowley's couplet as an il- weapons in the war he waged against
lustration of later date; but the slip the government of Walpole.
may be pardoned, for the argument

was ever complaining of cruelty while any thing was de- 1707–1709.
Æt. 40-42.
nied him, but when the lady ceased to be cruel she was to Ups and
downs of
Non-con-
formity.
be at his mercy; and so, as it seemed, every thing was to
be called persecution that would not leave the power to
persecute others. Very clear admission was at the same
time made, in this portion of the tract, of the growing
strength of Dissent in the press; and though·he refers to
De Foe as "the fellow that was pilloried — I forget his
name," and, the better to laugh at him, couples him with
Tutchin,* he also describes such writings as the *Review* De Foe's
political
writing.
and the *Observator* as having grown a necessary part in
coffee-house furniture, says that they seem to be leveled
to the understandings of great numbers of people, and believes them to be read at some time or other by customers
of all ranks.

When Morphew reprinted this tract in 1711, a few lines
of Swift's evident dictation were prefixed to the effect that
it had "ruined" the author with the then ministry, and
that a page "purely personal and of no use to the subject"
had been removed. This page can not now be found; but
a letter to the archbishop of the 8th of January shows its
object to have been to conceal the authorship, which even Swift's
devices to
conceal his
authorship.
from King himself, who is eulogized in it, Swift half af-
fects to withhold. "The author has gone out of his way
to reflect on me as a person likely to write for repealing
the Test, which I am sure is very unfair treatment. This
is all I am likely to get by the company I keep. I am
used like a sober man with a drunken face, have the scandal of the vice without the satisfaction." If the facts thus
far have been correctly stated, as my authorities probably
will be thought to establish, there could have been no
"ruining" in the case: but the tract could hardly fail to
strengthen against him that section of the ministry not
friendly to his claims. In his *Memoirs relating to the
Change*, he says that though he took all care to be private,

* From which Pope took his couplet—

. "Earless on high stood unabashed De Foe,
    And Tutchin flagrant from the scourge below."

yet he was guessed to be the author; the suspicion reached Lord Wharton, and he saw him no more till he went to Ireland. "At my taking leave of Lord Somers he desired I would carry a letter from him to the Earl of Wharton, which I absolutely refused; yet he ordered it to be left at my lodgings." What came of it will be told.

Swift lingered in London until March, but does not seem further to have troubled himself with public affairs. He was sitting to Jervas for his portrait, which was still unfinished when he left. He finished and received payment from Tooke for the editing of the final portion of Sir William Temple's *Remains*. He played piquet with Mrs. Long at Mrs. Vanhomrigh's, carefully recording his loss of sixpences. He passed some days with his whig friends, Sir Mathew Dudley and Frankland, the postmaster-general; staid another week with the Berkeleys; dined more than once with a great lover of Addison, and an "adorer" of Hunter, being himself "both a bel esprit and a woolen-draper," Will Pate;* and had been taken by Charles Ford to the operas, which were all the vogue in the winter of 1708-'9. But Swift had small enjoyment in music, and wrote to Hunter that he meant to set up by next winter a party among the wits that should run down such entertainments. We are nine times madder than ever, he said in a later letter, which also told his friend that the only book worth any thing the press had lately given them was a volume of poems by Prior. "The town is gone mad," he repeated to Philips in a letter not hitherto printed, "after a new opera. Poetry and good sense are dwindling like echo with repetition and voice. Critic Dennis vows to God that operas will be the ruin of the nation, and brings examples from antiquity to prove it. A good old lady five miles out of town askt me t'other day what these *uproars* were that her daughter was always going to." Poor Philips, who was still, like himself, the

---

* In the same letter which thus mentions Pate to Hunter, Swift adds: "The whigs carry all before them, and how far they will pursue their victories we under-rate whigs can hardly tell."

man of levees, the man of hopes, to whom he had admin- 1707-1709.
istered comfort under the fable of Sancho and his island, Æт. 40-42.
had lately asked him for another fable to reconcile him to Ante, 225, '6.
fresh disappointments. "I can fit you," replied Swift,
"with no fable at present, unless it should be of the man
that rambled up and down to look for Fortune; and at
length came home, and saw her lying at a man's feet who Favorites
was fast asleep, and never stirred a step. This I reflected of fortune.
on t'other day, when my lord treasurer gave a young fellow, a friend of mine, an employment sinecure of four
hundred pounds a year, added to one of three hundred
pounds he had before." There had since been another
illustration; though probably it did not occur to him, for
he was the last man to have made it a reproach to the
friend he loved. Addison's secretaryship of two thousand pounds a year had hardly been given him, when he
received in addition a patent appointing him keeper for
life of the Irish Records with a salary of near four hundred pounds a year.

Swift was now going back, after more than fifteen Swift's gain
months of suspense in England, to his income of three from the
whigs.
hundred pounds a year and his congregation of half a score
at Laracor; taking with him a small volume of *Poésies
Chrétiennes de Monsieur Jollivet* which he had begged and
brought away from Lord Halifax at taking leave of him,
and on the fly-leaf of which he afterward wrote that he
had desired my lord to remember it was the *only favor he
ever received from him or his party.* Whether or not he
took any thing with him also of the moral of his own fable
of Fortune, may be matter for conjecture. While he was
not soliciting, was it possible she might be near, and, when
he had ceased to look for her, be found lying at his feet?

Through the time of this weary waiting in London
down to that of his re-appearance there on the downfall
of the whigs, Swift suffered so much from the two terrible disorders that were more or less his life companions
(*ante*, 62-3), that this will be the proper place for a record
of some touching entries made in his note-books in regard

1707–1709.
Æt. 40–42.

to such illnesses. I have also subjoined, from the same small books of account and memoranda which have already supplied to my volume many important illustrations, a fac-simile of one of their pages. Upon it stands his outlay for December, 1708; and strangely yet sorrowfully characteristic, here, as on almost every page, are its trivial items of expenditure, with a dark background of pains and fears thrusting itself upon them.

Fac-simile of page of account-book, December, 1708.

(facsimile of handwritten account-book page, December 1708)

1708. " Nov. From 6th to 16th often giddy. Gd help 1707-1709.
me. So to 25th, less. 16th Brandy for giddiness, 2s. Brdy Æt. 40-42.
3d. Decr 5th Horrible sick. 12th Much better, thank God
and MD's prayrs. 16th Bad fitt at Mrs. Barton's. 24th
Better; but dread a fitt. Better still to the end." 1709.
" Jan. 24st An ill fitt; but not to excess. 29th Out of order. 31st Not well at times. Feb. 7. Small fitt abroad.
Pretty well to the end. March. Headache frequent. April
2. Small giddy fitt and swimming in head. MD and God
help me. August. Sick with giddiness much." 1710.
" Jany giddy. March. Sadly for a day. 4th Giddy from
4th. 14h Very ill. July. Terrible fitt. Gd knows what
may be the event. Better toward the end."

BOOK FIFTH.

WHIGS AND TORIES.

· I.

POWER CHANGING HANDS.

1709–1710. Æt. 42–43.

SWIFT had visited his mother in leaving Ireland, and 1709–1710.
Æt. 42–43.
again went to see her in returning. Her now failing
health might naturally suggest danger to his always
watchful affection for her, and his present visit was probably somewhat prolonged by fears that it might be the
last. He left London in April, but did not leave Leices- Last visit to
his mother.
ter till the end of June; though it appears from a letter
of Addison's that his friend had expected him in Dublin
before the close of the former month. For the later
weeks of this delay, however, a local ailment which prevented his getting on horseback was partly the cause.

Of what occupied him in the interval, beyond solicitude
and care for his mother, there is no direct evidence; but
as a note made before he quitted London shows that a particular piece,* to which circumstances had given personal

---

* It occurs in a list on the back
of a letter addressed to him at Lord
Pembroke's in Leicester Fields, and
presumably written in the closing
months of 1708, of Miscellaneous
Short Pieces which he proposed as
"subjects for a volume," comprising some of his earliest writings, and
some in contemplation but not written. Among the latter was the "Apology," though he could never have
meant to confess the authorship of
the *Tale* by including the Apology
for it in a volume known to be his;
and, besides a piece to be noted as
lost, another on the "Present Taste
of Reading," which was certainly

written and sent to Fountaine, and Short pieces
for a volume.
the piece entitled "Conjecture," are
not now discoverable. The contents
were afterward submitted to Benjamin Tooke, to whom, when sending
back to him the sheets of the Apology, he wrote at the close of June,
1710: "If you are in such haste,
how came you to forget the Miscellanies? I would not have you think
of Steele for a publisher" (editor, we
should say): "he is too busy. I will,
one of these days, send you some
hints, which I would have in a preface, and you may get some friend to
dress them up." Here are the subjects: "Discourse on Athens and

importance, was in his mind, and some letters to his book-seller after returning to Ireland make it clear that he had sent him this piece completed some months before, there is a fair presumption that it formed the occupation of his leisure while now in Leicester. Whatever the impression he might have brought away from London of the amount of zeal or of sincerity employed in pressing his claim to the bishopric, the ground taken for refusal of it remained; and though this assumed what he had never avowed, it was not the less his duty to show that in itself it was false. He wrote the Apology to repel the averment that the *Tale of a Tub* had been written by an infidel or scorn- er of religion ; and a remark to his book-seller shows some impatience that the publication of the edition in which it was to appear should have been delayed until the autumn of 1710. "I was in the country" (29th June, 1710) "when I received your letter with the Apology inclosed in it; and I had neither health nor humor to finish that business. But the blame rests with you, that if you thought it time you did not print it when you had it."

He was on the eve of starting for Ireland when, on the

13th of June, he wrote to Lord Halifax and to Lord Pem- 1709-1710.
Æt. 42-43.
broke. The first was a letter of compliment, written Letter to
Lord Hal-
ifax.
avowedly to beg some share in the memory of the person
addressed, and the countenance of his protection. As his
good offices had been promised,* they were challenged in
two particulars: the one that he should sometimes put the
lord president in mind of the writer, and the other that
he should himself duly, once every year, wish him removed
to England. He does not affect to conceal his "hate" of Desire to live
in England.
the place to which he is banished, or his belief that he
might live to some more useful or entertaining purpose if
he were permitted to reside in town ; or condemned to the
highest punishment on papists of having to live anywhere
within ten miles round it. But the postscript contains
the real gist of the letter :† "Pray, my lord, desire Dr.
South" (now on the verge of eighty) "to die about the
fall of the leaf, for he has a prebend of Westminster which
will make me your neighbor, and a sinecure in the country, both in the queen's gift, which my friends have often
told me would fit me extremely. And forgive me one
word, which I know not what extorts from me: that if
my lord president would in such a juncture think me
worth laying any weight of his credit on, you can not but
think me persuaded that it would be a very easy matter
to compass ; and I have some sort of pretense, since the
late King promised me a prebend of Westminster, when I
petitioned him in pursuance of a recommendation I had
from Sir William Temple." There could hardly be a Modesty of
claim to
preferment.
more modest statement of pretensions than this ; and, if I

---

* When Swift was afterward most
angry with Halifax, he said, commenting on Macky's character of him
as a great encourager of learning and
learned men, "his encouragements
were only good words and dinners,"
and in the present letter the dinners
are thus described : "Myself and
about a dozen others have kept the
best table in England, to which because we admitted your lordship in
common with us, made you our manager, and sometimes allowed you to
bring a friend, therefore ignorant people would needs take you to be the
owner."

† This is one of the letters before
named as now to be first correctly
printed from Mr. Kemble's collation.

1709-1710.
Æt. 42-43.

Reply of
Halifax.

read the words rightly, the feeling is unmistakably expressed in them that the failure hitherto to serve him had arisen rather from the not using, than the not having, means at disposal. Halifax did not reply until October, explaining the delay by his belief that Swift was to return to London with Addison; but his letter had at least plenty of "good words" in it. "I am quite ashamed for myself and friends, to see you left in a place so incapable of tasting you;* and to see so much merit, and so great qualities, unrewarded by those who are sensible of them. Mr. Addison and I are entered into a new confederacy, never to give over the pursuit, nor to cease reminding those who can serve you, till your worth is placed in that light it ought to shine in.   Dr. South holds out still, but he can not be immortal. The situation of his prebend would make me doubly concerned in serving you; and upon all occasions that shall offer, I will be your constant solicitor, your sincere admirer, and your unalterable friend." In the middle of the following month Swift thanked him for being pleased to remember a useless man at so great a distance, where it would be pardonable for idlest friends of his own level to forget him; and added that if the gentle winter should not carry off Doctor South, or the rever-

Reminder
to Lord
Somers.

sion of his prebend was not to be compassed, perhaps Lord Halifax might so use his credit, that, as Lord Somers thought of him last year for the bishopric of Waterford, so my lord president might now think of him for that of Cork, if the incumbent died of the fever he was under. There was no irony; but a gentle hint was conveyed, that what might be easy to an ex-minister without power, a

Of Ireland.

* Upon the back of the letter is written in Swift's hand, "I kept this as a true Originall of courtiers and court - promises."   A characteristic passage about Ireland, from his acknowledgment of it, may be subjoined: "I join with your lordship in one compliment, because it is grounded on so true a knowledge of the taste of this country, where I can assure you, and I call Mr. Addison for my witness, I pass as undistinguished, in every point that is merit with your lordship, as any man in it. But then I do them impartial justice; for, except the Bishop of Clogher and perhaps one or two more, my opinion is extremely uniform of the whole kingdom."

minister might find more difficult who had the means to give effect to his recommendation.

The letter to Lord Pembroke, which I found among the Narford MSS. with indorsement by Fountaine that the earl had sent it to him to read, began with punning allusions to his bodily ailment, into which he insinuates a regret that Ireland should now have another lord lieutenant.* He then says he has sent Sir Andrew Fountaine a very learned description that he hopes he has communicated to Doctor Sloane and Doctor Woodward, of an old Roman floor he has discovered in Leicester which was to be sold "a pennyworth;" but against buying which there were two objections: that it could not be taken up without breaking, and that it would be too heavy for carriage. He adds that Fountaine had fallen out with him because he could not prevail with a fellow in Leicester to part with three Saxon coins "which the owner values as I did my Alexander seal, and with equal judgment." The remark is followed by a pun;† as excuse for another, he desires to be made captain of a man-of-war of fifty guns for a fortnight, until he gets to Ireland; and the letter‡ closes with a sort of punning bonfire. "I beg your excellency will

* "I am inform'd you have been pleased to railly upon my misfortunes; because I have got an ailment incommodious for riding. But had your excellency been lieutenant of Ireland, if Pelion had been piled upon Ossa I would have been there before now."

† "There were some fellows here last year that could make medals faster than the Padua Brothers; and they dealt altogether in modern ones, and usually struck them upon the high road: I desire to know whether they were not properly Pad-way Brothers. I beg your excellency will send me a commission to be captain of a man-of-war for a fortnight till I get to Ireland. But I can do without it. For if the coasting privateers dare accoast me, I will so rattle out

your name, that it shall fright them as much as ever your ancestor's did at Boulogne. I always thought ships had rats enough of their own without being troubled with py-rats. Hence comes the old proverb: poison for rats and powder for pyrates. There is another proverb in your own calling which I suppose you know the original of: Ships when they are in dock are quiet, but at sea they sting all they come near. Hence came the saying, In Dock, out Nettle. I shall be at the sea-side in two days, and shall wish heartily for some of your snuff against the bilch-water."

‡ Addressed, "For the Rt. Hon. the Earl of Pembroke, Lord High Admirall &c. at his House in St. James's Square, London."

1709-1710;
Æt. 42-43.

order your fleets to beat the French this summer, that we may have a peace about Michaelmas, and see your lordship in Ireland again by spring. For which a million of people in that kingdom would rejoice as much as myself. Mr. Ashe assures me that whenever you come over, the whole island will be so inflamed with joy and bonfires, that it will all turn to Ashes to receive you."

Attentions
of Addison.

The day after these letters were written Swift left Leicester. A letter from Addison awaited him at Chester, "longing to talk over all affairs" with him, anticipating his friend's wish to have a ship at his disposal, and inclosing a direction to "the captain of the Wolf to accommodate him with all in his power:" failing which, a place was to be reserved in a government yacht.* He appears to have preferred the yacht, for, after staying a fortnight at Chester, he did not cross until the end of June. "Set sail from Darpool for Ireland June 29th 1709 at 3 a clock in the morning being Wednesday, lay that night in the bay of Dublin, and landed at Ringsend the next day at 7

Goes at once
to Laracor.

in the morning, and went strait to Laracor without seeing anybody, and returned to Dublin July 4 which was Monday following."† This agrees exactly with what is said in his *Memoirs relating to the Change*. "I stayed some months in Leicestershire, went to Ireland, and immediately upon my landing retired to my country parish without seeing the lieutenant or any other person, resolving to

Ante, 264.

send him Lord Somers's letter by post. But, being called up to town by the incessant entreaties of my friends, I went and delivered my letter and immediately withdrew.

---

* "The yacht will come over with the acts of parliament, and a convoy, about a week hence, which opportunity you may lay hold of, if you do not like the Wolf. I will give orders accordingly."—*Addison from Dublin Castle, 25th June*, 1709.

† From the same curious record in his note-books I take the route of his journey from Leicester to Chester:

June 14th: Left Leicester June 14th 1709. Journey to Chester. Diner &c. at Bruton-on-the-Hill, 2ˢ 10ᵈ. Stone, 6ˢ. Nantwich, 3ˢ 9ᵈ. Came to Chester 15th on Wednesday. At Chester to 19th 12ˢ 6ᵈ. Carriage 2 boxes, 14ˢ 6ᵈ. 26th Board Mⁿ. Kinalton's 10ˢ. 27th Boxes carrᵈ to Parkgate 2ˢ. 30th Ringsend."

During the greatest part of his government I lived in the country, saw the lieutenant very seldom when I came to town, nor ever entered into the least degree of confidence with him, or his friends, except his secretary, Mr. Addison, who had been my old and intimate acquaintance." He afterward reminded Esther Johnson that he had told her his intention so to live; and "you know I kept it; and, except Mr. Addison, conversed with none but you and your club of deans and Stoytes." She had reproached him for going straight to Laracor without coming first to see her in Dublin; and when next in London he remembered this, and promised her never to do it again. "I think it very hard," wrote Addison, disappointed in not seeing him at once, "I should be in the same kingdom with Doctor Swift, and not have the happiness of his company once in three days." Every part of his own statement is thus borne out by independent testimony; and to give countenance to party slander by reviving, even for the purpose of contradicting, any such averment as that he had turned savagely against Wharton only because Wharton treated with contempt intercessions made for him by Somers, is a grave injustice. Many imputations not ill founded are to be made against Swift, but that of having shown himself a sycophant or a slave is not one of them; and if satisfactory proof to the contrary has not here been given, the duty undertaken by the present writer is ill discharged.

That he was led thus to withdraw himself in a great measure from Dublin life by finding himself at odds with the policy of Lord Wharton's government, there can be little doubt; and his friendship for Addison, as well as his personal engagements with other members of the ministry, made his course a difficult one. Opening the Dublin parliament the month before his arrival, Lord Wharton had taken a decided tone upon "the necessity there was of cultivating and preserving a good understanding among all the Protestants of this kingdom," than which, perhaps, wiser counsel was never given; but Swift knew very well what

Margin notes:
1709–1710.
Æt. 42–43.
In retirement.

False charges.
See Scott, I., 97–103.

Objections to Wharton's government.

1709-1710.
Æt. 42-43. it pointed at, and was determined to continue his resistance to the repeal of the Test. He kept himself aloof, therefore, waiting his time.

It did not arrive that session: but there was to be a bill next year, it was said; and, immediately after Addison went back for the meeting of the English parliament, came the letter from Lord Halifax above quoted, and also Steele to Swift. a letter from Steele. "I assure you," wrote the good-hearted gazetteer, "no man could say more in praise of another than Mr. Secretary Addison did in your behalf at Lord Halifax's table on Wednesday last.... No opportunity is omitted among powerful men to upbraid 'em for your stay in Ireland.... I have heard such things said of that same Bishop of Clogher with you, that I have often said he must be entered *ad eundem* in our House of More of Bickerstaff expected. Lords.... The town is in great expectation from Bickerstaff.... I have not seen Ben Tooke a great while, but long to usher you and yours into the world. Not that there can be any thing added by me to your fame, but to walk bareheaded before you." All which seems to make it clear enough that if Swift was uneasy in what Henley called the inhospitable island* on which he had been cast, the great people responsible for casting or for leaving him there were uneasy too. Steele's letter mentions other things. He had received lately some *Tatlers* from the Vicar of Laracor, and he had heard of the great intimacy struck up between the Bishop of Clogher and the Irish The new Irish Secretary. Swift's note-books also tell us that he and Addison had passed several summer days at the bishop's houses in Clogher and Finglas; and that, both there and at Laracor, "little MD" was with them. "People of all

---

* Though six or seven years were to pass before De Foe's immortal masterpiece was written, there are whimsical foreshadowings of *Crusoe* in Henley's quaint letter: "You are now cast on an inhospitable island: no mathematical figures on the sand, no *vestigia hominum* to be seen; perhaps at this very time reduced to one single barrel of damaged biscuit...... Eat—do I live to bid thee! —eat Addison!! and when you have eat every body else, eat my lord lieutenant (he's something lean, God help the while)!"......

sorts," Swift wrote afterward of Esther Johnson, "were
never more easy than in her company.   Mr. Addison,
when he was in Ireland, being introduced to her, immediately found her out; and if he had not soon after left the
kingdom, assured me he would have used all endeavors to
cultivate her friendship."*   One habit in conversation she
had in common with Addison.   "Whether," says Swift,
"from her easiness in general, or from her indifference to
persons, or from her despair of mending them, or from the
same practice which she much liked in Mr. Addison, I can
not determine; but when she saw any of the company very
warm in a wrong opinion, she was more inclined to confirm them in it than to oppose them.   It prevented noise,
she said, and saved time."†   Nevertheless Swift hints that
though she did this herself, and liked to see it done by
Addison, he had known her very angry with some whom
she much esteemed (doubtless himself) "for sometimes
falling into that infirmity."   Perhaps her great friend's
touch was not so light as Addison's or her own.

The principal incident after Addison's departure was
the attack by Lady Giffard, who put forth a coarse advertisement in the *Postman* to the effect that in the last volume of her brother Sir William Temple's *Remains* his
Memoirs had been printed by Doctor Swift from an unfaithful copy.   Swift's reply has been given, disposing thoroughly of the charge; but he never forgave the wrong attempted to be done, and there is much significance in a remark which may here be added from his letter of the 10th
of November:‡   "Several of my friends in London sent

Margin notes:
1709-1710.
Æt. 42-43.
Addison and Esther Johnson.

Attack on Swift by Temple's sister.

Ante, 112.

---

* "All of us," he adds, "who had
the happiness of her friendship agreed
unanimously, that, in an afternoon's
or evening's conversation, she never
failed, before we parted, of delivering
the best thing that was said in the
company."

† This is the passage from which
Macaulay derived his remark on "one
habit" in Addison which he hardly

knew how to blame.   "If his first
attempts to set a presuming dunce
right were ill-received, he changed
his tone; 'assented with civil leer,'
and lured the flattered coxcomb deeper and deeper into absurdity."

‡ Wrongly dated "London" in the
portion of it printed by Mr. Courte-
nay.—*Temple,* ii., 243-'6.

1709-1710.
Æt. 42-43.
me that advertisement, but the packet coming to the secretary's office here, they were not conveyed to me till very
lately. The writer of the *Postman* pleads for his excuse
that the advertisement was taken in and printed without
his knowledge, and that he refused to repeat it, tho' urged
in your ladyship's name. He thought it too unchristian
for him to defend. But all that shall not provoke me to
do a disrespectful action to any of Sir William Temple's
Temperate reply. family, and therefore I have directed an answer wholly
consistent with religion and good manners.... I do not
expect your ladyship or family will ask my leave for what
you are to say, but all people should ask leave of reason
and religion rather than of resentment; and will your
ladyship think, indeed, that it is agreeable to either to reflect in print upon the veracity of an innocent man? Or
is it agreeable to prudence, or at least to caution, to do
that which might break all measures with any man who is
capable of retaliating?" Nor perhaps was this the only
subject, as another brief month brought other news from
England, that crossed his mind with uneasy sensation of
Exciting news from England. a power to retaliate. Early in December the first movement was made for impeachment of Sacheverell, and, the
whigs having taken thus to the luxury of roasting a parson, he must have felt that very soon would come the trial
of his own repeated notes of warning. The impeachment
began in February, sentence was given at the end of
March, and Harley was not only ready with his part, but
had forced his way behind the scenes. On the 11th of
April, Addison announced to Swift the approaching return of Lord Wharton and himself for the opening of the
Dublin session, telling him that in the satisfaction of again
seeing such a friend he lost all regret at leaving England,
that Steele and he had been often drinking Doctor Swift's
Favorite dish of Swift and Addison. health, and that he longed heartily to eat *a dish of beans
and bacon* with the best company in the world. "Your
friends at St. James's coffee-house are always asking me
questions about you when they have a mind to pay their
court to me, if I may use so magnificent a phrase. Pray,

dear Doctor, continue your friendship toward me, who loves and esteems you,* if possible, as much as you deserve." Swift never doubted it, or the continuance of his own part in their friendship; and it must have increased his difficulty, upon revival of last year's allusions to the Test in Wharton's address to the houses at Addison's return, in going again into opposition. But he did not hesitate; and to the first trial of party strength in election of a speaker, Brodrick having been made a peer, he contributed a letter without his name which had so much effect on the division that the bill was again withheld. The authorship was of course suspected.†

During these two months of April and May we have two glimpses of him at Laracor. On Sunday, the 17th of April, he wrote to tell the Dean of St. Patrick's that the ladies of St. Mary's, Esther Johnson and Rebecca Dingley, have arrived and delivered his commands, though Mrs. Johnson had dropped half of them by the shaking of her horse; that, as he expects soon to have these exiles from St. Mary's lamenting the flesh-pots of Cavan Street (the Dean's house), he is advising them to buy each of them a palfrey, and take a squire and seek adventures; and that for himself, he is just about to preach to his audience of fifteen, and is meanwhile quarreling with the frost for spoiling his poor half-dozen blossoms. "Spes anni collapsa ruit."‡ On Wednesday, the 10th of May, he writes

---

* Incorrectly, in all the printed copies, who "love and esteem" you.

† I possess the original of this tract in Swift's handwriting. It is excellently written throughout, and a couple of sentences will sufficiently show that it maintains the tone always taken by him on the Test question: "You know very well the great business of the high-flying whigs, at this juncture, is to endeavor a repeal of the Test clause. You know likewise that the moderate men, both of high and low church, profess to be wholly averse from this design, as thinking it beneath the policy of common gardeners to *cut down a hedge that shelters from the north*." In the printed copy it is "the only hedge;" and the numerous other more serious misprints suggest alarming considerations as to the condition of Swift's printed text generally. The remark applies equally, I regret to say, to the great number of printed letters which I have had opportunity of comparing with the originals.—*Ante*, 96–'7, etc.

‡ Those words are followed in the original by the subjoined, omitted in the printed copy: "Pray, sir, favor

1709–1710.
Æt. 42–43.
in his note-book, that between seven and eight that evening, in his chamber at Laracor, Mr. Perceval and Joe Beaumont being by, he received a letter from his sister inclosing one to her from Mrs. Worrall at Leicester, giving ac-
Swift's moth- count that his dear mother, Mrs. Abigail Swift, died that
er's death. morning, Monday, 24th April, 1710, about ten o'clock. " I
have now," this touching record closes, "lost my barrier
between me and death. God grant I may live to be as
well prepared for it as I confidently believe her to have
been ! If the way to heaven be through piety, truth, justice, and charity, she is there." The same note-book has
an entry which shows that she had been able to write to
her son during the month preceding her death ; and the
regularity of their intercourse in this way has pleasing il-
Letters writ- lustration in the same valuable records. In his account-
ten and re-
ceived in book for 1709 he sets down two lists of letters written
summer and and received; from the middle of June to the close of Oc-
autumn of
1709. tober, and from the opening of July to October 30th.
Here are the letters written : " June 13th, Lord Mountjoy,
Lord Halifax, Mr. Steele, Mrs. Vanhomrigh, MD. ; 24th
(inclosed to Reading), Mr. Tooke." (Those were " to 30th,
at Chester :") " Mother, Mr. Addison, Bishop Clogher."
(From " Ireland :") " July 8th, Mother ; 18th, Mrs. Barton, Sir A. Fountaine. August, Sir A. Fountaine, Mrs.
Barton ; 17th, Lady Giffard. Sept. 13th, Mother, Mr.
Tooke, Parvisol. Oct. 20th, Mr. Addison, H. Coote ; 30th,
Mr. Addison, Mr. Steele, Mr. Philips, Sir And. Fountaine,
Bishop Clogher." And here the letters received : " July
1st, Mrs. Barton, Sir And. Fountaine, Mishessy, Mr. Addi-
son (returned me from Chester), Lord Mountjoy. Aug.

Swift's lead-   me so far as to present my duty to   the employment of his parishioners,
ing parish-   my Lord Bishop of Cork : and I wish   which "for memory sake may be re-
ioners.   he knew how concerned I was not   duced under these heads : Mr. Perce-
               to find him at home when I went to   val is ditching ; Mrs. Perceval in her
               wait on him before I left the town." kitchen ; Mr. Wesley switching ; Mrs.
               This was Doctor Brown, ex-provost   Wesley stitching ; Sir Arthur Lang-
               of Dublin College, newly appointed   ford riching, which is a new word for
               to the see he had hoped that Somers   heaping up riches. I know no other
               and Halifax might have bestowed on   rhyme but bitching, and that I hope
               himself. In the same letter he gives we are all past."

6th, Sir A. Fountaine, Lady Giffard, Mother; 16th, Mr. Philips (Copenhagen), Mr. Tooke; 24th, Sir A. Fountaine. Oct. 23d, Sir A. Fountaine, Lord Halifax, Mr. Steele; 30th, Mr. Addison, Mr. Philips (from London), Sir A. Fountaine, Mother."* One of the letters thus received

---

* It may amuse the reader if, from the same curious and very interesting records, I show something of Swift's card-playing. Here is a note of his gains and losses as far back as 1702-'3, when his principal games were piquet and ombre, and his principal antagonists Perceval, Sterne (afterward dean), and the Bishop of Clogher :

1702–1703.	Lost.	£	s.	d.		Won.	£	s.	d.
Since Nov' 1ˢᵗ a bet		0	10	0	Feb. 11ᵗʰ Ombre		2	10	0
Feb. 10ᵗʰ Pick' with Mʳ Perce'ˡ		0	8	6	— 12ᵗʰ Picket		0	16	6
May 21ˢᵗ Pick' Perce'ˡ		0	4	0	Apr. 16ᵗʰ Omb' at Kⁿᵍᵉ		0	2	8½
Nov' 29ᵗʰ Ombre B. Clogher		0	4	6	— 17ᵗʰ Pick' wᵗʰ Dʳ Stⁿᵉ		0	1	0
	£1	7	0			£3	10	11¼

An entry as to the closing months of 1708-'9 shows the result of his games of piquet and ombre with Lord Berkeley at Cranford and Epsom, with Fountaine, Mrs. Barton, and Mrs. Finch, and with Mrs. Long at the Vanhomrighs' :

1708–1709.	Lost.	£	s.	d.		Won.	£	s.	d.
Nov' 22ᵈ to 27ᵗʰ Picq' at Cranford.	1	10	0	Nov' 5ᵗʰ Lᵈ B. & Ombr. at Epsom	1	1	6
December 2ᵈ Ombr. Lᵈ B. and Sʳ				Dec' 4ᵗʰ Bartous Ombre		0	2	0
A. F.		0	16	6	— 29ᵗʰ Piq' Mʳˢ Finch		0	0	6
Decemb' 6ᵗʰ Piqu' Lᵈ Berkly		0	8	0	Jan' 20ᵗʰ Ombrᵉ Long, Van Homᵗ	0	0	6

To this I add the entries covering his time in Ireland, after the stay with his mother at Leicester, from the autumn of 1709 up to the eve of his departure for London in August, 1710. This period includes for his principal antagonists, Perceval, a friend of his named Barry, Wesley, his curate Warburton, and the Vicar of Trim, the games played, doubtless, while he was at Laracor. There are also games with Ppt, Walls, Stoyte, Manley, the dean, and the bishop; and, besides ombre and piquet, they appear to have comprised basset, tables, and "whish:"

1709.	Lost.	£	s.	d.		1709.	Won.	£	s.	d.
Sep' 26ᵗʰ Ombr. Walls, Ombr.					Sep' 8ᵗʰ Ombr. for Ppt		0	4	0
morgᵈ before		0	1	1	— 9ᵗʰ Ombr. for Ppt		0	2	0
Oct' 5ᵗʰ Piq' Perce'ˡ		0	1	0	— 16ᵗʰ Ombr. Walls, Dean Sᵗ			
— 8ᵗʰ Piq' Barry		0	10	0	Ppt		0	0	8
— 8ᵗʰ Piq' Id		0	4	3	— 17ᵗʰ Ombr. Id		0	1	8
— 11ᵗʰ Piq' Id		0	1	1	— 2ᵈ Ombr. Id		0	2	10
— 15ᵗʰ Ombr. Barry's		0	5	7	— 24ᵗʰ Ombr.		0	2	0
— 18ᵗʰ Wesley		0	5	5	— 28ᵗʰ Ombr. Trᵐ Raymᵈ		0	1	10
— 19ᵗʰ Piq' Barry		0	2	2	Oct' 13ᵗʰ Piqu' Barry		0	5	0
	£4	18	4		— 24ᵗʰ Omᵇ Rayᵈ		0	0	8
	4	2	4	— 26ᵗʰ Piq' Barry		0	2	2
Won this year	£0	16	0	— 31ˢᵗ Bass' Raymᵈ		0	1	4

1709-1710. has a special significance. "Mishessy" was Hester Van-
Æt. 42-43. homrigh, who had thus early taken on herself to write;
nor was it her only letter. The spring of 1710 brought
another.

Sudden downfall of whig ministy.

Ten days before the first great blow against the whigs
was struck by the removal of Sunderland, Addison wrote,
in the old earnest strain, that he loved Doctor Swift's company, and valued his conversation more than any man's.
How keenly at the time his friend was watching affairs on
the other side appears in a passage of his letter to his publisher (29th June) about the proposed new edition of the
Tale of a Tub: "I have thoughts of some other work one

Thoughts of another book.

of these years; and I hope to see you ere it be long; since
it is likely to be a new world, and since I have the merit
of suffering by not complying with the old." Less than
a month later came another letter from Addison, the last
he wrote to his friend in the character of Irish Secretary,

Lost and won at cards.

1709.	Lost.	£	s.	d.
Novr 2^d Ombr. Perce^{vl} Barry.....		0	6	10
— 4th Piq^t Barry..............		0	2	2
— 9th Ombr and Piq^t Perc^{ll} and				
Barry.......		0	10	10
— 22^d to Decr 20th at Clogher				
with Bp. & Dean & Cards				
and Tables in all........		0	16	0

1709-1710.

	£	s.	d.
Decr 28th Tables Wesly..........	0	4	4
— 31st Ombr. Raym^d Morgan..	0	2	2
Jan^r 24th Ombr. Ppt. & Lei.......	0	1	4
— 20th Piq^t Bp. Cl.......	0	0	6
Feb. 3^d Ombr. Mrs Manley.......	0	2	9
— 6th Ombr. Mrs Manley........	0	1	1
— 7th Ombr. Walls*........./.....	0	2	10
— 13th			
— 18th Ombr. Ppt..............	0	0	11
Mar. 15th Tables Wesley.......	0	3	3
— 24th Basset Walls Ppt.......	0	0	8
— 27th Lost for Ppt.			
— 30th Lost for Ppt.			
Apr. 5th Ombr. Stu^s Walls........	0	0	5
May 18th Ombr. Barry, Percev^{ll}..	0	2	6
— 20th Ombre Barry, Percev^{ll}			
[the last]...............	0	9	2
June 8. Ombre, Walls............	0	4	2

1710.

	£	s.	d.
June 26th Om^r Walls. Manly......	0	3	11
July 22^d Ombr Punch Jo. Warb ..	0	1	2
Aug. 1st Ombr. Walls	0	0	0
— 7th P^d for Ppt. Walls, Ombr.	0	1	1
— 23^d Omb. Walls, Stoit.			

1709.	Won.	£	s.	d.
Novr 7th Omb^r Ray^d &c..........		0	2	7
— 8th Omb^r Percev^l Barry.....		0	5	8
" Ombr. and whish. Raym^d				
Morgan...................		0	2	4

1709-10.

	£	s.	d.
Decr 26th Tables Wesley..........	0	6	6
— 27th Ombre, Raym^d Morg^s..	0	1	1
Jan. 3^d Ombr. D. Sterne.........	0	2	5
Mar. 6th Bassett, L^{dy} &c..........	0	2	0
— 14th Bass^t Perc^{vlls}..........	0	0	6
— 21st Ombr. Raym^d Ppt......	0	4	4
— 22^d Ombr. Mrs Walls........	0	5	6
Apr. 6th Ombr. Manley Walls*....	0	3	2
June 13th Ombr. Mrs Tigh^e Bar^y...	0	6	6

1710.

	£	s.	d.
June 21st Ombr. D. St^e Walls.....	0	3	4
July 27th Omb^r Manl^y Ppt........	0	4	11
Augt 5. Ombre, Walls, Ppt........	0	1	4

transmitting to him, with the old earnest assurances, a let-
ter from Steele, which he fancies "he had my Lord Hali-
fax's authority for writing;" which has not itself survived,
but to which was doubtless applicable his own descrip-
tion of all the whig letters of the time. "I was a sort of
bough," he said, "for drowning men to lay hold of." The
only other notice he took of it was a dry intimation to the
secretary that he should take some occasion to let my Lord
Halifax know the sense he had "of the favor he *intended
me.*" A few days after his letter, a threatened dissolution
of parliament had recalled Addison suddenly to England
to provide for his election at Malmesbury; and when
Swift wrote to him, on the 22d of August, Godolphin had
broken his staff, the treasurership was in commission, and
the general whig overthrow was begun. During the sum-
mer months, while these great changes went on, he had
been keeping a strict silence; in which he persisted, even
against Fountaine's wish, that if he didn't break it, might
Parvisol break his snuff-box, his half acre turn to a bog,
his willows perish, and worms eat up his Plato! It was
very hard, Sir Andrew added, that though there might be
never a bishop in England with the wit of St. George
Ashe, nor ever a secretary of state with a quarter of Ad-
dison's good sense, therefore Swift could not write to those
that loved him as well as any Clogher or Addison of them
all.* The silence, nevertheless, was first broken to Addi
son. "I believe you had the displeasure of much ill news,"
Swift wrote, "almost as soon as you landed. Even the
moderate tories here are in pain at these revolutions, be-
ing what will certainly affect the Duke of Marlborough,
and consequently the success of the war. My lord lieu-
tenant asked me yesterday when I intended for England.
I said I had no business there now, since I suppose in a
little time I should not have one friend left that had any
credit; and his excellency was of my opinion." He then
asked Addison freely to advise whether it would be worth

Marginal notes: 1709–1710. Æt. 42–43. Drowning men. Fountaine to Swift. Doubts of the change.

---

* Addressed "At Mr. Curry's, over against the Ram in Capel Street, Dublin."

1709-1710.
Æt. 42–43. his while to go to England, or if there was any probability that the lord president might continue; and, complying with his friend's wish to know what still was in his
thoughts, mentioned Doctor South's prebend or sinecure,
Uncertain
of his own
course. and the place of historiographer. "But if things go on
in the train they are now, I shall only beg you, when there
is an account to be depended on for a new government
here, that you will give me early notice, to procure an addition to my fortunes." Of his friend's own fortunes he
added, with generous warmth, that every thing he might
wish for would still remain to him after office was gone.
"If you will come over again, when you are at leisure, we
will raise an army and make you King of Ireland." The
letter ends with a mention of books possessing still an interest for us. Bishop Clogher had shown him the small
Collected
Tatler. edition of the *Tatler*, where there was a very handsome
compliment to himself; but he could never pardon the
printing the news of every *Tatler*, and thought that Steele
might as well have printed the advertisements. "I knew
it was a book-seller's piece of craft to increase the bulk
and price of what he was sure would sell; but I utterly
disapprove it." Then comes a delightful passage about
Mrs. Man-
ley's Mem-
oirs. the picture of Addison in Mrs. Manley's "noble *Memoirs*,"
where the book is hit off with humorous precision in a single sentence. It seemed to him as if she had about two
thousand epithets and fine words packed up in a bag; that
she pulled them out by handfuls, and strewed them on her
paper; and that about once in five hundred times they
turned up right.

Swift was certainly still in doubt, when he wrote that
letter, whether or not he should go to England, though for
some weeks the thought had been in his mind that a sea-
voyage might be helpful to him. It has been seen how
much he had been troubled lately by his old enemies;
and, under like suffering many years later, he is found
writing to his friend Chetwode that a "hard journey"
from England had driven away, just then, both ailments
for a time. A like opportunity now unexpectedly arose.

Archbishop King had been in London the previous year, and at his return had recommended two Irish bishops whom he left behind him, Ossory and Killaloe, to keep watch over the subject of the first-fruits. But it had since occurred, both to him and the primate, in the new condition of affairs, that Swift, who had formerly rendered good service in the matter, ought again to be employed in it; and at their instance a proposal had been made to join him in a sort of formal commission with the two bishops in London. Such an arrangement was not agreeable to him; but, believing it to be merely a form, and that practically the "soliciting" would be left to himself, he accepted it; not sorry, at least, of the excuse for his journey. It was all so hurriedly arranged that the commission bore date on the very day Swift left, only nine days after he had written to Addison; and a brief sentence to the archbishop nine days later, which was the next day but one after he reached London, would perhaps express with some exactness the thought in his mind when he quitted Dublin: "I will apply to Mr. Harley, who formerly made some advances toward me; and, unless he be altered, will, I believe, think himself in the right to use me well."

1709-1710.
Æt. 42-43.
First-fruits commission.

Swift joins it: 31st Aug.

II.

OLD FRIENDS AND NEW.

1710. Æt. 43.

Swift's first three months in London in 1710, from the 10th of September to the 10th of December, prepared all that came in the three following years. Before they were over, he had disembarrassed himself of his old party relations, though retaining many of his old party friends; had cast in his fortunes with the ministry then supplanting Godolphin's; and, through Harley, had obtained the queen's concession of the boon for the Irish clergy which he had so long desired, for which he so incessantly had la-

1710.
Æt. 43.

First three
months in
London.

bored, and which it was the first object of his present visit to crave. These three changeful months, the prelude to three dazzling years, at once closed some chapters of the past and foreshadowed the future that was opening. They are described in the earlier letters of the Journal to Stella: not correctly so called, as I have said; because, at the time when the letters composing it were addressed to Esther Johnson and her companion, the name which eternally connects her with Swift had not been applied to her. Most certainly it was not used in any part of the letters themselves, nor had been previously in any known piece of writing concerning her.

Joe Beaumont accompanied him to the ship in which, attended by his servant Patrick, he embarked for England, having for fellow-voyagers his friend Lord Mountjoy, and the lord lieutenant. He reached Parkgate on Friday, the 1st of September, after a fifteen hours' sail; and in riding to Chester his horse fell with him. But the horse understanding falls very well, and lying quietly till his rider got up, there was no hurt. The first man he met in Chester, and introduced at his request to Lord Wharton, was his friend the Vicar of Trim, who with Mrs. Raymond had crossed on some law business; and he was so pressed by Lord Mountjoy, that Saturday afternoon, to begin the London journey at once, that, stealing time only to write a brief letter to Esther Johnson, with another to the Bishop of Clogher, and to pay a short visit to his coz Abigail, whom he found grown prodigiously old, they started next morning. Never, he told her, had he come to England in all his life with so little desire; and he had a perfect resolution to return as soon as he should have finished his commission, whether successful or not.

On Thursday, the 7th of September, after five days' travel (weary the first, almost dead the second, tolerable the third, and well enough the rest), Swift arrived in London. The fatigue had served for exercise, yet had not quenched the appetite for more exercise. Before Saturday was over he had conferred with some leading mem-

Ride to
Chester.

Cousin
Abigail.

Busy days.

bers of the whig ministry, among them the ex-lord-treas-   1710.
urer himself; had seen the Duke of Ormond, reported   Æt. 43.
likely to be the new lord lieutenant, and conveyed to him
messages from the new provost of the college; had visited
Steele, whom he found expecting to lose his place of gazetteer for attacking the tories; had seen his publisher, Ben
Tooke; had dined with his physician, Doctor Cockburn;
had passed Saturday afternoon with Sir Mat Dudley and
the son of the English postmaster-general, Will Frankland;
had met sundry other whig friends or associates at the
coffee-house that evening, among them Jemmy Leigh and
the painter Jervas; and on reaching home at night so act-
ively continued to employ himself, that by ten o'clock he
had written to Archbishop King and sent off his second
letter to Esther Johnson, and before going to bed had be-   Begins his
gun his Journals. Briefly I may add what that second   Journals.
letter contained.

Very cordial had been his reception from all private   Reception
friends. So much fatter and better was he looking, that   by friends.
Jervas had made him promise to sit for a retouching of
his picture, and already he is under engagement to Will
Frankland to christen the baby his wife is near bringing
to bed. The two days have not sufficed to carry him
round half his circle; but thus far all is as formerly, except that he may have lost a friend, and has certainly got
an enemy, at court—Lady Wharton having taken to laugh
at the royal circle, and old Lady Giffard having been much
received there. Jack Temple and his wife had passed by
him in their coach; but he took no notice, and is glad to
think he had wholly shaken off the family. · It is because
he will *not* see Lady Giffard that he has not yet seen Esther's mother; but he promises to contrive to see her in
the absence of the objectionable person. The whigs generally were ravished to see him, but as with the eagerness
of drowning men; for every thing was turning upside
down, and as every whig in great office would, to a man,
be infallibly put out, they were lavish of clumsy apologies
to their old champion in the matter of his preferment.

1710.
Æt. 43.
Exception
to the
greetings.
There was nevertheless one exception: the dry Godolphin
having shown him so much coldness that he was almost
vowing revenge. Perhaps it would again be as it had
been. Every body asked him how he came to be so long
in Ireland, as naturally as if London were his being, yet
no soul offered to make it so; and he protested he should
return to the canal at Laracor with more satisfaction than
he ever did in his life. Let them prepare, then. She and
Dingley are peaceably in his lodgings by this time, but he
Premature
resolve.
resolves to turn them out by Christmas; when he will
either have done his business, or found it not to be done.
And so, with a message to the provost, and his service to
the dean and Mrs. Walls and her archdeacon, he winds up
his brief dispatch just to tell her he is safe in London.
For "it is near ten," and he "hates to send by the bellman."

On the same night when that letter went, he began his
Journals, and their first entry recorded his intercession
with the English postmaster for a friend of Esther's, the
Irish postmaster Manley, whose office was greedily sought
in that shaking season for places, against whom there was
some charge of opening letters, and for whom there was
but little chance since Frankland himself was in danger.
Lord Somers was still lord president, though waiting only
the elections, a dissolution being now resolved, though the
Treason
against old
friends.
time was not fixed; but Swift, the day before he went to
him, fell in at "the club" with a discontented whig, Lord
Radnor, with whom for an hour and a half he talked treason heartily against the whigs, their baseness and ingrati-
tude. He came home afterward rolling resentments in
his mind and framing schemes of revenge; in fulfillment
of which he wrote some hints on that and on the following night, when he was discussing party changes even with
English and
Irish rabble.
his servant, Patrick. That worthy had taken occasion to
observe that the rabble in England were much more in-
quisitive in politics than the rabble in Ireland; and this
was his master's experience also, for he protests he never
saw so great a ferment among all sorts of people; and as
for Lord Wharton, who expected every day to be out, he

was working "like a horse" for elections. Next day, after
introducing Charles Ford to the Duke of Ormond, Swift
visited Lord Somers; from whose uneasy questioning,
which he appears to have thought but a part of the same
electioneering as Wharton's, he turned off and asked counsel as to the first-fruits. "I put him always off when he
began of Lord Wharton in relation to me, till he urged it:
then I said he knew I never expected any thing from Lord
Wharton, and that Lord Wharton knew I understood it
so." Upon this, Somers remarked that he had written
twice about Swift to Wharton, who both times said nothing at all to that part of his letter;* and, for himself, expecting every day for these two months to be out, his advice as to the first-fruits was that it would be much best
not to meddle with it till the existing hurry was over.
The interview was on the 12th, and it left Swift something depressed: "I protest upon my life I am heartily
weary of this town, and wish I had never stirred."

Two nights before, Sunday, the 10th, he had been at the
St. James's with Addison and Steele until ten o'clock (after dining with Lord Mountjoy in Kensington, where he
found his old mistress, Ophy Butler's wife, grown a little
charmless); and had advised Steele strongly not to "engage in parties." Next day he sat four hours to Jervas,
who gave his picture quite another turn; so that now the
painter himself approved it entirely, and only waited to
have the approbation of the town. "If I were rich
enough," says Swift, "I would get a copy of it and bring
it over."† That day he dined alone with Addison at his
lodgings, and sat with him in the evening. Four days
later, Addison, Colonel Freind, and himself, went to see

1710.
Æt. 43.

Interview
with Somers.

With Addi-
son and
Steele.

Sitting to
Jervas.
Ante, 240.

* Exactly confirmatory of what is
said, *ante*, 291.
† That masterly artist, Vertue, en-
graved very finely this portrait, as
well as Pope's by the same hand,
Jervas himself superintending the
work. "I intend this day," writes
Jervas to Pope, "to call at Vertue's,
to see Swift's brought a little more
like, and see what is doing to one
Pope."—*Supplement to Roscoe's Pope*,
13, in which a note attributes to
Kneller the Swift portrait spoken of!
But a worse-edited book than Roscoe's hardly exists in literature.

1710.
Æt. 43.
Lottery at
Guildhall.
the million lottery drawn at Guildhall; laughed at the jackanapes of Bluecoat boys giving themselves absurd airs in pulling out the tickets; afterward dined together at a country house near Chelsea "where Mr. Addison often retires;" and closed the night at the St. James's. Again, three days later, he dined alone with Addison at his Chelsea retreat; and getting home early, began, by way of help
No. 230.
to Steele, a letter for the *Tatler* about the corruptions of style and writing, which he wonders if Bishop Clogher will "smoke" for his. He had taken with him to that
Old class-
fellow,
Stratford.
last dinner, Mr. Stratford, the Hamburg merchant, his old school-fellow and college chum, whose name has been read immediately above his own on the university roll; believed to be at present worth a plum, certainly now lending the government forty thousand pounds, and a man of varied acquaintance. Swift had dined with him at a city merchant's four days before, when he first tasted Tokay, finding it admirable, but not to the degree he expected; and on the 17th they dined together at the country house of Will Pate, the learned woolen-draper. "Six miles here are nothing: we left Pate after sunset, and were here before it was dark." Yet the dinner cost him a venison pasty, to which on his return he found an invitation for that very day; and fancying it by the handwriting to be a letter from Mrs. Johnson, this proved a double disappointment.

He has not been unmindful meanwhile of his lady friends. Bull, the haberdasher on Ludgate-hill, a relative of the bishop who died not many days later, and a decided whig, had a hospitable home at Hampstead, and there at
Whig dinner.
dinner, besides Ben Hoadly, afterward bishop, and a great deal of ill (whig) company, he was delighted to find Lady Lucy and "Moll" Stanhope, and grieved to hear bad news of Mrs. Long's having broken up house and all being a
Ante, 242.
ruin with her. The news was confirmed a few days later, on his dining with a cousin, a printer, at whose house lodged Patty Rolt, another cousin, who had called on him
Ante, 37.
at his arrival. Then came, on the 19th, a pressing letter

from Lady Berkeley, begging him for charity to go and comfort her ailing lord at Berkeley Castle; and that was the memorable day when, without further waiting for the elections, the lord president, lord steward, and secretary of state, Lord Somers, the Duke of Devonshire, and Mr. Boyle, were turned out; to be shortly replaced by Lord Rochester, the Duke of Buckingham, and Mr. Henry St. John. Never had Swift remembered such bold steps taken by a court. He was almost shocked at it, though he did not care if they were all hanged. Strange will it be, he thinks, in the coming winter, to watch the struggles of a cunning, provoked, discarded party, and the triumphs of one in power; but thus far he means to be an indifferent spectator of both, and to return peaceably to Ireland when he has finished, successfully or not, his part in the affair he is intrusted with. One thing—the delay in dissolving parliament—had surprised him; but the day after remarking this, on the 21st, amidst great news from Spain, with Pampeluna taken by Staremberg, and King Charles and Stanhope at Madrid, the dissolution was announced, and Swift sent word of it to Esther Johnson from the St. James's coffee-house, where he had just received her first letter.

There are still a few vivid personal touches which belong to that week of party vicissitudes. Wonderful had been his own composure amidst the whig agitation. Lord Wharton, eagerly busy with elections in Bucks, had been sent for in violent haste by the Duke of Devonshire, but their projects were too late. Each day the coffee-house is shaken by fresh rumors, but Swift, not caring for them, comes "early home." One day the chancellor (Cowper) out, and Sir Simon Harcourt to succeed him; next day Sir Simon to be lord keeper; and two days later the great seal really in commission, and Sir Simon the new attorney-general. "Yesterday" the whig comptroller of the household, Sir John Holland, sent urgently to see Swift, which the latter had a mind to refuse, "but he is a man of worth and learning;" and following day ("pox on these declin-

Margin notes:
1710.
ÆT. 43.
Great ministers deposed.

Dissolution of parliament.

Law changes.

1710.
Æt. 43.
Pope's Duke of Chandos.

ing courtiers!") came a desire for his acquaintance from Brydges, paymaster-general; whom the queen herself, however, by message to the Duke of Shrewsbury, snatched out of the "declining" list. Swift was glad of this, because Brydges had promised him help in the first-fruits affair; and it was more than ever likely to be needed, for on the 18th there had been lost to him suddenly a great ally in the vice-treasurer of Ireland, Lord Anglesea, his leading tory friend. "I could hardly have a loss that could grieve me more." Bishop Bull, of St. David's, died

A lodging next door to Vanhomrigh's.

the same day. Three days later he went into lodgings in Bury Street, next door to Mrs. Vanhomrigh's, and the incidents that followed, up to the first memorable meeting with Harley, occupy his fourth and part of his fifth letter. On the 21st he was one of a dinner-party at the coffee-house with Will Pate, Will Frankland, the Florence envoy Molesworth, Stratford, Steele, and Addison, when a dinner for the same party, at Pate's country house, was appointed for the Sunday following. There are also dinners at Hampstead, with the Dean of Canterbury and Lady Lucy and Moll Stanhope; and with Frankland and his "Fortune," whom he finds not very handsome; and then

At Will Pate's.

another country dinner at Pate's, six miles away, from which he reaches home late, and is both weary and lazy, the day being hot as midsummer. Succeeding day, too,

At Mrs. Van's.

he continued so lazy that he went only next door to dine,* coming back at six to write letters. He dined with Sir John Holland, the comptroller, on the 26th, sitting with him till eight; and this was followed, on the first rainy day since he came, by a dinner at Frankland's, to "all our company," of the Will Pate set, "with Steele and Addison too." He dined next, "alone at her lodgings," where her uncle, Sir Isaac Newton, also lived, with his old friend, Mrs.

At Mrs. Barton's.

Barton; who gave him a bit of scandal about a lady of whose recent marriage Esther had questioned him, telling

---

* Mrs. Vanhomrigh's, though, apparently by mere accident, the name is omitted.

him " for certain " that the lady was with child when last   1710.
in England, and pretended a tympany, and saw every body;   Æt. 43.
then disappeared for three weeks, when, her tympany gone,
she looked like a ghost! And no wonder she married, is
his closing remark, when she was so ill at containing.

On Michaelmas-day he dined with Addison at his Chel-   Dining and
lampooning.
sea retreat, painter Jervas being asked to meet him ; and
on the morrow dined with Stratford at a tavern, where
Erasmus Lewis, just put in for one of the Cornish bor-
oughs, Dartmouth's under-secretary and a great favorite of
Mr. Harley's, was to have been, but was suddenly called
away to his chief at Hampton Court. Some hints had
already been dropped by Swift for carrying out schemes
of revenge suggested by his visit to Godolphin, and he
was not left in doubt as to the eagerness of the new ministers to enlist him in a service to which he is already
more than half inclined. Coming home after that dinner with Addison, he puts fresh touches to a lampoon
against the ex-whig chief ; which he had also worked at
after dining with Holland, another stanch whig, remarking then that it went on " very slow." A tory squib
began to take additional relish from a whig dinner.
Lady Berkeley had invited him to Berkeley Castle, and
Lady Betty Germaine to Drayton in Northamptonshire ;
but he would go to neither. " Let me alone," he adds ;
" I must finish my pamphlet." Ominous even is his remark on the weather as " a season of sudden changes."
Six days ago he was dying with heat, and to-day is a bitterly hard winter cold; but it is not of any suddenness
from heat to cold he has now to accuse the whigs. " It is
good to see what a lamentable confession they all make
me of my ill-usage, but I mind them not." The character   Character
given of him
to Harley.
given of him to Harley, he has heard, is that of a discontented person, used ill for not being whig enough ; and
from him he hopes for good usage. But the tories now
besetting Swift did not scruple to go farther. They dryly
told him he might make his fortune if he pleased ; but he
did not understand them, " or, rather, he *does* understand

1710.
Æt. 43.
Unusual
sensation
for Swift.

them." In other words, he listens in silence: "laughing," with a whimsical consciousness of former revolutionary habits, to see himself so "disengaged in these revolutions." Not in the social sense, however, as the reader observing his dinings-out will have guessed. It had cost him up to the 1st of October but three shillings in meat and drink since his arrival on the 7th of September, as thin as the town was; and now he has more dinners than ever, and more invitations than he can accept for his many pre-engagements. It is the foretaste of his new friends, with attentions doubled and redoubled from the old.

Lord Halifax had not been remiss in such courtesy. On that 1st of the month, Swift dined with the Florence envoy, Molesworth; leaving him early to go and sit with his

A rival
punster.

friend, Darteneuf, "the greatest punner of this town next myself;" and, earlier the same day, he had arranged to accompany the Portugal envoy to dine on the morrow with Halifax, who occupied lodgings at Hampton Court during repairs of his house there. On the 2d, accordingly, he finds himself at Hampton Court, "in a cruel hard frost with ice;" and, the queen being there, he went to the drawing-room before dinner, expecting to see nobody; but met acquaintance enough. He walked in the

Sights at
Hampton
Court.

gardens; saw the cartoons of Raffaelle; and closed the day by dining at Halifax's with Methuen, Delaval, and the ex-whig attorney-general; having great difficulty to get away, and resisting all my lord's importunities to wait till next morning, when he wished to show his house and

Dining with
Halifax.

park and improvements near the village. At the dinner Halifax began a health to Swift—"The Resurrection of the Whigs." But Swift refused it, unless he would add their "Reformation" too; and took that occasion to tell him he was the only whig in England* he loved, or had any good opinion of. While he was speaking one of his oldest whig friends may have been passing away, for it was the day

---

* Politician, or great minister, he | in Ireland," and so Swift would have means. Addison still was a "whig | called him.

of Lord Berkeley's death, of dropsy, at Berkeley Castle. "We left Hampton Court at sunset, and got here in a chariot and two horses time enough by starlight. That's something charms me mightily about London: that you go dine a dozen miles off in October, stay all day, and return so quickly. You can not do any thing like this in Dublin."

1710.
Æt. 43.

The great whig lord made one effort more. Swift had dined the day after with Lord Mountjoy at Kensington, had walked into town in the evening "like an emperor," and, having written his journal, had put out his candle, when his landlady came into his room with a servant of Lord Halifax's to desire he would go dine with him next day at his own house near Hampton Court; but Swift sent him word that he had business of great importance which hindered him. The important business was the introduction to Harley. On that morning he was taken privately to the minister, who received him with the greatest kindness and respect imaginable, and appointed him an hour on the following Saturday, when he was to "open his business" to him. Before the day closed, having in the interval dined with Delaval, the Portugal envoy, to meet Nic Rowe, the poet, and other friends, he had given to his printer the "lampoon" he had been busy with, and dropped some promise of "other mischief" in his heart; for if this particular piece hits, and he can find hints, he thinks he shall go round with them all. But as a set-off he was going in charity to send another *Tatler* to Steele, "who has been very low of late."

Halifax tries again.

Private visit to Harley.

Delaval called for him next morning to carry him to Sir Godfrey Kneller, who wanted to paint his portrait; but Sir Godfrey was out of town, and on their way back they came across a Westminster mob, the elections being now at their height, and the rabble crowded about their coach, crying, "A Colt! A Stanhope!" both being whig favorites, and they themselves crying as readily for either. "We were afraid of a dead cat, or our glasses broken, and so were always of their side." But the voters (who went to church, and had to pay for the war) were on the other

Westminster election.

1710.
Æt. 43.

Arrival of
Sir Andrew
Fountaine.

side, and Cross and Medlicott had a thumping majority. Again, that day, Swift dined at Delaval's; and in the evening, at the coffee-house, heard of the arrival in town of Sir Andrew Fountaine, who presented himself so early next morning in Bury Street as to catch Swift writing in bed. They went into the city together; dined at a chop-house with the learned woolen-draper; sauntered at china-shops and book-stalls; drank two pints of white wine at à tavern, and did not part till ten at night; when Swift, nevertheless, set to work in his lodgings to copy papers for his interview with Harley next morning. But he was thinking all the time of what every one told him about the

The elections.

elections, was wondering if the whigs still kept in their employments were meant to be a check on too large a majority of tories, and, none the brighter for his sauntering day, and the pint of white wine that had fallen to his share, blundered and blotted and tumbled asleep.

Then came the interview with the minister, to be presently spoken of, at which other things besides the first-fruits were brought up for discussion; and Swift was doubtless made thoroughly conscious that his old whig connection would not only be no disservice to him with Harley, but might be a help to those new friends. Prior had been won over, and Rowe, and there was a strong wish to be civil to Steele. During the week that followed his friendly compact with the tory leader, his intercourse

Writing
for Steele.

with whigs rather increased than lessened. On the 10th of October he was writing for Steele "*The Shower in London*," a masterpiece in its way; and he took two whig friends, Fountaine and Lord Mountjoy, to dine at an Irish whig friend's, Lord Mountrath, where he "sat till eleven like a fool," looking over Fountaine as he won eight guineas from Mr. Coote* at half-crown running ombre.

---

* This was the Mr. Coote afterward introduced by Swift to Pope in these terms: "Dear Pope, Though this little fellow be a justice of peace and a member of our Irish House of Commons, yet he may not be altogether unworthy of your acquaintance. J. S."—*From the Relation of Mr. Jones, of Welwyn, to Spence (Anecdotes, 266).*

Next morning "*The Shower*" was finished "all but the
beginning;" and to another paper in hand for Steele he
made some addition; dining afterward by Temple Bar
with Doctor Garth, to meet Addison, when their talk sug-
gested, doubtless, the reflection which he adds, that one
dull subject then swallowed up every thing ("your town
is certainly much more sociable"), for the only inquiry ev-
ery day was after the new elections. The tories were car-
rying it six to one. Addison's election, to be sure, had
passed easy and undisturbed; and if he had a mind to be
chosen king, Swift believed he'd hardly be refused: but
generally the whig party had been routed. They had
been sure of the four members for London, yet had lost
three out of the four. Onslow had lost Surrey, and they
were overthrown in most counties. For his own part, he
has done with them, and he hopes they have done with
the kingdom "for our time." She would ask how he
stood with the new people? Ten times better than he
did with the old, forty times more caressed. Everywhere
oozes out the confidence the new men were placing in
him. At Garth's dinner they had been talking of the
lord-lieutenancy, and Addison thought it would be in
commission; but on the last day of that week what he
had before told Esther Johnson came true. Wharton and
Addison were out, and the Duke of Ormond was viceroy.

"A silly thing" he did next day, which yet had some
attendant circumstances giving it claim to mention and re-
membrance. He had been all about St. Paul's and up at
the top, like a fool, with Sir Andrew Fountaine and two
more, who afterward led him to spend seven shillings for
his dinner. That was the second time; but he should
never do it again, though all mankind ("unconsidering
puppies!") should persuade him. One of the party was a
youth they were all fond of, about a year or two come
from the university—one Harrison; a little, "pretty" fel-
low, with a great deal of wit, good sense, and good-nature;
who was author of some "mighty pretty" things ("that
in your sixth *Miscellanea* about the 'Sprig of an Orange'

Margin notes:
1710.
Æт. 43.

One excep-
tion to the
whig rout.

Tory overt-
ures.

Up to the top
of St. Paul's.

Men of fash-
ion with
men of wit.

is his"); who had nothing to live on but being governor
to one of the Duke Queensberry's sons for forty pounds
a year; and yet the fashionable fellows were always invit-
ing him to taverns, and making him pay his club. With
himself, Swift adds, it was not much better; but he would
see them rot before they should continue to serve him so.
There was Lord Halifax always teasing him to go down
to his country house, at a cost to him of a guinea to the
servants and twelve shillings coach-hire; and he should
be hanged first. There was Anthony Henley, of the
Grange, making himself one of little Harrison's great cro-
nies, carrying him often to their six or seven shillings'
tavern-reckonings, and always making the poor lad pay

A protégé of
Swift and
Addison.

his full share. It vexed Swift to the heart; for he loved
the young fellow, was resolved to stir up people to do
something for him, and hoped, as he was a whig, to put
him on some of his own "cast" whigs. The sequel will
show how sincere this was, and how genuine the liking
professed. Addison had been Harrison's first patron, prais-
ing his verse and getting the tutorship for him; and, from
the first hour they met, Swift's kindliest consideration was
never wanting to the young man, for whom he was careful to practice what he so wisely preached. "A colonel
and a lord were at him and me to-night. I absolutely refused, made Harrison lag behind, and persuaded him not
to go to them. I tell you this, because I find all rich fellows have that humor of using all people without any consideration of their fortunes."

When next we see him, the morning after that day, a
more important whig than little Harrison, and more difficult to win over to the opposite ranks, is the object of his
solicitude. He has been two hours at the secretary of
state's office with Erasmus Lewis, talking politics, and discussing (perhaps a little prematurely) the chances of re-

Steele and
his appoint-
ments.

taining Steele in the office of stamped paper still held by
him. He had lost his gazetteership of three hundred
pounds a year by a paper which Anthony Henley had
written against Harley, who gave him the place, raising it

from sixty to three hundred pounds. That was "devilish
ungrateful," says Swift; but he hardly at the moment
saw the whole case. He had received a hint implying
more than seems at once to have been rightly understood.
He was told that he might save his old friend in the other
appointment, or, in other words, leave was given him to
"clear matters with Steele." Harley doubtless would Harley's
wish to re-
tain Steele.
have been glad to get Steele back, or any part of him
back, on any terms; but Swift, though at the time likely
himself largely to profit by this weak (or strong) side of
the minister's character, missed the explanation it afforded
in Steele's case of Harley's not unselfish interest in the
success of the "hint" he had given, and treated it too exclusively as for Steele's benefit alone. Dining next day
with another whig, Sir Mat Dudley, off he went to Addison after dinner, to offer the matter to him at distance as
the "discreeter person;" but party so possessed him (Swift How Addi-
son takes
Swift's in-
terference.
could think of no other explanation) that he "suspected
me," and would fall in with nothing. Was it not vexa-
tious, and when should he grow wise? He endeavored to
act in the most exact points of honor and conscience; and
his nearest friends, such as Addison and Steele, would not
understand it so. What must a man expect from his enemies?

Next day he dined with the Florence envoy, Molesworth, went thence to the coffee-house, where he punished
himself by behaving coldly to Addison, and so came home
to scribble. All he will do to keep up the coldness is but
the measure of what he will do to end it. He and Addi- Troubles of
friendship.
son were to dine together to-morrow and next day; but he
should not alter his behavior till Addison begged his pardon. They should grow bare acquaintance else. He had
become weary of friends; all but MD's were monsters.
Then came Mat Dudley's dinner on the morrow, when he
was again talking with Addison; but he left at six to go
to Harley, whom he found ill and gone to bed, "unless the
porter lied." Next day's dinner was with Addison's sis- Addison's
sister.
ter, "a sort of wit, very like him," though not such a fa-

1710.
Æt. 43.

1710.
Æt. 43. vorite with Swift, married to a prebend of Westminster, a Frenchman named Sartre, whose house and garden in the cloisters he thought delicious, but savoring of the monastic too much for him, and wanting the freshness of Laracor. Here were both Steele and Addison ; and the friends seem to have been much as of old, not quite "monsters" yet. Swift had heard that morning of the death of one of the Moor Park circle, "Mrs. Temple the widow," much to the "outward grief and inward joy " of the family ; and the following day he found himself in a nest of cousins that reminded him perhaps more forcibly of those early days.

Visit to Congreve. But first he had gone to see a very old friend and favorite, the author of the *Old Bachelor* and *Way of the World*. Congreve was now almost blind, had two cataracts growing on his eyes, and was never rid of gout; yet Swift found him looking young and fresh, and as cheerful as ever, though Congreve gave his visitor a pain in the great toe by merely mentioning the gout. "I find such suspicions frequently, but they go off again." Swift was older than his school-fellow by three years or more, but felt as if he were twenty years younger; and his dinners and wines have not yet the danger for him he was soon to City feasts. feel. He had yet no misgiving in dining at Stratford's in the city, with Burgundy and Tokay; coming "back afoot like a scoundrel;" then going to Addison ; and afterward making himself sick all night by supping with Lord Mountjoy. Not the less was he ready next day for a dinner with an Irish friend of Ppt's, Mr. Enoch Sterne, collector of Wicklow and clerk to the House of Lords, from which he was driven away early by a "prince of puppies, Col. Edgeworth;" then on the morrow he would dine again with Stratford at a young city merchant's, with Hermitage and Tokay ; and the following day, the 19th, when his letter was to go, he had dined in the city with Addison. 26th October. Nor should another city entertainment be forgotten, when, in what he called plaguy twelvepenny weather (had cost him ten shillings in coach and chair hire that last week),

he went to dine with his cousin, Patty Rolt; who lodged *1710.*
at Leach's, printer of the tory *Postman*, also his cousin *Æt. 43.*
with a pox! It is a theme of which his sarcasm never
tires, this prolific race of Swifts; all the sons of Godwin,
not to speak of numerous others, having been fertile of
offspring, and supplying him with an ever-springing mush-
room growth of kinsfolk. Oh oh! And Leach was his *Ante, 37.*
cousin, God knows how; and had married another of his
cousins; and now condescendingly offered to bring him
acquainted with the author of the *Postman*, a very ingenious man and great scholar who had been beyond sea; but
Swift was modest, and said maybe the gentleman was shy,
and so put it off. "And I wish you could hear me repeat- *Swift among his cousins.*
ing all I have said of this, in its proper tone just as I am
writing it, all with the same cadence, with oh hoo, or as
when little girls say, I have got an apple, miss, and won't
give you some." But the talk of this family party in the
city had turned much on bank stock and its extraordinary
profits, and through all his jeers at his cousins one sees (as
will hereafter appear) that he has been bitten by their talk.

There were but a very few days before the post would
claim his letter, and whig engagements were in every one.
Nic Rowe, the poet, had stood so well with the whigs at the *With Nic Rowe.*
time of Addison's Irish appointment, that he succeeded to
the place of under-secretary which Addison "had in England;" but as he was content to remain under the new
dispensation, Harley was only too glad to keep him, and
Swift called on him "at his office" on the 27th. There
he met Prior, who joined them afterward at dinner with
the under-secretary, and the whole three went later to "a
blind tavern," where they found Congreve, Sir Richard
Temple, Dick Eastcourt, the player (of whom Steele writes
so charmingly), and Charles Maine, over a bowl of bad
punch. Swift refused it; on which Temple sent for six
flasks of his own wine for him, and they sat till twelve.
Remembering the gouty twinge at Congreve's, however,
he was for that day abstemious. He was, nevertheless, at *With Garth and Addison.*
a hedge tavern next day with Garth and Addison (difficult

1710.
Æt. 43.

Hitting
Pembroke
with a pun.
to drop these whig friends, however short of one's expectation they may fall), going afterward to Harley, who was "denied or out;" then visiting Lord Pembroke just come to town, where they were very merry talking of old things, and Swift hit him with one pun; and, finally, weary of the coffee-house, closing the day at the lodging of his next neighbor, Ford (as near to him in Bury Street on the one side as Mrs. Vanhomrigh on the other), where he sat chattering "like a fool" till twelve. One discovers that some doubts of Harley in regard to finance had at this time occurred to him, and it was clear the whigs were counting on the new minister's inability to carry through his under-
An alarm.
taking. "God knows what will become of it. I should be terribly vexed to see things come round again: it will ruin the church and clergy forever: but I hope for better." Something was in this remark more than the friend to whom it was written could yet entirely comprehend. He had just spoken to her of a quasi-kinsman of his, an old whig partisan who had lately enlisted in the service of the tories;* but she had thus far received no direct intimation that he was himself to take such a turn, and to her these continued whig engagements might seem to make it hardly likely. But, though they filled the rest of this letter, it was not to close without revealing the change in himself that began to render such whig engagements wearisome.

One day he is dining with Addison, and on the next with Doctor Cockburn, coming home at seven, and Ford sitting with him till eleven. Next day again he dines at

---

* This was Doctor Charles Davenant, son of the celebrated Sir William, and uncle to the "little parson-cousin" (see *ante*, 156), who, to court the tories, had lately written a piece not inaptly named *Tom Double*, and who a few nights back had teased Swift at the St. James's to look over some writings of his; but Swift had avoided him and gone off with the comptroller to Sir Mat Dudley's for very good reasons: "The rogue is so fond of his own productions that I hear he will not part with a syllable;" to which he adds a very valuable hint of his own style: "The puppy uses so many words that I was afraid of his company." When Harley afterward would tease Swift, he attributed to Doctor Davenant, or the parson-cousin, what he knew that Swift had written.

Kensington with Addison and Steele, staying till nine, and going to the coffee-house plaguy weary, for " Col. Proud" was ill company, and he drank punch, and was made hot. Then he dines at Sir Richard Temple's with General Farrington, Congreve, and Vanbrugh, the latter and himself being only "civil and cold." Ppt would remember what he told her of his long quarrel about the verses on his house, Marlborough's wife having teased him about them, though a good-natured fellow. Yet again, the following day, he dines with Vanbrugh and Addison at the Portugal envoy's; Admiral Wager, Sir Richard Temple, and Mr. Methuen being of the party ; and himself stealing away at five, rather weary. And following this there is a supper at Addison's with Garth, Steele, and an Irish friend of Ppt's, Mr. Dopping, just come over. But the most whiggish and least agreeable entertainment of the whole was on that very 10th of October, at Lady Lucy Stanhope's, when they all ran down Swift's " Shower," and told Prior, whom they mistook for the author, that " Sid Hamet" was the silliest poem they ever read! Will Ppt wonder, after this, that he didn't dine there before; or that he don't like women so well as he did? " MD, you must know, are not women."

What MD was to him, supplying, if not woman, the place of all women, must now have illustration ; and, before the graver issues of this memorable London visit come to be related, the picture of Swift among old and new friends during its first three months must have by its side, for a companion picture, his confidences to Esther Johnson.

VOL. I.—20

(marginal notes)

1710.
Æt. 43.

Doubtless "Froud:"
ante, 172.

Swift and Vanbrugh.

Unexpected attack.

III.

ESTHER JOHNSON.

1710. Æt. 43.

1710.
Æt. 43.
PRESENTING thus, indeed, from his own letters, Swift's daily life at a momentous time, their disclosures would be incomplete, and her story for whom they were written would remain untold, if those portions of them more especially and exclusively meant for her, with their playful, pure, and winning tenderness, were left out of the record.

What Swift's
letters im-
plied.
Many were the grounds for pride in receiving them, but here must have been the most valued. Such letters from such a man were no ordinary tribute; but far beyond the magnitude or interest of the incidents related was the personal spell exerted over herself. To the girl who from her childhood had known the writer for playfellow, teacher, friend, and companion, their thousand innocent, half-childish, fantastic, fascinating touches of personal attachment may well have come to represent for her the charm and the sufficiency of life. Her own contentment that this should be so, there appears to be no reason to doubt.

Ante, 217.
Of the "little language" used in their intercourse something must now be said. Upon a previous page has been expressed the desire Swift had for a "life by stealth" between himself and her, or, in other words, for confidences the world was not to share; and there is nothing strained in the belief that there may in this be some remote shadow or fancy of the first intention with which they began to talk to each other in phrases special to themselves. Such
Ante, 122.
was the "little," or childish, language to which allusion has been made as perhaps dating from her girlhood at Sir William Temple's; which, when he spoke, he describes him-

self "making up his mouth" for, as grown people do
when they imitate children; and of which I have never
found the slightest trace except in his intercourse with her.
Extravagant as were his later interchanges of other kinds
of nonsense with Sheridan and his circle, there is no example of any thing resembling this; and as it does not
admit of doubt that he and Esther Johnson really talked,
as well as wrote, such particular silliness, it can not be excluded from any picture of the life they lived together.
But how make it out in any detail? It existed nowhere
but in the letters to her and Mrs. Dingley used in the preceding section, and forming what is called the "Journal to
Stella;" and those letters had been so printed that a dozen
childish words or so, dropped here and there, were all that
the editors had suffered to remain of what was once the
accompaniment of every entry in them of daily sayings or
doings. Any careful reader of the diaries, though he may
never have heard of the little language, sees at once that
the text must have been strangely meddled with. In the
first forty letters Swift calls himself Presto, and Esther
Johnson, Stella; though he never called Esther by that
name until long after all the letters were written, and
never at any time called himself by the other name, which
first appears in the twenty-seventh letter as the invention of the Duchess of Shrewsbury, who had forgotten the
English word and substituted her native Italian. In this
form were printed nearly two-thirds of the whole. But
in the last twenty-five letters both Presto and Stella dis-
appear; what Swift really had written, Pdfr for himself
and Ppt for his friend, take their place; and at beginnings
and endings, mornings and nights, of the journals of almost every day, traces unmistakably appear, not indeed of
the little language, but of a disjointed speech with which
some one has replaced it. Misgivings, unknown to the
editor of the first forty, had beset the editor of the last
twenty-five letters, though in actual publication the last
preceded the first; but both alike fail to express what the
language or the use of it was, and it seemed essential,

1710.
Æt. 43.

The "little
language."

First forty
letters.

Last twenty-
five letters.

properly to illustrate Swift's life, that attempt should be
made to obtain access to any originals of these famous letters that might still be in existence.

The success which attended this effort appears on a later
page, and from the section of restored passages entitled
Post, 425. "Swift's Unprinted and Misprinted Journals," the reader
will learn much.   He will see that in the earlier letters, on
all occasions, silent substitution is to be made of Pdfr and
Ppt for the "Presto" and "Stella" with which the first
editors unwarrantably replaced them; that Swift is himself throughout Pdfr, sometimes Podefar and FR, or other
fragments of what may be assumed to be Poor Dear Foolish Rogue; that besides Ppt, which presumably is Poppet,
or Poor Pretty Thing, it is also Mrs. Johnson, who is for
the most part designated by MD, My Dear, though this
occasionally comprises Mrs. Dingley as well; and that for
the latter lady exclusively D or DD, Dingley or Dear
Dingley, stands always; ME, or Madam Elderly, being
only now and then applied to her.   Other words or combinations of letters are explained in their place, and some
may not be perfectly deciphered; but in the restorations
given in my sixth book the little language first becomes
accessible in a form that makes any approach to being
complete or continuous.   "Do you know what," says Swift
to her, "when I am writing in our language I make up
my mouth just as if I were speaking it.   I caught myself at it just now."   All may now catch him at it, observing the passages recovered from the letters to Esther
Johnson.

Ever since he left Dublin his thoughts have turned to
her.   From Chester, in his first letter, he had prayed God
Almighty bless her, "bless poodeerichar MD," and she
was for God's sake to be merry, and "get oo health."
Every body else was to write to him under cover to Steele,
to save postage; but for hers he would pay at the coffee-
house, to get them sooner, till he should have tried the
other arrangement.   At present they occupy his lodgings

in Dublin; and if Mrs. Curry* makes any difficulty, he will quit them, and pay her from July. Ppt is, above all, to hold her resolution of going to Trim, and riding there as much as she can; and again, at the close, he prays God to bless her and her friend. 1710.
Æт. 43.
The ladies
in Swift's
lodging.

His solicitudes are renewed in his letter of the 9th, when he is anxious to hear of her being at Trim by the time she gets it, riding a little horse called Johnson after herself, "who must now be in good case." He then tells her his intention to write something every day to MD, and make it a sort of journal, and send it when full whether MD writes or not; and so "that will be pretty," and he shall always be in conversation with MD and MD with Pdfr. He thinks of her as dining at home, that Sunday when he writes, and "there was the little half-pint of wine," and they are to be good girls and all will be well. Next was his shaving-day (including often, in those times of peri-wigs, head as well as beard), and so, at seven in the morn-ing, she was not to keep him, for he could not stay, being also in a hurry to get to Jervas to sit, and pray let them dine with the dean, but not lose their money. In a few days he is speculating on the great deal of china he means to take them over, and, naming his own health as pretty well, prays God Ppt may give him a good account of hers. Then, on the very day when he changes his Pall Mall lodging for one in Bury Street, her first letter comes, and he thanks God for all being well. Hastening at once to seal up his own third, which he has brought to the St. James's coffee-house for the purpose, he stops just to send a message to his agent, Parvisol, about an offer for Ppt's horse. "Sell it with a pox!" he exclaims. "Pray let him know that he shall sell his soul as soon. What! Sell any thing that Ppt loves, and may sometimes ride? Let him sell my gray, and be hanged, but little Johnson is hers, and let her do as she pleases." Esther's
"little
Johnson."

What the
journals
were to be.

Her first
letter.

Little John-
son not to
be sold.

---

* Swift addresses this letter to her, | Fountaine, "Mrs. Curry's over against
as we have seen himself addressed by | the Ram in Capel Street."

1710.
Æt. 43.
Of course his fourth letter answers her first; but it answers also her second, which arrived five days later (the 26th); and what had been the contents of both we are at no loss to find from the hints, allusions, ejaculations, loving reiterations, boyish playfulness, manly tenderness, that come crowding upon us, overflowing and making themselves part of every most indifferent topic he talks about. For all his fears that there might be weariness at the plaguy deal he writes, it was clear that saucy MD "much thought" his paper was too small, and grudged his missing even space for a line. Saucebox! he calls her. That

He must tell where he dines daily.
she must, forsooth, know every day and each day where he dines! Such a stir and bustle with this little MD of ours! He was to write "constantly," forsooth. Every night, then, he must be writing. He can not put out his candle till he has bid them good-night. O Lord! O Lord! Ppt makes excuse for her handwriting, but he protests she writes like an emperor, only he is afraid it hurts her eyes—"take care of that, pray, pray, Mrs. Ppt." As to his own writing, she is to smoke how he widens the margin by lying in bed when he writes;* but he mustn't say

His letters to be always full.
good-night so as to lose a line, oh no, or MD will scold; and to his "good-night, sirrahs," he has sometimes to add "no, no, not night," because he is writing in the morning. But morning and night he is wholly MD's; and after wishing her a merry Michaelmas, he couples with it the last at Laracor and the next that is to come at his little goose's lodgings; and he calls her a brave boy, and a Mrs. Owl, and a little MD, and a Mistress Ppt.

One thing he finds to be wrong. They have not gone to Trim, and he does not like their reasons for not going; but they are in Pdfr's lodgings, and there is some project of the Bishop of Clogher's wife to take them for a visit to Ballygall, which he delightedly thinks will be a pure good place for air. They want him in some business of

---

* "My bed lies on the wrong side for me, so that" (now) "I am forced often to write when I am up."

Joe Beaumont's to get an order from the queen, which he laughs at for a jest: "such a combustion here that even in an affair concerning the clergy of a whole kingdom he is advised not yet to meddle, and will any body trouble the queen about Joe?" To their inquiries about his servant, Patrick, who had been discharged and taken back at their entreaty,* he reports him drunk about three times a week, and that he bears it, and Pat had got the better of him; but one of these days, when none of them are by to intercede, he will have positively to turn him off to the wide world. Many questions they have asked about Ppt's mother, whom he has been doing his best to contrive to see without seeing Lady Giffard; and the subject is resumed in her second letter, which reaches him before the reply to her first is gone, and which he begins to answer the night he gets it, as he lies in bed. "Here's a clutter! I've not seen your mother yet: my penny-post letter I suppose miscarried." So he wrote another, which brought a special visit to him next day from Ppt's sister (soon to change her name to Filby), "and she looked very well, and seemed a good modest sort of girl." Already he is preparing a box to go to Dublin: with chocolate for Ppt's health, and for Dingley "the finest piece of Brazil tobacco that ever was born." She wants him to consult some physician about his ears, but he does not think any lady's advice about his ears signifies twopence; and Radcliffe he knows not, and Bernard he never saw; however, in compliance to her he'll ask Doctor Cockburn. He promises he will eat no grapes: indeed, he eat about six the other day at Sir John Holland's, and would not give sixpence for a thousand, they are so bad this year. Nor will he drink any *aile*, by which he supposes her to mean *ale*, for he has good wine every day of five and six shillings a bottle. The ladies had got into some way of saving shillings, which he does not like (he connects it with their not go-

Marginal notes:

1710.
Æt. 43.
The queen and Joe!

Esther's mother.

Esther's sister.

See my Goldsmith, IV., ii.

Injunctions for diet.

---

* I quote from his note-book of the present year: "Patrick came to me the 2d time Feb. 9, 1709-'10."

1710.
Æt. 43.

ing to Trim); and it vexes him that Ppt should be a cow-
ard in a coach. As for the alleged robbery of Walls,
he says the archdeacon will certainly be stingier for sev-

Ppt's
punning.

en years upon pretense of it. Ppt had been punning.
"Why, it is well enough," he says: but he will not second
it, though he could make a dozen: he had never thought
of a pun since he left Ireland. · Yes, 'faith! he eagerly replies to a wish expressed by Esther and her friend in this
second letter, he *does* hope in God that Pdfr and MD

Her second
letter.

will be together this time twelvemonth! (And, O Lord!
he exclaims when he gets so far, how much Ppt writes!
Young women should not carry that too far, but be temperate to hold out.) Mr. Harley he is not to see for some
days yet. For Manley, on whose behalf they are again
strongly interceding, he will do his best. That he would
himself have small hopes from the Duke of Ormond, they
seem to have greatly feared. But why? he says to that.
"He loves me very well, I believe, and would in my turn
give me something to make me easy.... But I do not
think of any thing farther than the business I am upon."
He closes by satisfying her curiosity about the lodging in

His new
lodging.

Bury Street to which he removed a week ago. He has the
first floor, a dining-room and bed-chamber, at eight shillings a week: "plaguy deep," he adds, but he spends nothing for eating, never goes to a tavern, and very seldom in
a coach: yet, after all, "it will be expensive."

It was now the first week of October, and he tells her at
its close of a Sunday dinner, "as a spunger," with friends
known to her "that board hereabout" (Ford, Fountaine,
and Sir Charles Levinge); and in the evening Fountaine
would needs make Swift go with Ford and himself to sup
at a tavern, where they had a neck of mutton à la Mainte-

Debanch
with Fount-
aine.

non that a dog could not eat, and for two bottles of Portugal and Florence, among the three, had to pay each sixteen shillings; but if ever Fountaine catched him so again,
he protested he would spend as many pounds! And so
he came straight home; not fond at all of the St. James's
coffee-house, as he used to be, and hoping it might mend

in winter, every body now being out of town at elections, or not come from their country houses. He was not at all easy that night, the "ugly nasty filthy wine" turning sour on his stomach; but he was not so ill as to be prevented from dining next day with Sir John Stanley, Lady Stanley being one of his favorites. The day following, his fifth letter was to be posted, but he shall keep it till he can throw in a word about a dinner to which Harley, at their first interview, had invited him; and some addition from it may meanwhile be made to the more intimate privacies of the time it covers. Was he not bringing himself into a fine *præmunire*, he had said at its opening, to begin writing letters in whole sheets? And now he dares not leave it off. He can not tell if she likes these journal letters, he believes they would be dull to him to read them over; but perhaps little MD is pleased to know how Pdfr passes his time in her absence. He always begins his latest on the day its predecessor ends. All her commissions, to the most minute, he executes; describes what he means to do for Postmaster Manley, and how Southwell and Mr. Addison will see that Joe Beaumont's affairs are not lost sight of; and tells her even bits of indifferent gossip. "Smoke Pdfr writing news to MD." Bethinking him of some reproach of hers, well, he says, but he ought to write plainer when he considers Ppt can not read, and DD is not skillful at his ugly hand. "Do not lose your money at Manley's to-night, sirrahs," is his good-night as he puts out his candle. Another night he turns to read a pamphlet to amuse himself, and so prays God preserve their dear healths.

Often he gets into difficulty with unconscious repetitions. He will be far enough, is his exclamation, but he says the same thing over two or three times, just as he does when talking to little MD! But what cares he? They can read it, as easily as he can write it. (He thinks he has brought those lines pretty straight again; but he fears it will be long before he finishes two sides at this rate!) "An insipid sort of day," he closes one of his journals with,

Lady
Stanley.

Does she
like the
journals?

Does he
write plain?

or repeat
himself?

1710.
Æt. 43.

"nothing to remark upon worth threepence." Hopes MD had a better, with the dean, or the bishop, or Mrs. Walls. Is sure he had seen her, the night before, playing ombre at Manley's (roguishly altered to "last night but one" on tidings from Manley, before post-time, that she *had* then been so engaged); for he sat looking over her hand, and he tells her the mistakes she made. Busy next night for Harley, he could only heartily wish himself with them; and that he *would* be, as soon as he either failed in or compassed his first-fruits business. And so let them go to their cards, and their claret and orange at the dean's, and he will go write. He must, nevertheless, take up his diary again at day-break to wish them good-morrow; and very pretty he thinks it that he must be writing to young women in a morning, fresh and fasting, 'faith! But it is a foolish trick he has got. He must say something to MD whenever he wakes, even though it should only be "get you gone, you rogues," when he is busy. Yes, it would vex him to the blood if any of these long letters should miscarry : if they did, he should shrink to half sheets again, and half the journal would go too: "Ten days of Pdfr's life lost, and that would be a sad thing, 'faith and troth." Yet it sets him thinking, too, what scurvy company he'd be to MD when he went back. Why, they knew every thing of him already, and he should have nothing to say! Positively he'd tell them no more, or he should have nothing left, no story to tell, nor any kind of thing! He really thought, still, he should soon go back to her.

 · But by this time Harley's dinner is over; he has hurried home to put the finishing-stroke before his journals go; and so "puddled up" among papers was poor MD's letter, he means poor Pdfr's letter, he could not find it. Yes, here it is; and its last words are that he has dined with Harley, and hopes some things would be done, but must say no more, because the letter must be sent to the post-house, and not by the bellman. Again next Sunday, and he trusts to some good issue, he is to dine at Harley's. Then, by way of close, they are to imagine him, as soon as

Ante, 213.

"Fresh and fasting."

His life in his journals.

Sends off fifth letter.

ever he is in bed, beginning his sixth to MD as gravely
as if he had not written a word that month; fine doings,
'faith! Why, methinks he doesn't write as he should,
because he is *not* in bed: just see the ugly wide scrawl.
God Almighty ever bless them! Taking a last look at
the letter as he folds it up—'faith, 'tis a whole treatise.
He will go reckon the lines on the other sides. He *has*
reckoned them.... Seventy-three lines in folio, small
hand, on one side! And so goes his fifth letter.

Half an hour after its departure he had begun his sixth
with mention of his introduction, at that first dinner at
Harley's on the 10th of October, "with much compliment
on all sides," to Sir Simon Harcourt, the attorney-general,
and their discussion of the memorial to the queen, with
results to be presently related. He might at last believe,
indeed, that it needed nothing more to gain Fortune over,
since of no less a person than the first minister he could
add, "I am told by all hands he has a mind to gain *me*
over;" and though he lingered still among the whigs, and
helped the wits of the party, the whig ties will soon be
seen daily loosening, and his own resolve to have done
with them will not much longer be withheld. Meanwhile
he has to tell of the safe arrival of another letter from her
to which the journals he is now writing are to carry back
the answer.

He had dined in Addison's company with their old Irish
secretary, Ned Southwell, and walked afterward with Addison in the park, when, upon closing the day at the St.
James's, he had brought away a letter from the Bishop of
Clogher, and a packet under that gazetteer envelope which
she still sends hers by. This will inclose one, he is sure.
He opens the bishop's at once; but puts up Steele's envelope, visits a lady friend just come to town, and on getting home and into bed dandles and toys with the packet
that is to yield him so much pleasure, and prays God send
he may find MD well and happy and merry, and that they
love Pdfr " as they do fires." Oh, he will not open it yet:
yes, he will! No, he will not! "I am going; I can not

Margin notes:

1710.
Æt. 43.
Begins sixth.

Dinner at
Harley's.

Is Fortune
his at last?

1710.
Æt. 43.

Playful joy
on arrival
of letters.

Disappoint-
ments.

She asks
for more.

Transformed
"little lan-
guage."

stay till I turn over; what shall I do? My fingers itch!
And now I have it in my left hand; and now I will open
it this very moment!" He breaks the seal, and others
appear before that which he most desires. What is this?
Only some letter from a bishop perhaps, and of course too
late. Nobody's credit but his own should be employed
in that first-fruits matter now. Pshaw! It's from Sir
Andrew Fountaine. What! another? what Mrs. Barton
promised, he supposes? But no, she writes a better hand
(and he hopes Ppt will inquire for hers at Dawson's office
at the castle): *this*, by the scrawl, must be Patty Rolt's—
ah no! it is from poor Lady Berkeley, writ before my
lord's death, to invite him to Berkeley Castle that winter;
and how it grieved his heart! for she says, poor lady, she
hopes my lord is in a fair way of recovery. And then at
last came MD's, her number three, dated the 26th of September, though a letter from Manley of the 3d of October
reached five days ago. They had all lain a fortnight in
Steele's office, and forgot! Well, Steele was turned out,
and she was in future to direct to him under cover to
Addison.

And now he had settled himself to read her letter, what
was it? Why, it made him mad—"flidikins!" he had
been the best boy in Christendom, and there she came
complaining with her two eggs a penny! But, after all, he
thinks there *was* a chasm between his second and third;
yet, 'faith, he would not promise to write to her every
week; only every night he would write, and send it always when full, which would be once in ten days. Then
lovingly he turns the tables a little. If Ppt begins to take
up the way of writing to Pdfr just because it is Tuesday,
'egad, it will grow a task o' Monday! "But write when
you have a mind...... No, no, no, no, no, no, no, no.
Agad, agad, agad, agad, agad, agad, no poo poo stellakins!"
He is going to sleep, but must tell her first of what happened the night before her letter.* "Lord! I dreamed of

---

* At the close of my preceding | the "little language" is left by ruth-
page a slight mutilated fragment of | less editors, who have closed it with

Ppt so confusedly last night, and that we saw Dean Bol- 1710.
Æt. 43.
A dream.
ton and Sterne go into a shop; and she bid me call them
to her; and they proved to be two parsons I knew not;
and I walked about till she was shifting; and such stuff,
mixed with much melancholy and uneasiness, and things
not as they should be, and I know not how:" waking to
an ugly, gloomy morning. She had asked him what he
was writing. Only three things had he printed since he
came, but they had fixed on him fifty things. He tells
her all about "The Shower," hinting at others he "dare
not" send her; and he had a *Tatler* in hand which she and
Dingley would "smoke," as he had before referred to it.
Of the three printed things, the "Sid Hamet" lampoon was What he
has been
publishing.
cried up to the skies, though nobody at first (except Fount-
aine) suspected him; at least, they said nothing. Hadn't
he told them of a great man receiving him very coldly?
"that was he, but say nothing, it was only a little revenge.... I am not guessed at all in town to be the author; yet so it is: but that is a secret, only to you. Ten
to one whether you see them in Ireland; yet here they
run prodigiously." As a piece of writing, however, it was
not so good as "The Shower," which the people here called
his best thing, and so he thought it. Yes. Tooke was going on with his *Miscellany*, and he'd give a penny to include the Bishop of Killala's letter. Couldn't they con- *Ante*, 272.
trive to say to him that they wished the book-seller who
was putting "my things" together had that letter among
the rest? But they were not to say any thing of it as
from him. He forgot whether it was good or no, but having heard it much commended, perhaps it might deserve it.

 To continued inquiries after his footman, Patrick, for Patrick's
misdoings.
whom the ladies were frequent intercessors, he has no fa-
vorable answer. In three weeks he had been drunk ten
times. A few nights before he had himself come home
excessively late, and before going to bed had to pick off

---

a word, "Stellakins," which Swift | it was "Sluttakin," which he uses
could not have written. No doubt | for little slut.

the coals the extravagant whelp had just heaped on his fire. Only the night before he was home at nine, but the dog was abroad drinking, and he could not get his night-gown. No wonder, he adds, that he had a mind to turn the puppy away: but for yet a while this was not to be. Then he talks of the "little wooden box" that is to take the promised chocolate and tobacco; and winds up his letter with "pretty prattle for saucy little MD." She had been afraid these revolutions might hinder his business,

and was it certain the new people liked him, and couldn't he write a little plainer, and would it not be best that she should write on special days to him, and she had been sadly troubled by that weakness in her eyes. Revolutions a hinderance to him! Why, if it were not for revolutions one could do nothing, "though one is certain of nothing;" yet had he not said enough of how much better he stands

with the new people than with the old; and as for Mr. Harley, if he continued as he had begun, no man has been ever better treated by another. For her letters, she would find it best not to fix a particular day for writing; she was to write when she could, but, above all, she was not to hurt her eyes. And all that he writ she was not implicitly to believe; for his own letters (he wisely reminds her)

would be "a sort of journal where matters open by degrees;" and the event that must settle them was to come later. . . . Why, was that tobacco at the top of the paper, or what? He did not remember he slobbered. Yes, he would try to write plainer, for she must not spoil her eyes. He was afraid his letters were too long; so they must suppose one to be two, and read them at twice. And *this* she was not to read, the little rogue, with her own little eyes, but was to give it to Dingley, pray now, and he would after write as plain as the skies. (He must have his rhyme.) And let DD write and Ppt dictate—the saucy, little, pretty, dear rogues!

His seventh letter he began as usual on the day of the departure of his sixth, and it opened with an allusion which might have seemed to overpass the limits he strictly observed in such matters, but that doubtless it was only to be taken as a merry turn of speech. Oh, 'faith, he's undone! He has taken a larger paper than he wrote upon last. "And yet I am condemned to a sheet: but since it is MD, I did not value though I were condemned to a pair." From which he passes to his daily diary of dinners: not that it can be wit or diversion for her; but he fancies he shall some time or other like to know how he passed his life absent from MD.*

After meeting Harley at Erasmus Lewis's on the 19th of October, he dined with Mrs. Vanhomrigh (the first direct mention of her in these letters), and went afterward to see the Duke of Ormond's daughters, the youngest of whom was to be married " to-morrow " to the best match in England, Lord Ashburnham, twelve thousand a year and abundance of money; very sorrowful in the sequel, notwithstanding. Old friends and new still strongly contend for him. That evening he passed with Addison and Wortley Montagu over a bottle of Irish wine. Questions from her had shown him that his hankerings for such old associates, Steele among them, are not ungrateful to her; but though a doubt springs up now and then if the new ministers will hold, he takes good care that she shall hear of his continued eager welcome from them. Did any body else in Ireland really know of his greatness among the tories? Every body in London reproached him of it, but he heeded them not. And how did the things he named to her pass with Irish acquaintance? How was " The Shower " liked in Dublin? Here he never knew any thing pass better. Rowe and Prior praised it beyond any thing written of the kind: never such a shower since Danaë's! But, for their life, they were to say nothing of " Sid Hamet." Hardly any body suspected him for those lines, only it was thought that nobody but Prior or he *could* write them. There was also a punning ballad on the Westmin-

Margin notes: 1710. Æt. 43. — A sheet or a pair of sheets? — First mention of the Vans. — What about his published pieces? — Is he suspected?

---

* This came to be true; and when he was writing his *Memoirs of the* | *Change* and his *Last Four Years* he consulted these diaries.

1710.
Æt. 43.
ster election (a secret to all but MD), which cost him but half an hour, and " ran " though good for nothing. There is never really any pride in the "things." It is the sense of power reflected from them, the influence or personal consideration attending them. "If you have them not, I will bring them over." She had herself been guessing, and making wrong guesses. She had been making him responsible for what he has not written. He has not helped Steele to the extent she supposed. The *Tatlers* had been scurvy of late. One or two hints he might still send him ; but never any. more. He did not deserve it. He was governed by his wife most abominably. It was as bad a case as Marlborough's. "I never saw her since I came, nor has he ever made me an invitation. Either he dares not, or he is such a thoughtless Tisdall fellow that he never minds it. So what care I for his wit ? for he is the worst company in the world till he has a bottle of wine in his head." Reverting to her fancy that the *Tatler* of Ithuriel's Spear might be his, he calls it a puzzle between her and her judgment. In general she might be sure enough as to things, when they were what he had frequently spoken of ; but mere guessing was moonshine. "I defy mankind if I please. Why, I writ a pamphlet when I was last in London that you and a thousand have seen and never guessed it to be mine . . . and I have written several other things that I hear commended, and nobody suspects me for them."

Her interest in Addison, evidently much expressed in her letters, he satisfies by repeated and reiterated mention. As he sits down to answer her fourth letter, he tells her of Addison and himself dining with Lord Mountjoy, and going afterward to prolong their talk at the coffee-house, where it had been a full night. Next day he dined at Mrs. Van's (so for the most part he calls her), and after writing there a letter to "poor Mrs. Long," who had written to them, but was God knew where, and would not tell any body, he came home early and wrote till very late. On the next, which closed October with a fine day, Addi-

Marginal notes:
Guessing wrong.

Steele and his wife.

Unacknowledged pieces.

Mrs. Van and Mrs. Long.

son, Dick Stuart, brother to Lord Mountjoy, and himself 1710.
Æт. 43.
dined upon Addison's "treat;" and they were half-fud-
dled, but not he, for he mixed water with his wine, and
escaped between nine and ten, because that was the night
when "little MD's letter was to go off by the bellman."
And as it was to carry with it, besides the matters related,
his answer to her fourth, some hints of what she had written about may be added.

What then, in substance, were the points of her letter to Contents
of a letter
from Ppt.
which he replied? She had addressed him, "London, En-
gland," because he addressed her "Dublin, Ireland." Insolent sluts that they were! such was Ppt's malice. "She
had been suffering greatly from her eyes and head." What
should he do to cure them, poor dear life! her disorders
were a pull-back for her good qualities. "She had given
him a narrative, from Tisdall, of Convocation disputes."
Convocation, quotha! he thinks his own news better worth
sending than that! "And when would he be with them
again?" Be patient; in a month or two. "The Bishop
of Killala had not had his letter." He never writ to the A good
reason.
bishop, which he supposes was the reason the bishop had
not his letter. "Dean Sterne was so kind to them, and so
fond of Swift's letters." Fond as he was, he had not himself written; but he was kind where he knew it would
please most, and might make up, that way, his other usage.
"And has there been snow in England as with us here?
And he won't forget to send over a copy of Jervas's picture. And Poor John was gone. And Mrs. Perceval had
been in town, and Tighe was going to cross. And was
china really very dear: for they *should* like some salad Personal
news and
wants.
dishes, and plates, but nothing extravagant." (Dingley
here had thrust in a list of their wants.) To all of which
he replied with becoming gravity. No, they only had
snow for an hour one morning, but rather heavy. About
the picture, he would contrive to get a copy from Jervas;
for he would make Sir Andrew Fountaine buy one as for
himself, and would pay him again, and take it; provided
only he had money to spare on leaving London. Poor

John! Was he gone? Humm! And Madam Perceval had been in town, had she? Humm! And Tighe was to cross and be a trouble to him. *Indeed.* But Tighe should have little notice from him; and if they had *not* fallen out, it would have been the same. Let them go and be far enough, the negligent baggages, not to tell the people who were daily writing to him that he had no credit to do what was desired. Dingley's errand about the dishes should be done. He once had a fancy himself to resolve to go mad for china, but now it was off. Yes, yes, Dingley should have the dishes. He supposed they had named as much as would cost five pounds. There was also a postscript from Dingley about his writing plainer; about Ppt not being well with her eyes, which had prevented her writing as she wished; and about her own belief, as to himself, that if he took two or three "nut-galls" they would do him good. To which latter suggestion his reply is not complimentary, hinting that perhaps two or three "gut galls" might do as well for DD: but for Ppt he is full of concern. And her eyes and head are ill, poor dear life! He was almost crazed that she should vex herself for not writing. Couldn't she dictate, and not strain her little dear eyes? It was the grief of his soul to think she was out of order. If she *must* write, let her shut her eyes, and write just a line, and no more—thus, How do you do, Mrs. Ppt? That was written with his eyes shut. 'Faith, he thought it better than when they were open. And Dingley might stand by, and tell when she was too high or too low. To which he adds that they are to remember and inclose their letter to Addison, and (with a touch of remorse to his more elderly friend) as for DD's nut-galls —"what a clutter!"

The letter thus answered, he puts it up in the partition in his cabinet, as he always does every letter as soon as he answers it. "Method is good in all things. Order governs the world. The devil is the author of confusion. A general of an army, a minister of state—to descend lower, a gardener, a weaver— That may make a fine observa-

tion if you think it worth finishing; but I have not time." 1710.
It vexed him to send by the bellman, but he could put off ÆT. 43.
little MD no longer—"And you lose all your money at
cards, sirrah Ppt? I found you out—" He was only
staying till that ugly D was dry before he could fold up—
"don't you see it? Oh Lord, I am loath to leave you,
'faith, but it must be so till next time— Pox take that
D! I will blot it—"

There was reason for the blotting, not revealed until his
next letter: which began as usual on the day its predecessor went, and told them, what with his tender care he concealed from the close of his last when it might have led to
much unrelieved anxiety, that he had, sitting in bed that
morning, a fit of giddiness; but he hoped in God he should   Fit of gid-
not have more of it. He attributed it to late sitting and   diness.
writing on the previous night. He had taken brandy; he
never, now, eats fruit or drinks ale; and he has better
wine than they. The fit had troubled him sorely, he is at
no pains to conceal; and next night, without going to the
coffee-house, he came home at six, and writ not above forty lines ("some, inventions of my own; and some, hints"),   ·
and read not a bit, and all for fear little MD might be
angry; and he took four pills, which lay in his throat an
hour; and he supposed he could swallow four affronts as
easily. Next day, and day after, he had no giddiness. ·

Of politics, strictly speaking, out of all that was preparing and seething unseen, not much rises to the surface in
these earlier letters. He wishes her a merry new year on
the 1st of November ("you know this is the first day of   Old styles
it with us"), when he dined at Lord Mountjoy's with Ad-   of the year.
dison, and went at five to Harley, who could not see him,
but bid him to dinner on Friday, the 3d; when, accordingly, he went, dined, and was bidden again for the 5th.
Bishop Clogher had written to him, complaining of no letter, though long letters were written weekly to MD; why
did they tell him that? After the Sunday dinner he and
his host had sat together till seven, Harley saying all the
kind things in the world; and Swift believed he would

1710.
_Æt. 43._

Gossip of
Irish whigs.

serve him, if it were possible for him to stay in London. He affects still to think, however, that this will not be feasible; since he reckons that in time Ormond will be sure to give him some addition to Laracor. The whigs in Ireland had been saying to Ppt, forsooth, that he had come to England to leave them. But why should they think so? The dean knew he did not wish to come, and that he did all he could *not* to come. But who the devil cared what they thought—rot them for ungrateful dogs! he'd make them repent their usage before he left that place. "They say here the same thing of my leaving the whigs; but they own they can not blame me, considering the treatment I have had." She had asked him about St. John, and he tells her of a proposed dinner with him. It was to come off in a few days, to be at the secretary's own house, and Erasmus Lewis had told him that he'd like the company. But, before the dinner came for description, another letter, her fifth, arrived from Ppt, and he reproaches himself for having lost a little time in replying to it.

Answers
Ppt's fifth
letter.

Ante, 213.

Swift
at court.

He had been playfully telling his "little monkeys mine" before it came that he thought his writing was on the mend: "but methinks when I write plain, I do not know how, but we are not alone, all the world can see us. A bad scrawl is so snug, it looks like a PMD." It was a bit of the life by stealth he so much preferred. Hers arrived on the 3d, but he was then busy with other writing, and had not begun to answer it even on the 6th, when he was looking after Patty Rolt in the city, and taking a walk to exercise himself on his only disengaged day. For he has to tell her that dinners now were ten times more plentiful with him than in Dublin, or ever even in London. Next day was a thanksgiving-day, and, instead of answer, he treated her to a pure bite. He went to court, and saw the queen ("and I have seen her without one tory!") passing with all tories or ex-whigs about her, not one real whig; Buckingham, Rochester, Leeds, Shrewsbury, Berkeley of Stratton, Harcourt (now lord keeper),

Harley, Pembroke; and she "made me a courtesy, and *1710.* said in a sort of familiar way to Pdfr, *How does MD?* I considered she was a queen, and excused her." He does *A bite.* not miss the whigs, he adds, but has as many acquaintances at court as formerly. At last, on the 8th, when he has managed to steal away at five from the Portugal envoy's dinner, and has come home like a good boy, and has studied till ten, and has had a fire, oh ho! and now, finding himself snug in bed (" I have no fire-place in my bed-chamber, but it is very warm weather when one is in bed "), he has set himself to answer MD. The picture has another touch. He is wearing a " fine cap " made for him by Dingley, and it proves to be too little and too hot. She had lined it with *Writing* fur, and he wishes it far enough, for his old velvet cap is *In bed.* good for nothing, and he doubts if this has velvet underneath the fur. " I was feeling, but can not find." He'll have the fur taken off if there is velvet. And thus having settled his cap, he begins with a fervent thanks that the dear rogue's eyes were mending, and by an echo to what she had begun with. " Yes, 'faith, a long letter in a morning from a dear friend is a dear thing. I smoke a compliment, little mischievous girls, I do so."

Of sundry things affecting himself she had written, not always spelling correctly. Who were those *wiggs* that thought he was turned tory? Did she mean whigs? Which wiggs, and what did she mean? They expect he will tell them about their Vicar of Trim, Mr. Raymond. *Country vis-* Why, he knows nothing of Raymond: only heard once of *itor coming.* him since leaving Chester. Raymond, truly, was like to have much influence over him in London, and to share much of his conversation! No doubt he should introduce him to Harley, and the lord keeper, and the secretary of state.* If Mrs. Raymond was with child, he was sorry for it, and so, he believed, would her husband be. What

---

* Just as he closed he adds: " I had a letter just now from Raymond, who is at Bristol, and says he will be at London in a fortnight, and leave his wife behind him; and desires any lodging in the house where I am: but that must not be. I shall not know what to do with him in town."

did Ppt mean by "that boards near me, that I dine with now and then?" He knew no such person; he did not dine with boarders.* What the pox! They knew whom he had dined with every day since he left them, better than he did. They thought his lodgings dear? Impudence! if they vexed him, he would give ten shillings a week for a new lodging; and very likely he might have to do it, for already he was almost stunk out of Bury Street with the sink, which had helped him to verses in his "Shower."† Dingley was thinking of the (tory) world to come, and wanted the Westminster ballad; but it was not good for much, and she was to be patient till he went back. And the verger had been to her to say it was his turn to preach? Had he, indeed? "Lord bless me! my turn at Christ Church...and why to you? would he have you preach for me?" She had been urging him again as to her mother's affairs. Well, her mother had promised to see him on her return to town. Did Ppt think he could be so unkind not to see her, that she desired him in a style so melancholy? Then he told her more of his wish to obtain some investments for her in bank stock; and that though he could not make time to write to the Bishop of Killala, he'd take care of his as well as of Dingley's spectacles. But what did Madam Dinglibus mean by his fourth! Had not Ppt said, Goody Blunder, that his fifth was arrived? She frightened him till he looked back. He was writing then on Wednesday, the 8th, and meant

Uses of
a sink.

Turn to
preach.

"Goody
Blunder."

---

* He had forgotten. See *ante*, 312. Ford, Fountaine, and Levinge were the boarders, and not, as the editors supposed, the Vanhomrighs.

† "While rain depends, the pensive cat
    gives o'er
  Her frolics, aud pursues her tail no
    more.
  Returning home at night, you'll find
    the sink
  Strike your offended sense with double
    stink, etc."

It is difficult to resist the tempta-

tion of quoting from the most masterly description of its class in all the language; but I must give a couplet of humorous observation of this actual October, 1710, when the shower itself comes rattling down, clearing the streets; and the fugitives, by various fortunes led,

"Commence acquaintance underneath a
    shed:
  Triumphant tories and desponding
    whigs
  Forget their feuds, and join to save
    their wigs."

to keep his letter till Saturday, though he should write
no more; and if any thing came meanwhile from
MD, he would only say, "Madam, I have received your
sixth letter. Your most humble servant to command,
Pdfr."

1710.
Æt. 43.

Nevertheless, he did write more; and as he began next
morning, with his mouth full of water, he was going to
spit it out, because "how could he write when his mouth
was full?"... had she not done things like that, reasoned
wrong at first thinking? Much that was significant of unusual work in hand he hinted in his few following lines:
about not staying beyond seven at the coffee-house, but
coming home to his fire ("the maidenhead of my second
half-bushel") full of business and writing, making a great
deal of himself, now that MD was not there to take care
of him, and, in short, as he mysteriously adds, incessantly engaged from noon till night because of many kinds of
things. Then came what closed the diary of every day
before ruthless editors laid hands upon them—the never-
failing "Night, good-night," forever hemmed in and round
with his little language of endearment, to be read once
more only in the clusters of recovered passages of later
date at the end of my Sixth Book. "O Lord! if this
should miscarry, what a deal would be lost! I forgot to
leave a gap in the last line but one for the seal, like a
puppy; but when I am taking leave I can not leave a bit,
'faith." His editors had less scruple, and cut him off re-
morselessly at his "Paaast twelvvve o'clock, and so good-
night, etc." Next morning by candle-light the letter went;
and (for its final bit of news) she must know he was in his
night-gown every morning betwixt six and seven, and Patrick was forced to ply him fifty times before he could get
the night-gown on. And so now, for that while, he would
take his leave of his own dear MD. God Almighty bless
and protect dearest MD. Farewell, etc. (The reader must
always supply what his editors always omit.) "This letter's as long as a sermon, 'faith!"

Reasoning
wrong at
first think-
ing.

Close of each
day's diary.

Poet, 424.

Morning
habits.

Next day saw the beginning of Swift's friendship with

1710.
Æt. 43.

Henry St. John. He then first dined with him, and soon after had his help for an object long desired, and which the chief of the new ministry had at last placed within his reach.

IV.

A LONG-DESIRED OBJECT GAINED.

1710–1711.   Æt. 43–44.

1710–1711.
Æt. 43–44.

At the brief interview of Wednesday, the 4th of October, Harley had appointed Swift to go to him the following Saturday on the business for which he was joined in commission with other higher dignitaries of the Irish church, for the desired remission of first-fruits and tenths. Four in the afternoon having at last been fixed, he had to put off going with Doctor Garth, to dine near the Tower with one who had an employment there, a friend of his own and of the Bishop of Clogher, Charles Maine, Dick Eastcourt's patron, an honest, good-natured fellow, mightily beloved by all the wits, "and his mistress never above a cook-maid." Sorry to disappoint him, but unable that day to dine with any friend, Swift went instead to dine with Ben Tooke, and give him the ballad on the Westminster election, which already has been described as full of puns, but lost to us. Not finding him, however, off he went to a neighboring "blind chop-house;" dined for tenpence upon gill-ale, bad broth, and three mutton-chops; and then, it being his fate to be the same day a scoundrel and a prince, went "reeking" to the first minister of state.

A Mæcenas of the wits.

Scoundrel and prince.

. As he neared the door, he was thinking of that functionary of whom Jack Howe had said to Harley that if there were in hell a lower place than another, it must be reserved for his porter. He told lies so gravely, and with so civil a manner, that Swift was prepared to suspect every word. But the fellow told him no lie. He said his master had gone to dinner with much company, and would he return in an hour? Which Swift did, certain of then 1710–1711.
Æт. 43–44. hearing he had left; but dinner was just done, and as he stood in the hall out came Harley himself, took him into the dining-room, and presented him to the guests. Among them were Will Penn, the Quaker; Harley's son, and his son-in-law, " Lord Doblane, or some such name" (the name was Dupplin); and they sat two hours drinking as good wine as MD herself does. But the two hours following were more important. During these they were Harley and
Swift alone. alone, and the whole history of the first-fruits negotiations was related by Swift; the steps that had been made in it during the last three years; and all the difficulties that had arisen from lords lieutenants and their secretaries, who would not suffer others to solicit, yet neglected it themselves. The minister, hearing with patient attention the Vicar of Laracor thus tell his business, entered with all kindness into it; asked for his powers, and read them; read also a memorial which Swift had drawn up, putting it in his pocket to show the queen; told him the measures he should take, and, in short, said every thing Swift could wish, and more than he could have ventured to hope. There should be no interference from bishops or lords lieutenants: the act should be the queen's; and the credit given to where alone it was deserved. He should bring Swift and the secretary of state, Mr. St. John, acquainted; he called him by his Christian name, Jonathan; and The minister
calls the vic-
ar Jonathan. he spoke so many things of personal kindness and esteem, that the other was half inclined to believe what some friends had told him, that the ministers were ready and eager to do any thing to bring him over. One of Harley's remarks he thought a great piece of refinement. Being charged to call often, Swift spoke of being " loath " to give trouble in so much business as he had, and desired leave to attend the minister's levee; but Harley immediately refused, saying, "that was not a place for *friends* to come to."

So closed the memorable interview. " He has desired to dine with me (what a comical mistake was that!) I

1710–1711.
Æt. 43–44.

mean he has desired me to dine with him on Tuesday; and, after four hours being with him, set me down at St. James's coffee-house in a hackney-coach. All this is odd and comical, if you consider him and me. He knew my Christian name very well." And as, on reaching home that night, he could not help writing all about it to Ppt, even at the risk of being tedious, so neither could he forbear to think of that which, though published anonymously six years ago, people connected with his name, and had used to obstruct his advancement in the church. "They

Thinks of
the Tale of
a Tub.

may talk of the *You know what*, but, 'gad, if it had not been for that I should never have been able to get the access I have had; and if that helps me to succeed, then that *same thing* will be serviceable. But how far we must depend upon new friends I have learnt by long practice, though I think among great ministers they are just as good as old, ones." His wish to think them even better had thus early received strong confirmation.

First dinner
with Harley.

Of the Tuesday dinner, his first at Harley's, brief mention has been made. Sir Simon Harcourt was with them, and as to the memorial, he was able at once to tell Ppt that every thing was to be, not through their new lord lieutenant, the duke, but as a popular thing, conceded to himself, Doctor Swift. Nor were the arts of the consummate master of conciliation and compromise less successfully played off at the next dinner he gave to his new ally.

Second.

Just before had come out a Grub-street in verse on what for some time had been the town-talk against the ex-lord treasurer, of his having, in spleen at Harley's victory, ungraciously broken his staff, instead of having, as was customary, sent it back to the queen. It was not known until long afterward that Godolphin had done this at the queen's express desire.

> "No hobby-horse, with gorgeous top,
> The dearest in Charles Mather's shop,
> Or glittering tinsel of May Fair,
> Could with the rod of Sid compare.

> Dear Sid, then why wert thou so mad
> To break thy rod like naughty lad?
> You should have kiss'd it in your distress,
> And then returned it to your mistress."

1710–1711.
Æt. 43–44.
"Sid Ha-
met."

This was the "Sid Hamet" of which Ppt will very shortly deliver the opinion its author was so anxious to obtain from her. Hardly a better example could be given of Mrs. Johnson's keen yet kindly criticism. She thought it well enough, she said. It was the sort of piece an enemy would like, and a friend not; and of which both opinions would be changed on learning the author's name. It was a shrewder verdict than any he was to hear at Harley's second dinner.

Ppt's opinion of it

The day was Sunday, the 15th; Matthew Prior, whom St. John some time before had won over from the whigs, dined with them; among the guests also were Dalrymple, president of the Scotch Court of Session, and Benson, a lord of the treasury; and good news welcomed Swift as he entered. The queen had granted the whole prayer of his memorial for first-fruits and "twentieth" parts; it would probably be declared in to-morrow's cabinet; and he might hope to get even something of greater value. After dinner came in another ex-whig, his old friend, Lord Peterborough; "we renewed our acquaintance, and he grew mightily fond of me;" and what is this "Sid Hamet" I hear of? asked the eccentric warrior. Whereupon Harley repeated some of the verses, and then, pulling them out of his pocket, gave them to one of his guests to read, though they all had read them often. Then Peterborough insisted on reading them himself, and Harley bobbed Swift at every line to take note of their beauties, and Prior rallied Peterborough with having written them, and Peterborough declared them for a certainty to be Prior's, and Prior next turned them on Swift, and Swift knew them for Prior's, and in short "Sid Hamet" supplied the whole mirth of the evening. At nine o'clock both poets left; and sat at the Smyrna coffee-house until eleven, "receiving acquaintance;" prolonging the enjoyment, no doubt, which they

Scene at Harley's.

1710-1711.
Æt. 43–44.

State visit to the minister.

Handsome conduct of Harley.

had received at Harley's; and sitting attentive to their own applause.

Swift had a touch of disappointment the day following. He went early to Harley's in a chair, "and Patrick before it," a sort of state visit, with another copy of the memorial having additions from himself complying with some suggestion of the previous day; but the minister was "too full of business" to see him. He was going to the queen, and desired Swift to send up the paper, excusing himself upon his hurry. "I was a little balked, but they tell me it is nothing." He should judge by next visit; and, taking the precaution meanwhile to square matters "for a time at least" with a powerful personage, tipped Harley's porter with half a crown. Three days later he went to Lewis at Lord Dartmouth's office to know when he might see Harley; and by-and-by up came the minister himself, and engaged him to dine on the morrow. On the 21st, accordingly, he had his third dinner with Harley, who presented him to the Earl of Sterling, Lord Peterborough coming in the evening. Swift staid till nine before Harley would let him go, or tell him any thing of his affairs. Then he announced that all was settled, and would be signified to the bishops as done upon a personal memorial from Swift; and though an additional two thousand a year he had asked for could not yet be given, it might follow in time. Never was any thing compassed so soon, he averred with some truth; and done, too, by his own personal credit with Mr. Harley, who had been so extremely obliging that he "knew not what to make of it unless to show the rascals of the other party that they used a man unworthily who deserved better." In the second copy of the memorial before the queen, he told Esther Johnson he had spoken plainly of Wharton; and now in a month or two all would be over, he should have nothing more to do, and his "insolent sluts" were to tell him impartially, when the thing became known, whether the Irish public gave any of the merit to him or not. "I have so much that I will never take it upon me!"

A little exultation at such prompt success in a matter
so long in hand, and which had taxed to small effect suc-
cessions of viceroys and secretaries, was not unnatural;
yet Swift, who had written to the archbishop as soon as
he found success to be likely, had hardly written a second
letter announcing the success, imposing certain reserves
until official intimation should be sent, but telling him the
thing was done—that the bishops were to be a corporation
for disposal of the first-fruits, that the twentieth parts were
to be remitted, and that a letter from Secretary Dartmouth
would very shortly put the primate and himself in possession of all details—when a blow was struck at him from a
quite unexpected quarter. As soon as the news reached
Dublin that the Duke of Ormond was to be the new lord
lieutenant, the Irish bishops had met to discuss the advis-
ability of continuing the first-fruits commission as constituted; a majority leaned strongly to the belief that Doctor Swift's belonging to such a commission, considering
that he had been so long in supposed favor with the whigs,
might prejudice any chance of success with the tories;
and finally it was resolved to supersede the commission by
a formal representation from the entire Irish episcopate,
to be placed in the duke's hands, and by him submitted
to the queen. Doctor Swift was at the same time graciously requested not to discontinue his own solicitation.
Ormond's secretary, Ned Southwell (son of the Southwell
who was Temple's friend), told this to Swift, and showed
him the papers, a few days after he had dispatched his second letter to the archbishop giving account of what he believed to be the close of the affair. Almost at the same
moment, too, King replied to his first letter, confirming substantially all Southwell's statement; and "so," he wrote
to Mrs. Johnson, with pardonable indignation, "while their
letter was on the road to the Duke of Ormond and Southwell, mine was going to them with an account of the thing
being done. I writ a very warm answer to the archbishop immediately, and showed my resentment, as I ought,
against the bishops, only excepting himself, in good man-

1710–1711.
Æt. 43–44.

Good news
for the arch-
bishop.

Unlooked-
for blow.

Archbishop's
ill news.

1710-1711.
Æt. 43-44.
ners. I wonder what they will say when they hear the thing is done." Contrasting his own promptitude with what would have followed in the other case, he repeated a
What Ned
Southwell
thought of it.
remark of Southwell's that my lord duke had formerly had the matter three years in doing without any success, and that he "would doubtless only think of it some months hence when he should be going for Ireland."

However, Swift gave Esther Johnson free leave now to tell every one that the thing was really accomplished, and that Mr. Harley had prevailed on the queen to do it. For himself, as he hoped to live, he despised the credit of it, and desired she would not give him the less merit when she talked of it to any one. But though out of an excess of pride he said this, he was not the less eager to spite the bishops; and she was to be sure and have it spread widely abroad that all was due to Mr. Harley. "Never fear," he wrote afterward, as he began to measure the trouble he might have given her by the expression of his own, "I ain't vexed at this puppy business of the bishops, although I was a little at first." And then he laughingly tells her what his rewards will be. Harley will think Doctor Swift had received a favor, the duke that the Doctor had put upon him a neglect, and the Irish bishops that
"So goes
the world."
their vicar had done nothing at all. So went the world. But he had got above all that, with perhaps "better reason" than any of them knew; and so she should hear no more of first-fruits, dukes, Harleys, archbishops, and Southwells.

She was, nevertheless, to hear more before three days were past. Dining with Harley toward the close of November, he told the minister what the bishops had done, and the difficulty he was under; on which Harley bid him never bother himself, for that he would tell Ormond all about the business, and show him there was nothing to do. "So now I am easy, and they may hang themselves
"A parcel
of ungrate-
ful rascals."
for a parcel of insolent, ungrateful rascals." The minister told him on the same occasion that the queen's letter was

to go very shortly; and he was fain to tell his friend 1710-1711.
Æt. 43-44.
thereon, replying to reiterated "home" inquiries, that he
should then begin to think of returning; although "the
baseness of those bishops" made him love Ireland less
than formerly. Not yet, however, was the settlement to
be. Other things intervened; "mighty affairs, not your
nasty first-fruits;" and it was not until the continued delay had begun to compromise in Ireland the credit of the
assurances he had so confidently given, that he saw an absolute necessity for at once pushing the business to its
close. The end of December was now at hand, and in the Harley's
delays.
few past weeks St. John had given him proofs of a confidence in some points more absolute even than Harley's
own. He had no scruple, therefore, dining with the secretary, in taking him aside to complain of his chief having done nothing to forward the queen's letter for remission of the first-fruits, promised six weeks before; and·to
point out that he was himself in danger thereby to lose
reputation in Ireland. St. John, he adds, "took the matter right, desired me to be with him on Sunday morning,
and promised me to finish the matter in four days." In
four days they met accordingly, when St. John told Swift
it was to be done, not, as at first proposed, by a queen's letter, but by patent; and that Harley had desired assurance
to be given to him that the warrant for such a patent was
already drawn. It was to pass through several offices and
take up some time, because, in things the queen herself
gave, such "considerateness" was indispensable; but St.
John assured him it was granted and done, that it was First-fruits
finally re-
mitted.
past all dispute, and he desired Swift to be no longer in
any pain at all. The promises were kept, and the patent
was completed early in February.

Yet if Swift's pain was at an end in that matter, thus
brought at last to the issue long desired, there were others
in which his troubles were only beginning. The second
week of January had not passed before he was conscious
of "mighty difficulties" in the path of the new administration, and that his own way between its two chiefs would

1710–1711. not be very easy walking. "I told them I had no hopes
Æt. 43–44. they could ever keep in," is a remark in the letter to Esther
Johnson begun by him on the day after the first-fruits pat-
ent was completed.

V.

ROBERT HARLEY AND HENRY ST. JOHN.

1710–1711. Æt. 43–44.

1710–1711.   Swift's first two months in London had closed with his
Æt. 43–44. eighth letter to Mrs. Johnson, and he had then gone far to
settle much that before was undetermined. Up to its date
he was talking still (as upon provocation indeed he rarely
ceased to do, even in more triumphant days) of an early return to Laracor, with perhaps some addition to it through
the favor of the Duke of Ormond; but afterward, though
he repeated in sundry forms a desire and intention to go
back, there was little to show that he had really grave
thoughts in his mind of any such limit or bar to higher
expectations. The afternoon of the day when it had been
dispatched was that of his first dinner with Henry St.
John; his new party ties were soon to be fixed irrevoca-
bly; and formidable interruptions were to begin to even
the whig friendships it has been found so difficult to let
go. To the tories Swift had only hitherto given his giant
help now and then; even yet there was no alliance form-
Swift getting ally ratified; but after that letter left his hands he became
into harness. a continual worker on their behalf, and the reader has evidence before him in the preceding pages, until now not
obtainable in a form so complete, by which to estimate the
worth of the reproaches cast upon him for such advocacy.
If he had turned from men with whom he had in all things
cordially acted, to help men whom he had always as bitterly opposed, there would be little more to say; but when
he made his retort against the Irish bishops for the unmannerly treatment of him in their first-fruits commis-

sion, he scornfully reminded them that on the very ques- 1710-1711.
tion of the interests of the church, as to which they had Æt. 43-44.
withdrawn their confidence, he might at any time, if so The charge of rattling.
minded, have "made his market" with the whigs. This
should at least be remembered before he is charged with
having had no resource but to make his market with the
tories; and what is now to be said of the present leaders
of that party, of the position he was to take with them,
and of the kind of service he rendered them, will further
illustrate both his conduct and its motives.

The passage of the Godolphin ministry between the extremes of tory and whig has been seen at the various steps
of Swift's career. He never felt it to be safe during the Ante, 146.
prevalence of either, and he foretold its dangers the year
before it fell. As an avowed and decided whig administration it had not governed England for more than two
years, and its most dangerous enemy, less hopeful of success than perhaps at any previous time, was at a distance
from the scene of the long intrigue by which he had striven
to supplant its leading members, when the prosecution of
Sacheverell began. "The game is up," cried Harley, and Result of roasting a parson.
hurried back to London. In the brief six months which
were passed since then, a government believed to be powerful beyond precedent had been overthrown; the intriguer
was chancellor of the exchequer and chief minister; and
the young orator who had been his leading support in the
House of Commons, and allied with him throughout his
adventure, was principal secretary of state. It seems a
strange destiny that for so long a time had linked together in the same enterprise men so different in character and
intellect as Robert Harley and Henry St. John. But each
had need of the other, for success in a common desire; and
both largely profited by having the wit to see this, and the
good sense to turn aside from designs that would have made
them less mutually dependent. The object once achieved,
however, of which the pursuit had kept them united, they
could hardly less clearly have perceived that success would
divide them. Swift too soon became conscious of it.

Vol. I.—22

Macaulay's judgment of the two statesmen is briefly summed up. He calls Harley a solemn trifler, and St. John a brilliant knave. All that may be said in bar of the latter judgment does not need to involve any direct contradiction of it, but to the former large modifications are required. It was more than solemn trifling which for a dozen years in the House of Commons had so swayed the balance between two extreme sections as to prevent either from making itself predominant, and by which the toryism of Nottingham and Rochester was as much kept in check as the whiggism of Wharton and Sunderland. Of

Harley's
career.

puritan and republican descent, Harley had a family right to object to crown expedients and proposals; but, while every opposition party in its turn profited by his support, he was never identified with any single section of malcontents. The speaker in those days was practically also leader of the House; and when for the third time in succession Harley was chosen speaker at the meeting of William's last parliament, the cleverest had joined the stupidest in supporting him, and St. John seconded what the tory squires began. He was not an orator, as Swift himself admits; but he had the tact which eloquent men often want, of getting himself listened to on every occasion; such talents as he possessed he had assiduously cultivated; and his knowledge of parliamentary forms was unrivaled. That this was more than solemn trifling can be confidently said without affirming it to be eloquence, genius, or even statesmanship; but whatever it was, it was a thing

Product of
the Revo-
lution.

born of the Revolution. The man himself was one of its products; its principles were strengthened even by what he did in a contrary sense; his adroit management of parties at a critical time, secured the Act of Settlement against a time when his associates, if not himself, would fain have unsettled it; and as far as any single man could represent the Revolution, Harley did. As it trimmed between two parties, so did he; and in the two supports on which it mainly rested—parliament and the press—he found the agencies to which he most trusted. Upon some one ob-

jecting in his presence that the people of England would *1710-1711.*
never bear a bill which he meant to pass, Pope heard him *Æt. 43-44.*
reply that none of them knew how far the good people of
England would bear.   In very varied attempts upon this
problem, which the Revolution went a good way to solve,
Harley had been engaged all his life ; and the experiment
now in hand, the most difficult and dangerous of all, was
to make or to mar him finally.   According to Macaulay,
it did both.   It made him an earl, a knight of the garter, At the
lord treasurer, and master of the fate of Europe in a crit- summit.
ical hour; but it marred what had long been a high reputation by showing the possessor of it to be really a dull,
puzzle-headed man.   Yet, even if this were true, it is not
those who win their way to the summit, and only stumble
after reaching it, who are to be called unsure of foot.

Of the men who accompanied him on the way, sharing
his friendships and dislikes, and entering and quitting office with him, the only two of conspicuous ability were St. St. John and
John and Harcourt, and the name of Bolingbroke still re- Harcourt.
mains to us almost as famous in the literature as in the
history of England.   With Harley's third election as speaker, St. John's allegiance began, and up to the present time
it continued steady and unwavering.   He owed his place
of secretary of war perhaps more to Marlborough than to
Harley ; but the great soldier, when a question arose between the two, though he did not then doubt St. John's
loyalty to him, acted as if the Harley influence must necessarily be the stronger.   " By gaining Harley you will
govern the others," was his counsel to Godolphin when
beset with tory troubles ; and he would have been more
prudent for himself, if, as he watched the influence grow
into a danger, he had opposed it less directly.   Harley had
this much justification for the work now lying before him,
that it was the duke who had peremptorily turned *him*
out of office three years before ; but it is certainly to be
said of St. John that he had no justification whatever.   He St. John's
had never, during any period of his life thus far, received Marlbor-
any thing but kindness and confidence from Marlborough ; ough.

1710-1711.
Æt. 43–44.
during all the years in the House of Commons when he did the talking for Harley, he never committed himself to any expression of disbelief or distrust of the duke; and it was probably to avoid the necessity of taking public part against him, on Harley's dismissal at the opening of 1708, which led him to retire altogether from the House in resigning the war-office to Walpole. Nearly two years ear-

Duke's confidence in him. lier, Marlborough wrote to Godolphin that he was "very confident" St. John would "never deceive" them; and more than once in the two years while the duke had Somers, Sunderland, Halifax, and Wharton for his colleagues, St. John wrote hearty congratulations to him on his victories.* With a felicitous choice of phrase, he said, many years later, in his famous letter to Sir William Windham, that in the first essays he made in public affairs he "acted the part of a tory;" and he may perhaps have found some excuse for the tone he took at this time, in the belief that

Acting parts. the great general was only "acting the part" of a whig. But on both sides the acting is about to assume unusual earnestness, and the performers will have to face some sharp realities.

Swift's letters will from time to time reveal such of them as affected him personally, contributing to the story of his life; and these will be better understood by help of a brief general statement of the question which the political changes threw into greatest prominence, and around which the party passions on either side were to rage with the greatest fury.

Peace or war. At first it did not seem as if any possible question could arise between stopping and continuing the war. Distasteful in its origin and progress as it was to the tories, by its

---

* "I am very much obliged to you," Marlborough wrote to St. John on the 14th October, 1709, "for your congratulations and kind expressions on the late victory, the importance of which will, I hope, appear by its consequences, and that we shall enjoy the advantages of it. In the mean time I am very glad if that, or any thing else I can do, may prove the means of adding to your satisfaction, and particularly that you begin again to entertain more favorable thoughts of the world, in which you are qualified to do so much good." This was after Malplaquet.

conduct and successes opposition had been overcome, and its results had so exalted and strengthened Marlborough as to render him apparently independent of either party. He might have been so in reality if he had been less eager to get parliament to make him so, and if his wife had been less overbearing in support of such extravagant claims. His grasping wish to be made captain-general for life supplied the heaviest weapon employed against him. It seems doubtful if at first there was any intention to deprive him of his commands. Harley personally disliked him, but his hatreds were never very active; and if St. John on coming into power had any thought of his old chief, it was to induce him to resume his cast-off opinions, and prevail on him to lead the confederacy as tory·captain-general. He afterward very candidly declared, in his letter to Sir William Windham, that when he and Harley came to court they had just the same disposition as all parties before them had shown. The principal spring of their actions, he said, was to have the government of the state in their own hands; and their principal views were, the preservation of their power, great employments to themselves, and great opportunities as well of rewarding those who had helped to raise them as of hurting those who stood in opposition to them; though it was not the less true that with such considerations of private and party interest were intermingled others having for their object the public good of the nation, "at least what we took to be such." That the public good was secondary, is no unfair inference from these words; which the facts so far confirm that it was only when danger arose to "private and party" interests that the purpose began to be seriously entertained of striking down Marlborough and manœuvring for a peace.

At the outset, not sufficiently conscious of danger, the duke played into his enemies' hands by not only interfering to delay the resignation of Godolphin and other leading whigs, but by retaining his own command after even Godolphin's dismissal. If he had at once resigned, the new ministry could hardly have gone on without a com-

Margin notes:

1710–1711.
Æt. 43–44.

The duke's great falling.

Frank confession of ministerial policy.

Marlborough's mistake.

1710-1711.
Æt. 43-44.

promise; but the interval had enabled Harley to put a check on the extravagance of his followers during the arrangements necessary for complete transfer of the offices; and when Marlborough saw things more clearly, the resistance he offered came too late. The view Swift took from the beginning of the changes was, that the new men could not stand without a peace; and immediately after his first visit to Harley he wrote to this effect to the archbishop. What also he wrote of the first-fruits, we need not doubt, was the least important business transacted at that interview. A month before Swift reached London, St. John had started a weekly political broadsheet the same size as the *Tatler*, with the name of the *Examiner*, to which Prior, Atterbury, Doctor Freind, and Doctor King (who took quasi-editorial charge of it), had since contributed, and against which Addison had brought into the field his *Whig Examiner* with such damaging effect that the ministry were in ill case if better advocacy for them could not be found.* It is easy to understand, therefore, what Harley meant at the visit, when, with his fears that the ministerial majority in the Commons was too large, he coupled what he described as the exact parallel between his own case and his visitor's, that neither had been able to go all lengths with his party, and that for this reason "both had been ill-treated by the former ministry." The remedy he had himself found was open to his friend, and before a fortnight was past Swift had taken up the *Examiner*. Addison had laid down his† three weeks before. The

St. John
starts the
Examiner.

Swift takes
it up.

---

* It is, however, quite a mistake to say that St. John's attack on the war, and on Marlborough and his wife, to which the ex-chancellor, Cowper, replied (both letter and answer are in *Somers's Tracts*, xiii., 71, 85), was printed, as writers copying each other have averred, as the tenth number of the *Examiner*. The pamphlets were published independently, the one as a letter to the *Examiner*, commenting on the reasonings of that paper,

the other as a letter to Isaac Bickerstaff, Esq. (the *Tatler*), replying to the comment.

† The *Whig Examiner* was succeeded by the *Medley*, edited by Oldmixon, to which Mainwaring, Anthony Henley, Steele, Kennet, and other well-known ultra-whigs, contributed; which waged unceasing war against Swift's *Examiner* during the whole of his connection with it, and several months beyond; and which, having

friends never met in political conflict, as Johnson hastily
supposed.

It is not too much to say that no intelligible position
had been taken for the ministry in regard to a peace, either by themselves or their friends, until Swift thus entered the scene. The writers of previous *Examiners* had
only floundered about a meaning or a policy. Eager at
first to conciliate Marlborough, in one they wrote to prove
that his actions would be "guided by a nobler principle
than the little interests of any party;" in another, they denounced the intermeddlers, who strove to make the great
general uneasy in his commands, and persuade him to lay
down his commission; in a third, they did their best to **Its previous writers.**
make the Dutch unpopular, and inculcate the necessity of
taking a good peace as soon as it was to be had; in a
fourth, the ex-ministry were assailed for not having had
"twenty thousand more Englishmen in Spain;" in a fifth,
sundry reasons were given for "pushing on the war" with
the greatest possible energy, "in order to end it by a safe
and speedy peace;"* and all these veerings and varieties
of opinion were interlarded with indiscreet assaults on
revolution doctrines, which culminated in the last paper
before Swift took the pen (that of the 26th of October,
dropped from the series when reprinted) by an elaborate
argument to prove that the doctrine of non-resistance was
entirely consistent with the liberty of a free people. Nor
had the famous letter which St. John himself addressed **St. John's letter to the Examiner.**
to the writers, with all its spirit and vivacity, succeeded in
putting the question in any more acceptable form. It was

---

begun on the 5th of October, 1710, **Examiners and Medleys.**
closed with its forty-fifth number on the
6th August, 1711. Swift's first *Examiner* bore date the 2d of November,
1710, thirteen numbers having previously been published, and his last
was the forty-sixth number, issued on
the 14th June, 1711. Six numbers by
inferior hands (Mrs. Manley taking
charge of the publication) closed the

volume on the 26th July, 1711; and
with a second volume, which began
on the 6th of December, 1711, and
closed with its forty-seventh number
on the 23d of October, 1712, the *Examiners* ceased for that generation.

* Those five *Examiners* are dated
respectively the 3d, 10th, 24th, and
31st of August, and the 5th of October, 1710.

1710–1711.
Æt. 43–44. chiefly remarkable for its rash avowal of a belief that England had only a secondary interest in the war, and should never have engaged in it with the sacrifices and outlay of a principal; and by attacks still more inconsiderate, because calculated to strengthen France in any future negotiations, on the fellow-members of the confederacy of allies. Forgetting the congratulations he had himself poured out on Marlborough for his victories even so late as Oudenarde and Malplaquet (won at such cost of blood), the purpose of St. John's letter was in effect to declare that peace should have been made before Harley and himself left office in 1706; and its reasonings could have no practical result but to throw power into the hands of France.

Swift's first contribution. What all this wanted of a statesman-like quality Swift supplied. His first *Examiner* was a masterpiece. There was nothing violent about the war. A belief was expressed in the justness of its origin, while the admitted evils of its long duration were illustrated by the respective conditions into which the moneyed and the landed interests had been brought by it. The country gentleman was compared to a young heir out of whose estate a scrivener received half the rents for interest, having a mortgage on the whole; and it was shown that a few more years of war would reduce him to the condition of "a farmer at a rack-rent to the army and the public funds." There is no attack on the allies, and no playing into the enemy's hands: but the implication running all through the argument is a rooted belief that the main objects which justified the war had been obtained; and that to continue it for nothing but to drive the French king's grandson from the Spanish throne was, in effect, to begin a fresh war under new and Reasons for a peace. difficult conditions. If danger was possible on the side of France, it was more than probable on that of Austria; and the opinion which Swift certainly had held in favor of settlement on the terms proposed after the successes of 1709, pervaded this first *Examiner*. Its closing sentence embodied at once his opinion and his advice. He would have

parliament assist her majesty with the "utmost vigor" *1710-1711.*
till her enemies "*again*" should be brought to sue for *Æt. 43-44.*
peace, and until they "*again*" might offer such terms as
would make peace honorable and lasting. "Only with
this difference, that the ministry perhaps will not *again*
refuse them." The italics are his own.

In that spirit he had put on his armor for Harley and
St. John. What weapons he afterward employed, and for
what other objects, in the conflict of which he became the
principal champion, the event will show ; but this much is
at once to be said, that even in that age of infinitely varied
controversy there had been no such handling of matters
strictly political. With the statesman-like instinct of regarding questions not singly, but in their dependence or
incidence to others, which attracts one in Bolingbroke's
writing, there were qualities not in his or any one else's
pamphleteering. As marked an absence of all that might
weaken his argument as of every thing evasive in stating
it, unshrinking confidence that went at once against the
strongest positions of his adversary, humor that took its
highest relish from an imperturbable gravity, homely
words that struck like blows, short telling sentences, varied and always suitable illustration, a style of sense and
wit in equal proportions of vigorous reasonings and laugh-
able surprises, Swift's political writing had still for its *Swift's politi-*
prominent characteristic a simplicity of manner perfectly *cal writing.*
straightforward, with no pretenses whatever. It might
be of the date of yesterday, so modern are the turns and
phrases, if such authorship yet existed among us. No one
deserved less to have it said that he had hardly left his old
whig company before the most terrible of his invectives
against those former associates were heard. Swift was
not so clumsy at his own craft. Whether he deserted his
party or his party deserted him, it is certain that, with one
marked exception, he did not begin his work for Harley
by reviling the individual members of it. That was to
come later, in the heat of hard blows on both sides. For
the present Harley's tone is his ; and, saving the vigor and

1710–1711.
Æt. 43–44.

His early
Examiners.
vivacity, he writes like a moderate whig. He expounds the art of political lying, to show that its practice for twenty years had rendered friends and enemies no longer distinguishable; and incidentally he states that the inventor of lies, the devil, had been quite outstripped by the improvements of an eminent whig (Wharton) in this branch of the practice. In his succeeding paper he expressed a belief that no reasonably honest man of either side who looked into the disputes of religion and government that both parties were daily buffeting each other about, would find one point really material in difference between them; and in the same *Examiner* he put two significant questions, how certain great men of the late ministry (Marlborough and Godolphin) came to be whigs, and by what figure of speech certain others put lately into great employments (Shrewsbury and Somerset) were to be called tories? When, in another, he justifies the queen, as he would the owner of a mismanaged estate and establishment, for turning off the servants that had mismanaged

Personalities.

both, he is careful not to bring opinions into debate, and the sharpness of touch is within the limit of party warfare.* John the coachman (Marlborough), the steward Oldfox (Godolphin), and the clerks Charles and Harry (Sunderland and Boyle), are only charged with having run their mistress over head and ears in debt, though her tenants were punctual in paying rent, and she never spent half her income. He is for unsparing prosecution of the war till a safe and honorable peace can be had; and even

English commander and Roman general.

his famous comparison of the English commander's rewards to those of a victorious Roman general, the hundred-thousand-pounds post-office grant to the eight-pounds sacrificial bull, and the two hundred thousand pounds for Blenheim to the twopence for a Crown of Laurel, involved no personal attack on Marlborough. It was a bill of Ro-

---

* Even the "Bill Bigamy," by which he designated the ex-chancellor, Cowper, was not more of a scandal or libel in the common talk of that day than the "Cupid" applied to a statesman of ours; and it obtained a niche in Voltaire's *Philosophical Dictionary*, so widely was it known.

man gratitude put beside a bill of British *in*gratitude in
reply to loud complaints of the tory treatment of the English hero.

Five days after that *Examiner* appeared, Swift dined
once more with Halifax; crossing him in all his whig
talk, and making him come over to the other side. "I
know he makes court to the new men, although he affects
to talk like a whig." His first dinner with St. John had
been a fortnight before, when the only other guests were
Erasmus Lewis and Doctor Freind (for whom St. John,
who had been his fellow-student at Christ Church, had
great regard) "that writ Lord Peterborough's actions in
Spain." Harley was there before dinner, but could not
dine, and after dinner Prior came: when the secretary,
who had used Swift with all the kindness in the world,
took occasion to tell the rival poet that the best thing
he had read lately was not his, but Swift's, on Vanbrugh
("which I do not reckon so very good neither"). This
damped Prior's spirits a little, till Swift stuffed him with
two or three compliments; and as he sat there himself,
flattered and flattering, his thoughts went back to Moor
Park, and to the veneration he used to have for Sir William Temple because he might have been secretary of state
at fifty, whereas here was a young fellow hardly thirty in
that employment: the father still a man of pleasure walking the Mall,* frequenting the St. James's and the choco-

---

* St. John came of what Clarendon
calls a "mutinous family," but his immediate descent was from the younger and less mutinous branch, the St.
Johns of Battersea and Wandsworth.
Of the elder, the first who had the
title of Bolingbroke, created an earl
by James, and the second, who took
the title of St. John of Bletsoe, created
a baron by Charles, were both violent
parliamentarians; and on disappear-
ing from the scene, left the family
name to Oliver St. John. He bore it
only under the bar sinister, but carried
it to its highest fame; and from the
marriage of his daughter, when he
was Cromwell's chief-justice, thus
uniting the rebellious and the royalist
St. Johns as one family at Battersea,
sprung the father of the famous Henry
St. John. The grandfather, Sir Walter, did not die till 1708, when he was
eighty-seven; and his son, Sir Harry,
lived till he was ninety. He passed all
his life as he was passing it in Swift's
time. He was a lounger in the coffee-houses of the second Charles and
James, when he killed a baronet in a
night brawl. While his son rose to the
highest position in the state, and as

late houses, and the son principal secretary of state! Was not there something very odd in that? Though this was their first day of friendly intercourse, St. John already rivaled Harley in confidences; which he handsomely accounted for by repeating to Swift a compliment of Harley's, that from a man who had "the way so much of getting into you" there was no keeping any thing. "A refinement," Swift adds; "and so I told him, and it was so; indeed, it is hard to see these great men use me like one who is their better, and the puppies with you in Ireland hardly regarding me: but there are some reasons for all this which I will tell you when we meet." He was now more regularly working for them.

Matthew
Prior.

To their other ex-whig poet and workman he took very kindly, finding his foibles to be no indifferent help to his companionable qualities. They dined together next day at an eating-house with Erasmus Lewis for host, who sent his own wine and left early, the two poets sitting on until late, complimenting one another upon their mutual wit and poetry. Again they dined, three days later, with St. John at Harley's; and at the secretary's the day following, meeting among the guests Lord Orrery and the other

Lord Dartmouth.

principal secretary, Lord Dartmouth, who was a plain, unpretending, trustworthy man, whom nobody treated as of much account, and whose ignorance of French (which even Harley spoke clumsily) tended still more to throw all important affairs into St. John's hands. Harley could not dine; and, says Swift, "would have had me away while I was at dinner; but I did not like the company he was to have." The next evening, still with Prior, and joined by Lewis and Doctor Freind, he supped with "the ramblingest

Lord Peterborough.

est lying rogue on earth," as with a not unloving familiarity he calls Lord Peterborough. Afterward came another

suddenly fell from it, he continued to be a man of pleasure about town. That same son was under attainder when Walpole, to reward Sir Harry's easy whiggery, made him Viscount St. John with the barony of Battersea; and before he died, in 1742, he had been able to carry the indolent, careless, licentious life which he had lived through five reigns very far into a sixth.

dinner with St. John, at which the party, consisting of 1710-1711.
Æt. 43-44. Lord Anglesea, Sir Thomas Hanmer, Freind, Prior, and himself, sat till nine; when he closed the night by supper at his brother poet's lodgings, making a debauch off Prior's cold pie; "and I hate the thoughts of it, and I am full, and I do not like it." The same letter which tells all this to Ppt relates also an incident highly characteristic of his own ready sense and self-possession. Coming home from the tavern dinner with Lewis and Prior, a gentleman unknown stopped him in the Pall Mall; politely informed him that the queen owed him two hundred thousand pounds, and that he had two hundred thousand men ready to serve her in the war; and asked Swift's opinion, having been repulsed from seeing her by her people in waiting, whether it would be best for him to make another attempt that evening or to wait till to-morrow. Of course A madman
in Pall Mall. a madman, Swift at once saw, and with prompt sagacity got rid of him. "I begged him of all love to wait on her immediately; for that, to my knowledge, the queen would admit him; that this was an affair of great importance, and required dispatch; and I instructed him to let me know the success of his business, and come to the Smyrna coffee-house, where I would wait for him till midnight." Off he went, and so ended the adventure;* a coffee-house A coffee-
house chris-
tening. appointment more real and jovial being kept the night following at the St. James's, when he christened the child of the keeper of the house, Elliott, and "the rogue" gave a "most noble supper" in honor of the occasion, and Swift and Steele sat "late over a bowl of punch among some scurvy company."

The week or two that followed the meeting of the new parliament were important and busy ones. He began his tenth letter on the day† of the election to the speaker's

---

* Swift good-naturedly adds: "I would fain have given the man half a crown; but was afraid to offer it him, lest he should be offended; for, besides his money, he said he had a thousand pounds a year."

† Two days later, when he had gone to meet Harley in the Court of Requests, he saw "Jack Temple," and exchanged a few careless words with him.

chair of the high-church member for Oxford, Bromley,
when the footmen were to put up for their speaker Colonel
Hill's black Pompey, for whom Swift was engaged to use
his interest and get Patrick to collect votes. He had gone
with Charles Ford to see the Houses meet; but only seeing a crowd, they betook themselves to Westminster Abbey, where he sauntered so long among the tombs, he was
forced to go to an eating-house for his dinner. The queen's
speech that day was the first public appeal from the new
ministers; and Swift emphatically referred in his next *Examiner* to the several pledges it contained on their behalf
to bring forward needful measures of finance, to support
and encourage the church, to preserve the union, to maintain the indulgence to scrupulous consciences, to make
allegiance to the Hanoverian succession the condition of
employments, and to carry on the war with the utmost
vigor in order to obtain a safe and honorable peace, as the
confirmation in every point of what he had thus far put
forth in his *Examiners*. The same letter to Ppt contains
words of much significance. She had questioned him as
to some assurances which Patrick had sent over to Dingley. "What! O Lord!" is his reply. "Did Patrick write
of his master not coming till spring." Insolent Pat! He
know his master's secrets? No, as my lord mayor said,
"if I thought my shirt knew," etc. 'Faith, the master
would "come" as soon as it was in any way proper for
him to "come;" but, to say the truth, he was at present
a little involved with the ministry in some certain things
(this he told them as a secret); but as soon as ever he could
clear his hands, he would stay no longer. The present
men had a difficult task, and wanted him. Perhaps they
might be just as grateful as others; but, according to the
best judgment he had, they were pursuing the true interest of the public, and therefore he was glad to contribute
what was in his power.* "For God's sake, not a word of

---

* Something to the same effect was in a following letter, his correspond- ent having remarked that *some people* went to England who could never tell *when to come back*. Did she mean that, he asked, as a reflection upon

this to any alive." Under his own hand there is also a
statement of what had passed between himself and Harley
a few weeks back, before his engagements, only silently
understood till then, were formally undertaken. When
he supposed the first-fruits business to be finally settled,
he told the minister that he would very shortly be "intending" for Ireland; on which Harley frankly told him
that his friends and himself knew very well how usefully
he had written against measures proposed by the late ministry to which on principle he had been opposed, and this
had convinced them that he would not feel bound to continue to favor their cause simply because of his "personal
esteem for several among them." There was now entirely a new scene; but the difficulty to those who directed
it was the "want of some good pen" to keep up the spirit raised in the people, "to assert the principles and justify the proceedings of the new ministers." He then "fell
into some personal civilities which it will not become me
to repeat;" and closed by saying that it should be his particular care to "establish me" in England, and to "represent me to the queen" as a person they could not be without. "I promised to do my endeavors in that way for
some few months. To which he replied that he expected
no more, and that he had other and greater occasions for
me."* One thing the first minister had not said, but
Swift knew it very well, and St. John afterward charac-
teristically confessed it to him. "We were determined
to have you," he said. "You were the only one we were
afraid of."

Describing a dinner at Harley's a week or two later,
when Prior was present, but St. John did not come, though
he had promised, and had chidden Swift for not seeing
him oftener, the principal talk was about a "damned libel-

1710-1711.
Æt. 43–44.

Explana-
tions with
Harley.

Promises
exchanged.

Libelous
pamphlet.

Pdfr? Saucebox! He would go
back as soon as he could, and, he
hoped, with some advantage; unless
all ministries were alike, as perhaps
they might be.

  * My account is taken from *Mem-*

oirs relating to the Change, etc., in
which every statement that it is possible to test by other contemporary
evidence has been found to be singularly accurate.

ous pamphlet" against Lord Wharton, which had been
sent out by dozens to gentlemen's lodgings, nobody knowing author or printer. One or two had come to himself,
and he described it to Ppt as giving the character first and
then telling some of his actions, "the character very well,
but the facts indifferent." It was his own; and bad as
the libel was, the justification might be pleaded that what
it libeled was worse. Even Macaulay adopts the terse and
terrible description of Wharton which fell from Swift in
later years, " He was the most universal villain that ever I
knew ;" and other illustration may be spared. But though

Wharton's fame was unapproached, even in that day, for
lying, raking, and profanity, the whigs had few abler men
among them; none steadier to their principles, and none
that did so much to bear them up in desperate extremi-
ties. What had been saved to them in the last elections
had been almost singly his work; and to weaken his influence, for however short a time, was to damage their strongest bulwark. Affect him otherwise no man could. No
personal abuse ever moved him in the least. In the fourth
Examiner, under cover of a pleading of Cicero against
Verres, Swift had assailed without mercy his Irish government; and the only remark Wharton made upon it,
that it was "a damnable mawling," is repeated in the

"Short Character," with the addition that the writer had
entered on his delineation with the more cheerfulness because it was no longer possible either to make angry the
subject of it, or in any way to hurt his reputation. He
admitted his "good natural understanding, great fluency
in speaking, and no ill taste of wit," but declared him to
be without the sense of shame or glory, as some men are
without the sense of smell. It was not a humor to serve
a turn or keep a countenance, when Wharton showed indifference to applause or insensibility of reproach; it had
no grandeur of mind in it, or consciousness of innocence ;
it was the mere unaffected bent of his own nature.
"Whoever," Swift adds, "for the sake of others, were to
describe the nature of a serpent, a wolf, a crocodile, or a

fox, must be understood to do it without any personal love 1710–1711. Æt. 43–44. or hatred for the animals themselves."*

He was, nevertheless, a little disturbed when Mrs. John- A libel cried as Swift's under Esther's windows. son, anticipating the description he had sent her, wrote to tell him of a "scandalous" attack on their late lord lieutenant, which the newsmen had been crying as his under their windows. "As for the pamphlet you speak of, and call scandalous, and that one Mr. Pdfr is said to write it, hear my answer. Fie child! you must not mind what every idle body tells you. I believe you lie; and that the dogs were not crying it when you said so! Come, tell truth!" The Bishop of Clogher had before this taken the thing itself to her. "And so the bishop showed you a pamphlet. Well, but you must not give your mind to believe those things: people will say any thing. The Character is here reckoned admirable, but most of the facts are trifles. It was first printed privately here; and then some bold cur ventured to do it publicly, and sold two thousand in two days. Who the author is must remain uncertain. Do you pretend to know? impudence, how durst you think so?"

His eleventh letter took over his journals from the 9th to the 23d of December, and on the 12th he mentions having been at the secretary's office with Lewis when Lord Rivers came in, whispered Lewis, and then went Lord Rivers. up to Swift to desire his acquaintance, on which they

---

* The reader can compare this with Macaulay's famous character of Wharton (*Hist.*, vii., 80–'4). A sentence or two may be given. "To the end of his long life the wives and daughters of his dearest friends were not safe from his licentious plots. The ribaldry of his conversation moved astonishment even in that age. To the religion of his country he offered, in the mere wantonness of impiety, insults too foul to be described. His mendacity and his effrontery passed into proverbs. Of all the liars of his time he was the most deliberate, the most inventive, and the most circumstantial. What shame meant he did not seem to understand...... Great satirists, animated by a deadly personal aversion, exhausted all their strength in attacks upon him. They assailed him with keen invective: they assailed him with yet keener irony: but they found that neither invective nor irony could move him to any thing but an unforced smile and a good-humored curse; and they at length threw down the lash, acknowledging that it was impossible to make him feel." Macaulay's account of Wharton.

bowed and complimented a while, and parted. Rivers was not without distinction both in William's and Marlborough's wars; but Harley, who tempted him from the duke's side, had now made him constable of the Tower, and this was the beginning of some intimacy with Swift, which never improved into a real liking.* He probably had some hand in the decisive step which Swift mentions, the day after this meeting, as "the havoc making in the army;" when three of Marlborough's favorite general officers, Meredith, Macartney, and Honeywood, serving in Flanders at the time, were dismissed from their commands ("obliged to sell them at half value") for drinking destruction to the ministry, and offering indignities to a stick dressed up with a hat upon it, to caricature Harley. Even the duke's special friend, Cadogan, who led the van at Oudenarde, received what Swift calls a "little paring;" but he had not committed himself so deeply as his friends, and was only recalled from his civil employment. "His mother told me yesterday he had lost the place of envoy, but I hope they will go no farther with him."

A subject of stronger personal interest to Swift appears in his journal of the 13th. Dining that day with St. John, he asked him what Lord Rivers meant by telling him a couple of days ago he should be present "Sunday fortnight" to hear him preach before the queen; on which the secretary told him that, as a "pure bite," Harley and himself had imposed upon his father, Sir Harry St. John, and Rivers a belief that there was to be such a sermon next Sunday at St. James's; but that the preaching before the queen was no bite at all, for the ministers were resolved it must be. "The secretary has told me he will give me three weeks' warning, but I desired to be excused; and 'You shall not be excused,' said Mr. St. John. However, I hope they will forget; for if it should happen, all the

---

* Rivers, the reader need hardly be reminded, was the father of Savage, the poet. There is frequent mention of him in the journals, and a note of Swift's to *Macky's Memoirs* calls him "an arrant knave in common dealings, and very prostitute."

puppies hereabouts will throng to hear me, and expect 1710-1711.
Æt. 43-44.
something wonderful, and be plaguily balked, for I shall
preach plain honest stuff."* When the Sunday appointed
for the "devilish bite" came, Swift, after church, repaired to court (an ordinary custom with him) to "pick up" a
dinner; but the queen not being at church for her gout,
there was thin attendance, so he was fain to be content
with Sir Thomas Frankland and his eldest son, whom he
accompanied to dine at his son William's, in Hatton Gar-
den. "Abundance" of people had meanwhile gone in the Curiosity to
see Swift in
the pulpit.
morning to St. James's church to hear Swift preach,
"among them Lord Radnor, who never is abroad till three
in the afternoon;" while the object of all this interest had
passed a quiet day, had walked all the way home from
Hatton Garden at six on a "delicate" moonlight night,
had been denied to Vicar Raymond at nine in the midst
of some writing, and between eleven and twelve reported
himself to MD as in bed, dropping off to sleep, and intending to dream of his own dear roguish, impudent, pretty Ppt.

Next day he was hunting to dine with Harley, and next
day but one was again unsuccessful at the Court of Requests (the lobby of the House of Lords, a fashionable resort as well as a place for dining), and again the subsequent day; so he set off the following morning to the
minister's levee to vex him by saying he had no other
way of seeing him, whereupon Harley asked what had he

---

* Characteristic little incidents are
mentioned, two days after, touching
on his connection with Ireland. In
the tory excitements of Dublin there
had been an outrage on the statue of
the Deliverer, and Harley gave Swift
a paper about the college lads who
"defaced" the statue, wishing, as
Swift also did, one part of the sentence, that of "standing before the
statue," to be reprieved. That same
day Swift dined with his opposite
neighbor Darteneuf, and, coming
home, told Ppt he had been soliciting Care for an
old friend.
to get the Bishop of Clogher made
vice-chancellor of the college; but they
were all, and especially the Duke of
Ormond, set against him. In a later
journal he adds, however, "I have
got Mr. Harley to promise that whatever changes are made in the Council, the Bishop of Clogher shall not be
removed...... I will let the bishop
know so much in a post or two. This
is a secret; but...he has enemies, and
they shall not be gratified." *Ante*, 204.

1710-1711.
Æt. 43-44.

First family
dinner with
Harley.
to do there, and bid him come and dine on a family dinner, which he did, and it was the first time he saw Harley's wife and daughter. At five the lord keeper came
in, on which Swift desired to be presented to my lord
keeper, having only the honor to know Sir Simon Harcourt, "and so they laughed." But nothing more for the
present was said of that personal matter in regard to the
queen which St. John so determinedly had told him "the
ministers were resolved should be."

Such occasional notices from journals as will carry my
narrative very nearly to the close of February (1710–'11)
may sufficiently complete the picture proposed to be given
of these opening relations of Swift with the two leading
ministers. As intimacy with them grows more and more,
he has always a manifest apprehension of its growing less
and less with Addison. The evening of his dinner with the
secretary on the 14th of December had ended with a little
adventure. He left at eight, meaning to go on with his
letter; but Patrick asked to go out, and by-and-by up came
the girl to tell him a gentleman was below in a coach who
had a bill to pay him, so (caught in that ingenious trap)
Addison's
trap for
Swift.
he let him come up, and "who should it be but Mr. Addison and Sam Dopping from Dublin, to haul me out to
supper, where I have staid till twelve;" though he might
have escaped with help of Patrick, whom he had made as
expert in denying as Harley's porter himself. He talks
of other things, but still goes back to his old friend. "Mr.
Addison and I are different as black and white, and I believe our friendship will go off by this damned business of
party; he can not bear seeing me fall in so with this ministry; but I love him still as well as ever, though we seldom meet." Less agreeably the subject recurred next
day, when he dined with Lewis and Charles Ford, whom
he had brought acquainted, and Lewis told him "a pure
thing." The former "hankering" with Harley to save
Steele his other employment being known to Lewis, he
had himself taken occasion to say to his chief how gratefully Swift would take any kindness to the ex-gazetteer;

and the minister, not unmindful of some possible service 1710–1711.
to himself also, had thereupon appointed an interview, Æt. 43–44.
which Steele accepted, but nevertheless neither came nor Interference for Steele.
sent excuse. "Whether it was blundering, sullenness, in-
solence, or rancor of party, I can not tell; but I shall trouble myself no more about him. I believe Addison hindered him out of mere spite, being grated to the soul to
think he should ever want my help to save his friend; yet
now he is soliciting me to make another of his friends
queen's secretary at Geneva, and I will do it if I can. It
is poor pastoral Philips." The extent to which he is "falling in" with the new men has further illustration at the
opening of another letter, when he tells her "not to expect much from him that night: guess for why:" because
he was going to mind things, and mighty affairs, not her
nasty first-fruits. Those might stand aside for the present. What he was then to mind were other things of Business of moment.
greater moment; which she should know one day, when
"the ducks had eaten up all the dirt." So she was just
to sit still by him a little time while he was studying, and
not to say a word, he charged her; and when he was going to bed he would take both of them along, and talk
with them a little while. So there, sit there!

Christmas-eve was now come, and Swift hoped it would
be a merrier in Dublin than theirs in London, for it had
brought them bad news from Spain. Swift called at Bad news from Spain.
court on his way to church, and, the ill tidings having
come before he returned after service, "it was odd to see
the whole countenances of the court changed so in two
hours." As Sir Edmund Bacon was relating it to him, he
supposed the game in Spain to be played out; but it proved
to be not so bad, for the battle (that of Villa Viciosa) was
not absolutely lost, though neither Staremberg nor Ven-
dôme could be said to have won. It was remarkable, Peterborough's pre-diction.
Swift told Mrs. Johnson the day following, that Lord Peterborough should have foretold the loss of that battle
two months ago, one night at Harley's when Swift was
there, bidding them count upon it that Stanhope would

lose Spain before Christmas; and, though Harley argued
to the contrary, still holding to his opinion, giving them
reasons, and offering to venture his head upon it. Swift
was telling this to Lord Anglesea at court on Christmas-
day, when a gentleman near them said he had heard Peterborough say the same thing. To which Swift preg-
nantly adds that he had heard wise folks say an ill tongue
might do much, and it was an old saying (freshly invented): "Once I guessed right. And I got credit by't. Thrice
I guessed wrong. And I kept my credit on."

Boxing-day.   The next was Boxing-day, when, dining with printer
Barber in the city, and caught in the rain within twelvepenny length of home, he went to Harley's, who was away,
dropped his half-crown with the porter, and drove to the
St. James's, where the rain kept him till nine. By the
lord Harry, he exclaims at night, he shall be done with
Christmas-boxes! The rogues at the coffee-house had
raised their tax, every one giving a crown, and he gave
his for shame, besides a great many half-crowns to great
men's porters. There is a trouble with Convocation at
this time, which he is busy settling; and a couple of days
later he dined with Sir Thomas Hanmer to meet "the
famous Dr. Smallridge," when they sat till six. The day
following, St. John gave a dinner to Harley, Lord Peterborough, and himself, Lord Rivers joining them at night.
Lord Peterborough was to go to Vienna in a day or two,
and had made Swift promise to write to him; Harley left
St. John's at six; and what subsequently passed, when
Swift and St. the secretary and Swift were alone, shows that already he
John alone. thought the chief minister less of a business man even
than the younger minister. He complained to St. John
of Harley's dilatoriness, and obtained help to set matters
straight. "So I shall know in a little time what I have
to trust to." The talk that followed had much interest.
Arrival of The Duke of Marlborough was in England. In the few
Marlbor-
ough. days since he landed from Flanders, he had not only been
received by the queen, but visits of respect had been paid
to him by all the principal ministers, excepting only Har-

ley, and what ensued between him and the secretary had 1710–1711. Æт. 43–44. taken a tone of special confidence. St. John told Swift that the great soldier "lamented" to him his former wrong steps in joining with the whigs, and said he was worn out with age, fatigue, and misfortunes. "I swear it pitied me ; St. John's re-port of him. and I really think they will not do well in too much mor-tifying that man, although indeed it is his own fault. He is covetous as hell, and ambitious as the prince of it. He would fain have been general for life, and has broken all endeavors for peace to keep his greatness and get money. He told the queen he was neither covetous nor ambitious. She said, if she could have conveniently turned about she would have laughed, and could hardly forbear it in his face. He fell in with all the abominable measures of the Swift's misgivings. late ministry, because they gratified him for their own designs. Yet he has been a successful general, and I hope he will continue his command." That day he dined with Harley, where there was much company ; but, those thoughts still hanging about him, he was not merry at all, and he came away at six. Harley made him read a paper Prior and his verses. of verses by Prior, and he read them plain, without any fine manner ; and Prior swore he should never read any of his again, but he would be revenged, and read some of Swift's as badly. "I excused myself, and said I was fa-mous for reading verses the worst in the world, and that every body snatched them from me when I offered to be-gin. So we laughed."

Peterborough was now preparing for his mission to Vi-enna, to which the professed design was to bring the Em-peror and the Duke of Savoy to a better understanding, the real object doubtless being to give a too restless spirit something to occupy it. Swift was walking to St. John's on the 2d of January, having engagement to dine there, when, as he passed a barber's shop, Peterborough called Politics at a barber's. out to him from it, made him come in, and, after talking "deep politics" there, asked him to dine next day at the Globe in the Strand, when he would show him so clearly how to get Spain that it would not be possible to doubt it.

1710-1711. To the Globe accordingly he went, and found Peterbor-
Æt. 43-44. ough among half a dozen lawyers and attorneys and hang-
dogs, signing deeds and stuff before his journey, for he
was to start on the morrow. Among this scurvy company Swift sat till after four, but heard nothing of Spain;
only he discovered, by what previously had passed, that
Peterborough feared he should do no good in his present
enterprise. So they parted, and were to be mighty constant correspondents.

But in midst of his public talk he breaks out, " O Lord,
smoke the politics to MD." Well, but if she liked them,
he would scatter a little now and then; and his were all
fresh, from the chief hands. Indeed, he has been wondering he did not write more politics to her, for he could
make her "the profoundest politician in all the lane."

Examiners   She was to get the *Examiners* and read them. The last
and Tatlers. nine or ten were full of the reasons for the late change,
and of the abuses of the last ministry; and the great men
assured him they were all true. "They are written by
their encouragement and direction." He had not been
writing much else, and she was mistaken in her guesses
Steele in   about *Tatlers*. He did not write that on Noses, nor that
disfavor.   on Religion, nor had he sent Steele of late any hints at
all, for he had been asked by the ministers to give him no
more such help. But, by way of a final bit of politics in
Awkward   that letter, he tells them that some inquiries would very
necessity.   soon be made into the corruptions of the late ministry;
and, indeed, the present men must do it, to justify their
turning the others out.

Reading his journals from the 4th to the 16th of January, his correspondent would soon become conscious that
ministerial difficulties had not been lessening in those
twelve days. The nonsense of Convocation was making
troublesome the more important work in hand. He began by telling her that after dining with people she never
heard of, and it was not worth her while to know, "an
authoress and a printer," he had walked home for exercise,
and was abed by eleven; all the while he was undressing

"speaking monkey things in the air, just as if MD had *1710-1711. Æt. 43-44.* been by," and not recollecting himself till he got into bed. But even there his work pursued him. He had not fin- *Hard at work for St. John.* ished his morning sleep when there came from the sec-retary a summons so early and sudden he was forced to go without shaving, which put him quite out of method; however, he called at Ford's and borrowed "a shaving," and so made shift to get into order again. While with St. John, he spoke to him of a newspaper having reported Ppt's friend, Manley, as turned out, to which the secreta-ry's reply ("No: only that newswriter is a plaguy tory") *Tories plaguing their party.* showed that the ministerial troubles were by no means from whigs exclusively. A result of the conference was to send him next day to visit Dean Atterbury, the prolo-cutor of Convocation; and with this, by way of a "bite" for Ppt, he passes a pleasant jest on their friend Dean Sterne, lately chosen to the like office in Dublin. He had been, he said, to visit the dean—"or the prolocutor I think *A couple of deans and prolocutors.* you call him, do not you? Why should not I go to the dean's as well as you? A little black man of pretty near fifty? Ay, the same. A good pleasant man? Ay, the same. Cunning enough? Yes. One that understands his own interest? As well as any body. How comes it MD and I do not meet there sometimes? But do you know his lady .... a very good face and abundance of wit." "O Lord! whom do you mean?" "I mean Dr. Atter-bury, Dean of Carlisle, and prolocutor." "Pshaw, Pdfr, you are a fool; I thought you had meant our Dean of St. Patrick's." "Silly, silly, silly, you are silly, both are silly, every kind of thing is silly."

Next day he had again to go to the city after a "Grub" thing he was writing, and it was Twelfth-day, and very *Twelfth-day.* silly he thought the clusters of boys and wenches buzzing about the cake-shops like flies, and still sillier the fools that had let out their shops two yards farther into the streets all spread with great cakes frothed with sugar, and stuck with streamers of tinsel. After laying out eight-and-forty shillings in books at Bateman's, buying three little volumes of Lucian "in French for our Ppt, and so, and so," he dined at the post-office with Sir Thomas Frankland, finished his Grub thing, and came home. With a touch of bitterness, he tells her next morning that their new Irish chancellor, whom he had never seen, was just setting out for Ireland with a chaplain whom neither had he ever seen, one Trapp, a parson, a sort of pretender to **Reward for a pamphleteer.** wit, "a second-rate pamphleteer for the cause, whom they pay by sending. him to Ireland." That a first-rate pamphleteer would have to be satisfied with like payment was probably not then in his mind.

It was an anxious day that followed; but the evening brought some tender thoughts to relieve it all, and, coming home, he resolves to write them to her; and then says he, "No, no, indeed MD must wait;" and thereupon he was laying his half-written letter aside, but could not for his heart, though he was very busy, till he first asked her how she did since morning. "By-and-by we shall talk more, so let me lay you softly down, little paper, till then. So there—now to business. There, I say, get you gone: no, I will not push you neither, but hand you on one side—so. Now I am got into bed, I will talk with you." And then **St. John in trouble.** what weighs upon his mind comes out. Again that morning, in all haste, the secretary had sent for him, but he would not lose his shaving for fear of missing church, to which he could not go unshaved; and so they met afterward at court, and he had since dined with young Manley at Mat Dudley's, and so full is he of politics, so beset by misgivings which have been with him all the day, and which he can write easier to Ppt than to any body, that he pours them all out upon her.

Ministerial misadventures. He protested he was afraid they should all be embroiled with parties. The whigs, now they were fallen, were the most malicious toads in the world; and since the Villa Viciosa battle, the tories had had a second misfortune in the loss of several Virginia ships; so that he feared people would begin to think nothing thrived under this ministry; nor could he doubt that if the new ministers should

once be rendered odious to the people, the parliament
might be chosen whig or tory, as the queen pleased. Then
he thought his present friends pressed a little too hard on
the Duke of Marlborough. The country members were
violent to have past faults inquired into, and they had reason; but he did not observe the official men to be very
fond of it. In his opinion they had nothing to save them
but a peace; and as he felt sure they could not have such
a one as they were hoping, this of course would set the
whigs bawling what *they* could have done had they continued in power. He had told the ministry as much of all
this as he thought safe, and he meant to venture on saying a little more to them, especially about the Duke of
Marlborough. The whigs were at present giving out that
he intended to lay down his command: "and I question
whether ever any wise state laid aside a general who had
been successful nine years together, whom the enemy so
much dreaded, and his own soldiers can not but believe
must always conquer; and you know that in war opinion
is nine parts in ten." Then came what constituted always
his greatest dread: "The ministry hear me always with
appearance of regard, and much kindness; but I doubt
they let personal quarrels mingle too much with their
proceedings." Meantime, Harley and St. John seemed to
value as mere nothing, on their own accounts, what gave
him so much trouble. They were as easy and merry as
if they had nothing in their hearts or on their shoulders.
They were like physicians who endeavored to cure, but
felt no grief at whatever the patient suffered. Pshaw!
he interrupts himself, "what is all this?" And then he
would try to persuade himself that what he had written
was not the clear and piercing discrimination, which it too
truly was, of the principal dangers that hemmed Harley
and St. John round. The rock on which they were to split
at last had already become very visible to him. But he
swears his head is full, wishes he were at Laracor with his
dear charming Ppt, and so settles himself to sleep: his
first thought as he wakes being about the state affairs he

1710–1711.
Æt. 43–44.

had been writing overnight to MD. How did they relish it? Why, any thing that came from Pdfr was welcome, though really, to confess the truth, if they had their choice, not to disguise the matter, they had rather— "Now, Pdfr, I must tell you, you grow silly," says Ppt. "That is but one body's opinion, madam."

Once more he had promised to be again with St. John early that morning, but he was lazy and would not go, though he should be chidden; but what cared he, for only yesterday he had engaged to dine with Mr. Secretary, and he knew a brief delay could matter little for all the urgen-

Adventure at St. John's.

cy of affairs on hand. "Lord," he exclaims at night, "I have been with the secretary from dinner till eight, and, though I drink wine-and-water, I am so hot!" Lady Stanley had come in to visit the secretary's wife,* and, while he and St. John were together, "sent up" for Swift

Mrs. St. John.

to make up a quarrel with Mrs. St. John, whom he had not yet seen; and, would she think, that devil of a secretary would not let him go, but kept him by main force, though he told him he was in love with his lady, and it was a shame to keep back a lover. But all would not do. So at last he was forced to break away, when it was too late to go up; and "here I am, and have a great deal to do tonight, though it be nine o'clock:" but one must say something to these naughty MDs, else there will be no quiet. Once more with the early morning he was to see St. John, and failed; but the morning following he was with him, and also the next but one after, when he was made to

---

St. John's first wife.

* St. John's first wife was the daughter and co-heiress of Sir Henry Winchescomb, of a Berkshire family lineally descended from the famous Jack of Newbury, hero of so many ballads; and in her right St. John enjoyed the estate of Bucklersbury, which on her death in 1718 passed to her sister. It was not a happy marriage, nor, with the habits that continued to be St. John's during the eighteen years of its duration, from his twenty-second to his fortieth year, was it possible that it should be. But she did not leave his house until the autumn of 1713; she returned to him when he fell from power; she made strenuous exertions to get back his estates for him; and there are letters from her to Swift as late as 1716, not only doing her best to defend his honor, but speaking of him tenderly. Swift's liking for her is well justified.

promise to dine with him; which otherwise he must have done with Harley, whom he had not been with for ten days. "I can not but think they have mighty difficulties upon them: yet I always find them as easy and disengaged as school-boys on a holiday." There was the chancellor of the exchequer (Harley) with a deficiency of five or six millions, and stocks falling because the whigs would not lend a groat, having taken up the policy of Quakers and fanatics, that would only deal among themselves, while all others dealt indifferently with them. There was the secretary (St. John) under cross-fire of both Marlboroughs: the duchess offering, if kept in her employments, never to come into the queen's presence; and the duke, according to the whigs, declaring he would serve no more. "But I hope and think otherwise," says Swift, wishing to Heaven he were that minute with MD in Dublin, thinking the business he had undertaken to unravel might only perplex him more, already weary to very death of politics that gave him such melancholy prospects, and of which the worries and anxieties culminated that harassing night in an "ugly giddy fit" which suddenly assailed him.

Not many days after, weary still, he uses, in writing of the same subject, words claiming to be remembered. Bidding her adieu at the close of one of his letters, he gives her earnest injunction to love poor poor Pdfr, who had not had one happy day since they parted, as hope saved. "It is the last sally I will ever make, but I hope it will turn to some account. I have done more for these, and I think they are more honest, than the last;" he means the ministers. "However, I will not be disappointed. I would make MD and ME easy; and I never desired more." And he describes himself at the opening of his next letter as working every night from six to bed-time, in full favor with all the men in power, and having as little present enjoyment and pleasure in life as any body in the world.

But, as he so often and truly says, it is not in his nature thus far to cherish spleen or sadness, and even the morn-

1710-1711. ing after his giddy fit finds him in quite other mood. He
Æt. 43-44. is so far recovered that he can tell her his own enjoyment
Gross   of a "copy of verses" on St. John, indecent as the worst
language.   of Wycherley or Aphara Behn, and can count on her enjoyment of them too! He had been asking the secretary
about his and Harley's quitting office three years before,
on which St. John said that, meaning then to retire from
public life, a friend to whom he was expressing that intention, and his wish to have some lines to place over his
summer-house, shortly after gave him an inscription:

> "From business and the noisy world retired,
> Not vex'd by love nor by ambition fired,
> Gently I wait the call of Charon's boat,
> Still—"

His drinking and raking being expressed in the last line
with a profligate plainness to which decent print can not
lend itself, and for which it is only a poor excuse to say
that even delicate women could then listen unabashed to
the most intolerable grossness, that many of the worst passages in Swift's printed correspondence are in the letters
of high-bred, fashionable beauties, and that the teaching
of Addison and Steele on such points was but slowly mak-
Manners of ing its way. Swift adds that St. John swore to him he
the age.   could hardly bear the jest; for he did pretend to retire
like a philosopher, though he was but twenty-eight years
old. "And I believe the thing was true; for he had been
a thorough rake. I think the three grave lines do introduce the last well enough. Od so! but I will go sleep."
His next letter carried him to the close of January without any amendment yet perceptible in public affairs. The
fiddling and the burning went on together, and no one
could see the end. The morning of its second day was
passed in a pressing engagement with the secretary, and
they were to dine alone at Harley's on business of weight.
Ministers in From St. John's office, accordingly, they repaired to Har-
the midst of ley's, "and thought to have been very wise;" but deuce
trouble.   a bit! two or three gentlemen were there, this company
staid, and more came; and though Harley left his own ta-

ble at seven, the secretary and Swift staid with the rest of the company, drinking and talking and doing nothing, till eleven. Swift would then have had St. John leave, but he was in for it; and though he swore he would come away "at that flask," there Swift left him. "I wonder at the civility of these people: when he saw that I would drink no more, he would always pass the bottle by me, and yet I could not keep the toad from drinking himself, nor he would not let me go neither, nor Masham, who was with us." On reaching home, Swift found a pamphlet which had been sent to him, written entirely against himself, "not by name," but as the writer of something he had published very lately; yet as it was pretty civil, and affected to be so, he thought he would take no notice of it; and indeed he knew not what to say, nor did he care. He had not been so late in bed these two months as that night, for he now went earlier to bed than formerly; but the secretary was in a desperate drinking humor, and at their next meeting he had to sit later still. He went to him on the morning of the 24th about some urgent business, and, to his surprise, found a great whig with him. This turned out to be, as described by St. John, a creature of the Duke of Marlborough's, who had come to open matters as a go-between to try and make peace between the duke and the ministry; wherein his chances of success would be small. St. John came out of his closet to speak to Swift, and made him promise to come back and dine with him and Erasmus Lewis at three. But Lewis did not come till six, dinner being delayed thereby, and there they then sat talking and drinking, and the time slipped so, that at last, when Swift was "positive to go," it was past two o'clock in the morning! So he came home and went straight to bed. St. John would never let him look at his watch, and he could not imagine it to be above twelve when they broke up. Not till morning, therefore, could he bid her good-night, or tell her how he had passed that day; and though it was then near ten, he was still in bed.

Happily, before getting up on the morning of the visit

Margin notes:

1710–1711. Æt. 43–44.

St. John in a drinking humor.

At revel till two in the morning.

1710-1711.
Æt. 43-44.

to St. John preceding the last, he had answered the greater part of her letter point by point. "So now, my dearly beloved, let us proceed to the next;" and he notices additional subjects of which she had written. He was vexed they did not go into the country with the Bishop of Clogher, for, 'faith, it would have done them good, Ppt riding and DD going in the coach. As for his old friends she asked about, if she meant the whigs, they had not met lately, as she might find by his journals, except Lord Halifax, and

Lord
Somers.

him very seldom; Lord Somers never since the first visit, when he had done his best to involve him in a dispute as to Wharton; for he had been "a false deceitful rascal." This was a strong way of expressing resentments, which yet were not without some personal justification; for, though the charge implies no dishonor to the name standing justly highest in English constitutional history, it is to be said of the services rendered and received between Somers and Swift, as an individual account merely, that the balance is largely in Swift's favor. As for his new friends, he adds, they were very kind, and he had promises enough, but he did not count upon them; and, besides, his pretenses were very "young" to them. However, "we will see what may be done;" and if nothing at all, he should not be disappointed, although perhaps MD might, and then he should be sorrier for their sakes than his own. What sort of Christmas had he, she asked? Why, he had not had a Christmas at all. Had it really been Christmas of late? he never once thought of it. However, two or three letters ago he wished a merry Christmas to *them*, and sauce for the goose was sauce for the gander. (Did she see that he had been mending in his writing? but, 'faith, when Ppt's eyes were well he hoped to write as bad

Report as
to St. John
and Swift.

as ever.) Good lack for Ppt's news that Mr. St. John was going to Holland! Mr. St. John had no such thoughts to quit the great station he was in, nor, if he had, could "Doctor Swift" be spared to go with him. So much for politic Madam Ppt with her two eggs a penny! Then he tells her, forgetting he had told it before, what he has done about the box of things he had sent; but he is fretted, and "tosticated," and impatient, and vexed with other people's carelessness, so that he makes an allusion which MD might think indelicate, but "I mean decently, don't be rogues." 1710 1711. Æt. 43–44.

The whig company he finds so irrepressible turns up again in his next letter, when he has to tell her of another far from agreeable dinner at the once agreeable house in Hampstead, with Lady Lucy Stanhope and her sister, where he had not been this long time, as Ppt knew, and also knew why. She would remember the attack they had made on himself and Prior. They were, in truth, plaguy whigs, especially the sister, Armstrong; who was really the most insupportable of all women, pretending to wit, without any taste. There was the last *Examiner*, "the prettiest" he had ever read, with a character of the present ministry, and she was running it down! He left them at five, and came home. A little later in the same letter he, nevertheless, makes admission that the *Examiners* were thought objectionable by many besides Mrs. Armstrong. He mentions Prior as like to be insulted in the streets for being supposed the author, and that the last paper had cleared him. Nobody, he adds, really knew who the writer was but the few in the secret: he supposed the ministry and the printer. "Irrepressible" whigs. Ante, 305. Examiners out of favor.

All this had made it plain enough, as well to the ministers as to himself, that it was a service not without danger in which he was embarked on their behalf; yet nothing had again been hinted of the presentation to the queen promised by Harley, and the preaching before her settled by St. John, which were to give their champion a position among them to which at least he was entitled. It is possible that some uneasy consciousness of this, and a blundering wish to set it right in another way, may account for a mistake now committed by Harley which Swift strongly resented. Promises not kept.

The opening of his next letter showed that something was out of gear. Harley had sent to him on the 4th of

1710–1711.
Æt. 43–44.

February to ask if he was alive, and if he would dine the following day; which he did accordingly, Prior being of the company; but what he tells Ppt at night reveals that all had not gone pleasantly as usual. They did not sit down till six, and he had to stay till eleven; and henceforth he would choose to visit Mr. Harley in the evening, and would dine with him no more if he could help it.

Out of humor with Harley.

"It breaks all my measures, and hurts my health; my head is disorderly, but not ill, and I hope it will mend." Something more is disclosed next day, when he says that he refused to dine with Harley because they fell out the day before, and he was resolved not to see the minister again till he had made amends. Next day brought a letter from Harley to Lewis desiring to be reconciled; but Swift was deaf to all entreaties, and requested Lewis to let Mr. Harley know he expected further satisfaction. "If we let these great ministers pretend too much, there will be no governing them." Thereupon Harley laid some stress on Swift's again seeing himself, when he promised that every thing should be made easy; but Swift refused until satisfaction should actually have been given, and repeated his threat to cast off the minister. What had been done, in short, though intended as a favor, he had taken quite otherwise, both the thing and the manner having heartily vexed him; "and all I have said is truth, though it looks like jest." Harley's offense was having thrust a fifty-pound bank-note into Swift's hand by way of acknowledgment of his *Examiners*, and the money had to be taken back with apology for having offered it. Swift returned it through Erasmus Lewis, in a letter which Erasmus laid before Harley.

Harley's offense.

The same journals in which the incident is told describe Swift helping St. John in the impeachment on foot against "a certain great person;"* and mention his interference

---

* "Your Grace has heard," Swift writes to Archbishop King at this time, "there was much talk lately of Sir Richard Levinge's design to impeach | Lord Wharton; several persons of great consideration in the house assured me they would give him all encouragement, and I have reason to

with the same minister to endeavor to prevent an inten- 1710-1711.
tion he had that would utterly ruin Grub Street. He Æt. 43-44.
meant to tax all little printed penny papers a half-penny
every half sheet; and in spite of Swift, as we shall see, he
did it. Ppt did not hear, until the journals of his next
following letter reached her, that Harley had been taken
again into favor. On the 12th Swift was at the Court of The minister
Requests at noon, and there encountering the chief min- again in favor.
ister, whom he had been asked to meet that day at dinner
at St. John's, he "sent Harley into the house" to let St.
John know that Doctor Swift would dine with him if he
dined late; and dine together afterward they accordingly
did. He was at a dinner at Lord Shelburne's next day,
failing in an attempt to see Harley in the evening; and
it was not until after two days more he found the opportunity he wanted. On the 16th he caught the minister at
home after dinner, and they made up their quarrel, Swift
not leaving until late, and then with an invitation for the
following Saturday which had a special significance.

But "when was Pdfr likely to preach, and when was he Obstruction
to be presented to the queen?" The questions recurred in Swift's path.
still in MD's letters; and "they were fools," he replied.
He was upon another foot. Nobody doubted he could
preach, and he put it off as much as he could. As for the
queen, Mr. Harley of late had said nothing of presenting
him. "I was overseen when I mentioned it to you." The
minister had such a weight of affairs on him that he could
not mind all; but he talked of it three or four times "long
before I dropped it to you." Nor was it the weight of affairs only, or the factious proceedings of the whigs. There
were troubles nearer home. He told her in this letter of
the October club they were plagued with: a set of above October club.
a hundred parliament-men of the country who drank October beer at home, and met nightly at a tavern near the
houses to drive things to extremes. They wanted to call

know it would be acceptable to the court; but Sir Richard is the most timorous man alive, and they all be- gin to look upon him in that char- acter, and to hope nothing from him."

1710–1711.
Æt. 43–44.

the old ministers to account in the very way the new men most wished to avoid : "five or six heads" were what they wanted : and as to the means, they were utterly unscrupulous. The ministry were seeming not to regard them, yet one of them in confidence had hinted otherwise to Swift; and something would have to be thought on to settle things better.

Nor was even this all their danger. He would tell her, as a great secret, another grievous difficulty. The queen was not manageable. Sensible how much she was governed by the late ministry (their successors doubtless had made this very clear to her), she now ran a little into the other extreme, and on that point was become jealous even of those who got her out of the others' hands. So she stood between the ministry who were for gentler measures, and other tories who were for more violent. At the dinner the other day; Lord Rivers, talking to Swift, cursed the *Examiner* for speaking civilly of the Duke of Marlborough : and Swift happening to name this to the secretary, St. John blamed the warmth of that lord, and some others; and swore that if their advice were followed, the ministry would be blown up in twenty-four hours. Swift adds that he had reason to think immediate endeavor would be made, through persons likely to have means of persuasion, to prevail on the queen to put her affairs more "into the hands of a ministry" than she did at present; and there were, he believed, two men thought on, one of whom she had often met the name of in his letters. "So much for politics."

The afternoon before he told her this, Saturday, the 17th of February, Swift had dined with Harley upon the special invitation received as soon as their quarrel was made up. It was his first appearance at a dinner where he was afterward an invariable guest. "It is the day of the week that lord keeper and Secretary St. John dine with him privately ; and at last they have consented to let me among them on that day." The other secretary, Dartmouth, with Lord Rivers, joined them after Swift; and, "by degrees," Lord

The queen not manageable.

Swift admitted to the cabinet dinner.

Anglesea and the Dukes of Ormond, Shrewsbury, and 1710-1711.
Argyle; but the discussions became less important as the _Æt. 43-44._
numbers increased. Besides the Saturday, there was afterward a Thursday for "select company;" both had the
character of ministerial meetings; and the day when
Swift was first admitted to them was practically that of
his appointment as a minister without office. He signal-
ized it by some plain speaking. Though he rejoiced to
see them in such agreement, and that they loved one another so well, he told them he had "no hopes they could
ever keep in;" and he adds these memorable words:
"They call me nothing but Jonathan; and I said I be- Future
lieved they would leave me Jonathan as they found me, foretold.
and that I never knew a ministry do any thing for those
whom they make companions of their pleasures: and I
believe you will find it so; but I care not."

BOOK SIXTH.

BEING AN APPENDIX OF

BIOGRAPHICAL NOTES FROM SWIFT'S LETTERS TO ESTHER JOHNSON,

AND OF

PASSAGES IN THE LATER LETTERS CORRECTED AND RESTORED FROM THE ORIGINAL MANUSCRIPT.

I. Biographical Notes (November, 1710, to February, 1711).

II. Publication of the Letters containing the Journal to Stella.

III. Unprinted and Misprinted Journals of Swift.

I.

BIOGRAPHICAL NOTES FROM SWIFT'S LETTERS TO ESTHER JOHNSON.

11TH OF NOVEMBER, 1710—24TH OF FEBRUARY, 1710-'11.

IN the Fifth Book of this Biography use is made of the Journals of Swift contained in the first sixteen letters written from London to Esther Johnson, between the dates of the 9th of September, 1710, and the 24th of February, 1710-'11. But the latter half of the letters are employed for illustration of Swift's political career only, and to show the part he is about to play in the government of Oxford and Bolingbroke. Such of these journals as exhibit his private affairs exclusively are untouched, and I propose now to add, by means of a series of sketches each in its connection also as part of the continued story, what is contained in these last eight letters (from the ninth to the sixteenth both inclusive) of continued intercourse with friends, unceasing confidences to Esther Johnson, amusing anecdotes, characteristic personal ways and habits, wonderful pictures of the high and the low around him, and prodigious knowledge of humanity. Future reference to these journals would be in any case unavoidable; and to place the substance of them here will at once leave the main narrative undisturbed, and properly clear the ground for my second volume.

OF MONEY MATTERS; ESTHER'S, HER MOTHER'S, AND HIS OWN.

Coming home from his first dinner with St. John, he finds that at last Ppt's mother has written, and it was just as her daughter supposed. She could not leave Lady Giffard in a morning, and God knew when he should be at leisure in an afternoon. He wonders her mother should confine herself so much to "that old beast's humor." He can not in honor see Lady Giffard, and therefore could not go to her house; but he has written to the mother, reminding her of the £400 due to her daughter, and

LETTER IX.
Nov. 11-24.

LETTER
IX.
Nov. 11–24.

expressing his hope that Lady Giffard might consent to pay it
over for investment in Bank stock. Of his own "mighty desire"
to buy on the drop of thirty-four per cent. ("I was a little too late
for the cheapest time, being hindered by business, for I was so
wise to guess to a day when it would fall"), he tells her a few
days later. As soon as he could, he went into the city, and his
old school-fellow, Stratford, advanced him money to turn the opportunity to account. He had in Ireland £300; and stock to this
amount his generous friend, on his own mere word for payment
as soon as he could get the money over, had at once bought for
him; though every body else had told him "money was so hard to
be got here that no man would do it for me." The stock cost
only thirty shillings over the three hundred pounds, and he could
already get five pounds for his bargain. Then, in a few days,
came Ppt's mother to talk of the sum due to Ppt, which Lady
Giffard professed her inability at that moment to invest; and
upon her telling him that milady had a mind "to see him," he
told her what to say "with a vengeance," and the very thought of
it made him "writhe like a tiger"* in his bed.

OF AN OLD FRIEND, AND A CHRISTENING WITH CROMWELL'S DAUGHTER FOR GODMOTHER.

Nov. 12.

Ante, 242, 292.

This was a lazy day with him, beginning with a letter that had
given him discomfort from poor Mrs. Long, with account of her
present life obscure in a remote country-house, and how easy she
was under it, though it was as if Pdfr should be banished from MD
and condemned to converse with Mrs. Raymond. His dinner was
with Ford and Sir Richard Levinge "at a place where they board
hard by;" but, lazy as he was, he left early to write, and there he was
at home with a fire, spending his second half-bushel of coals ("I
have my coals by half a bushel at a time, I will assure you"); for
it had grown cold and frosty after a long fit of rain, and she must
give poor little Pdfr leave to have a fire morning and evening too,
and he will do as much for her. And so good-night. "Paaaaast
twelvvve o'clock!" It was the 13th when he so closed his diary,
and he had dined that day in the city, calling at "the great shop

---

* All the editors print this word "write." We have seen Macaulay's comparison of him to a "tiger" (*ante*, 100), but even that merciless critic would hardly describe him writing like one.

at Ludgate" to order spectacles for Mrs. Dingley and the Bishop LETTER
of Clogher, and going afterward to christen Will Frankland's child; IX.
Oliver Cromwell's daughter, Lady Falconbridge, "and extremely Nov. 11-24.
like him, by his picture I have seen," being one of the god-
mothers.*

OF THE NEW IRISH VICEROY.

Many things disturbed him during the second November week;
for it was then Ned Southwell told him of the Irish bishops having shown their want of confidence in him. That Duke Ormond *Ante, 333, 334.*
should even have accepted their memorial was something of an
offense to him. The duke was not a puppy himself, he remarks,
and it was a thousand pities he should have a natural affection for
puppies; but so it was, and he was going to take over with him for
chancellor as arrant a puppy as ever ate bread (Sir Richard Cox,
whom he dubs Sir Chancellor Coxcomb, who had been chancellor
from 1703 to 1707, but who did not live now to resume the seat).†
Nevertheless, Swift went to a public dinner on the 15th, "with fifty
other Irish gentlemen," which, at a cost of £300, the Londonderry
society gave to Ormond as the new lieutenant, stealing away (" it
was so cold, and so confounded a noise with the trumpets and
hautboys ") before the second course.

A PURCHASE USEFUL FOR LILLIPUT.

Other notes in this letter contain allusions that may hereafter
help to wind out raveled passages of his life. He was again at
the great Ludgate shop on the 14th, sorely tempted to buy a microscope if that virtuoso Ppt should consent: "not the great bulky
ones, nor the common little ones to impale a louse (saving your
presence) upon a needle's point; but of a more exact sort, and
clearer to the sight, with all its equipage in a little trunk that you
may carry in your pocket." He wound up the day, which he calls Nov. 14.

---

* The name was Falconberg. Her
husband, who died at the opening of
the century, had been raised to an
earldom by William. She was Cromwell's third daughter, and died in her
76th year in 1712.

  † When he afterward mentioned the
death, he did it (so strong and fre-

quent the habit with him) in the language which his editors never reproduce: but on this occasion Swift himself erased it and rewrote the words:
"'Faith I could hardly forbear our
little language about a nasty dead
chancellor, as you may see by the
blot."

an "insipid" one, by dining with Mrs. Vanhomrigh, and, after just
visiting the coffee-house, coming gravely home to work. He was
again in the city next day but one, dining with Manley, who entertained Addison, himself, and some other friends very handsomely. "I returned with Mr. Addison, and loitered till nine in
the coffee-house, where I am hardly known by going so seldom."
Addison and himself, he adds, met a little seldomer than formerly,
differing "a little" about party; although they were still at bottom as good friends as ever. Once more in the city next day with
Stratford and merchant friends, he dined and staid late, drinking
claret and Burgundy, and was impatient for MD's letter on getting
home. Another of the journals has a capital stroke of character
on the part of the optician of whom he was tempted to buy the
microscope. He had been there again to buy spectacles for Mrs.
Dingley and the Bishop of Clogher, when, to his amazement, the
optician wanted to give him the thirty-shilling microscope for
nothing. "I thought the deuce was in the man, but he said I
could do him more service than that was worth." And so, though
the gift was refused, and the microscope was bought and paid for,
Pdfr had in honor to recommend to every body's custom the dis-
creet, courteous, and scientific tradesman of Ludgate, who already so
cleverly had guessed the importance of a word from Doctor Swift.

ARRIVAL OF ESTHER JOHNSON'S SIXTH LETTER.

Four days later it came. Calling at the St. James's after his
dinner with St. John on the 22d, to examine the glass case for letters, he saw one to Addison which, looking like "a rogue's hand,"
he made the fellow give him, and he opened it before him, and
saw three letters all for himself, and came home with them.
"Well, and so you shall hear: well, and so I found one of them
in DD's hand, and the other in Ppt's, and the third in Domville's. Well, so you shall hear; so, said I to myself, what now,
two letters from MD together? But I thought there was something in the wind; so I opened one, and I opened the other; and
so you shall hear. One was from Walls. Well, but the other
was from my own dear MD; yes it was." And now his own
must go, or there will be "odd doings at our house," 'faith. But
he'd make "no other answer now;" no, 'faith, catch him at that!
and "never saw the like." He does not tell her next day where
he dined, but at night there is much tender playfulness. Of

course the letter of Walls was to ask intercession for somebody, LETTER IX.
Nov. 11-24.
and he has above ten businesses of other people already on his
hands. His time, nevertheless, is hers. Would she like to have
a short letter every week or a long one every fortnight? A long
one? Well, so it should be. Nothing but long ones did they
want; and now were they satisfied? No, he had had no fit since
the first. Soon after he closed this ninth letter, and its latest intimation may be given. Ppt's mother was going to send her
some plum-cakes and some wax-candles (a share of the cakes she
had sent him also); and they were to tell his sister, Mrs. Fenton,
that with the request she had sent him he would comply if possible; and his final entreaty, after hoping they had received two
several ten pounds he had sent them, and before sealing and sending his letter, was that they were to be good housewives, and that
Ppt was to walk for health whenever possible. "Have you the
horse in town? and do you ever ride him? How often? Con- Nov. 24.
fess. Ahhh, sirrah, have I caught you?"

VISIT TO LONDON OF DOCTOR RAYMOND, VICAR OF TRIM.
(Ante, 199.)

The Vicar of Trim's visit has been mentioned, and the story of LETTERS X. AND XI.
Nov. 25,
Dec. 20.
it may be completed here. Finishing his letter just sent off, he
told her that the doctor was come to town, but he had slipped
him off on some of his compatriots to show what was to be seen,
and he lends him Patrick. The unconscionable vicar, nevertheless,
desired to sit with him in the evenings, but Patrick has positive
orders that he is "not within." The next mention is very early
in his next letter, begun on the day he went with Ford to the
opening of parliament, when he staid so long among the aisles and
tombs of the abbey, and on coming home found himself with a
cold which he can only describe in a rhyme, He doesn't know how,
but got it he has, and is hoarse: he does not know whether it will
grow, better or worse. But Ppt's mother's cakes are good (one
of them serves him for breakfast), and he'll go sleep like a good
boy. That cruel cold kept him all next day in his night-gown,
reading, writing, and denied to every body; but at last Dr. Raymond called (and, for a reason* he had, was let up), who sat two

---

* His reason was amusing enough, | means he shall be used to have me de-
for he asked the vicar carelessly, How | nied to him, otherwise he would be
Pat denied his master, and whether | a plaguy trouble and hinderance to
he had the art of it? "So by this | me."

LETTERS
X. AND XI.
Nov. 25,
Dec. 20.
hours, drank a pint of fivepenny ale, smoked his pipe, and went away at eleven.   And let *them* go to their gang of Deans, and Stoytes, and Wallses, and lose their money.   Go, sauceboxes; and so, good-night, and be happy, dear rogues.   Sunday following he saw the doctor again, for that day he went to court (Sundays then were the court-days), and who should he see among the beef-eaters, staying for sight of the queen, but Raymond?   So he put him in a better place, made two or three dozen bows, left to go to church, and came back to pick up a dinner, which he did with Sir John Stanley, the two afterward visiting Lord Mountjoy and sitting with

Dec. 10.
him till near eleven.   The Sunday following he tells her more of their friend; how he has seen him twice a week, while dressing in the morning; how he has not been able to afford more time to him; and how poor Raymond had seemed to have no relish for London, and no wonder!   Some Templers were doing the civilities, and showing him about.   Next day he talks to them again of Raymond, whom he is "persuading" to leave, though he has lately gone out of his way to introduce him to solicitor-general Raymond (a relative).   Raymond's resolve to leave ("for fear his wife should be too far gone, and forced to be brought to bed here") had been shaken by the wreck of an Irish packet-boat, and hence the need of Swift's "persuasion."   Still, however, he staid on, calling (and being denied) on the 17th, but again calling, and being let up, next day, when Swift, Charles Ford, and their Irish friend, Dopping, were drinking bad claret and eating oranges, and Raymond told them all he should certainly leave "next day."   Nev-

Dec. 20.
ertheless, not next day, but the morning after, when Swift was up very early, and, having shaved by candle-light, was writing by the fireside, in came poor Raymond really to take his leave, being in truth summoned by high order from his wife, but pretending he had had enough of London.   Swift was a little melancholy to part with him, he had been so easy and manageable; but he was gone, and would save some lies a week to Patrick, who had grown so admirable at it he'd make his fortune by lying.   Not even yet, however, was the simply kindly Irish parson gone.   "At night, Dr. Raymond came back, and goes to-morrow.   I did not come home till eleven, and found him here to take leave of me."

IRISH OPINIONS OF HIS WRITINGS.   (*Ante*, 319, 320.)

In the second night's journal of his tenth letter he spoke of having heard from the Bishop of Clogher that they had bidden him read the London *Shaver*, and that they both swore it was Shaver, and not Shower. (" You all lie, and you are puppies, and can not read Pdfr's hand." Nevertheless, it was admired, forsooth. Why, the bishop said " he has seen something of mine of the same sort better than the Shower." I suppose he means the Morning* (verses also written for Steele); "but it is not half so good. I want your judgment of things, and not your country's. How does MD like it? And do they *taste* it all?" As for the bishop's conjectures of his share in the *Tatlers*, they were " out " entirely. He had other things to mind, and of much greater importance; else he had little to do to be acquainted with a new ministry who considered him a little more than Irish bishops did. The subject was afterward resumed with a remark that he supposed they thought it a piece of affectation in him to wish their Irish folks would *not* like his Shower: but they were mistaken. If he could have the general applause there, indeed, as he had here (" though I say it ") he'd be glad: but as he had only that of one or two, he would rather have none at all, but let them all be in the wrong. " But I am so tosticated with supper and stuff that I can not express myself." Why did not Ppt and DD tell their old acquaintance Griffyth that they fancied there was something in Sid Hamet of their friend " the Doctor's " manner? first spurring up his commendation to the height, as they served his poor uncle "about the sconce that I mended." (A lost anecdote of his favorite uncle William.)

LETTER X.
Nov. 25,
Dec. 9.

ANSWERS ESTHER'S SIXTH LETTER.

On the 29th he dined with Ford, coming early home; where, however, Ford followed, and " debauched " him to his chamber again with a bottle of wine till twelve. So he could not that night answer the saucy good dear letter. But he did so the night following, after some writing he had long neglected; dining with Mrs. Barton alone, sauntering at the coffee-house till past eight, and doing the other writing till eleven.   Nov. 30.

---

* Morning had appeared in No. 9, and the Shower in No. 238, of the *Tatler;* each introduced with one of Steele's happiest compliments to Swift, who, under the name of Humphrey Wagstaff, is described as "treating of every subject after a manner that no other author has done, and better than any other can do."

LETTER X.
Nov. 25,
Dec. 9.

Very charming then is his prittle-prattle over her letter, indulged before he goes to bed; rallying her still for not taking exercise enough, and reporting a late talk with her mother about it; telling her that, but for what she had herself written, what had been said to him of her health by a visitor from Ireland ("Smyth, of the Blind Quay") would have driven him distracted. He implored her not again to write until she was mighty, mighty, mighty well. in her eyes, and mighty, mighty sure it wouldn't do her the least hurt. "Oh, come, I'll tell you what; you, Mistress. Ppt, shall write your share at five or six sittings, one sitting a day; and then comes DD all together, and then Ppt a little crumb toward the end, to let us see she remembers Pdfr; and then conclude with something handsome and genteel, as ' your most humble cum dumble, or etc.'" She had told him of her winnings at cards; but he doubts. "Mrs. Walls, *does* Ppt win as she pretends?" "No, indeed, Doctor: she loses always, and will play so venturesomely how can she win?" "See here, now, are you not an impudent, lying slut?" But yet she was obedient, too. She had followed directions, and written with closed eyes. Yes, faith, Ppt wrote smartly with her eyes shut; all was well but the *w*. See how Pdfr can do it. "Madam Ppt, your humble servant." Oh, but one *may* look whether one goes crooked or no, and so write on. He would tell her what she might do: she might write with her eyes half shut, just as when one is going to sleep. There! he had done so for two or three lines now: it was but just seeing enough to go straight. Dingley's portion of the letter had volunteered regrets (which he calls "poligyes") for their frequent gadding from home, at which he laughs, liking nothing better; and Ppt had written something at which he threatens to break that young woman's head in good earnest. It was a "nasty jest" about Mrs. Barton. Unlucky sluttikin! But 'faith, he adds (reverting to her jest), he was thinking the day before, when he was with Mrs. Barton, of what Ppt said, and whether "she could break them or no." It quite spoiled his imagination.*

A sudden thought comes. Now should he tell them what! He had seen fellows wearing crosses that day, and wondered what

---

* The whole passage is obscure : the little language, that might have rendered it intelligible, having been struck out. But his correspondent was certainly not free from a habit very common then with women of birth and breeding.

was the matter; but just this minute he recollected it was little Pdfr's birthday. It was St. Andrew's Day. He had been resolving these three days to remember it when it came, but could not. "Pray, drink my health to-day at dinner; do, you rogues. Well now at last I have done with your letter, and so I will lay me down to sleep, and about fair maids, and I hope merry maids all." He did sleep about them, and woke wishing that Smyth of the Blind Quay were hanged; for he had been dreaming the most melancholy things in the world of poor Ppt, and was grieving and crying all night. "Pshaw, it is foolish; I will rise and divert myself; so good-morrow, and God of his infinite mercy keep and protect you!" The bishop had said in his letter they thought of going with him to Clogher; and he required them to go, I'pt on horseback and DD in a coach. "I have had no fit since my first, although sometimes my head is not quite in good order."

ROGUE STEELE.

Attention to a whig friend, Lord Shelburne, who had come over with other Irish acquaintance, the Pratts, occupied him all the day on which he was writing; for, calling to see them, they made him dine; and then he staid till eight, looking over them at ombre like a booby. That morning he had to describe to them the "impudentest" thing in the world that "Steele the rogue" had done; for out had come the *Tatler* with a letter which Swift had written and sent him, with intimation that Prior, as well as Rowe, was a party to it, and of course not signed, laughing at something in a recent *Tatler* about the propriety, now the Union was settled, of saying Great Britain instead of England even in private conversation; and the rogue had printed it with the signatures J. S., M. P., and N. R., which Congreve, with whom and Sir Charles Wager Swift dined that day at the Portugal envoy's, "smoked immediately."*

---

* It appeared in the 258th *Tatler*, and represented the writers at a coffee-house, where they met Mr. South British and Mr. William North Britain, and dined off North British collops, but were so much disturbed by children playing North British hoppers in the paved court outside, that they paid their North Briton as soon as possible, and came off in a coach to North-Britain-Yard; hoping that by thus describing their friends, Mr. English and Mr. William Scott, their Scotch collops, the children's Scotch hoppers, their own ("scot" or) share of the reckoning, and their abode near Scotland Yard, they would please Mr. Bickerstaff by the perfect accuracy of their new style.

AN EVENING AT HOME.

He came back at eight to do work, but could not at once set about it because that dog, Patrick, was not at home, and the fire was not made, and he was not in his gear. So, instead of writing an *Examiner*, he writes more at his tenth letter; looking over it and finding plaguy mistakes in words; and then comes Patrick; and at twelve he tells them he had been busy ever since, by a fire too, and now was got to bed. Well, and what had they to say to Pdfr, now he was abed? Come, now, let him hear their speeches. No, it was a lie, he was *not* sleepy yet. Let them all sit up a little longer and talk. Well, where had they been to-day, that they were but just that minute come home in a coach? What had they lost? Pay the coachman, Ppt. No, faith, not I, says Ppt; he will grumble. What new acquaintance had they got? "Come, let us hear!" Pshaw, so it was! He must be writing to those dear saucy brats every night, whether he would or no, let him have whatever business he will, or come home ever so late, or be ever so sleepy. So true was the old saying (that moment invented):

> Be you lords, or be you earls,
> You must write to naughty girls.

COFFEE-HOUSE ADVENTURES AND A TU QUOQUE.

Going to the Court of Requests to pick up a dinner (they had had the devil and all of rain, by-the-bye), he describes Anthony Henley laying hold of him and making him go dine at a tavern with him and one Colonel Brag, to meet Congreve, who didn't come. "Cost me money, 'faith!" They adjourned to the coffee-house, where Lord Salisbury, a high tory, came up mighty desirous to talk, and, while wriggling himself into Swift's favor, that dog, Henley, asked Swift aloud, to vex him, whether he would go to see Lord Somers as he had promised, "which was a lie." Two or three other such tricks Henley played the same evening, till there was nothing for it but to leave my lord and come home. And was it true, he asked Ppt when he got home, sharply reproving others for doing what he had done himself, that their recorder, and mayor, and fanatic aldermen had a month or two ago, at a solemn feast, drunk Mr. Harley's, Lord Rochester's, and other tory healths? The scoundrels! That he had himself not yet lost ground with the whigs for being supposed to have done the same thing, his next entry tells her. Congreve and Delaval had at last prevailed Lᴇᴛᴛᴇʀ X.
Nov. 25,
Dec. 9. on Sir Godfrey Kneller to entreat Swift to let Sir Godfrey "draw my picture for nothing; but I know not yet when I shall sit."

ARRIVAL OF ESTHER'S SEVENTH LETTER.

He dined with Ford that afternoon, and came home to work. Dec. 6. "But have you lost to-day?" Three shillings? "Oh fie! oh fie!" Still, whatever is in hand, he must call up l'pt to his fancy; he must talk to the saucy dear brat. And then, just as he is sending off his tenth, comes her seventh, quite pat; but he won't answer it, only he has not been giddy, and he is heartily sorry they do not go to Clogher, and so God Almighty protect poor dear, dear, dear, dearest MD. "Farewell till to-night. I will begin my eleventh to-night. So I am always writing to little MD!" His tenth went that day, but he does not yet think of answering her seventh. Having to write "idle things and twittle-twattle," four days pass before he begins any regular reply, though he has pleasant words in the mean while. For if he can only say MD is a dear saucy rogue, what then? Pdfr loves them the better for that. Or if he must go study, sirrahs, and call them rogues and sauceboxes when he has plaguy things to think about, that is all over when he gets to bed, for he can talk to them there, and think of nothing else. No, he will *not* answer her till he has leisure; so let other things go on as they will, what cares he? What cares saucy Pdfr? Yet still each night as it comes brings the question, *when* must he answer this letter of our MD's? There it was, lying slipped beneath his paper, on the other side the leaf. When? when? One of these odd-cum-shortlies he would consider.

PATRICK LOCKS UP HIS MASTER'S WORK.

He dined on the 9th with an old whig friend, Lord Abercorn, whom he wishes to serve, but fears 'tis too late, "by his own fault and ill-fortune." He attends court next day; sees again, without speaking to, the Duke of Richmond ("I believe we are fallen out"); dines with Sir Mathew Dudley; and after "a pure walk in the park," is at home at six for work. But he can do nothing; that scoundrel dog Patrick being out of the way, his work locked up, and himself forced to borrow coals, and not able to do any thing. So he takes up his Journal and talks to her instead. He tells her about Raymond, and of a violent storm last night; of the rumor of one of their packet-boats cast away, and in it Beau Swift (one of his own cousins, son of William); and of a question between the Bishop of Clogher and himself about the Laracor church bells ("he shall not cheat me of one inch of my bell-metal"). By which time Patrick has come home, and his master gets to "study" with his own ink and papers, and a new pen. Next evening, after dining with Mrs. Van, he again comes home for work, and finds the puppy Patrick has again locked up his papers and ink. However, it is not his intention to answer the saucy rogue's letter till he has leisure. But, after another word about Raymond, he tells her of his having had his stomach turned by a letter of Mrs. Long's from Lynn, containing no less than two "nasty jests with dashes to suppose them;" and he thinks she has been corrupted with vile conversation in that country town.

OLD WHIG CONNECTIONS.

He dined on the 12th with the Irish chancellor of the exchequer, Phil Savage, and his Irish club; he was with Sir Mat Dudley, too; and his thoughts, as they rarely failed of doing after whig companionship, turned to him whom he ever regarded as its *decus et tutamen.* "Mr. Addison and I hardly meet now once a fortnight. His parliament and my different friendships keep us asunder." As worth preserving is what he heard that day of Dudley having turned away his butler yesterday morning, the poor fellow dying suddenly in the streets the same night. "Was it not an odd event? But what care you! But, then, I knew the butler." That has a touching pertinence. Next day was appointed for him to go "trapesing" and sight-seeing with a whig family he had much liking for. It was a party for which Lady Kerry (a great favorite) and Mrs. Pratt had engaged him the pre-
Sight-seeing
with the
Shelburnes.
vious morning at tea; and at ten in the morning, from Lord Shelburne's house in Piccadilly, it started in three hackney-coaches: the first containing Lady Kerry, Mrs. Pratt, Mrs. Cadogan, and Swift; the second, Lady Kerry's son, his governor, and two gentlemen; and the third, misses and little master, the Shelburne children, with due supply of maids. They went first to the Tower, seeing all it had to show; visited Bedlam next, for its more terrible "sights;" dined at the chop-house behind the Exchange; called at Gresham College; and closed the night at the puppet-show, Swift depositing ladies and children home at eleven. "The

ladies were all in mobs—how do you call it? undressed; and it LETTER XI. Dec. 9-23.
was the rainiest day that ever dripped; and I am weary, and it is
now past eleven." Four days later, disappointed at Harley's, he
dined with his honest old whig physician, Doctor Cockburn, and at
night again saw Sam Dopping, being taken by Charles Ford "next
door" to drink bad claret and eat oranges with him; of which
indifferent repast we have seen that they permitted Raymond to
partake. He was too late for the Duke of Buckingham next day,
but he visited Mrs. Barton; and the day following he refused
Anthony Henley and every body in hope of Harley, so that at
last, not knowing where to go, he dined at Jemmy Leigh's lodging
on beefsteak, drank Ppt's health, and closed at a tavern with Ben
Tooke and Duke Ormond's secretary, Pontlack; drinking nasty
white wine till eleven, and coming home sick and ashamed on't.
The same ill-luck as to Harley pursuing him next day, and the
weather being "lovely," he went by water into the city, dined at
a merchant's house with Stratford, and walked back with an old
whig acquaintance, Colonel Caulfield. He calls his dining disappointments "coming down proud stomach."

ANSWERS ESTHER'S SEVENTH LETTER.

He began his reply on that day of the sight-seeing with the
Shelburne party, when, before starting, he could not help a little
talk to his saucy jades, just "a little snap and away." So let
them hold their tongues, for he must get up; not a word for their
lives! "How nowww? So, very well: stay till I come home,
and then, perhaps, you may hear further from me. And where
will you go to-day? for I can not be with you for those ladies.
It is a rainy, ugly day. I would have you send for Walls, and go
to the Dean's; but do not play small games when you lose."
And then comes advice about her way of playing ombre, already
quoted (ante, 213), all of it running over with delightful character; and then his unexpected full stop—. "Oh, silly! how I
prate, and can not get away from this MD even of a morning.
Go, get you gone, dear naughty girls, and let me rise." He would
have said it all the night before, but that Patrick had locked up
his ink again the third time last night. "The rogue gets the
better of me." Then he goes for his sight-seeing; and, weary as
he is that night, before he rises next morning the tender trifling
is resumed; and the loving shape it gave to pretty pictures of his

LETTER
XI.
Dec. 9–23.

fancy could hardly to himself be more vivid than it remains for us. "Let me see. Come and appear, little letter. Here I am, says he, and what say you to Mrs. Ppt this morning; fresh and fasting?" His health is the first matter, and upon this he re-assures her. Ah then, she *did* keep Pdfr's little birthday; would to God he had been with them! "Rediculous to think they *could* have forgotten it." *Rediculous*, madam! he supposed she meant *ridiculous*; let him have no more of that: it was the author of the Atlantis's spelling. And could Ppt read that writing of his without hurting her dear eyes? Oh, 'faith he was afraid not. "Have a care of those eyes, pray, pray, pretty Ppt." What she observed of his writing was perhaps well enough, that it might not be so well if he writ better; she was so used to his manner, she could turn the pot-hooks into letters and the letters into words. That sentence ends one side of the letter. The next begins, "Turn over. I had not room on the other side to say it, so I did it on this: I fancy that is a good Irish blunder." It was a grief to him they had not gone to Clogher. Ah, why did they not go, nautinautinauti-dear girls (he did not dare to say nauti without dear)? O, 'faith, they governed him. Seriously, he was sorry they did not go, as far as he could judge at that distance. But had her horse indeed been stumbling? He had been some time eager that she should have another horse; he would make Parvisol get her one. He always doubted that horse of hers. She was to let Parvisol sell him, and the other would be a present from himself. His heart ached when he thought she rode him, and he should never be easy till he was out of her hands. 'Faith, he had dreamed of horses stumbling five or six times since her letter. The animal was to "run" that winter if not sold.

Going through the subjects she had touched upon, he evidently thinks she makes it too much a merit in the Dean to have preached for him at Christ Church. And *did* the Dean preach for him? Very well. They could hardly have expected Pdfr to stand where he was and himself preach to them. No, the *Tatler* of the shilling was not his, more than the hint and two or three general heads for it. He had much more important business on his hands; and, besides, the ministry hated to think he should Hint to help
Steele no
longer. help Steele, and had made reproaches on it, and he had frankly told them he would do it no more. "This is a secret, though, Madam Ppt." *She* win eight shillings? She win eight fiddle-

sticks! She said nothing, 'faith, of what she lost. Yes, yes, he LETTER
was doing his best for Manley; and Mrs. DD was an unreasonable XI.
Dec. 9-20.
baggage. He was always in bed by twelve, he meant his candle
was out by twelve, and he took great care of himself. And so
they and the Dean dined at Stoyte's, did they? and Mrs. Stoyte
was in raptures that he remembered her? Why, then, he must do
it but seldom, or the raptures would go off! "But what now,
you saucy sluts! all this written in a morning!" I must rise and
go abroad. At night, however, before he can sleep, again they
are before him. Where did he leave off? Let us see. So, now
he has it. It was where somebody had been pleased to say that
some people went to England who could never tell when to come
back! But his rebuke to the sauceboxes for this has been told
(ante, 350.) Hussy Ppt! he knew that was a jest of hers about
poor Congreve's eyes; yes, she did jest, the hussy! but he would
bang her bones, 'faith. They had been hearing unpleasant gossip
about Steele. Yes, Steele *was* a little while in prison, or at least
in a spunging-house, some time before he came over, not since.
As for Convocation—a pox on their convocations! Lord! he exclaims next morning, what a long day's writing was his yesterday's
reply to them! Ah, but he had forgotten—Why did they leave
his picture behind them at the other lodgings? Forgot it? Well;
but let them pray remember it now, and not roll it up, did they
hear? but hang it carefully in some part of their room where
chairs, and candles, and mop-sticks would not spoil it, sirrahs!
No, truly, he would *not* be godfather to Goody Walls that bout, *Ante*, 200,
and he really hoped she would have no more. There'd be no 202.
quiet nor cards for that child, and he wished it out of the world
the day after the christening. And so there was an end of their
letter.

POSTSCRIPT OF THINGS REMEMBERABLE.

But no end to his tender playfulness morning and night, until
the time for closing his journal. It had still seven days to run,
and besides its pleasant daily greetings, of which something of the
substance can be guessed, though the form is gone, there are a
few more things to tell. What before he had mentioned of the
Bishop of Clogher's ill chance for the desired vice-chancellorship
(ante, 355), he confirmed on the 19th; when he told them of the
appointment of the Archbishop of Tuam, and that their friend had

Letter
XI.
Dec. 9-23.
"enemies" about the viceroy. While writing that, he gave them
a picture of Patrick folding up his scarf and doing up the fire
("for I keep a fire; it costs me twelvepence a week"), and desires
Talk at the
bedside.
them to be quiet till he is gone to bed, when they were to sit down
by him a little, and they would talk a few words more. Well,
now they were at his bedside, and now what should they say?
"How does Mrs. Stoyte? What had the Dean for supper? How
much did Mrs. Walls win? Poor Lady Shelburne!" (he had heard
of the dowager's death that day). Well, "go, get you to bed, sirrahs!" as he tells them he is just doing himself: but, with day-
break, he is talking to her again, and telling her about their Vicar
of Trim. How now, then, sirrah Ppt? he asks. Must he write so
much in a morning to her impudence?

> Stay till night,
> And then I'll write,
> In black and white,
> By candle-light,
> Of wax so bright,
> It helps the sight—

A bite, a bite! Marry come up, and what did Mrs. Boldface think
of his meeting and walking a turn in the park with "that beast
Ante, 127.
Ferris, Lord Berkeley's steward formerly," one of the personages
in Mrs. Harris's petition, whom he calls a scoundrel dog, but reports as married to a wife with a considerable estate in land and
houses about London, happy as an emperor, living at his ease at
Hammersmith, and a specimen of what her "confounded sect"
(sex) could do. Next night, after telling her this, he is very early
Dec. 22.
to bed, meaning to "sleep for a wager;" but he is first minded to
wish her a merry Christmas and a happy new year, and pray God
they might never keep them again asunder.

The following "dark" morning Patrick tempts him by a good
fire to leave his bed, and he wishes MD were by it or he by MD's.
And then, at last, comes the 23d, when his letter *must* go; and in
the morning he wakes wondering if the frame over the fire-place
at the coffee-house exhibited another letter from Ppt. He would
send by-and-by, and let her know. And so and so. Patrick
was gone on the errand. What would she say? Was there one
Wager
with Ppt.
from MD, or no? No, says Pdfr. Done for sixpence, says Ppt.
—He has won sixpence, he has won sixpence! There is *not* a letter for Pdfr! And so good-morrow; for he and Stratford are to

dine with Lord Mountjoy, and as he goes he prays God Almighty LETTER
to preserve and bless them. And when he comes back from din- XI.
Dec. 9-23.
ner " to study," he tells her of some better news from Spain (" our
news from Spain this post takes off some of our fears "), and that
Bank stock is so risen he might get twelve pounds for his bargain;
but he is troubled by Patrick, the puppy, being abroad, and how
shall he send his letter? He fills it meanwhile to the brim, pressed
down and running over, with tender words. "Good-night, little
dears both, and be happy, and remember your poor Pdfr, that
wants you sadly, as hope saved. Let me go study, naughty girls,
and do not keep me at the bottom of the paper. O, 'faith, if you
knew what lies on my hands constantly, you would wonder to see
how I could write such long letters; but we will talk of that some
other time. Good-night again, and God bless dear MD with his
best blessing; yes, yes, and DD, and Ppt, and ME too." . . .
And as he folds it up he has counted, besides postscript, one hundred and ninety-nine lines in it, which he had "a curiosity to
reckon." There was a long letter—longer than a sermon, 'faith!
And yet there is another word to put into it, about a letter from
his sister Fenton, which he will answer soon; and so his humble
service to Mrs. Walls and Mrs. Stoyte.

ILLNESS OF SIR ANDREW FOUNTAINE. (*Ante*, 176.)

His twelfth letter told her of increasing public as well as pri- LETTER XII.
vate engagements, but the politics and playfulness still went hand- Dec. 23,
Jan. 4.
in-hand, both attractive alike for her to whom both were addressed,
and neither interfering with the other. This letter was also unusually rich in individual anecdote, and in illustrations of manner
and character. Sir Andrew Fountaine had fallen ill, and so bad
was he on the 29th, after nearly a week's suffering, that he had
sent to Swift early that morning to have prayers, "which you
know is the last thing." He found the doctors and every body
in despair about him, and that he had settled all things; and when
he came out after reading prayers, the nurse asked him whether
he thought it possible poor Sir Andrew could live, for the doctors thought not. "I said I believed he would live; for I found
the seeds of life in him, which I observe seldom fail (and I found
them in poor dearest Ppt, when she was ill many years ago)."
He was right in his prediction. He was with the patient again
that night, finding him mightily recovered, and it was hoped he

LETTER
XII.
Dec. 23,
Jan. 4.

would do well, the doctor approving Swift's reasons: "but if he should die, I should come off scurvily." Next morning he had continued good news; and going later to read prayers again, he found Sir Andrew so far recovering as to desire to be at ease. He had given orders not to be disturbed. "I have lost a legacy by his living; for he told me he had left me a picture and some books." On New-year's-eve, however, Fountaine was still suffering, and Swift's first visit on New-year's-day was to inquire after him, when he was again better; and the following day he was mending much. Yet thoughts of his friend confused his dreams that night. 'Faith, he fancied he was to be put in prison, he did not know why, and he was so afraid of a black dungeon, and all he had been asking about Fountaine's sickness he thought was of poor Ppt; and the worst of such dreams was that one waked just in the humor they left one. Here was an impertinence! he exclaimed, opening his thirteenth letter. Sir Andrew's mother and sister were come above a hundred miles from Worcester to see him before he died, arriving but yesterday, when he must have been past hopes, or past fears, before they could reach him. Swift fell

LETTER
XIII.
Jan. 4–16.

a-scolding when he heard they were coming, and the people about him wondered at this, and said what a mighty content it would be on both sides that he should die when they were with him. But Swift, who believed him in a fair way to live, knew the mother for the greatest overdo on earth, and the sister, they said, was worse,

Family
mourners.

and so felt sure he'd relapse again among them. There was also the scoundrel brother, an ignorant, worthless rake, always crying in the outer room, and the nurses comforting him, and desiring him not to take on so, till Sir Andrew had fallen really into danger; and the dog remembered he should have all his estate if he died, and at last began to be consoled. Such was the condition of things at Fountaine's lodgings on the 4th. Then, three days later, came the housekeeper, Mrs. South, on her way to market, to whom Swift gave a New-year's gift of half a pistole, and who reported her master still in a fever, and might live or die, and the mother and sister actually arrived at the house, "so there is a lurry." It

Jan. 14.

is a week all but a day before Swift tells more; and then, saying it was spring with them already, and he ate asparagus the other day, and did she ever see such a frostless winter, he adds that Sir Andrew lay still extremely ill, and that it cost him, as it had done for three weeks past, ten guineas a day to doctors, surgeons, and apothccaries. On the day his letter was posted he visited the mother LETTER XII. Dec. 23, Jan. 4. and sister, finding the patient on the mend, though slowly, and later letters may be anticipated for the sequel. On the 9th of February he spoke of him as recovered, so that she might take back the sorrow she had just sent, and fling it to the dogs; two days after, he was reading prayers to him in the afternoon; on the 19th, when, having shipped off his mother and sister back to the country, he had just begun to sally out, Swift dined with him at Mrs. Van's; and again, a week later, they dined there together.

LORD HERBERT AND ANTHONY HENLEY.

I go back to the twelfth letter for a characteristic note on two LETTER XII. Dec. 23, Jan. 4. whig friends. Yes, yes, Madam Dingley was not to trouble herself; he had got another velvet cap. Lord Herbert had bought it, and presented it to him. It was ten days ago, when he was at breakfast with him, where he was as merry and easy as ever he saw him, yet had received a challenge half an hour before, and half an hour after fought a duel. Herbert was a friend of Anthony Henley, of whom Ppt wished to hear something, but he had nothing to tell of that " puppy " who had gone to the country for Christmas, except that he had lately got into a habit of coming up without his wife and keeping no house, but tempting his friends to eating-houses and the coffee-house; and Swift, growing tired of it, avoided him; upon which Henley, not able anyhow to get hold of him, sent him a message by Lord Herbert that he was " a beast " forever after the order of Melchisedek. Did she ever read the Scripture? It was only changing the word beast to priest. I will add the very attractive picture that closes this letter. When the day came for sending it, he would fain have more news to send. It was now thought Atterbury would be Dean of Christchurch, but the college would rather have Smallridge. But what was this to them? What cared they for Atterburys or Smallridges? No, 'faith, they cared for nothing but Pdfr. So he would rise and bid them farewell—and yet he was loath, with a great bit of paper yet to talk upon. So he tells them a couple of puns Ante, 206, 207. that he and Prior had made, and says it was really a shame that he did not remember to have heard one good one from the ministry. Still he can not leave off; he thinks he is bewitched to write so of a morning to little Ppt. " Let me go, will you? and I will come again to-night in a fine clean sheet of paper; but I can nor

LETTER
XII.
Dec. 23,
Jan. 4.
will stay no longer now. No, I will not, for all your wheedling!
No, no; look off; do not smile at me and say pray, pray, Pdfr,
write a little more. Ah, you are a wheedling slut; you be so.
Nay, but pray turn thee about, and *let* me go! Do: it is a good
girl; and do." A very tender, sweet picture that! And suddenly
his morning candle dwindles, and he is on the wrong side of the
curtain, and the dark comes upon him, and he can not see the
paper he writes upon, as, with service to Mrs. Walls and Mrs.
Stoyte, and once more God Almighty bless Ppt, he folds it up.

NEW *TATLER*, WITH "LITTLE HARRISON" FOR EDITOR.

LETTER XIII.
Jan. 4-10.
He tells her of this enterprise in his thirteenth letter. In its
predecessor's last journals he had told her of an evening at his
neighbor Darteneuf's to drink punch with Addison and little
Harrison, the young poet whose fortune he was bent on making
(*ante*, 300); and, mentioning that Steele also was to have been
there, but came not, "nor ever did twice since I knew him to any
appointment," he went on to give a reason that might at least
have excused his absence that day, and which has interest for us.
Last number
of Steele's
Tatler.
It was the day of the appearance of Steele's last *Tatler*. "You
will see it before this comes to you, and how he takes leave of the
world. He never so much as told Mr. Addison of it, who was
surprised as much as I; but, to say the truth, it was time, for he
grew cruel dull and dry. To my knowledge he had several good
hints to go upon, but he was so lazy and weak of the work, that
he would not improve them." The notion was doubtless started
that night, over Darteneuf's punch, of a new *Tatler*, with Harrison
at the head of it, and she was soon to hear of it again.

He told her on the 11th that some one had suggested a fresh
Tatler, and he was doing his best to give little Harrison the
chance. Something had been brought that evening for a first
number to come out next Saturday, and Swift had sent for a
printer (good-naturedly selecting one of his own irrepressible
"cousins"), and settled the matter between him and Harrison.
To follow Steele, however, was not easy; he doubted this thing
would not succeed, for what had been brought him was poor;
"and the scheme, being Mr. Secretary St. John's and mine, would
have done well enough in good hands." Harrison had just left
him as he wrote that, and he was tired with correcting his trash.
Two days after it came out, and Swift could only say there was not

LETTER
XIII.
Jan. 4-16.

much in it, but he hoped it might mend. Ppt must understand that already on Steele's leaving off there had two or three "scrub" *Tatlers* come out, and one of them held on still, being that day advertised against Harrison's, so that there would be disputes which was genuine, "like the strops for razors." But he was afraid the "little toad" had not the true vein for it. This he repeats after another three days, when he had given hints for a second number. The "jackanapes" wanted a right taste, and he doubted he would not do. This was but too true a prediction, and, notwithstanding Swift's help, the thing failed. How he yet does his best to prop it up appears frequently in the Journals. There is also a dispute with the printer he had specially recommended, and the incident and his manner of relating it are highly characteristic of him. Here came little Harrison yesterday, says he, to complain of the printer recommended for his *Tatler*, " and yet to see how things will happen," for that very printer was one Doctor Swift's cousin, his name Dryden Leach; had she never heard of Dryden Leach, he that prints the *Postman?* Oh, yes, he had told her (*ante* 303), but had forgotten. " He acted Oroonoko, he is in love with Miss Cross," and little Harrison had called him a coxcomb; very clearly not an unpardonable offense to Cousin Swift, who, on Mr. Leach coming to him a day or two later with a heavy counter-complaint vowing vengeance, answered gravely, got rid of him, and ordered Patrick to deny him ever after. But though he throws off the printer, he still tolerates his young friend, for whom he has a genuine kindness. There is an intercession for him with poor Congreve, now nearly blind, and just getting out of a severe fit of the gout, to whom Swift goes to sit of an evening; and he tells her that he got from his old school-fellow, by way of reward, a *Tatler* which, blind as he was, Congreve had written out as a help to Harrison, about a scoundrel grown rich, who went and bought a coat of arms at the Heralds' and a set of ancestors at Fleet-ditch. Another night we find him home early, expecting his little friend to get help for his Tuesday's number, having given him liberty to come two evenings in the week; but the jackanapes never comes; and he, expecting the toad, falls a-reading, having left off other business. When finally there is no more hope in the way of a new *Tatler*, he makes earnest intercession with St. John for Harrison, with what effect we shall see.

Congreve's
good-nature.

INCIDENT ON CHRISTMAS-EVE.

He had already announced to her his intention to change his lodgings in Bury Street. They had in them, he said, "a thousand stinks;" and this fact, which had enabled him to strengthen his verses on a London shower, had led to his being disturbed in more than one of his senses on Christmas-eve, for it brought the fear of fire. The little comedy will bear reproduction. He had come home early, and got into bed to go on with his letter to MD : for it was a maxim as old as the hills that you must always write to your MD's in bed :

> " The White and the Red, write to MD when abed ;
> The Black and the Brown, write to MD when you are down ;
> The Oak and the Willow, write to MD on your pillow."

On his pillow he had afterward turned to sleep, when—*what was that!* 'Faith, he must rise and look at his chimney in the next room, for the smell grew stronger and stronger. *Stay!* Well, he had been up and in his room, and found all safe, only a mouse within the fender to warm himself, which he tried to catch, and could not. Certainly he smelt nothing there. But it is not gone. Again he smells it, this time beyond a doubt in his bedroom, and at last he discovers the secret. Writing in bed, he had singed the woolen curtains. "Pdfr's plaguy silly to-night, is not he? Yes, and so he be. Ay, but if I should wake and see fire? Well, I will venture—and so"—he sleeps at last. A couple of days later he is sauntering about for a new lodging, having missed one "over the way" which he had bespoken, but not given earnest for, as Patrick recommended him to do, and so "the dog" let it to another. But he found one next day in St. Alban Street, where he paid the same rent (eight shillings a week) for an apartment up two pair of stairs, but with use of the parlor to receive persons of quality.

CHRISTMAS AND NEW YEAR.

All this was in the Christmas-time, when he is never tired of wishing Ppt a Merry Christmas, and many and many a one with poor Pdfr at some pretty place. On Christmas-day itself he was at church by eight, and received the sacrament ; came home by ten, and at two went to court, where it was a collar-day (" that is, when the Knights of the Garter wear their collars "); but the LETTERS XII. AND XIII. queen staid so late at sacrament that he came back to dine with his neighbor Ford, "because all people dine at home on this Dec. 23, Jan. 16. day." Which minds him of a pun he has made, that it was likewise a collar-day all over England, in every house, at least, where there was brawn. "That is very well," he says, complacently; and it encourages him to tell her of his pun about egoes, and to Ante, 206. twit the young women with pretending innocence that they may ask after "roguish" puns, and Latin ones too. But so open a winter as they had was very unlike Christmas. They had not had two frosty days; but it paid them off in rain, for they had not had three fair days these six weeks. One peculiarity of the season he would fain have them explain. He had called that day (the 27th) at one or two neighbors', hoping to spend a Christmas evening; but none were at home, they were all gone to be merry with others.* "I have often observed this, that in merry times every body is abroad: where the deuce are they?" So he went to the coffee-house, and talked an hour with Addison, who at last remembered to give him two letters (one of which was her eighth), which he could not answer that night; no, nor to-morrow neither, the young women might count upon that. He had other things to do than to answer naughty girls. An old saying and a true— "Letters from MD's must not be answered in ten days"—but a bad rhyme, he admitted. However, he has a better on New-year's-eve :

> " Would you answer MD's letter,
> On New-year's-day you will do it better,
> For when the year with MD 'gins,
> It without MD never lins."

—(He is comically careful here to explain that these proverbs have always old words in them ; *lins* is to leave off)—

> " But if on New Year you write nones,
> MD then will bang your bones."

---

* After two more days, when he dined with his quondam neighbor Ford, who always dined at home on opera-nights (do you know what *quondam* is, though ?), he protested he should not reply till next year. O lord—bo—but that will be a Monday next. Coda so, is it ? and so it is : never saw the like.—"I made a pun the other day to Ben Pontlack about a pair of drawers." Not now mentionable, though doubtless relished by her. "Pray, pray, DD, let me go seep : pray, pray Ppt, let me go sumber, and put out my wax candle."

LETTERS
XII. AND
XIII.
Dec. 23,
Jan. 16.

For New-year's-day accordingly he reserves the best of his rhymes, first wishing in prose his dearest pretty Ppt and DD a happy New Year, and health, and mirth, and good stomachs, and FR's company ("faith, I did not know how to write FR. I wondered what was the matter; but now I remember I always write Pdfr"); and then breaking out into a good-morrow, good-morrow, for his mistresses all: .

> " I wish you both a merry New Year,
> Roast beef, minced pies, and good strong beer,
> And me a share of your good cheer!
> That I was there, or you were here!
> And you are a little saucy dear!"

Again and yet again that New-year's-morning, he says good-morrow to his dear sirrahs, "one can not rise for your play;" and when returned home at night, his own charming play begins. Now let us come and see what this saucy dear letter says: " Come out, letter, come out from between the sheets: here it is underneath, and it will not come out. . . . Come out, again I say—so, then. Here it is. What says Pdfr to me, pray? says it. Come, and let me answer for you to your ladies. Hold up your head, then, like a good letter. There!" And he proceeds to answer it, first thanking her for having kept little Pdfr's birthday. Would to God he had been at "the health," rather than where he was, where he had no manner of pleasure, nothing but eternal business on his hands. He should grow wise in time—but no more of that! Only he said Amen with his heart and vitals to the wish that they might never be asunder again ten days to-gether while poor Pdfr lived! ————— The long line was put to put away sadness from what else he had to say. "I can not be merry so near any splenetic talk; so I made that long line, and now all is well again."

His birth-
day.

ECONOMIES AND DOMESTICITIES.

It was to be taken as settled between them that when they were silent all was pretty well, because that was the way he would deal with them; and, on the other hand, if there was any thing they ought to know "now," he would write by the first post, although he had written but the day before. The young women were to remember this, and God Almighty preserve them both and make "us" happy together; and they were to tell him always how accounts stood "between us," so as never to want, but LETTERS XII. AND XIII. Dec. 23, Jan. 16. to be paid long before it was due. "I will return no more money while I stay, so that you need not be in pain to be paid; but let me know at least a month before you can want." He was general pay-master, and evidence will hereafter appear that he in some way contributed to Ppt's income, as he certainly did to DD's; but that Mrs. Johnson was sensitive in this direction may be inferred from his present recurrence to what he had said about buying her a horse: "Pray, let Parvisol sell the horse. . . . I Meum and tuum. am glad you are rid of him, and was in pain while I thought you rode him; but if he would buy you another, or any body else, and that you could be often able to ride, why do not you do it?" Again he returns, before closing his letter, to money affairs, and the Lady Giffard debt, and something her mother has been blaming him about. "Now you are at it again, silly Ppt! Why does your mother say my candles are scandalous? They are good sixes in the pound, and she said I was extravagant enough to burn them by daylight. I never burn fewer at a time than one." There was another scandal about his fire. Well, well, he *did* keep a good fire. It cost him twelvepence a week, and he feared something more; and if they vexed him, he'd have one in his bed-chamber too. In the next letter, too, there are a few more homely notes. Pat's bills for coals and candles came sometimes to three shillings a week, for he kept very good fires, though the weather be warm; and Ireland would never be happy till they got some small coal, like the English: nothing so easy, so convenient, Small coal wanted in Ireland. so cheap, so pretty, for lighting a fire. They were not to forget to let him have accounts, that they might be paid their money betimes. There was four months for his lodging, that was to be thought on, too; and she was to go and dine with Manley, the "extravagant sluttikin," and not to fret, though it would be just three weeks to-morrow since Pdfr had a letter from her. The old farewell to dearest beloved MD followed, of course, with injunction to love poor, poor Pdfr, who has not had one happy day since he left them, and whose sole aim or care is to make MD and ME easy.

THE MISSING BOX. (*Ante*, 311, 318.)

Not long after his arrival in London, he had made up a little LETTER XII. Dec. 23, Jan. 4. wooden box for Dublin, in which he had sent sundry things to both Esther and her friend, including palsy-waters for Ppt's eyes, trusting it to their special friend, Enoch Sterne, and his troubles at its not arriving duly are incessant. He is grated to the heart at its not reaching them, because he thinks he discovers through her "little words" that she imagined he had not taken the care he ought. "I will never rest till you have it, or till it is in a way for you to have it. Poor dear rogue, naughty to think it teases me. How could I ever forgive myself for neglecting any thing that related to your health? Sure I were a devil if I did." (And he puts a great many stars after the word, as if to stand submissively apart.) See how far he was forced to stand from Ppt, because he was afraid she thought poor Pdfr had not been careful about her little things, when he was sure he bought them immediately according to order, and packed them up with his own hands, and sent them to Sterne, and was six times with him about sending them away. But she was little likely to join in such self-reproaches. All his life seems a care for her, and in every way he is eager to show it. A few days before he told her of an incident at court: A "fellow in a red coat without a sword" came up to him, and surprised him by asking how the ladies did. "I asked what ladies. He said Mrs. Dingley and Mrs. Johnson. Very well, said I, when I heard from them last; and pray when came you from thence, sir? He said, I never was in Ireland. And just at that word Lord Winchilsea comes up to me, and the man went off. As I went out I saw him again and recollected him. It was Vedeau with a pox. I then went and made my apologies—that my head was full of something I had to say to Lord Winchilsea; and I asked after his wife, and so all was well; and he inquired after my lodging, because he had some favor to desire of me in Ireland, to recommend somebody to somebody, I know not what it is." It was a "shop-keeper" named Vedeau, who, excited by the great duke's victories, had made over his share in the shop to his brother and taken up the trade of war, whom Mrs. Johnson and Mrs. Dingley had known at Farnham, and whom Swift is therefore thus eager to show attention to, interposing afterward, for her sake, more substantially to serve him.

CHARLES FORD AND ADDISON.

Charles Ford, already named, makes many pleasant appearances in the journals. One day they set apart for going into the city to buy books; but it was not altogether successful, for as they only had a scurvy dinner at the ale-house, Ford made him go afterward to the tavern and drink Florence (four-and-sixpence a flask, "damned wine!"), spending his money, which he seldom did, and passing an insipid day. Yet he preferred dining at Ford's the next, which was one of his opera days, sending excuse to Lord Shelburne; and four days later dined again at Ford's, going later to the coffee-house, where he had not been a week, and talking coldly a while to Addison. All their friendship and dearness were off; they were civil acquaintance; they talked such words, of course, as where they should meet, and that was all! He had not been at any house with Addison for six weeks. The other day they were to have dined together at the comptroller's, but Swift sent his excuses, being engaged to the secretary of state. Was it not odd? He knew well even then such strangeness could not last. "But I think he has used me ill, and I have used him too well, at least his friend Steele."

PATRICK AND HIS LINNET. (*Ante*, 311, 317.)

In the middle of January he was in the city to buy a new periwig; and telling her of it, and that it cost him three guineas, he cries out he is undone! But though he affects to say he thought it would be cheaper because it was bought of a "Leicester lad, who married Mr. Worrall's daughter where my mother lodged," Ppt would credit him with a kindlier motive, and think him all the richer for being so "undone." Another pleasant trait may be added, and especially for the fact that his blundering, lying, drunken, careless, incorrigible, easy, good-natured Patrick figures in it more creditably than usual. Going to the closet in his lodgings for some coals one night after Patrick was in bed, what should he discover but "a poor linnet," which Pat had consulted him about buying to carry over to Dingley! It cost him sixpence, and was tame as a dormouse. "I believe he does not know he is a bird," says Swift; does not know his advantage over humanity. "Where you put him, there he stands, and seems to have neither hope nor fear; I suppose in a week he will die of the spleen." Patrick advised with his master upon the purchase, but could not be dissuaded from his generous design to Dingley. "I laid fairly before him the greatness of the sum and the rashness of the attempt; showed him how impossible it was to carry him

LETTER
XIII.
Jan. 4–16. safe over the salt sea; but he would not take my counsel, and he will repent it." Though the bird occasions all sorts of trouble, Swift tolerates it. He had told them, he says in a subsequent journal, about Patrick's linnet for Dingley. It was very tame at first, and now was the wildest he ever saw. He kept it still in the closet, where it made a terrible litter. " But I say nothing: I am as tame as a clout." He reported the linnet still later as in full feather, the wildest ever seen, though bought for his tameness, and quite able to fly after them to Ireland: "if he be willing," adds Swift, to whom it is always matter of doubt if any thing or any body will ever willingly go over to Ireland.

THE ARCHDEACON'S WIFE. (Ante, 202.)

He can not close his letter without some good-humored jesting on Mrs. Walls, of whom he pretends to have heard surprising news when dining with Ophy Butler and his wife, and declares himself also to be quite certain that Ppt is that moment supping with the dean, after losing two-and-twenty pence at cards, and talking of their poor Mrs. Walls brought to bed of a girl that died two days after it was christened—but, "betwixt you and me," she was not very sorry; she loved her ease and diversions too well to be troubled with children. And really *has* she, he asks later, a boy or a girl? "A girl, hmm; and died in a week, hmmm; and *was* poor Ppt forced to stand for godmother?" Then he affects anger to be left so long without news from them, and says woe betide them, 'faith, for he will go to the toyman's here just in Pall Mall, who sells "great hugeous battoons;" yes, 'faith, and so he does! He thinks also of another punishment. Yes, he shall send his own letter away before hers comes; will send it two days sooner on purpose, out of spite, without its "third side;" and then her letter will come, and it will be too late, and he will so laugh, never saw the like. Will she not grumble for want of the third side, pray now? Yes, I warrant you; yes, yes, and she shall have the third when she can catch it. So, keeping his word, he whips his letter into the post-office as he returns that evening.

WAITING FOR A LETTER.

LETTER XIV.
Jan. 16–01. Very impatient he had become to hear from her, and one morning, immediately after breakfast, he starts off to the St. James's,

LETTER XIV. Jan. 16-31.

where the waiter comforted him by saying he had given Patrick a letter for him. Then he hunts for Harley at the Court of Requests and the treasury, and, after some time spent in mutual reproaches, is carried off to dinner by the minister, whom he left at seven, to come home and read MD's letter. The dog Patrick was abroad; but at last he returned, and Swift got his letter; and it was all in French, and subscribed Bernage; and, 'faith, he nearly flung it at Patrick's head. Yet it had a touch of Ppt in it, too. But for a glimpse of her name, indeed, he'd have put it in the fire. For Lieutenant Bernage was her friend, and had written to desire her recommendation to Doctor Swift to make him a captain, to which her cautious answer, " that he has as much power with Dr. Swift as she had," though it had brought upon him the present letter, seemed to him so notable, that, if she were here, he would present *her* to the ministry as a person of ability. However, for her sake, he'd speak to George Granville about him ; but Bernage was not again to bother him with letters when he is expecting them from MD. Next day, still no letter ; and so he fancies her, the saucy rogue, losing her money at Stoyte's. To let that bungler beat her—fie ! Ppt. Was not she ashamed ? Well, he forgave her that once ; but she was never to do so again—no, noooo ; kiss, and be friends ; and he bids them good-night in one long word, which in the morning he defies them to have read: " So good-night, myownlittledearsaucyinsolentrogues." Well, he repeats next day, when will this letter come from our MD ? To-morrow, or the next day, without fail ? Yes, 'faith, and so it is " coming." Meanwhile, the summer weather was gone ; and that being an insipid, snowy day, no walking day, he dined gravely with Mrs. Van ; and came home, and was got to bed a little after ten. For what was old Culpepper's maxim ?

> " Would you have a settled head,
>   I tell you, and I tell it again,
> You must early go to bed :
>   You must be in bed at ten."

Which made him all the fresher next morning in his new wig, " O hoao," visiting Lady Worsley ; then walking in the park to find Ford, whom he had promised to meet ; and, as they come down the Mall, who should appear but Patrick, pulling five letters out of his pocket. Reading the superscription of the first, Pshoh ! said his master. Of the second, pshoh again ! Of the third, pshah, pshah, pshah! Of the fourth, agad, agad, agad, he was in a rage! Of the fifth and last, O, hoooa! Ay, marry, this was something, this was our MD! "So truly we opened it, I think immediately, and it began the most impudently in the world, thus, *Dear Pdfr, we are even thus far.*" Now we are even, quoth Stephen, when he gave his wife six blows for one. Pretty even, indeed, that he should have their ninth four days after he had sent his thirteenth! But he would reckon anon about that with the young women, whom he calls (after the manner of Ancient Pistol) "huzzies base." Their friend Bernage he keeps steadily

in mind, though he affects to be at first a little careless. Next letter, he tells her that he has engaged to give St. John a memorial from himself to Duke of Argyle for her friend. "The duke is a man that distinguishes people of merit, and I will speak to him myself; but the secretary backing it will be very effectual." He was very busy that night as he wrote, but don't let them guess at what—impudent, saucy, dear boxes. He couldn't (at the end of a letter) say saucy boxes without putting dear between. "En't that right, now? Farewell. This should be longer, but that I send it to-night." So, laughing at the italics she *will* use, in feminine fashion, to emphasize her letters, he calls her silly, silly loggerhead.

ENJOYMENT OF WHAT ESTHER WRITES.

At the opening of his fourteenth letter, where he offers but poor account of the sum of his gains thus far from the "full favor" of the ministry, he had given her reasons why she should not fail in her letters. Pdfr ben't angry; 'faith, no, not a bit; only he would begin to be in pain next Irish post, except he sees MD's little handwriting in the glass frame at the bar of St. James's coffee-house, where Pdfr would never go, but for that! Pdfr is at home, God help him, every night from six till bedtime; and has little enjoyment or pleasure in life at present. As hope saved, nothing gives him any sort of dream of happiness, but a letter now and then from his own dearest MD. He loves the expectation of it; and when it does not come, he comforts himself that he has it yet to be happy with. Yes, 'faith; and when he writes to her, he is happy, too. It is just as if methought she were here, and he prating to her, and telling her where he had been. Well, says she, Pdfr, come, where have you been to-day?

Come, let's hear, now. And so then he answers: "Ford and I
were visiting Mr. Lewis and Mr. Prior; and Prior has given me
a fine Plautus; and then Ford would have had me dine at his
lodgings, and so I would not; and so I dined with him at an
eating-house, which I have not done five times since I came here;
and so I came home, after visiting Sir Andrew Fountaine's mother
and sister; and Sir Andrew is mending, though slowly."

LAUGHS AT *HER* ANSWERS, AND DESCRIBES HIS OWN.

In his fourteenth letter also he replies to her ninth, and wishes
them both to think of the country for summer, and to tell him if
the apples from Laracor were good for any thing. What! the
Wallses at Donnybrook with them! Why, wasn't she brought
to bed? They were to give his service to Mrs. Stoyte and
Catherine; and let Catherine *get the coffee ready* against he went
over, and not have "so much care on her countenance;" for all
would go well. As for their "Mr. Bernage, Mr. Bernage, Mr.
Fiddlenage," who sends him three letters successively, he has told
Ppt what he shall do; and she is to draw it up into a handsome
speech, and repeat it to her friend. As to what she says about
leaving a good deal of Pdfr's tenth unanswered—impudent slut!
When did she ever "answer" his tenth, or his ninth, or any other
number? and who asks her to answer, provided only she writes?
He defied the devil to answer his letters, except a question now
and then which he'd be glad she replied to; but he afterward for-
gets, and she never thinks of. He'd never love answering again,
if *she* talked of answering. Answering, quotha! pretty answerers,
truly. And now he had done; and his *was* an answer! for he
laid hers before him, and looked and wrote, and wrote and looked,
and looked and wrote again. So, good-morrow to his madams
both, and he would go rise.

INVENTION OF OLD RHYMED PROVERBS.

There is no channel through which Swift is so fond of suggesting or insinuating the advice he desires to impress as what he calls
ancient proverbs, or sayings in rhyme, which he plentifully invents
at the moment he may want them. He has to take Ppt to task
for writing on thin paper. Why, didn't she know a common caution that writing-masters gave their scholars? she must have heard
it a hundred times! It was this (invented, of course, then and

there—they are at hand, and authors for them, in every conceiv-
able emergency) :

> "If paper be thin, ink will slip in ;
> But if it be thick, you may write with a stick."

Again, as he comes to the close of a letter, and is looking over it
before going to bed, he finds it pretty near the bottom of the
second folio page, and, replying to their wish to have it entirely
filled, he thanks them for nothing, but he doesn't think he'll write
on the other side. 'Faith, if he would use them to sheets as broad
as the room, they'd expect such from him always! They took no
heed of the old saying, Two sides in a sheet, And one in a street,
though it was but a silly old saying, and so he'd go to "seep, and
do you so too." His rhymes may be the most incoherent in the
world, but he must have them. "I did not get home till nine, and
now I am in bed to break your head." He can not resist them,
reason or no reason. He will tack them on to the most matter-
of-fact remark, as in that just cited, or where he tells her that he
writes "just to let her know how matters go, and so, and so, and
so." One phrase in the little language he is fond of, and first in-
troduces thus : "And so, good-morrow, little sirrahs, that is for the
rhyme." But, as the reader observes, the rhyme has been spoiled
by disappearance of the little language, or it would have run—
"And so

> "Dood mollah
> Little Sollah !"

SICKNESS AFTER ST. JOHN'S REVEL. (*Ante*, 354.)

After the post-midnight revel at St. John's, there is a blank of
four days (26th to 29th), the first in his journal, during which he
had been so lazy and negligent he could not write. His head,
since a previous attack a fortnight ago, was not in order; not
absolutely ill, but giddyish, and made him restless. He walked
every day, and took Doctor Cockburn's drops, and was trying
some bitter drink twice a-day, which Lady Kerry had sent him.
He wished he were with MD. He longed for spring, and good
weather, and then he would go over. His riding kept him well in
Ireland. He was very temperate, and eat of the easiest meats, as
he was directed; and hoped the malignity would go off; but one
fit shook him a long time. And then, as he seals up his letter on

the 30th, he gives them good-night, "My dears," with injunction LETTER XIV. Jan. 16-31. to love Pdfr, and be healthy, and God Almighty bless them both, here and ever, and poor Pdfr. Afterward, he re-opens the letter to put in two bills of exchange: six fishes for Ppt, and six fishes for DD, to be placed to the account of their humble servant, Pdfr. His opening of his next letter shows him in trouble still from his health and the weather. His head confounded every thing; often he could not scribble even his morning lines to MD, and, with his occasional giddiness, he found the late dining of the ministers a thing to be avoided. He began (on the 31st) by saying it was Ford's birthday, and he had refused the secretary to dine with Ford. For the time, they were in as smart a frost as he had seen, delicate walking weather, and "the canal and Rosamond's Pond full of the rabble, sliding, and with skates, if you know what those are." Patrick's bird's water freezes in the gallipot, and his own hands in bed. He was next morning with poor Lady Kerry, whom he found much worse in her head than himself. With his always shrewd wisdom, he adds that they were so fond of each other because their ailments were the same. Did not Madam Ppt know that? Had he not seen her conning ailments with Joe Beaumont's wife? He was very busy that day, and having to go into the city, he walked, because of the walk, for Pdfr's health was to be taken care of for poor little MD's sake; but he walked plaguy carefully, for fear of sliding against his will.

WRITING IN BED.

They had asked him not to write in bed at night. No, no, he LETTER XV. Feb. 1-10. did not now read or write after going to bed. The last thing he did "up," was to write something to our MD, and then get into bed, and put out his candle, and so go sleep as fast as ever he could. But in the morning, as she knew, he did write in bed sometimes. An instance follows: "Morning. 'I have desired Apronia to be always careful, especially about the legs.' Pray, do you see any such great wit in that sentence? I must freely own that I do not. But party carries every thing nowadays, and what a splutter have I heard about the wit of the saying, repeated with admiration about a hundred times in half an hour! Pray, read it over again, and consider it. I think the word is *advised*, and not *desired*. I should not have remembered it, if I had not heard it so often. Why—ay—" On which the truth blurts out, that the

LETTER
XV.
Feb. 1-10. words were part of a dream he had that moment waked with in his mouth; and happy as a child at play, and calling on his two rogues to admit the success of his "bite," he is very soon at his daily walk in the park, defying every thing but actual rain. Did they know what the weather had "gone and done?" he asked that night on his return. They had a thaw for three days; then a monstrous dirt and sleet; "and now it freezes, like a pot-lid upon our snow." He had dined with Lady Betty Germaine; and there, with other business enough to do, did he sit like a booby till eight, looking over her and another lady at piquet.

LIVING WITS, AND A DEAD ONE.

LETTER XVI.
Feb. 10-24. In the middle of February, he had an evening with enjoyment in it he thinks memorable, when, after going into the city for a walk, and failing to find the person he meant to have dined with, he came back, and called at Congreve's, and dined with him and Dick Eastcourt, and "laughed till six;" the only drawback being that Congreve's nasty white wine gave him the heart-burn. He adds a note on the death of Doctor Duke, who had died suddenly, and whom, a few days later, Atterbury and Prior went to bury. "He was one of the wits when we were children, but turned parson, and left it, and never writ further than a prologue or recommendatory copy of verses. He had a fine living given him by the Bishop of Winchester about three months ago. He got his living suddenly, and he got his dying so too." He was a friend of Otway's, and Johnson has given him two pages in his *Lives*.

ANSWERS ESTHER'S TENTH LETTER.

LETTER XV.
Feb. 1-10. On the coldest day (it was the 8th of February) he had felt that year, Harley, meeting him in the Court of Requests, asked him how long he had learned the trick of writing to himself? He had seen Ppt's letter through the glass case at the coffee-house, and would swear it was Swift's hand, and Ford was of the same mind. "I remember others have formerly said so too. I think I was little MD's writing-master?" Meanwhile, her letter has not been forgotten. "Come, where is MD's letter? Come, Mrs. Letter, make your appearance. Here am I, says she, answer me to my face." And this he proceeds to do, first regretting she had his twelfth so soon, and fearing that at the moment he was replying to her tenth, she would have got his fourteenth; for his wish was

always to have one letter from Pdfr reading, one traveling, and LETTER XV. Feb. 1–10. one writing. As to the missing box, he has nothing to reply but that, oh, 'faith, they had too good an opinion of his care; he was negligent enough of every thing but MD; yet he should have one more tug for it. Yes, yes, yes, the plague was done with. (There had been a touch of plague at Newcastle, and Harley, at Swift's instance, had ordered certain medical sanitary measures.)   So, twelve shillings was charged for mending his strong box! for a farthing's worth of iron put on a hinge, and gilded! Let her give the man six shillings, and he would pay it, and never employ him again.   And her sight was still ailing? Poor Ppt's eyes, God bless them, and send them better.   She was to pray spare them, and write not above two lines a day in broad daylight.   Poor dear Ppt, how durst she write those two lines by candle-light, bang her bones! Madam DD was to be sure and tell him how Ppt looked. A handsome young woman still? What! was not Mrs. Walls's business over yet? Would she never have done with it? Why, Ante, 213. he had hoped she was up, and well, and the child dead, before this!   Then he talked of their accounts, and trusted they were good managers, and that, when he said so, Ppt would not think he intended she should grudge herself wine.   But going to those expensive lodgings required some fund, or they might be drained "as poor as rats," and for some reasons he wished they had staid till he went over; and the country might be necessary, too, for poor Ppt's health; but they were to do as they liked, and not blame Pdfr.   Then he restates, as to their letters, that he will write when he can, and so should MD; and upon occasions extraordinary he would write, though it were but a line; and when either he or they had not the letters to the time, they were to assume all was well; and so that was settled forever, and they were to hold their tongues.   "Well, you shall have your pins; but for the candle-ends, I can not promise, because I burn them to the stumps."   Then, 'faith, it occurred to him his letter should go off to-morrow.   Answering theirs had filled it up so quick, and he did not design to use them to three pages in folio, no, nooooh!   So much for one morning's work in bed.   They wanted politics, but, 'faith, he could not think of any; and so, come, they were to sit off the bed, and let him rise. Would they?

Letters
XIV.–XVI.
Jan. 16,
Feb. 24.

THE WINTER OF 1710–'11.

It was a hard winter, and some notices from the three latest of the letters will show its trying changes during the first two months of 1711.   On the 24th of January he tells them he had dined at Ford's because it was his opera day, and it snowed, and was so terribly cold he did not care to stir farther.   All night the storm went on, and in the morning it was "vengeance" cold.   He began to write in bed, but could not write long; his hands would freeze. "Is there a good fire, Patrick?   Yes, sir.   Then I will rise: come, take away the candle.   You must know I write on the dark side of my bed-chamber, and am forced to have a candle till I rise, for the bed stands between me and the window, and I keep the curtains shut this cold weather.   So pray let me rise; and, Patrick, here, take away the candle."   He dined that day with Doctor Cockburn, whom he liked better than his company, who were mainly "a parcel of Scots;" so he should not be in a hurry to dine there again.   The storm went on.   They were now in high frost and snow, and the largest fire could hardly keep them warm.   It was very ugly walking.   A baker's boy broke his thigh yesterday. He was careful himself to walk slow, make short steps, and never tread on his heel.   Then he tags his proverb, declaring it to be a good one the Devonshire people had:

> "Walk fast in snow,
> In frost walk slow,
> And still as you go
> Tread on your toe.
> When frost and snow are both together,
> Sit by the fire and spare shoe-leather."

Ante, 214.

Starving, starving, uth, uth, uth, uth, uth! is his morning salutation.   Did not they remember he used to go into their chamber of a cold morning and cry uth, uth, uth?   "Oh, 'faith, I must rise; my hand is so cold I can write no more."   Very difficult walking he found it that day, when Doctor Stratford and he had to dine with merchant Stratford in the city, but he preferred to walk for exercise in the frost, not knowing that it had *given* a little (" as you women call it ") and was become something slobbery.   Before he returned he had absolutely gone and called at Lady Giffard's house to see Ppt's mother, and had got from her some more palsy-water to replace that sent by the unlucky box (suspected to be lying at Chester, but all inquiry still unavailing); and he would feeling it to be less cold than yesterday, but in came a printer have begun to answer some of her letter next morning in bed,

LETTERS
XIV.-XVI.
Jan. 16,
Feb. 24.

about some business, and staid an hour, and then he got up; and then came in Ben Tooke; and then he shaved and scribbled; and it was such a terrible day he could not stir out till one, and then he called at Mrs. Barton's, and they went together to Lady Worsley's, where they were to dine, and where they heard of the young Lord Berkeley going to marry the Duke of Richmond's daughter Louisa.

Still the bad weather enters largely into every journal. At the beginning of February, after telling her that Patrick had been out of favor these ten days, his master talking " dry and cross " to him, and calling him " friend " three or four times, he adds that he is going to see Prior, who was to dine with him at Harley's, so he couldn't stay " fiddling and talking " with dear little brats in a morning; and it was still terribly cold. He wished his cold hand were in the warmest place about them, " young women;" he would give ten guineas upon that account with all his heart, 'faith! Oh, it starved his thigh: so he'd rise and bid them good-morrow. " Come, stand away ; let me rise. Patrick, take away the candle. Is there a good fire?—So—up a dazy." The day following was the queen's birthday, and such a hurry with it, so much fine clothes, and the court so crowded that he did not go there. Then the frost suddenly disappeared. It thawed on Sunday and so continued, though ice was still on the canal (not Laracor, but St. James's Park), and boys sliding on it. . . . But when was he to answer MD's tenth?—why, one of these odd-cum-shortlies. Next day, when he and Ford dined with Lewis, they had a monstrous deal of snow again, and, besides walking till he was dirty, it cost him two shillings in chair and coach.

" Friend "
Patrick.

And so, thaws notwithstanding, the trying cold continues, and through the greater part of his last February letter to beyond the middle of the month his entries repeat still the same story—that it had rained all day and was now ugly weather: rain, rain, mixed with little short frosts: terrible rain sometimes, followed by terrible snow, and then fine; and so up to the 22d, when it snowed prodigiously, and was some inches thick in three or four hours. Then next day the snow was gone every bit, but remains " of great balls made by boys;" and it ended with fine sunshiny frost and

Letters
XIV.-XVI.
Jan. 16,
Feb. 24.
cold. All which cost him shillings in coach hire (they were not to call them thirteens), and he had an accident in a chair. The chairmen that were carrying him to dinner at Lewis's squeezed a great fellow against a wall, who wisely turned his back, and broke one of the side-glasses in a thousand pieces. " I fell a-scolding, pretended I was like to be cut in pieces, and made them set down the chair in the park while they picked out the bits of glasses: and when I paid them I quarreled still, so they dared not grumble, and I came off for my fare: but I was plaguy afraid they would have said, 'God bless your honor, won't you give us something for our glass?'"

CHANGE AT LAST.

At last, however, there had come a real change, and Swift notes the days as being fine and long, and he tells them of his walking as·much as he can for his little disorders toward giddiness (for he has no actual fits); and how Lady Kerry is the same, only far worse; and how, on the·first morning of Lent, Lord Shelburne, Lady Kerry, Mr. Pratt, and he went to Hyde Park instead of church, to which, till his head was settled, he thought it better not to go. It would be so silly and troublesome to go out sick. The following day, too, he walked purely about the park, and being pressed to go with Leigh and Sterne, whom he met, went with them to dine; but meeting a worthless Irish fellow, one H——, waiting to form one of the party, he refused to stay; then tried Harley's (whom he had hunted for at the Court of Requests in the morning), but he was dining out; and finally dined at Sir John Germaine's, finding Lady Betty just recovered of a miscarriage. Upon which he takes occasion to .describe his writing an inscription for Lord Berkeley's tomb; and reminds them of the
Young Lord
Berkeley
and his wife.
young rake, his son, the new earl, who married (as he has told them) the Duke of Richmond's daughter. They were coming to town, and he predicts they'll be parted in a year. "You ladies are brave, bold, venturesome folks; and this chit is but 17, and is ill-natured, covetous, vicious, and proud in extremes. And so get you gone to Stoyte to-morrow." He whispered something afterward about a project he had (with Lewis) to get £500 without obligation to any body, which was to be a secret till he saw his dearest MD. His head was still a little disordered before dinner, but he walked stoutly and took pills. Then he began to look for

letters from certain ladies that live at St. Mary's and are called in Letter XV. Feb. 1-10. a certain language our little MD: "no, stay;" he won't expect for six more days! that'll be three weeks; "ain't I reasonable?" But the weather vexes him still. The morrow proved to be such a terribly rainy day he could only dine with his neighbor Van, where Sir Andrew Fountaine dined too; for Sir Andrew, to whom he was so lately reading prayers, had now begun to sally out, having shipped off to the country his mother and sister. He still is doing his best for her friend Bernage. Colonel Masham and his wife's brother, Colonel Hill, were backing St. John in recommending Swift's suit to Duke of Argyle, and the duke was reported to have said that he only wished the favor asked by Doctor Swift ten times greater! But, anxious as he is to help her, he won't have her tell him stories; and when she attempts a parallel from Dublin to his description of the London storms, he is amusingly incredulous and intolerant. She tells him in one of her letters of a tremendously high wind in Dublin that had blown down their chimney and carried it next door, and he protests it to be quite incredible. Hurricane, forsooth! she was a pretending slut. There had been nothing extraordinary that way in London, and he'd rather there were not. . . . As for their chimney falling down, the Lord preserve them. He supposed they only meant a brick or two. That must be a damned lie of their chimney being carried to the next house with the wind; and they were not to put such things upon him, but keep a little to possibilities. ("My Lord Hertford would have been ashamed of such a stretch.") They should take care what company they conversed with, for when one got that faculty it was hard to break one's self of it.

WALKING FOR HEALTH'S SAKE.

The rain necessarily interfered with many of his ordinary en- Letter XVI. Feb. 10-24. joyments, but he tells her specially of one fine evening, when, after he and Fountaine had dined with the Vans, he walked with Prior in the park. Whenever, indeed, it was not raining, now the days were long enough, he betook himself to walking in the park after dinner; and he calls it a remedy strange in its uses. For Prior, who generally had a cough "which he calls only a cold," walked to make himself fat, and Swift to make himself lean; and so they walked the park together. And one of these evenings

Letter
XVI.
Feb. 10-24. Prior took him to the Smyrna coffee-house, where they saw four or five Irish parsons, very handsome, genteel fellows, having nothing to do in Ireland. But this is a busy time with him, as she will infer from his visits to ministers in much haste and at untimely hours, when he may not walk, but (as to my lord keeper's) must pay two shillings for coach-hire. Walk, however, he does whenever he can, for the sake of his head; and he goes to dine with Lord Shelburne, that he and Lady Kerry may "con ailments" together, "which makes us very fond of each other."

A COMFORT IN SICKNESS AND HEALTH.

Letter XV.
Feb. 1-10.
• While his head still troubles him, he tells her of a comfort he had received through Ford: two letters sent from the coffee-house, one from the Archbishop of Dublin, and the other from—who did she think the other was from?—well, he would tell them both, because they were friends: why, then, it was, 'faith, it was, from his own dear little MD, number ten. "Oh, but we'll not answer it now! No, noooooh, we'll keep it between the two sheets. Here it is, just under: oh, I lifted up the sheets, and saw it there: lie still, you shall not be answered yet, little letter; for I must go to bed, and take care of my head." He is continuing his care next morning, for he avoids going to church. But he felt so much the better for Lady Kerry's "bitter," that he went later, and dined with Addison at his lodgings. He had not seen him these three weeks; they were grown quite common acquaintance; yet what hadn't he done for his friend Steele? The last time he saw Harley, the minister had reproached him with having offered, for his pleasure, to be reconciled with Steele, who, nevertheless, never came to the appointment made. Harrison, whom Addison recommended to him, he had induced the secretary of state to promise to take care of; and he had so represented Addison himself to the ministry, that they thought and talked in his favor, though before they hated him. "Well, he is now in my debt, and there is an end; and I never had the least obligation to him, and there is another end."

OLD SCENES AND FRIENDS RECALLED.

Letter XVI.
Feb. 10-24. As he is about to shut up this letter, he can not resist the quaint personal talk, the whimsies and fancies that crowd his pages with jokes and mystifications about their friends, with touching remi-

niscences of pleasant days past in Ireland, and with hopes of some still to come. Snow once more was falling, which he declares to be a great mistake, when he is so terribly in need of good weather; but it clears, and he sees that he shall have his walk. So, being fine again, they were to get them gone to poor Mrs. Walls, who had had a hard time of it, but was now pretty well again. He was sorry it should be a girl, and pitied the poor archdeacon for looking so miserable when they told him, and asked how much it had cost Ppt to be gossip? They were to be sure and go, but not to stay out late, and catch cold, for he wanted to see them at night. At night, accordingly, he resumed, and told them how much he required good weather; and how plaguy busy he should be, he prettily says, if he were at Laracor now; cutting down willows, planting others, scouring his canal, and every kind of thing. Then comes what has already been partly used (*ante*, 198), but this one repetition will perhaps be forgiven. If Raymond goes over this summer, MD is to submit, and make them a visit, "that we may have another eel and trout fishing, and that Ppt may ride by and see Pdfr in his morning-gown in the garden, and so go up with Joe to the Hill of Bree, round by Scurlock's Town. O Lord! how I remember names! 'Faith, it gives me short sighs; therefore, no more of that, if you love me." Speculations on the arrival of her next letter are then taken up; and if it should come on that 23d, he did not mean to answer it, but only to say, Madam, I received, etc., and so, and so. But whether it appears or not, he will certainly post his next evening, as sure as they're alive, and they'll be so ashamed; for if he were to reckon like them, he'd say he was six letters before them—this being sixteen, and theirs ten; but he reckons theirs sent as eleven, and his received as fourteen. And it's fine, cold, sunshiny weather; and he wishes Ppt to walk in "your Stephen's Green" as he does in "our park." It's as good as our park, "but not so large." And, 'faith, this summer they and he would take a coach together, for sixpence, to the Green Well, the two walks, and thence all the way to Stoyte's. His hearty service to Goody Stoyte; and Catherine is to be sure and get the coffee ready, and remember all his injunctions. He hopes Mrs. Walls had good time. "How inconsistent I am! I can not imagine I was ever in love with her!" And so he prattles, and mystifies them. And, as his paper is closing, he doesn't care how or in what hand he writes. And the letter was just a fort-

Right margin note: LETTER XVI. Feb. 10-24.

night's journal. "Yes, and so it is, I am sure, says you, with your two eggs a penny. ' Lele, lele, lele. O Lord! I am saying there, there to myself in all our little keys." (A broken-off morsel of the " little language.") And talking of keys, he told her that the dog Patrick had just broken the key-general of the chest of drawers with six locks, and he had been " so plagued " to get a new one, besides his good two shillings! And still the tender talk interlaces itself all through his ordinary or extraordinary utterances. What were they that moment doing? Gaming and drinking, he supposed; fine young-lady diversions! Well, he wished for them Seville oranges from London, and for himself some Dublin wine! In London were the finest oranges, twopence apiece; and the basest wine, six shillings a bottle. But it was not of *that* wine they'd have half a hogshead when he got back to Ireland; and he'd treat MD at his table in an evening, oh hoa! and laugh at great ministers of state!

THE VANHOMRIGHS. (*Ante*, 243.)

I close with such notices as these last eight letters contain of Swift's visiting at Mrs. Vanhomrigh's. Though the time is brief, the visits are not infrequent, and will surprise the readers of Lord Campbell's *Lives of the Chancellors* who may happen to remember what is said in the memoir of Lord Cowper (v., 279): " In perusing the Journal to Stella, it is curious to observe that, in the minute and circumstantial accounts he gives of all his other visits, he studiously and systematically suppresses his visits to Mrs. Vanhomrigh, and his acquaintance with her daughter!" I was myself so surprised to read this, that I had the curiosity to count the number of mentions made of such visits throughout the journals, and I found that, besides allusions to her in which she is not expressly mentioned, Mrs. Vanhomrigh appears by name no less than seventy-three times. It can not be said that this was an error committed in haste, which the author had not the opportunity to correct; for my quotation is taken from the latest of many editions of a still popular book.

The first mention to be recorded here, is where he says he had closed an insipid day (14th November) by dining with Mrs. Van, just visiting the coffee-house; and coming gravely home. The 3d of December marks also a day when he had " no adventure," simply dining with Mrs. Van, and studying. Four or five days

later he dined again with her, having a request to prefer "to desire LETTERS
them to buy me a scarf, and Lady Abercorn is to buy me another, IX.-XVI.
Nov. 25 to
to see who does best; mine is all in rags." Again he dined with Feb. 24.
her on the 11th, having to "study" in the evening. And on the
19th he thought to have dined with one of the ministry, but he
had to "come down, proud stomach," for it rained, and Mrs. Van's
was nigh, and he took the opportunity of paying her for the scarf
she bought him, and then dined with her. Twice he and Fountaine dined with her in February, on Sir Andrew's recovery from
his bad illness; and when he discovers that by accident, after his
post-midnight revel with St. John, he had dropped four dinners
from his journals at the close of January, before he closes his
fourteenth letter he remembers these four dinners to be accounted
for thus: "Yesterday, at Mr. Stone's, in the city; on Sunday, at
Vanhomrigh's; Saturday, with Ford; and Friday, I think, at Vanhomrigh's." A more important reference is in a following letter.
Having printer's business on hand, he walked into the city with Feb. 2.
Ford; then to buy books at Bateman's, where he laid out twenty-
five shillings on a Strabo and an Aristophanes, mentiqning, incidentally, that he had now got books enough to make him another
shelf, and meant to have more, "or it shall cost me a fall;" and as
they came back, they drank a flask of right French wine at Ben
Tooke's chamber; and when he got home, he had a message, at
which the reader may pause and reflect a little. It was from Mrs.
Vanhomrigh, who sent him word that her eldest daughter was
taken suddenly very ill, and desired Swift would come and see
her. He went, and found it was a silly trick of Mrs. Armstrong,
Lady Lucy's sister, who, with Moll Stanhope, was visiting there.
"However, I rattled off the daughter." Raillery would, perhaps,
be the polite phrase for rattling. There is also after this a special
visit named to Mrs. Vanhomrigh's, on her daughter's birthday, the
14th of February, when he and Ford kept it by dining there, and
spending the evening drinking punch, which was their way of
beginning Lent. At last these frequent visitings begin to stir
curiosity a little over in Ireland, and in one of her letters I'pt remarks about the Vanhomrighs (of whom neither she nor himself
had known any thing while yet their home was in Dublin), that
they were not people "of consequence," were they? To this he
makes no immediate reply; though he mentions, upon his return
at night, his having dined that day with his neighbor Van, it being

LETTERS
IX.-XVI.
Nov. 25 to
Feb. 24.
such dismal weather he could not stir farther. But his next letter answers the question : " You say they are of no consequence.
Why, they keep as good female company as I do male. I see all
the drabs of quality at this end of the town with them. I saw
two Lady Bettys there this afternoon : the beauty of one, the
good breeding and nature of the other, and the wit of either,
would have made a fine woman." The one was Lady Betty
Butler, and the other Lady Betty Germaine.

II.

PUBLICATION OF THE LETTERS CONTAINING THE JOURNAL TO STELLA.

1710–1713.   Æt. 43–46.

1710–1713.
Æt. 43–46.
THE opening of the second section of my Fifth Book explains
in what way inquiry into the times and circumstances of the publication of the letters containing the Journal to Stella became a
necessary part of the illustration of Swift's life, and I now state
the results of the investigation given to it.

The first public allusion to them was in Mr. Deane Swift's
Essay (1755), where extracts are given from a collection of
" thirty-eight " of the early letters (the actual number was forty),
Mrs. White-
way and her
son-in-law.
which had been lent him by his mother-in-law, Mrs. Whiteway,
" who found them accidentally, about half a year ago, among a
parcel of papers given to her by the Doctor in the year 1738.
The rest of them, which are supposed to be about twice as many "
(they were only twenty-five), " are in all probability in the hands
of those who are in the possession of the Doctor's effects. But
Mr. Swift" (the writer), " although he had frequently solicited
the favor within these last three years, never could get a sight of
them ; notwithstanding that he himself was the person who saved
them from being utterly destroyed in the year 1741." At Mrs.
Johnson's death, the letters had gone back to Swift, who used
them for reference in his *Four Years*, his *Memoirs relating to that
Change which happened in Queen Anne's Ministry in the year* 1710,
and other writings on the queen's reign ; and the later letters had
probably been mislaid when the earlier were given to Mrs. Whiteway.   Mr. Deane Swift believed them to have passed into the

hands of the executors, with one of whom (Delany) he had a personal feud; but this did not prove to be so.   Doctor Lyon, who had charge of Swift's person in his last illness, had either received them as a special gift, or found them among the mass of papers of which he took possession at the death; and by him they were ultimately handed over to his friend, Mr. Thomas Wilkes, of Dublin.

1710-1713.
Æt. 43-46.
Doctor Lyon and Mr. Wilkes.

It was not until 1766, when eleven years had passed, that either collection was heard of again.   Hawkesworth then published, in continuation of his edition of the works issued ten years before, three volumes of letters, "from 1703 to 1740," describing them as "a present from the late Doctor Swift to Doctor Lyon, a clergyman of Ireland for whom he had a great regard," and as disposed of to the London book-sellers by Mr. Wilkes, who had obtained them from Doctor Lyon.   Among them were the twenty-five letters comprising the close of the Journal to Esther Johnson; of which Hawkesworth quite justly remarked, that "from them alone a better notion may be formed of Doctor Swift's manner and character than from all that has been written about him."   He was conscious, at the same time, that to have printed them required an apology, so very private was much contained in them, and the date still so recent.   "It may, however, be presumed," he says, "that the publication of letters is not condemned by the general voice, since a numerous subscription has been lately obtained for printing other parts of the Dean's epistolary correspondence by a relation, who professes the utmost veneration for his memory."   In this, he referred to an issue by subscription in the previous year (1765), from the publishing-house of Mr. Johnston, of Ludgate Hill, of two volumes of miscellaneous prose pieces, poems, and letters "collected and revised by Deane Swift, Esq., of Goodrich, in Herefordshire."

The later letters published first.

The fifty-one letters to Esther Johnson, completing the Journal, were, nevertheless, not part of that book; but Mr. Wilkes's example was not lost upon its editor, who in the following year placed in Mr. Johnston's hands a new series of as many letters, "from 1710 to 1742," as Wilkes had transferred to Hawkesworth.   These were similarly issued to subscribers, in three volumes, in 1768, and the most interesting of them were those that contained Swift's Journal, from its opening in 1710 to its entry of the 9th of February, 1711-'12.   Mr. Deane Swift had, however, treated

Publication of the earlier letters.

1710-1713.
ÆT. 43-46.

the text much less reverentially even than his predecessor; though Nichols mistakenly supposed* that what in the Hawkesworth book had been left in place of the "little language," which, though often ungainly, was better than entire suppression, indicated not alone negligent transcription, but an awkward eagerness to be "more polished" than the original. There can be no doubt, on the contrary, that of the two publications, Hawkesworth's had

Differences in the printing.

a far greater resemblance to the original, and was much less "polished," than Mr. Deane Swift's. There was in it no adoption of such words as Prestoor Stella, before either had been invented, and when neither could possibly have been used; but the correct Pdfr and Ppt were uniformly given. There are terrible omissions and mistakes in it, and the desire to retain the meaning, in abolishing the form, of the "little language" fails altogether; but though the folly of objecting to the language, because of its difficulty or uncouthness, was common to both editors, Hawkesworth really did attempt to deal with it, while Mr. Deane Swift shirked it altogether. Nor could Mr. Deane Swift, who had also before him the example of what Hawkesworth (or Wilkes) had done, even plead the excuse of its not having occurred to him that there might be a possible importance in retaining the most obscure allusions. A reference full of meaning, in the Journal of the 3d of November, 1710, illustrates Swift's fanciful liking for their very obscurity. "Methinks," he says, when he writes plain, he doesn't know how, but he and she cease to be alone, and all the world can see them, whereas "a bad scrawl is so snug, it looks like a PMD;" and this elicits the remark, by way of note, from Mr. Deane Swift, that "this cipher stands for Presto, Stella, and Dingley; as much as to say, it looks like us three, quite retired from all the rest of the world."† One might imagine, after this, that there ought to be some meaning in what, with much complacency, is thrown out

Editorial "trouble."

in another note, about the "infinite trouble" which "this 'little language' that passed current between Swift and Stella has occasioned in the revisal of these papers."‡ But, alas! there is no

---

* See Preface to second edition (1708), i., xlii. Or see first edition, ii., xxv.-vi.

† See Mr. Deane Swift's *Miscellanies and Letters*, iv., 78, published by Johnston, of Ludgate Hill.

‡ See Mr. Deane Swift's *Miscellanies and Letters*, iv., 113. As Charles Lamb said of the whitewasher of Shakspeare's bust, "Methinks I see him at his work, the trouble-tomb!"

trace of trouble except in the way of omission, which, from com- 1710-1713.
parison of his letters as printed with the originals of Hawkes- Æt. 43-46.
worth's, he evidently on all occasions ruthlessly resorted to. For
in this also the two editors contrast unfavorably, that any trace of Contrasts of
Mr. Deane Swift's originals, excepting only the first letter, is now editorship.
not discoverable; whereas all the letters printed by Hawkesworth
were deposited in the British Museum, and remain still accessible
there. In the dedication of the letters to Lord Temple, Mr. Wilkes
had stated that this course would be taken, and he kept his word.

Discovery of the fact some years ago enabled the present writer
to make careful collation of twenty-four of the last twenty-five
letters, and of a twenty-fifth (forming, strangely enough, the first
of the series, that which stands No. 54 having been unfortunately
lost); and hence the means now afforded of restoring the part of Original text
the Journal they comprise to the condition in which it was when partly re-
it left Swift's hands. My first intention was to have used in this stored.
place only so much of the corrected text as would exhibit the "little
language;" but, on reflection, it seemed desirable at once to print
all the restored passages, reserving such comment as they suggest
to the portion of the narrative into which they fall in point of
date. Much will be thereby submitted to the reader in which he
can not yet take interest, or find to be entirely intelligible; but
we are already in the thick of the incidents and interest of which
the earlier letters tell the story, and to bring now upon the scene
the Journal as it was actually written, though only in its later
portions, will in the end increase not the interest only, but the
intelligibility of every part of it. As it is, we have had great need
to know what the "little language" really was, and here it will be
found. It is accessible only in the restorations I am about to
make, in any form that makes distant approach to being complete
or continuous. "Do you know what," says Swift to his corre- How Swift
spondent, "when I am writing in our language, I make up my spoke the
mouth just as if I were speaking it. I caught myself at it just "little lan-
now." All may now catch him at it, observing the recovered pas- guage."
sages from the letters to Esther Johnson.

A word must be added to what has been said (ante, 307-8) on
the fanciful substitutes for names. The two collections of letters
were first brought together, and printed in proper sequence, under
the title they have borne ever since, in Sheridan's edition of 1784; Name of
but the name then given, as already remarked, never occurs in the Journal first
invented.

originals.   Combinations of letters, frequently hard to decipher, and often bearing manifestly more than one meaning, are used both as proper names and as terms of endearment, of greeting, or farewell.   As I have said, he is himself throughout Pdfr, sometimes Podefar and FR, or other fragments of what may be assumed to be Poor Dear Foolish Rogue.   She is Ppt, presumably Poppet, or Poor Pretty thing; but MD, My Dear, is also for the most part her designation, though it occasionally comprises Mrs. Dingley, who has the further designation of ME, Madam Elderly; D or DD, Dingley or Dear Dingley, standing only and always for her exclusively.   The letters for Farewell, FW, are for Foolish Wenches as well; and Lele, which means often both "Truly" and "Lazy," is also still more frequently used as a mere "There, there," though it seems to have, in addition, other meanings not always discoverable.   Any absolute certainty of translation is, indeed, not possible with several of these whimsical combinations, and in regard to some, the attempt will be best made as they occur.   The "little language" strictly is much more definable; being generally, as I have said, what a child might turn ordinary speech into, whether from imperfections of childish utterance or mere habit continued from childhood.   Every restored passage is preceded by the passage as printed, taken from the latest of Scott's editions. Some of the mere errors in deciphering or printing the MS. will be thought minute; but even the apparently most trifling of those retained, out of the very many it was not possible to include,* have a certain importance; and as far as possible all are italicised in my extracts from the printed version.   In those extracts, italics also indicate the perversions of the "little language" from the orignal text, and the substitutions for it of ordinary language.   The altered words, and the sentences replacing the "little language," are thus always marked in the extracts from Scott, and in the corresponding extracts from *Original MS.* the entire sentences, as well as single words dropped altogether from the print, will as invariably be found.   No italics are employed in the manuscript restorations; but in the Scott extracts note is made of some of the principal omissions afterward silently supplied.

---

* I have not even attempted here to correct the mispointing, though a | mere comma misplaced will often wholly alter the sense.

III.

UNPRINTED AND MISPRINTED JOURNALS.

CHESTER, SEPTEMBER 2D, 1710. *Scott*, ii., 7.

THE first man I met in Chester was Dr. Raymond. He and Mrs. Raymond were here about levying a fine, in order to have power to sell their estate. I got a full off my horse. . . . Let all who write to me inclose to Richard Steele, Esq., at his office at the Cockpit, *Many* near Whitehall. My Lord Mountjoy is now in the humor that we *omissions.* should begin our journey this afternoon, so that I have *stolen* here again to finish this letter. . . . You will send it her inclosed and sealed. God Almighty bless *you ;* and, for God's sake, be merry, and get *your* health. . . . If Mrs. Curry makes any difficulty about the lodgings, I will quit them. · The post is *just* come from London, and just going out, so I have only time to pray to God to bless *you*, etc.

CHESTER, SATURDAY, SEPTEMBER 2D, 1710. *Original MS.*

"The first man I met in Chester was Dr. Raymond. LETTER 1. He and Mrs. Raymond were come here about levying a *Addressed* fine, in order to have power to sell their estate. They *"To Mrs. Dingley at* have found every thing answer very well. They both *Mr. Curry's* desire to present their humble services to you. They do *house over against the* not think of Ireland till next year. I got a fall off my *Ram in* horse. . . . Let all who write to me inclose to Richard *Capel Street, Dublin, Ire-* Steele, Esq., at his office at the Cockpit, near Whitehall. *land."* But not MD. I will pay for their letters at St. James's *Indorsed by Swift "1st* coffee-house, that I may have them sooner. My Lord *MD received this Sept. 9.* Mountjoy is now in the humor that we should begin *—Letters to Ireland from* our journey this afternoon, so that I have stole here *Sept., 1710,* again to finish this letter. . . . You will send it her *began soon* inclosed and sealed, and have it ready so, in case she *after the change of* should send for it: otherwise keep it. I will say no *ministry.—* more till I hear whether I go to-day or no: if I do, the *Nothing in this."* letter is almost at an end. My coz Abigail is grown pro-digiously old. God Almighty bless poo dee richar MD: and for God's sake be merry, and get oo health. . . . If Mrs. Curry makes any difficulty about the lodgings, I will

1710-1713.
Æt. 43-46.

quit them; and pay her from July 9 last, and Mrs. Brent must write to Parvisol with orders accordingly. The post is come from London, and just going out, so I have only time to pray to God to bless poo richar* MD FW FW MD MD ME ME ME."

9TH FEBRUARY, 1711-'12. *Scott*, ii., 494.

... Nothing to *dear charming* MD, *you* would wonder. ... I dined to-day with Sir *Mathew* Dudley. ... We *can get* no packets from Holland. ... Another cold, *but* not very bad.

Original MS.

LETTER 41.

Addressed to "Mrs. Johnson at her lodging over against St. Mary's Church, Dublin, Ireland." Indorsed by her "Rec^d March 1," and by Swift "Letters from Pdfr. to MD."

"... Nothing to deerichar MD, oo would wonder. ... I dined to-day with Sir Mat Dudley. ... We can yet get no packets. ... Another cold, not very bad. Nite, Nite, MD."

10TH FEBRUARY, 1711-'12. *Scott*, ii., 495.

I saw Prince Eugene at court to-day very plain. He is plaguy yellow, and *literally* ugly besides. The court was very full, and people had their birthday clothes. (Omission.) I was to *have invited* five; but I only invited two, Lord Anglesey and Lord Carteret. Pshaw, I told *you but* yesterday.

Original MS.

"I saw Prince Eugene at court to-day very plain: he's plaguy yellow, and tolerably ugly besides. The court was very full, and people had their birthday clothes. I dined with the secretary to-day. I was to invite five; but I only invited two, Lord Anglesey and Lord Carteret. Pshaw! I told you this but yesterday. Nite dee MD."

11TH FEBRUARY, 1711-'12. *Scott*, ii., 496.

... It is so very late; but I must always be, late or early, MD's, etc. (Omission.)

Original MS.

"... 'Tis so very late; but I must always be oors dee MD late or early. Nite deelest sollahs, MD, Pdfr's MD."

---

* In the "poo dee richar," "poo richar," and such combinations, I can not find that the "ri" has any other meaning than to connect "poor dear charming," the "poor charming," and so on. Sometimes a "mi" takes the place of "ri," and may stand for "my charming," just as the editors thought "ri" added to "dee" might stand for "dearie."

1710-1713.
Æt. 43-46.
Letter 41.

12th February, 1711-'12.   *Scott*, ii., 496.
... three colds successively; I hope I shall have the fourth.   Three messengers *come* from ...   I shall know more.   (Omission.)

Original MS.

"... three colds successively; I hope I shall have the fourth. Euge, euge, euge.* Three messengers came from ...   I shall know more to-mollow. Nite dee MD."

13th February, 1711-'12.   *Scott*, ii., 497.

You *have not* troubled me much. ...   Pray have *you got your apron,
Mrs.* Ppt? ...   Go to bed. ...   *Night, dearest* MD.

Original MS.

"You han't troubled me much. Pray have oo got oor aplon, Maram Ppt? ...   Go to bed, Ppt. Nite deelest MD."

14th-16th February, 1711-'12.   *Scott*, ii., 498.

To-day I published the Fable of Midas. ...   I know not how it will *take;* but it passed wonderfully at our society ...   here is *a* six days' journal, and no nearer the bottom. I fear these journals are very dull. *Note my dullest lines.* 15 *Feb.* Busy till two *in the* after-noon. 16 *Feb.* *Night, dearest* MD.

Original MS.

"To-day I published the *Fable of Midas.* ...   I know not how it will sell. But it passed wonderfully at our Society ...   here is six days' Journal, and no nearer the bottom. I fear these journals are very dull. Nite my deelest lives. 15 *Feb.* Busy till two afternoon. 16 *Feb.* Nite dee logues."

17th February, 1711-'12.   *Scott*, ii., 500.

Sir Andrew Fountaine and I went and dined with Mrs. Vanhom-righ. I came home at six, and have been very busy till this minute, and it is past twelve, so I got into bed to write to MD. (Omissions.) We reckon the dauphin's death will *set* forward the peace a good deal.

Original MS.

"Sir Andrew Fountaine and I went and dined with Mrs. Van. I came home at six, and have been very busy till this minute, and it is past twelve, so I got into bed to write to MD MD, for we must always write to MD MD,

---

* Intended to express his cough.

1710–1713. MD awake or asleep. We reckon the dauphin's death will
Æt. 43–46. put forward the Peace a good deal. . . . Go to bed. Help
Letter 41. pdfr. Rove pdfr. MD MD. Nite darling rogues."

18TH FEBRUARY, 1711–'12. *Scott*, ii., 501.

Received a letter from *the* Bishop *of* Clogher. . . . I am not *near*
so keen about other people's affairs as Ppt used to reproach me
about. It was a judgment on me. Hearkee, idle dearees both, methinks I begin to want a *letter* from MD.

Original MS.

"Received a letter from Bishop Clogher. . . . I am
not now so keen about other people's affairs as saucy Ppt
used to reproach me about: it was a judgment on me.
Hearkee, idle dearees both, methinks I begin to want a
Rattle from MD. . . . Nite deelest MD."

19TH FEBRUARY, 1711–'12. *Scott*, ii., 501.

I told him of four lines I writ extempore with my pencil, on a
bit of paper in his house, while he lay wounded. . . . They were inscribed to Mr. Harley's physician thus:

Many omis-   "On Britain Europe's safety lies;
sions here.   Britain is lost, if Harley dies.
               Harley depends upon your skill:
               Think what you save, or what you kill."

He designs that the lords of the cabinet . . . should dine that day
with him [the anniversary of Guiscard's attempt]: however, he has
invited me *to dine*. I am not *yet* rid of my cold. . . .

Original MS.

"I told him of four lines I writ extempore with my
pencil on a bit of paper in his house, while he lay wounded. . . . Shall I tell them you? They were inscribed to Mr.
Harley's physicians. Thus: On Europe Britain's safety
lies; Britain is lost if Harley dies.* Harley depends upon
your skill: Think what you save, or what you kill. . . . Are
not they well enough to be done off-hand, for that is the
meaning of the word extempore; which you did not know,
did you? . . . He designs that the lords of the cabinet . . .
should dine that day with him [the anniversary of Guis-

* By an odd mischance Swift here | struction of his meaning. It will be
made the mistake of transposing Brit- | observed that the lines run on in his
ain and Europe in his line, to the de- | MS. as if prose.

card's attempt: "him" is written "them" by mistake] 1710-1713.
Æt. 43-46.
Letter 41.
however, he has invited me too. I am not got rid of my
cold. ... Nite, MD."

20TH FEBRUARY, 1711-'12.   *Scott,* ii., 502.

I have been *terribly* busy ... and I wanted some very necessary papers, which the secretary was to give me, and the pamphlet must *not be* published without them. ...

Original MS.

"I have been horribly busy ... and I wanted some very necessary papers which the Secretary was to give me, and the pamphlet must now be published without them. ... Nite DeeMD."

22D FEBRUARY, 1711-'12.   *Scott,* ii., 503.

I assure *you, it is very late now;* but this goes to-morrow: and I must have time to converse with *our little MD. Night, dear MD.*

Original MS.

"I assure oo it im vely rate now: but zis goes to-morrow, and I must have time to converse with own deerichar MD. Nite dee deer sollahs."

23D FEBRUARY, 1711-'12.   *Scott,* ii., 504.

I am going out, and must carry *this in my pocket* to give it at some general post-house. I will talk further with *you* at night. I suppose in my next I shall answer a letter from MD that will be sent me *on Tuesday.* On Tuesday it will be four weeks since I had your last. ... Farewell, MD. (Omissions.)

Original MS.

"I am going out; and must carry zis in my Pottick to give it at some general post-house. I will talk further with oo at night. I suppose in my next I shall answer a letter from MD that will be sent me. On Tuesday it will be four weeks since I had your last. ... Farewell, mine deelest rife deelest char Ppt, MD MD MD Ppt, FW, Lele MD, ME, ME, ME, ME aden, FW MD, Lazy ones, Lele, Lele, all a Lele."

23D-24TH FEBRUARY, 1711-'12.   *Scott,* ii., 504.

LETTER 42.
Addressed
"To Mrs.
Johnson at

After having *disposed* my last letter in the post-office. ... But what care *you* for all this? ... *Night, dearest rogues.* 24 *Feb.* I have writ much for several days *past:* but I will amend. ...

1710-1713.
Æt. 43-46.
her lodging
over against
St. Mary's
Church, near
Capel Street,
Dublin, Ire-
land."

Original MS.

"After having disponed my last letter in the post-office. . . . But what care oo for all this. . . . Nite deelest logues. 24 *Feb.* I have writ much for several days together, but I will amend."

24TH FEBRUARY, 1711-'12.   *Scott*, ii., 505.

But *pray let us know a little of your life and conversation.* Do you play at ombre, or visit the dean, and Goody Walls and Stoytes and Manleys, as usual? I must have a letter from *you.* . . . This is sad *stuff to write; so night,* MD.

Original MS.

"But pay, deerichar MD, ret us know a little of oor life and tonvelsasens. Do you play at Ombre, or visit the Dean, and Goody Walls's and Stoyte's and Manley's, as usual? I must have a letter from oo. . . . This is sad stuft to rite: so Nite MD."

25TH FEBRUARY, 1711-'12.   *Scott*, ii., 506.

There *was* half a dozen ladies riding: . . . then I went to visit Perceval and his family, whom I had seen but *once* since they came to town. They *are going to Bath* next month. My third cold . . . did I tell you, that I believe it is Lady Masham's hot rooms that *give* it me? I never knew such a stove. . . . *Night dear MD.*

Original MS.

"There were half a dozen ladies riding. . . . Then I went to visit Perceval and his family, whom I had seen but twice since they came to town. They too are going to the Bath next month. . . . My third cold . . . did I tell you that I believe it is Lady Masham's hot room that gives it me? I never knew such a stove. . . . Nite deelogues."

26TH FEBRUARY, 1711-'12.   *Scott*, ii., 507.

I was again busy with the secretary. (Omissions.) We read over some papers, and did a good deal of business. I dined with him.

Original MS.

"I was again busy with the Secretary, giving help promised, iss oo Ppt, and we read over some papers, and did a good deal of business; and I dined with him."

1710-1713.
Æt. 43-46.
Letter 42.

27TH FEBRUARY, 1711-'12. *Scott*, ii., 509.

It is pretty late now, *young women ;* so I bid *you night, own dear, dear little rogues.*

Original MS.

" 'Tis pretty late now, ung oomens, so I bid oo nite own dee dallers."

28TH FEBRUARY–1ST MARCH, 1711-'12. *Scott*, ii., 508.

I have been packing up some books in a great box. . . . This is a beginning toward a removal. I have sent to Holland for a dozen shirts, and design to buy another new gown and hat. I will come over like a Zinkerman.*. . . *29th Feb.* The court may want a majority *at* a pinch. *Night, dear little rogues.* Love Pdfr. *1st March.* I went into the city to inquire after poor Stratford, who has put himself a prisoner into the Queen's Bench, for which his friends blame him *very* much, because his creditors designed to be very easy with him. He grasped at too many things together. . . . I gave him notice of a treaty of peace, while it was a secret, of which he might have made good use, but that helped to ruin him ; for he gave money, reckoning there would be actually a peace *for* this time, and consequently stocks rise high. Ford narrowly escaped losing £500 by him, and so did I too. *Night,* my two *dearest* lives MD.

Original MS.

" I have been packing up some books in a great box. . . . This is a beginning—towards a removal. I have sent to Holland for a dozen shirts, and design to buy another new gown and hat. I'll come over like a zinkerman. . . . 29 *Feb.* And the Court may want a majority upon a pinch. Nite deelest logues. Rove Pdfr. 1 *March.* I went into the city to inquire after poor Stratford, who has put himself a prisoner into the Queen's Bench, for which his friends blame him much, because his creditors designed to be very easy with him. He graspt at too many things together. . . . I gave him notice of a Treaty of Peace, while it was a secret, of which he might have made good use, but that helpt to ruin him. For he gave money, reckoning there would be actually a Peace by this time, and consequently stocks rise high. Ford narrowly 'scapt losing £500 by him, and so did I too. Nite my two deelest lives MD."

* The editors supposed Zinkerman (which they printed in capitals) to mean some outlandish or foreign dis-tinction ; but it is the "little language" for "gentleman."

1710-1713.
ÆT. 43-46.
Letter 42.

3D MARCH, 1711-'12.   *Scott*, ii., 511.

Pray tell Walls that I spoke to the Duke of Ormond . . . about his salary from the government for the tithes of the park, that lie in his parish, to be put upon the establishment. (Omissions.) I dined in the city with my printer, with whom I had some small affair. I have no large work on my hands now. I was with lord treasurer this morning, and *what care you for that?* You dined with the dean to-day. Monday is parson's holiday. *And you lost your money* at cards and dice; *the giver's device.* So I'll go to bed. *Night,* my two *dearest little rogues.*

Original MS.

"Pray tell Walls that I spoke to the Duke of Ormond . . . about his salary from the government for the tithes of the park that lie in his parish, to be put upon the establishment; but oo must not know zees sings, zey are secrets; and we must keep them flom nauty dallars. I dined in the city . . . with my printer, with whom I had some small affair: but I have no large work on my hands now. I was with Lord-Treasurer this morning, and hat care oo for zat: oo dined with the Dean to-day. Monday is Parson's holiday, and oo lost oo money at cards and dice, ze Givör's* device. So I'll go to bed. Nite my two dee litt logues."

6TH MARCH, 1711-'12.   *Scott*, ii., 514.

Society's
dinners.

Lord Orrery is to be president next week; and I will see whether it [dinner] can not be cheaper; or else we will leave the house. (Omission.) Lord Masham made me go home with him to-night to eat boiled oysters. Take oysters, wash them clean; that is, wash their shells clean; then put *your* oysters *in* an earthen pot, with their hollow sides down, then put this pot *covered* into a great kettle with water, and so let them boil. *Your* oysters are boiled in their own liquor, and† not *mix* water.

Original MS.

"Lord Orrery is to be president next week; and I'll see whether it [dinner] can not be cheaper; or else we will

---

* The word in Swift's MS. is certainly Givör, but I can not explain it other than by supposing it to mean that Evil One, who, as he elsewhere said, is more than usually busy on parsons' holidays.

† This not being intelligible to the editors, they correct in a note, "*and* should be *do*;" but Swift wrote quite intelligibly. I may add that in the entry of the 4th he mentions having nothing on his hands to write, and says it is a great comfort to him "now that" he can come home and read; but commas are thrust between the words so as really to alter their sense.

leave the house. Pidy pdfr, declest sollahs. Lord Masham 1710-1713. Æt. 43-46. Letter 42.
made me go home with him to-night to eat boiled oysters.
Take oysters; wash them clean; that is, wash their shells
clean; then put the oysters into an earthen pot, with their
hollow sides down; then put this pot into a great kettle
with water, and so let them boil. The oysters are boiled
in their own liquor, and not mixt water."

8th March, 1711-'12.   *Scott*, ii., 515.

Pray read the Representation; it is the finest that ever was writ.—
Some of it is Pdfr's style; but not *very* much. . . . I must go this
moment to see the secretary, about some *business;* so I will seal up
this, and put it in the post. (Omissions.) Farewell, *dearest* hearts
and souls, MD.

Original MS.

" Pray read the Representation. 'Tis the finest that
ever was writ. Some of it is Pdfr's style; but not vely
much. . . . I must go this moment to see the Secretary
about some businesses. So I will seal up this, and put it
in the post my own self. Farewell, declest hearts and
souls MD. Farewell, MD MD MD, FW FW FW, ME
ME, Lele Lele Lele, Sollahs, Lele."

8th-10th March, 1711-'12.   *Scott*, iii., 3-9.

What Joe asks is entirely out of my way. . . . I know not who is Letter 43.
to give a patent; if the Duke of Ormond, I would speak to him
(omission), but good security is all. . . . Did I tell you of a race of Addressed "Mrs. John-son at her lodgings over against St. Mary's Church, near Capel Street, Dublin, Ire-land;" and Indorsed "October, 1711. 43. Mar. 30."
rakes, called the Mohocks, that . . . slit people's noses, and *bid* them,
etc. *Night, sirrahs, and love* Pdfr. Night, MD. 9 *March.* . . . So I
dined with Mrs. Van*homrigh*. . . . Lord-treasurer is better. *Night,
my own two dearest* MD. 10 *March*. It is now six weeks since I had
your number 26. I can assure *you* I expect one before this goes, and
I will make shorter days' journals than usual, 'cause I hope to fill up
a good deal of *this* side with my answer. . . . We shall have rain
soon, I *suppose.* Go to cards, *sirrahs, and I to sleep.* Night, MD.

Original MS.

" What Joe asks is entirely out of my way. . . . I know
not who is to give a patent; if the Duke of Ormond, I
would speak to him; and if it comes in my head I will
mention it to Ned Southwell. They have no Patent that
I know of in such things here; but good security is all. . . .
Did I tell you of a race of rakes, called the Mohocks, that
. . . slit people's noses, and beat them &c. Nite Sollahs,

Vol. I.—28

1710–1713.
Æt. 43–46.
Letter 43.
and rove Pdfr. Nite MD. 9 *March*. So I dined with Mrs. Van. . . . Lord Treasurer is better. Nite, my own two delights, MD. 10 *March*. 'Tis now six weeks since I had number 26. I can assure oo I expect one before this goes; and I'll make shorter days journals than usual 'cause I hope to fill up a good deal of t'other side with my answer. . . . We shall have rain soon, I dispose. Go to cards, sollahs, and I to seep. Nite MD."

11TH–12TH MARCH, 1711–'12.   *Scott*, iii., 6.

Lord treasurer has lent the long letter I writ . . . and I can't get Prior to return *it*. *I* want to have it printed, and to make up this Academy for the improvement of our language. 'Faith, we never shall improve it so much as FW has done; *shall we?* No, 'faith, *our richer Gengridge. So night, my two dear little MD.* 12 *March*. Here is a young fellow has writ some Sea Eclogues, Poems of Mermen, resembling pastorals *and* shepherds. . . . *Night, dearest* MD.

.   *Original MS.*

"Charming language." "Lord Treasurer has lent the long letter I writ . . . and I can't get Prior to return it; and I want to have it printed, and to make up this academy for the improvement of our language. 'Faith, we never shall improve it so much as FW has done; sall we? No, 'faith, oor is char gangridge! So nite my two deelest nauty nown-MD. 12 *March*. Here is a young fellow has writ some Sea Eclogues, Poems of Mermen, resembling pastorals of shepherds. . . . Nite dee litt MD."

13TH–14TH MARCH, 1711–'12.   *Scott*, iii., 9.

The nights are now dark, and I *came* home before ten. *Night, my dearest sirrahs.* 14 *March*. He has argued with me so long upon the reasonableness of it, *and* I am fully convinced it is very unreasonable.

Original MS.

"The nights are now dark, and I come home before ten. Nite, nown deelest sollahs. 14 *March*. He has argued with me so long upon the reasonableness of it, that I am fully convinced it is very unreasonable."

15TH–16TH MARCH, 1711–'12.   *Scott*, iii., 10.

I heard at dinner, that one of them [the Mohocks] was killed last night. We shall know more in a little time. I *do not* like them *as* *to men.* (Omission.) 16 *March.* Lord Winchilsea told me to-day at court, that two of the Mohocks caught a maid of old Lady Winchilsea's, *at* the door of their house in the park, *with* a candle, and had just lighted out somebody. They *cut all* her face, and beat her without any provocation. . . . *How shall* I have room to answer *your letter when I get it, I have* gone so far already? *Night, dearest rogues,* 18 *March. Young women,* it is now seven weeks since I received *your* last; but I expect one *next packet* . . . so I wish *you* good luck at ombre with the dean. *Night.**

1710–1713.
Æt. 43–46.
Letter 43.

Original MS.

" I heard at dinner that one of them [the Mohocks] was killed last night. We shall know more in a little time. I don't like them. But the more I lite MD. 16 *March.* Lord Winchilsea told me to-day at court, that two of the Mohocks caught a maid of old Lady Winchilsea's just at the door of their house in the park, where she was with a candle, and had just lighted out somebody. They all cut her face, and beat her without any provocation. . . . How sall I have room to answer oo Rattle hen I get it? I am gone so far already. Night, deelest logues MD. 18 *March.* Ung oomens, it is now seven weeks since I received oor last; but I expect one next Irish packet. . . . So I wish uu good luck at ombre with the dean. Nite nautyes nine."

19TH–20TH MARCH, 1711–'12. *Scott,* iii., 13.

. . . it cost me above a crown. I don't like it, as *my* man said. . . . It is a great *stir* this, of getting a dukedom from the king of France. . . . *Night, dearest little* MD. 20 *March.* Some will do, and some will not do: *that's wise, mistresses.* . . . I made our society change their house, and we met *together* at the Star and Garter in the Pall Mall . . . when all have been presidents this *turn.* . . . *Night, dearest.*

Original MS.

" . . . it cost me above a crown. I don't like it, as the man said. . . . 'Tis a great air, this of getting a Dukedom from the King of France.† . . . Nite deelest michar MD. 20 *March.* Some will do, and some will not do. That's ise, maram. . . . I made our Society change their house,

---

* In this entry there is mention of Mrs. Perceval's "young" daughter having the small-pox, which is misprinted "youngest."

† Lord Abercorn had asked Swift to "get him the dukedom of Chatellerault from the King of France."— See a note by Scott, iii., 13–14.

and we met to-day at the Star and Garter in the Pall
Mall ... when all have been presidents this time. ...
Nite, deelest, nite."

21st March, 1711-'12. *Scott, iii., 15.*

Now I will answer MD's *letter*, N. 27; you that are adding to your
numbers and grumbling, had made it 26, and then *altered* it to 27. ...
O, the sorry jades, with their excuses of a fortnight at Baligall, seeing their friends, and landlord running away. *O what a trouble and
a bustle! Beg your pardon, mistress: I am glad you like the apron:*
no harm, I hope. And *so MD* wonders she has not a letter all the
day; *she will have it soon.* ... The deuce he is! ... You may converse with those two nymphs if you please, but — take me if ever
I do. *Yes, 'faith, it is delightful* to hear that Ppt is every way Ppt
now. ... The session, I doubt, will not be over *till the* end of
April. ... I wish I were just now in my *little* garden at Laracor. ...
Hold *your* tongue, *you* ppt, about colds at Moor Park! the case is
quite different. ... *Good morrow, little sirrahs.* ... Lady Masham's
young son is very ill, and she is *sick* with grief. Night, my own two
dearest saucy dear ones.

Original MS.

"Now I will answer MD's Rattle, No. 27. You that
are adding to your number and grumbling, had made it
26, and then cobbled it to 27*. ... O, the sorry zade, with
her excuses of a fortnight at Baligall seeing their friends,
and landlord running away. ... O Rold, hot a cruttle and
a bustle! ... Bed ee paadon Maram; I'm drad oo rike so
aplon; no harm, I hope. And so maram MD wonders she
has not a letter at the day; ow'll have it soon, mum. ...
The D— he is. ...† You may converse with those two
nymphs if you please, but the d— take me if ever I do.
Iss, 'faith, it is delighttull to hear that Ppt is every way Ppt
now. ... I doubt the Session will not be over till towards
the end of April. ... I wish I were just now in my garden

---

* In the same entry as to letters
under and overdue, Swift says he
"ought to consider that this was
twelve days right," to which he puts
himself a marginal note to say he
means "writing;" which the editors
print thus, "I ought to consider that
this was twelve days right, writing!"
  † The exclamation relates to Dilly
Ashe's marriage; after which he hints

at a friend of hers, Enoch Sterne
(printed simply "Sterne," as if it
might be the dean), not being very
well-behaved as to women, and that
it may cost his wife (I quote Scott's
text) "a — (I don't like to write
that word plain)." *Like* should be
care, and the word is written plain
enough.

at Laracor.   Hold oor tongue, oo Ppt, about colds at Moor   1710-1713.
Park!   The case is quite different. . . .   Dood mollaws   Æt. 43-46.
michar sollahs. . . .   Lady Masham's young son is very ill,   Letter 48.
and she is out of mind with grief.   Nite, my own two
deelest sawcy dee lit ones."

22D-23D MARCH, 1711-'12.   *Scott,* iii., 18.

I will immediately seal up this, and keep it in my *pocket* till evening, and *then put it in the post.* . . .   Pray send (blank) that I may
have time to write to (blank) about it. . . .   Farewell, *dearest dear* MD,
and *love* Pdfr dearly.   Farewell MD MD MD &c. *there, there, there,
there, there, and there, and there again.* . . .   So *you* know it is late
now. . . .   Night, my *dearest* MD.*   23 *March.* The court serves me for
a coffee-house; once a week I meet *an* acquaintance there, that I
should not otherwise see in a quarter. . . .   Can DD play at ombre
yet, enough to *hold* the cards while Ppt steps into *the* next room?
Night, *dearest sirrahs.*

Original MS.

" I will immediately seal up this, and keep it in my pot-
tick till evening, and zen put it in ze post. . . .   Pray send
Pdfr the ME account that I may have time to write to
Parvisol about it. . . .   Farewell deelest deel MD, and rove
Pdfr dearly dearly.   Farewell MD MD FW FW FW ME
ME ME Lele Lele Lele   Lele Lele and Lele   and Lele
aden.

" So oo know 'tis late now. . . .   Night, my own two
deelest nautyes MD.   23 *March.* The court serves me for
a coffee-house: once a week I meet acquaintance there,
that I should not otherwise see in a quarter. . . .   Can DD
play at ombre yet?   Enough to hode the cards while Ppt
steps into next room?   Night, deelest sollahs."

26TH-27TH MARCH, 1712.   *Scott,* iii., 21.

Our Mohocks . . . cut people's faces every night, *but* they shan't
cut mine. . . .   27 *March.* Society day, you *know; that's* I suppose.
Dr. Arbuthnott was president. . . .   *It is late, sirrahs.   I am not drunk.*
Night, MD.

Original MS.

" Our Mohocks . . . cut people's faces every night. 'Faith,
they shan't cut mine. . . .   Nite MD.   27 *March.* Society

---

* These words follow a passage | stead of " them," but not necessary to
turned into nonsense by " him " in- | be given.

1710-1713. Day. You know that, I suppose. Dr. Arthburnott* was
Æt. 43-46. president.... 'Tis rate, sollahs; I an't dlunk. Nite MD."

28th March-8th April, 1712. *Scott*, iii., 22.

Letter 44.   ... Routing among my papers. ... (Omission.) Domville is going
———   to Ireland. ... 29 *March*. I'll try to go to *sleep*. ... I'll *write* no
Addressed   more now, but go to sleep, and see whether *flannel and sleep* will cure
"To Mrs.   my shoulder. *Night dearest* MD.. 30 *March*. I was not able to go to
Rebecca   church or court to day (omission). ... It makes me think of *poor*
Dingley, at   Ppt's bladebone. ... It has rained terribly *hard* all day. ... 31
her lodgings
over against   *March* to 8 *April.* (Illness.) The spots increased every day, and *red*
St. Mary's   little pimples. ... I have been in no danger of life, but miserable
Church, near   torture. (Omission.) So adieu, *dearest MD, FW, &c. There, I can*
Capel Street,
Dublin, Ire-   *say there yet, you see.* Faith, I don't conceal a bit, as hope saved. ...
land." In-   *Are you not* surprised to see a letter want half **ɩ** side ?
dorsed by
Mrs. John-
son, "44.
April 14."   *Original MS.*

"... Routing among my papers. I have a pain these
two days exactly upon the top of my left shoulder. I fear
it is something rheumatick. It winches now and then.
Shall I put Flannel to it ? ... Domville is going to Ireland.... Nite MD. 29 *March*. I'll try to go seep. I'll
rike no more now, but go to sleep, and see whether sleep
or flannel will cure my shoulder. Nite deelest MD. 30
March. I was not able to go to church or court to-day, for
my shoulder. ... It makes me think of poo Ppt's bladebone. ... It has rained terribly all day.... Nite deelest.
31 *March* to 8 *April.* (Illness.) The spots increased every
day, and bred little pimples.... I have been in no danger
of life, but miserable torture. I must not write too much.
So adieu, deelest MD MD MD FW FW ME ME ME!
Lele—I can say Lele yet oo see—'Faith, I don't conceal a
bit, as hope saved. ... An't oo surprised to see a letter
want half a side ?"†

24th April, 1712. *Scott*, iii., 25.

Letter 45.   'Tis this day just a month since I felt *the pain*. ... I advised the
doctor to *use* it like a blister ... went out a day or two, but confined

---

* So Swift first spells the name of
one of his dearest friends.
† The last words are added in the

folding of the third page of the letter.
The entry preceding is in a very weak
and tremulous hand.

myself two days ago. I went to a neighbor to dine, but yesterday   1710–1713.
again kept at home.   To-day I will venture abroad, and hope to be   Æt. 43–46.
well in.a week. (Omissions.)   Farewell, MD &c.
                                                                      Letter 45.

Original MS.

" 'Tis this day just a month since I felt a small pain. . . .
I advised the doctor to raise it like a blister . . . went out a
day or two; but confined myself again. Two days ago, I
went to a neighbor to dine; but yesterday again kept at
home. To-day I will venture abroad a little, and hope to
be woll in a week. . . .   Farewell, MD MD MD ME ME
ME FW FW ME, ME."*

10TH MAY, 1712.   *Scott*, iii., 26.

No, *simpleton :* it is not a sign of health . . . she [his sister] has been   LETTER 46.
once since I recovered. . . .   This is a long letter for a *sick* body. . . .
He tells *me* Elwick has. . . .   Ppt does not say one word of her own
little health. I am angry almost; but I won't, *because she is a good
girl in other things. Yes, and so is DD too.* God bless MD, and FW,
and ME, *and* Pdfr too. Farewell MD, MD, MD, Lelc. I can say Lele
yet, young women ; yes I can, well as you.   ·

Original MS.

" No, sinkerton, 'tis not a sign of health. . . .   She [his
sister] has been once here since I recovered. . . .   This is a
long letter for a hick body. . . .   He tells me one Elwick
has . . .   Ppt does not say one word of her own little
health. I'm angry almost; but I won't: 'sause see im a
dood dallar in odle sings. Iss, and so im DD too. God
bless MD and FW and ME, ay and Pdfr too. Farewell
MD MD MD FW FW FW ME ME ME.
" Lelc. I can say Lele—It, ung oomens, iss I tan, well
as oo."†

---

* This letter 45 is very brief; so   † This letter 46, though longer
altered in the writing by illness as   than the last, is as languidly and
hardly to be recognizable for his;   tremulously written ; but is ad-
and is addressed, in another hand,   dressed by Swift "To Mrs. Ding-
"To Mrs. Johnson, at her lodgings   ley, at her lodgings," etc. Mrs.
over against St. Mary's Church, near   Johnson's indorsement is "46, May
Capel Street, Dublin, Ireland." It   15."
has indorsement by Mrs. Johnson,
"45, May 1."

1710-1713.
Æt. 43-46.
Letter 47.

Addressed
to "Mrs.
Dingley,"
with Mrs.
Johnson's
indorse-
ment: "47,
June 5."

31st May, 1712.   *Scott*, iii., 29.

I never wished as much as now, that I had staid in Ireland; but the die is cast, and is now a spinning, and till it settles, I can not tell whether it be an ace or a size.   (Omission.)   The moment I am used ill, I will leave them . . . but I will take MD in my way, and not go to Laracor like an unmannerly *spreenckish fellow*. . . .   I will give you a note for it on Parvisol, and *beg your pardon* I have not done it before . . . so I *hear*. . . .   I'll say no more to *you to-night, sirrahs, because* I must send away the letter, not by *the* bell, but early; and besides, I have not much more to say at *this present writing*.   Does MD never read at all now, *pray?*   But *you walk prodigiously, I suppose — You* make nothing of walking to, to, to, ay, to Donnybrook.   I walk *as* much as I can. . . .   I suppose I shall have no apples this year neither. *So* I dined the other day with Lord Rivers, who is sick at his country house, and he showed me all his cherries blasted. . . .   Night, *dearest sirrahs;* farewell, *dearest lives, love poor pdfr*.   Farewell, *dearest little* MD, MD, MD, FW, FW, FW, ME, ME, Lele, ME, Lele, Lele, *little* MD.

Original MS.

"I never wished as much as now that I had staid in Ireland; but the die is cast, and is now a spinning, and till it settles, I can not tell whether it be an acé or a sise. I am confident by what you know yourselves, that you will justify me in all this.   The moment I am used ill, I will leave them . . . but I will take MD in my way, and not go to Laracor* like an unmannerly spreemikich† farrow." . . .   I will give you a note for it on Parvisol, and bed a paadón I have not done it before. . . .   So I heecar. . . . I'll say no more to oo tonite, sollahs, 'sause I must send away the letter, not by bell, but early: and besides, I have not much more to say at zis plesent liting.   Does MD never read at all now, pee?   But oo walk plodigiousry, I dispose—oo make nothing of walking to, to, to, ay, to Donnybrook.   I walk too as much as I can. . . .   I suppose I shall have no apples this year neither.   For I dined t'other day with Lord Rivers, who is sick at his country house, and he showed me all his cherries blasted. . . .   Night, declest sollahs; farewell declest rives; rove poo poo Pdfr. Farewell declest michar MD MD MD, FW FW FW FW FW.   ME ME.   Lele ME, Lele lele michar MD."

---

* As she formerly reproached him for having done.

† Spreemikich is for splenetic;—

"spreenckish," in the print, does not represent it at all.

17TH JUNE, 1712. *Scott*, iii., 32.

I feel [still in the shoulder] *violent* pain. . . . I dined with the Duchess of Ormond at her Lodge near Sheen, and thought to get a *boat as* usual. I walked by the bank to Kew, but no boat, then to Mortlake, but no boat, and it was nine o'clock. At last a little sculler called, full of nasty people.

Original MS.

"I feel [still in the shoulder] constant pain. . . . I dined with the Duchess of Ormond at her lodge near Sheen, and thought to get a boat back as usual. I walked by the banks to Cue,* but no boat; then to Mortlack,* but no boat; and it was nine o'clock. At last a little sculler called, full of nasty people."

1710-1713.
Æt. 43-46.
LETTER 46.
Addressed
to "Mrs.
Rebecca
Dingley,"
with indorse-
ment by Mrs.
Johnson,
"48. June
23."

17TH JUNE, 1712. *Scott*, iii., 33.

And first. I did not relapse, but *I came* out before I ought. . . . The first *coming* abroad, the *first going abroad*, made people think I was quite recovered. . . . Well, but John Bull is not *wrote* by the person you imagine. (Omission.) It is too good for another to own. Had it been Grub Street, I would have let people think as they please; and I think that's right: is not it now? so flap *your* hand, and make wry mouths *yourself*, saucy doxy. Now comes DD. Why *sirrahs*, I did write in a fortnight. . . . I need not tell *you* why. . . . So Ppt designs for Templeoag (what a name is that!). Whereabouts is that place? I hope not very far from (blank). Higgins is here. . . . I *can not be* the least bit in love with Mrs. Walls—I suppose the cares of the husband increase with the fruitfulness of the wife. I am *glad at heart* to hear of Ppt's good health : *please to* let her finish by drinking waters. I hope DD had her bill, and has her money. Remember to write a due time before *the* money is wanted, and be good *girls, good* dallars, I mean, and no crying dallars. . . . So, now *your* letter. . . . You see I can answer. . . . Well, but now for the peace : why we expect it daily; but the French have the *stuff* in their own hands. . . . I think Ppt should walk *to* DD, as DD reads to Ppt, for Ppt *you* must know is a good walker; but not so good as Pdfr. . . . Farewell, dearest MD, FW, ME, &c. (Omissions.)

Original MS.

"And first, I did not relapse, but found I came out before I ought. . . . The first coming abroad made people think I was quite recovered. . . . Well, but John Bull is not writt by the person you imagine, as hope —— It is too good for another to own. Had it been Grub Street, I would have let people think as they please; and I think

"As hope"
for "as I
hope to be
saved."

---

* So spelled by Swift.

1710-1713.
Æt. 43–46.
Letter 48.

that's right: is not it now? So flap ee hand, and make wry mouth ooself, saucy doxy. . . . Now comes DD. Why sollah, I did write in a fortnight. . . . I need not tell ee why. . . . So Ppt designs for Templeoag (what a name is that!)—whereabouts is that place? I hope not very far from Dublin. Higgins is here. . . . I am not the least bit in love with Mrs. Walls. I suppose the cares of the husband increase with the fruitfulness of the wife. I am grad at halt to hear of Ppt's good health: pray let her finish it by drinking waters. I hope DD had her bill, and has her money. Remember to write a due time before ME money is wanted, and be good galls, dood dallars I mean, and no crying dallars. . . . So, now oor letter. . . . You see I can answer you. . . . Well, but now for the Peace. Why, we expect it daily; but the French have the staff in their own hands. . . . I think Ppt should walk for DD, as DD reads to Ppt. For Ppt, oo must know, is a good walker; but not so good as Pdfr. . . . Farewell, deelest lole, deelest MD MD MD—MD MD—FW FW FW—ME ME Lele me Lele me Lele me Lele Lele Lele me."

1st July, 1712.   *Scott*, iii., 86.

Letter 49.
Addressed to Mrs. Dingley. Indorsed by Mrs. Johnson, "49. July 8."

I never was in a worse station for writing letters than this [Kensington], (omission) for I go to town early. Mrs. Bradley's youngest son is *to marry* somebody worth nothing. . . . Mr. Secretary will not take the title of *Bolingbroke*. . . .

Original MS.

" I never was in a worse station for writing letters than this [Kensington], especially for writing to MD, since I left off my journals. For I go to town early. Mrs. Bradley's youngest son is married to somebody worth nothing. . . . Mr. Secretary will not take the title of Bullenbrook. . . ."

1st July, 1712.   *Scott*, iii., 40.

Go, get *you* gone, and drink *your* waters, if this rain has not spoiled them, saucy doxy. I have no more to say to *you* at present: but *love* Pdfr, and MD, and ME. And *Pdfr will love Pdfr*, and MD, and ME.

I wish you had taken *an* account when I sent money to Mrs. Brent. I believe I have not done it a great while. (Omission.) Farewell, dearest MD, FW, ME, &c.

1710–1713.
Æт. 43–46.
Letter 46.

Original MS.

" Go, get ee gone and drink u waters, if this rain has not spoiled them, saucy doxy. I have no more to say to oo at present, but rove Pdfr, and MD, and ME ; and Podafer will rove Pdfr, and MD, and ME. I wish you had taken any account when I sent money to Mrs. Brent. I believe I ha'nt done it a great while ; and pray send me notice when ME wants me to send. She ought to have it when it is due. Farewell, dearest MD FW FW FW ME ME ME."

17тн July, 1712. *Scott,* iii., 41.

Poor Master Ashe has a *bad* redness in his face . . . his face all swelled, and will *break out* in his check, but no danger. . . . Pdfr has writ five or six Grub Street papers this last week. Have you seen Toland's Invitation to *Dismal,* or Hue and Cry after *Dismal, or* Ballad on *Dunkirk, or Agreement* that *Dunkirk* is not in our Hands ? Poh! you have seen nothing. . . . Parvisol . . . tells me there will be a *septennial* visitation in August. I must send Raymond another proxy. So now I will answer *your letter.* . . . Yes, *Mrs.* DD, but *you* would not be content with letters from Pdfr of six lines, or twelve either, 'faith . . . (I am now sitting with nothing but my *bed*-gown, for heat). Ppt shall have a great Bible (omission), and DD shall be repaid her *other* book; but patience; all in good time : you are so hasty, a dog, would, &c. So Ppt has neither won nor lost. Why, *mun,* I play sometimes too at picket; that *is* picquett, I mean. . . . Why, pray, madam philosopher, how did the rain hinder the thunder from doing any harm ? I suppose it *squenched* it. . . .

Letter 50.
Addressed
to Mrs.
Dingley.
Indorsed by
Mrs. Johnson, " 50,"
July 23."

Original MS.

" Poor Master Ashe has a sad redness in his face . . . his face all swelled, and will break in his check, but no danger—Pdfr has writ five or six Grub Street papers this last week. Have you seen Toland's Invitation to Dismal, or Hue and Cry after Dismal, or a Ballad on Dunkirk, or an Argument that Dunkirk is not in our Hands ? Poh! you have seen nothing. . . . Parvisol . . . tells me there will be a triennial visitation in August. I must send Raymond another proxy. So now I will answer oo Rattle. . . . Yes, maram DD, but oo would not be content with letters from Pdfr of six lines, or twelve either, faith . . . (I am now sitting with nothing but my night gown, for heat). Ppt

shall have a great Bible. I have put it down in my mem-
landums, just now. And DD shall be repaid her t'other
book. But patience; all in good time: you are so hasty,
a dog would, &c. So Ppt has neither won nor lost. Why,
mum, I play sometimes too at picket; that is, picquet I
mean. . . . Why pray, madam philosopher, how did the
rain hinder the thunder from doing any harm? I suppose
it Ssquenched it. . . ."

17TH JULY, 1712. *Scott*, iii., 42.

So here comes Ppt *again* with her little watery postscript. *You
bold drunken slut you!* drink Pdfr's health ten times in a morning!
you are a whetter, *faith*. I sup MD's fifteen times *every morning* in
milk porridge. *There's for you now—and there's for your letter*, and
every kind of thing—and now I must say something else. You hear
Secretary St. John is made Viscount *Bolingbroke.*

Original MS.

"So here comes Ppt aden with her little watery postscript. O Rold, dlunken srut, drink Pdfr's health ten
times in a morning! You are a whetter. 'Faith, I sup
MD's fifteen times evly molning in milk porridge. Lele's
fol oo now, and lele's fol u Rattle, and evly kind of sing;
and now I must say something else. You hear Secretary
St. John is made Viscount Bullinbrook."*

19TH JULY, 1712. *Scott*, iii., 43.

I could not send this letter last post, being called away before I
could finish it. . . . I am now in bed, very *lazy* and sleepy at nine. . . .
It is late, and I must rise. Don't play at ombre in *your* waters, *sirrah.* Farewell, dearest MD. (Omission.)

Original MS.

"I could not send this letter last post, being called away
before I could fold or finish it. . . . I am now in bed very
easy and sleepy, at nine. . . . 'Tis late, and I must rise.
Don't play at ombre in the waters, sollah. Farewell, deelest MD MD MD ME FW FW ME ME ME Lele Lele
Lele."

---

* It is not till he has written the word five times he gets it right at last. Bullenbrook, Bullinbrook, Bul-linbroke, Bulingbrook, Bullinbrook, bring him at last to Bolingbroke.

7TH* AUGUST, 1712. *Scott,* iii., 44.

1710-1713.
Æt. 43-46.
LETTER 51.
Addressed to Mrs. Ding-ley, and In-dorsed by Mrs. John-son, "51. Aug. 14."

I *received* your No. 32 at Windsor; I just read it, and immediately sealed it up again, and shall read it no more this twelve month at least. The reason of my resentment *is,* because you talk as glibly of a thing as if it were done, which, for aught I know, is farther from being done than ever. . . . I believe you fancied I would *not affect* to tell it you, but let you learn it from newspapers and reports. *Remember* only there was something in your letter about ME's money, and that shall be taken care of. (Omission.) Have you seen the red stamp the papers are marked with? Methinks the *stamping it* is worth a halfpenny. . . . Dilly is just as he used to be, and puns as plentifully and as bad. The two brothers see one another; *and* I think not the two sisters. . . . Won't *you see poor Laracor?* . . . Pray observe the cherry-trees *in* the river walk; but *you* are too lazy to take such a journey. (Omissions.) Poor Lord Winchilsea is dead. Farewell, dearest MD, FW ME, Lele, *rogues both; love poor Pdfr.*

Original MS.

" I had your No. 32 at Windsor; I just read it, and immediately sealed it up again, and shall read it no more this twelvemonth at least. The reason of my resentment at it is, because you talk as glibly of a Thing as if it were done, which for aught I know is farther from being done than ever. . . . I believe you fancied I would affect not to tell it you, but let you learn it from newspapers and reports. I remember only there was something in your letter about ME's money; and that shall be taken care of on the other side. . . . Have you seen the red stamp the papers are marked with? Methinks it is worth a halfpenny the stamping it. Dilly is just as he used to be, and puns as plentifully and as bad. The two brothers see one another, but I think not the two sisters. . . . Won't oo see pool Laratol? . . . Pray observe the cherry-trees on the river walk; but oo are too lazy to take such a journey. . . . And pray send me again the state of ME's† money; for I will not look into your letter for it. Poor Lord Winchilsea is dead. . . . Farewell, deelest MD MD MD FW

---

* Had written 17th, and writes above his correction of it, "Podefar was mis'-ken."

† Had written MD's—which he changes to ME's.

1710–1713.   FW FW ME ME ME ME ME, Lele logues both, Rove
Æt. 43–46.   poo pdfr."*

15th September, 1712.   *Scott*, iii., 47.

LETTER 52.   Nothing at all is, nor I don't know when any thing will, or
whether *any* at all, so slow are people at doing favors. . . . The
Addressed to   dean never answered my letter, *and* I have clearly forgot whether I
Mrs. Ding-
ley, and in-   sent a bill for ME in any of my last letters. I think I did. . . . I wait
dorsed by   here but to see what they will do for me; and whenever preferments
Mrs. Johu-
son, "52.   are given from me, *as* * * * *said*, I will come over.
Oct. 1, at
Portraune."   *Original MS.*

" Nothing at all is, nor I don't know when any thing
will, or whether ever at all, so slow are people at doing
favors. The Dean never answered my letter, though. I
have clearly forgot whether I sent a bill for ME in any of
my last letters. I think I did. . . . I wait here but to see
what they will do for me; and whenever preferments are
given from me, as hope saved† I will come over."

18th September, 1712.   *Scott*, iii., 49.

The doctor tells me I must go into a course of steel, though I have
not the spleen; for that they can never give me, though I have as
much provocation to it as any man alive. . . . My Lord Shrewsbury
is . . . to be Governor of Ireland. . . . The Irish Whig leaders promise
great things to themselves from *this* government; but *great* care shall
be taken, if possible, to prevent them. . . . She [his sister] is *retired* to
Mrs. Povey's. . . . Parvisol keeps me at charges for horses that I *never*
ride: yours is *large*, and will never be good for anything. . . . Pray
God preserve MD's health, and Pdfr's, and that I may live *free* from
the envy and discontent that attends those who are thought to have
more favor at *court* than they really possess. Love Pdfr, who loves
MD above all things. Farewell, *dearest*, ten thousand times *dearest*,
MD, FW, ME, Lcle.

Original MS.

" This doctor tells me I must go into a course of steel,
though I have not the spleen; for that they can never give
me, though I have as much provocation to it as any man

---

alive. ...   My Lord Shrewsbury is ... to be Governor of 1710-1713.
Ireland. ...   The Irish Whig leaders promise great things Æt. 43-46.
to themselves from his government: but care shall be Letter 52.
taken, if possible, to prevent them. ...   She [his sister]
is returned to Mrs. Povey's. ...   Parvisol keeps me at
charges for horses that I can never ride: your's is lame,
and will never be good for any thing. ...   Pray God
preserve MD's health, and Pdfr's: and that I may live
far from the envy and discontent that attends those who
are thought to have more favor at courts than they really
possess. Love Pdfr, who loves MD above all things. Farewell, deelest, ten thousand times deelest MD MD MD FW
FW ME ME ME ME Lele Lele Lele Lele."

9TH OCTOBER, 1712.   *Scott*, iii., 54.

I loved the man [Earl Rivers], *but* detest his memory. ...   I had LETTER 53.
poor MD's letter, No. 32, at Windsor; but I could not answer it *then;* ——
Pdfr was very sick then: besides, it was a very inconvenient place to Addressed to
write letters from. *You* thought to come home the same day. ... Mrs. Ding-
I am now told Lord Godolphin was buried last night.—O poor ley, and in-,
Ppt * * * (Omissions.) ...   I hoped Ppt would have done with her dorsed by
illness: but I think we b**oth** have *the* faculty never to part with a son,' "53.
disorder for ever; we are very constant. I have had my giddiness Oct. 18, at
twenty-three years by fits. Portranne."

Original MS.

" I loved the man [Earl Rivers] and detest his memory...
I had poo MD's letter, No. 3 ,* at Windsor; but I could
not answer it there. Poo pdfr wem vely hick then: and
besides, it was a very inconvenient place to send letters
from. Oo thought to come home the same day. ...   I
am now told Lord Godolphin was buried last night.—O
pooppt, lay down oo head aden—'faith I ho dove u—I
always reckon if oo are ill I shall hear it; and therefore
hen oo are silent I reckon all is well. ...   I hoped Ppt
would have done with her illness, but I think we both
have that faculty never to part with a disorder for ever.
We are very constant. I have had my giddiness twenty-
three years by fits."

---

* A blank after 3: exact number forgotten. It was 32.

11TH OCTOBER, 1712.   *Scott*, iii., 55.

How the deuce came I to be *so exact* in *your* money?   Just seventeen shillings and eightpence more than due.   I believe you cheat
me.   (Omissions.)   Ppt makes a petition with many *apologies.* . . .
It is my delight to do good offices for people who want and deserve
it, and a tenfold delight to do it to a relation of *Ppt*, whose affairs
Pdfr has so at heart.

*Original MS.**

" How the deuce came I to be so inexact in ME money?
Just seventeen shillings and eightpence more than due: I
believe you cheat me.   If Hawkshaw doesn't pay the interest, I will have the principal.   Pray speak to Parvisol,
and have his advice what I should do about it.   Service to
Mrs. Stoyte and Catherine and Mrs. Walls.   Ppt makes a
petition with many apolozyes. . . .   It is my delight to do
good offices for people who want and deserve, and a tenfold delight to do it to a relation of Ppt's, whose affairs
she has so at heart."

11TH OCTOBER, 1712.   *Scott*, iii., 56.

That is enough to say when I can do no more; and I beg *your*
pardon a *thousand* times, that I can not do better. . . . O, 'faith, *young
women*, I must be *ise, yes*, 'faith, must I; else *we shall* cheat Pdfr.   Are
you good housewives and readers?   Are you walkers?   I know you
are gamesters.   Are you drinkers?   Are you—*hold*, I must go no
farther, for fear of *abusing fine ladies.* . . .   Parvisol has *not* sent. . . . I
am just going out, and can only bid you farewell.   Farewell, dearest
little MD, &c.   (Omissions.)

Original MS.

" Zats enough to say when I can do no more; and I beg
u pardon a sousand times, that I can not do better. . . . O,
'faith, ung oomens, I must be ise; iss, 'faith, must I; else
ME will cheat Pdfr.   Are you good housewives and
readers?   Are you walkers?   I know you are gamesters.
Are you drinkers?   Are you —— O Rold, I must go no
farther, for fear of aboosing fine Radyes.   Parvisol has
never sent. . . . I am just going out, and can only bid oo
farewell.   Farewell, dearest ickle MD MD MD MD FW
FW FW FW ME ME ME ME Lele deer me Lele lele
lele Sollahs bose."

---

* Prefixed to 11th October are the words "Ppt FW," the only instance
before a date.

1710-1713.
Æt. 43-46.
Letter 55.

Addressed to
Mrs. Ding-
ley, and In-
dorsed by
Mrs. John-
son, "Nov.
26. Just
come from
Portrannc."

15th November, 1712. *Scott*, iii., 62.*

The dog Mohun was killed on the spot; and, while the Duke† was over him, Mohun *shortened* his sword, stabbed him in at the shoulder to the heart. The Duke was helped toward the cake-house by the ring in Hyde Park. . . . You have heard the story of my escape in opening the band-box sent to *the* lord-treasurer . . . but so it pleased God, and I saved myself and him; for there was a *bullet-piece.* . . . *Night, dearest sirrahs, I'll go to sleep.* . . . 10 *Nov.* . . . The *coroner's* inquest on the duke's body is to be to-morrow. And I shall know more. But what care *you* for all this? *Yes, MD is sorry for Pdfr's* friends. . . . 17 *Nov.* . . . I had been with Lady Orkney, and charged her to be kind to her *sister in* affliction. . . . 18 *Nov.* The Duchess is mightily *indisposed* . . . else I shall not have time; lord-treasurer usually *keeps* me *so* late . . . the exactness I used to *write to MD.* (Omissions.) Farewell, *dearest little MD,* &c. Smoke the folding of my letters of late.

Original MS.

"Cheese-
cake house."

" The dog Mohun was killed on the spot; and while the duke was over him, Mohun shortening his sword stabbed him in at the shoulder to the heart. The duke was helped toward the cake-house by the ring in Hyde Park. . . . You have heard the story of my escape, in opening the band-box sent to Lord Treasurer . . . but so it pleased God, and I saved myself and him; for there was a bullet apiece. . . . Nite dee Sollahs. I'll go seep. 16 *Nov.* The crowner's inquest on the duke's body is to be to-morrow; and I shall know more. · But what care oo for all this? Iss, poo MD im sorry for poo Pdfr's friends. . . . 17 *Nov.* . . . I had been with Lady Orkney, and charged her to be kind to her sister in her affliction. . . . Nite nite deelest MD. 18 *Nov.* The duchess is mightily out of order . . . else I shall not have time; Lord Treasurer usually keeping me too late . . . the exactness I used to write to MD with. Farewell declogues, deelest MD MD MD, Rove Pdfr, MD MD ME ME FW FW FW ME ME ME Lele me, me. Smoke the folding of my letters late."

---

* Letter 54, from 28th to 30th October, and addressed to Mrs. Johnson, is not among the originals in the British Museum; but it is a specimen of the careless printing of all the editions ("continue" for "contrive," and many other errors), as will be seen from my collation of it. Letter 55 describes the fatal duel of the Duke of Hamilton, a familiar friend of Swift's, with Lord Mohun.

† The duke had just been proposed for embassador to France, and wanted Swift to go with him as secretary— of course he could not be spared.

1710–1713.
Æt. 43–46.
Letter 56.
Addressed to
Mrs. Ding-
ley. In-
dorsed by
Mrs. John-
son, "56.
Dec. 18."

12th December, 1712.   *Scott*, iii., 68.

Here is now a *strange thing; a letter from* MD unanswered. . . .
Why could it not be sent before, *pray* now? . . . I will *renew* my
journal method next time. . . . O! Ppt I remember your reprimanding me for meddling in other people's affairs: I have enough
of it now, with a *vengeance*. God be thanked that Ppt *is better of
her disorders*. God keep her so. . . . Sir Richard Levinge, *stuff*, and
Pratt, more stuff. . . . Abel Roper tells *me* you have had floods in
Dublin; no, *have* you? Oh ho! Swanton seized Portraine, now I
understand *you*. Ay, ay, now I see Portraine at the top of your
letter. . . . Heigh! do *you write by candlelight! naughty, naughty,
naughty dallah, a hundred times for* doing so. . . . My brother Ormond sent me some chocolate to-day. I wish you had share of *it,
they* say it is good for me, and I design to drink some in *the* morning. . . . I have given away ten shillings to-day to servants.
(Omission.) *What* a stir is here about your company and visits!
Charming company, no doubt: *now* I keep no *company*, nor have I
any desire to keep any . . . my only *debauch* is sitting late *when* I
dine. . . . Well, *then, you* are now returned to ombre and the dean,
and Christmas; I wish *you* a very merry one; and pray don't lose
your money, nor play upon Watt Welch's game. *Night, sirrahs, it is
late, I'll go to sleep;* I don't *sleep* well, and therefore never dare to
drink coffee or tea after dinner: but I am very *sleepy* in a morning.
This is the effect of *wine* and years. *Night, dearest* MD.

Original MS.

"Here is now a stlange ting: a Rattle from MD unanswered. . . . Why could it not be sent before, pay
now? . . . I will resume my journal method next time. . . .
O! Ppt, I remember your reprimanding me for meddling
in other people's affairs: I have enough of it now, with a
wannion. . . . God be thanked that Ppt im bettle of her
disoddles: pray God keep her so. . . . Sir Richard Levinge, stuff, stuff; and Pratt, more stuff. . . . Abel Roper
tells us you have had floods in Dublin; ho, brave you!
Oh ho! Swanton seized Portraine; now I understand
oo. . . . Ay, ay, now I see Portraune* at the top of your
letter. Heigh! do oo rite by sandle light, nauti-nauti-
nauti dallar a hundled times fol doing so! . . . My brother Ormond sent me some chocolate to-day. I wish you
had share of it. But they say 'tis good for me, and I
design to drink some in a morning. . . . I have given

---

* It will have been observed that she so dated her own. He is al-
she so spells the word in her indorse- ways glad to have a hit at her mis-
ments of her letters, and doubtless spelling.

away ten shillings to-day to servants: 'tan't be help if one
should cry one's eyes out. Hot a stir is here about your
company and visits! ... Charming company, no doubt.
I keep no company at all, nor have I any desire to keep
any. My only debauching is sitting late where I dine.
Well zen, oo are now returned to ombre and the dean,
and Christmas; I wish oo a very merry one; and pray
don't lose oo moneys, nor play upon Watt Welch's game.
Nite Sollahs, 'tis rate. I'll go to seep. I don't seep well,
and therefore never dare to drink coffee or tea after dinner: but I am very seepy in a morning. This is the effect of time and years. Nite deelest MD."

1710-1713.
Æt. 43-46.
Letter 56.

13TH DECEMBER, 1712.   *Scott, iii., 73.*

I am so very *sleepy* in the *morning* that my man wakens me above
ten times; and now I can tell *you* no news of this day. (Here is a
restless dog, crying cabbages. ... I wish his largest cabbage were
sticking in his throat.) I lodge over against the house in Little
Rider Street, where DD lodged. *Don't you remember, mistress?* ...
We shall have a peace very soon; the Dutch are almost entirely
agreed, and if they stop we shall' make it without them; that has
been resolved. ... One Squire Jones, a scoundrel in my parish, has
writ to me to desire I would engage Joe Beamont to give him his
interest for parliament man for *him:* pray tell Joe this; and if he
designed to vote for him already, then he may tell Jones that I received his letter, and that I writ to Joe to do it. If Joe be engaged
for any other, then he may do what he will: and Parvisol may say
he spoke to Joe, *and* Joe is engaged. ... It *is* ten o'clock ... and
I must be abroad at eleven. Abbé Gautier sends me word I *can not*
see him to-night; *p— take* him! ... I am glad to hear *you* walked
so much in the country. Does DD ever read to you, *young woman?*
O, 'faith! I shall find strange doings *when I come home!* ... Farewell, dearest MD, FW, ME, Lele. (Omissions.)

Original MS.

"I am so very seepy in the mornings that my man
wakens me above ten times; and now I can tell oo no
news of this day. (Here is a restless dog crying cabbages. ... I wish his largest cabbage were sticking in his
throat.) I lodge over against the house in Little Rider
Street, where DD lodged, don't oo lememble maram? ...
We shall have a Peace very soon. The Dutch are almost
entirely agreed; and if they stop, we shall make it without them. That has been long resolved. One Squire

1710-1713.
Æt. 43-46.
Letter 56.

Jones, a scoundrel in my parish, has writ to me to desire I would engage Joe Beamont to give him his interest for parliament-man for Trim; pray tell Joe this; and if he designed to vote for him already, then he may tell Jones that I received his letter, and that I writ to Joe to do it. If Joe be engaged for any other, then he may do what he will: and Parvisol may say he spoke to Joe; but Joe's engaged.... It im ten o'clock ... and I must be abroad at eleven.... Abbé Gautier sends me word I can't see him to-night; pots cake him!... I am glad to hear oo walked so much in the country. Does DD ever read to you, ung ooman? O, faith! I shall find strange doings hen I tum ole!... Farewell, deelest MD MD MD ME ME ME FW FW FW Lele."

18TH AND 19TH DECEMBER, 1712. *Scott*, iii., 76.

Letter 57.
Addressed to
Mrs. Ding-
ley, and in-
dorsed by
Mrs. John-
son, "57,
Jan. 13."

It cost me nineteen shillings to-day for my *club dinner;** I don't like it.... 19 *December. How agreeable it is in a morning for Pdfr to write journals again!* It is as natural as mother's milk.

Original MS.

"It cost me nineteen shillings to-day for my club at dinner; I don't like it, sirs.... Nite, dee sollahs. 19' *Dec.* Ay, mally, zis is sumsing nite for Pdfr to write journals again! 'Tis as natural as mother's milk."

23D DECEMBER, 1712. *Scott*, iii., 80.

This morning I presented one Diaper, a poet [author of *Sea Eclogues*] to Lord Bolingbroke.... I have contrived to make a parson of him, for he is *half one* already, being in deacon's orders, and serves a small cure in the country; but has a sword at his *tail* here in town. It is a poor, little, short wretch, but will do best in a gown, and we will make lord-keeper give him a living.... Don't you see how curiously he [Tom Leigh] *continues* to vex me; for the dog knows, that with half a word I could do more than all of them together.... *Night, dearest sirrahs! I will go to sleep.*

---

* "Club dinner" and "club at dinner" are two very distinct things. In the same letter he says he "proposed" their society meetings to be "only once" a fortnight: of which "only" is dropped out of the print, and "propose" put for the right word. In the entries to the 23d the mistakes in the print are unusually numerous, but not very important. The "little language" of farewell, closing each day, is invariably omitted, with the oo and oors for you and yours, and the "dee" before MD).

Original MS.

1710-1713.
Æt. 43-46.
Letter 57.

" This morning I presented one Diaper, a poet [author of *Sea Eclogues*] to Lord Bolingbroke. . . . I have contrived to make a parson of him, for he is half a one already, being in deacon's orders, and serves a small cure in the country ; but has a sword at his [word not printable] here in town. . . . 'Tis a poor, little, short wretch, but will do best in a gown ; and we will make Lord-keeper give him a living. . . . Don't you see how curiously he [Tom Leigh] contrives to vex me ; for the dog knows that with half a word I could do more than all of them together. . . . Nite, dee Sollahs, I'll go seep a dozey."

25TH DECEMBER, 1712. *Scott*, iii., 82.

(Omissions.) I carried Parnell to dine at Lord Bolingbroke's. . . . *Night, dear rogues.*

Original MS.

"All melly happy Tismasses—melly Tismasses—I said it first—I did—I wish it a sousand times, zoth with halt and sole ! I carried Parnell to dine at Lord Bolingbroke's. . . . Nite dee logues."

26TH DECEMBER, 1712. *Scott*, iii., 82.

I dined with lord-treasurer, who chid me for being absent three days. Mighty kind, with a p—; less of civility, and *more of* interest ! We hear Macartney [second in Hamilton duel, and £700 offered for his capture] is gone over to Ireland. Was it not comical for a gentleman to be set upon by highwaymen, and to tell them he was Macartney. Upon which they brought him to a justice of peace, in hopes of *a* reward,* and the rogues were sent to gaol. Was it not great presence of mind ? But may be you heard *of* this already ; for there was a Grub-street of it.

Original MS.

" I dined with Lord-Treasurer, who chid me for being absent three days. Mighty kind, with a p—; less of civility, and more of his interest ! We hear Macartney [second in Hamilton duel and £700 offered for his capture] is gone over to Ireland. Was it not comical for a gentleman to be set upon by highwaymen, and to tell them he

---

* The *a* for *the* in this passage, the reader will not fail to observe, makes all the difference.

1710-1713.
Æt. 43-46.
Letter 57.

was Macartney; upon which they brought him to a justice of peace, in hopes of the reward, and the rogues were sent to gaol. Was it not great presence of mind? But maybe you heard this already; for there was a Grub-street* of it."

27th–30th December, 1712.   *Scott*, iii., 84.

Well, go to cards, *sirrah* Ppt, and dress the wine and *orange, sirrah Me*, and I'll go *sleep*. *It is late. Night*, MD. 29 *Dec*. . . . I dined in the city upon the broiled leg of a goose and a bit of *bacon*, with my printer. . . . *Night, dear rogues*. 30 *Dec*. I suppose this will be full by Saturday. (Omission.)

Original MS.

"Well, go to cards, sollah Ppt, and dress the wine and olange, sollah Me, and I'll go seep. 'Tis rate. Nite MD. 29 *Dec*. . . . I dined in the city upon the broiled leg of a goose and a bit of brawn, with my printer. . . . Nite two dee litt logues. 30 *Dec*. I suppose this will be full by Saturday: iss it sall go."

1st–2d January, 1712-'13.   *Scott*, iii., 85–87.

A great many new years to dearest MD. Pray God Almighty bless *you*, and send *you* ever happy. . . . But burn politics, and send me from courts and ministers! *Night, dearest little* MD. 2 *Jan*. Go and be *merry, little sirrahs*.

Original MS.

"A sousand melly melly new years to deelest michar MD. Pay God Almighty bless oo, and send oo ever happy. . . . But burn politics, and send me from courts and ministers! Nite deelest own michar MD. . . . 2 *Jan*. Go and be melly, oo little Sollahs."

3d January, 1712-'13.   *Scott*, iii., 88.

I came back just by nightfall, cruel cold weather. (Omission.) I'll take my *leave*. I *forgot* how MD's accounts are. . . . Go, play *at* cards. *Love* Pdfr. Night, MD, FW, ME, Lele. The six odd shillings, tell Mrs. Brent, are for her new year's gift. (Omissions.)

Original MS.

"I came back just by nightfall, cruel cold weather. I have no smell yet, but my cold's something better. Nite

---

* A flying-sheet or pamphlet always called a Grub-street by Swift. In the print of the two following entries, some words are omitted,

"terrible dry" made "terribly dry," with other mistakes not necessary to the sense.

dee sollahs, I'll take my reeve. I forget how MD's ac-
counts are. . . .   Go, play cards and bo melly, deelest
logues, and Rove Pdfr.   Nite michar MD FW oo roves
Pdfr.—FW, Lele lele, ME ME, MD MD MD MD MD
MD MD FW FW FW ME ME FW FW FW FW FW
ME ME ME.   The six odd shillings, tell Mrs. B——, are
for her new year's gift.   Lele, lele, lele and lele."

1710-1713.
Æt. 43-46.
Letter 57.

4TH AND 7TH JANUARY, 1712-'13.   *Scott*, iii., 89.

Lady Mountjoy told me that Macartney was got safe. . . .   Others
say the same thing.   (Omission.)   After church to-day, I showed
the Bishop of Clogher, at court, who was who.   *Night, my two dear
rogues.* . . .   *7 Jan.* Played at ombre with Mrs. Van*h*omrigh. . . .   I
have got *weak* ink, and it is very white. . . .   I'll go to *sleep*.

Original MS.

Letter 59.

Addressed to
Mrs. Ding-
ley, and in-
dorsed by
Mrs. Johu-
son, "59.
Feb. 4. Of
Lord Peter-
borow's re-
turn."

" Lady Mountjoy told me that Macartney was got safe. . . .
Others say the same thing.   'Tis hard such a dog should
escape. . . .   After church to-day, I showed the Bishop of
Clogher at court who was who.   Nite my two dee logues
and lastalls. . . .   *7 Jan.* Played at ombre with Mrs. Van. . . .
I have got new ink, and 'tis very white. . . .   I'll go to
seep.   Nite MD."

12TH-14TH JANUARY, 1712-'13.   *Scott*, iii., 95-97.

I bought Plutarch, two volumes, for thirty shillings, &c.   Well, I'll
tell *you* no more; *you* don't understand Greek. . . .   So *night, own dear
dallars*.   *13 Jan.* . . . sat with Lady Orkney till twelve.   (Omission.)
The parliament was. . . .   *14 Jan.* . . . so we laughed, &c.   *Night,* my
own *dearest little rogues*, MD.

Original MS.

" I bought Plutarch, two volumes, for thirty shillings,
&c.   Well, I'll tell oo no more; oo don't understand
Greek . . . so nite nown dee dallars.   *13 Jan.* . . .   Sat with
Lady Orkney till twelve: from whence you may conclude
it is late, Sollahs.   The parliament was. . . .   Nite dea MD.
14 Jan. So we laughed, &c.   Nite my own deelest richar
logues MD."

15TH AND 16TH JANUARY, 1712-'13.   *Scott*, iii., 97, 98.

" . . . people seeing me speak to L. T* *causes* a great deal of teasing.   I
tell you what comes into my head, that I never knew whether *you*
were Whigs or Tories, and I value our conversation the more that it

never turned on that subject. I have a fancy that Ppt is a Tory, and a *rigid* one. I don't know why; but methinks she looks like one, and DD a sort of a trimmer. 16 *Jan.* ... because I have much business. So my journals shall be short, and *Ppt* must have patience.

Original MS.

" . . . people seeing me speak to L. T^r causes me a great deal of teasing.—I tell you what comes into my head, that I never knew whether MD were Whigs or Tories, and I value our conversation the more that it never turned on that subject. I have a fancy that Ppt is a Tory, and a violent one;* I don't know why; but methinks she looks like one: and DD a sort of a trimmer. 16 *Jan.* ...'cause I have much business. So my journals shall be short, and MD must have patience. So nite dee Sollahs."

18th–21st JANUARY, 1712-'13. *Scott,* iii., 99–101.

Go to cards, *dearest* MD. 19 *Jan.* A poor fellow called at the door where I lodge, with a parcel of oranges for a present for me. I bid my man *learn* what his name was, and whence *it* came . . . and not to let him leave his oranges. ... Let them keep their poison for their rats. I don't love it. (Omission.) That blot is a blunder. *Night, dear* MD. 20 *Jan.* Tom Leigh must go back, which is one good thing *to* the town. 21 *Jan.* This letter *shall* not go till Saturday ... so you must know I expect *a letter very* soon, and that MD is *very well;* and so night, dear MD.

Original MS.

" Go to cards, Sollahs, and nite MD. 19 *Jan.* A poor fellow called at the door where I lodge, with a parcel of oranges for a present for me. I bid my man know what his name was, and whence he came . . . and not to let him leave his oranges. ... Let them keep their poison for their rats. I don't love it. Nite dear MD—drowsy, drowsy, dear—[here comes a blot scrawling in a line across page] —That blot is a blunder. Nite dea MD. 20 *Jan.* Tom Leigh must go back, which is one good thing for the town. Nite MD. 21 *Jan.* This letter sall not go till Saturday... so oo must know I expect a Rattle vely soon ; and that MD is vely werr ; and so nite dee MD."

* This was banter. She had no violent predilections; but such as they were, they were whig, and derived from himself. He has another al-lusion later, with less tone of banter; but evidently replying to some gentle intimation from herself. "'Faith, I never knew MD's politics before."

23D AND 24TH JANUARY, 1712-'13. *Scott*, iii., 101, 102.

Dr. Pratt and I sat this evening with the Bishop of Clogher, and played at ombre for *threepence*. That I suppose is but low with you. I found, at coming home, a letter from MD, No. 37. I shall not answer it *this* bout, but will the next. I am sorry for *poor* Ppt. Pray walk *if you* can.... (Omission.) Night, MD. 24 *Jan.* I have just time to send this without *giving it* to the bellman. (Omission.) My second cold is better now. Night, dearest little MD, FW, ME, Lele.

1710-1713.
Æt. 43–46.
LETTER 39.
Addressed to Mrs. Ding-ley, and in-dorsed by Mrs. John-son, "59. Feb. 2d. Death of Secretary Harrison."

Original MS.

" Dr. Pratt and I sat this evening with Bishop of Clogher, and played at ombre for threepences. That I suppose is but low with you. I found at coming home a letter from MD, No. 37. I shall not answer it zig bout, but will the next. I am sorry for poo poo Ppt. Pray walk hen oo can.... Pay, can oo walk oftener—oftener still?... Nite dear MD. 24 *Jan.* I have just time to send this without going to the bellman. Nite deelest richar MD. Sawcy deelest MD MD MD, FW FW FW, ME ME, Poo Pdfr, Lele lele lele. My second cold is better now.... Lele lele lele lele."

25TH AND 26TH JANUARY, 1712-'13. *Scott*, iii., 103.

My little pamphlet is out: 'tis not politics. If it takes, I say again you *shall* hear of it. (Omission.) 26 *Jan.* This morning I felt a little touch of giddiness, which has disordered and weakened me with its ugly remains all this day.

Original MS.

"My little pamphlet is out: 'tis not politics. If it takes, I say again you sall hear of it. Nite deelogues. 26 *Jan.* This morning I felt a little touch of giddiness, which has disordered and weakened me with its ugly remains all this day. Pity Pdfr."

27TH–30TH JANUARY, 1712-'13. *Scott*, iii., 104, 105.

I know not what to judge. Night, my own dearest MD. 28 *Jan.* I was to-day at Court, where *the* Ambassador talked to me as if he did not suspect any design in burning d'Aumont's house: but Abbé Gautier said ... d'Aumont had a letter the very same day, to let him know his house should be burnt, *and tells* several other circumstances. 29 *Jan.* ... Well, but I must answer *your letter, young women :* not yet; *it is late now*, and I can't *find* it. 30 *Jan.* ... He [little Harrison] must be three or four hundred pounds in debt at least. *Poor* brat ! Let me go to *bed, sirrahs. Night, dear* MD.

1710-1711.
ÆT. 43-44.

Letter 59.

Original MS.

" I know not what to judge. Nite my own dearest
MD, rove pdfr. 28 *Jan.* I was to-day at court, where the
Spanish ambassador talked to me as if he did not suspect
any design in burning d'Aumont's house: but the Abbé
Gautier said ... that d'Aumont had a letter the very same
day to let him know his house should be burnt. And they
tell several other circumstances. ... Nite dear MD. 29
Jan. ... Well, but I must answer oo Rattle, ung oomens:
not yet: 'tis rate now, and I can't tind it. 30 *Jan.* ... He
[little Harrison] must be three or four hundred pounds in
debt at least, the brat! Let me go to ed Sollahs. Nite
deerichar MD."

1ST FEBRUARY, 1712-'13. *Scott*, iii., 107.

Here is a week gone, and one side of this letter not finished. O,
but I *will* write now but once in three weeks. *Yes*, 'faith, this shall
go sooner.... I spoke to *the* Duke *of* Ormond ... of Irish affairs ...
will speak to lord-treasurer to-morrow that we three may *settle* some
way or other. (Omission.) .

Original MS.

" 'Faith, here's a week gone, and one side of this letter
not finished. O, but I write now but once in three weeks.
—Iss, 'faith, this shall go sooner.... I spoke to Duke Ormond ... of Irish affairs ... will speak to Lord Treasurer
to-morrow that we three may settle them some way or
other. Nite, sollahs both, rove Pdfr."

3D AND 4TH FEBRUARY, 1712-'13. *Scott*, iii., 108, 109.

Sat till twelve with the Provost and Bishop of Clogher. (Omission.) 4 *Feb.* My head is still in no good order. I am heartily sorry
for Ppt. I am sure her head is good for (blank). I'll answer more
to-morrow. Night, dearest MD.

Original MS.

" Sat till twelve with the Provost and Bishop of Clogher
at the Provost's. Nite MD. 4 *Feb.* My head is still in no
good order. I am heartily sorry for poo ppt I am sure: her
head is good for something. I'll answer more tomollow.
Nite two dee Sollahs. Nite MD."

5TH FEBRUARY, 1712-'13.   *Scott*, iii., 109.

1710-1713.
Æt. 46-46.
Letter 59.

I must go on with *your* letter.   I dined to-day with Sir Andrew Fountaine and *the* provost, and played at ombre with him all the afternoon. ˙ I won, yet Sir Andrew is an admirable player.   Lord Pembroke came in, and I gave him three or four scurvy Dilly puns, that begin with an *if*.   Well, but *your* letter, well, *let* me see.—No, I believe I shall write no more this good while, nor publish what I have done.   (Omission.)   I did not suspect *you* would tell Filby. *You* are so (blank) Turns and visitations—what are these ?   I'll preach and visit as much for Mr. Walls.   Pray God mend *people's* health ; mine is but very indifferent.   I have left *off* Spa water ; it makes my *legs* swell.   *Night, dearest* MD.

Original MS.

" I must go on with oo letter.   I dined to-day with Sir Andrew Fountaine and provost, and I played at ombre with him all the afternoon.   I won, yet Sir Andrew is an admirable player.   Lord Pembroke came in, and I gave him three or four scurvy Dilly puns, that begin with an *if*.   Well, but oor letter, well, ret me see.—No.   I believe I shall write no more this good while, nor publish what I have done.   Nauty Ppt, oo are vely tempegant.*   I did not suspect oo would tell Filby.   Oo are so recise ; not to oor health.   Turns and visitations—what are those?   I'll preach and visit as much for Mr. Walls.   Pray God mend poo Ppt's health ; mine is but very indifferent.   I have left Spa water ; it makes my leg swell.   Nite deelest MD."

6TH-8TH FEBRUARY, 1712-'13.   *Scott*, iii., 111.

This is the queen's birthday, and I never saw it celebrated with so much *hurry* and fine clothes. . . . I passed the evening at Mrs. Vanhomrigh's, and came home pretty early, to answer *your letter* again. . . . *You* did well to let Parvisol make up his accompts.   All things grow dear in Ireland, but corn to the parsons. . . . *Night, dearest rogues*, MD.   7 *Feb.* Colds ! we have been all dying with colds ; but now they are a little *off*, and my second is almost off. . . . So now I have answered *your letter* . . . and I'll say no more but bid *you night, dear* MD.   8 *Feb.* I was to see Lady Worsley to-day. . . . She lodges in the very house in King Street, between St. James's Street and St. James's Square, where *DD's* brother *bought* the sweetbread, when I lodged there, and *DD* came to see me.   Short (blank) Night, MD.

* Termagant.

1710–1713.
Æt. 43–46.
Letter 59.

Original MS.

" This is the queen's birthday, and I never saw it celebrated with so much luxury and fine clothes. . . . I passt the evening at Mrs. Vanhomrigh's and came home pretty early, to answer oo Rattle again. . . . Oo did well to let Parvisol make up his accounts. All things grow dear in Ireland, but corn to the parsons. . . . Nite deelogues. 7 *Feb.* Cold! why we have been all dying with colds; but now they are a little over, and my second is almost off. . . . So now I have answered oo Rattle, . . . and I'll say no more, but bid oo Nite oo deelogues MD. 8 *Feb.* I was to see Lady Worsley to-day. . . . She lodges in the very house in King Street, between St. James's Street and St. James's Square, where MD's brother brought the sweet-bread, when I lodged there, and MD came to see me. Short sighs. Nite MD. Poo pdfr."

13TH AND 14TH FEBRUARY, 1712-'13. *Scott,* iii., 113, 114.

I sent to see how poor Harrison did, and he is extremely ill: and I *am* very much afflicted for him, *as* he is my own creature. . . . I am *much concerned* for this poor lad. . . . Night, dear MD. 14 *Feb.* No loss [little Harrison's] ever grieved me so much; poor creature! Pray God Almighty bless *poor* MD.

Original MS.

" I went to see how poor Harrison did, and he is extremely ill, and I very much afflicted for him, for he is my own creature. . . . I am in much concern for this poor lad. . . . Nite Ppt, nite deelogues, Nite. 14 *Feb.* No loss [little Harrison's] ever grieved me so much: poor creature! Pray God Almighty bless poor ppt, poo MD."

15TH-19TH FEBRUARY, 1712-'13. *Scott,* iii., 115-117.

LETTER 60.
Addressed to
Mrs. Ding-
ley, and in-
dorsed by
Mrs. John-
son, "60.
Mar. 7."

15 *Feb.* I am come home very melancholy, and will go to bed. *Night, dearest MD.* 16 *Feb.* I have been reading *a book* for amusement. 17 *Feb.* Lord Bolingbroke is sending his brother to succeed *Mr.* Harrison. . . . I *lost* my money at ombre sadly; I make a thousand blunders *at* . . . . I play *but* threepenny ombre; but it is what you call running ombre. 18 *Feb.* I believe she [Harrison's mother] is an old devil, and her daughter a (blank). 19 *Feb.* . . . so *night,* dear MD.

Original MS.

" I am come home very melancholy, and will go to bed.

Nite MD, my own deelest MD Ppt. 16 *Feb*. I have been reading a foolish book for amusement. 17 *Feb*. Lord Bolingbroke is sending his brother to succeed poor Harrison. . . . I lose my money at ombre sadly; I make a thousand blunders. I play putt [*sic*] threepenny ombre; but it is what you call running ombre. 18 *Feb*. I believe she [Harrison's mother] is an old devil, and her daughter no better. . . . Nite MD. 19 *Feb*. . . . so nite, dee Sollahs, nite."

1710-1713.
Æт. 43-46.
Letter 60.

20TH AND 21ST FEBRUARY, 1712-'13. *Scott*, iii., 117.

Good *lack!* when I came home, I warrant, I found a letter from MD, No. 38; and *you* write so small nowadays. I hope *your* poor eyes are better. . . . I will speak to Mr. Griffin to-morrow, about Ppt's brother Filby, and desire, whether he deserves or no, that his employment may be mended, that is to say, *if I* see Griffin; otherwise not; and I'll answer *MD's letter when I* Pdfr think fit. *Night,* MD. 21 *Feb*. Methinks I writ a little saucy last night. I mean the last (blank)* I saw Griffin at Court. . . . If I knew *where* to write to Filby, I would. . . . I dined with lord treasurer and seven lords to-day. You know Saturday is his great day. I sat with *them till* eight.

Original MS.

"Good luck! when I came home, I warrant I found a letter from MD, No. 38; and oo write so small now-oo-days, I hope oor poor eyes are better. I will speak to Mr. Griffin to-morrow, about Ppt's brother Filby, and desire, whether he deserves or no, that his employment may be mended. That is to say, if I can see Griffin; otherwise not; and I'll answer oor Rattle hen I Pdfr think fit. Nite dee MD. 21 *Feb*. Methinks I writt a little saucy last night. I mean the last word, God 'give me. I saw Griffin at Court. . . . If I knew how to write to Filby, I would. . . . I dined with Lord Treasurer and seven lords to-day. You know Saturday is his great day: but I sat with them alone till eight."

24TH FEBRUARY, 1712-'13. *Scott*, iii., 120.

But I'll go to-morrow; for Lady Catherine Hyde and Lady Boling-

---

* He meant, of course, the "when I | that a blank should be left in place of think fit;" and it is incomprehensible | the "last word," written quite plainly.

1710–1713.
Æt. 43–46.

Letter 60.

broke are to be there by appointment, and I *lifted* up my periwig, and all, to make a figure. Well, who can help it? Not I, vow *to Heaven! Night*, MD.

Original MS.

"But I'll go to-morrow; for Lady Catherine Hyde and Lady Bolingbroke are to be there by appointment. And I listed up my periwig and all, to make a figure. Well, who can help it? Not I, vow to Nite MD."

27TH AND 28TH FEBRUARY, 1712–'13. *Scott*, iii., 122, 123.

Sir Thomas Hanmer has my papers now. (Omission.) *You are now* at ombre with the dean, always on Friday night with Mrs. Walls. . . . *Night, dear* MD. 28 *Feb.* . . . And now I must bid *you* farewell, dearest rogues. God bless dear MD; and love Pdfr. Farewell MD, FW, ME, Lele.

Original MS.

"Sir Thomas Hanmer has my papers now—And hat is MD doing now? Oh, at ombre with the dean, always on Friday night with Mrs. Walls. . . . Nite own deo litt MD. 28 *Feb.* And now I must bid oo farewell, declest richar Ppt. God bless oo ever, and rove Pdfr. Farewell MD MD MD, FW FW FW FW, ME ME ME, Lele lcle."

3D–5TH MARCH, 1712–'13. *Scott*, iii., 124, 125.

Letter 61.

Addressed to Mrs. Dingley, and indorsed by Mrs. Johnson, "61. Mar. 27."

I walk when I can, but am grown very idle; and, not finishing my thing, I *ramble* abroad and play at ombre. 4 *March*. Night, dear MD. 5 *March*. Night, MD.

Original MS.

"I walk when I can, but am grown very idle; and not finishing my thing, I gamble* abroad and play at ombre. 4 *March*. Nite poodeerichar MD. 5 *March*. Nite Sollahs."

6TH MARCH, 1712–'13. *Scott*, iii., 126.

I was to-day at an auction of pictures with Pratt, and laid out *two pounds five shillings* for a picture of Titian, and if it were a Titian it would be worth twice as many pounds. . . . I was at lord-treasurer's levee with the provost, to ask a book for the college.—I never go to his levee, unless *it be* to present somebody. (Omissions.)

Original MS.

"I was to-day at an auction of pictures with Pratt, and laid out forty-four shillings for a picture of Titian, and if it

---

* "Gambol" he means. He spells it "gamble" for a pun.

were a Titian it would be worth twice as many pounds. ....
I was at Lord Treasurer's levee with the provost, to ask a
book for the college. I never go to his levee, unless to
present somebody. For all oor raillying, saucy Ppt, as
hope saved I expected they would have decided about me
long ago; and as hope saved, as soon as ever things are
given away, and I not provided for, I will be gone with
the very first opportunity, and put up bag and baggage.
But people are slower than can be thought. Nite MD."

1710-1713.
Æt. 43–46.
Letter 61.

Important
omissions
restored.

7TH MARCH, 1712-'13. *Scott*, iii., 127.

I knew MD's politics before, and I think it pretty extraordinary,
and a great compliment to you, and I believe never three people conversed so much with so little politics.... O yes, things *are* very dear.
DD must come in at last with her two eggs a penny. There the
provost was well applied. ... I was not at court to-day, a wonder !
Night, dear MD. Love Pdfr.

Original MS.

" 'Faith, I never knew MD's politics before, and I think
it pretty extraordinary, and a great compliment to you ;
and I believe never three people conversed so much with
so little politics. ... O yes, things very dear. DD must
come in at last with her two eggs a penny. There the
proverb was well applied. ... I was not at court to-day.
A wonder ! Nite Sollahs. Rove poo Pdfr."

9TH MARCH, 1712-'13. *Scott*, iii., 128.

Lord-keeper is suddenly taken ill of a quinsy, and some lords are
commissioned, I think *lord treasurer*, to prorogue the parliament in his
stead. You never saw a town so full of ferment and expectation.
Mr. Pope has published a fine poem, called Windsor Forest. Read
it. *Night*, MD.

First men-
tion of Pope
in Swift's
letters.

Original MS.

" Lord Keeper is suddenly taken ill of a quinsy ; and
some lords are commission, I think Lord Trevor, to prorogue the parliament in his stead. You never saw a town
so full of ferment and expectation. Mr. Pope has published a fine poem called Windsor Forest. Read it. Nite,
MD."

1710-1713.
Æt. 43-46.

Letter 61.

I went to look *on* a library I am going to buy, if we can agree. I have offered a hundred and twenty pounds, and will give ten *pounds* more. Lord Bolingbroke will lend me the money. I was two hours poring *over* the books. (Omission.) *Night, MD.* 11 *March.* Sir Andrew Fountaine invited the provost and me to dine with him, and play at ombre, when I fairly lost fourteen shillings. *It* won't do.... Went out four matadores and a trump in black, and *yet* was beasted. *Very sad,* 'faith! *Night, my dear rogues, MD.*

Original MS.

"I went to look over a library I am going to buy, if we can agree. I have offered a hundred and twenty pounds, and will give ten more. Lord Bolingbroke will lend me the money. I was two hours poring on the books. How do oo do, Sollahs? Rove Pdfr, poopdfr. Nite MD MD MD. 11 *March.* Sir Andrew Fountaine invited the provost and me to dine with him, and play at ombre, when I fairly lost fourteen shillings. 'Faith, it won't do. Went out four matadores and a trump in black, and was beasted. Vely bad, 'faith, of Pdfr. Nite deelest logues. Nite MD."

I had much discourse with the Duke of Ormond this morning, and am driving some points to secure (blank). I left the society at seven.... *Night, dear* MD. 13 *March.* ... This letter shall not go to-morrow. No haste, *young women;* nothing that presses.... *Night, dear* MD. 14 *March.* I doubt I shall not buy the library; for a *roguish* book-seller has offered sixty pounds more than I designed to give... and so *good night.* Love Pdfr and MD. 15 *March.* Ppt may understand me.... Brevets are commissions. Ask soldiers, *dear sirrahs.* Night, MD.... 16 *March.* Night, MD. 17 *March.* Night, MD. 18 *March.* Night, MD. (Omission.)

Original MS.

Important restoration.

"I had much discourse with the Duke of Ormond this morning, and am driving some points to secure us all in the case of accidents, Ppt. I left the Society at seven.... Nite, own dee MD. 13 *March.* This letter shall not go to-morrow. No haste, ung oomens; nothing that presses.... Night, logues. 14 *March.* I doubt I shall not buy the library; for a roguey book-seller has offered sixty pounds

more than I designed to give. . . .   And so dood nite, 1710-1713.
sollahs all.   Rove Pdfr.   Nite MD.   15 *March*. Yes, ppt, ÆT. 43-46.
oo may understand me. . . .   Brevets are commissions. Letter 61.
Ask soldiers, dull sollahs.* Nite MD.   16 *March*. Nite,
deo MD.   17 *March*. Nite deelest sollahs, 'tis rate.   Nite
MD.   18 *March*. Nite my own deo sollahs.   Pdfr roves
MD."

19TH-21ST MARCH, 1712-'13.   *Scott*, iii., 133-135.

The Bishop of Clogher has made an *if* pun, that he is mighty proud
of, and designs to send it over to his brother Tom. But Sir Andrew
Fountaine has wrote to Tom Ashe last post, and told him the pun,
and desired him to send it over to the bishop as his own ; and, if it
succeeds, it will be a pure bite. The bishop will tell it us as a wonder, that he and his brother should jump so exactly. I'll tell you the
pun :—if there was a hackney coach at Mr. *Pooley's* door, what town
in Egypt would it be? Why, it would be *Hecatompolis*; *Hack at
Tom Pooley's*. *Silly,* says Ppt . . . *what care you?* *Night*, MD.   21
March. I'll keep the letter in my *pocket,* and give it into the post myself. . . . Farewell, dearest MD, FW, ME, Lele.

Original MS.

" Bishop Clogher has made an If pun, that he is mighty
proud of, and designs to send it over to his brother Tom.
But Sir Andrew Fountaine has wrote to Tom Ashe last
post, and told him the pun, and desired him to send it over
to the bishop as his own ; and if it succeeds, 'twill be a pure
bite. The bishop will tell it us as a wonder, that he and his
brother should jump so exactly. I'll tell you the pun. If
there was a hackney coach at Mr. Polley's door, what town
in Egypt would it be? Why, it would be Hecatompolis;
Hack at Tom Polley's. Silly, says Ppt . . . hat care oo?
Nite, darling dea MD.   21 *March*. I'll keep the letter in
my pottick, and give it into the post myself. . . . Farewell,
deelest MD MD MD, FW FW FW, Ppt, ME ME ME,
Lele—Lele logues."

---

* He calls them " dull," because he | a maid of honor *passée,* that since she
does not fancy they will understand | could not get a husband, the queen
a joke he tells them of Duke Disney, | should give her a brevet to act as a
an old battered rake (" not an old | married woman.
man, but an old rake"), who said of |

1710-1713.
Æт. 43-46.

Letter 62.

Addressed to
Mrs. Dingley, and Indorsed by
Mrs. Johnson, "62.
Apr. 13."

21st-25th March, 1712-'13. *Scott,* iii., 135-138.

I wish I could have done better, and hope *that you* will take what can be done in good part, and that *Ppt's* brother will not dislike it. *Night, dearest* MD. 22 *March.* Pray remember Eltee. You know the reason. L. T. and Eltee *are* pronounced the same way. Stay, it is *now* five weeks since I had a letter from MD. I allow *you* six. You see why I can not come over the beginning of April; but as hope saved, it is not Pdfr's fault (misplaced). Whoever has to do with this ministry can fix no time ; but as hope saved, it is not Pdfr's fault. (Omission.) 23 *March.* I endeavor to keep a firm friendship between the Duke *of* Ormond and Eltee. *You* know who Eltee is (or have *you forgot* already ?)... I'll go *sleep. Night, dearest* MD. 25 *March.* ... the weather is so bad. Is it so with *you? Night, dear* MD.

Original MS.

"I wish I could have done better, and hope oo will take what can be done in good part, and that oor brother will not dislike it.—Nite, own dear MD, Ppt. 22 *March.* Pray remember Eltee. You know the reason. L. T. and Eltee pronounced the same way. Stay, 'tis five weeks since I had a letter from MD. I allow oo six. You see why I can not come over the beginning of April. Whoever has to do with this ministry can fix no time. But as hope saved, it is not Pdfr's fault. Pay don't blame poo Pdfr. Nite, deelest logues MD. 23 *March.* I endeavor to keep a firm friendship between Duke Ormond and Eltee. (Oo know who Eltee is, or have oo fordot already?). ... I'll go seep. Nite, deelest MD. 25 *March.* ... The weather is so bad. Is it so with oo, sollahs? Nite, nite, own MD."

27th March, 1713. *Scott,* iii., 139.

An Essay on
the Different
Styles of
Poetry, Inscribed to
Lord Bolingbroke.
" Published
this day by
Ben Tooke."
London
Gazette of
21st-24th
March,
1712-'13.

Parnell's poem is mightily esteemed ; but poetry sells ill. I am plagued with that (blank) poor Harrison's mother.... I went afterward to see a famous moving picture, and I never saw any thing so pretty. You see a sea ten *inches* wide, a town *at the other hand,* and ships sailing in the sea, and discharging their cannon. You see a great sky, with moon and stars, &c. I am a fool. *Night, dear* MD.

Original MS.

"Parnell's poem is mightily esteemed ; but poetry sells ill. I am plagued with that devil's brood, poor Harrison's mother. ... I went afterwards to see a famous moving picture, and I never saw any thing so pretty. You see a sea ten miles wide, a town on t'other end, and ships sailing

in the sea, and discharging their cannon. You see a great
sky with moon and stars &c. I'm a fool. Nite, dee
MD."

29TH AND 30TH MARCH, 1713. *Scott,* iii., 141.

. . . The altar [at Chelsea Hospital] put me in mind of Tisdall's
outlandish *mould* at your hospital for the soldiers. . . . Have *you* such
weather? Night, MD. 30 *March.* . . . I paid the hundred pounds   :
this evening, and it was a *great* surprise to the receiver. *Night,* MD.

Original MS.

". . . The altar [at Chelsea Hospital] put me in mind of
Tisdall's outlandish would* at your hospital for the soldiers. . . . Have oo such weather? Nite dee dee MD.
30 *March.* . . . I paid the hundred pounds this evening,
and it was an agreeable surprise to the receiver. Nite,
dee MD."

31ST MARCH-5TH APRIL, 1713. *Scott,* iii., 142-147.

Sir Andrew Fountaine invited *the* Bishop of Clogher and me, and
some others, to dine where he did. . . . This evening Lady Masham,
Dr. Arbuthnot, and I, were contriving a lie for to-morrow,† that
Mr. Noble, who was hanged last Saturday, was recovered by his
friends. . . . *Night,* MD. 1 *April.* Addison is to *have a play* on
Friday in Easter week: 'tis a tragedy, called Cato; I saw it unfin- First night
ished some years ago. . . . *Night, dear* MD. 2 *April.* I never saw of Cato:
such *a* long run of ill weather in my life. *Night, dear MD.* . . . 4 Tuesday,
April. This Passion-week, people are so demure, especially this last 14th April.
day, that I told Dilly, who called here, that I would dine with him,   .

---

* So Swift writes in his MS.: probably so spelling accidentally the word
in his mind—wood. The gift mentioned in the next entry had been
intrusted to Swift for a "very deserving," but "poor and sickly," person, who was quite unknown to the
giver, but whose position Swift had
described.

† Among the papers at Narford,
strange to say, I found in Swift's
handwriting the very "lie" thus prepared to turn into April-fools the
friends who might be credulous
enough to believe it. A curious
interest is imparted to it by the fact
that in the famous scene of *Marriage*

à la Mode, where the seducer is es- April Jest
caping through the bed-chamber win- (MS.).
dow after murdering the husband,
Hogarth had in his mind this very
Noble, whose profession was the law,
and who was hanged for committing
murder in precisely those circumstances. Swift's MS. runs thus:
"Do you know that Mr. Noble was
but half-hang'd, and was brought to
life by his friends, but was since seiz'd
again, and is now in a messenger's   .
hands at the Black Swan, in Hol-
born? This was talked all over the
Court last night." Swift had, of
course, given this copy to Fountaine.

and so I did, 'faith; and had a small shoulder of mutton of my own bespeaking. . . . 5 *April.* Lord Abingdon *had* like to have snapped me for dinner, and I believe will fall out for refusing him; but I hate dining with *him, and* I dined with a private friend. Night, MD.

Original MS.

" Sir Andrew Fountaine invited Bishop Clogher and me, and some others, to dine where he did. . . . This evening Lady Masham, Dr. Arbuthnot, and I, were contriving a lie for to-morrow, that Mr. Noble, who was hanged last Saturday, was recovered by his friends. . . . Nite dee MD. 1 *April.* Addison is to have a play of his acted on Friday in Easter week : 'tis a tragedy called *Cato ;* I saw it unfinished some years ago. . . Nite, dee MD. 2 *April.* I never saw such long run of ill weather in my life. Nite dee logues &c. &c. 4 *April.* This Passion-week, people are so demure, especially this last day, that I told Dilly who called here, that I would dine with *him,* and so I did, 'faith; and had a small shoulder of mutton of my own bespeaking. Nite dee MD. 5 *April.* Lord Abingdon was like to have snapped me for dinner, and I believe will fall out for refusing him; but I hate dining with them, and so I dined with a private friend. Nite, dee MD."

It is rainy weather again; *never saw the like.* This letter shall go to-morrow; remember, *young women,* it is seven weeks since *your* last, and I allow *you* but five weeks; but *you* have been galloping in the country to Swanton's. *Pray* tell Swanton I had his letter: *night, dear* MD. 7 *April.* I have not been abroad, *you* may be sure; so I can say nothing to-day, but that I *love MD better than ever, if possible.* . . . *Don't* this perplex you? *What* care I? But *love* Pdfr. Farewell, dearest MD, FW, ME, Lele. . . . *Night, dearest little MD.* (Omission.)

Original MS.

"It is rainy weather again; nevle saw ze rike. This letter shall go to-morrow; remember, ung oomens, it is seven weeks since oor last, and I allow oo but five weeks; but oo have been galloping in the country to Swanton's. Oh, pray tell Swanton I had his letter. . . . Nite, deelest MD. 7 *April.* I have not been abroad, oo may be sure; so I can say nothing to-day, but that I rove MD Ppt bottle

zan ever if possibere. . . . Does this perplex you ? Hat   1710-1713.
care I ? But rove Pdfr, sawey Pdfr.   Farewell, deelest   Æt. 43–46.
MD MD MD FW FW FW ME ME ME Lele. . . .   Nite,   Letter 62.
dee Sollahs.   Late.   Rove Pdfr."

8th-10th April, 1713.   *Scott,* iii., 149-151.

Lord Cholmondelcy is this day removed. . . . I dined with lord-   Letter 63.
treasurer, and did the business I had for him to his satisfaction. I   Addressed to
won't tell *you* what it was. (Omissions.) 9 *April.* . . . [The Duchess]   Mrs. Ding-
told him stories, which the weak man believed, and was *converted.*   ley, and in-
10 *April.* I had a great deal of business to-night, which gave me a   dorsed by
temptation to be idle, and I lost a dozen shillings at ombre, with Dr.   Mrs. John-
Pratt and another. (Omission.)   Night, MD.   son, "63.
                                                                                        May 4."

Original MS.

" Lord Chomley (the right name is Cholmondelcy) is this
day removed. . . . I dined with Lord Treasurer, and did
the business I had for him to his satisfaction.   I won't
tell oo what it was. So much for zat.   9 *April.* . . . [The
Duchess] told him stories, which the weak man believed,
and was perverted.   Nite MD.   10 *April.* I had a great
deal of business to-night, which gave me a temptation to
be idle. I lost a dozen shillings at ombre, with Dr. Pratt
and another. I have been to see t'other day the Bishop
Clogher and Lady, but did not see Miss.   Nite, dee MD."

13th-22d April, 1713.   *Scott,* iii., 153-157.

I bid Mr. Lewis tell my lord-treasurer, that I *take* nothing ill of
him, but his not giving me timely notice, as he promised to do, if he
found the queen would do nothing for me... stay I will not; and so
believe for all *our* (blank) *you* may see me in Dublin before April
ends. . . . *What* care I ? *Night, dearest rogues,* MD.   14 *April.* . . . And
so he will *say* for a hundred nights.   15 *April.* Lord Bolingbroke
made me dine with him to-day. I was as good company as ever:
and told me the queen would determine something for me to-night...
Night, dear MD.   16 *April.* Out came lord-treasurer, and said ... that
I must be *Prebendary* of Windsor. . . . *Night, dear* MD.   19 *April.*
After dinner Mr. Lewis sent me *word,* that *the* queen staid till she
knew whether the Duke *of* Ormond approved of Sterne for *a*
bishop. . . . Night, MD.   20 *April.* I can't tell. *Night, own dear* MD.
22 *April.* I hate this suspense. . . . *Night, dear MD.*

Original MS.

" I bid Mr. Lewis tell my Lord Treasurer, that I took
nothing ill of him but his not giving me timely notice, as

1710-1713.
_Æt._ 43-46.
Letter 63.

he promised to do, if he found the Queen would do nothing for me. .... Stay I will not; and so I believe for all oo sawcy ppt can say, oo may see me in Dublin before April ends. .... Hat care I? Nite, deelest rogues. Nite MD. 14 _April._ .... and so he will for a hundred nights. Nite, dee MD. 15 _April._ Lord Bolingbroke made me dine with him to-day (I was as good company as ever), and told me the Queen would determine something for me to-night.... Nite, deelest MD. 16 _April._ Out came Lord Treasurer, and said ... that I must be Prebend of Windsor.... Nite, own dee MD. 19 _April._ After dinner Mr. Lewis sent me a note, that Queen staid till she knew whether the Duke Ormond approved of Sterne for bishop. .... Nite deelest MD. 20 _April._ I can't tell. Nite, dear de Rogues. Nite MD. 22 _April._ I hate this suspense. Nite, dee logues. Poo pdfr."

23d April, 1713.   Scott, iii., 157.

I must finish the book I am writing, before I can _go_ over; and they expect I shall pass next winter here, and then I will drive them to give me a sum of money. However, I hope to pass four or five months with MD _whatever comes of it._ (Omission.) I received _yours_ to-night; just ten weeks since I had your last. I shall write next post to Bishop Sterne. Never man had so many enemies _in_ Ireland as he. .... The Archbishop of York, my mortal enemy, has sent, by a third hand, that he would be glad to see me. Shall I see him, or not? I hope to be over in a month, and that MD, with their raillery, will be mistaken, that I shall make it three years. I will answer _your letter_ soon; but no more journals. I shall be very busy. Short letters from henceforward. I shall not part with Laracor. That is all I have to live on, except the deanery be worth more than four hundred pounds a year. Is it? If it be, overplus shall be divided (blank) beside usual (blank). Pray write to me a good-humored letter immediately, let it be ever so short. This affair was carried with great difficulty, which vexes me. But they say here, it is much to my reputation, that I have made a bishop, in spite of all the world, to get the best deanery in Ireland. _Night, dear MD._

Original MS.

" I must finish the book I am writing, before I can come over; and they expect I shall pass next winter here, and then I will drive them to give me a sum of money. However, I hope to pass four or five months with MD, and whatever comes on it MD's allowance must be increased,

and shall be too, 'faith! iss truly. I received oor dee Rattle
No. 39 to-night; just ten weeks since I had your last. I
shall write next post to Bishop Sterne. Never man had
so many enemies of* Ireland as he. . . . The Archbishop
of York, my mortal enemy, has sent by a third hand that
he would be glad to see me. Shall I see him or not? I
hope to be over in a month, and that MD with their raillery will be mistaken, that I shall make it three years. I
will answer oor Rattle soon; but no more journals. I shall
be very busy. Short letters from henceforward. I shall
not part with Laracor. That is all I have to live on, except the deanery be worth more than four hundred pounds
a year. Is it? If it be, overplus shall be divided between
MD and FW, beside usual allowance of MD dee rogues.
Pray write to me a good-humored letter immediately, let
it be ever so short. This affair was carried with great
difficulty, which vexes me: but they say here 'tis much to
my reputation, that I have made a bishop in spite of all
the world, to get the best deanery in Ireland. Nite, dee
dee Sollahs."

(margin notes: 1710–1713. Æt. 43–46. Letter 64. Important passage restored. Interesting words supplied.)

24TH–27TH APRIL, 1713. Scott, iii., 158–160.

I forgot to tell you, I had Sterne's letter yesterday, in answer to
mine. (Omissions.) I made mistakes the three last days. . . . 25
April. I know not whether my warrant be *got* ready from the Duke
of Ormond. I suppose it will by to-night. I am going abroad, and
will keep this unsealed, till I know whether all be finished (blank).
I had this letter all day in my pocket waiting till I heard the warrants were gone over. . . . I think to take a hundred pounds a year
out of the deanery, and divide between (blank) but *will* talk of that
when I come over. Night, dear MD. Love Pdfr. 26 *April.* Yesterday I dined with lord-treasurer . . . and was so bedeaned! The Archbishop *of* York says, he will never more speak against me. . . . I
have given Tooke DD's note, to prove she is alive. (Omissions.) 27
April. Farewell, MD, FW, ME, Lele. (Omissions.)

Original MS.

"I forgot to tell you, I had Sterne's letter yesterday
in answer to mine. Oo performed oor Commission well,
dood dallars both. I made mistakes the three last days.

---

* He means Irish enemies; enemies belonging to Ireland.

1710–1713.
Æt. 43–46.
Letter 63.

25 *April.* I know not whether my warrant be yet ready from the Duke Ormond. I suppose it will by to-night. I am going abroad, and will keep this unsealed, till I know whether all be finished.—Morn^g· dee Sollahs.—I had this letter all day in my pocket, waiting till I heard the warrants were gone over.... I think to take a hundred pound

Important passage restored.

a year out of the deanery, and divide it between M. and Pr. and so be one year longer paying the debt;* but we'll talk of zis hen I come over. So Nite, decre Sollahs. Lo Pdfr. 26 *April.* Yesterday I dined with Lord Treasurer, and was so bedeaned! Archbishop York says he will never more speak against me.... I have given Tooke DD's note, to prove she is alive. I'll answer oor Rattle and addle soon. 27 *April.* Farewell, deelest deelest. Nite MD MD FW FW FW ME ME ME Lele lele."

16TH MAY, 1713. *Scott,* iii., 160.

LETTER 64.

Addressed to Mrs. Dingley, and indorsed by Mrs. Johnson, "64. May 2."

I will write to Parvisol ... and a blank for whatever *fellow the* last dean employed.... Tell Raymond I can not *succeed to get him the* living of Moimed.... Take no lodging for me. What? at your old tricks again? I can lie somewhere after I land, *and care* not where, nor how. I will buy your eggs and bacon (blank) your caps and Bible; and pray think immediately, and give me some commissions, and I will perform them. (Omission.) The letter I sent before this was to have gone a post before; but an accident hindered it: and, I assure *you, I am very angry MD did not write to Pdfr,* and I think *you* might have had a dean under your girdle for the superscription.... Farewell, dearest MD, FW, ME, Lele. (Omission.)

Original MS.

"I will write to Parvisol ... and a blank for whatever fellow it is whom the last dean employed. ... Tell Raymond I can not succeed for him to get that living of Moimed. ... Take no lodging for me. What? at your old tricks again? I can lie somewhere after I land, and I care not where, nor how. I will buy your eggs and bacon, DD, and, dee deelest Ppt, your caps and Bible. And pray

---

* "The debt" is explained by what he had written in his Journal of 23d of April: "I thought I was to pay but six hundred pounds for the house; but Bishop Clogher says eight hundred pounds. First-fruits a hundred and fifty pounds, and so with patent a thousand pounds in all. So that I shall not be the better for this deanery these three years."

think immediately, and give me some commissions, and I
will perform them, as far as a poo Pdfr can. The letter
I sent before this was to have gone a post before; but an
accident hindered it: and, I assure oo I wam vely akree
MD did not write to *Dean* Pdfr, and I think oo might
have had a Dean under your girdle for the superscription. . . .   Farewell, deelest MD MD, MD FW FW FW
MD MD MD Lele."

1710-1713.
Æт. 43-46.
Letter 64.

CHESTER, 6TH JUNE, 1713. *Scott*, iii., 162.

I resolve on Monday to set out for Holyhead, as weary as I am . . .
'tis good for my health, *man*. When I came here, I found MD's letter of the 26th of May, sent down to me. Had you *written* a post
sooner, I might have brought some pins: but you were lazy, and
could not write your orders immediately, as I desired you. I will
come, when God pleases; perhaps I may be with you in a week. I
will be three days going to Holyhead; I can not ride faster, say *what
you* will. I am upon Stay-behind's mare. . . .   I will lodge as I can;
therefore take no lodgings for me, to pay in my absence. The poor
dean can't afford it. . . .   Farewell, MD, FW, ME, Lele, &c. (Omissions.)

Lᴇᴛᴛᴇʀ 65.
Addressed to
Mrs. Ding-
ley, and in-
dorsed by
Mrs. John-
son, "65.
Chester let-
ter."

Original MS. (Chester.)

". . . I resolve on Monday to set out for Holyhead, as
weary as I am. 'Tis good for my health, mar'm. When
I came here, I found MD's letter of the 26th of May, sent
down to me. Had you writt a post sooner, I might have
brought some pins: but you were lazy, and would not
write your orders immediately as I desired you. I will
come, when God pleases; perhaps I may be with you in a
week. I will be three days going to Holyhead. I can
not ride faster, say hat oo will. I am upon Stay-behind's
mare. . . .   I will lodge as I can; therefore take no lodgings for me, to pay in my absence. The poor Dean can't
afford it. . . .   Farewell, MD MD MD FW FW FW ME
ME ME ME Lele lele lele Logues and Lads bote fair and
slender.

Restora-
tions.

"I mightily approve Ppt's project of hanging the blind
parson. When I read that passage upon Chester walls, as
I was coming into town, and just received the letter, I said
aloud Agreeable Witch."

INDEX.

END OF VOLUME I.